# THE LAST
# TALES OF THE
# SHADOWMEN
## Volume 20: Fin de Siècle

# also from Black Coat Press

# THE LAST
# TALES OF THE
# SHADOWMEN
## Volume 20: Fin de Siècle

edited by
**Jean-Marc & Randy Lofficier**

essays & reminiscences by
**Stephen R. Bissette, Neil Gaiman, Stuart Gelzer, Robin Hobb, Stephen Jones, K.A. Laity, Randy Lofficier, Tim Lucas, Frank J. Morlock, Kim Newman, Sharan Newman, Henry Lion Oldie, David J. Schow, Michael Shreve, John Skipp, Brian Stableford, Antifas de Torquemada, Rob Walton, Lance Weiler, Douglas E. Winter** and **Thomas Yeates**

stories by
**Jason Scott Aiken, Tim Newton Anderson, Jean-Michel Archaimbault, Matthew Baugh, Atom Mudman Bezecny, Thom Brannan, Nathan Cabaniss, Bill Cunningham, Matthew Dennion, Paul Di Filippo, Brian Gallagher, John Gallagher, Martin Gately, Lex Gil, Micah S. Harris, Travis Hiltz, Riley Hogan, Matthew Ilseman, Rick Lai, Roman Leary, Sean Lee Levin, Jean-Marc Lofficier, David McDonald, Rod McFadyen, Nigel Malcolm, Xavier Mauméjean, William Patrick Maynard & Anna Victoria Maynard, Jess Nevins, Christofer Nigro, John Peel, Neil Penswick, Anthony Perconti, Dennis E. Power, Pete Rawlik & Sal Ciano, Josh Reynolds, Chris Roberson, Robert L. Robinson, Jr., Frank Schildiner, Artikel Unbekannt, Nathalie Vidalinc** and **David L. Vineyard**

cover by
**Raphael Del Rosario**

A Black Coat Press Book

*Dedicated to Terrance Dicks.*

*Thanks to Steve Bissette, without whom…*

All stories & essays Copyright © 2023 by their respective authors.

Cover and back cover illustration Copyright © 2023 Raphael Del Rosario.

Visit our website at www.blackcoatpress.com

# Table of Contents

# *Introduction*

Welcome to the 20th and final tome of *Tales of the Shadowmen*—a very special volume gathering many of our past and present collaborators, as well as a few extra surprises.

When we began soliciting contributions for this book, the one question that was asked the most frequently was—not surprisingly—*why*? Why stop now? It is a fair question, one that deserves an equally fair answer, and we're going to try to answer it as honestly as we can in this introduction.

As is often the case, there isn't a single answer, but many. In no particular order, these are:

*20 years is a good run.* Except for George R. R. Martin's *Wild Cards*, we can't think of any other thematic anthology series that has lasted for twenty years. We are both very proud of having carried that torch for so long, but...

*Not getting stale.* ...After twenty volumes, a certain lassitude has begun to set in. So we thought it was important to end on a high note rather than run the risk of becoming stale and repetitive.

*Mission accomplished.* Our primary goal when we launched Black Coat Press way back when in 2003, in the wake of our much-praised McFarland book on French Science Fiction,[1] was to introduce heretofore unknown classics of French popular literature to the English-speaking public. We did it through translations, non-fiction books (such as *Shadowmen* 1 and 2), and various thematic anthologies, including *Tales of the Shadowmen*, which was meant to be a playful sandbox for writers to discover these works.

If French characters such as Arsène Lupin, Captain Nemo, Fantômas, Judex, Robur and Rouletabille, to name but a few, were already known to a certain section of the English-speaking public, due to earlier translations or film adaptations, we are enormously proud to have introduced such massively important characters as the Black Coats, Doc Ardan, Doctor Omega, Felifax, Harry Dickson, Madame Palmyre, the Nyctalope, Sâr Dubnotal, the Vampire City and many others to our American audience.

To quote John Clute's *Encyclopedia of Science Fiction*: "*Due primarily to* [Black Coat Press], *it has become clear to English-language critics and readers that French SF is not a counter-tradition conditional upon the central flow of SF in the UK and America, but an extremely formidable tradition in its own right.*" And the same is also true of French popular literature.

---

[1] Now updated and rereleased by Black Coat Press in four volumes entitled *The Handbook of French Science Fiction, Of French Fantasy & Supernatural Fiction, f French Fantastic Cinema* and *Of French Fantastic Radio & Television.*

To illustrate this point, we asked a number of fellow professionals what role or influence a work of French fiction might have played in their creative life, or even simply to share a personal reminiscence of the same. The results have been endlessly fascinating, and are presented here in what must surely be a unique collection of essays in the annals of literature.

So: Mission Accomplished!

*Discovering New Talent.* A secondary objective in launching *Tales of the Shadowmen* was that we hoped to discover new writers who would then go on to bigger and better things. And, boy, were we not disappointed! We're not going to name here each and every author for whom *TOTS* was but the first step in an otherwise distinguished career (with the exception of the wonderful Frank Schildiner who has since become a steady provider of a series of thrillers drawing their inspiration from French classics), but our roster of authors has become quite illustrious over the years. However, with the advent of self-publishing on the internet, the role of a "paper" book like *TOTS* has decreased and become far less useful than it was twenty years ago, which brings us to...

*We're not getting any younger.* When we began planning our first volume of *TOTS* in 2004, just before relocating from Los Angeles to a small village in Southern France, we had just turned 50. Simple arithmetic will tell you that, *"twenty years later"* (to borrow Alexandre Dumas' famous phrase), we're not quite as energetic as we used to be, and while there are still many adventures to be had (we hope!), and many villains left to be conquered, these two Musketeers also aspire to a quieter and more restful life.

So here we are then, with this last volume of *Tales of the Shadowmen*, ready to rest on our laurels.

Our eternal gratitude to the brilliant twenty artists who have graced our covers: Juan Miguel Aguilera (#18), Michel Borderie (#13), Fernando Calvi (#2), Jean-Claude Claeys (#8), Christine Clavel (#6), Phil Cohen (#7), Daylon (#3), Raphael Del Rosario (#20), Mariusz Gandzel (#11), Mike Hoffman (#12), José Ladrönn (#4), Nathalie Lial (#9), Aurélien Maccarelli (#19), Mandy (#17), Mike Manley (#1), Stephan Martiniere (#15), Jean-Michel Nicollet (#10), Florine Rétoré (#14), Daniele Serra (#16), and Alan Weiss & Lovern Kindzierski (#5).

Before closing, we would be remiss not to acknowledge those contributors who have sadly passed away in the intervening years: Robert Sheckley—his contribution to Volume 1 might well have been the very last story he wrote—, our very dear friend and mentor, *Doctor Who* writer Terrance Dicks, the everenthusiastic Alain le Bussy from Belgium, Joseph Altairac, Nicholas Boving and Paul Hugli. May their stars always shine bright in the firmament of the Shadowmen!

Jean-Marc & Randy Lofficier

# ESSAYS & REMINISCENCES

## *Stephen R. Bissette*

Before I was 8 years-old, I'd already read and reread the *Classics Illustrated* comic book adaptations of many of the Jules Verne novels, prompting me to read English language translations of *Journey to the Center of the Earth, 20,000 Leagues Under the Sea,* and *Mysterious Island* soon after. They were initially a slog, tough going for a young reader, but I stuck with it and quickly came to love Verne's novels. Seeing the film versions as a kid fueled my seeking out all the Verne novels I could find in our local library, or on the paperback racks. I remember having the first in-depth discussion I'd ever had with an adult (in this case, one of my elementary school teachers) about a movie after the Cy Endfield/Charles Schneer/Ray Harryhausen film version of *Mysterious Island* was broadcast on prime-time CBS-TV, and my teacher was surprised that I'd read the novel beforehand. She took me quite seriously then; we discussed the differences between the novel and the film, which I'd have to cite as the beginning of my thinking analytically about any sort of media, really.

I also discovered Jean Ray before I was a teenager. My formal introduction to Jean Ray was around the age of 12, when I lucked into a copy of the American paperback *Ghouls In My Grave* (translated by Lowell Bair; Berkley, New York, 1965). But as my friend Richard Gagnon later pointed out to me, I'd actually been exposed to Ray's work earlier, when I was 7 years-old, via the uncredited "lift" of one of Ray's short stories by comics writer John Stanley in the Dell Comic *Tales from the Tomb* (1962, the story "The Mudman"). Ray was as vital a writer to my preteen growing love of horror fiction as were the works of Poe, Matheson, Bradbury, and Lovecraft.

It was cinema that brought me to Cocteau and Franju, specifically films shown on television—movies shown on the French Quebec TV station Channel 10, CFTM, out of Montreal. One afternoon while randomly switching through the TV stations we received via antenna in northern Vermont, I was instantly fixated by the surprising image of a cat-like being with glowering eyes: Jean Marais as the Beast in Cocteau's *Beauty and the Beast*! I had no idea what I was watching at first, but couldn't look away, and despite not understanding a lick of French (though my mother and her sisters, my aunts, spoke it fluently), didn't change the channel until the movie was over. That was it, I was hooked. The most singularly terrifying French film I saw at too-young-an-age was the Quebec-made *La Petite Aurore: L'Enfant Martyre* (1952), but not because it was a

9

horror film: it was a relentless account of child abuse, inflicted on the titular waif until she died (!). Soon after I caught Franju's *Les Yeux Sans Visage* on Channel 10, too—after having seen a late-night English broadcast of the same film under its US title, *The Horror Chamber of Dr. Faustus*—and was shocked to see footage not included in the American broadcast (the uncut facial-removal surgical sequence). That was that; I was thereafter addicted to scouring the *TV Guide* for any genre fare on Channel 10, though I still didn't understand French. I watched many French films and TV shows, including my first viewing (sans subtitles) of Franju's *Judex* (1963) and the non-genre (but still borderline-horrific) *La Tête Contre les Murs* (1958). I adore Franju's films, and Raymond Durgnat's book *Franju* (1968) was the first book I ever purchased about a filmmaker.

I also had a rich teenage exposure to the work of Georges Méliès (thanks to Blackhawk Films collections, which I purchased via mail-order in 8mm, three Méliès shorts to a reel, and his longer one-reel masterpieces like his 1912 *À la Conquête du Pôle*, which I watched over and over), which places Méliès right up there as well. Thanks to cinema texts I'd read like Arthur Knight's *The Live-liest Art* and especially Carlos Clarens' seminal *An Illustrated History of the Horror Film,* I fully understood the importance of Méliès to the genre I still love best, making the continuing access to his films via the Blackhawk 8mm and Super 8 releases an inspiration.

I could go on and on (Henri-Georges Clouzot! Robert Enrico's *Au Cœur de la Vie*! Pierre Boulle! Jean Bruller aka "Vercors"' *Les Animaux Dénaturés / You Shall Know Them*) but I won't; those hit me in my later teenage years and my early 20s, along with my first reading of Gaston Leroux and others. I should mention a University of Vermont showing of Clouzot's *Les Diaboliques* (1955) having an almost life-altering impact comparable to that of my early exposures to *La Belle et la Bête* and *Les Yeux Sans Visage*. Of course, having a stunningly beautiful college-age blonde woman (whom I did not know) sitting to my immediate left, impulsively digging her fingernails into my arm (drawing blood) as she screamed aloud when dead-eyed Paul Meurisse rose out from the bath water—that *may* have had something to do with the lasting impression the film made upon gawky high schooler Steve. She apologized, but she needn't have!

In terms of comics—*bandes dessinées*—I'd have to cite the first Hergé's *Tintin* and René Goscinny and Albert Uderzo's *Astérix* translations I discovered at our local library as a kid, though the first *bandes dessinées* that *really* blew me away and influenced me were the stories and artwork in *Métal Hurlant,* which my college friend Jack Venooker had mail-ordered from Bud Plant. That wasn't until 1974 or '75, though, when I was 19 years-old. Jack gave me the initial run of issues as a gift when I left Vermont to join the pioneer class (Class of 1978) of the Joe Kubert School of Cartoon and Graphic Art, Inc. and I turned some of my classmates on to *Métal Hurlant* as well, just before the American edition *Heavy Metal* hit the newsstands.

10

## Neil Gaiman

When I was 14, I went to France for two weeks: I stayed with old family friends. There were adverts everywhere for *Métal Hurlant*. I bought a copy which I still possess, and borrowed others.

It was the best comic I had ever owned, partly because of my schoolboy French. I could not understand a lot of the strips, particularly Moebius's *Airtight Garage*, which was, I knew, because they were too complicated and too adult, too smart and too intelligent.

I knew that it was possible to make comics for adults then. Those issues of *Métal Hurlant* became inspirational. One day I would make comics that deep, that smart, that well-written.

(Years later, I read a translation, and learned that the comic was stream of consciousness surrealism. But it didn't matter. The damage had been done.)

## Stuart Gelzer

Growing up bilingual in an American family but in a francophone country (Cameroon), for me the experience of learning to read in French was synonymous with learning to read at all. As the youngest child of five, my incentive for proving I could read a whole French book by myself was to be given my own books, rather than having to read and reread books belonging to my older siblings. The first French book that was truly mine, I got for my fourth birthday: *C'est moi le chien,* by Albertine Deletaille: "*Le chien, c'est moi, Azan. Je suis beau. Le garçon, c'est mon maître. Je l'aime...*" No, I don't have it memorized (though I probably did at one time); somehow, across the decades and the countless moves to homes on four continents, I've managed to hang onto it—and half a dozen other childhood French favorites—and it's open in front of me now in New Mexico.

Of course what I was really eager to read was *Tintin*; before then I'd been looking at the pictures in our old cloth-spined copies and basically making up the dialogue in every frame. But once I demonstrated that I could read *Le Secret de la Licorne* from cover to cover by doing so aloud to my parents, they rewarded me with my own copy of the sequel, *Le Trésor de Rackham le Rouge.* And after that, there was no stopping me—*Astérix, Lucky Luke, Tanguy & Laverdure,* all followed in the years to come: the world of serious (all right, semiserious, or at least adult-worthy) French *bande dessinée* that has no parallel in English.

In school, though I attended a local Cameroonian elementary school entirely in French, I was zipping through (and a little bored by) much less challenging material, the only example of which I've saved is *Boucles d'or et Pomme d'api,* a first-grade primer by Fernand Nathan: "*Connaissez-vous mes petits amis, Boucles d'or et Pomme d'api? C'étaient deux jumeaux qui dormaient dans le même berceau...*" Meanwhile at home I'd moved on: Hachette's *Bibliothèque Rose* didn't satisfy me long, but the *Bibliothèque Verte* was a perfect match, and I plunged into impressively thick books with no pictures, from one kind of classic—Alexandre Dumas, whether *Les Trois Mousquetaires* or *Le Comte de Monte-Cristo*; Jules Verne, though oddly more of the conventional adventures like *Michel Strogoff* than the science fiction—to another, more modern kind of classic, the *Michel* series by Georges Bayard, starting with *Michel mène l'enquête.*

It was one of those Hachette *Bibliothèque Verte* books that I read when I was about twelve—actually a two-volume set, and you can imagine how grown-up I felt about that—Paul Féval's "cape and sword" epic *Le Bossu,* which I rediscovered decades later... and when I found out there was no English translation, I instantly set about correcting that terrible omission personally.[2]

So my childhood foundation in French literature was not just the vague sentimental background for my turn to translation in my sixties, it was the direct inciting spark.

---

[2] *The Hunchback*, Black Coat Press, ISBN 978-1-64932-066-7.

## Robin Hobb

My introduction to French literature happened at a very early age. First, of course, were the fairy tales in my father's lavishly illustrated books from his childhood. I did not, of course, think of *Little Red Riding Hood* or *Sleeping Beauty* or *Puss in Boots* as French stories. They were MY stories, from a wonderful place and time called Once Upon a Time. When I consider them now, it is something of a marvel that stories so far from me in time and place still spoke to me so strongly.

But it was not just the fairy tale books in our family book cases that influenced me. In a handsome black binding with a color cover, there was a book called *The Mysterious Island* by Jules Verne. N C Wyeth was the illustrator for that edition and W.H.G. Kingston was the translator. I will forever owe a debt to whoever bought my father such lavish books! The story was captivating. Prisoners escaping together in a hot air balloon, only to be marooned on a Mysterious Island where they used all the skills of engineers and sailors to create a safe haven for themselves. Everyone in the party has something to contribute to their survival, and the statement it made about race was a very important one for that time.

Our family had inherited a lovely set of small books bound in red leather. The covers felt wonderful to touch, and they were the perfect size to carry about. They had been my grandmother's, and included not only *The Three Musketeers* but the sequels, *Twenty Years After* and *Ten Years Later* (*The Vicomte de Bragelonne*). Those volumes are still on my shelves. Many years later, when I first met Steven Brust, we were delighted to discover that not only did we both love those same stories, but that it was the same translator in the books we had! (And I am away from my home right now, of I would try to honor that translator by name!)

In short, due to the wonderful work of translators, I had access to "international literature" at a time when I didn't even know it was international. It is a tribute to those story tellers and writers that their work spoke to a kid growing up in the 50s and 60s United States. Could Verne or Dumas have ever imagined that when they were penning those tales? Let alone that sitting at a laptop keyboard, all those years later, the thought of those tales still makes me smile. Pencroft, D'Artagnan, Aramis, Athos, Porthos, Cyrus, Neb—thinking of them is like thinking of old friends.

## Stephen Jones

I don't really remember all that many Belgian horror movies.

Of course, there's Harry Kümel's *Les Lèvres Rouges* (aka *Daughters of Darkness*, 1971) in which Delphine Seyrig's luminous lady Dracula stalked the winter-chilled streets of an out-of-season Ostend. Or Jean Brismée's *La Plus Longue Nuit du Diable* (aka *The Devil's Nightmare*, also from 1971), which featured Erika Blanc's sexy succubus preying on seven guests in a Gothic castle.

Both of these are terrific films, but they seemed a bit too obvious to me. So, in the end, I decided to go with a perhaps lesser-known title from just over a decade earlier.

*Le Moulin des Supplices* (aka *Mill of the Stone Women*, 1960) is not strictly a Belgian movie. Instead, it's one of those curios 1960s hybrids—a European co-production involving a number of different countries, in this case Italy, France, Holland and Belgium, the latter apparently used for location filming.

Directed by Italian Giorgio Ferroni (a journeyman whose only other notable genre credit is the 1971 vampire movie *Night of the Devils*) and shot in a striking Technicolor palate by cinematographer Pier Ludovico Pavoni that recalls the work of Mario Bava, the opening credits claim the film is based on a short story by "Peter van Weigen" from the book *Flemmish Tales*, although no such author or volume is known to exist. This was a ploy often used by filmmakers to give their productions greater verisimilitude.

In fact the screenplay, co-penned by director Ferroni and bevy of other uncredited scriptwriters, is set in 19th century Holland, where Hans van Arnhim (French leading man Pierre Brice) arrives at an old windmill to research an article to mark the centenary of a creepy carousel of female statues maintained and added to by sculptor and art professor Gregorious Wahl (stage actor Herbert Böhme, a sort of German Donald Wolfit).

The writer soon meets and falls in love with Wahl's beautiful but sickly daughter Elfie (Italian actress Scilla Gabel, a former stand-in for Sophia Loren), who is kept isolated from the outside world by her father and live-in physician Dr. Loren Bohlem (Wolfgang Preiss, Germany's "Dr. Mabuse" himself).

Meanwhile, local women continue to mysteriously disappear around the old mill house.

Before you can say *Eyes Without A Face* or *House of Wax*, and after a lot of atmospheric creeping around cobwebbed crypts and hallucinogenic close-ups of the sinister statues, it will come as a surprise to no one to learn that Wahl and the doctor are kidnapping the young women and draining their blood to transfuse it into Elfie to keep her alive. The sculptor then encases the victims' corpses in wax to display as part of his macabre tableau.

When their nefarious deeds are discovered, the movie ends with the obligatory climax-by-fire as the windmill and its carousel of death are engulfed in flames.

Trust me, it's a lot better than it sounds.

In fact, when it opened in Italy in 1960 as *Il Mulino Delle Donne Di Pietra*, the movie grossed more than that year's better-known releases, *Black Sunday* and *Atom Age Vampire*.

As with many of these pan-European productions of the time, the film exists in various different versions, including the regular 96 minute original and English-export version, a shorter French-language cut with alternative footage, and the re-edited American version released in 1963 by the obscure Parade Releasing Organization with different dubbing and additional special effects. All these versions, and much more, can be found on the 2021 limited edition Blu-ray boxed set from Arrow Films with a new audio commentary by Tim Lucas.

It should also be noted that the undeniably eye-catching American one-sheet was definitely an improvement over the artwork used on some of the original European posters.

Mostly forgotten today, *Le Moulin des Supplices/Mill of the Stone Women* may not be ranked along with some of the better-known European horror movies of the early 1960s, but it still stands up as an interesting curio that in the hands of a more visionary director such as Mario Bava or Riccardo Freda might well have been considered a classic of the genre.

## K.A. Laity

Probably my first memory of anything Belgian or French was in the pages of the *Children's Digest*. My grandparents bought me an annual subscription since I was mystifyingly bookish. The magazine contained a variety of things every month, but the real treasure was it serialized *Tintin*. I knew nothing about the comics. My first experience was joining *Tintin in Tibet* in media res, but its impact was immediate and I was hooked.

Years later when I first went to Belgium, I got the biggest thrill at *Le Centre Belge de la Bande Dessinée* seeing the *Tintin* rocket ship there in the lobby of Horta's beautiful *Art Nouveau* building, then all of Hergé's sketches that seemingly impossibly transformed into the clean lines of the strip. And of course buying Tintin merch with my faves Milou and Captain Haddock.

I know the surrealists got in there somehow, but I suspect that was first through Dalí appearing on American talk shows. That first trip to Bruxelles cemented my fascination with Magritte as well as introducing me to Wiertz, for whom I continue to evangelize. The museum made in his studio is absolutely stunning. I had of course seen reproductions of Magritte but it is nothing like seeing the paintings face to face. I suspect he's the reason I have such a fondness for the remake of *The Thomas Crown Affair*.

I know I discovered French films in the 70s, likely in some attempt to either understand sex or the sophistication denied me by growing up in the hinterlands of the Midwest. I loved Gerard Depardieu in *Get Out Your Handkerchiefs* so much I convinced my brother to come see *Mon Oncle d'Amérique* with me and wow, he has never let me forget that surreal experience. French film criticism—especially on noir—has continued to be an important thread in my writing.

It seems weird that despite growing up next to Canada with grandparents who lived there part of the time I never got around to properly learning French until fairly recently—and entirely to study the Surrealists. My only explanation (despite learning nine or ten languages for my PhD) is that I find non-WYSIWYG languages endlessly frustrating. No wonder so much French language humor lies in homonyms. *Petit à petit, l'oiseau fait son nid.*

17

## Randy Lofficier

Almost twenty-six years ago I set out to teach myself French. I started out with reading magazines, specifically *Elle*, which in France is a weekly. I mostly read the ads, because they were the easiest things to understand. But after several months of application, I finally began to realize I could read the articles as well. I moved on to comics, a natural choice in our household.

Then, one day, I felt that I had mastered enough of the language to tackle something meatier: a novel.

Why did I choose *Phantom of the Opera* [3] as my first novel? To be honest, I can't remember today. Perhaps because it was there. Perhaps it was because I thought I knew it from having seen the various film adaptations. However, it doesn't really matter, because tackle it I did.

The first thing that astonished me was how modern the prose read. It didn't feel like a book that had been written almost a hundred years earlier. The second thing that grabbed me was that the story was far more than what the various films had shown. There was a depth to Erik's character that was totally lacking in anything I had seen. The truly monstrous nature of his being, as reflected in the horror of his face, was brutally chilling.

The hero, Raul, was quite a wimp and Christine was foolish and naïve. But Erik was evil and devious, totally convinced of the righteousness of his actions. As I learned about him through the Persian's narrative, I felt that I could believe that he had truly existed.

Like E. L. Doctorow after him, Gaston Leroux had ably blended fact and fiction in a way that increased the reality of the horror. It was hard to realize that none of what was described in the book had actually happened. Also, because he was a journalist, the language is crisp and punchy, not flowery. Those elements combined to make it a gripping read that drew me in without giving me a moment's pause.

And perhaps that is what made it truly horrific, the feeling that I was reading about possibly real events. I could see the Rat Catcher and his herd of vermin as they ran beneath the streets of Paris. I wanted to see the vast lake where Erik lived. I was fascinated by the City that was the Paris Opera.

How was it possible that a chandelier had not fallen during a major performance, injuring dozens of people? Was the Opera filled with secret doorways and passages? I truly wanted to believe that it was.

I was doubly shocked when I eventually took a look at the version of *Phantom* that was available in English. All the power of the language was miss-

---

[3] Black Coat Press, ISBN 978-1-932983-13-5.

ing and it had become turgid and heavy. Of course, it was also clear to me that the various adaptations of the book onto film had missed the essential core of Erik. He was not a tragic hero, but instead, a true villainous monster. His soul was even more corrupt than his flesh. Totally ignored is the fact that, because his exterior was hideous from birth, he was rejected as a human being by everyone he met, including his parents. The innate cruelty of mankind was as responsible for his later actions as he was himself. By pretending that, like Quasimodo, his perverted exterior hid a heart of gold, the unpalatable truth is never exposed: Erik has no heart. It was crushed into a small hard stone before he ever left the land of childhood.

I know that for most people, *The Phantom of the Opera* is the story of doomed romantic love. But for me it will always remain a powerful tale of fear and brutality. I've read it several times over the years and I never fail to come to the final pages without a sense of true horror having touched me once again.

## Tim Lucas

The genesis, research and writing of my critical biography *Mario Bava: All the Colors of the Dark* occupied my inner life almost entirely between the ages of 15 and 51. Throughout that time I felt spiritually Italian and focused mostly on Italian cinema, because I needed to know not just about Mario Bava but everything that surrounded Mario Bava. As soon as my work was completed with the book's publication in 2007, my inner life almost immediately became predominantly French in its interests and obsessions.

In my late teens and twenties, when I first began working toward writing novels, my heroes were predominantly French (in translation) and British. I was particularly drawn to the practitioners of the *Nouveau Roman* (Alain Robbe-Grillet especially, but also André-Pierre de Mardiargues, Nathalie Sarraute, Marguerite Duras and eroticists like Pauline Réage, Violette Le Duc, and Jean de Berg). Robbe-Grillet continues to be a major source of inspiration, my favorite novelist. Because I am restricted to reading these writers in English, there tend to be some gaps in my reading and understanding of the whole arc of their careers; I am especially unhappy that only one volume of Robbe-Grillet's three-volume autobiography has been translated. I have tried to compensate for the books I can't read by collecting them in their original language.

At some point after the Internet came into my life, along with sources like ebay and abebooks, I became newly obsessed with French pulp and crime and mystery fiction, especially of the 19th and early 20th century. I began collecting the works of Gaston Leroux, the *Fantômas* novels of Pierre Souvestre and Marcel Allain, Maurice Leblanc, Arthur Bernède, and also the more contemporary thrillers of Boileau-Narcejac—again, always in translation. Again, being limited to what is available by these authors in English has always been a problem. For example, I've never been able to read *The Midnight Lady* (the first volume of the English translation of *La Reine du Sabbat*, released only in the UK and very, very rare) so I used Google Translate to read that portion of the novel from a French ebook! It wasn't entirely satisfactory but it gave me enough to proceed with the second half, which I owned as *The Missing Archduke*. I should also mention that I was very impressed by Jacques Sternberg's novel *Toi, Ma Nuit* which was published in English as *Sexualis 95*.

But my greatest, most overwhelming enthusiasm came at the end of 2018 when I innocently decided to read Jules Verne's *In Search of the Castaways (The Children of Captain Grant)*, which became one of the most absorbing and thrilling reading experiences of my life. I fell in love with Verne as I have with few other writers—from the Earth's Core to the ring of space surrounding it.

Here is a man that took our entire world as his subject when it could still only be most thoroughly explored in a virtual sense, through maps and literature.

I had previously read *The Green Ray* (mostly in response to the Eric Rohmer film, to understand more about its inspiration), which I liked, but it didn't prepare me for what was to come. I began to study and realized that Verne's early editions—in French *and* English translation—were the real fore-runners of the Hollywood blockbuster. They were beautifully bound and illus-trated in ways that seemed to capture their original moment in time. So I began to collect them—not only the most beautiful English editions I could afford, but also as many of the Hachette first edition replicas as I could find and import, be-fore transcontinental shipping charges became prohibitive. I've shared photos of my Verne collection with other such collectors and they tell me my collection is of museum quality. I own some titles in more than one translation, as translation is a bitter issue with Verne—and all the more reason for me to have the original texts on hand.

In terms of film, my French heroes are Franju, Feuillade, Clouzot, Cocteau, Rohmer, Godard, Chabrol, Méliès, and also the Polish expatriate who made some of their best work in France—Kieslowski, Zuławski, Polanski. Also Jacques Champreux for his superb adaptation of *Judex* for Franju, the TV mini-series *Les Compagnons de Baal*, and his embodiment of the "Man Without a Face" in Franju's *Nuits Rouges*. My favorite actor is Jean-Louis Trintignant, my favorite actresses Isabelle Huppert, Bernadette Lafont and Edith Scob.

It may seem somewhat off the mark, but I'm also very fond of Eddie Con-stantine movies (and wrote the introduction for his daughter's biography of him) and the music of Françoise Hardy.

I feel there is still so much to discover in all of the French arts!

## Frank J. Morlock

I wasn't much interested in literature of any sort until my Senior year in High School. I had five years of French and four years of German, and I frankly preferred German because I am of German descent on my father's side. It was my best language. In the Summer between graduating from High School and entering College, I discovered literature in a big way. I read *War and Peace*, and T. Wolfe's *Look Homeward Angel*, and these two books had an enormous impact on me that lasted to this day (I was 16 and now I'm 62.) I also discovered Drama, which has become the form of literature I prefer. I read *The Red Robe* by Eugène Brieux which was a very powerful play about a murder trial in France, and I also read Stendhal's *The Red and the Black* in translation, and Dumas *père*'s *The Three Musketeers* in one night. (I began it around eight in the evening and finished it at 4 the next morning.) I read a couple plays by Racine and Corneille in French, but that was all.

Years went by, and, one day after I had just graduated from Law School, quite by accident. I met my old High School French Professor who had retired. We talked for a bit and he said to me, "If you've kept your French up for six years you will never forget it." I had, and he was right.

Again, nothing to report for many years. Then. one day. when I was in my 30s, I was teaching a course in Legal Research to Paralegals at the University of Maryland Library. After giving my students an assignment, I wandered around the stacks and came across a small book of plays by a writer named Charles Dufresny who I had never heard of. The first play in the book was called *The Spirit of Contradiction*. It was short, about 30 pages-long, and had been printed on very high quality vellum paper. I think it was published in the 1800s and was about the size of my hand. I started reading it and I thought it was the funniest thing I'd ever read in my life. It's about a woman whose sole pleasure in life is to thwart the desires of her husband, and daughter, and anyone else who happens to be around. They know her tricks and are very careful to conceal their desires. But she knows they know and is very wily in unraveling their efforts to conceal their desires. It was written in 1700. I thought it as funny as anything Molière had ever written.

I decided to translate this play. It was short, no long speeches. A piece of Cake! Two months later, I finally finished it. Now I can translate twenty pages in a day. But like anything else, you have to struggle to do it before it becomes easy. So, in my late 30s, I began translating books from French. I started with 18th century plays to be sure they were out of copyright, and also because it was hard to find more recent authors. The University of Maryland's Rare Books Department had quite a few .titles I became interested in; also Johns Hopkins Uni-

22

versity, which I visited when I drove up to see my mother in Boston, my home town. I would stop at Yale and find some very good material as they have a huge collection.

Eventually, I began to publish these translations with Wildside Press and then Black Coat Press. I believe that, in the 30,000 plays published in French during the 19th century, there is a wealth of literature largely forgotten, even by the French themselves, that compares favorably with the most famous novels and novelists. Stendhal, Vigny, Balzac, Dumas *père & fils*, Hugo, Sand, Flaubert, Zola, Maupassant, the Goncourts, Verne, and many others all wrote a significant number of plays. And other writers also penned some excellent adaptations of great novels, and they also wrote some truly ingenious melodramas. They adapted not only French novels, but English novels such as Clarissa Harlowe, Tom Jones, Pickwick and others. (Not to mention excellent French adaptations of Shakespeare.)

Nowadays, much of this material is available online at Gallica and the Internet Text Archive, and more recently a French site called Theatre Documentation. com which only collects French language scripts and has over 6,000 plays that are downloadable.

The last forty years of my life have been enriched by translating numerous masterpieces undeservedly forgotten. Of the 36,000 plays written in the 19th century, maybe 200 had been translated before my efforts. Alas, not too many people are interested, but that's as may be. The pleasure is the same in recreating a great work of art even if it remains in the shadows.

# Kim Newman

My first experience of French (well, Belgian) popular culture came in the early 1960s, when I was about four or five—I think I probably learned to read from a couple of albums of Hergé's *.Tintin*, which my parents read to me from, pointing to the word balloons as I looked at the pictures.

The first of the albums we had was *The Secret of the Unicorn*—part one of a two-part story completed in *Red Rackham's Treasure*, which I didn't get to for some time (perhaps years). A very early memory is of a brief sequence (pp 32-33 in the edition I now have) where lookalike policemen Thompson and Thomson (Dupond and Dupont in French) pursue a well-dressed pickpocket and get caught up in his morning coat (which contains clues)—with Thompson (or is it Thomson?) running into a lamp-post at the end of the encounter. What struck me as a child was the particular blue gloom, which felt a lot like British London weather—though, when Tintin & Co visited Britain in *The Black Island*, the album had to be redrawn for UK publication to eliminate inaccuracies.

I had a sense of Tintin not being English==he wasn't like Enid Blyton's *Famous Five*, with whom I didn't get on as a child, or the children in *Five Children and It* or the Narnia books, which I loved (still do)—but thanks to the very tactful, inventive translations (by Leslie Lonsdale-Cooper and Michael Turner) the supporting cast were more relatable... Captain Haddock swearing about "blue blistering barnacles," Professor Calculus with his plum-bob and ear trumpet, the formidable diva Signora Bianca Castafiore (the only significant female character in the series).

I was naturally drawn especially to the more fantastical adventures—the mummy-like curse-spreading Inca priest of *The Seven Crystal Balls/Prisoners of the Sun* is impish and terrifying; the two-part *Destination Moon/Explorers on the Moon* at once full of nuts-and-bolts 1950s science fiction and colorful whimsy (and beards); the final perfect page of *Tintin in Tibet* with the yeti left behind after the expedition goes home still strikes me as masterly; the rather melancholy near-apocalypse of *The Shooting Star* springs mushroom-related weirdness on the reader; and, at the end of the run, Hergé has Tintin mixed up in an enigmatic von Däniken-ish alien encounter of *Flight 714*.

I read (and reread) all the available albums in the 1960s, and followed the five-minute episodes of a cartoon serial squeezed into the BBC's children's programming schedules (narrated in the export version either by Paul Frees or by someone doing Paul Frees' voice)—which ran over and over, until the slot was filled by another gallic import blessed with an inventive English translation, *Le Manège Enchanté*—reimagined by Eric Thompson as *The Magic Roundabout*.

UK kids' TV drew a lot on European material in the 1960s, screening Eastern European fairytales in the *Tales From Europe* slot—every kid my age remembers being .frightened by the East German *The Singing, Ringing Tree*— and *Tintin* and *The Magic Roundabout* were joined by the epic-length serial adaptation of *Robinson Crusoe* (with a memorable, melancholy theme) as a trifecta of across-the-channel influences.

## *Sharan Newman*

I have long been under the spell of France. There is no one reason for this. When I was in graduate school, most of my colleagues preferred medieval England, either Normans or Saxons but, apart from the food and wine being better, I yearned to delve into the medieval history of France.

In my first undergraduate medieval history class, I fell in love with Peter Abelard. By the time I came to my senses, I had discovered the enchantment of Heloise and her world, much less rarified than that of the philosophers. I soon moved to the twelfth century, based myself in Paris and have lived there for the most part, ever since.

While breaking stereotypes from history, the French people I met also taught me how diverse and similar we are. The countryside lured me with ancient mysteries, spirits of Gauls and Greeks and secret heretics.

France has given me a life-long career. I receive knowledge from voices whispering in Old French and Occitan. Every time I go there, I find something new and enchanting. However long I live, it will call to me. *Du fond du coeur, Merci.*

## Henry Lion Oldie
### (Dmitry Gromov & Oleg Ladyzhensky)

Even though there are two of us (we are long-time friends and co-authors), our acquaintance with the works of French writers happened in approximately the same way. It started with the novels of Jules Verne, when we were nine years-old in elementary school. A couple of Verne books were found in Dmitry's home library. Oleg was luckier—shortly before this, his parents miraculously managed to acquire a signed collection of Verne's works.

The first were *The Children of Captain Grant, Twenty Thousand Leagues Under the Sea, The Mysterious Island...* And that's it, we were lost! We dived headlong into the world of these wonderful novels, like the *Nautilus* into the depths of the ocean, and did not want to surface. We wanted more, more! But we must say that it was problematic to buy good books freely—not only those of Jules Verne—in the Soviet Union, where we were born. It was not for nothing that we said that Oleg was very lucky in this case: truly interesting and fascinating books were in short supply. Public libraries and friends with whom we regularly exchanged books "to read" helped out. We ended up reading *The Fifteen-Year-Old Captain, Five Weeks in a Balloon, From the Earth to the Moon* and *Around the Moon, Journey to the Center of the Earth, Robur the Conqueror, The Begum's Five Hundred Million*, and many more. Brave heroes, the spirit of search and adventure, scientific discoveries and inventions, exotic countries, underwater travel—what else could little boys need?

A little later, we became acquainted with the novels of Alexandre Dumas, both in the same way: some were found in home libraries, the rest were borrowed from friends or public libraries. Of course, Dumas's first book we read was *The Three Musketeers*. Our friends and we became obsessed with musketeers. We made wooden swords, staged duels and collective battles, imagining ourselves on the streets of Paris, which they saw "live" only many years later, as adults. *The Three Musketeers* was followed by *Twenty Years Later, The Count of Monte-Cristo, The Lady of Monsoreau, The Forty-Five...* (By the way, in our trilogy *Alumen*, which we co-wrote with Andrey Valentinov, Alexandre Dumas appears as a character.)

In parallel with Dumas, we discovered the works of Georges Simenon—his detective stories featuring Police Commissioner Maigret. And we became afflicted again. We even kept special notebooks where we wrote down all sorts of strange and suspicious incidents—at least, from our point of view,--in great details. We collected "evidence", imagining ourselves as detectives...

Later, there was Francis Carsac with his wild imagination, astronauts and space pioneers, adventures and battles, other planets and races: *Those From Nowhere, This World is Ours, The Mountains of Destiny, The Lion's Parasites, The Robinsons of the Cosmos, Runaway Earth*... Also J.-H. Rosny Aîné, Louis Boussenard, Robert Merle and *Malevil* and *The Day of the Dolphin*, Gérard Klein, Jean Ray, Pierre Boulle and *Planet of the Apes*, Bernard Werber...

Of course, our acquaintance with French writers was not limited to fantasy and adventure: Guy de Maupassant, Honoré de Balzac, Gustave Flaubert, Stendhal... And much later, already in adulthood, we became acquainted with great pleasure with the wonderful novels of Pierre Lemaître.

Without a doubt, the books of French authors have had a considerable influence on us as writers. Not only them, of course, but them too.


*Translated by Patrice Lajoye.*

## David J. Schow

This might seem to be a rather convoluted film-to-literature timeline, but I think most of our modern conception of tales horrific can be credited to the febrile imagination of two seminal founding figures, both women. (Edgar Allan Poe is genre-ubiquitous, of course, but he didn't come along until much later—the mid-1800s, to get precise.)

Mary Shelley is obvious. But before her came Gabrielle-Suzanne Barbot de Villeneuve with *Beauty and the Beast (La Belle et la Bête)*,[4] first published in 1740. Villeneuve (1685-1755) was born and died in Paris.

Romances with monsters are evergreen. I realized this while tracking the inspiration for *Creature From the Black Lagoon* (1954), which was very obviously sired by *King Kong* (1933), itself a monster-movie spin on Villeneuve's immortal source tale; it's even called out by name, with "Beauty" being the timeless Woman in White that persisted not only through *Creature*'s world-famous one-piece bathing suit, but Marilyn Monroe's evocation of it (and reference to it) in Billy Wilder's *The Seven-Year Itch* (1955). That makes it doubly interesting that the "female lead" in *La Belle et la Bête* is simply named "Beauty," whose merchant father loses his fortune (and the means to support his family) in a maritime disaster—the sea takes everything away from him.

---

[4] Black Coat Press, ISBN 978-1-61227-626-.

## Michael Shreve

I have always been an avid reader. As a kid I devoured sci-fi, fantasy, horror, crime, any kind of pulp fiction I could find. I rode my bike down to the public library, then soon around to used bookstores to feed my favorite hobby. One day, I brought home a weird book, _Heartsnatcher_, by a weird guy named Boris Vian. What the hell was that? Fantasy? Not like I'd ever read. Just plain weird. But intense. I liked intense. The scarier, weirder, more outlandish the better.

See, as a kid I was reading things I probably shouldn't have, that I didn't fully understand. But I couldn't help it, I liked Poe, not the Hardy Boys. I got bored with Tolkien, but I was fascinated by Mervyn Peake. My attention wandered during Asimov, but you couldn't tear me away from P.K. Dick. And French fiction, I found, was more to my taste.

But I didn't go through the typical Jules Verne stage. I was reading Philip José Farmer and through him discovered the crazy adventure of Ironcastle by J.-H. Rosny _aîné_. And really, the "Planet of the Apes" was a book? I had to read it. Lo and behold, Pierre Boulle, a French author. I somehow encountered René Barjavel and his speculative visions. Then there was the twisted _New Bodies for Old_ (a.k.a. _Doctor Lerne_ )[5] by Maurice Renard. Little by little, more and more, I was hooked.

Unfortunately, the lack of translations kept most of this treasure trove hidden from me until years later when I taught myself French. At the time, however, I imagined that the kind of stories that were ignored or rejected in the US were normal and popular in France. For me they were (and continue to be) more stimulating to my intellect, more challenging to my preconceptions and more politically engaged, intriguing in the way they so often mix/subvert/transcend genres, break the mold as it were, to open up new vistas for the imagination. Indeed, unearthing some new French author has always been a breath of fresh air.

---

[5] Black Coat Press, ISBN 978-1-935558-15-6.

## John Skipp

Aside from the obvious heavyweights, I gotta lead with Jacques Brel. Or, more to the point, the American Film Institute's film version of *Jacques Brel Is Alive and Well and Living in Paris*, which I saw in my high school senior year (at the fancy little York Country Day School in Pennsylvania, where I went after quitting high school proper, and where I met Craig Spector, who'd just been kicked outta his).

As fate would have it, I was *incredibly* stoned when we showed up at the York Mall for this screening. And it struck me that this was one of those early 70s films where the entire cast and crew were every bit as high as I was. These very stagily-staged sequences anticipated the music videos that would be emerging soon, vanguarded by artists like Kate Bush. And there was a swooshing delirium to the visual delivery, very much in keeping with the melancholy waltzes and march-to-war bombast of the orchestrations.

But it was the music that killed me. Those incredible songs. They said Brel was the Belgian Bob Dylan, which is apt only in the measure of their brilliance. But Brel's music was a trillion times more sophisticated, drawing from French pop and cabaret roots rather than the jangle of folk acoustic guitar. And the stories were heartbreaking, mesmerizing, hilarious deep dives into the lives, deaths, and dreams of common people with infinite longings, often thwarted.

And there was one song in particular, *The Soldier*, in which a monument to our fallen war dead suddenly comes to life, in a park surrounded by hippies, and starts telling them to get the fuck off his lawn. In the process, we see the lying, cheating, dishonorable little man he was in life, who knows he does not deserve to be this statue. Shamed by the hypocrisy of the monument he's become. And that the kids aren't the problem. Just his own self-hate.

The song is so incredible. Such a perfect work of *Twilight Zone*-ian horror. And it's just one of seeming dozens, each more brilliant than the last. To this day, Jacques Brel is one of my favorite songwriters. And definitely takes this cake.

Speaking of the American Film Institute, this same series released *Rhinoceros* by Eugène Ionesco, the absurdist playwright and proto-Bizarro, reuniting *The Producers* stars Gene Wilder and Zero Mostel. The movie is swell. But the real thrill for me was that I'd appeared in the stage play a couple years earlier, in a junior high school production. (I played the "Elderly Gentleman".) In its tale of rampaging fascist conformity, as everyone transforms into the titular horned behemoths, I helplessly saw the parallels to our own time. And adored this work of giddy, galumphing nightmare art.

31

We'll wrap up quick with Robert Enrico, who directed the sublime film version of Ambrose Bierce's *An Occurrence at Owl Creek Bridge*. When this appeared in *The Twilight Zone*'s final season, it perfectly evoked the longing, the rallying spirit, and the short sharp shock of Bierce's breathtaking story.

And speaking of short stories: Guy de Maupassant. That motherfucker could write.

## Brian Stableford

The work that probably offers the best representation of the genre called *roman scientifique* is a book that attempted to conceive a similar genre in slightly different terms: Félix Bodin's *Le Roman de l'Avenir*.[6] It was not published posthumously, although that was a close-run thing, but it is something of a mess, having been hurriedly put together as a portmanteau text by a writer who knew that he was not going to be able to bring it to anything resembling a satisfactory condition, but who was desperate to get something into print in order to establish a claim of priority. Bodin was not the first person to end up in that predicament.

Cyrano de Bergerac, who produced by far the most important and influential precursor of the genre in *L'Autre Monde*, battled with all his might to finish it while on his death-bed. He appears to have succeeded, but his success was partly cancelled out because half of the manuscript was stolen and destroyed by someone who thought it ought not to exist, and the rest was only published posthumously in bowdlerized form.

Nicolas Restif de La Bretonne, who produced by far the most adventurous and ambitious work in the genre written in the eighteenth century similarly spend his last few active years desperately trying to get the relevant work he had done into print. In the end, he managed to get part of it into print—the part that was, unfortunately, still a messy and unsatisfactory portmanteau text—while the more coherent and presumably better part, *L'Enclos et les oiseaux*, was lost forever, because Restif had exhausted all his resources publishing previous works and nobody else cared enough to preserve it.

The surviving fractions of those three endeavors—the incomplete *L'Autre monde*, the unsupplemented and unsatisfactory *Les Posthumes*[7] and the incomplete *Le Roman de l'Avenir*—are the truly revealing exemplars of the genre retrospectively assembled as the ancestry of Vernian *roman scientifique*. They are its true classics, its hard-won and partial victories over adversity—or, more accurately, the survivors that made its defeat by adversity a little less than total.

---

[6] *The Novel of the Future*, Black Coat Press, ISBN 978-1-934543-44-3.
[7] *Posthumous Correspondence* (3 vols.), Black Coat Press, ISBNs 978-1-61227-513-0, 978-1-61227-514-7 and 978-1-61227-515-4.

## Antifas de Torquemada

The moment I found out that the French *avant-garde* was crazy about a certain shape-shifting, murderous, thieving demon[8] from the *belle époque*, I felt compelled to summon him. Tim Lucas[9] supplied the incantations, Project Gutenberg[10] opened the doors to the first six circles of his particular hell, and when I realized that Fantômas had laid his foul eggs inside my brains it was too late to stop them from hatching.

Shortly afterwards, I stumbled upon the 1980 *Fantômas* TV adaptation[11] and that was all I had to go on for over a decade. Sadly, digital versions of novels seven through forty-three of the series are nowhere to be found, personal shipping between the EU and my Andean hometown was impossible until recently, and most of Fantômas' original exploits have never been issued in the US[12]. However, this handful of pages and pictures harbored worlds within worlds[13].

Their vastness notwithstanding, after years of carefully visiting and revisiting these few tales, I managed to suss out three of their main features[14].

1. They disregard genre conventions. Take *The Exploits of Juve*[15]: it features a rigorous forensic investigation that eventually leads to Fantômas' pet, a monstrous yet portable snake capable of crushing human bodies into an unidentifiable jelly. Surely this viscous yarn cannot be cleanly filed under "detective fiction," "science fiction," or "horror?"

2. They imbue impalpable fancy with the immediacy of palpitating flesh. Fantômas' murders are constantly described, in the books, as both invisible hex-

---

[8] Cf. Audureau, A. (2010). *Fantômas: Un mythe moderne au croisement des arts*. PU Rennes.

[9] http://www.fantomas-lives.com

[10] https://www.gutenberg.org/ebooks/author/32911

[11] *Fantômas*. Created by Claude Chabrol and Juan Luis Buñuel, A2, Gaumont Television, Portman Film, 1980.

[12] Christophe Gans' abandoned a movie project that could have changed this. Hopefully Wassim Beji will soon pick up where he left off: https://www.allocine.fr/film/fichefilm_gen_cfilm=146592.html

[13] Francis Lacassin beautifully extolls this boundlessness in Allain, M. & Souvestre, P. (1987). *Fantômas: Édition Présentée et Établie par Francis Lacassin*. Éditions Robert Laffont, S.A.

[14] The disguises and identity thefts that pervade the whole series are such a well-known staple of popular fiction that they fall outside of the scope of this article.

[15] Souvestre, P.E. & Allain, M. (1917). *The Exploits of Juve*. New York, NY: Brentano's.

es and festering ravages, and they somehow never fail to strike inspector Juve and ace reporter Fandor, his brilliant pursuers, as criminal masterstrokes. The entire third novel is built around Fantômas' superb ability to hide his finger-prints... by wearing the skin of his victim's hands.

The television show is dotted with head-on collisions between ethereal fancy and visceral immediacy. In fact, whenever horrific –perhaps lifelike?– corpses appear on the screen they are enveloped in unsettling, repetitive sounds reminiscent of breaking waves, nightmare flotsam washed up on the shore of crude wakefulness. I suppose Claude Chabrol and Juan Luis Buñuel, brought up as they were in the midst of several surrealist revolutions, had a knack for this sort of thing.

3. They are bristling with incidents. Dire events such as explosions, dis-memberments, train wrecks, home invasions, thefts, arrests, interrogations, dragnets combine with mundane minutiae, like champagne dinners, walks in the park or surgery, to bury any conceivable leads until their catastrophic conclu-sions, or maybe the next few installments, partially clear the fog of war. Judging from their unruly trajectories, it seems the main characters of the series have no precise objectives other than amusing themselves or wreaking havoc on their enemies' plans.

It is possible to take apart any given Fantôplot and rearrange or expand up-on its components. This is why the show manages to be true to its sources de-spite – or is it because of?– adding unwarranted complications to them, such as Fantômas pretending to be deaf under the guise of Dr. Chaleck[16], and letting go of memorable plot points altogether, such as a fully furnished elevator mimick-ing a fully furnished office[17]. As long as the zany turn-of-the-20th-century news ticker keeps on dragging our heroes and antiheroes along at top speed we will be within the confines of an authentic Fantômas story.

Marcel Allain and Pierre Souvestre, by stringing together sensational odds and ends without much forethought, cooked up a grand *modular* narrative sand-box for us all to play with several decades before William S. Burroughs or Julio Cortázar. Thanks to the generous help of friends and mentors, like the infamous Professeur Bissette, whose support and incredible gifts have kept me on the right track, I have mustered the courage to tinker with the Fantôsphere to create my very own fantomastic guignols. May the emperor of crime, the master of fear, the grand torturer, sow this same pestilence within you all.

---

[16] "L'étreinte du diable." *Fantômas*. Created by Claude Chabrol and Juan Luis Buñuel, A2, Gaumont Television, Portman Film, 1980.
[17] Allain, M. & Souvestre, P. *The Corpse Who Kills* (2008).(Candice Black, Trans.). Solar Books. (Original work published 1911)

## Rob Walton

I didn't just read *Asterix* by René Goscinny & Albert Uderzo for the first time. I experienced it. For a kid raised on North American comics discovering *Asterix* was like discovering plutonium. In the very first panel of *Asterix* I beheld the seemingly impossible. *Asterix and the Laurel Wreath* opened on a panorama of Rome itself. Forget Jupiter, Uderzo was my god. As if the perfection of architectural drawing weren't enough, the locations were populated by fully rendered and perfectly delineated characters. This was a fully formed world far beyond the mean streets of New York City where costumed heroes rarely strayed beyond their five square city blocks of Queens. After *Asterix* I couldn't look at comics in the same way. I couldn't think of them in the same way either.

*La Planète Sauvage* (*Fantastic Planet*, 1973), directed by René Laloux and based on a novel by Stefan Wul, is a film that continues to inhabit my imagination after forty years. When it was released in Canada in the mid-1970s, the press campaign naturally drew comparisons and differences to Disney's standard fare. Simply put, *Fantastic Planet* was something new: Animation for an "adult" audience (which included teenagers). Adding to the film's mystique was its art house venue in the long gone second floor theater of Toronto's Cinecity.

Did I "get" *Fantastic Planet* on first viewing? No. I left the theater confused, dazzled and obsessed with its hallucinogenic, dreamlike images. Alan Goragueur's unforgettable soundtrack was on auto-replay in my brain. The ethereal mood of *Fantastic Planet* never left me and I remain under its spell. Its influence still reverberates beneath the surface of my recently published 2023 work [*Bloodlines*] with its mixture of philosophy, mysticism, dreamscapes and chilling horror.

Like many kids in the 1960s, my first exposure to French literature (or any literature) came from reading *Classics Illustrated*. While I enjoyed Jules Verne's fantasies, it was Victor Hugo's Quasimodo that made the most significant impression. No one would dare classify *Notre-Dame de Paris* as genre fiction (except under its more popular English title, perhaps), but hunchbacks have long held their place next to vampires, werewolves and re-animated monsters. I don't know when the trope of the monster-with-a-heart began, but it certainly finds mature expression in Hugo's creation.

Like many other kids, I went on to read the novels the comics were based on and Hugo did not disappoint. The last paragraph of *Notre-Dame de Paris* remains a favorite in all of literature (preserved faithfully in the comic). Hugo pays off subplots in a heartbreaking fashion. Such payoffs are a staple in the classical arts whether in Greek Tragedy, Shakespeare, or Warner Brothers' animation (Think of Wile E. Coyote running into his own previously defective steel wall trap he'd set up at the beginning of "Stop! Look! And Hasten!") It's a lesson I carried into my writing and comics as well. There was no better teacher than Hugo.

# Lance Weiler

My first exposure to French cinema was *Weekend* (1967) by Jean-Luc Godard. It was unlike anything that I had ever seen. I was 17 at the time and I stumbled into a retrospective of 60s cinema at an art house theater in Philadelphia. I was immediately struck by the biting satire, the visceral quality of the storytelling, the late 60s style and the political commentary. *Weekend* introduced me to subtext. That more could be happening beyond what I was seeing or hearing. It felt like a fever dream. The chaos, the color, the sound or the lack of sound. Even the graphical approach to the titling. That was when I first started to become aware of the power of an aesthetic.

Godard would leave an indelible mark on me. *Weekend* was seared into my brain. I became obsessed with his work especially the films that he made in the 1960s. *Breathless* (1960), *Contempt* (1963), *Band of Outsiders* (1964) and *Alphaville* (1965) are all films that I love. Only later would I start recognizing the impact and influence of Godard on my work.

But it wasn't my films as much as it was the way it impacted the art I was making with emerging media. Work that is and will continue to be difficult to define because it defies form. In a sense it's the experimentation and the rejection of linear narratives found in Godard's work that I feel most connected too.

His own affirmation sums it up: "…a film should have a beginning, a middle and an end but not necessarily in that order." That's something that I've adopted within my own work. It brings a freshness and freedom that challenges the convention of what a story can be while also feeling timeless.

For instance, *Weekend* still feels as relevant today as when I first saw it over thirty years ago. The commentary on consumption, alienation, class, and excess still rings true. After seeing *Weekend* for the first time I took a deep dive on Godard. I watched and read anything I could get my hands on. Today I find myself longing for a discovery like the moment I wandered into that screening of *Weekend*. A chance encounter became a portal to a cinematic world, an introduction to the French New Wave.

## Douglas E. Winter

Prominent among my childhood memories are the Saturday nights spent in the care of my grandmother. Those nights were special because Grammie Winter allowed my brother and me to watch *Wrestling at the Chase*, beamed live from across the river in St. Louis on KPLR-TV, and then (often with a ghost host) a horror or science fiction film—a fundamental building block for my lifetime passion for science fiction, *Kaiju* films, adventures with Aztec mummies, Hammer horrors, and more. And it was there, one Saturday afternoon as my grandmother cooked dinner, that I may well have realized there was a distinctly European genre of fantastic film.

Now of course I'd seen, on television and at our only movie theatre, the visions (as imported, if not intended) of Mario Bava and his Italian compatriots, but the lead actors were often American, the settings typically historical, the vibe Anglo-American. On that day, however, squinting into a twelve-inch black-and-white screen poised on a kitchen table, I saw Jesús Franco's quirky spy-fi frolic *Cartes sur table* (1966) under its Anglicized title, *Attack of the Robots*. Showcasing the craggy mug of Eddie Constantine, the seductive charm of Françoise Brion, and the sinister scowl of Fernando Rey, this Spanish-French coproduction tipped me headfirst into an enduring love of Continental genre film.

At university I would discover—on big screens-- y Four Horsemen of French fantastic cinema: Cocteau's *Le Belle et la Bête* (1946), Franju's *Les Yeux Sans Visage* (1960), Resnais and Robbe-Grillet's *Last Year at Marienbad* (1961), and Godard's *Alphaville* (1965). Soon I was devoted to the novels of Robbe-Grillet, who remains among my very favorite writers. I embraced Roman Polańksi's *The Tenant* (1976), and its source novel, Roland Topor's *Le Locataire* (1964).

My ever-expanding trove of paperbacks included Jean Ray and (typically in "year's best" compilations) the weird Lovecraftiana of Eddy C. Bertin.

And that was only the beginning.

## Thomas Yeates

In the early 1970s the world of comics was expanding. There was even a whole store I'd heard of devoted to comics, not just a spinner rack in a drug store or standing shelves in a supermarket. In 1971, I visited that store, it was in San Francisco. Other stores were trying to open up. Comic book conventions were happening, spreading across the nation. It would have been in this environment that I first heard about comics produced in France and Belgium.

French films must have been on television on occasion as I had a sense of them and I'd seen stills of Cocteau's *Beauty and the Beast*. The spectacular Disney film of Jules Verne's *Twenty Thousand Leagues Under the Sea* was a favorite since childhood. We all knew of him and of his many titles like *Off On A Comet* through the *Classics Illustrated* line of comic books. Many years later, when VHS tapes were available, the French thriller *Diabolique* was one of my first.

By 1976, when I attended the Joe Kubert School, I'd been to Europe, seen *Astérix*, Hergé, and some painted comics, but it was Joe Kubert who really turned me on to the French and Belgium comics. One story was that the printing presses in Europe had been destroyed in World War II, so they had all new presses with modern tech making it possible to print comics of much higher quality than in the USA, where we still used worn-out old printers. Joe Kubert had visited Europe, met the artists, seen the huge strides the art of comics had made in Europe, and his enthusiasm was palpable to us his students. Most memorable to me was probably *Arzach* by someone mysteriously named Moebius. Richard Corben was doing fantastic full color comics painted with an airbrush in the underground comics, and there were other examples of real visionaries in U.S. comics but they were the exception. Then the French comics magazine *Métal Hurlant* began appearing in rare sightings. Then *Heavy Metal* started up, and the far-out comics of France and Belgium, were on newsstands in the USA.

# STORIES

*It is the first time one of our authors taps into the universe of Prosper Mérimée (1803-1870), a French writer of the Romantic era, best remembered for his novellas* Carmen *and* Mateo Falcone, *about a Corsican man who kills his son in the name of justice (1829)...*

## Jason Scott Aiken: *The Hunter and the Grubber*

*Corsica, April 6, 1814*

Mateo Falcone set his jaw as he examined the scorched corpse on the charred forest floor. Trying to show the greatest amount of dignity to the deceased as possible, he continuously pushed the thought of succulent cooked beef to the back of his mind. He finally retrieved a gray bandanna from his pocket, tied it behind his ears and unrolled it, covering both his mouth and nose. The face mask only marginally aided in diluting the morbidly appetizing smell.

At his feet lay the remains of Colona, a fellow shepherd. Where his wrists and ankles should have been were iron manacles attached to chains which were fastened to iron spikes that penetrated deep into the ground. The man had no chance of escape when the fire came for him.

Just below the Colona's feet, carved into the forest floor was a crude symbol depicting the head of a goat with large dots interspersed among the outlining lines. Falcone's eyes narrowed, realizing his friend Colona was a casualty of not just one war, but two.

"So, good Orlandi, did you happen to see what fiend did this to our friend?"

Orlandi, who was taller than Falcone, but not as robust, nodded. "Yes, sir, but I was too slow to help Colona. I tried to reach him, but the fire had already spread." Orlandi lifted up his burned palms to Falcone. "There was no getting through that wall of flames, sir."

"Fear not, Orlandi, your honor remains intact. No one will question your efforts, my friend. But I hope you have a description of the assailant."

"Even better, sir, I have a name for you. During the occupation, while you were away, I often saw him spending his time at the tavern. He's about your height, but he's a lean specimen. The dog was even wearing his uniform when he struck the match that ended poor Colona. I heard him laugh while he mocked poor Colona, too. He said, 'You farmers love to burn the forests to improve your soil, I'm just doing my part before we leave this dung heap of an island for good.'"

Falcone gripped his rifle so tightly he thought he felt the wooden stock crack. "What is this bastard's name, Orlandi?"

"His fellow soldiers called him Sergeant Kurtz, but I never learned his full name. He was often seen using his position to take advantage of the local women. I saw him shoot a young son of one woman who tried to extract a vendetta against him. He was merely a boy and stood no chance. Kurtz was quick with his pistol."

"Kurtz, meaning short in stature, or it could even be interpreted as grubber or foot soldier. Well, he certainly has my attention."

"What do you mean, sir?"

Falcone shook his head. "Nothing, Orlandi. It's nothing, my friend. You're aware of the meaning of my name are you not?"

"Yes, sir. Falcone means falcon."

"Indeed it does, but another interpretation is hunter, as this Sergeant Kurtz will soon be made aware—if he isn't already."

"But the British occupation is over, they left the island hours ago once the French infantry came ashore. He's probably out on the open sea and returning home. How do you hope to reach him?"

"Don't worry, Orlandi, *we* have eyes everywhere."

*(Decrypted Correspondence)*

*June 26th, 1816*
*Dear Mr. Hunter,*
    *Grubber spotted at the Carson Estate in Oxfordshire. I took the liberty of sketching his appearance for your reference. Please find it enclosed. He appears to be quite friendly with the Carson family (who, to my knowledge, are not part of our conflict) and is settling in. I've watched him over the last two evenings and he's always the last to turn in. He'll be in your talons if your wings are swift enough.*
    *Kind regards,*

*E.Q.*

*Oxfordshire, August 6, 1816*

Mateo Falcone watched his prey light his tobacco pipe from afar. Even on the darkest of nights his eyes remained peerless. The orange glow brought his mind back to the scene on Corsica over two years ago and he raised up his rifle and sighted it in on Kurtz. The hunter's desire for revenge was still just as potent as the day he had discovered his friend's corpse, but he wasn't going to cowardly assassinate him from afar. He lowered his rifle and decided he would wait. He wanted to speak to him before he killed him. Now he just had to be patient and wait for Kurtz's companions to retire for the evening. So he stayed in position, ever vigilant, ever watchful.

*August 7, 1816*

Shortly after midnight a storm, one of the many during the past year, could be heard in the distance. Kurtz's companions stood up and bid him good night. Falcone watched as he put his feet up on the table and leaned back in his chair staring in the direction of the gathering storm clouds.

Knowing this was his chance, Falcone stood up, adjusted his gray coat, and slung his rifle over his shoulder. He checked his surroundings, there was no one else visible to his keen eyes. So he walked silently and purposefully toward the gardens of the Carson Estate. Although the years had been long, the time it took to close the distance between he and his prey felt even longer. Falcone felt as though he were moving in slow motion right up until the time he stood no more than twenty paces from his prey and announced himself.

"Sergeant Kurtz, I presume?"

Kurtz removed his feet from the table, but kept his hands behind his head. He stood up and faced Falcone, his eyes seemed to twinkle upon seeing him. "Oh, my good man, you must be Mateo Falcone. I've been wanting to meet you for a long time. But the war is over and I'm out of the army, drop the Sergeant. You can call me by my given name Alfred."

"*One* war is over. The other remains ongoing. In either case, we are still enemies."

"Indeed." Kurtz brought his hands out in front of him and removed his gloves. On the back of his right hand was a more detailed illustration of the symbol left on the forest floor in Corsica. A goat's head surrounded by a pattern of stars.

"Very brazen, Kurtz. Do your betters know you flaunt your involvement so openly?"

Kurtz ignored the query and cracked his knuckles. "I was actually hoping to run into you on the island, but you were suspiciously absent during the occupation. Tell me, hunter, just what were you up to?"

"Unlike you, Kurtz, I don't talk so openly about my activities. But needless to say, had I known a dishonorable urchin such as yourself was on my island, I would have returned immediately to dispatch you. Why kill Colona? Especially in that manner? What did he do to you?"

"Nothing, my good man. But we were withdrawing and you had yet to return home. I had to leave you a message. You see, I only volunteered for the

Corsican occupation to have a chance at you, hunter."

"I thought as much, grubber. I've been told that within your organization I'm a highly valued target."

"Oh, you are, but I'm not that concerned with the desires of the higher-ups. You killed someone important to me five years ago in Paris."

Falcone shook his head. "Unfortunately, that doesn't narrow things down a great deal. That was a productive trip. Nevertheless, it appears we have the opportunity to settle this now. Let us do so with honor. I see the pistol on your hip. You may load it at your leisure."

Kurtz smiled. "My pistol is already cocked and loaded."

"As is the rifle over my shoulder."

"It's going to take you longer to bring that long barrel up, hunter. Are you sure about this?"

"A suitable handicap, grubber. It should make things as fair as possible, given my skill."

For a split-second, Falcone could see the specter of doubt cross Kurtz's face, before the man laughed it off.

"So when do we start?"

"When you reach for your pistol. But I must warn you, I don't miss."

Kurtz's hand whipped down at his pistol with precision, but Falcone was just too fast. If anyone were to see the duel from the side, the blurred movement of his Baker rifle barrel would have resembled a quarter of a circle in shape. Just as Kurtz's pistol was clearing the holster, Falcone drilled him squarely in the chest. Kurtz was blown back off his feet and splayed out across the grass, his pistol falling from his grasp.

Falcone spun around at the sound of footsteps. Standing there in a sleeping shirt was a young boy who couldn't have been any more than seven or eight years-old. His handsome features were reminiscent of Kurtz's, but Falcone recognized the boy's eyes immediately. They were dark gray, the exact shade of color as Nicoletta Savoli, the brilliant Italian woman he killed while in Paris. This boy had to be her son. No wonder Kurtz had wanted him dead.

"I don't know how much your father told you, but consider this advice. Stay with the Carsons for as long as they'll have you. You'll have a better life than your father did. Than I do. Than any of *us* do."

The boy looked at Falcone then over at the corpse of his father. "No! Papa! Someone help!"

Falcone cursed himself for being sentimental, he ran past the boy and darted for the woods bordering the estate. While running he could hear the grounds coming to life and it wasn't long before he heard the sound of pursuing horses. While he was fast, his legs were short and he couldn't eat up the distance like a person of greater stature could. It wouldn't be long before they were on him. Out of the corner of his right eye, he spotted movement near a tree and thought he had been discovered. He reached for his knife at his belt before a young woman emerged from the darkness.

"Hunter, come! Come!" The young woman beckoned him.

Seeing no other choice, Falcone took her outstretched hand and she led him into the forest. She moved through the trees as though she was a creature of the woods; the darkness did not seem to bother her in the slightest. It wasn't long before the sounds of the approaching men faded off into the distance.

The woman slowed her pace and whispered, "We're almost there, hunter. A derelict foraging hut is just ahead. No one associated with the Carsons should be aware of it. We can take refuge there until morning."

The woman was true to her word, the hut appeared to be ancient and in disrepair. Falcone thought it better shelter than nothing as the storm finally appeared. As rain pummeled down on them, the two crawled on their hands and knees through what was left of the entrance.

They moved around pieces of broken furniture within then sat upright and put their backs against the hut walls to rest.

"So, my good woman, do you plan on telling me your name?"

"Elizabeth Quatermain, sir, *née* Clarke, of Kane's line, at your service."

"Kane—meaning *the* Kane, the warrior?"

"A bastard line, sir, but yes. He's my ancestor. But I like to think of myself as more of a healer these days. I spend most of my time at the church tending to the sick and impoverished."

"A noble undertaking as I've ever heard. You may not carry a sword or pistol, but trust me, you do all your ancestors proud young lady."

"I'm not so young anymore, hunter. I have three sons already. Although I've been ordered to conceive a fourth. Tonight."

Falcone was taken aback by this. "Are you serious? They want us to..."

"Yes. I understand that you have been blessed with a daughter, but they want another male with your talents. Now if you don't mind, we'd better get to it. I take it I'm acceptable?"

"Why, yes, but my wife and I are already planning on having more children. This is so sudden."

"I've come to find that life always is, hunter."

*(Decrypted Correspondence)*

*January 14, 1835*
*Monsieur Hunter,*

*The higher-ups have dispatched me to the Dark Continent where I've taken up the guise of an arrogant Bonapartist who enjoys the spirits. As part of my duties, I've been tutoring young A.Q. He's inherited your peerless eyesight and prodigious marksmanship, as well as the cleverness and kindness of his late mother. But I'm afraid the latter trait makes him entirely unsuitable to carry on in your footsteps as our organization's hunter.*

*You see, for such a small young man, his heart is just far too large.*
*All the best and good hunting,*

*Monsieur Leblanc*

*It is well known that the Surrealists—an artistic movement created in 1917 by Guillaume Apollinaire—were fond of outrageous, amoral, larger-than-life characters such as Fantômas or the Mysterious Dr. Cornelius. In the story that follows, Tim Newton Anderson brings them into the universe of the Shadowmen...*

## Tim Newton Anderson: *The Exquisite Corpse*

*Paris, 1924*

"Mandrin is all very well, but he is not Fantômas or even a Vampire. I want exquisite horror mixed with the fantastic. I want a Maldoror or Melmoth. I want the savage beauty of a straight razor to the eyeball or the transgressive elegance of a dead god," said André Breton.

The surrealists were returning from the cinema for a nightcap at *Les Deux Magots* to discuss the film they had just seen and plan for the opening of their Surrealist Research Bureau the next day. The cobbled side streets of the Rive Gauche were slick with rain and petrol spills made rainbows beneath their feet. Above their heads the rain sparkled in the streetlights.

As they turned into the Rue Saint Benoit, they saw their rivals sitting outside the Café de Flore. Yvan Goll was talking animatedly with Tristan Tzara, Pierre Albert-Birot and Francois Picabia. Despite the sound-deadening effect of the rain, Goll looked around when he heard Breton's voice and leapt to his feet.

"How dare you call yourself Surrealists," he yelled. "You are not worthy to lick the boots of Apollinaire, much less seek to take forward his legacy."

"Guillaume was a friend and a mentor," replied Breton. "He bestowed the mantle of surrealism on my shoulders. We will trounce any imposters with our art and actions, and if necessary, with our fists."

He started to run towards the Café de Flore, and, after a second, Louis Aragon, Antonin Artaud. Paul Eluard and Robert St Onge raced in his footsteps, splashing water from the pavement as they charged.

It was not the most elegant display of pugilism the Boulevard Saint-Germain had ever seen. Neither group included seasoned fighters, or even expert brawlers in their number, but all had had some training due to their military service and all were fired up with passion.

Breton faced off against Goll and took a stance he had seen Arthur Cravan adopt. His punches had more power than accuracy, but they landed more often than Goll's counter attacks. The friends of both parties decided on less conventional tactics and grabbed chairs and bottles from the tables, swinging wildly with their improvised weapons. Here too, a lack of technique and experience meant the blows that did land did little real damage, although Artaud's poor health meant that even glancing impacts jarred his body. But no matter what injuries they suffered, both groups were fighting for their beliefs and their loyalty to their friends, and would not fall back from the engagement.

By now, a crowd had gathered, unfurling umbrellas when they couldn't crowd under the café's canopy. Most had no idea who the brawlers were, or why they were fighting, but arbitrarily picked a side to cheer, and one bystander, who still wore the uniform of the Parisian Apaches, started taking bets on who would win. Every Parisian loved the Grand-Guignol and this was good free entertainment.

The fight ended when Breton knocked Goll to the ground with a blow to the nose that spurted blood and left him lying winded in a puddle.

"Withdraw your manifesto, and acknowledge we are the true Surrealists," said Breton, still holding his fists ready to resume the fight.

"Never," said Goll. "We are the first and only legitimate Surrealist group. This fight changes nothing."

"Wait until tomorrow," said Breton. "You will see what true Surrealists do. I may be willing to accept some of your members into our movement, but you are dead to me. Tomorrow belongs to me."

Albert-Birot and Picabia had also been knocked to the ground, but the others had stopped fighting when Goll was felled. The three collapsed poets pushed themselves back to their feet and Goll's group slunk off into the night. Aragon, Artaud and St Onge slapped each other on the back and walked out of the rain onto the *Magots'* terrace to order drinks from the waiter who had been cheering them on a few seconds before. Breton was still standing in the downpour watching his rivals retreat. He knew this was just one skirmish in the battle for acceptance, but he had his plan of action and knew he would prevail. He had already started drafting his own manifesto, and tomorrow the Bureau would open to the world.

Belphegor had entered the Charles X rooms in the Louvre in disguise. Breaking in to steal the golden scapula sought by the alchemists would not be easy. Security had been ramped up during the invasion of Paris by visitors to the Olympic Games in the summer, and had not gone back to the previously relaxed standards. Truth be told, the days when someone could sneak in and steal the *Mona Lisa* were long in the past. There was no chance of grabbing the prize during the day, and the extra locks that had been fitted and additional guards meant night would also be tricky. The scapula was displayed in a glass case in the center of the first room in plain sight from the guard station.

Belphegor had already planned a way of staying in the museum after the doors closed for the night, having scoped out a hiding place in a cleaning cupboard on the same floor, but there would have to be a distraction to get the guards out of the way for the theft and the getaway.

As Belphegor planned the heist, they noticed an additional problem. On the far side of the room Leo Saint Clair, a.k.a. the Nyctalope, had just entered the exhibition.

Like many others across the globe, Belphegor had heard of the crime fighter. His exploits had been widely covered in the world's press, and his associates presented as formidable a challenge as the man himself. Belphegor wondered if he knew the miraculous properties of the rare meteoric gold that had been used in the creation of the scapula. The combination of radiation and otherworldly bacteria in the meteorite that had created the Kamil Crater had given special powers to the line of Pharaohs which had unified Egypt and made them seen godlike to their subjects. Little wonder they worshipped the sun after the gold that had fallen from the sky boosted their physical and mental abilities.

Belphegor had learned about meteoric gold from the Black Coats who had been trying to steal a critical mass of the metal for 100 years. Belphegor had also heard rumors that a meteor had also been responsible for the creation of the vampire race and that Edison had used it as a source of power for the android Eve he had created.

The Nyctalope also had his eyes on the scapula, although he was simultaneously scanning the room noticing the number of attractive women who were browsing the items on display. He was well aware of the powers of the meteoric gold, or Radiant-Z as his father had called it, from personal experience. He knew what it could do in the wrong hands. The Martians had used its radioactive properties extensively and he had used his adventures in Africa and Asia to check for meteor strikes to prevent the gold to be taken by malefactors.

As well as the colossal statues and carvings and household items from Ancient Egypt, there was jewelry made from the fused glass found at meteor sites which supported the theory they had benefitted from the power found there.

Across the room a young woman was looking intently at one of the cases of jewels. Leo walked over and introduced himself.

"They are beautiful," he said. "As are you."

She smiled and brushed her blonde hair back from her face. Leo loved his wife, but things had been difficult between them after the birth of their second child. He was sure Laurence would understand that a man such as himself could not be bound down to a single woman, although he had been careful to keep his affairs from her. There was no point in causing her unnecessary suffering.

"They are beautiful," the woman said. "Do you know much about them?"

"The glass is of a type only used in Egypt," he replied. He had used his full name in introducing himself and was surprised she had not associated it with his identity as one of mankind's greatest heroes. "Perhaps you would join me for a drink and we could discuss it further?"

"I'm afraid I already have an appointment," she said. "However, if you would like to take my card, perhaps we could meet up another time?"

The card said that she was Simone Desroches and was an actress and a film-maker. That made her even more interesting. Leo was sure that a serial based on his exploits would be a major success, like those based on other contemporary heroes and villains, and he had already had discussions with Louis Feuillade about the possibility.

Simone excused herself and walked over to one of the other exhibits. Leo shrugged and brought his concentration back to the task in hand. Part of his unique powers came from the meteoric gold powering his artificial heart. He thought of himself as a trusting person, but he was worried that others may have discovered the secret and he had heard rumors that there were villains intent on collecting the gold. This scapula was one of the most obvious sources and he wanted to make sure its security was watertight. It looked safe, but perhaps he needed to try and stage a theft himself to test how hard it would be to steal it.

He left the room, intending to talk to the head of security for the Louvre and tell them of his plan. They should be grateful. If he could break in, then so could others.

Belphegor watched as the Nyctalope left the exhibition. His conversation had revealed little of the reason for his visit and it would be worrying if he was aware of Belphegor's plans. If so, then something was needed to neutralize that threat. It may also be too dangerous to proceed with the initial plan for concealment.

André Breton was almost pleased by the turnout at the opening of the Surrealist Research Centre. There were not enough of the general public for his liking, but at least there were plenty of journalists in attendance, and he was sure that would lead to more people coming along and detailing their dreams. He and his friends had developed a range of techniques for making the unconscious immanent in their writing, but to truly bring about the surrealist revolution, the whole world had to be awakened. The bourgeois were trapped inside social norms and only breaking their minds free could affect a similar transformation in society. This was not just art for art's sake.

Breton recognized many of the press corps present. He was surprised to see Feéix Fénéon, as he regarded him as hopelessly out of touch with modern movements in art. He was also surprised to see a number of journalists he associated with crime reporting rather than art, like Jacques Bellegarde, Phillipe Roget, Jerôme Fandor, Phillipe Guérande, and Joseph Joséphin. There were other artistic movements Breton considered a crime against good taste, but surely not his own. He had tried to talk to Fandor about the adventures he had had chasing Fantômas, but the journalist disliked Breton's adulation of the criminal and complained about inaccuracies in the stories and films about him.

As well as the press, there were other attendees he recognized, like his friends Adrienne Monner and Sylvia Beach. However, there was an attractive woman near the entrance talking to Robert St Onge whom he did not know, but would very much like to. She looked too fashionable to be an artist. but could be a wealthy collector, or even a publisher. Either was good.

Breton left Aragon and Eluard to deal with the media and walked across to the door to interrupt the young poet's conversation.

"I hope my colleague has been explaining the importance of our work here," he said. "We aim to capture the dreams of the city and transform them into art."

The young woman introduced herself as Simone Desroches.

"Surely the dreams of the masses are too mundane to make art," she said. "I have found even the most interesting people become boring when they try and tell you a fascinating dream they had. We all share the same boring round of flying, being naked in public, or being frozen to the spot."

"But there is gold among the chaff," said Breton. "Freud tells us what treasures lie buried in our minds, and his colleague Jung suggests we all share a collective unconscious."

"Mademoiselle Desroches would be interested in making dreams real," said St Onge. "She works for the cinema."

Breton was even more interested now.

"I agree, films can show us the splendid monsters that are inside all of us," he said. "My writing can only reach a small, although discerning, percentage of the population, but a film could bring our vision to all."

"Precisely why I am here," said Simone. "I adored the vision of René Clair's Dadaist *Entr'acte* with its vistas of a mysteriously empty Paris. I had an idea which you may be interested in helping me realize."

"And would we get the credit for the collaboration?" asked Breton.

"Absolutely," said Simone. "I would want everyone to know your part in the enterprise."

"Perhaps we could discuss this further over a meal," said Breton. "It sounds fascinating."

Robert St Onge was having a coffee outside the *Deux Magots* on the evening after the launch of the Bureau. Although he believed in Surrealism with all of his heart, he was getting slightly frustrated with Breton's iron grip on its direction. It wasn't so much a disagreement about what Breton wanted, more that you were only allowed to contribute if it matched his vision.

Robert would have liked to contribute to the manifesto that was being prepared, but felt he was not fully accepted into the inner circle. He believed that Surrealism was for all and shared Breton's wish for a bomb that would turn the world into a miraculous place. Instead, he had reconciled himself to seeing the marvelous in the mundane.

As he sipped his café, a man came over and asked if he could share the table. He had the most extraordinary eyes Robert had ever seen: bright golden with an inner light. He was tall and muscled and looked out of place amongst the bourgeois families and impoverished artists who made up the rest of the clientele. He looked like a walking statue, Rodin's rather than the Chinese ones that adorned the cafe.

"I hope you don't mind," the man said, introducing himself as Leo Saint-Clair.

"Not at all," said Robert. "Glad to have the company."

He noticed the man was staring over at the Café de Flore, where Breton was talking with Simone Desroches. The Surrealist leader had given instructions to the others to give him and the actress some privacy.

"She is a beautiful woman," Robert said. "And by all accounts a very talented one."

"I'm sorry," said Saint-Clair. "I was hoping to have dinner with her myself but I see she has another companion."

"André can be charming when he wants to be," said Robert. "And many find his intensity attractive. Although you seem quite intense, yourself."

"I am primarily focused on my mission in Paris," Saint-Clair replied. "I believe there is about to be a theft at the Louvre and I am determined to thwart it."

"You are a detective, then?" Robert asked.

"No detectives could do what I do," said Saint-Clair. "You wouldn't believe the things I have seen and done."

"You will find I have an open mind and a vivid imagination," Robert replied. "I am a surrealist and our creed is that the inner and outer worlds are more startling, beautiful and terrible than most people imagine. I am surprised to hear you suggest the Louvre may be plundered. Surely security there is impregnable."

"There are many criminal geniuses in the world and nothing is beyond their twisted ambition. Lucifer. Zigomar. Satanas. Not to mention all the anarchists and communists who want to overturn the world's governments."

*I hope he never mentions that to Breton if they meet*, thought Robert. Breton was almost as passionate about communism as he was about Surrealism.

"Personally, I wouldn't mind if a lot of the work on display in the Louvre vanished to free us from the dead weight of the past," Robert said. "Although we have a lot to learn from African and Chinese art."

Saint-Clair's look told Robert he didn't share his passion for other cultures.

"If you are guarding the treasures of the Louvre, what are you doing here?" Robert asked.

Saint-Clair tuned and stared at St Onge.

"Gathering intelligence," he replied. "None of the usual suspects seem to be involved. The Vampires have been crushed. Fantômas has disappeared. Countess Cagliostro is believed to be dead. And Lupin has no need for meteoric gold. There must be a new evil genius at work."

Robert was confused and excited in equal parts. This man was discussing these fabulous criminals Robert only knew from lurid press articles and unauthorized biopic films about their exploits as if he knew them personally. He wanted to question the man more but Saint-Clair stood up and strode off without saying good-bye.

Robert looked across at the neighboring café and saw that Simone had also left and Breton was walking across to join him.

"I have the most marvelous idea," he said as he sat down. "Simone has access to *Ayahuaca*, a potion which gives people fantastic visions. Tomorrow, we will introduce it into the City's water supply. All of Paris will see the world the way we do. How can anyone resist joining our movement when they also see the world full of luminous wonder? Even Fantômas never dreamed of such an outrageous plan!"

"Is it safe?" asked St Onge.

"Aragon and I will try the potion for ourselves first," Breton said. "We will be pioneers—psychonauts if you will—the forerunners of the magical."

"If you think it is safe, I will join you," said Robert. "There will certainly be danger from the act, and you will need one person with a clear head to carry it off."

Breton did not look convinced, but reluctantly agreed. It was an opportunity too great to squander.

Belphegor had seen the Nyctalope sitting at the café table and thought it a good opportunity to try out the new plan of attack at the Louvre. The initial scheme had involved hiding inside at closing time, but the thief had then discovered one of the security guards had money problems and was amenable to bribery. At a pre-arranged signal, he was to leave a window unlocked on the ground floor while on his rounds, and it was an easy matter to slip inside, covered in black clothes and a specially designed mask, and ascend to the Charles X gallery. The guard had also been happy to detail the patrol schedule so Belphegor could get there without being seen.

The cabinet containing the scapula was alarmed, but Belphegor was an expert in electricity and set to bypassing the system. A simple cut of the cord would set off the alarm as much as breaking the glass. Belphegor had planned on using an electromagnetic pulse to disable all of the building's systems but it was not yet complete and this was too good an opportunity to miss. A bull's eye lantern was perfect for finding the right display without being seen by outside observers.

Belphegor had just taken a glass cutter from a bag of tools when there was a noise from behind.

"I was expecting a gang," said the Nyctalope. "You must be especially bold to attempt this on your own."

Belphegor had no illusions about who would win in a fight and threw the lantern at the crime-fighter. It may do little physical damage but would provide enough time to flee. The criminal had memorized an escape route and raced off in the darkness.

To the thief's surprise, the Nyctalope was equally unfazed by the darkness and chased at an amazing speed. Belphegor knew a large statue stood to the left and grabbed and pulled it with a burst of strength born from desperation. The thief's shoulders and biceps sent a burst of agony to the brain, but it wobbled and then toppled on top of Saint-Clair. To Belphegor's surprise, the Nyctalope seemed hardly stunned, although it slowed him down enough for the criminal to make an escape into the next gallery.

Saint-Clair was surprised when he entered the next section—the thief was nowhere to be seen. His enhanced vision scanned the room but could find no trace of the intruder. Two doors led off the area, but when he looked through both, there was no sign. He decided to go to the nearest guard post and instigate a thorough search.

After five minutes, Belphegor decided it was safe to push open the lid of the sarcophagus used as a hiding place. It was imperative to get back to the open window and escape immediately. The theft would have to wait until the next night when the diversion would be in place. In the meantime. something had to be done about the Nyctalope.

As he walked across Paris the next day, Robert St Onge was glad he had declined the offer of trying the drug. He had seen Breton and Aragon when they were drunk and this had made them even more unmanageable. The *Ayahuaca* was contained in a wooden beer barrel which they were pushing through the streets in a painter's cart, but Breton and Aragon would regularly let go of the handles and wander off to pursue some errant vision. So far, the barrel had almost toppled three times into the street.

At one point, St Onge had bribed a street urchin to stand guard over it while he dragged Aragon out of an arcade where he was ranting about the beauty of the commonplace. A window full of stamps was full of exquisite portraits of surrealist heroes and a stuffed fish had transformed into a luminous white whale, which Aragon was convinced was his spirit animal.

Breton, meanwhile, was staring with a frightening intensity at every woman who passed. As the women crossed the road in fear, he shouted after them that they were his muse and must become his mistress. He claimed each head was surrounded by an orb of glowing gold and their features had all morphed into those of his ideal woman. Robert was worried their antics would draw the attention of the gendarmerie and get them all arrested.

What should have been a twenty-minute walk to the Parc des Buttes-Chaumont took over an hour. Dusk was falling and Robert tried to steer his comrades and the cart away from the promenading families and lovers.

"Look at the temple over the lake," said Breton. He was transfixed. "It is the playground of the gods. I can see Athena and Apollo dancing in the last rays of the sun, and hear the music of Pan and Orpheus wafting through the air on the perfume of the plants. The trees are gyrating in sympathy and waving their branches to conduct the symphony."

"Do not look there," said Aragon. "See the waterfall and the grottos. The dead are rising, clawing their way through decades of detritus to reclaim their world. The hanged man of the Tarot has sacrificed himself for our sins even more than Jesus. This world now belongs to the crucified thieves and not some biblical fraud."

Robert was exasperated.

"Have you two forgotten why we are here?" he asked. "I need help tipping this barrel into the river so it can enter the water supply. We are supposed to be creating a masterpiece of surrealist film as the drugged Parisians fill the streets. I'm sure no film-maker will ever want to work with us again if we mess this up. This is supposed to be the ultimate surrealist act, not a day outing for your minds."

Breton seemed to rouse himself enough to pay attention to the young poet, although his eyes were still only partly focused.

"The water of life," he exclaimed. "The water of new life. The holiest of communions—the transubstantiation of the mind. We must act!"

He spun round on his heel, but stumbled and continued spinning like a wheel as he tried to regain his balance. The spiraling motion across the grass carried him across to the cart which he knocked over, spilling out the barrel. The barrel with the drug-infused water started rolling down the grassy bank towards the river.

"Stop it, Louis," shouted St Onge. "If it reaches the water, it will just float off."

To Robert's surprise, Aragon drew a bull-nosed pistol from his coat pocket and fired it at the barrel, striking it three times. It did nothing to stop the trundle towards the water, but when it fell in, liquid started gurgling from the newly-acquired holes and left a rainbow trail like gasoline as it was borne along with the current.

Robert St Onge spun his head from side to side and spotted a park-keeper running towards them. It was always the plan to claim credit for the results of their actions, but as a result of opening up minds through their art, not poisoning Paris' water supply. He grabbed Aragon by the arm and started dragging him away. It was more important to get him to safety as he was the one with the gun and, in his present state of mind, there was no telling what he might do with it. Thankfully, Aragon complied like a child being led by its mother and happily skipped along as St Onge led him away from the guard.

Robert looked over to see what was happening with the barrel. It was almost around the bend in the river and had sunk well into the water. The liquid inside must be being displaced with water from the river. It would not sink completely but at least it was less obviously visible.

The getaway was made even easier because Breton ran over to the park keeper and embraced him warmly, almost tipping both of them onto the grass.

"My brother," he exclaimed. He gave the man a long kiss on the lips. Robert vowed never to mention this, given his leader's hatred of homosexuality. "I love you. You are a rainbow come to life. Light shines from your pores."

The man was stunned and stood like a statue as Andre turned and danced off across the grass. Robert hoped Breton would make it home safely as shepherding Aragon to safety would be enough of a challenge. At least, they had succeeded in their mission.

The Nyctalope stood behind a sarcophagus, scanning the room. He had frightened off the thief the previous evening, but knew he would be back. This was no common villain seeking some artworks they could sell to wealthy collectors. He was after a very specific prize because of its unique properties rather than its monetary value. The police could deal with the common criminal, while his unique talents were saved for the uncommon. The mad megalomaniacs and scientific geniuses intent on upending the social order he had dedicated his life to upholding. Surely, this crook was one of those.

He had made sure the lights were switched off so that his unique night vision would provide the advantage. It had come at a considerable cost, but as Nietzsche said, whatever does not destroy us makes us stronger. It was incumbent on the superman to protect society.

The villain must have been wearing soft-soled shoes as he had no warning of his approach before a figure appeared in the doorway. Even with his super-sight, it was hard to make out details as they were clothed completely in black. The painted mask which obscured their face looked like the visage of a demon or pagan god. He would wait until they had approached the cabinet before pouncing as he did not want to miss this opportunity to capture him.

"You can come out into the open if you like," said the figure. "That is, if you can." There was a device in the thief's hand instead of a gun and he flicked a switch on the top. The Nyctalope heard a soft buzzing and felt a vibration in his chest. Then his heart seemed to stop and he slumped to the floor.

"It's a broadcast power device I developed from a prototype by Tesla," said the thief. "I installed it this afternoon, dressed as a janitor. The Louvre worries a lot less about people bringing things in than taking things out. I connected it to the golden scapula as a power source. It sends a powerful electromagnetic pulse which shuts down any electrical devices.—like your artificial heart."

"You murderer," exclaimed Saint-Clair.

"Not necessarily," the thief replied. "I know you have been trained in the eastern arts and if you use them, you can slow down your bodily functions and go in a fugue state like a yogi. You should be able to preserve your life long enough for the custodians to come and switch off the machine."

"But you cannot take the scapula to which it is connected without running the risk of releasing me," said Saint-Clair.

"Very true," replied the thief, taking off her mask to expose the head of a young woman. It was Simone Desroches. "But I've decided I no longer require it. To become Belphegor, the master criminal, what I need is money. Lots of it. Because for a woman, money is independence. Playing at being weak—a muse or a mistress—can be fun, but only if you have a choice. I quite liked Simone because she had some freedom, but you and that fool Breton would have been happier if she had less."

The Nyctalope was conflicted between saving himself and bringing Belphegor to justice. He tried to force his unwilling arms to reach out and draw his gun from his belt. Belphegor watched him struggle and when he finally drew his weapon, she stepped over and lifted it from his fingers, throwing it across the room. She then walked back to the display cabinet and lifted a large bag from behind it.

"Have a fun night, and good luck," she said. "I'm now about to loot as much ordinary gold and jewels as I can before the guards make their round. When I overheard them earlier, they said they would skip this section as it was safe in your hands. In the future, always have a backup plan."

Belphegor gave an ironic bow and walked out of the gallery. Saint-Clair tried to shout, but did not have the energy to fill his lungs properly. What was important now was survival, and he fought to quiet his mind and body and put himself in a trance.

Robert St Onge had been at the Surrealist Research Center for two hours when André Breton arrived, looking tired and emotional.

"I was expecting the Center to be full of people detailing their electric dreams," he said. "A cataclysmic chaos. Surely their visions were glorious enough to want to share with the world?"

"About that," said Robert, smiling. "Feel free to throw me out of the movement, but I couldn't do it. The sort of visions we share are not for everyone. I substituted a different substance in the barrel. It was that film-maker who gave me the idea based on *Entr'acte*."

He picked up a newspaper and showed it to Breton. The front page trumpeted a story about a mass outbreak of food poisoning which had emptied the city's streets.

"Not actually poison," Robert said. "Just a strong laxative. If we were not to expose them to wonder, at least, we could purge them of their bourgeois tastes and refresh their palettes for more refined fare."

"And you believe we should be associated with the toilet in the mind of the public?" asked Breton.

"As your hero Jarry would say: *Merdre*."

*The exploits of Chevalier Bruno Coqdor (and his pet pstor Râx) by Maurice Limat was one of the most popular space opera series published by Editions Fleuve Noir between 1964 and 1987, comprising nearly 50 volumes. In 2007-09, the undersigned plotted a sequel trilogy for our French sister imprint Rivière Blanche, excellently scripted by Jean-Michel Archaimbault, himself a noted French author. For this last volume of* Tales of the Shadowmen, *it seemed appropriate to ask Jean-Michel to write a story (again based on an idea by Yours Truly) featuring a crossover between the indomitable Chevalier and E.E. "Doc" Snith's* Skylark, *a series also published in France by Rivière Blanche in a translation edited by Jean-Michel...*

## Jean-Michel Archaimbault: *When Worlds Collide*

### (based on an idea by Jean-Marc Lofficier)

### The 22$^{nd}$ Century

The spherical ship emerged from total darkness into a dim explosion of white light. Its single passenger couldn't believe his eyes when he saw the vast galaxy that lay ahead of him, and towards which his ship was now hurtling.

"The Milky Way! So the Masters of the Island have sent me home after all?"

Had the Tyrants of Andromeda used the AKKA weapon or a terrifying disruptor to break the boundaries of space-time? That question would remain, for the moment, unanswered. Nor was it possible to estimate the duration of his journey.

But a spirit as strong, as determined, combative and devious as that of the newcomer would never give in to surprise, worry or discouragement. Pragmatism, a thirst for action and opportunism always prevailed in him. Now that he was back, he had gained a different perspective. All he had to do was adapt his plans.

Beneath the Asgard crater of Callisto lay the High Security Internment Center of the Martervenux federation—its most sophisticated and inviolable prison. The inmates locked up in its force-field cells embodied the quintessence of criminality; all intelligent species and all categories of crime combined.

The individual registered there as INFER-XBO-125 might have looked like an Earthman of European origin, but he was at least two hundred years-old, now that the 22nd century was coming to a close. His manners, his behavior and many of his attitudes were dated, but his scientific, technological and astronautical knowledge had impressed even the most eminent scientists who had questioned him since his incredible capture.

INFER-XBO-125 had appeared out of nowhere, unknown to all Marterve-nux and alien databases. In just a few months, aboard his seemingly invulnerable and elusive spaceship, he had left a trail of evil deeds throughout the galaxy. The media had nicknamed him the "Black Bird" and he would surely go down in history as the most dangerous pirate of all time.

Interpol/Interplan had used up all its resources, energy, and motivation in a futile chase to apprehend him. Many agents, under the direct command of Director Robin Muscat himself, had been lost or driven mad. To add insult to injury, the Black Bird also possessed psychic powers.

Only one man had the ability to stop him: Chevalier Bruno Coqdor, the green-eyed lawman with his own array of superhuman mental powers. And he had succeeded brilliantly, after one of the most frenetic, hallucinatory and perilous adventures of his already long and proud career. Thanks to him and his faithful *pstor* Râx, the bat-bulldog from far-off planet Dzô, an inconceivable catastrophe had been averted *in extremis*.

"We'll never know how this devil of a man learned of the existence of our captive chronon and what prompted him to want to get his hands on it! I can only imagine what he might have done with it, had you not caught him in time, Bruno!"

That anguished comment was made by Dr. Stewe, the keeper of the unfathomable Zero Particle, stored in a ten-dimensional Pyrian box, the only thing capable of containing that time-annihilating grain of nothingness. Still, it shed no light on the Black Bird's plan. But in the end, it was enough that the chronon had been recovered. The universe was safe again.

During his few weeks on Callisto, INFER-XBO-125 had agreed to explain the most recent events. His ship had initially resurfaced near the perigalactic cluster M79-PG, on the opposite side of the Milky Way from the Sol System. It had been transported there by the mysterious interdimensional beam known as the "Great White Beam." It had traversed that obscure, impenetrable void located at the edge of the space-time continuum, where parallel, higher and lower universes met. The Masters of Andromeda had clearly known how to get rid of undesirables! But *which* Andromeda?

Often, the man's heavy-lidded eyes, framed in an austere, dark face with jet-black hair and beard, appeared veiled in eternal regret and unfathomable bitterness. *I won't tell them why I needed the Zero Particle!* he thought. *To change the past, resurrect the woman I loved... To become myself again... This aborted dream is mine alone!*

The multiversal red notice had arrived on Interpol-Interplan's encrypted terminal via the channel of the "Small White Beam," now domesticated by the Martervenux' best scientists. Very few were ever received. But if a criminal wanted elsewhere was caught there, a transdimensional gateway in a special

Callisto bunker could be activated to send him home as soon as contact was established.

A contingent of armed guards escorted Chevalier Bruno Coqdor, Râx and INFER-XBO-125 through the prison complex. As soon as they entered the small hypogeum housing the gateway, the interdimensional interface was activated and began shimmering in hypnotic undulations.

Silently, the Chevalier stared at the man dressed in an old-fashioned and yet technologically advanced spacesuit who had just emerged from the gate. Next to him, Black Bird froze.

"Richard Seaton!" he exclaimed. "So it was you who warned these people..."

"Who else could have done it, Blackie," replied the other man. "You know that I've never stopped following you, wherever you are in space, time, or dimensions. My condolences, by the way, for Stephanie's untimely death... You certainly made amends before you left, but that doesn't mean I can trust you blindly and forever... The proof is in what you did here!"

Dr. Marc C. DuQuesne had lost yet another game, and, with this final defeat, had given up all hope.

"We could have turned a blind eye," Seaton continued, "and not tried to get you back, but you would have continued to enjoy yourself to your dark heart's content at the expense of the good folks of this universe. Now that they've caught you, you're our responsibility. So..."

At these words, DuQuesne turned pale and glared at Coqdor's pet.

"And I would have gotten away with it too, if it weren't for your meddling *pstor*!" he swore.

Stroking Râx's head, the Chevalier burst out laughing.

"To have your behind bitten by a *pstor* is indeed not very glorious. And quite painful too..."

For a moment, Seaton joined in the laughter. Then he turned towards DuQuesne.

"If you hate monsters, Blackie, come and help Kinnison and I fight a real green one, on a universal scale..."

"Are the Chlorans back?"

"Of course not! But someone has decided to bottle up our major cities. This new foe is at least as vicious as you are."

"The more the merrier," quipped Blackie. "Will you be joining us, Chevalier, with your rabid beast? Who knows, its jaws might come in a handy..."

Coqdor smiled, but declined the invitation. Other galaxy-spanning missions awaited. The farewells were brief, but courteous. Seaton crossed the gateway first; and in Marc C. Duquesne went.

*Translated by Jean-Marc & Randy Lofficier.*

*With his usual panache, Matthew Baugh brings together the cosmic horrors of H.P. Lovecraft and the more mundane, but equally terrifying, bloody carnage of World War I...*

## Matthew Baugh: *The Staffel From Yuggoth*

### (from an idea by Greg Gick)

*France, The Western Front, 1917*

Biggles squinted into the rising sun as his Sopwith Camel soared over the lush French farmland. He knew he was heading east. Aside from that, he didn't have a clue where he was. His dawn patrol squadron had tangled with an exceptionally tough pack of Heinies. The Fokkers had all been piloted by aces, and he thought he'd identified the aircraft of von Stalhein, Stachel, and Kessler. The only one he could be sure of was Heinrich von Fruelich. The baron had gotten on his tail, and Biggles had only shaken him after a long series of twists and turns had carried him miles off course. Now, he was lost and getting low on fuel. He only hoped that Algy and the rest of the squadron had fared better and were safely headed home.

Lost or not, he knew that continuing west would only take him into German territory. He brought the Camel around in a wide turn. As he did, he spotted the flash of guns to the northwest. He pulled out a spyglass and placed it to his eye. He could see planes dogfighting in the reddish light, and his heart pounded faster. Could that be the rest of the 287, still dealing with the Heinies? Either way, his duty was clear; he turned his ship toward the conflict and made best speed. Drawing closer, Biggles saw that the besieged aircraft were SPADs, meaning it must be an American squadron. The German planes were strange, though; small biplanes, quicker and more agile than anything he'd seen.

The Yanks were showing some splendid flying, but it wasn't helping. The Heinies could climb faster, turn tighter, and outperform any maneuver they tried. Biggles cut north until he had the rising sun at his back, then swooped in to rescue a SPAD desperately trying to shake one of the little planes. He swooped down on them, catching the Heinie by surprise and stitching a line of holes down the fuselage with his twin Vickers guns.

The little plane nosed up, climbing out of his line of fire with impossible quickness. Biggles pulled back on the stick for all he was worth but couldn't match his foe. The little plane climbed almost vertically. As it approached the stall point, it arched back into an Immelman turn and rolled to bring Biggles into its sights. Tracer rounds flared past him, perforating his wings. Biggles threw his stick left into a wingover that turned him 180 degrees and out of danger. It would have shaken most pursuers, but the little plane was on his tail a moment later.

Biggles banked into a circling turn, and the little craft matched him. There was no way for him to turn tightly enough to shake this little devil of a pilot. Fortunately, as if reading his mind, the Yank pilot joined the circle chase in a Lufbery. As the Heinie lined up Biggles in his sights, he put himself in the American's line of fire. The pair of Vickers opened up, and the mysterious plane began to trail smoke. Its engine sputtered to a stop a moment later, and it fell like a broken kite.

The Yank gave a thumbs up, and Biggles returned the gesture with a grin. Turning to the control panel, he saw that his tank was almost empty. One of the German's rounds must have punctured his petrol tank. He signaled the American that he was heading down and saw the pilot signal understanding.

A field left fallow gave him a safe landing strip, and as he climbed out, he saw the SPAD touch down behind him. It rolled to a stop as he climbed out and looked his plane over. A moment later, the Yank doffed helmet and goggles and trotted over.

With a grin, Biggles strode to meet him and clasped his hand.

"Good show, that," he said. "You sure saved my bacon."

"And you mine," the Yank replied. "That was some damned fine flying!"

"Thanks! Name's Bigglesworth, by the way. 'Biggles' to my friends. You've more than earned the right to use it."

"Glad to know you, Biggles. I'm Jack. Jack Powell."

"The one they call the 'Shooting Star'? I'm glad to know you."

Jack glanced at a nearby hill. A trail of smoke climbed above it.

"That Heinie nearly put paid us both," he said. "Suppose we should see if he survived."

Even if he didn't, I want to look at that little ship he was flying. Something like that could change the course of the war.

The two climbed the hill and found the smoking wreckage of the plane. As they approached, they saw it was even smaller than they'd thought and looked more like a big toy than a warplane. But that wasn't the strangest thing about it.

"There's no cockpit," Jack said.

Biggles swallowed. The eeriness of a pilotless aircraft spooked him. It was unnatural.

"Looks like some sort of hatch where there should be one," he said.

The two moved closer and found that the hatch was a thin affair made of aluminum. They pried it open and found a cavity where a metal cylinder sat. It was about ten inches high and ten in diameter. Biggles didn't recognize the metal, but it must have been something amazingly tough, for it bore the marks of his bullets, none of which had managed to puncture it.

Wordlessly, the two men stared at the strange object.

"Those levers on the top," Jack said. "I'll bet we could open it."

Biggles nodded. He didn't want to see what lay inside. He couldn't remember anything he'd ever wanted less. But an invention this deadly demanded an investigation.

"For king and country," he muttered.

He grasped one of the levers with both hands, and Jack did the same. The men exerted themselves for several moments until the levers flipped to an open position. There was a hiss of escaping pressure; then the lid came off. Inside, the cylinder was filled with a thick, transparent fluid and, suspended in its midst, floated a human brain!

Biggles touched down on the British wing command airstrip. He left his Camel with a pair of mechanics who wheeled it to the hanger and headed toward a cluster of Quonset huts that he assumed housed the staff. As he crossed, he heard a glad cry. Turning, he saw a man jogging toward him. It was the Yank, Jack Powell. He grinned and shook the smaller man's hand warmly.

"So, they've got you down here too," Jack said.

"They have, and I'm glad of the break in routine. What's this all about, do you suppose?"

"It's very hush-hush," Jack replied. "But between you and me, I'd say it has to be something to do with the you-know-what we pulled out of that Heinie ship."

Biggles nodded, sobering up.

"I'd half convinced myself I'd imagined that. Wish I had, really. It was pretty ghoulish, like something straight out of M.R. James."

"Or H.G. Wells," Jack said. "It made me think of one of those Martian war machines somehow."

"I hope they tell us what's at the bottom of it. I don't like the thought of Fritz sending more of those damned machines after our boys."

As they spoke, a tall British pilot stepped out of one of the huts and headed toward them.

"Are you chaps Bigglesworth and Powell?" he asked.

The two saluted and nodded in the affirmative.

"I'm glad to meet you," the man said.

He was a beautiful lad, Biggles thought. Tall and lithe with black hair and grey eyes. He was probably only a year older than them, but not yet twenty. Despite this, he had the most powerful grip Biggles had ever felt. It was like shaking hands with an orangutan.

"I'm Jack Clayton," the young man said. "Pleased to meet you both. You need to head on inside. Major Brand's waiting on the two of you. He's doing a briefing in the second hut over, straight through the back."

They found Brand, where Clayton had told them. The major was a tall gaunt man with a hawk's beak nose and the weary look Biggles had seen on the face of so many senior officers. The stress of sending young pilots to their deaths had made him twenty years past his actual age. The other ten men were dressed as pilots. They were French, British, and even a lone Italian. Brand acknowledged Biggles and Powell with a curt nod, and they found a couple of unoccupied chairs.

"Right, that's all of us, then," Brand said. "You may have heard rumors of the newest super-weapon Jerry's turned loose on us. Well, here's where you get the real story and it beggars anything we've ever seen."

"I dunno," a tall American flyer with an impressive mustache said. "My old squadron went up against those giant bats Herr Doktor Krueger created a while back. I don't see how anything could top that."

A tall man in a French uniform sitting in the front row stood and turned to face the flyers. His face was grim, and when his eyes passed over Biggles, he seemed to feel a tingle as if the man's gaze were electrically charged.

"This is not the work of Krueger nor of any merely human intelligence. We are up against the inventions of extraterrene science."

"What?" A British flyer said. "Men from Mars?"

A nervous chuckle passed through the room, though the Frenchman's arresting gaze quickly silenced it.

"Not men," he said. "Not from Mars either, though I fear that the day we must defend against that quarter may not be far off. No, *mes amis*, what we face now is an alliance between the Boche and the inhabitants of the ninth planet, named Yuggoth by its inhabitants."

The pilots were silent, expressions of disbelief frozen on their faces.

"It's true!" Powell was on his feet now, looking around the room with a fierce intensity. "I don't know about other planets and such, but what we fought... It wasn't from this world. I don't even know how to tell you. Biggles was there. He saw it, too."

Reluctantly, Biggles rose to his feet. Between them, he and Powell managed to get the whole story out, ending with their discovery of the disembodied brain. The others looked at them with a kind of blank astonishment. Finally, the same American spoke.

"The Devil, you say. That's impossible."

"Gentlemen," the tall French pilot said, "we have the brain in question, along with the mysterious cylinder that held it."

"Bosh!" the American replied.

"That's quite enough, O'Malley," Brand snapped. "This is real, and you will believe it. That is a direct order! Am I clear?"

"Yes, sir!" O'Malley said, though with no enthusiasm.

"Moreover, you are to refrain from discussing this with your friends or squadron members. This is most secret." Brand looked around at the men with an intense gaze.

"Our agents on the ground have discovered the base these 'brain-fighters' operate out of," the Frenchman said. He moved to a map hanging on the room's back wall and indicated a point that had to be a hundred miles behind enemy lines. Biggles felt a cold wash of fear as he looked at it.

"Maggiore," a little Italian pilot whose name was Pagot said. "Even if we count this as a suicide mission, how can we reach this place? The Boche will shoot us to pieces before we are halfway there."

"That I leave to Captain Saint-Clair," Brand said, nodding to the French pilot.

"We fly tonight at midnight," the man said. "There is no moon, so the German spotters will never see us."

"But how will we navigate?" Powell said. "You can't fly a mission like this with just a compass."

"I will guide you in," Saint-Clair replied. "I assure you, the darkness will not be an issue."

Brand ran through the plan with them. The planes were painted black and would have difficulty keeping up with each other in the darkness, but they should be invisible to the ground batteries. The only difficulty would be the brain-driven fighters when they got close to the target. The devilish craft were faster and more maneuverable than anything they had. To make things even more difficult, the mysterious metal of the brain cylinder was stronger than hardened steel. Though less than an inch thick, it could deflect even heavy machine gun fire. There was no chance of disabling the pilots. The only way to stop the brain-ships was to cripple the engine or tear up the wings.

A tall American in his mid-twenties spoke up.

"Tell us more about this metal."

"That is a perceptive question, Captain Strange," Saint-Clair said. "It is called *tok'l* and is found only in several places on earth. There is a mine in Germany, which is why the Mi-Gou have allied with the Boche. They..."

"Captain Saint-Clair," Brand said. "I must remind you that we are not to divulge all the details of this mission, only what the pilots need to know!"

"General staff be damned!" the Frenchman snapped. "It's obvious that our target should be the *tok'l* mine, not the factory. Only that will remove the Mi-Gou from the fight."

"It doesn't matter what you think," Brand shot back. "We both have our orders, and this sort of insubordination will not be tolerated. I should throw you in the stockade for that outburst. Just be thankful your special skills are needed for this mission."

Saint-Clair scowled, but fell silent.

Brand stepped up and pointed to a spot about fifteen kilometers south of the mine.

"This is the airfield they are operating out of. We want to bomb the airfield first and take out as many of the little devils as we can while they are still on the ground. Our main objective is a repurposed bicycle factory about three kilometers from that. If we can cripple that, they won't be able to build any more of their fiendish machines for weeks."

He glanced at Saint-Clair, who returned a bitter scowl.

"We're using two bombers of Captain Saint-Clair's design," Brand said. "He and his crew will be on one, Strange, you'll fly the other, Powell and Bigglesworth will be your gunners. The rest of you are flying escort. Any questions?"

"I'd like to ask Saint-Clair where he got all this information about this strange metal, the ninth planet, and all that," Strange said.

"Didn't you hear?" Saint-Clair said. "Need to know and all that."

"Who is Kalakaperi of the Pfifltriggi?"

Saint-Clair's eyes widened slightly, then narrowed.

"You're a man of hidden depths, Captain Strange," he replied. "I'll thank you to keep clear of me. I have reasons to dislike your kind."

"Spooky one that Frenchie," Powell said.

Biggles took a bite of steak and nodded. He had gotten an early sleep and joined the others for a late supper before their mission. Also at the table were Pagot, Powell, and Clayton.

"They call him the Nyctalope," Clayton said around a mouthful of rare meat. Biggles didn't mind a rare bit of meat, but the Englishman's steak looked like it had made only a passing acquaintance with a cooking flame.

"The Nyctalope?" Biggles repeated.

"Means something like 'night vision,' doesn't it?" Powell asked.

Clayton nodded.

"People get all sorts of strange nicknames in war, don't they? I'm called 'Killer,' and Powell here is 'Shooting Star.' How about you, Bigglesworth?"

"Nothing quite so dramatic, I'm afraid. They just shortened me down to 'Biggles.'"

"Well, if you believe all the stories about him, our man Saint-Clair can see in the dark. More than that, he has an artificial heart and ages much more slowly than the average man."

"And he claims to have been to Mars," Powell shook his head. "We have a lunatic leading us behind enemy lines."

"Not a lunatic," Biggles said. "After all, he doesn't claim he's been to the moon. He'd be more of a…"

"Martia-tic?" Powell suggested, and Clayton and Pagot laughed.

"I wouldn't be so quick to write Monsieur Saint-Clair off," Clayton said.

"Do you believe the stories?" Powell said.

Clayton shrugged and smiled pleasantly.

"They wouldn't be the strangest I've heard. Some of the stories the chaps tell about me are just as strange."

He gulped down the last of his steak.

"Well, I'd better be off. I'm flying a mission of my own. My partner is one of those spooky types, like Saint-Clair, and I don't want to keep him waiting."

"What do they call him?" Biggles asked.

"Allard? He goes by the Dark Eagle." Clayton grinned, and it seemed to Biggles that this man wasn't actually intimidated by anyone.

Clayton rose and shook hands all around. He hesitated as Strange entered the room and took a tray.

"Speaking of nicknames, here comes the man with the best of the lot."

"What's that?" Biggles asked.

"They call Captain Strange the 'Brain Devil.'"

Then Clayton was off. A moment later, Captain Strange took his seat and started in on his dinner. The conversation died as the rest of the men at the table watched. After several moments, he sighed, put down his utensils, and looked at the others.

"Yes, Biggles, they call me the Brain Devil, and you've already guessed why in the briefing."

With a start, Biggles realized Strange had answered his unspoken question.

"Wh-what?"

"I read minds," Strange explained. "I learned it when I studied in Tibet. I can tell you that your friends were both thinking of their sweethearts just now. Mr. Powell's young lady is named Sylvia, and Signor Pagot's is a singer named Gina."

Pagot startled visibly, and Powell's face turned ashen.

"Assuming that's true," Biggles said, "what was that whole to-do between you and Saint-Clair?"

"I was feeling him out," Strange said. "He really has been to Mars. Or, if he hasn't, he has the most vivid hallucinations of any man I've ever known."

Powell frowned, looking skeptical.

"Then that bit about Kakapalakikaki of Poofiloofakaboofa...?"

"Kalakaperi of the Pfifltriggi," Strange corrected with a faint smile. "An alien scientist he met on the red planet."

"What I want to know is what he's got against you?" Biggles said.

Strange's features sobered.

"I don't know. When he said he didn't like 'my kind,' I had the strong sense he had met other mind-readers before, and those encounters have left him with a lot of anger and mistrust. He's got a remarkably disciplined mind and has been hiding his thoughts from me since the briefing."

"Can't say I blame him," Powell said. "Mucking around in someone else's brain. It's unnatural. Ah, no offense, Strange."

The Brain Devil shook his head.

"I understand, Powell. And you're probably right, that's all that it is. Still, I plan to keep an eye on our mysterious ally."

Biggles strained to keep an eye on the dim blobs of light ahead. The two bombers were painted a matte black but with a small patch of phosphorescent paint atop each wingtip so they could keep track of each other. The fighters had no such markings, and Biggles had no idea if all the smaller planes were still with them. It was easy to imagine some getting lost in the endless darkness around them. Aside from the infrequent glow from a farmhouse, he couldn't even tell up from down. It took nerve to keep on course and faith in the pilots that they weren't heading into the side of a mountain.

"You don't seem to think much of Captain Saint-Clair?" he asked.

He had found that, by shouting, he could converse with Strange over the noise of the engines.

"I think he's arrogant, secretive, and thoroughly convinced of his superiority," Strange replied. "I also think he's fearless, highly intelligent, and patriotic to a fault. I doubt we'll ever become bosom chums, but that's not what this is all about."

"No, sir, I suppose not."

He knew Strange was right. As much as he loved the chaps in his squadron and admired the men on this mission, Biggles understood that one had to work with every ally. The price of personal likes and dislikes was much too high, and so, every man aloft was a brother. At least, that was how it had to be until the war was over. After that, well, he'd have to wait and see.

"There!"

Strange thrust out an arm. Following it, Biggles saw some faint lights from a series of buildings.

"The factory?"

"Yes!" Strange shouted. "And that means the airfield should be…" He shifted his arm a few degrees. "…Right over there and a little ahead. Signal Powell to be ready."

Biggles blew into a speaking tube, then listened for the answer.

"Yes?"

"Be ready; we're almost over the target."

"Understood. We will turn their 'bicycles' into little pieces."

Closer and closer they came. The airfield was blacked out, but they were flying low enough that Biggles could see the outlines of buildings.

"Listen!" Strange's voice cut the air like a pistol shot. Biggles strained for a moment, then he heard it. The sound of aircraft engines, but not at the pitch of the Spads, Camels, or the big bombers. A high-pitched sound that he had heard once before.

"The devil-planes!"

The first of the little craft rose out of the darkness, its twin guns stitching lines of fire at them. A line of tracer bullets sliced across the wing less than a meter from Biggles. He fired after the little plane as best he could, but it lost itself in the night.

"How can they see us?"

"Not sight," Strange yelled back. "Some other form of perception."

Two more of the little craft bore down on them from behind. Biggles spun his gun to a rear-facing position and opened fire. He didn't think he hit either plane but came close enough to make them veer away.

A ball of flame lit up one of the buildings below. Powell had scored a hit on one of the hangers. Three more explosions followed in quick succession, though Biggles couldn't see what damage they caused.

The big plane stayed steady and on course. Biggles, used to the evasive maneuvering of his Camel, felt like a sitting duck waiting for the hunter's bullet. Still, he knew that Strange was flying as the mission required him to, staying the course to deliver the bombs on target.

Biggles saw burning buildings and planes on the ground now. At his four-o'clock, a SPAD went down in flames. Another limped away from the fights, trailing smoke, a pair of the little aircraft in pursuit. His allies were losing the battle.

"Dammit!" Strange said.

Biggles glanced over, and Strange pointed to the south, where a large aircraft could be seen leaving the fray.

"Saint-Clair is running away?" Biggles said.

"No. The fool is heading toward the mine," Strange yelled back.

Three of the little planes shot past them, guns blazing. Biggles targeted them with his Vickers guns and was confident he hit one, but the plane didn't falter or fall. Two lines of bullet holes opened in the canvas over the bomber's fuselage, and he heard the engine falter.

"We're hit," Strange shouted. "Hold tight; I'm going to try to put us down!"

The bomber nosed down as Strange fought for control. Biggles watched him momentarily, calculating the odds of anyone landing a ship this big on a dead stick. He'd never heard of anyone doing it and figured the chances were close enough to zero that it didn't matter. He turned his attention to his guns and singled out one of the approaching Boche aircraft. He fired a continuous burst, not worrying about conserving ammunition. He was rewarded by a burst of flame from the tiny craft's engine. The propellor slowed to a stop, and the devil-plane went into a spinning nosedive.

"You're not so invulnerable after all," he whispered.

Biggles scanned the sky for other enemies, but none were at hand. He saw several SPADs and Camels fleeing west, the devil-planes in pursuit. The sight made his heart sink, though he understood. With both bombers lost, there was no reason for the fighters to remain. He offered a brief, wordless prayer that they make it home safely.

There were several moments of near-silence as the battle moved away from them. He could still hear the guns firing, but as they moved farther away, the sound took on a dreamlike quality. Without the vibration of the bomber's engines, there was no sense of motion other than the icy wind. The darkness enfolded the bomber, and it seemed like they would fall forever through the void.

The illusion was shattered as the bomber struck the ground. Strange had managed to touch down on the landing gear, but their descent had been too steep and much too fast. The impact stunned him, and the big plane rolled forward a few meters before overturning, struts bending and cables snapping around him. The last thing he was aware of was the sudden smell of petrol fumes and a flicker of orange light as flames spread.

Biggles came to in a narrow bed, hardly more than a cot, in a large and pleasant room. He'd seen its like before in the manor houses of England, converted to wartime service as field hospitals. His head was wrapped in bandages, and he ached all over, but he couldn't feel any serious injuries. He tried to sit up, but a surge of dizziness and nausea forced him back. He closed his eyes and let his consciousness slip away.

When he woke again, he could look around without the vertigo. He saw that the room was quite large, holding five other cots like his, only two of which were occupied. Powell's form filled one bed while Strange lay in the other. Powell wore a cast on one leg while Strange seemed uninjured but wore a strange metal skullcap outfitted with radio tubes and coils of wire.

Two young men, German by the look of them and dressed in long white labcoats, moved about the room, performing various small tasks. If they noticed that Biggles was awake, they didn't seem interested.

He sat up and then started to rise. That caught the attention of one of the men who approached the bed, staring blankly.

"Remain still," the man said.

"See here," Biggles said. "If I'm a prisoner of war, I have certain rights. I demand—"

"Remain still," the man repeated, drawing a small pistol from his lab coat.

Biggles froze. The man didn't seem to be a soldier, but his blank expression and monotone voice gave the impression that he was somehow not human. He didn't doubt the robotic man would shoot him without a pang of conscience. He relaxed but remained sitting.

"Do you mind me asking where I am?"

There wasn't even a flicker of response from the man.

"This is a field hospital? Are there any more of my squadron here? How's Powell doing? And what's that fancy get-up on Strange's head?"

The gun never wavered, and the man barely blinked.

"Now, see here—" Biggles leaned forward and raised a finger.

"Remain still."

Biggles relaxed again. If talking wouldn't work, he could at least study the man and learn what he could. Surely, if that detective chap in *The Strand* could deduce someone's profession, personal likes, and history from a few inconsequential clues, he could do the same.

After a tense ten minutes or so, he decided that wasn't true. The man's clothes were neither brand new nor old. They had a few small stains that could, have been blood but could just as easily have been tea, gravy, or whatever the Heinies ate. He had an average build, and a few small scars and callouses adorned his hands, so he clearly worked with them. What kind of work was unclear, and Biggles silently cursed Dr. Watson's stories and their smug assumption that you could tell one callous from another. If anything, he knew less about his captor than when he had first seen him.

"Could I trouble you for something to smoke?"

"Remain still."

"Excellent, Heinrich," a new voice said. "You can resume your regular duties."

The newcomer was a small man in his seventies, mostly bald and wearing a pince-nez. His blue eyes twinkled, and he wore a delighted smile. Biggles could picture him living in a hollow tree somewhere in an enchanted forest. Without a flicker of expression, Heinrich pocketed the pistol and resumed puttering around the room.

"Herr Bigglesworth," the gnomish man said in English. "I'm so happy to see that you are awake. How are you feeling?"

"Aside from being confused, having had a gun stuffed in my face, and needing a smoke, I seem fine."

"Good, good. You were quite concussed when they brought you in, but the Mi-Gou know just how to give you a swift and full recovery. Their knowledge of the human brain is most remarkable."

"Is that what you're doing with Captain Strange?" Biggles nodded toward his friend.

"It was not necessary. Your Captain Strange has a remarkable constitution and came through your crash-landing with only minor injuries. A most remarkable bit of flying, I have to say."

"And Powell?"

"Sedated for now. His leg was badly broken, a compound fracture. We are treating it with a drug the Mi-Gou developed that causes the bone to re-knit at a highly accelerated rate. Unfortunately, the healing process is painful, so I thought it better to keep him under for the time being."

"You didn't say what that electrical tiara you've got Strange wearing is for, doctor..."

"Forgive my manners. I am Karl von Junzt, at your service." The little man gave a bow. It wasn't the stiff, military bow of the Prussian academy but the polite bow of a host to an honored guest. "That 'electrical tiara'—a charming description—is even more wonderful than a healing device," he continued. "It is a glimpse of paradise, a gateway to a fuller and happier life than you can imagine. It's something I offer to all my subjects before the transition. You, too, will experience this before long, and I know it will bring you great joy."

"What the deuce are you talking about?"

"How to explain?" von Juntz's features clouded in thought, and his eyes lit up. "Of course. You have no reason to trust me, though I bear you nothing but goodwill, but you admire Captain Strange. He can tell you."

With the help of Heinrich and another robotic orderly, von Juntz deactivated the device and removed it from Strange's brow. The American's eyes flickered open, and he blinked rapidly.

"K-Karol?"

"Please relax, Herr Strange," von Juntz said. "The weakness and the confusion will pass momentarily. It's only a side-effect of the treatment."

"Treatment...?"

"He had you hooked into some sort of brain-machine," Biggles said. "Are you alright, captain?"

"Brain-machine? But I... I was in Mecklenberg, and Karol... where is Karol?"

"Mecklenburg." von Juntz smiled. "A lovely region. Don't worry, Herr Captain, your lover waits for you there, and you can rejoin her shortly."

"You hypnotized him with that machine?" Biggles said.

"Nonsense! You weren't hypnotized just now, were you, captain?"

"I...." Strange took a moment to focus. "No, I wasn't hypnotized. I was there; it was real, then I was here."

"It's a trick," Biggles said. "That machine made you think you were somewhere else, but you were here all along."

Strange shook his head.

"I was there. , it was real. As real as this place is."

72

Von Juntz smiled like a proud father.

"Precisely! We think the reality is in this crude material stuff around us, but that is simply an illusion. Reality is in the mind, and nothing is real until it is perceived in the mind. We usually think that the world is what our senses tell us it is, but our senses fool us. Any competent magician can fool a thousand people by making them think they see, hear, or feel what is not actually there. No, my young men, the senses are liars, and we must not trust them. The only way to know reality is directly, through the mind."

"The machine planted those images directly into my brain?" Strange said.

"Very clever," von Juntz replied. "However, your insight does not go far enough. The device allowed you to enter a world of pure mentality, a world every bit as real as what you think of as the real world. Every blade of grass, every drop of water, everything your senses could detect was exactly as real as it is in this world. Your brain responds to it in exactly the same way."

"What about Karol?" Strange asked.

"Her as well. If you hold the hand of the young woman, the sensation is exactly as if you do it in this world. If you kiss her lips, it is the same."

"But she wasn't really there."

"Yes? And could you tell any difference? The fraulein doktor was true to your memories in every way, was she not?"

Strange was silent. After a moment, von Junzt shrugged.

"She was not in the mental world at the same time you were; that is true. However, your experience of her was no different than if she had been. Still, I can appreciate the appeal of both of you experiencing that world together. Do not be afraid; I see the time coming when she will be there with you, both young and deathless."

"What do you mean?" Until now, Biggles had been silent, not knowing what to say in this surreal conversation.

"This is a gift to the entire world, Herr Bigglesworth. In return for allowing them access to the precious *tok'l* metal, the Mi-Gou have given us the technology to live free of our bodies and their limits. To cast off corruption and experience life for untold centuries."

"Living as brains in bloody vats?" The idea nauseated Biggles.

"No, Herr Bigglesworth, living in perfect bodies in the world of the mind. Brains can be preserved almost indefinitely in the *tok'l* metal cylinders, requiring only a minimum of nourishment and care. No longer will human beings suffer from famine and disease. No longer will illness, deformity, or injury disable a man from living the life he desires. When people submit to the device—and they will gladly—the world will become a paradise!"

"But for now, you still send the disembodied brains of men to their deaths," Strange said.

Von Juntz nodded, looking sorrowful.

"This is the sad reality of war. However, this is destined to be the last war humanity will ever fight. With the technology the Mi-Gou have given us, Germany and her allies will sweep across the earth. Then we will offer a war-weary population the chance to become immortal, living in a world where there is no war nor any cause for war."

"Madness," Biggles said.

"Not madness, but salvation," von Juntz replied.

"Your salvation is built on lies," Strange interjected. "I could hear them while I was connected to the machine. Your pilots don't know what is happening to them. The German pilots, thinking they were still in their bodies, healthy and whole, despite remembering they were shot down in flames."

"Would you have me tell them differently?" Von Juntz raised his bushy eyebrows. "What is the purpose of telling a man his body was crushed and burned beyond repair if you can give him a life of perfect health? Would you have me be so cruel?"

"What about the allied pilots?" Strange asked. "Whenever they go out, they think they're fighting the Central Powers. You've tricked them into betraying their nations and killing their brothers."

"It is necessary if we are to bring the blessings of the Mi-Gou to the world." Von Juntz shook his head. When he spoke again, his voice was subdued. "I hate that I must do this, but such things are necessary in a time of war. Can you tell me you would not do the same?"

Strange glared at the man. He didn't speak, but Biggles did, with a passion.

"You're bloody right. I wouldn't do it! Twisting a man's mind to make him do your dirty work, it's disgusting. And this whole unnatural business; I won't rest until you, the Mi-Gou, and all your plans are broken into little pieces."

"I see," von Juntz said. "You are a passionate man of limited imagination. I had given Captain Strange a taste of the mental world to persuade him to join my cause. Alas, his unique mental sensitivity has persuaded him otherwise. With you, Herr Bigglesworth, I can see there is no point. You should prepare yourselves, my friends. When I return, we will begin the surgery."

The scientist left the room, leaving Biggles and Strange under the watchful eye of Heinrich and another man with a matching labcoat and pistol. Strange stared at the men while Biggles tried to devise some sort of escape plan. The men had a level of concentration he had never seen before, and all he could think of was to leap at them. He would be killed, but he might create enough of a distraction for Strange to jump the men.

"Don't try it, Biggles," Strange said. "These men are inhumanly precise. You can't distract them."

Even having seen Strange's eerie powers in action, Biggles started. Much as he was coming to admire the man, this mind-reading unnerved him.

"Are they the 'Mi-Gou' von Juntz was going on about?"

"No. They're human enough, in body at least, but their minds are gone. I've tried reading them, but there's nothing there, just a hint of something inhuman. I think they're being controlled."

Biggles sat up and clenched his fists in impotent rage.

"Remain still," Heinrich said.

"Witty conversationalists, though," Biggles said.

Strange chuckled.

"You know, Bigglesworth, I really appreciated your little speech. I have to admit, von Juntz was starting to get to me. He believes in everything he says, and it starts to seem reasonable after a while. I've always prided myself on giving a fair ear to whatever the other chap says, but that can be a fault. Anyway, you pulled me back."

"Well, I... I guess I just got mad."

"Righteous anger. If this is it, I'm glad to have you with me."

Biggles felt his face turn warm.

"That isn't what worries me. I've made my peace with going down fighting the Boche, but the thought of getting shut in a pickle jar and trying to shoot down the chaps in my squadron..."

Strange nodded.

"I'm with you. When the professor comes back, we need to attack him. We don't have a chance of surviving, but if we can take him out with us, that's worth something."

"Should you be talking about this plan with Heinrich and Heinrich 2 listening?"

"They're focusing on keeping us from doing anything, but they aren't aware of what we're saying. Isn't that right?" Strange raised his hands over his head.

"Remain still."

The door opened to admit von Juntz, and Biggles tensed his body, preparing to attack. Then he saw the form of something massive and inhuman filling the doorway behind the professor. Strange screamed in agony, clutching his head with both hands. Biggles wanted to scream with him, but couldn't stop staring dumbly at the creature. It was as big as a large man, but it was more crustacean than anything else in form. The thing had limbs, six or eight, he thought. It held two like arms and stood on the rest. Its entire body was covered in a coral-pink carapace except for a pair of folded membranous wings and a mass of short antennae where a head should be.

He wanted to leap at the thing but couldn't make his body respond. Something about it was so wrong that he couldn't move any closer to it. His revulsion at the thought of touching it was so strong that he wanted to vomit.

There was a loud chattering noise from the hallway outside, and the monster's body began to convulse. Heinrich and the other man moved as one, trying to get past, yes, the inhuman thing. He recognized the sound now, a Bergmann MP 18. He had seen one of the new weapons—a submachine gun—demonstrated several months ago. Smaller than a rifle, it fired pistol-caliber ammunition at a frightening rate of speed. Bullets chopped through the creature's pink carapace, causing a foul-smelling green ichor to flow from a dozen wounds.

The thing collapsed, the antennae on its "face" flashing different colors, and Biggles saw that Saint-Clair held the submachine gun. He fired his last few rounds into Heinrich's body. The other man aimed at the Nyctalope and fired several times before Biggles, shaking off his paralysis, tackled him from behind. They hit the ground, and Biggles got a grip on the man's gun wrist. They struggled over the weapon, and Biggles realized the muzzle was turning inexorably toward him. Whatever had made Heinrich and his companion into robotic puppets had also increased their strength past normal human levels. Their struggle had left Biggles on his back, with the German pinning him. He had both hands on the man's wrist, but still, the muzzle slowly shifted in line with his face. It would be over in a moment, and there was nothing he could do about it.

A pistol went off, and blood sprayed across Biggles's face. The guard's body convulsed once, then went limp. Biggles pushed out from under it and saw the Nyctalope holding a Ruger semiautomatic pistol. The tall man turned to face Professor von Junzt, who cowered against the room's back wall.

"Please, don't kill me," the little man said. "You have no idea what humanity stands to lose if I—"

The Nyctalope's pistol fired, but as it did, Philip Strange sprang at him, deflecting his aim. A hole appeared in the wall next to the professor's head, and he yelped.

"Blast you, Strange," Saint-Clair swore.

"We need him," Strange replied.

"Captain Saint-Clair," Biggles said, struggling to his feet. "I don't know where you came from, but you saved us."

"How is it you're alive?" Strange asked.

"I never reached the mine. Those devil-planes shot me down half a kilometer from the target. My crew was lost, but I had brought an experimental parachute with me and managed to jump to safety. I came back here to see if any of your group had survived. I hoped we could steal a plane from the air base and try again."

76

Strange managed a half-smile.

"You're still determined to finish the mission, even after all this?"

"I'd like to, but I fear it is impossible," Saint Clair said. "I've scouted the base. There are perhaps thirty of the little planes, though they are useless to us. There's no place for a pilot to sit, let alone controls a human can operate. There are some Fokkers. We could steal a couple of those and perhaps make it back to our lines."

"If our own allies don't shoot us down," Biggles remarked.

"Nevertheless, it's the only plan open to us." Saint Clair picked up the pistols Heinrich and the other guard had carried and handed them to Strange and Biggles. As he did, Biggles saw a dark stain on his leather jacket and two holes where Heinrich's bullets had struck.

"You're hurt," he said.

"I have a stronger constitution than most men. I should be able to fly back to base. Now, come on."

"What about Powell?" Biggles demanded.

"Leave him," the Nyctalope said. "An unconscious man is dead weight, and we cannot afford that."

"We can't leave him," Strange said.

"Sentimentalism, captain? I expected better."

"It's not that," Strange replied. "It's the gadget von Junzt had me hooked into. If I could hear the thoughts of all the pilots, perhaps they could hear mine as well. They don't know what's been done to them. If they did…"

"If they did, they might want revenge." The Nyctalope smiled grimly. "Very good, Strange. Perhaps we can finish this mission after all."

"There," von Junzt said as he finished a final adjustment.

For all his disdain for the physical world, the little man was terrified. He knew he could exist free from pain and injury in the mental realm, but a bullet through the brain would take that possibility away from him forever. He had chosen to help them rather than face that inevitability.

Strange took the device and was about to place it on his head when the Nyctalope caught his arm.

"Von Junzt, are you certain this won't harm him?" he asked.

"I think so," the German answered.

"I want certainty."

"So far as I know, it should be fine," von Junzt replied, "but I have never used an adjustment like this before, and I have never worked on a subject with Captain Strange's unique gifts."

"I'll take the chance." Strange settled the device on his head like an oversized crown. Several electrical sparks flickered across the device, but there was no other sign that it was functioning.

"What do you see?" Saint-Clair asked.

"I'm at a sidewalk café in Wismer," Strange replied. "It's an autumn day, and everything seems normal. It's you and your world that seem like the dream, Saint-Clair."

"Can you hear the voices of the other pilots?"

"Yes. They're stronger this time. Clearer."

"Good. Now, professor, tell him how to turn the mental world off."

Biggles half listened as he worked on reviving Powell. Slapping the man hadn't been much use, but splashing his face with cold water was showing some results. His eyes flickered open, and they took several moments to focus.

"Where are we?" he asked.

"We've been captured by the Boche," Biggles answered. "Don't worry, we're getting out. Can you walk?"

Powell lurched to his feet and, after several tentative steps, nodded.

"Good!" Biggles said. "Are you up to an escape?"

"You'd better believe it!" Powell winced as he lowered his wounded leg.

"Are you sure?" Biggles inquired.

"A little thing like this isn't going to stop me. I'll see you in Paris and dance with more mam'selles than you," the other replied with a grin.

Biggles helped the younger man out of the room and down the stairs. Von Juntz followed, and the Nyctalope brought up the rear, guiding Strange with one hand and holding a pistol on the scientist with the other.

As they reached the ground floor, two more white-coated men fired on them. Biggles swore as a bullet cut a shallow gash in the side of his neck, then returned fire. His automatic barked thrice before the first man went down. Saint-Clair came alongside him and dropped the second man with a single shot.

"Get their guns," the Nyctalope commanded.

Biggles and Powell moved to obey. As they did, a klaxon sounded.

"Damn," swore Saint-Clair. "We'll have to fight our way to the airstrip."

He let go of Strange, who sat on the stairs, and moved to the front door. He peered through the curtains, then bashed out a pane from the window and began to fire. The roar of rifles answered him.

"How many?" Biggles inquired, moving next to Saint Clair.

"I make it three squads of rifles."

"And us with four pistols," Powell said, grinning. "Well, let's let the Heinies know they've been in a fight."

Biggles and Powell took up flanking positions at the room's windows.

"Don't waste ammunition," the Nyctalope added.

Biggles thought that comment was unnecessary but said nothing. A large clock in the foyer told him it was just past 11:00, and the dark sky outside meant late evening. That was fortunate for them, for the almost moonless night made it hard for the riflemen to target them. The Nyctalope, on the other hand, picked off man after man with uncanny accuracy.

"Amazing!" Biggles said.

"Not good enough." The Nyctalope turned toward von Juntz, who crouched against the wall. He fired once before Powell or Biggles could react, and a small, neat hole appeared in the scientist's forehead.

"Good Lord, man!" Powell said.

"He was a prisoner!" Biggles added.

"His knowledge was too dangerous to let him live. We don't have the luxury of being gentlemen in this situation."

Saint-Clair turned back to his post at the door as Biggles fought down a queasy feeling. He'd learned that war was ugly, but this was something new to him. He could see that Powell felt the same. Glancing back, he saw that Strange hadn't reacted to the situation. He sat, holding the sides of the strange helmet, a look of concentration on his face.

The Nyctalope pulled the trigger of his pistol, and the hammer fell on an empty chamber.

"Both of mine are empty," he said. "What about you two?"

"I've got three left," Biggles replied.

"Five here," Powell echoed.

The Nyctalope held out a hand, and Powell handed him his pistol.

"Looks like our last stand," Powell said. "I've got to say, I'm awfully proud to go out with the three of—"

"Listen!" Saint-Clair said.

It took Biggles a moment to recognize the sound of aircraft engines. Not the thrum of Camels or Fokkers but the higher pitched while of the little devil-planes' engines.

"What the deuce?" he said.

The sound became the shrill whine of planes diving and was joined by the terrifying chatter of machine guns. For a moment, Biggles thought the fighters were attacking the building, but then it became clear that was not happening.

"They're strafing the Germans," Saint Clair said. "Strange, is this your doing?"

The American nodded but clearly didn't want to break his concentration by speaking.

"They're going around for another strafing run," Saint Clair said. "When they do, follow me and stick close."

The Germans went to ground when the devil-planes returned. A few fired at the escaping pilots, but none of the shots reached their mark in the dim light. They made their way to the airstrip as quickly as they were able. Fortunately, the cover provided by the devil-planes kept their pursuers at bay. They came to the field to find a dozen Fokkers unattended.

"Can you fly with that thing on?" Saint-Clair asked.

"I'll have to, won't I?" Strange replied. "We can't give up our escort."

"Look there!" Powell said, pointing to another plane. This was a Halberstadt CL II, an older fighter with a second seat for a gunner.

"Good," the Nyctalope said. "Biggles, you take Strange in the Halberstadt. Powell and I will escort you. Strange, you know where we are going?"

"I do."

"Will they cooperate?"

"They know what's been done to them now," Strange replied. "They'll do anything to have their revenge."

They had been airborne for less than five minutes when the little planes caught up. Biggles felt a prickling in his neck and scalp. He understood the need to have this horrible craft with their disembodied pilots with them, but their presence gave him a sense of dread. It wasn't just the thought that they might turn on him at any moment. It was their wrongness, the idea of living men stolen from their bodies. He wanted to be far from here, where he could try to forget. He wanted this to be some horrible dream.

As Saint-Clair's plane dipped toward the ground, he was pulled from his thoughts. He couldn't see the mine entrance but knew where it must be and followed the Halberstadt down. Around him, the little planes began to dive, quickly passing him, and then the Nyctalope. The first plane struck the mine entrance and burst into flames. A second later, another of the devil-planes hit, then another, then another. With each impact, the conflagration grew.

Biggles pulled back on the stick and circled. The last of the devil-craft slammed into the flaming wreckage, obscuring the mine entrance. The surrounding forest had caught fire, and the conflagration threatened to grow out of all control. Perhaps the mine could be reclaimed one day, but he didn't see how. Would that be enough to convince the Mi-Gou to leave this world alone? He hoped so. He wondered about the pilots, allied and German, who had given their lives for this victory. It had taken a horror from another world to get warring earthmen to come together. Would they do so again, or would humankind always fight among themselves?

He didn't know the answers, and the questions made him weary. He shifted his attention to the controls. He and his comrades had survived and were headed home. For today, that was enough.

*A figure like Gaston Leroux's Erik (a.k.a. The Phantom of the Opera) casts long shadows in the dark world of the Shadowmen. In the story that follows, Atom Bezecny investigates some of these tragic characters...*

## Atom Mudman Bezecny: *The Society of the Phantom*

It was commonly believed that the hidden passages and chambers beneath the Paris Opera had been sealed away forever. They had certainly been sealed away from the conscious memory of the people of Paris—the popular chatter about the Phantom of the Opera had been washed away long ago by the tides of fresh gossip. But in spite of this forgetfulness, or because of it, the Phantom's secret lair had survived, and now, it served as an altar to the memory of the deceased Erik.

Like any other altar, secret devotees of the altar's subject flocked to its hallowed steps. The grave of the famous Phantom could have been a place of worship for any number of persons: there were architects, who admired Erik's skills in the art of construction; there were musicians, who admired his compositions; and of course, there were criminals, who admired his mastery of traps and deadly weapons. But the Society of the Phantom, which came into being in the first half of the 20th century, was comprised of those who shared a certain physical trait with the tormented haunter of the dark. They were all facially deformed.

Seven figures sat around an oval desk in what had once been had the Phantom's famous "shrinking room." At the head of the table was their Chairwoman, Mrs. Eugenia Ronder. She was a strong woman and a proud leader, and like all those present, she presented her scarred visage without a veil. Each of those present were pitiably disfigured, but Mrs. Ronder possessed hardly even a hint of what had once been her face. Instead she bore a reddish mass out of which two dark holes stared, holes which were the remains of eyes.

At her side was Baron Adelbert Gruner, a colleague of hers; they had become acquainted due to having an associate in common, namely a famous detective with whom they had once been involved. Gruner's injuries were also quite complete, as he had suffered a devastating acid attack. But there was still more to see of him than Mrs. Ronder.

Joining them was a supposed former colleague of Erik's, René Marot. Beside him was the once-famed wax sculptor Ivan Igor. Igor was a relative newcomer to the Society, having taken the seat of his distant relative, Henry Jarrod, who was once the order's toast.

Also present were Captain Roger Vigers, an English *gueule cassée* from the Great War; Janos Szabo, an ill-fated Hungarian; and Nora Goodrich, a noted American chemical researcher victimized by a faulty compound. The Society was a multinational *mélange* which welcomed diverse outlooks.

All of them had found a newfound beauty in the universe upon hearing the tale of Erik. Erik, who had been a genius of many disciplines, who was a great romantic, who was a modern tragic figure such that Shakespeare would write of. He was their hero. True, he had done terrible things and tried to do more, but he understood something they'd all learned the hard way: that in a world that loathed those who had been wounded and deformed, there was no such thing as law or justice.

They would find a way to get back at a society that punished them for their suffering, even as Erik had revenged himself upon the world of the unblemished. That was the purpose of each of their secret meetings.

A great part of Erik's revenge was achieved by tackling life with a certain profound-if-tragic *joie de vivre*. They all knew he had found a strange delight in his clashes with Raoul de Chagny and the Persian, a delight born of his true love for Christine Daae.

Each of them had adopted this joyfulness, this trickster spirit, this love of the shadows; and this outlook had broadened their lives. In the course of this improvement, these survivors of mutilation had adopted a different kind of spirit entirely. Specifically, by means of psychical seances, they had learned how to call forth the ghost of Erik himself. Out of respect for his desire to rest in peace, they only roused him lightly, and for brief periods of time. But in those brief moments, they had gained much wisdom, and learned to live by his post-mortem edicts.

This meeting in particular was to be very special indeed.

"Tonight is the night, my friends," Mrs. Ronder began. "Tonight, the Master has promised to reveal to our Society the fate he has planned for us. He has been refining us all for a divine purpose. We have glimpsed the artistic beauty of his soul and it has inspired both hope and terror in us. Now we shall learn what we have been reaching towards all this time."

"At last!" Gruner proclaimed. "At last we shall see what future awaits us— and if the world is to change to take on a portion of our twisted image."

"The Master will give meaning to our lives," Ivan Igor agreed.

Slowly, the members of the Society took each others' hands, forming a circle—but an incomplete one. There was a chair at their table which they kept empty in honor of their deceased members. Presently, the chair served as a memorial to the late Pretty Boy Murphy of Laredo, Texas. The missing link formed by that seat would be filled by Erik.

As the psychic focus of each of the members filled the room, Mr. Szabo and Ms. Goodrich gasped. They felt a cold, solid hand embrace their own. The room darkened as the table's candles flickered. In the dark, the Society members could see the faint silhouette of a man: a man whose face was like a naked skull, who stared at them with ghoulish yellow eyes.

*Greetings, my faithful*, the wraith of Erik intoned.

"Greetings, O Master!" they cried.

*You have come as I have requested.*

"We have, Master!" Mrs. Ronder declared. "We have heeded your word, and now await your ultimate and final instructions!"

*I knew that I could trust your loyalty,* Erik hissed. *You have, in turn, earned my faithfulness for all time.*

"What do you command of us, sire?" asked Janos Szabo.

*You have all proven yourselves worthy of my legacy. You have shown me your reverence for beauty, you have shown me your kindness, and also, you have shown me not a little guile. And so you will be the sons and daughters which life never allowed me. You will carry my word and my name into the world.*

There was a great exuberance in the room.

"We are to inherit your legacy?" Marot whispered. "What does that entail, Master?"

*You are to go out into the world and become new Phantoms. You are to haunt the theaters of this world, as I once did. It is my will that the Phantom be a part of every drama, every romance, every tragedy. You will lurk in the shadows, and you will guide young women towards the peak of their artistry. You will safeguard your lairs with traps and weapons. You will be assassins.*

*You are not my first apprentices, and you shall not be my last. My legacy is eternal...* Don Juan *Forever* Triumphant.

*That is my command to you. Wear your masks. And haunt.*

The Society had their orders.

They set out into the world, to carry out their grim but joyous assignment.


At least one of the newborn Phantoms had haunted theaters before. René Marot had had a career in the London Opera House before being forced to move on to work in the fleapit theaters of Paris, the poor man's Grand Guignols. After being defeated there, he had retreated to the shrine of Erik, where he was surprised to find friends.

Now he moved on to the Bijou Theater in London, where he terrorized the movie-going guests of a man who, as it happened, was an international spy. Marot fared no better at the Bijou than he did in London or Paris, as he was only able to linger a few months before the British government learned about the owner Karl Verloc's fifth column tendencies. In a long series of events, Verloc perished, and the theater was abandoned, leaving Marot high and dry—but he lingered in the darkness, hoping that the next owners would reopen it as an entertainment establishment

He underestimated the ruthlessness of Scotland Yard. Detective Sergeant Spencer, who had helped defeat the foreign agent, returned to the Bijou to see if any other terrorists were hiding anywhere in the Bijou. He overcame Marot's traps and arrested this new "Phantom." British Intelligence was unable to determine any usefulness for Marot during interrogation, and he was unable to convince them he was not a terrorist. He was sentenced to death and quietly executed, though rumors stated that, before his death, he fathered a son christened Charles Larousse with a young French female prisoner. This son ostensibly achieved the rank of Chief Inspector among the Paris police.

Baron Gruner took up residence in the Freiburg Tanz Akademie in Germany, not far from his family estates in Austria. The rehearsal stages the dancers graced were his theater of choice.

He was, like Marot, unable to secure his own personal Christine. This was because he found himself continually haunted by a Phantom of his own: the Phantom of a woman. He believed at first that she was a mortal woman, perhaps the headmistress of the Akademie. Then he wondered if it was perhaps the Winter woman responsible for his injuries, stalking him for some reason.

But soon, he determined that this spectral woman was something else entirely. Something that filled him with a deep abiding dread. He knew that one day he would probe too deeply into the Akademie's forgotten catacombs and not come out again.

He was not wrong.

This experience was not too dissimilar to what Janos Szabo faced at the Metropol Theatre in Berlin. Janos' attempts to seduce a young woman and become her teacher were spoiled by the fact that he was constantly harassed by a strange figure dressed in black. This figure also wore a mask, but his mask chilled Janos to the bone. Whether this man was deformed behind that mask, he never knew. He didn't want to find out. He avoided him whenever he could.

When the Metropol started displaying another mask in the lobby, a mask that looked like the face of a demon, Janos had had enough. Not only did it suggest that the staff were aware of him in some sense, but he was losing too much sleep staying there as it was thanks to the Man in Black. He fled the Metropol, and instead moved to London, where he was last known to have found an unlikely wife in stage actress Eve Gill.

Ivan Igor traveled to Australia for his haunting. He sought out Melbourne's Princess Theatre as his target, most famously striking terror into audiences during a production of *Doctor Omega and the Thirteen Bees to Gloomsday*. The Princess Theatre would close down in the early '70s, but some productions were still rehearsed within its empty skeleton; this was how Igor met and fell in love with Helen Selleck. Helen, née Cathy, was an actress who was severely traumatized by witnessing the death of her mother as a child. Unfortunately, people around her had a tendency to die from being slashed and stabbed with broken glass—the same means by which her mother died. Igor was one of many victims of this curious phenomenon.

Roger Vigers and Nora Goodrich didn't fare much better.

Captain Vigers traveled to the Spotlite Theater, run by one Austin Johnson, and also wound up the victim of an insane killer—the theater's former owner.

Nora chose an abandoned theater in Italy to seek out a student. The ruins of this theater housed rehearsals much as the broken-down Princess did. Unfortunately, Nora arrived to the theater at the same time that it was under attack by Irving Wallace, the Night Owl Killer, and she fell victim to Wallace's rampage.

It seemed that sinister forces both old and new had already nested in the dark hollows the young Phantoms sought out. Ancient evils and nascent madnesses alike had lashed out at them bitterly, like a cave bear waking up scared and hungry.

They say that the Paris Opera is still haunted by a Phantom.

They say Eugenia Ronder yet lives, perhaps with many spawn of her own, in the ancient and revered catacombs. They say she has learned to play *Don Juan Triumphant.*

They say that when people catch her unmasked, her maimed face is smiling.

*Thom Brannan & Matthew Baugh penned a Judex story (which is alluded to here) for our collection* The Shadow of Judex. *Thom now returns to the dark-clad avenger in this tale, which pits Judex and a most unexpected ally against another creature of the night...*

## Thom Brannan: *Holy Water*

*Paris, 1925*

The man in the overcoat and slouch hat stood atop the wall surrounding the Père Lachaise Cemetery and observed the ceremony from afar. His friend—or better, his acquaintance, as friendship was a thing hard to come by in his line of work—Matthieu Cordère was being buried today, his life snuffed out twelve hundred miles away, on the battlefield of Fort Zinderneuf in Morocco.

He was too far away to hear anything the priest was saying, and that was fine. He'd heard it before; he'd said it before. He was no stranger to death. He had been both judge and executioner, and he carried the name Judex. His presence at the ceremony would have caused a stir, in either his work clothes or not, as he and Matthieu traveled in vastly different circles, most of the time.

The ceremony wasn't why he was there, anyway. Not really. He looked back at the sun as it neared the horizon, then checked his watch. Time was close, and he was prepared to spend the night, or however long would be needed.

The details of Matthieu Cordère's demise were confused and contradictory, and the story set a fire in Judex's mind. Most of it could be discarded, but the sole detail which snagged like a hook in his brain was the massive blood loss reported. Matthieu hadn't been done in by the curved edge of a Rif *koummya*, but instead by a bullet from a captured Spanish rifle. But his body was almost entirely drained of blood.

Judex turned to watch the sun again.

He'd dealt with this once, six years before, when an aging actress had committed herself to the dark. He'd followed the trail of bloodless bodies and hard-won clues to her apartment door, and sent her into the nether.

Judge. Jury. Executioner.

The service was over before long, and the small crowd of friends and family dispersed. Even now, seven years after the end of the Great War, people had experienced so much death, they fell back into old patterns without realizing. A survival mechanism, no doubt.

Matthieu Cordère had been one of Judex's network of underworld spies and informers until he wasn't. The lure of another war, this one fought beside the Spanish on the northern corner of Africa, had successfully snagged his spirit. Full of dreams of success abroad, which would surely translate into prosperity at home, he left to serve under the Lion of Verdun.

And now, he was under the soil of Paris, France.

Full dark was nigh. The cemetery was as empty as night would have it, and the sun was no longer loitering near the horizon. By the time Judex reached the fresh dirt of the grave, it would be as dark as it gets. Judex stepped lightly off the wall, into the cemetery, and walked with purpose towards the grave of his ally. As he neared, he opened his overcoat, exposing the red lining within, and drew a pistol with his left hand. In his right, a rapier with a basket hilt and over-sized, straight quillon.

Judex would not, he found, have long to wait.

A mist grew from the rough rectangle of earth; it swirled and rose, gathering to itself substance and color, until the form of Matthieu Cordère stood before him, resplendent in the military uniform in which he had been buried. The face was the same, in essence, but the eyes and mouth which had been lit with good humor, even in dark times, were now hard and cruel.

"Judex," Matthieu hissed, and he smiled, baring elongated, exaggerated canines. "Have you come to welcome me back to Paris?"

In response, Judex held up the sword, and Matthieu laughed.

"Is that what you think? I'm afraid I am quite beyond having to fear that trinket."

The newly-risen dead man took a step forward, and Judex whirled the sword, planting it point-first in the dirt. Matthieu looked at it again and recoiled, for the sword with its oversized quillon had formed an effective cross. Matthieu's arms came up to shield his face, as if from a blow. He snarled and rushed to get around the sword, but Judex matched him step for step.

The right hand which had held the sword now held a stake.

Fear crept into Matthieu's voice. "You know. How did you already know?"

With silence as his only answer, Matthieu threw himself, with all his new speed, around the sword-cross, only to find himself impaled upon the stake in Judex' hand.

The man in black and red drove his former friend to the ground, then raised his foot and stamped the stake once, twice, until it bit dirt. Matthieu thrashed and his mouth worked, but no sound issued.

Retrieving the sword, Judex stood above his fallen comrade and whispered a prayer, one he feared would go unanswered. The sword rose and fell, almost as if on its own, and the head of Matthieu Cordère separated itself from his body. Judex dropped the sword and reached into an inner pocket, retrieving a small pile of holy wafers. He put them in Matthieu's mouth, and turned to dig the coffin back up. It was going to be a long night.

"Vampires," he cursed.

Judex rested in the shadows of the ruined keep which stood above his hidden lair and watched the sun come up. His blood had cooled considerably through the strain and effort it had taken to re-inter Matthieu, and he felt himself again.

Vampires. He'd only had one encounter with their type before, and it had been enough to last the rest of his life. It had marked him so thoroughly, the odd aspects of Matthieu's death report had called him to the cemetery with no question as to what he was facing.

But now that the work was done, and his former associate was at peace, the questions started. Why Matthieu Cordère? What advantage could be had by turning a *légionnaire* and sending him back to France?

The rising sun was now bright enough to force Judex to look away. As he did, he caught a glimpse of the sun reflecting in a shard of glass, ricocheting off in a dozen directions.

"How many more?" he muttered to himself.

Gathering his dark coat around him, he descended into the ruined castle, past open areas and through hidden doorways which only he knew, down to his lair below. The question drove him, how many more? He would have to be crafty; his military contacts at the moment were few and far-between. France's intervention on behalf of Spain in the Rif War had shuffled personnel around in a way for which he had not yet compensated, and his usual drops were no longer working.

"Vampires," he muttered again.

No matter. If the death and turning of his man was just a one-off, a coincidence which could not be accounted for, then all the better. A fiend in Morocco was not his concern. But it bore investigation, and this was not a matter Judex would take lightly. He was the only creature of the night France could stand.

Judex closed his eyes and conjured the image of Matthieu Cordère in his uniform. Medals just so, ribbons in order. Brass buttons on blue, red slacks, puffed and stuffed into high black boots. No, that would not do. If he were to get into any place where they held the medical records he needed, he'd have to either be an officer or a doctor. Of the two, a doctor would be easier, but without the authority he would require to infiltrate army headquarters in Paris. Ah, the knife edge of uncertainty.

His attaining of Matthieu Cordère's papers had been a fluke, but Judex believed no more in coincidence than he did the man in the moon. No, providence had handed him this mission. He'd do whatever he must to see it through.

He whirled and entered his closet, mind on the items he would need to do it right.

Colonel de Saint-Avit was at his wits' end with this pompous, puffed-up jaybird who had breezed into his records depot without so much as a *Bonjour*. The boy at the front had kicked this civilian interloper upstairs to him as soon as he could, and De Saint Avit was wishing he had an upstairs to kick this man, as well. But, as it were, his was the uppermost stair.

"Please, Monsieur Lavigne, explain once again?"

The civilian sighed and looked so wearily at him that the officer felt a momentary pang of regret. Then he caught himself... no, no, *he* was in the right here!

"Colonel, I'm afraid I only have the patience to go through one last time, and then I shall have to report in defeat to Marshall Pétain himself that I was unable to complete this one simple task he assigned me."

The colonel straightened at this casual mention of the Commander-in-Chief of all French forces in northern Africa. He resolved to handle this carefully.

"If you please," he said, "my ears are not what they used to be, especially after the shelling at Reims."

Monsieur Henri Lavigne executed a most elegant shrug. "That's war, it cannot be helped." The man leaned forward, placing his lips closer to Colonel de Saint-Avit's ear. "The Inspector-General has given me a most peculiar assignment, you see. He has heard through the grapevine that our sacred dead are being used to smuggle *items* into France from Morocco, but only those who have died in a certain way. He did not confide to me all the details, for he knows I am not one to bear up under such grotesqueries, but he did tell me what to look for. All I need from you, Colonel, is to allow me access to your files."

The officer leaned back and felt himself reddening. That was *all* he needed? He felt himself begin to sputter, and the civilian leaned forward again.

"I have this," he said, presenting a small envelope. It had a red wax seal on it, with the Great Seal of France thereon embossed. Colonel de Saint-Avit broke the seal and read the short missive within.

*31 October 1925*
*It is by my order and the good of the state that the bearer of this has done what he has done.*

*PÉTAIN*

De Saint-Avit felt himself deflating, and he handed back the small envelope. "This way, if you please, Monsieur."

Judex brooded in his lair, his notes spread out before him on the desk. He had taken quite the chance with Colonel de Saint-Avit, but he knew from his short research the man was not much of a reader. He cast a quick glance over at his Henri Lavigne costume draped over a chair and allowed himself a small smile. He was back to brooding before he knew it.

Nineteen others, all from the lower strata of French society, all shipped back home drained of blood. The official causes of death were wide and varied, but every one of them had come back with uninjured faces. It was infiltration, of course, but to what end? And who was the puppeteer, pulling their strings?

The pictures of the nineteen men were laid out on the desk, and Judex picked each up, one by one, committing their faces to memory before placing them on the wall. Nineteen fledgling vampires to find, each with the strength of many men and all the gifts the devil had to offer. As inured as he was to the darker aspects of the life he'd chosen for himself, he had had this particular nightmare for weeks after his last encounter with the undead. And here it was, on his desk and on his wall, come to life.

"Vampires," he cursed again.

Individually, he had a chance against the fiends, but if they were in any way congregated, he knew his death would be a foregone conclusion. No, no, physical confrontation was out. Judex would bet on himself against almost any man, but this was more than he could handle himself. Not without a plan. Not without nested plans, contingencies within contingencies.

But first, information.

The cemetery vexed him, in particular. As far as he knew, it was still consecrated ground. What could have happened to make it unhallowed? He made a note to contact a priest. He had the interment locations of all nineteen men, but too much time had passed to count on finding all or any of them there.

On the next wall, he pinned up a map of Morocco. He grimaced and took it back down. Over a quarter million square miles, that was no good. He went back to the reports and compared locations, then rifled through his maps. He found two maps, one of Fez and one of Meknes, and put them up side-by-side, positioned such that their respective locations and distances would be accurately mirrored on his wall. He then took twenty flags, one for each possible vampiric death, and placed them on the maps. When he was done, he took a step back and looked at the maps. Not enough.

Judex referenced the reports and then numbered the flags in the order of the deaths as they were reported.

And there it was.

Concentric waves of deaths, first in Fez, then in Meknes, but a definite pattern. And from that, Judex found a spot in the center of it all in each city. He marked both and stepped back again, smacking his fist into his hand, a sharp sound in the gloom. This was no time to travel, so Morocco would have to wait. Fortunately, the plot extended here, to Paris, with the nineteen fledgling vampires he knew of. He could poke this end of the hornet's nest and see what came flying in from Africa.

Judex dismissed that wall for now and turned back to the nineteen. He marked their burial locations in his mind and considered.

He'd need to contact more than one priest, then.

Or perhaps, one very special priest.

Jacques de Trémeuse stood before the Institut Catholique de Paris, hoping his contact in the Faculté de Théologie got his missive in time to prepare for him. Jacques knew there was a priest on loan from the Netherlands, Lankester Merrin, a visiting exorcist. This suited Jacques' purposes like a glove.

His contact, Father Comusse, stepped outside and beckoned him over. Jacques followed the priest into the school and they made a beeline for the faculty quarters, moving directly to the reading room.

"Monsieur de Trémeuse, you will have the room for fifteen minutes. I could arrange for no more on such short notice."

Jacques clapped the priest on the shoulder. "Nonsense, my friend. If I cannot convince *this* man in fifteen minutes, I could not convince him in fifteen days."

"*Merci, bonne chance.*"

Taking a deep breath, Jacques opened the reading room door and stepped in. Father Merrin sat in a richly upholstered chair, perusing a leatherbound edition. The title was mostly obscured by his grip on the book, and all Jacques could see of it was *Vermiis*. Father Merrin turned a sun-browned, high-planed face up to him and closed the book.

"Monsieur de Trémeuse, I presume?"

Jacques nodded one time, quietly surprised at the man's lack of an accent. "I am, Father. I have come to you today to talk about... well, Father, I cannot beat around the bush. Paris is about to have a serious vampire incursion, and I cannot handle it on my own."

Father Merrin took this in without any of the outrage or incredulity Jacques had feared.

"On your own, you say. Who are you, to have to stem this tide in the first place?"

"If it becomes necessary for you to know, you will know, Father. That is all I can say for now."

With a knowing smile, Father Merrin picked up a pipe from the small circular table next to him.

"You'll be the judge of that, eh?"

Jacques returned the smile. "Father Comusse hints too much."

"What is it you need from me, Monsieur de Trémeuse?"

Jacques leaned forward and unfurled his plan for the priest.

Two men in black approached the Père Lachaise Cemetery that night. One, a priest, Father Merrin. The other, Judex, in a black suit and oilcloth duster, slouch hat obscuring most of his face in the gloom. Practical in all things, he had eschewed his normal cloak for the greater storage available with the coat.

Also, it looked like rain.

"I'm not a bishop," Father Merrin muttered.

"You've already said," Judex answered. "We shall have to trust that the

Lord above will grant some mercy in this battle against the undead." He shifted inside his large coat. "Though, He knows well enough I shall not be surprised if He does not."

Father Merrin opened his valise and cast a wry smile at Judex. "Mysterious ways, *Monsieur le Juge*. Mysterious ways." He pulled an old and worn book from his bag, along with an eyeglass case. "Shall I begin?"

Judex remained on the alert, eyes and ears strained to their maximum. "Do as you must, please. And best were it done quickly."

Grunting with good humor, the priest turned toward the recently disturbed sod of Matthieu Cordère's final resting place. He launched into a Latin liturgy, and Judex tuned him out. There was one other grave in this place they had to visit, and then it was on to a different cemetery.

The first grave went quietly enough, with only a short interruption by a homeless man, looking for a place to lay his head for the night. He shuffled off quickly enough, and then Judex led Father Merrin to the next plot.

Here, as soon as the priest began his incantation, a streak of blue and red came out of the brush. Judex managed barely to intercept the fledgling vampire, only knocking him off his course. Father Merrin continued undisturbed, and Judex knew he'd gotten the right man for the job.

Reaching into his greatcoat, Judex drew one of his Steyr automatics. The vampire laughed at this, and he bared his chest for the black-clad vigilante.

Thunderous gunfire drowned out the Latin rite, and the vampire laughed again. "Was that supposed to hurt, you fool?"

With a Parisian shrug, Judex thumbed the switch on the side of his gun and his remaining rounds fountained out. From his left-hand pocket, he withdrew another stripper clip of ammunition and reloaded the gun.

"Try again?" he asked the vampire, who had come within ten feet of him.

The vampire straightened, considering. "You are a valiant one! Your blood will make me strong! Come, foolish brave heart. Do as you must to meet your end with dignity."

Judex bowed his thanks and unloaded the gun into the vampire's chest. These rounds tore into the undead body, ejecting fluids and steam as they expanded and tumbled through the supernatural flesh.

The vampire collapsed, trying to scoop its blood back into the open chest cavity. Father Merron's Latin faltered at the sight of this, but he turned away and continued his work.

"Express bullets," said Judex to the vampire, "filled with a drop of holy water each, fashioned from colloidal silver."

The vampire sputtered.

"*That* was supposed to hurt," Judex continued, holstering his gun. He drew a foot-long stake from inside his coat, along with a short-handled sledgehammer. A blow from the sledgehammer ceased the vampire's jerking for a moment, more than long enough for the man in black to set the stake and pound it into place. He laid these to the side and drew his rapier from under the coat, then decapitated the vampire.

Father Merrin finished his liturgy and stooped to assist Judex with his cleaning up. "I had no idea you were carrying around so much," the priest said.

"The burden I carry is heavy," Judex said. "Compared to that, these are but a trifle." He sheathed his sword and collected his implements from the priest. "We have a long night ahead of us. We must get moving."

Father Merrin gestured to the corpse. "And this?"

"I have men on the way. They'll be behind us all night."

He turned and stalked away, the priest shaking his head in his wake.

Judex stood watch as the priest did the sixth grave of the night and considered this as an untenable situation. There had been no interference since the last, and he knew that somehow, word had gotten to the rest of them. Was it a feeling they had? Did they share some kind of telepathic communication? Or was it just the luck of the Devil?

There was no telling, and this would be the last time they did it at night. Waiting for one vampire to show up was bad enough; if they showed up in force, as he feared, it would be his nightmare come to life.

Judex had divested himself of the cross-carved bullets which had had no effect on the vampire. The holy silver, though, he kept those close at hand and vowed to make more of them. Father Merrin had seemed skeptical when he was blessing the colloidal silver mix, but the results spoke for themselves.

The exorcist finished this last grave for the night, and Judex hustled them both back to his sleek black modern car. The sun was on the rise, but that didn't mean much to Judex. Some vampire lore said they, the undead, could not operate during the daytime, but other accounts merely downgraded their powers under the light of the sun. Preferring to fail safe, Judex acted as if the latter were true until proven otherwise.

They had arranged for the priest to have a short leave of absence from the Institut Catholique de Paris for at least a fortnight. After they dealt with the remaining graves in Paris and the outlying areas, the good father was going to take a train to Marseilles, and here, a steamship south. As it were, they powered towards the Château-Rouge, where Judex maintained his hidden lair. The mutual decision was made to sleep until noon, then take the rest of the available daylight to get as much done as they could.

That night, though, Judex had plans. The idea of this many vampires moving in at once had been simmering in the back of his mind, and he thought he had an avenue of investigation which would yield results.

He sent the priest off to rest and himself turned in. Sleep was elusive, but Judex turned to breathing techniques he'd learned early in his career, for his mind was almost always in turmoil. Injustice felt like an interminable condition, and the fight wore at him like the tide eroding away a rock. He had had his justice against the man who'd set him on this path, but there was always something. Judex closed his eyes and sleep overtook him.

In his guise as M. Vallieres, which he had not worn for some time, Judex made his way into the Centre des Impôts Fonciers. He went straight for the busy clerk and cleared his throat. The man looked up from his paperwork and adjusted his glasses.

"Yes, can I help you?"

Judex cleared his throat again. "I have come to view the *plans cadastraux*, my good man."

The clerk reached for his visitor registry. "May I ask the purpose for this?"

"Once upon a time, I was the right-hand man for the banker Favraux. He, as you may know, died under less than honorable circumstances, and we all thought everything was behind us. Unfortunately, it appears some of the land transactions which were under his auspices have recently come under suspicion, and to clear my own conscience, I have come to research the *lieu dit* and *bornage* of the properties in question."

The clerk was already filling out the registry. "Land registration research, check. Sign here, *Monsieur*."

Judex signed the book with a flourish and returned it.

"That way," the clerk said, pointing, attention already back on his papers.

Judex turned away, a wry smile on his face. It appeared his efforts to disguise himself were unnecessary. He went into the land registry and looked for the most recent purchases, in particular those made in bulk by one party. In less than an hour, he had tallied several dozen property transactions to investigate. The purchases made by individuals he thought he could perhaps ignore; if he were up against an older vampire with money to burn and financial savvy of the ages, he was sure any purchases would be made through shell companies. However, he was not ignorant of their mesmeric powers, so all of these would bear research.

He pocketed his list and took a last look at the large map of Paris hung in the room. *I will find you*, he thought, *and I will serve justice.*

With a short glance at the clerk, still absorbed in his paperwork, Judex left the Centre des Impôts Fonciers and headed to the offices of Alfred Cocantin, a private investigator with whom he had often collaborated. He and his adopted son, Petit Jean, have been instrumental in several of Judex' successes.

He found them in a celebratory mood, having just concluded some investigation or other. While Cocantin was still a passable investigator, the real energy in the office came from the son these days. The orphan he'd taken in had been instrumental in organizing Judex' eyes and ears with the youth of the street, and he was not shy about using them for his own ends.

They noticed him in the room at the same time. Jean (no longer Petit Jean or The Kid) remained cool, but Cocantin shuddered in his chair as he almost always did.

"Never will I become accustomed to the way you just appear, M. Judex," he said, "but come, join us! We are celebrating the successful conclusion to my final investigation as the head of the agency."

Judex held in his surprise. Somehow, it felt as if he'd never considered that Cocantin might retire one day, but he had already been past middle age when they started working together.

"Congratulations," Judex said after a moment. "I shall send for champagne, provided we all live through what is coming next."

Jean sat up straight, all mirth gone, and Cocantin's joviality faded almost as quickly. "Tell us," they said.

As quickly as possible, Judex filled them in on what he knew and what he needed to know.

"Vampires, again," Jean said. He wiped his mouth with the back of his hand. "I suspect it won't be over as quickly as last time."

"It will not."

Jean nodded. "Fear not. The eyes and ears of the street shall not fail you. Nor ourselves; truth be told, the element of self-preservation will light fires under some feet which money would not otherwise move."

Judex clapped the young man on the shoulder and turned to leave. He stood outside their door for a moment, slightly regretting the ice-cold water he'd thrown on their celebration, but the dark would not rest.

Father Lankester Merrin stepped off the steamship in the port of Casablanca with his single bag and looked immediately for transportation. He wished for his part in this to be over as quickly as possible. Yes, he had made it his career to face down Evil, but the method he'd chosen (or which had been chosen for him) was very rigid and well-documented, with rites and rituals and rules. This new darkness was amorphous and chaotic; there were still rules, but Father Merrin didn't know them as well as he ought.

He was about to step up to a carriage when a voice stopped him.

"*Monsieur l'Abbé*, it is not that one you want."

Father Merrin turned to find a wizened old man behind him, dressed in a white linen suit, holding a cane before him and leaning on it with both hands.

"Chevalier Auguste Dupin, at your service," the older man said with a very slight bow. "I have been wondering when the Judge would send somebody. I have been waiting at the port for a week." A smile took some years off the old man's face. "He must be busy."

The priest extended a hand. "Father Lankester Merrin," he said. "How did you know he would... that I would... did he wire you a message?"

A glint of amusement came into Dupin's eyes, but he shook his head. "I am tempted to show off, but we have very serious business to attend. Come this way. I have arranged for very fast transport to Fez."

Dupin set off at a rapid pace for such an old man, and Father Merrin found himself stumbling to keep up. More than anything else at the moment, he was confused. It was as he had just thought: chaos.

On the ride to Fez, which took two days with horse and driver changes, Dupin and Merrin exchanged their stories, and the priest was at first skeptical that the old man had deduced what was happening from the few clues he'd given at the start of his story, but after the detective had elaborated on his process, the priest was a believer.

"It was fascinating, to put myself in the mind of such a predator," he said as they neared Fez.

"Yes, well," Father Merrin said, "I am thankful that such is not my purview." He shuddered. "Not with my foes."

"Surely," Dupin said, "that would be the ruin of anyone in your profession. As would be an excess of empathy. There, I feel, we are alike."

Father Merrin wondered what the wizened detective meant by this, exactly, but decided he did not want to know. The man came off as a bloodless calculating machine, highly amused by his own deductions. Whether that was true would be determined by more time spent in his vicinity, but the priest wasn't sure he had the stomach for that. There was quite enough on his plate.

Dupin knocked his cane on the deck of the carriage. "Best to approach the property during the daylight hours, I believe. Have you brought the necessary implements of destruction?"

The priest gathered his valise closer to him. "Destruction, no. My best offense is a God defense." He looked out the carriage window. "How much longer until we arrive?"

"Presently," the detective said. "Oh, we're almost there."

The two days after the priest had left had been interminable, as far as Judex was concerned. He had sifted through all the land deals by then and knew all the players; this information might not be pertinent for the vampire menace, but one never knew when a nugget of knowledge might come in handy. Nonetheless, he felt as if he were in his overpowered car, spinning his wheels in autumn mud.

Jean crept into Judex's study, and the vigilante thought he'd never been happier to see him.

"What news from the street?"

With a wide smile, the brash young man handed over a list. All but four of the properties had been crossed off the list.

"These are the ones you want," he said. "Nobody in or out for days, except some uncouth lookin' deliverymen, packing large wooden boxes."

Judex grunted. "Dirt, no doubt. Thank you. And thank your urchins and ruffians, as well." He tossed a heavy leather purse to the young man. "Keep them away from those buildings. Yourself, as well."

The smile ratcheted down several notches. "I can help! You saw how good I did—"

"No," Judex interrupted. "That was one vampire. This is twenty, if their chief is already in France. Absolutely not."

"Come on, you're not going up against twenty of them, not by yourself. Just the one last time almost left you dead, and if it weren't for me—"

"If it weren't for you, I'd be dead. Or worse. I know." Judex sighed. "And if anything happens to me, it would happen to you, too. And if that comes to pass, who would be there to act as avenger?"

Jean pursed his lips. "That's pretty low, boss. And yet."

"And yet," Judex repeated. "Besides. I won't be on my own." He patted the side of an ammunition box next to his desk. "Father Merrin has left me an equalizer."

"We could all go," Jean said, trying his final gambit. "The whole lot of us. Maybe there's twenty vampires, but the streets are endless."

"The streets are in enough danger, from within or without. No. You keep everybody clear of these properties, and I will do what needs to be done."

Jean, defiant, tossed a jaunty salute to the dark figure on his way out, and Judex, in silence, watched him go. Perhaps it had been a mistake to bring up the possibility of him having to avenge his death; he had no wish for any others to have to walk the same path as he. But it did the job, and he was sure Jean would keep himself clear, if for only that reason. Must there always be a Judex?

He shuddered.

The time was late, and he was not rested. Judex knew he'd have to get an early start on the day to hit all of these places while the sun shone bright. Luckily, he had not spent all of his time poring over papers and land deeds.

He stood and hefted a valise of stakes, dowels of wood half a meter long and sharpened to pitiless spikes. He snatched up the box of special 9mm ammunition for his Steyr-Hahns. He already had his sword in the car, as well as several other small devices and incendiaries.

It was going to be one hell of a day.

Father Merrin approached the house as the sun was rising. He had his valise slung across his back and a great crucifix in his hands, as provided by the increasingly insufferable Dupin. The priest checked himself. The detective had an impressive skill, and Merrin found himself more in awe of the deductions made and the steps taken in complete confidence of his predicted outcomes. The prepared travel means and materials he had ready, even knowing ahead of time that he, Father Merrin, would be a priest, a Jesuit, specifically. He was unnerved, and thus found himself easily prone to disliking Dupin.

With that bit of navel-gazing out of the way, Merrin proceeded to the front door.

The house was seemingly untouched by the turmoil in Morocco, which also unnerved the priest. He pushed the square door in the vaguely bullet-shaped door frame and it swung open on silent hinges. The interior was dark, all windows covered in heavy drapes, high ceilings disappearing into shadow. The profusion of slim columns brought to mind pairs of giant fangs.

Taking a deep breath, Father Merrin closed the door behind him and advanced into the house. He lit the brand-new flashlight provided by the detective, and its weak yellow light was welcome.

The spaces were completely bereft of furnishings. No decorations on the walls, no tables or chairs, not enough things in the house to fill even a small wagon. The priest ventured from empty room to empty room, drifting deeper and deeper into the house.

He came to the last room and took hold of the ringed door handle. In his right hand, he held his large crucifix, and the flashlight hung from his teeth by its brass ring. He took a deep breath and pushed the door open.

In the center of the room lie an ornate casket, somewhere between an oversized aquarium and an infant's coffin of etched glass and carved ebon wood. For reasons unfathomed, it brought to Father Merrin's mind the Ark of an obscene Covenant. Eternal life, inverted to represent centuries of bloodshed.

Within the glass walls of the casket lie a man, a pale man, with a full head of auburn hair, long sideburns down to the edge of his jaw. He wore garb native to Morocco; he was dressed in soft-looking black cloth, embroidered at the sleeve ends and hem in white, with matching pants. Over this, he wore a white robe in opposition, black embroidery on the trim. Low slippers sat on his crossed feet. Father Merrin looked at all this, and when he brought the flashlight back to the face, the eyes were open and fully black.

The priest took a stumbling step back as the figure rose in the glass casket. An arm pushed open the thick metal lid, which must have easily weighed several hundred pounds, and the vampire stood.

The gun-barrel eyes landed on the priest's, and the vampire smiled.

"Apologies for the state of my house. We are in the process of relocating to far friendlier climes. And you are?"

The priest extended the crucifix. "I am Father Lankester Merrin, empowered by His Holiness Pius XI to—"

The vampire blurred from standing in his coffin, holding up the lid, to standing a meter from Father Merrin. The *clang* of the falling coffin lid cut off whatever else the priest was going to say.

"Ah, of course," the vampire said. He bowed. "I am Lord Ruthven, at your service." He winked, the sclera in his all-black eyes clearing to white. "And you're going to have to deliver your name with more conviction if you want people to believe you."

The phrase shook the priest out of his shock. His grip on the large crucifix strengthened, and he raised the flashlight in a steady hand.

"And where, good priest, are your weapons? How are you to destroy my flesh and release my soul?"

"I—"

The door to the room opened behind them. Both Merrin and Ruthven looked to see Dupin standing in the doorway, cane before him.

"I take it we're to the point where the father has admitted he's brought no weapons?"

Father Merrin gaped at him and Ruthven laughed.

"I suspected as much. *Permettez-moi.*"

His left hand came up with a .45 Colt 1911, and he fired four times. The vampire, who hadn't moved, looked at Dupin with amusement on his face.

"Your turn, priest!" Dupin near-shouted.

Merrin snapped out of his state of shock and saw the gaping hole in the glass of Lord Ruthven's casket.

"Oh," he said.

Loathe to throw it, Father Merrin dipped into his pocket and launched something at the hole in the coffin. Ruthven caught it and immediately let it fall from a smoking hand.

"Eucharist, I believe," Dupin said, as the priest threw three more. They sailed into the coffin and landed inside. Ruthven looked from the holy wafers to Father Merrin as Dupin changed magazines.

Snarling in his momentary defeat, for that was his only resting place in the entire house, Ruthven blurred away, slamming into the heavy metal and glass casket. It screeched away from them, revealing a heavy trapdoor set into the floor. He wrenched it open and dropped into darkness, the wooden trapdoor slamming behind him.

"Come," Dupin said, "we should get away while we can. The vampire is temporarily inconvenienced by this, but he was on his way to France anyway, we've only accelerated his timeline. But fear not, dear priest, I have prepared for this moment."

Spinning on the detective, Father Merrin was close to losing his composure. "How?"

Dupin shrugged eloquently. "How would I know where he lived without knowing everything else, dear sir? Before I approached you in Casablanca, I sent off some papers which I had been preparing for just this moment. All of Lord Ruthven's assets are now, through admittedly less than legal channels, mine. And since that does not confront me very much, I have arranged a dirigible for your return to Paris."

Father Merrin was still in shock. "You what?"

Dupin smiled. "*Allons-y!*"

Judex hammered home the seventeenth stake of the day and fell back, sweating and exhausted. He was in the sixth of seven properties, and he had not moved quickly enough. The sun was fast on its way down, and there were still two vampires left to behead. He had planned his route and... *dispatch* duties in excruciating detail, but even his iron thews were paying for the lack of rest. He'd pushed himself like this before, but never against such implacable foes. He'd been too slow to stake and dismember the last houseful of the undead, and now he was out of time.

The three vampires he'd just staked to their coffins were still to have their heads removed. He still had enough of the eucharist to do the job, but he was fatigued to the point where he was requiring more than one blow to sever the necks completely.

It was just too much for one man.

Judex shifted his hands on the hilt of his sword, renewing his grip and his resolve. He would complete this portion of his task, and then he would gird himself for what came with the nightfall. His gloves felt as they'd been soaked through with blood and sweat, even though he'd been extremely careful. With only a slight tremor in his arms, he lifted the sword and brought it down. Once, twice, three times.

Satisfied with his cuts, he wiped the blade and sheathed the sword before taking a wobbly step towards his black valise of items blessed by Father Merrin. He had rifled through it and found the holy wafers when the sun finally set. He felt the change from day to night, somehow, and hurried to stuff the wafers into the mouths of the severed heads.

That sorted, he retreated to the corner of the large room in which he had been working and squatted down, his back to the wall. Judex knew not if the vampire corps had any kind of telepathic communication, if the two remaining vampires would know their brethren were gone from the nighttime world, but if they did, it was only a matter of time before they came looking for the reason.

He resolved to be ready if they did.

Judex was practicing breathing exercises to remain awake and alert when he heard a sound in the house. The breathing had helped to rejuvenate him some small amount, but he was still enormously tired. Stifling a groan, he stood and unholstered his matching Steyr-Hahn pistols. Suddenly, he was no longer alone in the room. He hadn't heard a door or window open, but a man stood in the middle of the room, looking down at his headless cohorts.

"I can smell you, you know," he said. "You reek of sweat and self-assured righteousness. And... what is that, gun oil?"

Judex raised the automatics, fingers on the triggers.

The vampire moved, and Judex' first two shots missed their marks entirely. He fired three more times, not yet feeling the iron grip on his wrists, forcing the barrels upward. The vampire was there, in his face, bared fangs dripping with something clear and viscous. Judex pushed with all his considerable might, but it was like trying to arm-wrestle a marble statue.

"Are you curious as to how it's going to sound when I crack open your sternum to remove your still beating heart, fool?"

There was a loud *crack!* and the vampire twitched. He and Judex looked down together to see a brightly polished metal arrow protruding from the vampire's chest.

"If *you* were curious," Jean Cocantin said from the doorway, "that was the sound of a W.W. Greener harpoon gun."

He yanked, and suddenly Judex felt his hands free. He wasted no time, aiming and pouring his last few rounds into the writhing vampire. When the slides locked back, he dropped the guns and drew his sword, rushing forward to decapitate the vampire.

Once the head sprang away from the body, he relaxed and let the sword fall from his tired hands. Dragging, he retrieved his pistols and ejected the empty magazines to reload.

"You're not going to yell at me about showing up?"

Judex sighed. "You've been behind me all day, just waiting for a chance to show off." He looked up at Jean. "How did you know the harpoon wouldn't get me, too?"

"Huh?" Jean said, the smile slipping a notch.

Shaking his head, Judex got slowly to his feet. "We have to find the final vampire. It might show here, or—"

"Oh!" Jean said brightly. "The Grands-Champs Faction just radioed in. They got him as he left the house, about ten minutes after this one." He pointed to the recently severed head.

Judex looked up at Jean. "How did your street urchins afford a radio transmitter?"

"Secrets are exciting, aren't they? What's next, boss?"

Peeling his gloves off, Judex snatched up his sword and indicated the pile of severed heads. "Gather those up. Wafers in that new one. They all go in the bag. We'll burn them at the Château-Rouge." He finally grinned. "Are you still glad you followed along?"

Jean slung the harpoon rifle on his back. "You just have to *win*, don't you?"

When Judex and Jean returned to the Château-Rouge, they found Father Merrin waiting for them. The priest quickly told of his encounter with Auguste Dupin and their subsequent face-off with Lord Ruthven.

Judex sat on his desk and removed his slouch hat.

"A dirigible." He rubbed his face with his hands, which he had dry-scrubbed in a bucket of sand several times while the priest talked. "There is no rust on the Chevalier. He must be very old by now. You've beaten this Lord Ruthven to Paris by at least a full day, thanks to him. This is good." He passed a hand over his eyes, realizing how fully tired he was. "I have a plan. There is one property left which is still available. The rest, we have cleansed of his filth and salted against him. I have a plan for the last building. Are you ready to hear it?"

Jean and the priest looked at each other, then back to Judex.

"*Allons-y*," the priest said.

Judex stood in the center of a wide-open space in the last building, waiting for the sun to go down. He was rested, he was well-fed and felt limber. It was a good night of sleep; there were nightmares, but that was the norm for him. He'd led a life full of danger and placing himself in the path of Evil, a little bit of nighttime terror was to be expected. The priest and Jean and his army of urchins had been busy through the day, and he was ready.

They were ready.

He reflected on waiting for the sun to go down, was it only a little over a week ago? Waiting on the wall of the Père Lachaise, waiting to see if his suspicions were correct. And now this, the closing of the circle.

The energy in the room changed as the sun dipped below the horizon. From the grate in the middle of the floor rose a mist which grew and ballooned to almost fill the space before it condensed to manlike proportions. It became solid, and before him stood Lord Ruthven.

The vampire was resplendent in his fashion. He wore a charcoal frock coat with just a hint of blue over a dark brown vest. A high-collared white shirt was accentuated by a black cravat, studded in the center with a gem of some kind. A gold watch chain hung at his waist, and he held a Cahill hat in black. It was slightly behind the times, but it fit with the vampire's looks and demeanor.

Judex felt the vampire's eyes looking him over, taking in the suit, the cape, the slouch hat.

"*Monsieur le Juge*, I must presume," Lord Ruthven finally said. "I have followed your career with interest, knowing this moment must eventually come. You have my respect."

Judex tilted his head in acknowledgment.

"Then you must know, Lord Ruthven, how much preparation means to me. And so, sir, you have a choice."

Lord Ruthven smiled. "I am riveted."

"Just so," Judex said. "Your fledgling brood is no more. Whatever plan you had to seed yourself in Paris is over. All you have left to your name is this building in which we stand, and I would wager you know next to nothing about it."

Bemused confusion crossed the vampire's face. "This is a very confusing threat. Or are you stalling?"

"Stalling? No. This is a warning, Lord Ruthven. You will leave Paris and all of your machinations for France will cease. Otherwise…" He held up a lighter.

The toothy smile returned to Lord Ruthven's face. "You're going to burn this place down, with me in it? And yourself, as well? This is again, a very confusing threat."

Judex sighed. "This building, my lord vampire, has a history from before you bought it through your shell corporations. It was a textile factory, and the previous owner was forward-thinking in technology and safety, if not business. You should be able to see now, with your enhanced vision, the light web which emanates from where I stand."

"I can."

"Excellent. This building was retrofitted with a firefighting system from Grinnell Co., an outfit in America which installs automatic sprinkler systems. Very modern."

The vampire wrinkled his eyebrows.

"Yes, still a warning," Judex said. "The priest you met the other day, he's been very busy while you slept in your mound of dirt. Every entrance and exit to this building has been sealed against your kind, from the windows to the doors to the ventilation to the waterways. For benefit, the previous owner had a survey done, updating the architectural blueprints, not for such an occasion, but we would be foolish not to take advantage."

"So I'm trapped in here," Lord Ruthven said, the smile slipping, "with you."

"My lord vampire, I am no fool. I know it is I who is trapped in here with you; however, if anything happens to me, my associate outside will do what I cannot. The web you see stretches from where I stand to all of the fire detectors in this vast space. The web is made of short-time safety fuse, black powder core in yarn sleeving. If I were to light it, you might be able to snuff some of it before it reached the detectors, but not all of them. And if any of them go off?" Judex shrugged. "All of the sprinklers go off."

"Water?" Lord Ruthven asked. "Perhaps my estimation of your abilities was wrong."

"I have done physical battle with the undead, My Lord, and I am sure you outclass them all. And so, I must take a different tact." He gestured upwards. "Holy water," Judex said, his voice strengthening. "Gallons and gallons of holy water, and you with no way out. We don't burn together, as you first thought. We both get very wet, and I watch you die—perhaps your final death."

Lord Ruthven seemed to thrum, moving without moving, and the full force of his attention was on Judex now.

Judex bowed. "You come from a time before, where your word was your bond. Take this opportunity to leave Paris, to leave France, and to never return. If you give me your word."

Judex put out his right hand. The left flicked the lighter, holding it perilously close to the web of fuse.

Lord Ruthven stared, and finally sagged.

"The world is changing, my dear vigilante," he finally said. "The Great War has come and gone, and there will be another. Technology proliferates at a frightening rate, even for one such as I. I was hoping, through a new brood of my own kind, to gain some foothold in this new world, but you have put me in check. What shall I do, my fellow creature of the night?"

"You've very wise," Judex said. He did not waver. "What do you have in mind?"

Lord Ruthven smiled. His teeth were very white and very sharp in his face.

"I think, *Monsieur* Judex, I shall close the circle."

He rushed at Judex, and the man in black lit the web of fuses. Like an explosion of light rays, fire spread to each sprinkler head as Ruthven drove Judex to the ground.

Judex tried to hold back the hands which held him by the neck, but he might as well have been trying to lift a tree from the ground. The water started coming down, and the vampire screamed and streamed as it hit him, but he kept the pressure on. Judex slammed his fists into the undead forearms and elbows, tried strikes at the vampire's neck, all to no avail. The world started to go dark, and all the while the vampire screamed.

As his vision dimmed to a single point, all he could see was fangs.

Later in the day, Judex awoke on his own. He was in a bed at the Château-Rouge. He recognized he was in the small medical room he kept for emergencies. Next to him in a chair slept Father Merrin, an open Bible in his lap.

He grunted, and the priest woke up, catching the Bible before it could fall. Judex grunted again, trying to ask a question, but nothing came out.

"It is done," the priest said. "We did as you said, waiting a full ten minutes before going in. You were under a pile of clothes, with no sign of the vampire. We brought you here and Monsieur Cocantin had a doctor in tow to look at you. You cannot speak right now, but that will pass. There is blood in your eyes from the pressure, but that will clear, as well. All in all, things went well."

Judex nodded, closing his eyes. When he opened them again, the shadows had shifted and the priest was in a different set of clothes.

"I'm headed back to the Institut for a respite from my respite," he said, a smile on his face. "You're improving with rest." Father Merrin stood and extended his hand. "Thank you, Monsieur de Trémeuse. My chosen profession has little in the way of actual combat with specters of Evil, combating instead the small ways in which men harm themselves and each other. It is, in short, a very frustrating way to live. This, as dangerous as it was, was a welcome reminder that things could be worse."

Judex forced himself upright to take the priest's hand. He stayed that way until the man was out of the room, then he laid back on his pillow. He was quiet, by nature, so this was alright by him. He watched the window, enjoying the clear blue sky he could see. As it darkened, Paris came to life, and he pondered what Lord Ruthven had had to say about technology and war. And he agreed.

He watched the sun go down and started planning for what was next to come.

*Despite the undisputed slickness of the new* Mission Impossible *films, they don't make thrillers the way they used to in the 1970s. Fortunately, Nathan Cabaniss is here to remedy this by crafting slick action-packed yarns that bring together a surprising coterie of the best heroes and villains of the times...*

## Nathan Cabaniss: *Get Fantômas*

*Tangier, 1970*

There was a creak in the floorboards, and the old man opened his eyes. Instinctively, his hand went to the Luger pistol beneath his pillow, fumbling with the safety catch as he untangled himself from the sheets. He didn't dare turn on the lights, didn't bother with his slippers... He padded barefoot across the room, careful to make as little sound as possible.

He paused at the door of his bedroom, listening for any further signs of the intruder. He lived in a humble flat that used to be a café on the outskirts of the city, nice and quiet and out of the way, but that also made him an easy target for squatters—vagabonds on the so-called "hippie trail" that stretched from Europe to South Asia. They occasionally knocked on his door, English and American children who stank of Arab dope, thinking the café was still in operation. All the old man had to do was show them a glimpse of his Luger, and that prompted them to be quickly on their way.

Not hearing any more sounds in the hallway outside his bedroom, the old man stepped quietly across the threshold, Luger poised and at the ready. He didn't think any of the hippie children would be bold enough to break into his house while he was sleeping, but he wasn't prepared to take any chances.

As soon as his foot touched the floorboard on the other side, he felt a cold bite of metal against his throat. The sharpened tip drew a dab of blood, which felt like a bead of sweat running down his neck.

"*Graf* Hugo von der Drache," a voice called out, in tones as smooth as silk. "What a pleasure to meet you."

The old man was shocked, his mouth going dry at the mention of that ancient name—one he himself hadn't heard spoken aloud in years. "How do you know that name?"

"*You can only hide your sins for so long before they catch back up with you,*" the voice replied in German, before switching back to English as easily as slipping on a pair of worn slippers: "MI6 thought you were killed in that submarine, but you and I know better, don't we?"

A gloved hand emerged from the shadows and took the Luger from the old man's grasp. He didn't try to resist. After years of cheating death, having to constantly look over his shoulder, cover his tracks—this was finally the end. He found himself feeling an odd sense of calm. There was something almost soothing in knowing all of that was behind him now. "Who are you?"

The knife disappeared from his throat, and a figure materialized from the shadows... almost growing out of them. The old man couldn't help but gasp at the sight. What stood before him had the general shape of a man, but it couldn't possibly be human...

It wore an all-black suit with leather gloves, but the head... *the head* was smooth and featureless. The gargoyle-like face had a wide-set nose and piercing blue eyes that burned like the last embers of a dying fire. The thin slit of a mouth curled up at the end, and the old man realized the thing was *smiling* at him.

"You don't need to worry about who I am," it said, pointing the Luger at the old man, "all that need concern you is what I want."

"I have nothing of value..."

"My dear Count," the creature continued, voice never wavering from its smooth, easy tenor. "We both know that isn't true."

"Believe what you want," the old man said, finding his spine. He didn't care if the thing before him was a demon from Hell, come to drag him down into the flames. He was tired of playing games. "Have a look around for yourself. There's nothing here."

The gargoyle-faced thing raised its knife again, and the old man flinched. Amused, the creature merely tapped his forehead with the blade's tip. "What I want is in here. You may be old and feeble now, but I know you've still got it tucked away up there somewhere."

"I don't know what you're talking about..."

"You once had various plans for specialized, long-range missiles. You even bragged they would soar high enough rake the Moon... How it must have rankled you to see the Americans touch down upon its surface not even fifteen years later."

"That's impossible," the old man said. "Those plans were lost years ago. I couldn't possibly recreate them from memory..."

"I have ways of extracting information that would surprise even an ex-Nazi like you. You're going to tell me everything," the gargoyle man said, the thin slit of a smile growing wider as it spoke, "and then you're going to die."

*Two Years Later*

"Agent N-3, confirm channel is secure..."
"This is N-3. Call sign NYW-41-46-86."
"Channel secured. What's your position?"
"Still in the nest."
"The birdie?"
"Hasn't flown the coop, as yet."

"Copy. Maintain position and keep a close watch. With any luck, the threats are all a load of bunk, anyway."

"We can only hope. N-3, out."

The line went dead after a click. Nick Carter allowed himself the luxury of looking up from the telephoto lens, satisfied that nothing exciting would happen for at least the next few minutes. After a full day of nonstop meetings, Senator Thomas Jordan had seemed to settle in for the night: relaxing in a lounger while listening to music, only getting up to change out records once they finished playing. The curtains to his room were drawn (his accompanying Secret Service had done that much right, at least), but Carter found a spot in the adjacent building that give him the perfect line of sight to Jordan's lounger, visible through a thin gap.

He'd been vacationing in Rome, working on his tan and buying drinks for women, when AXE called him back in for a special assignment in London. It wasn't a big deal, as he was already in Europe, and starting to feel a bit antsy, anyway. He'd already had a big assignment in the U.K. within the last year, and this was nothing more than a glorified babysitting job.

Carter didn't know why Johnson needed the extra protection from AXE when the Senator already had his own detail, not to mention the MI5 agents he clocked posted up in the immediate area; surely that would be enough bodies for a visiting politician. There had been an attempt on Jordan's life during his presidential run in '59, though, so Carter guessed they were taking no chances when they got wind of another threat.

He checked the lens again: the esteemed Senator was still sitting in the lounger, and was now enjoying a cigar. Wishing he had one of his own, Carter lit up a cigarette instead. He ought to just go over there and ask Jordan for one of those stogies; the Senator owed him a whole case for going to all this trouble, by Carter's reckoning. More than likely his Secret Service boys would call him crazy and throw him back on the street. Hardly anyone even knew the existence of AXE, outside the President of the United States. The tattoo of a blue axe just above his right elbow was supposed to identify him as an agent, but what good did that do, when no one knew the agency existed in the first place?

Just then, Carter heard the noise—something like an ice pick poking a hole in a frozen lake. His eyes went back to the lens, and saw a hole in the window pane, perfectly placed between the gap in the curtains. In the room, Senator Thomas Jordan was slumped over in his lounger, unmoving; a red stain growing on his chest. There was a flurry of movement, hard to make out in the gap of the curtains. A pair of hands pulled the Senator out of his chair to the floor. The Secret Service was doing their job, locking the area down, but from what Carter could tell, it was already too late.

The MI5 agents outside must have heard, too, as they blew their cover to rush the building. Carter didn't think twice. He broke down the lens and tripod, started taking apart the rifle he had set up in case he needed to take care of any immediate threats. That was something he knew he'd have trouble explaining—the angle of the shot through the gap in the curtains meant it had to come from the building across the street, and before long he'd have agents swarming him, wondering why he was posted up in that very same building...

He could take the lead and search the building for the shooter, but more than likely they'd fled as soon as they took the shot. No, it was better to get out while he could, then he'd check in with AXE and see where things stood.

As if reading his mind, a voice crackled on the radio, not even bothering with proper protocol: "What the hell's going on out there, N-3? Did you take a shot?"

"Negative," Carter growled, a little incensed. *Why would they even ask that question?* "It wasn't me."

"Chatter over the wire is saying the shot came from the building across the street..."

"Why the hell would I shoot a man I'm supposed to protect?"

There was a long, uncomfortable silence. The hair on Carter's arms stood on end. Something wasn't right.

"Hold position and await further orders."

"There's no time. MI5's about to be up my..."

"*Hold position*, N-3. That's an order."

The line clicked off. Carter froze in place, trying to decide what to do next and running out of time. Why would the agency want him to stay in place at such a critical moment? He went back over the previous conversation in his head, taking note of the tremble in the operator's voice. They were nervous, indecisive... *Did they actually think he had* killed *Jordan?* It was too much to process in too little time, with every second bringing him closer to having to make a cataclysmic decision to prevent being arrested on foreign soil.

Finally, the radio crackled back to life. Different voice, this time: "Nick... Listen, we think the best course of action is for you to surrender yourself to the authorities there. Just cooperate for now, and we'll get this all straightened out later. Bring you back home, safe and sound..."

That was when Carter knew. They were hanging him out to dry... *Someone had set him up.*

He killed the radio and drew Wilhelmina, his modified Luger pistol. He left his gear where it was and headed for the door. First course of action was to get clear of this building, get as far away from the scene as he could. Where he went after that would have to be a decision for another guy to make, one who wasn't currently across the street from the scene of a murdered politician...

Checking that the hallway was clear, he left the room he'd been posted up in for the better part of the night. It was an office building, and had been empty since close of business earlier that day. He ran to the stairwell, hoping it would remain empty in the time it'd take to clear the seven floors to the ground.

As soon as he started his descent, he heard them: footsteps, coming from the bottom of the stairwell. Could be the overnight cleaning crew, just getting in now to start their rounds through the building. He chanced a glimpse over the railing, saw they weren't carrying cleaning supplies.

"Hold it right there! Move and we shoot!"

Carter took off the other way, heading up the stairs. They opened fire on him, trying to bring him in the hard way now. He fired a couple warning shots from Wilhelmina back at them, disabusing them of the notion. He didn't want to off some poor schmuck who was just earning a paycheck, but he also didn't want to walk out of here in handcuffs.

The only exit now was the roof. He didn't know what he'd do when he got there or what he'd do after that, but he was sure of one thing…

Nick Carter was going to find the son of a bitch who set him up.

The noise of the club was blaring. The bartender asked him what he wanted for the second time.

"Single malt," he yelled over the noise. It was an expensive choice, but he allowed himself the luxury. Tyrone Tackett was a stranger in a strange land, dealing with jetlag and a growing headache, but he'd been paid a healthy sum to cross the Atlantic and take the job. He could afford to drink the expensive stuff for the duration of his stay.

The bartender gave him his drink, and he slunk off to a booth in the corner. He wished he'd kept looking for a more quiet place, but he was tired of tramping down London streets, needing to take the edge off after an eleven-hour flight. Besides, the two pubs he'd tried previously seemed to stop as soon as he stepped through the doors, all eyes on him like he was the ghost of Al Jolson. Maybe they weren't used to seeing such a fly-ass brother with an actual sense of fashion. Or maybe they were just a bunch of old racists. Either way, Tyrone wasn't eager to stick around and find out. At least in this place, the clientele was much younger, and wouldn't have given a damn if he were green and had antenna sticking out of his head.

Tyrone took a generous pull of the single malt, felt himself begin to relax as it went down smooth and easy. This was what he thought the life of a professional killer was when he was younger, based on what he read in cheap novels and movies at the drive-in. Travelling the world, living in luxury as you took out high-profile criminals and corrupt dictators; not being asked to knock-off some old lady and her kids for a buck-fifty, all because they happened to be in the wrong place at the wrong time. Tyrone hadn't sunk quite that low, but he was far from a saint.

But *this*… This was something different entirely. He was skeptical of the offer at first, thinking some crank had gotten a hold of his number, until the money came over the wire. Twenty-thousand American dollars, with the promise of sixty more upon arrival; plus all travel expenses covered, offered by some cat calling himself "Gurn." It was hard to say "no" after that. It might as well have been a paid vacation.

Taking another sip of his drink, he happened to look across the room, and caught a pair of eyes checking him out. Honey-brown eyes, with lashes that ran for days. Her hair was done up in an afro, and she wore a leopard-print pantsuit, hugging her so tight it didn't leave much to the imagination.

Seeing she had his attention, she gave him a glimpse of her pearly whites. Tyrone smiled back, but stayed sharp—he was here on someone else's dime, after all, and an expensive one, at that. No telling who might come sniffing around.

They played a game of eyes for a while, checking every so often to make sure each still had the other's attention. Tyrone had to admit: he wouldn't mind getting to know this one better. There was no reason he couldn't enjoy himself while abroad, but at the same time, there was also no reason to wind up with a bullet between his eyes in a tangle of bed-sheets.

She was the one to make the first move. She sauntered over to him, hips swaying for all they were worth. She was a tall one—had to be over six feet, and moved every inch of that frame like a pro, in total control of her every gesture. When she spoke, her accent was American. "Good to see a fellow Yank."

"How'd you know I was American?"

"I can always tell. It's a vibe."

*Sure you can*, he thought.

"You mind if I join you?" Whatever her game was, he had to find out one way or another, so Tyrone shrugged and motioned for her to sit.

She took the seat across from him, sitting her handbag on the table. Tyrone knew enough to know it was an expensive one. "You here for business, or pleasure?" she asked.

Tyrone smirked. "You tell me, mama."

She laughed at that, and Tyrone felt himself melt a little at the sound. What he'd give to be a normal dude now, his only worry being whether or not he remembered to pack his rubbers.

"I'm here for work," she said. "I'm a model."

He could believe that. She was a fox, no doubt. "You been in anything I would have seen?"

"Mostly magazines. I do the odd commercial, here and there." She shrugged it away like it was no big deal. "I can't say I love it, but I do get to travel the world. Meet interesting people..." She smiled at him again, turning the charm up to eleven. "What about you? What do you do for a living?"

He once met an ex-Mafioso who shared his profession that used to tell people he *"painted houses."* It was a little too on-the-nose for Tyrone, but he liked the idea of being considered an artist. "Guess you could say I'm a painter."

She didn't say anything at first, holding his eyes like she was studying him for a test later. Then, out of nowhere, she burst into laughter. It wasn't the gentle, flirty titter of before. This one sounded more like she was laughing *at him*.

He didn't like that. "I say something funny?"

"Oh, Tyrone," she said, raising his hackles. "Where'd you get that one from? The TV?"

Tyrone's smile was gone. "I don't remember telling you my name..."

She smirked at him, but it wasn't flirty this time. Tyrone started from his seat, but the woman pulled a gun from her handbag, showing him the business end of the barrel.

"The name's Cleopatra Jones," she said, "and I'm afraid you're in over your head, sugar."

"C will see you now, Sir."

Neil Burnside nodded at the secretary, and entered the office of the head of all British Intelligence.

"Neil." The man behind the old oak desk closed the blotter of files before him. "Close the door, why don't you?"

Burnside did as he was bid, pulling the leather-bound door shut. The new C hadn't been in office for very long, only recently appointed after a scandal brought down his predecessor. He was a relic, but also a first-rate spy. The two shared a history, and Burnside knew he could trust him with his life if it came to it, but he also guessed it was only a matter of time before the old man crumbled in his new position; such was the way with men of any integrity in this profession. Still, it was good to have someone capable in the big seat, for a change. Among the relics, he was certainly a better choice for leadership than that boob from the Double-0 section.

"C," Burnside replied as he took his place, standing at the foot of the desk. "Or do you still prefer 'Control?'"

"I'd prefer 'George.' Or 'Smiley,' at the very least." C closed his eyes and rubbed the bridge of his nose. "Take a seat. You're making me nervous."

Burnside again did as he was bid, fearing he was in for a long one. He was a highly-trained operative of the Special Operations Section, known colloquially around MI6 as a "Sandbagger." C had requested to meet with Burnside personally; called him into his office, no less. He didn't know why, but considering C had bypassed Burnside's immediate superior completely, he guessed it wasn't anything good.

He waited for C to continue, but the old spook merely removed his glasses. He wiped the smudges on the glass away with his tie, looking very deep in thought all the while.

Burnside waited as patiently as he could before getting to it: "Forgive me for asking, Sir, but... Why am I here?"

"I need someone I can trust."

"You don't trust D-Ops?"

"I don't trust him to do the job *right*." C finished with his spectacles. He put them back on and looked Burnside in the eye. "The situation is rather... delicate."

"What is it?"

"The American politician who was killed last night."

"I thought Five would be taking the lead on that..."

"Suspect number one is a foreigner. Interpol's issued a red notice, so we'll be kindly offering our services to MI5."

"They love that, no doubt. What's the name?"

"That's where it gets complicated. It's an American." C opened the file again, flipping through the assembled documents. "Name's Nick Carter. The red notice lists him as freelance, but our intel places him as an operative for some agency called AXE... one of these offshoot spy factories the Americans are so fond of these days. He holds the rank of 'Killmaster.'" C couldn't help but sneer at that last bit.

"How quaint," Burnside said. "Have you spoken with Langley?"

C frowned. "They claim they don't know any operative by the name of 'Nick Carter,' and deny all knowledge of the existence of any organization known as AXE."

Burnside nodded. *Typical.* The CIA could talk all they wanted to about the "Special Relationship," but only held to it when it benefitted *their* country. "So what are we thinking? Agent gone rogue?"

"It seems that way." C became contemplative, fumbling with his glasses once more. "Or at least, that's what we're being led to think."

Burnside raised an eyebrow. "Surely the Americans wouldn't kill one of their own..."

"Ask JFK." C paused, placing his elbows on the desk and lacing his fingers together. "I don't know, Neil, but I do have questions. Something about this stinks to high heaven, and I fear we're only at the starting line."

Burnside didn't say anything for a time. It was an odd affair. As far as he knew, the American politician had been visiting the U.K. for the most rudimentary of diplomatic functions. *"Strengthening the bond between our two countries,"* and the like—little more than a convenient excuse to give the U.S. Senator a holiday.

Whatever the angle was, Burnside couldn't yet see it from his vantage. "What do you need me to do?"

"Find Carter, first and foremost."

Burnside nodded. "When I find him, should I... ?"

"Absolutely not," C said, shutting the door on that subject quite definitively. "This could go any number of ways. Perhaps Carter's gone rogue, perhaps he was acting on orders... Perhaps he was framed as part of a larger plot. Whatever it is, I need you to get to the bottom of it, Neil. *Quietly*. We can't do anything to jeopardize the Special Relationship."

"Forgive me, Sir, but it sounds like the Americans already have…"

There was the sound of a latch being undone, and the heavy metal door opened with an ancient, rusty creak.

"Right this way," the man on the other side said. He wore a brown fedora with a tweed coat, his face accentuated by a pair of square glasses and a thin mustache. When he spoke, it was English with a French accent. "You're the last to arrive."

Tyrone nodded, and stepped through the door. They were underground—possibly somewhere in the London sewer system, given the dank atmosphere and the pungent smell. Tyrone didn't know, as he'd been brought here blindfolded. He tried his best to relax and remain calm, but his nerves were already shot, and the twenty-minute trip with his eyes covered hadn't helped. This was a world to which he was unaccustomed to, with rules and rituals that made sense only to the initiated. Every step was one filled with danger, but he had to go through with it. Tyrone didn't have any other choice.

As they walked through a damp tunnel, the Frenchman attempted to strike up a conversation. "Tackett, isn't it? I'm called Joubert." Tyrone didn't say anything, so Joubert continued: "You're from California, yes?"

"That's right," Tyrone said, annoyed. He wasn't eager to strike up a conversation.

"I hope to visit some day. California looks so lovely in your American movies…" Tyrone didn't provide any further comment, hoping to kill any chitchat before it started. It worked: they walked the rest of the way in silence, Joubert leading Tyrone further underground.

They reached the end of the tunnel, which fed into a larger area. It seemed to be some manner of pumping station that was no longer in use; a cold, wet place that echoed with dripping water and other tinny, indistinct sounds.

A crowd was gathered therein, with faces from all across the world. Killers, thugs, assassins… Tyrone put on his best hard face, trying to keep his cool. "Join the crowd," Joubert said with another self-satisfied smirk. "The show is set to start soon."

Tyrone took a spot toward the back of the room, more than aware that he was being watched. Eyes from across the room sized him up, determining who would come out on top if they wanted to groove.

Joubert stepped upon the raised platform at the head of the room, joining a white woman with long, blonde hair. She held a coiled whip in her gloved fist and wore a leather, bikini-style outfit. There was another standing with them, a large Chinese man with muscles that bulged like a modern-day Hercules.

Joubert nodded at the woman, who uncoiled her whip and gave it a sharp crack. The room halted, everyone inside appearing to hold their breath. Another emerged from behind the three on the stage, seemed to materialize out of nowhere from the shadows.

It was another woman, this one with dark hair and softer features than the blonde with the whip. She wore a pale blue dress, and moved to the head of the platform with uncanny grace. Something about her seemed not quite human— she looked like she was floating when she moved, ghostly and ethereal.

"Our host thanks you all for accepting his invitation," she said, her red lips parting into a smile. "While he regrets he cannot attend in person, he has elected me to speak on his behalf. My name is Lady Beltham, and it is my pleasure to welcome you all into a brave new age. The age of Fantômas..."

The woman on the stage continued her spiel, but Tyrone found it hard to pay attention. He couldn't say he dug this scene at all, but it's not like he'd had much choice...

"*Believe me when I tell you, Tyrone,*" Cleopatra Jones had told him the other night, after leading him out of the night-club at gunpoint, "I'm doing you a favor."

Tyrone did what she told him. He thought maybe if he waited, he could get close enough to snatch the pistol away from her and knock her out cold before she knew what hit her, but the woman kept enough distance between them the whole time.

"Yeah, you're just full of generosity tonight," Tyrone said, eyeing the gun-barrel pointed directly at him.

"Sorry, but I have to make sure you behave while we hash some things out."

"Just who the hell are you, anyway?"

"I already told you who I am..."

"That's not what I mean. Why do you give a damn about my business?"

"It's my job," Cleo said simply.

"What, you a cop or something?"

"Or something," she said, before stopping him in front of a brand-new Corvette Stingray, parked on the street. Even under the circumstances, Tyrone had to admit it was a nice ride. She opened the passenger door for him, and then got behind the wheel, gun on him the whole time.

"We going somewhere?" Tyrone asked.

Cleo didn't start the engine. Instead, she leaned back against the car door, keeping her gun where it was. "You're being set-up, Tyrone," she said, fixing him with a hard stare. "They paid you all that money to come out here and take a fall."

Tyrone narrowed his eyes. "What do you mean?"

"Why do you think they brought a low-rent hood from Oakland across the Atlantic? You think you're that special? They want you to do their dirty work, and then take the heat off them when you get caught."

Tyrone paused, thinking it over. He didn't want to look a gift horse in the mouth when the offer first came through, but now he had questions. "Why should I trust *you*?"

"I've got no reason to lie to you."

"Easy to say when you're the one holding the gun."

Cleo paused for a moment. "You're right," she said, before putting the piece away. "I can't make you do anything. You wanna leave right now, feel free. But just know: you go through with this job, you'll be taken for a punk."

Tyrone gritted his teeth, feeling like he was being drawn further into a trap. The cheese was right there, but so was the spring. He was too far in now, anyway; he had to know the score before he could make his next move. "Ticket's paid for," he said, relenting. "Might as well stick around for the main event."

Cleo was quiet for a time, her eyes going distant. "I got one name for you: *Fantômas*."

"Name means nothing to me."

"It should. He's the cat who brought you out here. Been around for the better part of this century. Wrote the book on murder, extortion and terrorism. I've been chasing him the last couple years, after I stumbled onto the body of some old Nazi in Tangier, who once tried to bomb London... I believe he was killed by Fantômas. He's planning something big, but I don't know what, just yet." Her long lashes parted as she locked eyes with Tyrone. "That's where you come in."

Tyrone shook his head, grunting out a laugh. It was typical... The more time he spent wandering God's Green Earth, the more apparent it became how the world really worked. Everybody had a game, and everything had its price. That's all people were to each other, when you got right down to it. Just means to an end.

"Something funny?" Cleo asked.

"Not at all," Tyrone said. "Look, I don't know what you want me for. All I know is I was promised eighty large to come over here and do a job. No details 'til I met my contact, where I'd receive further instruction."

"That's perfect, actually. We get a wire on you going into that meet, and we'll have a better idea at what Fantômas is planning..."

"'We' nothing. You think I'm gonna walk anywhere wired up, you're out your mind..."

"Like I said before: nothing's stopping you from leaving this car and going about your business. But you do that, then nothing's stopping *me* from hauling your ass away to a deep, dark hole where you'll never see the sun again."

"I call 'bull' on that," Tyrone said. "So far, all I've heard is nothing but hot air."

"It'll be easy. All it takes is one phone call to my boss."

"Who's that? J. Edgar Hoover?"

"Try the President of the United States."

Tyrone raised an eyebrow. "Face facts, Tyrone, baby," she said with a smirk, "you don't have a choice."

And just like that, Tyrone found himself in some godforsaken *sewer*, a wire riding up his crotch in a roomful of the most dangerous killers on the planet.

"*Our mission is twofold,*" the fancy woman on the stage continued, and Tyrone snapped back to the present. He got that feeling he used to get in school, when he wasn't paying attention and hoped the teacher wouldn't call his name. "Each of you will be assigned a target. The elimination of each target will weaken faith in the various espionage and spy organizations of the world, leading them to doubt and mistrust one another. Then, Fantômas will deliver the *coup de grace...*"

Tyrone tried to pay attention, but he found the words washed over him like driftwood from a sinking ship—passing him by as he drowned, but giving him nothing to grab onto. He could always try and get away. Everyone's attention was focused on the makeshift stage. The room was full of shadows. He could slip into any of them and disappear into the night, Miss Cleopatra Jones be damned. Anything to get out of this nest of vipers...

"I call our first assassin to the stage," Lady Beltham said, beckoning to the audience with a slim white hand. "Bring forth the Jackal."

A man in dark glasses weaved his way through the crowd, dressed in an equally dark pea-coat and ascot. He stepped on the stage, and Lady Beltham moved aside as the large Chinese man, whose name was Bolo, frisked him, and Tyrone felt his stomach drop. That settled it—Tyrone *had* to get out of here, right this instant.

With everyone's attention fixed to the platform ahead, Tyrone took a few tentative steps backwards. On the stage, Bolo found a pistol and knife on the assassin. He turned to Lady Beltham, and she nodded. The Chinese man gave the Jackal back his weapons, and motioned for him to stand in place behind Lady Beltham.

Tyrone continued to inch his way backwards, subtly searching the room with his eyes for an exit whilst trying not to grab the attention of the crowd surrounding him...

Just then, he locked eyes with Lady Beltham, whose red lips curled into a smile that was anything but welcoming.

"*You,*" she said, pointing a slender finger right at Tyrone. "You're next."

Burnside lifted up from a crouch, his knees popping as he rose, not feeling any better than he had before deciding to send new flames of pain shooting down to his feet.

He looked over the room once more, seeing if there was anything in the three bodies arranged on the floor that he might have missed. They were all male, athletically-built with brutish faces. Possibly European, but they were lacking identification, so it was hard to say. Burnside suspected a few of them had faces that would show up on Interpol's Red List, but identifying them would take *days* at the very least, and he didn't have that kind of time.

Whoever was here had torn through all three like a hurricane. Burnside knew in his gut it had to be Carter (only an American could be so trigger-happy), but the assassin left no trace. He'd taken them all out with kill-shots to the heart, leaving no casings or wild shots in the walls. Ballistics could always try the bullets in their corpses, but Burnside suspected that would lead nowhere, too. Carter was a professional killer, and knew how to get away with murder in just about every country on the planet.

With a sharp inhale, Burnside left the room, nodding to the Scotland Yard Inspector as he passed. The Inspector tried to stop him, desperate for anything he could use, but Burnside cut him off with a shrug, telling him he'd let him know if anything came to light, knowing good and well that nothing would.

He left the building through a rear exit, bringing him out into the wet English night. The pavement of the alley shined with tacky Soho neon of the street just ahead, like all the sex shops and clip joints lining the streets had been poured into a container too small to hold them and were now spilling over its edges. Burnside pulled a cigarette from the pack he'd hidden in his coat pocket. The wife had been nagging him to quit, but the marriage was on its way out, so he allowed himself the vice. It's not like he'd be home any time soon, anyway... one of the many reasons she had decided to call it quits.

She'd accused him of being married to the Service instead, and Burnside found it hard to disagree. He couldn't say it was love that kept him tied to Queen and Country, but it was certainly a stronger pull than anything he'd ever felt for any woman. Put simply, somewhere out there, there were people doing wrong, and Neil Burnside couldn't rest until he'd put a stop to it. He'd like to say it was it some noble quest for justice that made him this way, but deep down he knew it was more selfish than that: Burnside had to outsmart the bastards, plain and simple.

As he started to light the cigarette, Burnside felt something metal press into his back.

"No sudden moves, Mack," a voice called from the shadows. A voice with a distinctly American accent.

Burnside didn't raise his hands, but he held them open at his sides. "Come back to admire your handiwork, Carter?"

"You're Burnside, right?" Carter replied. "With MI6?"

"We prefer 'SIS,' actually," Burnside said, trying to think of a way out of this. "Why don't you put the gun away? I'm not armed..."

"Not until I have a few assurances."

Burnside sighed. "It would make things a whole lot easier if you'd turn yourself in. If you're innocent, we can get it sorted..."

"Not so fast," Carter said, cutting him off. "If I come in, it's on *my* terms, and my terms only. I need a helping hand here, not a pair of handcuffs."

Burnside turned around slowly, his hands still open at his sides. "So let me help you."

Carter paused, keeping his gun trained as he weighed his options. Burnside took the opportunity to study him carefully. He matched the description Burnside had been given: handsome in a rugged, very American way, with hardened lines around his grey eyes and a cleft in his chin.

After a moment, Carter let the gun drop to his side. "I'm going to trust you on this, Burnside. All I ask is that you trust me, too."

"Of course," Burnside lied, lowering his hands as casually as he could. "So... where do we go from here?"

"Everything's so complicated, like a knot with too many tangles." Carter holstered his pistol, rubbed at the side of his temples. "Do you have a place I can get cleaned up? Maybe take a shower, cool my heels for a bit?"

"I know of a safe-house nearby. There's an apartment we rent for surveillance purposes."

Carter nodded. "After I get freshened up, get a chance to get my head right, then we can talk about me coming in..."

Burnside looked him over. Carter certainly looked the worse for wear. His clothing was roughed up—torn and haggard, with parts of it rust-colored and caked with dried blood. Burnside took particular notice of a tear at the elbow which cut through Carter's jacket and shirt sleeve, wide enough to show off a white patch of skin beneath. Seeing this immediately gave Burnside pause.

"Let's get to it, then," Burnside said, leading them towards the Soho streets ahead, trying to think his way out of what was almost certainly a trap...

Whoever it was standing before him, it wasn't Nick Carter.


"*You... you're next.*"

Lady Beltham's slender finger was pointing directly at Tyrone, and everything in the room seemed to come to a sudden halt. All eyes turned to him, the crowd parting for him like he was Charlton Heston at the Red Sea. It was like they all knew exactly who he was and why he was here, naked and stripped of everything except for the wired bug running between his legs and taped to the small of his back.

His mouth dry, Tyrone attempted to swallow as nonchalantly as he could, but it came out in an awkward cough. Realizing he couldn't delay this, he slowly made his way to the platform. Not that it would matter in few seconds anyway... everyone's suspicions would be well and fully raised at that point.

Tyrone found himself at the foot of the platform before he knew it. He took another glance at the figures on-stage before stepping up. Tyrone reckoned he could pull his pistol and take out Lady Beltham the quickest, but he also didn't want to give the dominatrix to her left any chance to use that whip. The well-dressed Joubert was probably armed as well, so he'd have to deal with him before he pulled heat. And he didn't want to give the giant any opportunity to clear the stage and get his hands anywhere near him; he was big enough that Tyrone was sure he'd have to empty half a clip before the big man would go down and *stay* down.

Of course, all of that was assuming no one in the crowd of killers and assassins would take a swing at him, either. He could hope that they would wait for their checks to clear before rushing to the aid of their employers, but he was in a room full of the most deadly individuals on the planet, all of them primed and ready to get in on the action. No matter how he played his hand, the odds were against him.

Tyrone took his first hesitant step onto the platform, unable to draw the moment out any further.

"Tyrone Tackett," Lady Beltham said. "Are you committed to our cause?"

His mouth dry, Tyrone could only nod.

"Let us see, then," the Lady said. "Bolo."

The large Chinese man approached Tyrone, motioning for him to raise his hands.

*This was it...* it was now or never. Tyrone started to raise his hands, planning to pull his pistol and put one in the big dude's head before anyone knew any better...

Suddenly, the Jackal leapt forward, drawing a Luger and grabbing Lady Beltham by the waist. Before anyone could do anything, he was holding her in front of him, pressing the barrel of the Luger hard into her cheek...

"Anyone moves, and this one gets a new hole to breathe out of."

The three others on the stage tensed, ready for action. The blonde woman in the leather getup uncoiled her whip, poised like a panther ready for the strike.

"I said nobody moves..."

"You're not the Jackal," Lady Beltham said.

"And you're not a Lady," the man with the Luger said. "Tell your friends to back it up."

Tyrone froze where he was, unable to get a handle on how the situation was developing. Everyone was focused on the fake Jackal and his hostage. The question was... were they so distracted that Tyrone could slip away without notice? Moving so slowly as to be barely perceptible, he took a single step backwards...

"You must know there's no way out of this," Lady Beltham said, smiling devilishly in spite of the gun barrel against her cheek. "At least, not alive..."

"If I go, you go, sister."

"Is that what this is, then? An elaborate suicide?"

"I want the big man himself," the fake Jackal said. "I want Fantômas."

119

"*I'm already tired of this,*" Lady Beltham sighed under her breath, before addressing the crowd: "A million dollars to whoever brings me this man's head!"

Tyrone heard a roomful of clicks and metallic scrapes, the sound of the gathered killers and assassins all drawing their weapons at once.

Tyrone sighed. *So much for waiting for the checks to cash...*

"It's just up here," Burnside side, pointing out the safe-house to his companion.

"Nick Carter" nodded, following along for now. It was a risk, leaving his back open on a man with a gun, but it's not like Burnside could do anything about it otherwise. He was unarmed himself, and besides, he'd prefer to find a way out of his current predicament without turning things into the O.K. Corral.

All he had to do was get whoever this was into the safe-house apartment, let him think he was safe. Then Burnside could think of a way out of this, get some help... but there were too many questions left unanswered in the meantime.

"You say you think you were set up," Burnside threw over his shoulder as they walked, trying once again to get a better feel for where he stood. "Why would someone want us to think you killed that Senator?"

"How should I know? I've just been trying to *survive*, man."

"And that was what happened to those men in Soho," Burnside said. "Just you... surviving."

"What do you think?"

"I just want to get a clear picture. In order to help you, I'm going to need all the facts I can get..."

"Look, buddy, we can talk it all over as soon as I've had a shower and a chance to think straight. Then I'll tell you everything you want to know."

*Ah... so that's it, then.* The imposter *wanted* to be brought to the safe-house. Why was that, Burnside wondered. Unable to put the pieces of the puzzle together fully, he decided it was time for a curveball.

Burnside stopped, turning around apologetically. "You know what—this probably isn't a good idea."

"What do you mean?"

"I'll be completely honest with you," Burnside said, attempting sincerity. "The room's probably bugged. As soon as we enter, my superiors will know we're there."

"So? If it's bugged, let 'em listen. All they'll hear is the truth."

"Yes, but they're focused on bringing you in, no matter what. They won't care what you have to say..."

"Let's just get inside, yeah? All I need is..."

"A shower and a chance to think straight." Burnside smirked. "Yes, you may have mentioned it."

"I say something funny?"

"Not at all. I just find it odd that you're willing to come in now, after refusing an offer from your own agency..."

"What, you think I'm leading you into some kind of trap? It's *your* safe-house."

"And you're the one with the gun."

They stood in the chill night air for a solid minute, each sizing the other up. Almost as if a switch was flipped, Carter's expression changed from an angry scowl to a bemused smirk. "I think that's enough verbal gymnastics for one night, Mr. Burnside. Don't you?" His voice changed, losing its hard-edged Yank tenor and becoming something infinitely smoother, more seductive. The accent was now French.

"You're not Nick Carter."

"I'm not? What a disappointment..."

"Carter has a tattoo on his inner elbow," Burnside said, nodding at the tear in the imposter's jacket. "When choosing your disguise, perhaps next time don't take your coat off a dead man. Was it Carter's?"

"Carter is beyond my grasp at the moment. But never fear... I'll find him, all in good time."

"So it's you, then?"

The imposter raised an eyebrow, bemused. "I'm afraid I don't follow..."

"The man behind the curtain," Burnside said. "The one calling all the shots."

The imposter chuckled as he pulled a silencer from his pocket, and screwed it into the barrel of his pistol. "Let's go inside, shall we?"

"No, I don't think that will be happening now."

"Either way suits me fine. Nick Carter's gone rogue... If he executes a British spy in the street, it only helps me."

"But then everyone will know that spy is dead, and thus no one will be able to impersonate him down at Century House." The imposter's smile dropped, his eyes going cold. "What, you think I didn't know? You seem to be a master of disguise, whoever you are. You won't kill me unless you're sure you can take my place."

"*I'm also good at improvising,*" the imposter said. Something about the timbre of his voice, the way his eyes wouldn't catch the light... Burnside felt the hairs on the back of his neck stand up on end. "Come now, Burnside. You can't talk your way out of this one. You're dying tonight—in that, you have no choice. But how messy it gets will be entirely up to you..."

Burnside had to admit: his chances weren't good. The Nick Carter imposter was right. He could talk all wanted, but no matter how clever he was, none of that would stop a bullet. All he could do now was keep the imposter from taking him inside. The safe-house was indeed bugged, but by the time any help could arrive, he'd be dead.

Just then, the sound of an engine roared from the other side of the street. Both men turned in time to see a Corvette Stingray take the corner, barreling right toward them. The imposter raised his pistol, but machine gun fire filled the night. Concrete exploded at their feet, and Burnside and the imposter dove on opposite sides of the street as the Stingray flew between them.

The imposter fled down a dark alley as the Stingray's tires squealed to stop, the barrels of two machine guns smoking from within the headlights. There was a woman at the wheel, wearing a leopard skin cat-suit like some tart from the cover of a magazine. She pulled a revolver and had the door open in a flash, throwing bullets into the alley after the Carter imposter.

There were no groans of pain or thuds of impact from the darkened alley. There was no sound whatsoever.

"*Damn*," the woman said, lowering the smoking revolver to her side.

Burnside pulled himself up from the street. The woman turned, quick as a cat, and Burnside raised his hands slowly. She gave him the once over with her eyes, before putting the revolver away.

She gave Burnside a sly smile. "You need a ride, honey?"

At a loss for words, Burnside could only nod. "I suppose so…"

The woman jumped back in the Stingray, the engine still purring. "Well, hop in. Looks like we got a long night ahead of us…"

Burnside was now completely lost. "I'm sorry… who are you again?"

"Don't worry, sugar," Cleopatra Jones said, her long eyelashes batting a thousand. "I'm the cavalry."


Nick Carter couldn't catch a break. As far as nights went, he'd certainly had better.

He held the woman by the waist, the barrel of Wilhelmina at her cheek. The three assassins on the stage were coiled like springs, ready to pounce at the first opportunity they had. And now, the rest of the crowd were eager to get in on the action, drawing their weapons after Lady Beltham's offer. Turns out Carter was worth one million U.S. dollars… he would have been flattered, if he hadn't found himself fighting for his life.

He only found out about this gathering not even five hours previous, after taking care of a roomful of Albanian gangsters. They were all in the employ of this Fantômas the Lady mentioned earlier, orchestrating the murder of Senator Jordan and putting the frame on Carter. The AXE agent was beginning to suspect it was Fantômas himself who had pulled the trigger. It was all part of some larger plan, turning the governments of the world against each other and kicking off some new world war or another, but Carter couldn't say he was too concerned with the specifics. All he wanted to do was to put Fantômas in the ground…

A prospect that was looking less and less likely as the night wore on. The blonde with the whip let it uncoil at her side, ready to strike. If Carter was going to make a move, it had to be now. He let go of Lady Beltham and pushed her into her three bodyguards, before sticking his hand down his pants and reaching between his legs. That's where he kept Pierre, his third and most dangerous weapon. He twisted the egg-shaped capsule and threw it at the Lady's feet, before holding his breath and leaping off the platform.

Lady Beltham took the first whiff and collapsed instantly, foaming at the mouth. The others seemed to cotton what was going on, covering their mouths and putting distance between themselves and Pierre.

"*Gas!*" the Frenchman shouted, pulling a handkerchief and covering his nose and mouth as he ran from the stage. The room erupted like a bomb. No one tried to stop Carter as he carved a path through the crowd of assassins, each of them now more worried about the colorless, odorless gas that was quickly spreading through the room. A few gunshots went off, everyone shouting and trying to break through the chaos. Carter made his way through the throng as bodies crashed and tripped over themselves, not above putting a few down with Wilhelmina when they got in his way. Many of them had already hit the ground, their eyes bulging and foam sputtering from their lips.

Finally, Carter made it to the tunnel where they had all entered. He got the heavy door open and latched it behind him, the door sealing the air behind him. He let his breath go and took a few more deep breaths to get his lungs back into rhythm. Using Pierre was always a zero-sum game, as likely to kill Carter as it was his intended victims. This little revenge of his was turning out to be more trouble than it was worth.

Carter leaned his head against the rusted metal door, still catching his breath. "*Fantômas,*" he whispered to himself. That was all that mattered. He chanted the name over and over again in his head, until it burned like a rash that wouldn't stop itching. He stood up straight again, tightening his grip on Wilhelmina. The anger surged through him like a rush of adrenaline, ready to carry him to gates of Hell itself, if that's what it took.

Getting his hands on Fantômas... that was all that mattered now.

He took off down the lengthy tunnel, trying to remember the way out. He'd counted his steps before when they brought him down blindfolded, but the tunnels were dark and twisting—likely dug years ago and built over so much, no one even knew they were here. An urban tangle beneath one of the largest cities on the planet.

A cough just ahead brought him to a full-stop. The barest sliver of light showed a turn in the tunnel just ahead, and Carter could hear shuffling noises emanating from the corridor around the bend. Just some bum who'd made his home underground... or something worse? Carter readied Wilhelmina, began easing his way along the tunnels' edge...

Without realizing it, the barrel of Wilhelmina scraped against the tunnel walls, resulting in a brief shriek of metal on metal. The shuffling around the corner stopped, and the tunnel was deathly silent. Carter waited, listening for the slightest scuffle. Nothing moved on the other side. Maybe it wasn't anything to worry about, just the sounds of an especially large rat who got out of there as soon as he heard someone coming.

A dark figure sprung around the corner. Carter couldn't make out any features, but he could make out the outline of the gun in its hands…

He didn't think twice. Carter pulled the trigger, and gunshots bounced off the tunnel walls.

The Stingray took another wild turn, tires screeching in the London night, as Burnside gripped the dashboard to keep from being tossed about like a ragdoll. "Can't you keep this thing bloody *straight?*"

Cleo kept her cool behind the wheel, tries screeching as she took the next left. "You don't like it, you can always call a cab."

"London isn't made for this kind of driving…"

"We don't have time. I lost audio as soon as he went underground," she said, motioning to the radar screen that folded out from the center dashboard. "The signal's weak, but I can still track the bug I put on him. I have to pull my asset out of there…"

Burnside glanced at the dashboard, the blinking dot on the cathode-ray screen awkwardly jutting out from the collapsible panel. "Does this tell us where he is?"

"Not exact coordinates, but it'll let us know when we're close."

Burnside couldn't help rolling his eyes. It was patently ridiculous, the type of nonsense the boob from the Double-0 section wasted his time with. Equally ridiculous was the woman's story, but a call to her from the car phone confirmed she was an American agent, so he had to believe her. At the very least, her story backed up Carter's innocence, so that matter could be put to bed. Now it was simply a matter of finding the "Killmaster" before he wrecked half the country on his mission of vengeance.

"You really have no idea what this Fantômas is up to?" Saying the name out loud made him feel like a fool, but remembering the deep voice and the cold eyes from earlier, Burnside found himself involuntarily shudder.

"The Nazi he killed in Tangier was a rocket scientist who tried to bomb London in the fifties, so two guesses what he's up to now…"

Burnside considered the pieces laid before him, but none of them added up to a sum he could make any sense of. "If he's planning a missile strike, then why assassinate a U.S. senator?"

"That's what I'm hoping my asset can tell us… if he's still alive."

"Assuming he hasn't turned tail and run off himself…"

"Relax, Jeeves. This cat's from Oakland… they don't fold easy."

*If he's smart, he will,* Burnside thought, but said nothing aloud. *Fantômas…* it couldn't possibly be the genuine article, could it? If the geezer was still alive, he'd have to be well over a hundred years old. No way someone that old could stage something of this scale; no way the man he met earlier was the terror of Paris from the early part of the century. Yet Burnside kept thinking of that cold stare, those eyes that didn't seem to catch the light, and couldn't help but wonder...

When Cleo spoke, Burnside had to keep himself from jumping in his seat: "When you talked to your people earlier, did they give you an idea on how long it would take to rally the troops?"

"I didn't have much to give them. All I've seen is a single man, and I can't tell them my only lead is a terrorist from eighty years ago. The threat of a missile strike might get their attention, but I'd need hard proof for them to mobilize, and by that time, it'll probably be too late."

"*Goddamn red-tape,*" Cleo said.

"You're really acting on your own?" Burnside asked. "No agency to back you up, if you need it?"

"Just me and my signed letter from the President. I'm afraid I don't play well with others."

Burnside grimaced. "All those Yank agencies: the IMF, UNCLE, Omega Sector... Not one of them would take you?"

"Not many of them take an interest in the types of cases I handle," Cleo said. "Too many white knights... emphasis on the 'white.'"

Burnside sighed. "You're probably better for it. All those departments, conflicting agendas... You'd more than likely wind up like Carter, left hung out to dry whenever you became an inconvenience."

Cleo didn't say anything. Burnside looked out the window at the empty streets as they whizzed by, calculating their odds. "So, it's down to us, then. The cavalry..."

"Looks like," Cleo said. "*Ride 'em hard, cowboys.*"

She whipped the wheel again, causing Burnside to bump his head against the window.


Tyrone looked down at himself, didn't see any holes. His ears were ringing, his eyes dotted with spots from the muzzle flashes, but he was otherwise intact.

When he looked back up, the cat who shot at him was doing the same, checking himself over. Despite the brief exchange of gunfire, neither man had a scratch.

The man's gun was back up in a flash, ready to correct his previous mistake. Tyrone took his finger off the trigger, immediately raised his hands in a show of good faith. "Okay, whoa... *time out.*"

"This game doesn't have time outs."

Tyrone had to think fast, find a way out of this one now. The man before him was the fake Jackal, the imposter who had unknowingly saved his life earlier, only to put it back in jeopardy by dropping the gas bomb. He'd gotten lucky breaks all night; might as well go for one more. Trying for a gamble, he played the only card he had: "You want Fantômas, right? I think I know where he is... Or at least, where he's going to be."

This appeared to catch the man's interest, if only in stopping him from punching holes in Tyrone like a piece of Swiss cheese for the moment. "You got two minutes to give me something that'll stop me pulling this trigger."

Tyrone spilled it all, quick and clean as he could. As he said the words, he found himself not believing them, even though he'd spent the better part of twenty-four hours *living* it. The fact that he'd survived being put on display before a room filled with the deadliest assassins in the world was wild enough, but managing to escape what came next was a whole other experience...

As soon as the bodies starting dropping like flies, he'd taken a last gulp of air and darted for the exit. But the room was too chaotic, too many falling bodies and clenching hands, desperate to cling onto whatever life they had left, however long they could. Running out of air fast, Tyrone wouldn't be able to reach the only exit he knew of in time. But then, Lady Luck pulled him out of another one. Out of the corner of his eye, Tyrone saw Joubert and the other two, the dominatrix and the giant, exit through a hidden door in the wall. He made a mad dash after them, seeing his only chance swing away like the door closing after the three disappeared through the hidden passageway...

Tyrone pulled his piece as he dove at the wall, sliding along the ground like he was going for home plate. Just as he reached the hidden door, he slid the barrel of the pistol in the crevice, stopping the door before it closed all the way...

When Tyrone finished his story, the man didn't pull the trigger, but he didn't lower his gun, either.

"It's Tyrone, right?"

"That's right. Just like the actor who played Zorro."

"You followed all three of them without being spotted?"

"Wouldn't have been able to get away if they did."

The man didn't move for what felt like a long time, his gun still trained on Tyrone. The Oakland hitman took a sharp breath through his nose. This had to be it, then. *Oh, well...* When you got down to it, Lady Luck only has so many cards she can deal out.

Without warning, the man finally lowered his gun, keeping his gaze fixed on Tyrone.

"Take me back there."

"This is the place?"

"The best place to enter, near as I can figure," Cleo said, closing the door of the Stingray behind her.

"This is the Wapping Power Station," Burnside said, looking the old building over.

"Doesn't look like it's powering much..."

126

"Old hydraulic power lines," Burnside said. "They were largely phased out after the city went electric. These lines haven't been in use for decades."

"Sounds like a handy way of getting around without being noticed." She pulled her revolver and checked the cylinder, reloading the empty chambers. "Sure I can't interest you?"

"Not allowed the use of firearms on domestic soil."

Cleo shook her head. She reached into the Stingray, punching in a combination in the glove box. When she popped back out, she tossed a small Walther pistol to Burnside.

"Sorry, Jeeves, but I'm not going in there 'less I know my partner's got enough heat to back me up."

Burnside frowned, putting the pistol in his coat pocket. "I'd rather have this resolved without any fireworks…"

"Then you're in the wrong business," Cleo said, snapping the chamber of her revolver shut.

Carter followed Tyrone into the darkness, just enough light in the deep tunnel to make their way without tripping over each other.

Tyrone Tackett… low-level hood from the States. He'd fed Carter some line about working undercover, even going so far as to show him the wired bug running between his legs. Carter didn't know what to believe, honestly. He half-expected to be walking into a trap, but he didn't mind: so long as it put him within shooting distance of Fantômas. Still, Tackett had managed to survive thus far. Might be he'd come in handy, if the fight proved to be more than Carter could handle.

Tyrone then stopped, turning to Carter as he said, "I'll be honest: this next part ain't much fun."

He reached up and grabbed the lowest rung of a ladder, leading into a vertical tunnel above them. This one was barely big enough to fit Carter's shoulders, but he followed Tyrone up as the rusty ladder creaked against their weight.

"*I don't like the sound of that,*" Carter said.

"Told you it wasn't fun."

They continued their climb at a steady clip—not wanting to risk the ladder by going too fast, but also not wanting to spend any more time on it than they absolutely had to. They had to pause as one of the posts holding the ladder to the wall broke loose, causing the ladder to sway for a moment.

"Tell me we're almost to the top…"

"Only a few more steps."

They continued on, the ladder creaking more than ever against their weight. It held until they reached the top, where the vertical tube fed out onto another tunnel, this one with metal grate flooring. Tyrone helped Carter up to the new level, where the two of them had to crouch, the ceiling above their heads only four feet up from the grate floor.

The two took a moment to catch their breath and steady their hands. "Not outta the woods yet," Tyrone said, as he crawled along the grate floor. Carter followed him once more, and before long, a light appeared just ahead. Tyrone led them out of the tunnel into a large underground cavern. The grate flooring they crawled on turned out to be a narrow catwalk, suspended in the air roughly fifty feet up from the floor below them.

The cavern was massive, housing ancient machinery that no longer worked alongside brand-new computer terminals built over them. Below them, the Frenchman, the blonde and the giant from earlier were moving around the consoles, checking readouts and fiddling with knobs and dials.

"Didn't see anyone else when I followed them here earlier," Tyrone whispered, "but I figure the big man's bound to show up sooner or later."

But Carter stopped when he saw the adjacent cavern, this one larger and deeper than the one they were currently in. A smooth, tower-like cylinder stretched the length of it, so tall that its top and bottom were obscured from view. He felt his stomach drop at the sight, the situation now much more complicated than he realized.

"How far are you willing to go with this?" Carter asked Tyrone, also keeping his voice low.

"What do you mean?"

"That's an intercontinental missile housed in that silo," Carter said. "I'm guessing it's carrying a nuclear payload."

Tyrone looked at the missile, and turned gray in the harsh floodlights that illuminated the caverns.

"You want out, that's okay," Carter said. "You can head back the way we came... no harm, no foul. But if you stay, I need to know you can handle yourself; I can't risk having an amateur cock things up. Not with everything at stake..."

Carter watched Tyrone as he weighed his options, conflicted. Just as he thought he could see veins in his forehead about to pop, Tyrone looked up at him. "Count me in."

"All right, then," Carter said, pulling Wilhelmina from her holster. "Here's the plan..."

Tyrone watched Carter get into position, attaching his nylon cord to the catwalk and leaning out over the edge. Tyron pulled his own piece and got ready, himself, clipping his cord into place and trying not to look at the fifty-foot drop beneath him.

There was no question about it—the dude was certifiable. If Tyrone had any sense, he would have taken up Carter's offer to leave and got right the hell out of there, but the Oakland hitman hesitated. He supposed that, deep down somewhere, he didn't want to let Cleopatra Jones down. But Tyrone also couldn't deny the feeling that this was *important*. Nuclear missiles didn't just

128

spring up out of the ground, and the thought of one in the hands of someone like Fantômas was enough to keep him around, no matter how much he was desperate to get out and leave all this madness behind. Thinking about it, Tyrone had to suppress a shiver; he couldn't believe he almost *worked* for the man.

Carter gave Tyrone the signal, and both men attached descenders to their respective cords. Carter produced a stun grenade he called "Pepito" (the headcase had a name for all his weaponry, far as Tyrone could tell), pulled the pin and tossed it down, easy as a bean-bag.

Pepito landed right in front of Bolo, the giant. Before he could do anything about it, the grenade went off—Tyrone covered his eyes before the flash, but nothing could be done about bang. Ears ringing, Tyrone opened his eyes in time to see Carter zipping down his nylon cable, firing away all the way as he went. Tyrone followed suit, taking Joubert in his sights as he loosened his descender and felt the pull of gravity. He fired at the French assassin to no avail—every shot went wide, giving Joubert enough time to dive behind one of the consoles.

Tyrone did likewise as soon as he hit the ground, looking around to see where Carter was as the cavern filled with gunfire. It was about then that Tyrone felt himself get pulled off his feet as something grabbed him and threw him across the room. He lost his grip on his pistol when he hit the ground, tried crawling back to it as soon as he got his wits about him…

But as soon as his hand touched the grip, a large boot kicked the gun spinning away from him. Tyrone looked up to see Bolo standing over him, soot stains on his face from the stun-grenade. He didn't look too happy about it.

The giant made a fist, and the next thing Tyrone knew, the world went black…

Carter had the Frenchman pinned behind one of the consoles, the two of them at a stalemate. Any time either would pop up, the other would put them back in place with a quick exchange of gunfire.

Carter decided to take a chance. He popped a few warning shots from Wilhelmina, before leaping from behind his own cover. The leap brought him into a barrel roll, bringing him close enough to the Frenchman to almost touch. Before he could do anything about it, Carter kicked the pistol out of his hand, had him dead to rights with Wilhelmina…

The air split in a thundercrack as Carter felt a bee-sting in his wrist, causing him to lose Wilhelmina. The blonde woman gave another crack of her whip, this time drawing blood on Carter's cheek.

"Boys and their toys," she said, smiling coldly as she brought her whip back for another crack. But something snagged her whip, yanking it back and causing the blonde to fall off her feet.

Puzzled, Carter watched as a woman with an afro appeared behind her, gripping the cracker of the whip in one hand, a hand-cannon of a revolver in the other. "Party's over," she said, leveling the revolver at the blonde. "Although you're awful under-dressed for the occasion…"

Before Carter could get his bearings and properly assess how the new pieces on the board were changing the game, his solar plexus exploded, knocking him back a few steps.

The Frenchman lowered his foot in a dramatic fashion. He took a fighting stance, clearly enjoying himself. The new pieces on the board would have to wait—Carter flicked his wrist, and out popped Hugo, the thin stiletto blade he kept in his shirt sleeve.

The Frenchman smiled. "A fellow connoisseur of the blade," he said, producing a knife of his own from a sheath at his ankle. "It's so rare to meet colleagues with common interests…"

With that, he lunged at Carter, knife glinting as it came straight for his throat…

Burnside kept to the shadows while the collection of circus freaks duked it out on the cavern floor. He and Cleo had made considerable progress on their descent through the dank tunnels, following the tracer on Cleo's asset, when they heard gunfire echoing in the distance. All they had to do then was follow the sounds, and Cleo had wasted no time once they got to the open cavern, jumping into the action without a second thought…

Cleo seemed to have subdued the dominatrix-looking blonde for the moment, while a large man pummeled another—Cleo's asset Tyrone, presumably. Two others were also engaged in a knife fight. Burnside clocked Nick Carter immediately, although he couldn't get a make on his well-dressed opponent. Both seemed equally matched, circling each other and lashing out like tigers swiping their claws.

Burnside had the Walther Cleo had given him in his pocket, but he wasn't eager to jump into the fray like his new partner. Being a hero was more than likely to get you killed, and Burnside wouldn't be much help to anybody in that state. Much more pressing was the adjoining cavern, dug far deeper into the Earth than the one they currently occupied, and the monolithic object it held. He had a guess as to what that was, and if his hypothesis was correct, this was far more important than winning a mere fistfight.

While the others were preoccupied, Burnside slipped over to the largest of the consoles. On the screen was a digital readout, the image of a crude world map. A circular target blipped over the corner of North America, the location unmistakable: New York City.

The pieces came together then, as Burnside's mouth went dry. The assassinated senator. The monolith in the adjoining cavern. A nuclear payload launched from Great Britain, into the heart of the biggest metropolis on the planet…

*My god*, Burnside thought. *He's going to start World War III.*

When Tyrone came to, Bolo was still standing over him. His face felt like used leather, swollen and sore as the skin tightened at the rush of blood. Still dizzy, Tyrone snapped awake when he saw the giant winding his fist up for another round.

He managed to get his arms up over his face before the blow connected, for all the good that did. His forearms exploded with fire, and he wound up smacking himself in the face as the blow connected. Still, it was enough to keep him cogent, and he was able to roll away, putting some distance between himself and Bolo.

Having a second to look around, he saw his pistol on the ground, just a few feet away. He pulled himself along the floor, reaching out to grab the piece, his fingers just inches away…

Tyrone yelled as a giant boot came down on his hand. He didn't know if it was broken, but he heard something pop. Bolo picked him up by his hair, wrapping a massive arm around his neck and pulling tight. It was like being trapped by a python, as Tyrone felt the life being squeezed out of him as a bicep the size of a softball crushed his larynx.

Just as spots were dotting the corners of his vision, the air split in a series of pops. The arm let go immediately, and Tyrone took in a lungful, never noticing how sweet the air tasted before.

He looked behind him. Bolo stumbled backwards, two holes in his chest. He looked up disbelievingly, still stumbling backwards, unable to stop himself, until the giant stumbled into the silo housing the missile, falling out of sight.

Tyrone turned to look the opposite way, and couldn't believe what he was seeing, thinking for a moment he might be hallucinating due to a lack of oxygen. "Told you I'd take care of you," Cleo said with a smirk, a revolver smoking in her hand.

The celebration was short-lived. The blonde woman beneath her swept her leg in an arc, knocking Cleo off her feet. As soon as she hit the ground, the blonde kicked out with her heel, tearing open the skin above Cleo's eyelid with its pointed tip. She kicked Cleo's gun away and retrieved her whip, giving it another crack now that it was back in hand, eager to use it once more…

His face still throbbing, Tyrone picked himself up off the floor, grabbing his pistol in the hand that still worked. *He should've never gotten on that goddammed plane…*

Carter was starting to tire out, and could only hope his opponent was feeling the same. They'd been at it for a while, neither man yet drawing blood as they sliced the air with their knives. Their duel had brought them closer and closer to the cavern's edge, which dropped precipitously into the silo housing the nuke.

His fatigue probably explained why Carter fell for the Frenchman's feint, leading to a lazy thrust that left him wide open. The Frenchman slid his thigh behind Carter's knee, taking him off his feet and putting Carter on the ground.

Split seconds now. His blade was diving straight for Carter's throat. Without thinking, Carter swiped Hugo wildly, hitting pay-dirt when it struck meat, implanting in the Frenchman's ankle. His opponent grunted, causing his knife to waver as it came down. Carter rolled out of the way just in time for the blade to stick in the ground.

Carter took the opportunity to put his boot in the Frenchman's face, knocking him back a pace. Able to catch his breath, he took stock of his surroundings: the two women were fighting it out over the blonde's whip, a battered Tyrone making his way over with a gun in his hand. The blonde noticed him approach, and whipped the gun away. Carter didn't see any sign of the giant, but there was a new player, this one wearing a frumpy suit and overcoat and losing his hair, standing over one of the consoles with furrows in his brow...

"I've had fun, my friend," the Frenchman said, pulling himself up from the ground, "but I'm afraid I must bring our dance to its conclusion..."

He pulled Hugo out of his ankle with a wince, pointing the blood-stained stiletto blade at Carter as he approached. Carter had run out of weapons, readied himself to deal with a blade with nothing but his bare hands, but then he saw it. A gun lay on the ground few paces away, one of the many kicked away during the fracas. He dove for it, taking the pistol with ease and rolling up with it pointed straight at the Frenchman. His opponent didn't have any witty *repartee* then... Carter pulled the trigger twice, and the Frenchman went down.

Carter whipped the gun over to the remaining players. The man in the frumpy suit was frantically working the controls, so pale he almost looked like a ghost—he didn't appear to be working for Fantômas, and didn't look like much of a threat, anyway. Carter instead turned the pistol on the blonde with the whip, who was now cracking it back-and-forth, keeping Tyrone and the other woman at bay. Carter leveled his pistol at the blonde, who had her back to him. Shame to take her out in such a way, but you didn't get points taken away for ungentlemanly conduct in this game...

A searing pain shot him in the chest. Carter looked down, saw a knife sticking out of him, held by a black-gloved hand. Looking back up, Carter saw something that wasn't quite a face, but that still smiled at him through a thin slit. Looking into its eyes, Carter didn't see any hint of life. The featureless, unsightly green face was the last thing he saw before the curtains drew and world faded out, smiling like the star of the show taking his final bow...

Burnside worked his way through the controls of the console, trying to figure if there were any way to shut down the whole system powering the silo. Near as he could tell, it looked like the target coordinates were set and couldn't be reversed, with the launch sequence activated via remote. Burnside supposed he could always destroy the console, hope that would be enough to shut the whole thing down. He pulled the pistol from his pocket, took aim at the machinery before him...

"You'll find that to be of no use, Mr. Burnside," a voice called out from across the room, bringing everyone to a stop.

Burnside looked up to see a black, barely-human shape standing next to Carter, who was making a sound like he'd had the breath knocked out of him. The devil twisted the knife in his chest, as Carter continued making that horrible gasping sound, desperate for a breath that never came.

Grinning, Fantômas pulled the knife free, and Carter fell into the silo behind them. In his other hand, he held a remote. "No matter what you do to that console, I control the missile with *this*."

Burnside stepped away from the console hesitantly, placing his pistol back in his coat pocket. Cleo, the blonde and Tyrone ceased their scuffle, drawn instead to the new drama playing out before them.

Burnside approached Fantômas, still keeping a wide gulf between them. "This was your plan, then? Engineer a war between the UK and the US?"

"Among others. There's always money to be made in a war..."

"No," Burnside said, narrowing his eyes. "I don't think so. Money's not what you're after... not really."

"Oh? Don't keep it a secret... I do so love being analyzed by others."

Burnside kept his cool, presenting himself as unflappable. Trying not to show the slightest hint of panic as he thought of a way out of this. "I imagine you have grand designs on uprooting systems and exposing the flaws therein. You like bending things to your will, thinking you have some manner of control over the world and everything in it. But really, you're nothing more than a common thug."

At that, Fantômas' smile grew wider. "A common thug who's been at this decades before you were born."

"I don't think so," Burnside said, as casually as if he were discussing the weather with co-workers. "You're not the real Fantômas—merely an imitator."

"There's no way you'll ever know, though, is there?" the devil said. "There's no way to prove I'm *not* who I say I... *Stop that right now!*"

Burnside turned to see Cleo reaching for her fallen revolver. The blonde snapped her whip, but Cleo caught it before the crack. She yanked the other woman forward by her whip, giving her an elbow beneath her jaw and knocking her out cold.

"*Anyone else moves and I push the button,*" Fantômas said, raising the remote to show he meant it. Everyone did as he commanded, staying absolutely still.

Out of options, Burnside tried a gamble. "You know, I'm thinking I rather want you to push that button."

This caught Fantômas off-guard. "What?"

"You really think America doesn't have defenses in place that would shoot that missile down before it ever reaches their soil? This is a cold war between nuclear superpowers. Everyone's prepared."

"They can't stop *this*," Fantômas said, becoming more agitated. "This is the finest intercontinental missile yet manufactured. Undetectable by radar, with precautions for any anti-aircraft protections..."

"We'll see," Burnside said. "It's also rather naïve of you to assume the two won't be able to figure out what's going on immediately. Once they bring down that nuke over the Atlantic, you can be sure they'll take the proper precautions in investigating the crash. They'll figure out it's based on the late Drache's design, and then it's only a matter of time before they'll be able to put two and two together. That's the problem with world domination," Burnside said with a smirk. "Not terribly feasible in the real world."

Now visibly angry, Fantômas was almost shaking. He had no response, for once having nothing to say. *A sliver of doubt...* that was all Burnside needed.

"Don't believe me? Prove me wrong, then," Burnside said. "Go ahead and launch it."

"You're willing to risk everything on a hunch, then? You're absolutely confident the Americans can shoot it down before it hits New York?"

"No, but getting you talking about it bought enough time for my colleague to get into position..."

Before Fantômas could react, a whip cracked and the remote leapt from his hand. Burnside snatched it from the air, turning a key and disarming the missile. Cleo coiled the whip in her hands. "Cutting it kind of close there, Jeeves."

Tyrone appeared on the other side of Fantômas, leveling a pistol at him. "After carefully considering your offer of employment, I think I'm gonna pursue other opportunities."

His inhuman face twisting in rage, Fantômas produced a black, marble-shaped object and threw it at the floor. In an instant the room was filled with black smoke, blotting everything from vision. Burnside drew the pistol from his coat. He could hear his comrades coughing, but they sounded further and further away. Burnside tensed, ready for anything, imaging Fantômas' blade coming for him like it had Carter. Slitting his throat, piercing his vital organs... His hair stood on end.

Slowly, the smoke began to clear. All Burnside saw now were Cleo and Tyrone. Then a whisper seemed to come from nowhere, small enough as to be almost inaudible: "*Watch your back.*"

He whipped around, pistol at the ready, but nothing was there. Fantômas was gone.

A mountain of paperwork was laid on the table in front of Burnside, large enough to make a considerable *thud* upon impact.

"These are just the preliminaries, Sir," the clerk said.

"Of course they are."

The clerk departed the room, passing by Cleo entering with cardboard cup-holder filled with coffee. "Catching up on your crosswords?"

"Laugh all you want," Burnside said. "Half of this is yours."

"Surely it can wait a few days. We did save the world, after all."

"Our superiors would disagree. How else are they going to make themselves feel useful, if they can't discern whether or not it was justified firing your gun at a green-faced ghoul?"

Cleopatra set a coffee down next to his pile. "No sign of Fantômas, or the blonde honey with the whip," Cleo said. "They also didn't recover any other bodies from the site."

Burnside grimaced. *Typical.*

Cleo handed another cup to Tyrone, who was having trouble keeping his eyes open, leaning back in a chair in the corner of the room.

"You handled yourself all right back there…"

"My face feels like a piñata."

"You're good in a scrap, quick on your feet… You ever think about putting those skills to good use?"

"What, work for Uncle Sam?" Tyrone looked up at her, smirking. "That mean we get to work together again?"

"Sorry, sugar," Cleo said. "I already got a man. Come to think of it, the two of you do share a passing resemblance…"

"Can't blame a brother for asking." Tyrone shrugged. "I dunno. I'm not sure all this is my bag."

"I'm serious. You could do a lot of good if you came on board. A lot better than you could out on the street, anyway. You're better than that, Tyrone."

Just as Tyrone was about to answer, the clerk popped her head in the doorway again, getting their attention. "Mr. Tackett? You have a phone call from the states."

"I'm not agreeing to anything," Tyrone said as he got up, following the clerk out the door.

"You get a recruitment bonus for each wayward soul you bring in?" Burnside said, without looking up.

"Don't be an ass. I'm just trying to help the man."

"Help him by what, turning him into a spy? He probably makes more in his current profession. All of it tax-free."

"Come on. You know that's not the reason we do what we do…"

"Isn't it? It's just a job, like any other. We're all working for a pay check."

"If that's how you feel, then why keep doing it?"

Burnside paused, thinking. "It's all I know how to do, at this point."

The two of them fell silent. Rain tapped lightly against the window outside.

"You think he'll be back?"

"He just went to answer the phone."

"That's not who I meant…"

Burnside sat his pen down, staring off into space. "He's just a man in a Halloween get-up, whoever he was. Thinks he's cleverer than he is. That's all."

"He almost changed the world with the push of a button…"

"And we stopped him," Burnside said. "It was destined to happen, because of the nature of *who he was*. He couldn't help but fail in the end, because we ultimately are who we are in the end, and nothing else."

Just then, Tyrone came back in the room, looking hollowed out.

"Tyrone? What's the matter?"

When he spoke, he sounded like he'd just seen a ghost: "I'm gonna have to head back to California. My brother's dead."

*On June 14, 1940, Paris was occupied by the Nazis after the Wehrmacht had blitzed their way through Northern France. A curfew was in effect from nine p.m. to five a.m., and the city went dark under German control—or at least, the Resistance led them to believe it was so...*

## Bill Cunningham: *The Midnight Train to Paris*

*"He who contemplates the depths of Paris is seized with vertigo. Nothing is more fantastic. Nothing is more tragic. Nothing is more sublime."*
Victor Hugo

*July 9th, 1940. 23:00 hrs. Five kilometers outside Paris.*

The agony raced up and down my side as my blood poured out of the wound. Some Jerry sniper was indeed a sure shot as he clipped my left flank tearing off a good chunk of flesh. It felt like a single shot so maybe he was just lucky. A clip of gunfire roared through the night as the ground troops tried to get a bead on me. I unbuckled my chute and crawled through the field grass. Bullets were hitting all around me. I suppose that's what one gets when you parachute into occupied France on a Top Secret mission.

*Snap!*

Someone was behind me, but I couldn't get their scent. The wind was everywhere, and the odor of gunpowder didn't help. I pulled my pistol, but my hand was already wavering and my vision was blurry. What in bloody hell was wrong with me? Then I found myself surrounded.

A small contingent: a woman, a black fellow, and two others. My French has never been superb, but I could understand them clearly enough. If the black fellow didn't clinch it, the French did. These weren't Nazis.

"Look at him. He's done for."

"Pick him up."

"*Madame*, please... let us just go. Leave him to the Boche. He is dead, he just doesn't know it."

The black fellow looked me up and down, as he turned and fired at the tree line. He looked at me again. He wasn't sure.

"I'll make it," I managed to croak. There was blood in my mouth. I had to get under cover so I could recover. "Just get me the hell out of here."

The black man looked at the lady and nodded his head.

To the frogs' credit, they managed to get me under cover quite quickly. We just had a little to go to reach the tree line. The gunfire clipped the ground around us, but never seemed to draw a perfect bead on us. These people seemed to know their way around. I guess I'll have to trust them. Too bad I'm not in the trusting business.

"We're moving too slow. The Jerries are catching up."

The pale lady picked me up in a Fireman's Carry and ferried me to the forest edge while the black gentleman and the two others laid down cover fire. How the hell she picked up a 13-stone man, I don't know. She wasn't even breathing hard. I must be hallucinating…

She turned my head to hers and said, "You're not hallucinating. Now be quiet, *Monsieur*. We have work to do. Serious work, *oui*?"

I didn't have time to answer her, so I just whirled my pistol around and fired. Behind her an SS soldier dropped to the ground. The lady smiled. She had a curious smile, but it was her eyes that fascinated. They were amber in color, as if a flame burned within. Hypnotic. Then she whispered, and it was the only sound in the world.

"*Merci, Monsieur.* Let's see if I can return the favor, *non*?"

She turned and fired her broomhandle Mauser into the shadows opposite us. I heard a distinct *thud* as one of her shots hit flesh and bone. The three others came running up behind us and relieved the lady of her burden, namely me. Not a good way to start a job. M, what the hell have you gotten me stuck into?

We kept moving back and forth—animals running from their predators—as the wound continued burning into my side. I could hear their boots trudging over the forest floor as we hurried to safety. We were through the trees and into the dark when we came out onto a narrow dirt road.

The black man smiled a big toothy smile as he and his fellow resistance fighter carried me to a small delivery lorry. They deposited me in the back and rolled a canvas over me. The last thing I saw was his smiling face, and his words, "Welcome to Paris."

*July 10th, 1940. 03:00 hrs. 84 Avenue Foch, Paris.*

"Idiot!"

Lieutenant Sturmer stood at stiff attention in front of the *Kommandant*. Beside him stood one of their best snipers, the man who had shot the parachutist.

The *Kommandant*'s face never came out of the shadows thrown by the small desk lamp. The whisper of his voice was a razor held to Sturmer's throat. He had seen others fail this dark *Kommandant*, never to be seen again.

"You were ordered to capture the spy, and bring him directly to me!"

"*Herr Kommandant*, we were there as you ordered—ready to strike—when he was spirited away by the terrorists. I don't know how they did it; it was as if the shadows themselves wrapped around them."

"And now they're roaming the countryside… free!"

"I wouldn't say that, *Herr Kommandant*. Flick!"

The sniper snapped to attention, and reached into the small pouch on his belt. He pulled out a shiny object and placed it on the *Kommandant*'s desk. He then stepped back into perfect attention. Sturmer looked at Flick; he was a good soldier.

The *Kommandant* studied the shiny object on his desk, but didn't touch it. A low chuckle escaped from his darkness. Perhaps Sturmer hadn't failed him after all.

"You hit him?"

"*Jawohl, Herr Kommandant,*" gulped Flick. "Wounded, not killed. But I do not understand the need for silver bullets."

The silence after his query was deafening.

"You will leave us, Sturmer." It wasn't a command, more a statement of fact. The *Kommandant* was like that—what he stated as fact *became* fact. Cold, impenetrable fact. Sturmer pitied Flick for what was going to happen next.

Sturmer offered, "We have the *Gendarmes* contacting all the hospitals and Doctors' offices. Also, all of the Veterinary clinics." That last bit seemed to amuse the *Kommandant* slightly, though it was always hard for Sturmer to tell.

The *Kommandant* said, "There is much more at hand." It meant that Sturmer was to return to him later with a report on his progress, and the *Kommandant* expected progress. Flick didn't make a sound, couldn't make a sound as Sturmer brought himself to attention, saluted, and then exited the room.

*July 10th, 1940. 03:15 hrs. Somewhere under Paris.*

I was on a table somewhere. I could just tell that much. I must have passed out. The smell was wet. There was a small lamp off to the side casting shadows along stone walls, and there was a painting on the wall...

"We aren't in the sewers? But the tunnels..."

"*Oui, Monsieur,* they are nearby. Creatures like us feel very much at home in the underground of Paris. Few venture down into the darkness, and many of the tunnels have long been forgotten. While the Boche occupies the above, we occupy the 'Invisible City' you see here."

"But all this?"

"It is a long story, and one told by one who lived it."

He motioned to the flickering stone walls around us and smiled. I could discern elegant furniture and fanciful decor on the walls. Wherever I was, this person's "home" was exquisitely decorated. I looked up to see one of the Resistants who had pulled me out. He was stripped to the waist and wore a mask over his mouth. There was a shiny scalpel in his hand.

"These are things we will talk about later. For now, I must remove the bullet in your side."

"It hasn't...?" That wasn't good.

"*Non*. It is still inside you. There is no exit wound. Now, be quiet. You've lost a lot of blood. I must get it out. I do not have chloroform. I am waiting for our man to bring me some."

I laid back and turned my head. There, staring at me were the black man and the woman with the flaming eyes. The look on their faces told me this was touch and go. No exit wound, *eh*? That *was* a most unusual bullet.

"Forget the chloroform," I said as I looked into her eyes. "Let's get on with it. We don't have time."

"But, *Monsieur*!"

"Get on with it! The Nazis are going to be watching anyone buying medical supplies. Tell your man to stay away. He'll lead them right to us."

The woman nodded and one of the soldiers ran off.

I kept my head turned and stared at her red eyes as the scalpel descended. Someone grabbed my bloody shirt and made a gag, but my eyes were still locked with hers.

My barely muffled screams echoed off the stone walls as I felt my blood spill out onto the floor.

*July 10th, 1940. 03:15 hrs. 84 Avenue Foch, Paris.*

Sturmer left the *Kommandant*'s office and made his way down the hall of the building at 84 Avenue Foch, the headquarters of the *Sicherheitsdienst*—the SS. It was still early and dawn had not yet crept past the Arc de Triomphe. Sunlight would never penetrate these recesses of the building, buried as they were. While the more public activities of the SS were going on above, the very secret operations of Sturmer's unit were kept in the shadowy concrete "caverns" below.

It was no secret that the Führer had done extensive research into the myths and legends of the Aryan race. He had teams racing the globe obtaining religious and occult artifacts. He even had archeological teams digging up remains in Egypt, Peru, and even the dark mountains of Transylvania. What that research entailed, and how it affected the *Kommandant*'s operations here in Paris remained a mystery to Sturmer. In fact, everything about what he and the *Kommandant*'s other select men were doing was a mystery.

None of the other divisions of the SS acknowledged their existence. Reports of any and all activities from the Interrogation, Wireless, and the *Standartenführer* Helmut Knochen's divisions of the SS landed in his office. He read them all dutifully and reported their intelligence to the *Kommandant*. However his commander seemed to already know what the reports said before Sturmer gave them. As if he were testing his hold over Sturmer by reading his very thoughts. And the *Kommandant* had a hold over him. Iron strong. He just had to make sure it didn't become as tight as the grip that was surely around Flick's throat.

Climbing the stairs, Sturmer reached the basement elevator of the building and stepped inside. It was the only light in this area of the floor. He had left Flick with the *Kommandant*, back in the darkness, and the mere thought filled him with chills. He knew he would never see his loyal sniper again. An excuse would be made, papers filed of a transfer to the Russian front for the official record, but only here in the dim light of the elevator could Sturmer relax just enough to ponder the grim fate of the soldier. By morning a replacement would be chosen and brought into the fold. Another square to add to the patchwork quilt that was the mystery of their mission there in Paris.

Sturmer reached the ground floor of the building, and stepped out of the elevator's cage.

"Lieutenant! Lieutenant Sturmer!"

He turned at the mention of his name and was greeted by *Standartenführer* Knochen's secretary, Hans Kiefer, whose hand gripped a black folder. Sturmer stiffened at the presence of his superior officer. "How may I help you, Major?" He liked Kiefer, as he didn't treat Sturmer as a subordinate officer. More of a colleague, a fellow soldier in the battle to save the Fatherland from her enemies.

"Glad I caught you. There is a report that's come in from the Vélodrome d'Hiver. The preparations that were ordered by the Reichsführer-SS of the Medical Corps are in progress for your tests. We have tasked the *Gendarmes* to begin rounding up the *Juden* soon. Ahead of schedule."

Sturmer held his reaction in check as he accepted the folder. "Ahead of schedule? Thank you, Herr Major. I will see to it that my *Kommandant* knows of your timely assistance in this matter. I am certain he will be pleased."

The Major smiled and nodded. "Heil Hitler!" he saluted.

"Heil Hitler!" echoed Sturmer, wondering what exactly was ahead of schedule, and why that made his blood run cold. It was yet another bit of patchwork he would have to resolve if he was to survive.

*July 10th, 1940. 03:30 hrs. Somewhere under Paris.*

"Raaaaaargh!" I screamed into my gag.

Doctor Génessier motioned over the rest of his team that had kept me alive thus far. "Hold him down! I have to open the wound more to get at the bullet. Horrid thing!"

"What is it?" asked the red-eyed lady as she placed her hands on my shoulders and pushed. The black man and the other fellows went to my now-thrashing legs and held them down.

"Hold him down!" said the doctor. "Now let me get in there! This is more than just a bullet!" He held his scalpel to the hole and sliced.

I screamed again and raged against the hands holding me down. My mouth was dry and my sinews stretched and crackled. It was happening. The beast was coming. I looked at the lady's eyes, and could see her curiosity there.

The doctor dropped the scalpel and grabbed some pliers. He plunged them into the bloody wound. I kicked and sent one of the men flying back into the darkness, hitting the wall with a thud. The black man redoubled his efforts to hold me down and motioned for another man to come and take my other leg.

"Hold. Him. Down!" screamed the doctor. " I can't get the forceps around the bullet, and the wound..."

"What?!" I yelled. My mouth was bared and my fangs grew.

"The wound seems to be closing around the bullet like it was burning!"

The red-eyed lady (I really would have to learn her name) held me down and turned my head to face her. I roared again.

"Ssh..." she whispered.

My eyes found her red ones. Pools of fire they were. Warming and calm.

"*It's all right*," she whispered again. No, wait. Her lips weren't moving. How?

"*Never mind that. Look into my eyes. You feel nothing.*"

"I feel nothing." I could feel my muscles relaxing. *God, her eyes...*

She smiled a bit. Someone else would have missed it. Her red lips parting and displaying ivory white teeth. Matched to her fair skin. All framed with her luscious dark hair. "*Merci, Monsieur*" were her words that filled my head.

"That's good. Keep him calm."

I heard a small click as he fished around in my guts. A few more times sent me into spasm.

"Raaaaaaaaaaaaaaaarrrrgh!"

Doctor Génessier, brilliantly, didn't falter. He yanked... hard! The bullet pulled out of my side with a small geyser of blood. More spilled down the table and onto the floor. The doctor didn't miss a beat. He held up the bullet. He dabbed the wound with some gauze, but it was already... repairing itself.

The bullet lay on the floor bubbling in the small pool of blood. It was silver, and etched with some sort of markings. Runes.

My blood coalesced backward, pulling itself off the floor and back toward my side. I shook violently, my breath came back to me in gulps. My skin reddened as my veins bulged in my arms and chest. Then I howled, and collapsed.

Though my conscious mind was off, my subconscious was very aware they stood around me in stunned silence. All of my blood flowed back into my body, and my wound sealed itself, leaving a small bruise. This was going to have to be a long briefing to explain this.

"He's a *loup-garou!*"

Okay, maybe not so long. Brilliant.

*July 11th, 1940. 18:00 hrs. Budapest Station, Hungary.*

The Budapest station was smoky, steamy and smelled of the worst of humanity. The couple standing on the platform, a man and a woman in their late

30s waited impatiently. Both were dressed in their travel finery, and clutched their tickets and documentation. They had hoped to catch this last ride on the Orient-Express in Vienna, but the border closings and reallocations made that impossible.

Therefore the couple had to detour to Budapest where they would travel through the heart of the Fatherland all the way to Paris. This detour added two days to their schedule, with all of the security stops and border checks, but placed them on the train before the "Package"'s arrival in Munich. Fortunately, those delays and other barriers to success had already been foreseen.

Under normal circumstances this would have been an impossible journey. However, the gentleman still had family connections in Heisse-Weimar and used them surreptitiously to obtain the necessary travel documents for himself and his sister under false identities. With some additional forged documents along with a few bribes, they were now the fully-documented Matthias and Sophia Dietrich who were on their way to Paris from Hungary to receive the legacy of their long lost uncle who made a fortune for himself, but died leaving no heirs. The Dietrichs were traveling to ensure they could bring the good fortune back to the Fatherland.

The fiction, while solid, supported as it was by all of the appropriate German government and National Socialist Party documents, was nonetheless a bitter pill for "Sophia" to swallow. She had no desire to be there other than to resolve the matters that stood before them. The sooner this dark business of theirs was completed the better. She tapped her foot nervously until her brother took her arm and wrapped it around his. This gave her only a slight sense of calm.

She recalled when her estranged brother appeared at her door a fortnight ago. It was a short two days after the death of her husband Jérôme Fandor—the love of her life—of a heart attack. Her brother's words were clear that the death of her husband—despite the physician's proclamation that he had died from a simple heart attack—was not "natural causes." He then intimated that her son, whom she had sent for, but had not heard from, was being held to ensure her cooperation, and that his survival depended on it.

"You monster," she yelled, "How can you casually threaten your family like this?"

He pulled a leather envelope out of his jacket pocket, untied it, and handed it and its documents over to her. The breath caught in her throat as she read the words on the parchment.

"But..."

"It would seem, dear sister, that I am not *quite* the monster you think. Whoever has my nephew has plotted this most carefully and completely."

"Whoever? Look at this. We know who has kidnapped my son."

The papers slipped out of her hands and fell to the floor. In the corner was a small thumbprint of blood. There was a familiar small scar on the red print, and beside it was the florid handwritten "F." There could be no doubt as to from whom this document came—the calligraphy was too perfect and all too familiar.

*Fantômas.*

"When do we leave?" she whispered.

Now the pair, the brother Vladimir and sister Heléne—children of the notorious Lord of Terror—were standing on the platform to board the train that would send them hurtling toward their fate and the fate of Heléne's son.

*July 11th, 1940. 1900 hrs. Somewhere under Paris.*

"I am here to facilitate the extraction of a high value scientist and his equipment."

The words left my lips with a smack as I chewed on the rare steak they had prepared for me. It was good meat. They must have a good source on the black market to serve the German guests upstairs. "The Jerries want him. We need to keep him and his invention out of Hitler's hands."

I sat at the table that had, hours before, served as my surgery. All eyes were on me, especially the red ones. It didn't affect my appetite. "My name is Major John Talbot, but for the purpose of my covert mission, you may call me *Jean.* Or *Sir.*"

"So, we are to take your orders, *Monsieur*?"

"For the duration of this mission, yes."

A mumble crept out of the darkness.

"I'm sorry, I didn't quite catch that."

The soldier who had held my legs down stepped into the light. "I am Pierre Martin, a soldier for a Free France, a member of the Resistance and I do not follow the orders of a monster like you."

"Oh sure you do, Monsieur Martin." With that I stood up from the table, and unleashed the beast within me. My jaw and skull cracked and shifted while hair sprouted across my body. My fingers and toes bled as my claws came out. My forearms bulged and my legs twisted. I inched toward him like the hungry wolf I am, arched and ready to strike, to kill. My growl filled the air.

This Martin trembled in fear, so thick I could smell it on him, but he stood his ground. "Every time you obey those Godless Nazi hordes out there. Every time you don't rise up and strike back. Every time you allow them to dictate who and what you are…" I growled at him.

"I fight for France!"

"Good, because I have a fight for you. Let me be clear, if we don't get this man and his invention out of Nazi territory, France and the rest of the world are lost."

"That's enough!" The red-eyed lady placed her hand on my furry chest and pushed effortlessly. I recoiled five feet. I'd forgotten she's stronger than she

144

looks. No wonder M wanted me to team up with her. That wily trickster. Her red eyes flared and yes, I could see the ivory of her... *fangs*?

Oh, that explained much.

What good is a secret army with one monster behind enemy lines when you could have two creatures of the night? Again, brilliant, M. My hats off to you. I smiled, though I suppose to her and the rest I was simply bearing my fangs. I wasn't about to clarify the situation.

I called on my human self and drove the beast back down. Guns were at the ready. Hmmm... these Frenchies were better trained than they looked. They weren't too thrown by my lupine good looks.

"There are swastikas all over Paris. Are you going to stand for it, or are you going to use every weapon you have to send those Nazi bastards back to hell?" I let that sink in for a moment. "If you follow me, I will help you kill more Nazis than you ever thought possible." That did it. They looked at one another deciding their fate.

The lady looked at Bullard, the black man, and then Pierre Martin. Then they all lowered their weapons and retreated into the shadows. *Now we were getting somewhere.*

As they left, I could finally focus my senses to discern clearly the shape of the vast underground room I was in. It wasn't a sewer despite the cacophony of smells. It was more of an archive of a bygone era—an underground museum. Large block walls with Gothic arches for support were adorned with rare works of art. Windows looking back into the Renaissance. A tapestry hung from one wall with a large "F" emblazoned on it. Louis the XIVth furniture was neatly arranged about the place. This was a *pied-à-terre,* not a sewer. The lady saw my surprise at our surroundings.

"Tell me about this place," I said, as I sat down to finish my meal.

"When I was much younger, I was a member of a gang of thieves called *Les Vampires.* We were notorious and very successful. No bank, no jewelry box was safe from our acrobatic and criminal skills. We were the scourge of Paris. The pride of the Apaches. Oh, to be that young, foolish, and notorious again."

I looked her over. She didn't look over 25. Must have been a hell of a life if she's already mourning her lost youth. Then I gazed into her eyes, surrounded by such darkness. She of the Amber Eyes.

"One night we were contracted to steal specific *objets d'art* from a certain personage who was rumored to be deceased." She motioned around the apartment, "This chamber was the secret home of..."

"Fantômas."

"Yes. You know of him, the Emperor of Crime?"

I'd heard of him.

"He was nothing... and *everything*. More myth than reality. More evil than can be conceived by ordinary humans." The very words made her tremble.

"And?" The words, as soon as they escaped my lips, unleashed something in her. She looked at me with her blazing red eyes. Then she calmed.

"Yes. Nothing and everything. We Vampires infiltrated this secret fortress and recovered the religious artifacts for our client. However, Fantômas guarded his secrets well. He incorporated several fatal traps into the structure. Two of our criminal brothers succumbed to their embrace. Those of us who survived made our way out through the passageways to the surface. As we left one of several secret exits he built into this headquarters, we were confronted by Fantômas himself... Whoever, whatever he was, he was darkness incarnate. Even myth does not begin to reveal the mysteries that are Fantômas."

"One of our kind then." She shrugged her shoulders. "Obviously you made it out."

"I did, but not so obviously. He attacked us with a ferocity I have never seen before. Moving with such swiftness and bloodthirsty cruelty. He killed my comrades and was then on me like an animal unleashed. I found myself screaming, frightened beyond belief... to even breathe. Then, when I awoke, it was three days later."

"You became Irma Vep in more than just a name." She hung her head then lifted it to reveal her red eyes and fangs.

"An ironic joke. Irma Vep—Vampire. But I have yet to feed. I am alive, human... yet not. Were I to take blood, or if I were killed, I would condemn myself to eternal life on my death. As it is now, I am living a cursed existence. Constantly keeping myself in check."

I looked at her like I was looking into a mirror. The wound that had been pouring blood out of my side must have been like ringing the dinner bell, yet she held her own. Good girl. I spoke up.

"I know something of that. My 'curse' was inherited. Just lucky, I suppose. The first male born of the house. He is cursed with the beast within. Condemned, driven to a frenzy to kill when the Moon is full. No one knows why anymore. Supposedly it was a witch, but I have a hard time believing any woman would be that upset at a Talbot."

"Don't be so sure."

*Touché.* "Outside the influence of the Full Moon, I control the change." As a demonstration, I held up my hand and grew my claws out from bloodied fingertips. "My family had me declared dead. The estate was closed. My kin was driven out and scattered to the winds. The Talbots are no longer spoken of except in whispers. My family name is now a curse."

She stepped closer to me. "To those that know, and there are still some here in this great metropolis who touch that supernatural darkness, my name is used to frighten children."

I could smell her perfume, and the blood that was on her boots. My blood. She looked at me... no, it was more like she looked through me. I blinked.

"To the cursed then," I offered as a mock toast. She didn't bite. "You seem to have made a go of it. Establishing your headquarters here…"

"It seemed logical. Fantômas was nowhere to be found, and the Resistance needed a place of safety. A secret to guard secrets—especially mine. Because I was all that was left of the Vampires, I took their treasure and financed Eugène Bullard's purchase of the nightclub above, *Le Grand Duc*. Before the Nazis took over the city, we gathered criminals from all across France to join us. To them, fighting the Nazis or the Police was the same. Pierre, the young man you growled at? He is a master safecracker. Others are confidence men and women, cut-purses, cutthroats, even prostitutes who have had their heads shaved by the locals as horizontal consorts to the *Boche*. They are very effective at ferreting out intelligence. The Germans drop their guard around women who have "proven" their loyalty to them. I am their protector. Their Madame."

"And do they know what you are?"

She raised an eyebrow, but shook her head. "Not all. Just the most-trusted who have access to this chamber. To those like Pierre, my supernatural abilities enhance my criminal ones, all to their benefit."

"So, they turn a blind eye, and keep your secret."

"Yes—and they also work upstairs in the club. Gathering intelligence from the Nazi officers who frequent our exclusive establishment. You would be surprised at how a good drink, a good meal, and some companionship loosens their tongue."

"And of course, M knew all about this…"

"*Bien sûr*. Your friend plays a formidable game of chess. He is positioning his pieces," she said flatly. "How long have you known him?"

I wasn't about to answer that question. "So Paris is our field of battle then. At least, for this mission. Oh, and M is most-assuredly no friend of mine. People like me—we don't have friends."

She held her arm up and gestured to the doorway. "If you have no friends then, what do you have?"

I grabbed a shirt off of the back of a chair and pulled it on as we made our way up the stairway. "We have people who aren't trying to kill us… for the moment, anyway. Now let's get stuck in. There's much to do."

With a new understanding of our situation, I laid out the plan.

*July 12th, 1940. 14:00 hrs. Munich Hauptbahnhof. Germany.*

Vladimir had allowed Hélène to enter the train's roomette first and seat herself next to the window. From Budapest to Munich, she stared out the window, lost in the darkness outside. As the Express pulled into the Munich *Hauptbahnhof*, she could see the darkness was deepening.

Nazi Soldiers and Munich *Polizei* were everywhere, checking each passenger's paperwork as they boarded the cars. Large red banners emblazoned with the swastika flapped back and forth in the wind. Hélène was reminded of the falcons that her father used to hunt on their quiet estate in South Africa. The birds of prey would swoop down from above and slash with their claws. Gripping their meal with their iron talons, they would take to the sky and then deliver their feast to their master. He would allow them to feast, to keep them wild, but under his control. He would laugh under his hood and marvel at his minion's ferocity. Such was Fantômas's style of parenting.

When she broke ties with her father, Hélène and her lover, Fandor, traveled a long way in their lives, both physically and metaphorically, leaving behind all the death and destruction wrought by the Lord of Terror. It had not been easy, for she was her father's daughter. Iron-willed, cunning, and yes, even deadly. She came by her death's-head tattoo honestly. He taught her all she held dear until Fandor had opened her heart to the possibility of something new.

*"Entschuldigen Sie, Madame und Herr. Dürfen wir sitzen?"*

Vladimir and Hélène saw an elderly gentleman at the door holding the hand and guiding a young girl who clutched her doll tightly. The man was in a slightly stooped position and the girl seemed overwhelmed by the activity outside their car. "Certainly," Hélène found herself saying.

The man guided the little girl to the window seat opposite Hélène while he stowed his suitcase in the overhead shelf. He couldn't quite get it up high enough and with a quick nudge by Hélène, Vladimir stepped up to help the old man. *"Danke, mein herr."* The two men sat down.

The old man saw to his charge, and settled back into his seat. The little girl nudged her elder and he bent down as she whispered in his ear. The old man smiled and looked over to Hélène. "My granddaughter is curious about your finery, Madame. She would like to know how such a wonderful lady as yourself and your companion come to be on this train to Paris. I am Richter Baumann and this very curious little one to my right is my granddaughter, Anneke. We are both pleased to have you as our traveling companions."

Hélène smiled at the girl, who cautiously smiled back.

"I am Matthias Dietrich, and this is my sister Sophia," said Vladimir in a tone that said he was volunteering nothing further.

Hélène leaned forward slightly and looked at the waifish Anneke. "That's a very pretty doll. She must be very precious, you hold her so tightly." She smiled again.

"My mother gave her to me," said the girl barely above a whisper.

"And where are your parents?"

"They are both gone. They were in Austria," said Baumann as if that explained everything.

"We are now going to Paris where we shall start our new life together, eh *liebchen*? I am to take a position in the Department of Medicine at the Sorbonne University."

Hélène's smile disappeared as she was reminded that her own husband and son were gone. One taken from her by her father, and the other held captive to coerce her to board this train, and complete some arcane mission. Her son would be yet another innocent victim in the long struggle she had endured with her father—if she failed in her mission. She felt sympathy for the child. She too was trapped in something not of her own making.

But as she settled back in her seat, something nudged her in the back of her razor-sharp mind. The dreaded Fantômas was thought to be long dead. Obviously, and yet again, he had faked his death to escape justice. She dove into that thought, weighing all the possibilities and dismissing the ones that fell outside the twisted ego of her father. It was certainly plausible that Fantômas had come out of "retirement," killed her husband and kidnapped her son. It was equally plausible that Vladimir was doing this in his father's name as some sort of plot of his own devising. Perhaps to re-establish her father's network with him as the new "Emperor of Crime?" But how did this fit with the old man and child before her? Certainly it was no coincidence that they were all together in the same compartment. Why was Fantômas forcing her and Vladimir to escort them to Paris? What threat awaited them all in the City of Lights that had become the City of Darkness?

No matter what the threat, Hélène would have to be wary if she was to recover her beloved son. These days, threats were like Nazis: they were everywhere, seen and unseen.

While Vladimir's eyes darted around the roomette, uncomfortable with their traveling companions, Herr Baumann sat reading the morning copy of the *Volksblatt* declaring the "Great German Victory" as their forces moved west. Seated quietly next to him, Anneke played with her doll. She looked up at Hélène and smiled. Unable to help herself, Heléne smiled back.

*July 12th, 1940. 18:00 hrs. Somewhere under Paris.*

"You're certain these will work?," I asked as I loaded several small ingenious charges into my bag.

Eugène Bullard loaded several similar charges into his bag and sealed it. The "bags" were form-fitting affairs with two straps to hold them in place around a thief's chest, side, or back. A simple adjustment of the strap placed the bag exactly where he needed it most—for throwing grenades, for drawing a machine pistol, or stuffing francs inside during a heist. The whole affair was light, compact, and hid well under a trench coat. "We used them last year to help several of our friends escape prison, and join the Maquis. They will do the job... if we knew what that job was, Talbot."

There it was. The man's mind was faster than he ever let on—until it suited him. I'd read his file. He was an American negro born from two slaves. At age 11, he'd run away from home and managed to survive on his own in the American South for six years. He stowed aboard a German freighter, came to Europe and bounced around until he joined the French Foreign Legion. He was wounded at Verdun and taken back to Paris to recover. On a bet, he'd joined the *Aéronautique Militaire* despite the color of his skin and had become a fighter pilot. With multiple commendations and air victories, he'd tried to enlist in the American Flying Forces when they joined the war, but they wouldn't accept a black man into their ranks. Now, by some weird twist of fate, he was here in Paris. Fighting yet again.

"I'll let you know when it's time to know. We just need to get through the city to our destination."

"Already done. Why all the secrecy? And why has Madame taken off?"

"It's no coincidence that I was hit with a silver bullet, laced with arcane druidic runes. The Jerries were waiting for me, and they knew what would work against me."

Bullard paused, then narrowed his eyebrows. "You think one of us is a traitor?"

"The thought had crossed my mind as I was bleeding out on the table."

"And Madame?"

"She is Stage One of the plan." I looked him over as he simply nodded his head. "You are taking this all in stride. Working with a vampire and a werewolf fighting the Nazis?"

Bullard sighed and thought for a moment. "I have traveled much, seen much, know much. This I know—a quote by King Francis the first: 'Paris is not a city; it is a world.'" Bullard smiled that smile of his and went back to work. It was then I knew. If any of us knew what it was to be cursed, it was the man who stood before me. He knew the true way of the world.

*July 12th, 1940. 21:00 hrs. Châlons-sur-Marne.*

Irma Vep felt one with the night. The Cathedral Saint Etienne gave her an unobstructed view as she awaited the whistle of the Orient-Express to signal departure from the Châlons-sur-Marne stop. They were approximately two hours outside Paris, and the Germans instituted a stop there before entering the great metropolis, fearful that the Resistance may try and sabotage the train from various points throughout the Alps. They also off-loaded cargo destined for various gun emplacements around Paris and across the countryside. They were very efficient that way.

And very predictable. This was adding another hour to their trip.

The cold night wind whipped at her bat-winged cloak, but didn't affect the woman. From behind her ebony hood mask she kept her red eyes focused on the activity on the platform. SS Soldiers inspected the undercarriage of the train as others made their way through each car inspecting everyone's paperwork, and searching through all compartments of the seventeen cars. The last three cars of the train were the baggage cars for luggage and shipping. These went through an especially rigorous inspection.

Sturmer directed the Teutonic troops to review the manifests thoroughly. From this distance, Irma Vep couldn't hear his orders, but she could see the soldiers' reactions. Their lives depended on following them to the letter. They worked swiftly, but precisely. Sturmer double-checked their work then called them to assemble.

The clock tower began ringing. It was nine o'clock. That put the famous train in Paris at midnight. Right on schedule for their mission.

And that's when she spotted *it*.

Sturmer ordered the troops off the platform and to board the train, then boarded himself.

Then, notable not for being seen, but for being a void, a long shadow glided aboard behind the Lieutenant. If she had blinked, her red eyes would have missed it. But it was there and oh so familiar. The darkness slid aboard just as the whistle blew.

This was unexpected, but not unwelcome. She shivered, but not because of the night air. Irma Vep was hungry. Her nostrils flared and her eyebrows furrowed, giving her the fierceness of her flying namesake. She stood atop the steeple and opened her arms. Her cloak with its bat-wing shape caught the wind and she leapt off the steeple!

Plunging downward, faster and faster toward the plaza below, she arched her back, focused her thoughts, and her "wings" caught the draft and held her aloft! Part physics, part supernatural energy she swept upward in a high arc and glided across the night sky. To anyone observing, she would be yet another night time predator in the sky. In her case, she was a predator who had a train to catch.

The Express was just pulling out of the station in a cloud of smoke and steam as her dark wings flew through the night and landed on the top of the exiting train. Irma Vep clung tightly to the roof and crawled delicately like a spider toward one of the gangway connections.

As the train picked up speed, she tightened her already steely grip and made her way to one of the spaces between cars.

She neared the edge of the car roof and peered down to the gangway below. The roar and *click-clack* of the train filled her ears as the train sped up. There on the platform was a SS soldier, his *Karabiner* 98k rifle at the ready. The young man peered back and forth from the platform, his body shifting to the rhythm of the train's movements across the track.

Irma Vep pulled back, grabbed one of the roof's side rails and silently swung herself over the edge and onto the platform rails. She crouched and balanced uncannily on the now roaring train's rail behind the soldier. She twisted her head back and forth, and looked him over with her red eyes. Heard the breath in his lungs, heard the beating of his heart, and saw the pulsing of blood in his neck.

Oh, yes, that neck. She could feast on that neck. But she held herself in check. She wasn't here for that.

The engine roared, the whistle blew, and the train picked up even more speed. Then, unfortunately for him, the soldier turned and saw two red eyes staring back at him. Before he could even scream, Irma Vep's arm lashed out and struck him in the chest with the force of a sledgehammer. He flew backwards off the train, landing with a crunch against a building, his neck broken in the impact. Irma Vep turned, ready to see if she had been discovered.

No, she was still one with the darkness.

The train's whistle sounded as it pulled out of Châlons-sur-Marne and raced back toward Paris. Phase One was in progress, and Irma Vep was now on the hunt. But the clock was ticking, and she had to hurry if she were to succeed.

*July 12th, 1940. 21:30 hrs. The Orient-Express.*

The door slid open and Sturmer stepped inside their car. Two soldiers, rifles at the ready, stood behind him. The threat of their presence was clear.

"Your papers, *bitte.*" Sturmer wasn't asking. He pulled a notebook and pencil from his pocket and awaited their identification.

Hélène kept her eye on Vladimir as he reached into his coat pocket. One of the soldiers moved his rifle over to cover the dark-eyed man. Vladimir took the hint and pulled his paperwork with two fingers and gently held his identification up for inspection. Sturmer took them and reviewed them with a trained eye.

Hélène reached for her purse at her side and carefully pulled her paperwork, making sure not to make any sudden movements. As she handed over her papers, she glanced over at Baumann who was likewise very cautious. Anneke sat in her seat staring at the guns menacing her grandfather.

"Grandfather?" she asked nervously.

"Hush, child. *Alles ist in ordnung,*" said the old man. He handed over their papers.

"I will determine that..." Sturmer consulted the paperwork, "...*Herr Doktor.*"

"*Danke, Leutnant.* I am certain you will find my and my granddaughter's papers in order."

Sturmer looked over each of their documents and returned them one by one. Vladimir's, Hélène's, Anneke's, and then Baumann's. Just as he was handing over the man's papers, Sturmer pulled them out of reach.

"It is a pleasure to finally meet you, Herr Doctor Frankenstein!"

*July 12th, 1940. 2140 hrs. Gare de l'Est. Paris.*

We shook back and forth in the back of the lorry as our cadre made its way to the Gare de l'Est, the final stop for the Orient-Express, and one of the few hubs of activity during the Paris night. We were all outfitted as the night cleanup crew for the station. Pierre Martin had a cousin (doesn't everyone?) who worked at the station and made arrangements to get us in to empty the trash, mop the floors, and clean the bathrooms. The Jerries liked their trains to run on time and their stations to be spotless. That's exactly what I was counting on.

Our lorry turned to the entrance and stopped. A fat SS soldier, a Sergeant, ordered us out of the back and to line up next to the truck. His sidekick was a Vichy police officer. He kept his pistol in its holster, but at the ready while the fat bastard checked our papers. Pierre knew the Vichy *flic* and chatted him up a bit. Apparently, most of our crew got food poisoning from some sort of bad cream sauce. That's why we were the new faces. The fat Nazi wasn't as easily convinced.

"What about the *schwarze*, here?" he asked. He meant Bullard.

Fatty pulled up Bullard's papers. These Jerries were thorough.

"He's from the French Antilles."

"*Oui, Monsieur.* I was a woodcutter in the Martinique," said Bullard. His accent was perfect.

Let me guess, our pilot, soldier, nightclub owner spent some time in the Caribbean too.

"What brought you to Paris, *Schwarze?*" This Nazi was getting on my nerves. He was costing us time.

I gave him a stare, but he was too busy browbeating Bullard who gently put a hand on my arm.

"There was no more wood to cut."

The reply hung out there for a second then Bullard smiled.

The Nazi looked at the Vichy officer and laughed a good belly laugh. The Fat Sergeant had enough.

"All right you *Froschfresseren*, get to work!" The Vichy officer looked at me funnily, and I simply took back my paperwork and nodded my head.

Pierre put his hand on my shoulder and whispered, "That's my other cousin."

He smirked and we all turned and made our way through the iron gates surrounding the station. We were inside. Now we had to make sure that we had a proper British greeting in place before midnight.

*July 12th, 1940. 21:45 hrs. The Orient-Express.*

Irma Vep climbed in through the window and landed silently on the floor of the baggage car. She turned her attention to the door, creeping up to the frame and focusing. She tuned out the roar of the train. There! There was just one soldier behind the door. She could hear his heartbeat. She slid the bolt on the door

153

to make sure she wasn't disturbed. But even with the door locked, Irma Vep was wary and filled with dread. Where was the darkness that was Fantômas, the one who had cursed her?

But she had work to do if she was to meet her deadline. Talbot had given her a manifest number and she had to find the crate that matched it. She moved along the heavy wood inspecting them each for a matching number. One by one, she checked the numbers precisely and moved along. Then, towards the back section of the car was the crate she sought—success!

*Braaaaaaap! Braaaaaaaap!*

Bullets ripped into the wood frame of the door followed by the butts of rifles splintering the heavy oak. She flipped out of the way as bullets ripped their way inside. Irma Vep had no time. She pushed the large crate back into place and lifted one of the smaller crates back on top of it. Then she turned back toward the door, leaving her bag off in the corner. "Let's have at it then."

*Craaaaaaash!*

The door burst inward and several SS soldiers stormed inside with their rifles firing. Irma Vep, eyes aglow, was at the back and ran at them dodging their bullets. She leaped up and ran along the wall and launched herself into the two soldiers at the front of the assault. She grabbed the first, who screamed in shock at the frenzied animal before him, and threw him back into his compatriots. Bullets ripped through his body as they kept firing. Their screams of "*Monster! Monster!*" filled the car.

Irma Vep leapt back up to the ceiling, and grabbed the electrical conduit for support. Her leg shot out and caught one of the soldiers on the chest spinning him off into the gangway. She turned and caught the other with her fist sending him to the floor with a broken jaw.

Then something grabbed her around the neck and threw her back down the car and into the crates! She hit the wood with a crunch and she could feel her ribs give way. Stunned, she looked up to see... nothing?

Yes, there was nothing, but cold darkness and pain before her. It was *him*!

Her fangs extended from her gums and she leapt back into the fray! High into the air she rose and kicked out against the dark. Her foot connected with something, but it felt like kicking into mud.

*Kick! Kick! Kick!* But nothing seemed to connect to her target. Then its shadowy arm shot out and slapped her across the room!

If she had been any less prepared for it her neck would be broken. As it was, Irma Vep collided with the floor, splintering the wood. That was when she saw it. Her bag of explosives sat in the corner. The darkness moved toward her and it was... laughing?

"*Ha ha ha... so good to see you again, my child.*"

Irma Vep crawled to her feet and hissed at the shadowy figure before her as her red eyes blazed. Her intentions were clear; she poised for the attack. She reached down and pulled her gun.

154

*"Oh, so naive."*

She smiled. "Not anymore. I see it now. To fight a monster requires another monster."

She whirled and aimed her broomhandle Mauser. Fired a single shot at her bag on the floor.

If one had been looking at the train as it roared across the track along the French countryside, one would have seen a massive thunderstorm of fire as it blew out of the second to last car on the line. The baggage cars buckled and ripped away in a fireball, leaving one half of the baggage car attached. Crates and bags were launched across the landscape pulling the fire along the track and down the hillsides into the water below. The last car, twisted and aflame, dug into the tracks and flipped end over end, then skidded to a stop.

As the Orient-Express, under strict orders from the SS, continued on her race to Paris, with one half of a smoking baggage car still behind her.

*July 12th, 1940. 21:55 hrs. The Orient-Express.*

Vladimir was already moving as the flash of light from the explosion reached their car followed by the concussion. Their windows exploded inward unleashing a storm of heat and glass shards. Hélène threw herself over the child Anneke as the tiny razors flew through the air. The soldiers withdrew back into the passageway as Vladimir and Sturmer struggled. Vladimir reached into his boot and pulled out a silvery stiletto. He made a backward slash, but the SS Lieutenant dodged it, and responded with a concussive punch to Vlad's ribs.

Her brother recoiled and pummeled the young officer with shots to his ribs. The officer roared and grabbed Vladimir's dagger hand. He expertly twisted Vladimir's arm and wrapped him in a bear hug. Hélène heard the cracking of Vladimir's ribs and reached for her own dagger attached to a garter sheath along her inner thigh. She whipped her blade across the room catching the one SS soldier in the eye.

Sturmer and Vladimir grunted at each other, twisting each other back and forth. The pair landed on Frankenstein who struggled to get them off him, and away from his granddaughter and Hélène. The second soldier raised his rifle, but Sturmer called out, "Stay back! He's mine!" The surprisingly agile German twisted Vladimir yet again and wrested his weapon from him. He raised his arm high, dagger in hand.

Hélène shouted as Sturmer plunged the dagger into Vladimir's side and threw him to the ground! Anneke screamed in terror at Vladimir's face which was frozen in shock. Then he looked at his sister, smiled, and died silently.

As more soldiers arrived, Hélène clutched the small Anneke to her.

Sturmer motioned fiercely to his men. "Take them to the forward compartments and see to it they are guarded securely or you'll pay with your lives. Is that understood? I'm going to inspect the damage to the baggage cars after I radio in our situation to the train station."

Anneke, silent through most of this bloodshed, suddenly piped up. "The baggage cars? Grandfather, our things!" Frankenstein stood up as the Nazis guided them out of the roomette.

"Do not be afraid, little one. Everything will be alright. We must be brave." He clutched his side where the two men had collided with him.

But the frightened little girl clung ever-so-tightly to Hélène as they marched out. She was aware, just as Hélène was, that the old man was lying. Everything wasn't going to be alright.

*July 12th, 1940. 22:30 hrs. Gare de l'Est. Paris.*

Sturmer's radio alert came over the airwaves with the greatest of dispatch. The Orient-Express had been attacked and now was racing toward Paris at full speed. The radio operator hit the alarm switch and sirens rang out. Talbot, just outside the room, emptied a trash can, staying out of the way of the platoons responding to the alert. As the troops raced noisily down the passageways, Talbot reached into his bag and pulled one of the bombs, placing it underneath the trash can next to the radio room.

Talbot checked his surroundings then slipped inside the radio room.

"*Stoppen! Sie haben keine Berechtigung, sich in diesem Bereich aufzuhalten!*"

Talbot locked the door behind him. "*Oh, ich glaube nicht, dass das deine größte Sorge ist.*" With that, Talbot unleashed the beast within himself and leapt at the screaming operator. He ripped into the operator's throat and the man gurgled and collapsed to the floor. Talbot concentrated and caged the beast inside him. Blood dripped down his chin like a good pint. He wiped his chin on his sleeve, and sat at the operator's station. He adjusted the dials, changing the transmitting frequencies to another predetermined setting that was monitored by the Allies. He keyed his microphone and began.

"*Catcher to Dugout. Come in Dugout. Bring in the Outfield. Repeat. Bring in the Outfield. Ball is headed toward the Catcher's Mitt,*" he said with a grin, "*and the Crowd goes wild.*"

Talbot, being Scottish by birth and raised in England, had no idea of the intricacies of American baseball other than what that lovely American nurse in Purfleet had told him. Of course, he was locked up in a cell, and she was under strict instruction not to engage with him, but his puppy dog eyes did work wonders. She had nothing to worry about as the chains he was locked up with were the densest of steel.

When all was said and done, Talbot confirmed over the radio that Dr. Frankenstein, the object of their mission, was headed to Paris on the Express. He

156

didn't know the details of the explosion on the train, but he had other concerns. Allied bombers were headed their way!

*July 12th, 1940. 22:40 hrs. The Orient-Express.*

The SS soldiers trudged down the speeding train's passageway guiding the elderly Dr. Frankenstein, Anneke, and Hélène toward the forward cars. They stopped three cars behind the engine and the soldiers placed them in their roomette. A soldier positioned himself next to the windows with the shades already drawn. Another stood by the door, and two more were outside in the passageway. They were going nowhere, except to Paris.

*July 12th, 1940. 22:50 hrs. The Orient-Express.*

Sturmer made his back through to the smoky wreckage being pulled behind the remaining fifteen cars of the Orient-Express. While the last car went off the tracks and flipped end over end, this car was a gaping black maw clinging to the rest of the train. The wind roared past him, and Sturmer was amazed at how lucky they all were. If the bomb had gone off in any of the middle cars the Express would have run off the tracks and crashed.

Now, with the one and a half of the cars gone, the heaviest cars at that, the train was racing ever faster toward her dark fate. Sturmer turned back toward the cars when an arm shot out of the smoky dark and gripped him by the throat!

"Herr *Kommandant*... Aargh!"

*"I am so gratified you're delighted to see me, Sturmer. Rest assured it would take more than an exploding bomb to destroy me. I am... hard to kill. You would do well to remember that. It has been the downfall of others before you."*

"We have Dr. Frankenstein. We await your command, *Mein Herr*." The words choked out of Sturmer's mouth.

*"Get word to our troops in the area. I want all of the material in the baggage car recovered..."*

*"But, Herr Kommandant ..."*

*"Sturmer! You will recover every scrap. No matter how small, no matter how insignificant, every bit will be retrieved and brought to me... or else."*

Sturmer nodded his head and exited, secure in the belief that nothing was ever what it seemed.

What could the *Kommandant* want with blown up wreckage?

*July 12th, 1940. 22:55 hrs. Gare de l'Est. Paris.*

Sirens wailed like banshees all over the chaotic Paris night. The Allied bombers were flying overhead. Searchlights and gun emplacements around the city limits were at full alert. Word had already gone out over the radio and via phone: "Prepare for an air raid." Units were recalled to help with the gun emplacements outside the city. I liked German predictability. Now the train station would be manned with a minimal number of troops.

The Resistance and I headed toward the shelters with the rest of the workers in the station. As everyone else entered the shelter door, I checked my watch then looked around.

Pierre walked up and nodded his head. Everything was in place. The fireworks were about to begin. Then I sent him and the rest off for their part in the mission. They had a rendezvous to keep.

I entered the shelter and locked the door. All around me were soldiers taking cover. Young soldiers and old Sergeants, and a few officers. Brilliant. I like killing Nazi officers.

I unleashed my beastly alter ego as I locked the door. At first, they didn't see me. Then the old fat Sergeant at the gate turned and saw me. He was first to scream.

The screams echoed with gunfire and the spilling of blood.

Oh, yes, there was plenty of blood. I made sure of that.

*July 12th, 1940. 23:00 hrs. The Orient-Express.*

Hélène held the little girl tightly to her chest. Anneke was buried face down, crying into her little doll. The soldier at the window motioned at the little girl, "Shut her up." Hélène patted her back as the soldier snarled at them. Then she calmly whipped her arm upward launching a small dagger at the soldier. The razor-thin missile slid into his throat, cutting off his voice box. He choked and leaned forward.

The soldier at the door moved forward, but Hélène was ready for him. She flipped her other wrist at the man and her blade hit her second target—the man's eye. He fell over dead, twitching.

Baumann (for it was still hard for Hélène to believe this kindly old gentleman was truly the infamous Dr. Frankenstein) looked at the two wounds from the blades and murmured, "Some sort of poison?"

Hélène picked up Anneke and was already checking the door. "Yes, Doctor. One of the special blends from my family. Very effective." She gestured to the soldier's throat which was already marked with a purple blotchy mass.

Then she turned to Anneke, got down on her knees and looked the little girl right in the eyes. "I shall need you to be very brave, little one. Do you understand?" The little girl's eyes took on a fierce determination, far beyond her years. She nodded. Then Hélène asked, "How are you, Doctor?"

Baumann/Frankenstein rose from his chair and held himself upright. He was shaky, but rallying. "I think it is time we took our leave of this place and escort my granddaughter to safety, yes?"

Just then, an experimental M64 500 lb. aerial bomb was dropped on the hillside next to the train tracks. The windows shattered as the train ground to a halt.

Sturmer grabbed one of the soldiers by the collar. "Get up to the engine car and get this train moving. We are sitting ducks if this train isn't moving!" The soldier saluted and dashed for the car. Sturmer looked outside to see the aftermath of the bomb... bomb? Singular? But there were multiple aircraft overhead. There would not be just one bomb. This was a diversion!

He turned and raced down the passageway toward the only thing that mattered.

*July 12th, 1940. 23:10 hrs. The Orient-Express, approximately four kilometers outside Paris.*

"Step down now, darling," said Frankenstein to his granddaughter. The little girl took her grandfather's hands and calmly took the steps down to the grassy plain along the Orient-Express's tracks. Hélène stood watch with another blade in hand as she climbed off the train and motioned for them all to head toward the forest.

Frankenstein clutched his side, but pointed at another angle away from the dense wood. "No, over there it is better! I thought I saw a small bridge. We can hide under it." Anneke grabbed her grandfather's hand and guided him in that direction. He was clutching his side harder and harder as they moved across the soft soil. It made for heavy moving. Hélène, eager to just get away before the Nazis pursued them, acquiesced. They had to hurry. Clinging to the shadows of the hillsides, the trio headed off into the darkness.

Too close behind, Sturmer and a squad of four soldiers exited the train. Sturmer ordered them to fan out and find any trace of them. He left them with the following orders as he ran off in his own direction, gun drawn, "By order of the *Kommandant*, they are to be captured, not killed! Your lives are forfeit if any harm should come to them!"

Above them, a long shadow cast across the landscape then faded back into nothingness.

*July 12th, 1940. 23:30 hrs. Approximately three kilometers outside Paris.*

Hélène lifted Anneke out of the creek bed and onto the bank. The cover was good with a stand of trees dappling the light from the road above the bridge. For the moment, they were hidden. Hélène then helped Frankenstein from the muddy waters. They caught each other's gaze and volumes of thoughts raced between them. Frankenstein smiled the grim smile.

159

"This is an unusual match."

"Chess, my dear. The Game of Kings."

"Is that how you see yourself then? A King?"

"No. I am a simple student. One whose curiosity knows no bounds. I am one who would walk with gods. There are those who would use that knowledge for their own ends."

"Arrogant then. I am familiar with arrogance, hubris."

Frankenstein smiled again. This time it was the smiling of knowing. "Your father," is all he said. But that was enough.

"Do you know what Fantômas has done with my son?" she asked flatly.

"I like your directness, *Frau* Fandor. Let me be equally direct. See to it that we reach Paris, and all will be revealed," he replied just as flatly. "Remember, in this game we play, nothing is ever as it seems."

Hélène, accustomed as she was to the machinations of her father, then realized how she had been used. That, even though she questioned the source of these machinations, she allowed her true blind spot—love—to draw her here to the point where she held a blade in her hand and could do nothing. Not only that, but she now had to use all the deadly skills her father endowed her with in order to save the man who killed her husband and kidnapped her son.

Frankenstein saw the multitude of questions and conundrums that haunted her. In a moment of either great pity or razor-sharp sarcasm he coughed, then offered, "Best not to think too hard on it my dear. It is far more complicated than we have time for. After all, we have an appointment at the Paris train station."

Anneke, holding onto her doll, stood in the tunnel and pointed. "I think I see lights. Is that Paris?"

"Yes, my dear. Let's keep moving, " said Frankenstein. "We have an appointment to keep at midnight."

Hélène watched behind them as Frankenstein and his granddaughter joined hands and walked through the tunnel under the bridge. He held his side as step-by-step they moved closer to the lights of Paris.

None of them noticed the darkness that creeped across the night, hunting them.

*July 12th, 1940. 23:55 hrs. Gare de l'Est. Paris.*

The Beast, as I called myself when I took my werewolf form, crawled out of the shelter. I was a frenzied animal, gulping for air and covered in Nazi blood. The killing lust was upon me. I could taste, smell, hear, feel everything around me. I raised my throat and howled.

Overhead, the Allied aircraft were selectively dropping their bombs, attacking the gun emplacements. Their explosions of fire and fury tore through the night lending a soft glow to the landscape outside of Paris. I grinned as I released my inner fury and returned to my human form the way M had taught me. Then I glanced at my watch. It was almost midnight.

"Oh, bollocks," I yelled and ran for the train tracks. I dove down in the massive trench cutting its way through the station. I hugged the concrete wall as the first of our bombs went off.

The radio room was the first explosion, cutting off the Nazis from seeking shelter in the station. The bomb tore through the concrete and steel, shattering the glass. Those who were positioned outside and within the buildings screamed through the flames and thought the Allied planes hit their target.

Suddenly, a Nazi soldier landed behind me and hugged the wall as I had. The young man, who didn't look old enough for the army, looked up to see a fierce, blood-soaked man. I smiled, which in retrospect probably wasn't the right thing to do. Wide-eyed, the soldier screamed and ran off.

*July 13th, 1940. 01:05 hrs. Approximately one kilometer outside Paris.*

The trio of escapees could hear the explosions go off before they crested the hillside. As they reached the top, the soft glow became a blazing inferno of explosions. They were close now, about a kilometer away. Soon it would all be over... that was good because the way Frankenstein held his side, he needed some sort of medical attention.

"Stop right there!"

Behind them, Sturmer and a soldier had caught up with them. Hélène placed herself between Sturmer and her charges, right in the line of fire. Anneke clung to her grandfather's leg in fear. "Grandfather?" she whined. The old man however was having his own problems. He was covered in sweat and each step of his was like hauling wet concrete. He was dying.

Hélène held up her blade. "Don't do this. I am charged with their protection, and I cannot let you do this." She arched her stance as her father had taught her, readying herself for battle.

Sturmer smiled. "And I cannot allow you to do that, my daughter." With that, he reached up and removed his SS officer's cap. Then, he gripped his forehead and removed his face!

*Fantômas!*

The soldier behind Sturmer stepped forward into the glow and removed his helmet.

*Vladimir!*

Hélène was in shock. She lowered her blade slightly, and took a step forward. Fantômas held up his hand, then pointed toward...

Frankenstein coughed, then clutched his side. Then Hélène knew. The good doctor had been poisoned! She turned and looked at Vladimir with a questioning look. Vladimir simply smiled and held up a needle. Hélène rewound their conflict in the train car in her mind. Vladimir and Sturmer... no, Fantômas

161

had collided with Baumann... no, Frankenstein. Vladimir must have injected him then.

Hélène surmised a yellowish purple mark was growing on Frankenstein's skin. She looked at the weakening doctor. She could see it in his eyes.

Anneke looked at her grandfather, then at the stone-faced mask of Fantômas. "What did you do to him?!"

"I simply changed the rules, my child," said the Emperor of Crime, "My Master needs you and your... unique technology for his purpose. If you wish to live you will come with me."

Hélène's ears pricked up... *Master? Every day of her life that she had known him, the great Fantômas never, ever, had acknowledged that anyone was his master. What was going on here?*

"He knows where my son is, Father. Force his tongue!" Hélène's words made her tremble.

"All in good time, Hélène. There is another bit of business that *must* come first." Fantômas pulled his pistol, and held it steadily on the coughing man. "Now we have you. We have your granddaughter. Where is your equipment? You do not have long now, Doctor! Surely you realize your escape plan with the Allies is over."

The old man pushed his granddaughter away and stood alone on the bank. Behind him, the explosions were still going off around Paris giving his now twisted frame a soft orange halo.

"I learned of your master's plans for me, and how he was sending you to capture me and my granddaughter." He looked at the little girl cowering off to the side. He looked into her eyes. "I owe you so much, you made me better." He smiled a 'thank you' and then turned his attention toward Hélène... "I needed a champion. Someone who could counter every move of your father. My mistake was not identifying the viperish nature of your brother. I am sorry. I cannot allow my work to fall into his master's hands. I have seen the gods he worships, and they are dark indeed."

A single tear ran down Hélène's cheek.

Suddenly, a cloak of darkness passed her eyes and onward onto Vladimir. It vibrated in and out of sight as it wrapped itself around the soldier. Vladimir struggled but the shadows had a grip on him like a python. Then, as if emerging from the darkest of night, the pale face of Irma Vep—she of those blazing red eyes, those gleaming ivory fangs—ripped into Vladimir's neck sending a geyser of blood onto the ground.

She was already moving when Fantômas pulled his trigger. As she hit him, the bullet left the chamber, hurtled past Hélène's face, scarring her cheek, and found its target. A small round hole opened on Frankenstein's forehead and exploded out the back of his skull. His body collapsed to the ground, and Irma Vep whirled around a second time and struck Fantômas with all her might, cracking his ribs and sending him flying ten feet away into the dirt.

He didn't move. Irma turned her attention back to Hélène and the girl. She became less a living shadow and more of a figure dressed in black leather beyond understanding.

Hélène screamed, "No!" But she wasn't screaming over her father. It was a scream of frustration as she saw her only hope to see her son again bleeding into the ground. She fell to her knees near the bloody Frankenstein. All of her hopes were dashed. She would never see her son again.

"Get up!" said Irma.

Hélène hazily crawled to her feet. Anneke ran to her side. Clung to her like she clung to her doll earlier.

"Hélène, what will happen to us?" cried the little girl. Hélène picked her up, held her tight.

"What about my father?"

Irma Vep smiled slightly. She didn't bother to turn her head and said, "He's already gone."

Thinking that he had passed away, Hélène looked over to where the Lord of Terror had landed to find nothing. He had already disappeared!

"You don't seem to have any concern for your brother," said Irma.

"Leave the bastard to the wolves," was all Hélène could manage. She grabbed her scarf and wiped the blood off her cheek.

Irma tilted her head and listened to the night. "Hurry, we have to go. The *Boche* are coming. Get over the hill. The Allies are waiting for you in the forest."

The trio began running up the hill and across the fields just in time. Gunshots echoed in the dark and bullets struck the soil around where they had just stood. Irma looked back at their pursuers and yelled at Hélène and Anneke, "Keep running to the trees! I'll hold off the soldiers!"

And then she became a shadow and melted away.

Hélène, seeing the gunfire from the distance, held Anneke tightly and broke out into a run.

A squad of SS soldiers formed a line across the field and advanced toward their target. They fired as accurately as they had been trained, but they were still too far away, and too much darkness between them for precision. Their Sergeant called for double-time and the troops broke out into a run. They would soon catch up and capture their prey.

"*Vorstoßen*," screamed the Sergeant, urging his squad to advance. *"Wir können sie nicht entkommen lassen!"* It was at that precise moment, when the last syllable of his rallying cry erupted from his throat, that Irma Vep, a Child of the Night, grabbed his head and twisted his skull off completely! The Sergeant's torso stood upright while his heart pumped blood onto the grass from the stump that was his neck. The man's head, lying on the ground, stared wide-eyed up at his body in shock. Then his torso fell and lay next to it.

But Irma Vep paid no attention as she was already moving on to her next kill.

As he ran, Private Willi Herold could feel he was being stalked somehow. He grew up in countryside like this in the German-speaking Sudetenland of Czechoslovakia. He had hunted with his father, and grandfather and knew when he was predator and when he was prey. He called out to his squad mate, "Franz?" Where was he? He was supposed to be on his left with the other three in his squad.

Herold could no longer hear them, but he did see something in the distance. Something white and flowing? A scarf? Meyer stopped and sighted his rifle at the bright spot. He controlled his breathing, and inched his finger onto the trigger.

He could hear his Sergeant screams into his ear at basic training, "Don't grip the trigger so hard, and quit jerking it back! Do you pleasure your girlfriend like that? Poor girl!" Over and over the gruff Sergeant would tell them, "Take better care of your rifle than your girlfriend. There will always be another girlfriend, and rest assured she won't save your life like your rifle."

Herold sighted the flowing white object. He had a killshot.

Then for whatever reason—instinct, precognition—he turned and fired to his right. The bullet flew through the air and struck Irma Vep right in her chest. She hit the ground, shocked that she'd been shot, and shocked it was by a rosy-cheeked boy soldier!

Herold, the boy soldier, stood his ground, ejected his shell and set another in the chamber. Irma Vep stood and glared at him with her eyes. Her burning, red eyes. He stiffened, mesmerized on the spot as Irma Vep, Lady Vampire sauntered over to him. He began to sweat as she walked around him contemplating where she would start…

*"Raaaaaaaaaaargh!"*

The beast leapt in front of her and grabbed her arm. She struggled, but Talbot, the wolf-man, held on. She snarled, "Let go! Don't you understand? It takes a monster to stop a monster!"

Talbot, unafraid of what he saw of himself there, looked directly into her hypnotic orbs.

"No."

She looked back at him and wiped blood red tears from her eyes. Her eyes dulled in color and her fangs, once ready to rip the young soldier's life from his throat, retreated. Talbot softened his look and then let go of her arm. "Let's get out of here. We don't have time for you to play with your food."

"Always the joker, Major Talbot," she blubbered. She wiped her eyes again, sniffed and composed herself. "How do you do it, Major? How do you stand being a monster?"

Talbot looked at her. "Character is what you are in the dark, milady." He let the words hang there. "Now let's go. Bullard is waiting for us with the lorry."

"You mean, the *camion*."

"Whatever Madame wants."

The pair took off toward the forest. They could already hear their men.

"Thank you, Major."

"Whatever for?"

"Well, if you had been an American, you would have tried to make me feel better instead of letting me feel what I needed to."

*Thirty-Six Hours Later. Somewhere under Paris.*

"Bollocks!"

"Is that a quote?"

I paced around the chamber like an animal in a cage. In my hand was a radio message from London informing me of my new orders. Her Ladyship Irma Vep couldn't be bothered to turn around from the work she was doing, and the other two—Fantômas' daughter and Frankenstein's grandchild—were off in the corner reading one of the books off the shelf. "Are you listening to me?"

"I can hear you, as you well know, Major. No need to howl."

"Thanks to the brilliant job we have done here of *not* recovering Dr. Frankenstein, and actually blowing to bits whatever he was working on..."

"Which couldn't be avoided as you well know..."

"Yes, so you say. Blow it all up. Keep it out of the hands of the forces of darkness..."

*"Non. The* Darkness."

"Whatever her Ladyship says."

She turned around and walked over to where I stood.

"And what, pray tell, is the bad news, *Monsieur*? Because the only thing I can think of that would make matters worse would be for you to remain here in Paris." Then she smiled.

"How the hell did you know that? That's exactly what my orders say. The Germans were up to something and so was Fantômas. London wants to know what and to put a stop to it!"

Irma Vep walked over to the settee where the ladies were reading. They both looked up at her. "There is still much we must learn, Major. Hélène has already shown us this." She placed her hand toward the painting on the wall, then passed her hand right through it. It was some sort of an optical illusion, invisible until you actually touched the painting. Irma reached around inside then pulled.

The wall behind her opened up into another chamber filled with all sorts of equipment and chemicals. An extensive laboratory for the Emperor of Crime!

Hélène seemed ashamed at the sight, but said nothing. Anneke looked at the glassware and chemicals as if they were new toys.

"We have many secrets to uncover, Major."

"Well, I suppose if you can put up with another guest, I will find a cozy spot to curl up and sleep."

"We will make allowances. See M. Bullard about a uniform."

"Uniform?"

"I understand there is a need for a *serveur* upstairs in the night club."

Damn you, M. I hate you.


Irma Vep retired to her own chamber, deep within the rock, and Talbot went up to find Bullard. Anneke leaned back on the settee and sighed. Hélène closed the book they had been reading. She was silent and still. Anneke could tell she was still in shock and mourning for her husband and her lost son.

"Please, dear Hélène. Don't be sad. Given that you have aided me so very much, I will help you. I will restore your lost son to you..."

"Anneke, please! How can a little girl be so cruel!"

"I will be what I want when I want, and you will not interrupt me again!"

Hélène recoiled slightly. This wasn't the tone of a little girl, but that of...

"Yes, you're beginning to see now, aren't you my lovely Heléne? Here, let me convince you..."

Anneke gently held her hand, smiled, and placed it on the back of her head. "Feel around." Hélène moved her fingers delicately through the child's hair. Then she felt it. Puzzled, she moved her finger softly along a scar hidden under the little girl's hairline. It was a long scar from what had to be a complex surgery. Hélène jerked her hand away as if she had been burned. She was horrified at the thoughts that were now running through her mind. Anneke nodded her head. "Yes, darling Hélène, nothing is ever what it seems, and what you are thinking is true. The old man was not my grandfather. He was my *disguise*. Please allow me to introduce myself properly. I am Dr. Victor Frankenstein, and if you have any hopes of ever seeing your son again, then you will do as I order and protect me at all times. Is that understood?"

Hélène, still in shock, found herself nodding her head.

*July 16th, 1940. 08:00 hrs. Four kilometers down river from Châlons-sur-Marne.*

"What is it, son?"

The young farmer used his rake to latch onto the crate jutting out of the thick mud on the bank of the river. He pulled mightily and only managed to lift it slightly onto shore. "I don't know, Papa! It's some sort of crate. Maybe it's from that explosion the other night? Here, help me get it up! It might be valuable."

The older farmer got down from their wagon and came over to the bank. "It might be trouble."

The young man pointed to the side of the crate. The pair looked down at the *Boche* markings. The two looked at one another and rolled up their sleeves. They pulled and grunted their way up onto the harder soil. The young man stooped down to get a better look at the markings. He wiped away the mud caked on the wood. "Some of the wood is broken here, Papa..."

Then, just as he wiped away the last of the mud and removed the broken board, a pale, scarred arm shot out the crate and grabbed him by the throat!

*"Aaaaaaaaaaaaaaarrrrrrrgh"*

His father grabbed the young man and pulled him back. The two men collapsed in the mud as another fist tore through the crate. Then someone... *something* kicked the crate shattering it. A tall figure, misshapen and scarred, suddenly stood above them. Wires and tubes adorned his body, injected into key points on the monster's frame. And indeed, he was a monster, stitched together in a pattern indicating haste not aesthetics.

The Creature looked down at the river and caught his reflection in the shiny water, then he collapsed.

*July 16th, 1940. :1900 hrs. SS Headquarters. 84 Avenue Foch, Paris.*

"I am sorry to report that we have yet to recover the contents of the baggage car, *Mein Herr*." Major Hauptmann stood before the *Kommandant*. He was nervous, but stood firm at attention. He was well aware that Lieutenant Sturmer had been transferred to the front lines of battle.

The *Kommandant* gestured to the chair in front of his desk. Hauptmann politely sat down, but kept his formal military bearing. He had not yet been placed, "at ease." The *Kommandant* leaned forward into the light of the small desk lamp. His piercing eyes never left Hauptmann's. "I do not accept failure from my subordinates, Hauptmann. What do you intend to do about finding my equipment?"

Hauptmann reached into his folio and retrieved a formal military order. "I have taken the liberty of placing more troops on standby. If you would sign this order, it will double the number of soldiers involved in the search. In addition, we will have aerial reconnaissance at your command, providing our intelligence unit with photographs to chart all of the wreckage and determine the path of the currents. We will search all farms and buildings in the area. It is now simply a matter of time, *Kommandant*."

Satisfied for the moment, the *Kommandant* signed the paperwork, and then stamped it with the seal of his office. He left the paper on the desk and sat back out of the light. "Leave now."

Hauptmann stood up at attention, and retrieved his orders. He studied the florid signature for a moment then asked, "If one may ask, sir, what is the correct pronunciation of your family name. So that I may properly address you?"

The *Kommandant* leaned back into the light, his eyes aglow.

*"Alucard. I am Kommandant Alucard."*

*Often hailed as the best French science fiction writer of the early 20th century, Maurice Renard coined the term "Scientific Marvel Fiction" to pen a series of gripping, ground-breaking stories that owe as much to Edgar Allan Poe as they do to H.G. Wells. Until Black Coat Press published five volumes collecting the classic works of this pioneering giant of French science fiction, Renard was best known to the English-speaking public for his thrice-filmed thriller,* The Hands of Orlac. *Matthew Dennion's tale takes its inspiration from* Doctor Lerne *(1908), a novel dedicated to Wells, which features a mad scientist who performs organ transplants not only between men and animals, but also with plants and even machines...*

## Matthew Dennion: *A Greener Future*

*California, 1969*

My name is Nicolas Vermont and my thoughts are currently weighing heavily on me. As I sit here in the twilight of my life, I am faced with an important decision that could lead to great horror being unleashed on the world, or perhaps set into motion events that were destined to happen for the preservation of it. The question is, what forms of life will my decision preserve? Will it help all manner of life or simply a form of life that has existed long before the first animals crawled and swam on the planet? Will my decision lead to helping mankind live in harmony with the world or will it lead to the world turning on its most dangerous inhabitants?

In the past, the knowledge that is in my care has led to many terrifying events. Due to the fact that many horrific events have been centered around it, I have had trepidation about sharing it with others. Still, once, a long time ago, a great man told me that, for better or worse, I would know when the time to pass such knowledge had arrived. As I look at the two letters on my desk, I wonder if that time has come. In hopes of helping me to make my decision, I cast my thoughts back to events which served as a prelude to my current conundrum...

It was the summer of 1918. My heart was racing as I pulled the car to a stop in front of a massive estate. While the reputation of the man who was said to inhabit it was part of the reason for my elevated heart rate, I would be lying if I said that it was the only cause of my distress.

Another reason for my excited state was the fact that my former lover, the woman who had broken my heart and left me for another man, was sitting next to me. The fact that I had not driven an automobile since the unfathomable events which had occurred around my last vehicle also bothered me. I had to

169

constantly reassure myself that this car was not vexed by the same sinister forces that had possessed my earlier automobile over a decade ago.

The car itself may not have been cursed, but I was certain that those same forces had returned to haunt me once again. With a heart filled with both longing and regret, I walked around and opened the door for Emma.

Despite how she had walked away from our relationship as if it were but a mere trifle had shattered my heart, I still had strong feelings for her. While her manipulative nature was now known to me, I was still extremely attracted to her. Her skills as a lover were matched by no other woman I had ever met. Her sheer beauty could only have been equaled by Helen of Troy herself. Thus, when she came to me looking for help, her beauty, and the circumstances surrounding her plight, caused me to give her shelter for at least a night while I considered her tale.

After the horrific events she recounted, I found myself in a position where I was honor-bound to help her resolve her situation. As such, we immediately began seeking assistance, and, after numerous stops, had ended our journey here.

We were walking up to the house when Emma grabbed my arm and stopped me.

"Nicolas, are you sure that this Sâr Dubnotal will be able to help us?" she asked. "I still feel that Doctor Ardan would be the individual most capable of assisting us with the matter at hand."

I sighed and did my best to respond in a manner of becoming a gentleman.

"My dear, you heard what Doctor Ardan's associate said about him having a family affair to attend to in Central America. He also noted that our, er, situation might well require expertise outside the realm of the Doctor's expertise. Besides, knowing your proclivities toward attractive men, I'm sure that part of your interest lies more with his physique rather than his scientific abilities. But if it helps, from what I've heard, I doubt that even your methods of seduction would have worked on a man of his moral fiber."

Emma pouted. "They were effective enough on you! I would also suggest that Ardan's associate would have done anything I asked as well."

My body shivered as I recalled the effect her sexuality had on me. I pushed the thought aside and focused on the task at hand.

"I've learned from our previous liaison what it means to be involved with you. And for Ardan's associate, given his ape-like appearance, I'm not sure he's not a man who's had his mind grafted into the body of a gorilla."

Our conversation came to an end as we reached the door of the great estate. I had scarcely knocked on the door when it was opened by a servant who ushered us into a study and informed us that his master would soon meet with us. I was surprised that no introduction on our part was needed, but given the nature of the individual we were seeking out, upon reflection, it seemed quite natural.

A moment later, the imposing and powerful form of Sâr Dubnotal entered the study. The man both inspired and terrified me. His appearance was a unique blend of a well-built Frenchman and a Hindu. Beyond his physical attributes, he gave off a sense of power and mystery. One look at Emma's hungry eyes told me that she was taken with the enigmatic figure as well.

The Psychagogue bowed as he introduced himself.

"Good evening. I am Sâr Dubnotal. I sense that you are in grave need of assistance. How may I aid you?"

I stood up and went to shake his hand, but after seeing how he had introduced himself, I bowed instead. I then began recanting the nature of our current plight.

"My name is Nicolas Vermont. This is Emma Bourdichet. We have a strange story that is filled with horror and nigh unbelievable acts done to man, beast, and even plants. I am the nephew of Doctor Frédéric Lerne, and Emma was formerly his ward. A year ago, I went to spend the summer with my uncle. It was during that time that I met Emma and fell in love with her. At the time, I thought she was being kept as some kind of prisoner. This assumption turned out to be only partially true..."

I wiped the sweat from my brow as the events of the past ran through my mind. "The truth was that Doctor Lerne was experimenting with grafting the parts of men, beasts, and plants together. This included swapping the brains of both men and animals. I myself had my brain put into the body of a bull while the creature's brain was put into mine. Thankfully, after the creature in my body attempted to kill itself, the Doctor put my brain back in my original body. I thought this would be the end of the horror, but sadly, it was only the beginning. At some point, one of Lerne's assistants, Otto Klotz, saw an opportunity to profit from Lerne's work. He had the other two assistants, Ronald LeBay and Alex Olsen, put his brain in Lerne's body and killed him in the process. He sought to gain my uncle's fortune and control of Emma.,,"

I looked over at Emma to see her ravenous eyes staring at the Sâr. I ignored her lustful gaze and continued my tale.

"We only discovered this after Klotz seemingly died in Lerne's body. We then sought to leave and escape the horror which had occurred there but found that Klotz had taken the Doctor's work to another level. He had mastered not only putting a man's brain into another body, but also transferring a man's very consciousness into a separate object. He was able to not only transplant his mind into plants, but even a mechanical apparatus such as my automobile! Emma and I discovered this when my car began to operate itself with us in it!"

I looked over at my former lover with that same combination of yearning and pain in my heart as I told the next part of our story.

"Afterward, Emma left me for a former lover, a boxer named Alcide. I was able to return the car to my uncle's estate and kept it there for several years, locked in a box. Klotz would often spur his engine and try to break out, but eventually he seemed resigned to his fate.

"I thought he would stay there until one day a strange odor came from the box. I went to investigate and found the car half-melted into the ground and the very grass and foliage around it had grown into the vehicle. I thought this was the end of Klotz. That is, until the other day when Emma and Alcide were attacked by a man and, of all things, an ape!"

Emma feigned a swoon as I told this part of the story. It was obvious she was trying to gain the sympathy of the mystic but, to his credit, Sâr Dubnotal's eyes remained fixed on me. Seeing this, I continued the tale.

"Emma recognized the man as LeBay. The ape, whom we assume was Olsen's mind in an ape's body, tried to capture Alcide and Emma. Being a huge man and a boxer, Alcide was able to hold off Lebay and the ape, long enough for her to escape and come to me for help. I can only assume that what I thought was a decaying car surrounded by overgrowth was actually Klotz's consciousness somehow merging with the plants. It must have been through this method that he escaped his prison and rejoined with his cohorts.

"That was when the situation became dire. Emma came to what was formerly Doctor Lerne's house to find me. She told me what happened. We both guessed that Klotz, still enamored with Emma, had succeeded in transferring his consciousness into Alcide's body in order take her, either by her own accord or against her will.

"That very night, we heard a strange cracking of trees accompanied by terrible roars. When we learned the nature of these sounds, we were dumbstruck. Not only did Klotz in Alcide's massive body appear out of the woods, but so did the ape, now with a thick layer of tree bark attached to his body. Aside from that, Klotz had also learned of the adventures of my uncle's neighbor, Monsieur de Gambertin, who lived on the other side of the forest that bordered our property. Gambertin had discovered a living megalosaurus! This beast now had LeBay's mind in it, and was also covered in tree bark!

"Klotz demanded to have Emma now that he possessed a body she could love. He also insisted that I give him what remained of Lerne's fortune. If his demands were not met, he threatened to send LeBay and Olsen, now in the bodies of the hybrid wood-ape and the megalosaurus, to kill me and take Emma by force. If we ran, he vowed to use Lerne's knowledge to create an army of chimeric animal-plant creatures to hunt us down.

"I had my rifle ready and fired upon the beasts, but, with their tree bark armor, the bullets didn't harm them. Emma and I ran to my car and we tried to flee, only to find a hulking figure composed entirely of foliage in front of us. I can only assume that this muck monster was another of Klotz's men whose mind he put into some form of vegetation to also carry out his bidding!"

Exhausted, I slumped down into a chair.

"For the two days since that terrifying encounter, we have been on the run, trying to seek help from men of renown. We first reached out to Doctor Francis Ardan but he was away. Given the somewhat supernatural nature of our tormentors, one of his assistants first contacted Flaxman Low. Low wanted to help us, but said that his expertise was purely in the realm of the supernatural, but this case was a mixture of science and magic. You see, we're not only dealing with the physical removal of brains from one body into another, but also the transfer of consciousness from men to plants and machines. Low suggested that you were the only person who has sufficient mastery of both science and sorcery to help us. Who knows what kind of monsters Klotz will create… I fear that if he is not stopped, he will send more creatures across France in search of Emma. Aside from the danger to her, I fear for the lives of innocents who may get in the way."

Emma stood and threw herself at Sâr Dubnotal. She wrapped her arms around the mystic and gazed into his eyes with her seductive stare. My heart sank as I watched her attempting to use her sex appeal to entrap yet another powerful man in her amorous spell. To my surprise, the mage glared at her, and with God as my witness, I swear I saw his eyes light up with flames as he addressed my former lover.

"Remove your arms from my body! I am not a man who shall fall for your feeble attempts at seduction."

With the look of scorned puppy, Emma pulled away from the sorcerer. Sâr Dubnotal then looked at us.

"There is an aura coming off the two of you that suggests you are involved in events which extend beyond the immediate horror you both face. I shall assist you in ridding the world of this evil. We shall leave post haste to address the threat posed by Klotz. You two shall come with me. Madame, these fiends are after you, and the best way to protect you is for you to stay by my side. Your presence will also draw them to us. If we approach them on their own terms, we will reduce the chances of others being injured as they pursue you."

The great psychagogue then turned toward me. "There is a role for you to play as well, but I can't fully discern what it is yet. When the time comes, I am sure it will present itself. Together, we shall meet this threat and end it."

Seeing the determination in his face gave me a renewed sense of self-confidence. I offered to drive us right away, but Sâr Dubnotal declined to use my vehicle. He suggested we should take his automobile as he had cast spells over it that would protect it from having the consciousness of man placed inside it. Emma and I agreed and made our way to the Sâr's vehicle.

Night had fallen once again as we approached my residence. His driver, Frank, stopped several miles from the house. At that point, the mystic told him to wait there while the rest of us proceeded on foot through the forest that surrounded my property. Sâr Dubnotal then removed a vial from within the folds of his clothing. He sprinkled its contents over the three of us. He said that it would prevent any animal from detecting our scent until we had reached our target.

Despite his presence, I must say that my mind was filled with trepidation as we made our way through the woods. The sights of the wood-megalosaurus, the bark-ape, and the grotesque plant creature that we had encountered were still fresh in my mind.

We were walking at a quick but quiet pace when Sâr Dubnotal suddenly threw his hands up and motioned for us to stop. He then gestured to remain silent as he scanned the trees. The mage slowly spun in a circle before his keen eyes settled on a spot to our right. He then lifted his hands into the air as a massive creature emerged from the stygian darkness.

As it moved out from behind the leaves that were obscuring it, the moonlight revealed it to be the walking mound of grass, leaves, and muck that we had encountered when we had initially fled. Emma screamed at the sight of this walking nightmare and ran behind Sâr Dubnotal. I tried to remain brave and stood my ground out of a sense of chivalry, but was forced to back away from the monster as he shambled closer to us.

I looked over at Sâr Dubnotal expecting to see the same grim determination I had seen on his face when he'd first agreed to help us. But to the contrary, the man's demeanor suggested feelings of curiosity, sympathy, and. dare I say. respect as he looked at the monster.

He addressed us as he walked toward it. "I do not think this creature was created by Klotz. He is something more." He then spoke to the beast in a kind voice. "I sense that you are not a threat, but perhaps serve a great purpose. May I lay my hands upon you and join our minds so that we may understand one another?"

The monster did not respond, but simply remained still as the mystic placed his hand on the muck-encrusted creature. After a few seconds, Sâr Dubnotal removed his hand and nodded at the now seemingly benign creature. The mage turned to Emma and I and relayed what he had learned.

"It is as I thought. This being is not a creation of Klotz. He is known as the Heap. He was created by Mother Nature herself from the remains of a pilot who once went by the name Baron Eric von Emmelman. He functions as the current Guardian of the Green. He protects all plant life on the planet and helps to maintain the balance between they and animal life. Klotz's grafting of plants into humans and animals has caused a disruption that, if not addressed quickly, will have catastrophic consequences. The Heap is here to put an end to these atrocities—and to Klotz. He has agreed to work with us toward that end.

"While his presence here validates my suspicions about the direness of the situation, we are fortunate to have him. The Guardian of the Green is traditionally one of the most powerful beings on the planet. With him by our side, our chances of vanquishing Klotz's unnatural forces are greatly increased. Come! We haven't a moment to waste!"

174

As we approached my house, I whispered to Sâr Dubnotal, "Sir, I thank you for your assistance in this matter. I want to help as much as I can, but at the same time, I also wish to protect Emma. I think this could be the role you mentioned earlier. If I can make it to my gun room, I can arm myself and..."

The Sâr held up his hand to stop me and replied, "No. I shall protect the woman. Through the Heap, I have now divined what your role in this matter is, and it is two-fold. First, you must destroy your uncle's greenhouse and laboratory. The experiments he started and which Klotz continued must be put to end. Should the plant life continue to be perverted in this manner, Mother Nature herself might intervene utilizing methods that will have grave consequences for the future of mankind."

I nodded. "I shall destroy the laboratory and the greenhouse. What is my second task?"

"Doctor Lerne's notes and his formula for bonding man to plant—you must preserve these. While Mother Nature does not wish Klotz or any human to bond with plants, she herself will use this formula to create future guardians like the Heap."

The mage looked me in the eye and spoke directly. "In the future, many savants and mystics will reach out to you regarding Lerne's work and its application to their own endeavors. You will have to decide to whom to give your uncle's notes."

"How will I know to whom I'm supposed to give this knowledge?"

"The Green will work through you. You shall simply have a feeling that sending your work to certain people is what you are supposed to do. From there, Mother Nature will shape their work into what is required. The stoppage of the current experiments and the preservation of future studies are of the utmost importance—even more so than protecting Emma, or our own lives."

I nodded that I understood, then asked, "Through contact with the Heap, you're able to see future events?"

"Not with clarity. I can only see glimpses of Mother Nature's plan, but I can see the aspects I just mentioned are pivotal for her future plans. I do not envy the position you will be in, Monsieur Vermont. Mother Nature knows what is best for life, but she does not favor one form of life over another. Your decision will have a profound effect on plant and animal life, including humans, when the time comes."

Our conversation stopped when a roar echoed across the sky. Sâr Dubnotal nodded. "We are close. I can sense great death around this place. Is there a graveyard or cemetery around here?"

"Yes. On the side of the house facing the forest, there's a graveyard of past subjects that Doctor Lerne and Klotz experimented on. The bodies of many animals are interred there, as well as several human bodies, including that of Lerne himself. There's even some dinosaur fossils akin to those that Gamberdin found on his own property."

"Good. The Heap and I shall make our stand there. Emma, you stay behind us as we engage these villains." Sâr Dubnotal looked at the Heap. "The key will be to keep Klotz and his men occupied while I devise a spell to force them back into their original bodies." He then looked at me. "You know what you need to do. Now, let us meet our enemies."

Through the trees, I saw Klotz in Alcide's body, and the two bark-covered monstrosities. I was trying to gather my courage as Sâr Dubnotal strode out of the forest with the Heap next to him and Emma directly behind them.

The sight of the imposing Heap caused even the megalosaurus to take a step back as he beheld the marsh monster. Klotz was moving closer to his ape companion when he noticed Emma. The scoundrel smiled as he saw the object of his lust.

With Klotz's thoughts fixed on Emma, I seized my opportunity and broke for the garage which held the kerosene I used to heat the house. As I ran, I could hear the exchange between the sorcerer and the body-snatcher.

Klotz mocked Emma. "I see, my love, that you have found another fool to help you." He then looked at the Heap. "Is that another of your former lovers? Has Nicolas transferred his mind into that rotting pile of leaves in a vain attempt to stop me? Leave these fools behind! Save them, and countless others, from undue suffering. Be with me! We both know how fond you are of this body."

I snatched up the kerosene and every match I could find as I heard the mage respond. "I am Sâr Dubnotal! Leave these unnatural bodies you possess! Forsake the insane science you have been using! Leave this woman in peace or face my wrath, as well as that of nature itself!"

Klotz laughed and turned to his armored ape and saurian. "Destroy these fools and bring me my bride!"

I came out of the garage to see the ape leaping toward the Heap. He brought his full weight crashing into the plant creature and caused it to fall to the ground. The primate then began pounding the Guardian into the soil. I had nearly reached the laboratory when I saw the earth behind the ape suddenly beginning to rise. Before my very eyes, the Heap had restored himself and risen again. The muck monster then wrapped his arms around the chimeric beast and wrestled him to the ground.

When I entered the greenhouse-laboratory, I began dispersing the kerosene as I watched the confrontation through the windows. The bark-encrusted megalosaurus roared and began making his way toward Sâr Dubnotal. Rather than running, the mage placed his hand on the ground and said the words. "*Klaatu barada nicto!*"

To my astonishment, the very dirt on which the mystic stood began to shift. I saw all manner of bones bursting out of the soil. The skeletons of men, bulls, dogs, birds, horses, goats. and even the fossils of several dinosaurs. Rose up. As if this sight was not astonishing enough, what happened next nearly transfixed me to the point that I almost forgot my mission. Sâr Dubnotal began

176

moving his hands around and his motions caused the bones of the various beasts to begin to combine into a single colossal creature.

Not only was I stunned by the event, but so were Klotz and even LeBay inside the megalosaurus. Both of them stood still as the ghastly skeletal creature took form. The only creatures not affected by the event were the Heap and the ape as they continued to jockey for position.

Sâr Dubnotal constructed a skeletal figure that had legs and tails of a long-ago deceased iguanodon. The horror's body was a mixture of the thick ribs and the spines of numerous bulls and horses that had been experimented on. It had two long arms that were made up of the legs of rams and sheep and ended into the thumb-clawed hands of the iguanodon. The beast's skull was that of a bull with its long horns protruding out of its heads. From its back, the wing bones of countless birds connected to form two sets of skinless wings that connected to its spine.

The cadaverous creature unleashed a horrible moan at the megalosaurus and charged it as the Heap rose again, lifting the ape high over his head. The muck monster tossed him into a nearby tree as the wood covered saurian and the skeletal abomination tore into each other like lions battling for the rights to a pride. The Heap grabbed onto the dinosaur's tail when the ape jumped onto his back and pulled it off his cohort.

I moved to the desk where Doctor Lerne had kept his notes. I was stuffing them in my pocket when I saw Klotz, in Alcide's herculean body, approaching Sâr Dubnotal and Emma. The psychagogue still had his hand on the ground as the giant loomed over him.

Klotz mocked him. "It seems that our monsters are engaged in a standoff. That leaves only you and I to fight for this woman."

Sâr Dubnotal dug his hands into the dirt as he responded. "There is another one other here who has a particular interest in seeing you pay for your misdeeds."

I gasped in disbelief. Emma fainted and fell to the ground. Klotz screamed in horror, as Sâr Dubnotal pulled his hand from the soil with his fingers wrapped around the decaying but reanimated face of Doctor Lerne himself. He then released his hold on Lerne's head as the zombie pulled the rest of his rotting corpse out of the ground on his own accord.

While Alcide's body was twice the size of Lerne's, the revenant seemed to be imbued with supernatural strength as he grabbed the giant and forced him to the ground. I saw the undead Lerne lean in toward Klotz's face. When worms began to squirm out of the Doctor's skeletal mouth and empty eye sockets, I was forced to turn away. I moved to the door and struck a match that sent the whole laboratory aflame.

Emma was still unconscious behind Sâr Dubnotal as the mage appeared to be meditating. I ran over and revived her. She wrapped her arms around me, thanked me, and gave me a passionate kiss. Despite our history, I confess that at the moment, I once more fell for the enchantress.

Our kiss came to an abrupt end when the Heap slammed the wood-ape down next to Sâr Dubnotal. The mystic kept his eyes closed as he placed his hand on the ape's head and spoke a word I could not even begin to pronounce. The beast howled for a moment before its body went limp.

With the wood-ape dispatched, the Heap once lumbered over to the warring skeletal chimera and the wood-covered megalosaurus. The two leviathans were still engaged in a struggle in which neither of them seemed to gain the upper hand. The Heap grabbed the saurian's leg. We watched as the plant life around him seemed to be pulled into the creature's body.

The muck monster tripled in size and then threw his gargantuan body over the dinosaur. The living mudslide buried the plant-beast and covered his face. The skeletal horror then added his own weight to the Heap's by climbing on top of the saurian.

The Heap moved a small amount of plant life away from the creature's leg. Once the megalosaurus was restrained and his outer layer was exposed.,Sâr Dubnotal walked over to the creature and placed his hand on it. The sorcerer repeated the odd word he had used to disable the ape. As the word left the mage's mouth, the megalosaurus roared and then fell still.

The Heap slid off the dinosaur and returned to his normal size. The monster then began walking over toward the battling Lerne and Klotz. Using Alcide's size and boxing skills, the body-snatcher had gained a small advantage over my undead uncle. Klotz was about to strike Lerne when the Heap grabbed his right hand and forced the boxer to the ground. Klotz's left hand was then snatched by Lerne. Together, the zombie and the swamp monster forced the giant to his knees.

Klotz struggled to free himself as Sâr Dubnotal approached him. The sorcerer once more had fire in his eyes as he yelled at Klotz. "Where is this man's mind?"

Klotz laughed. "Do you think I would leave any chance of Emma's lover returning to his body? I destroyed his brain the moment it was taken out of his body."

Upon hearing this proclamation, Emma buried her sobbing face into my shoulder. Sâr Dubnotal placed his hand on Klotz's forehead. "Then there is no need to keep you in this world as your body is long decayed. I send you to whatever destination awaits you in the afterlife."

The mystic placed his hand on Klotz's head. The body-snatcher screamed as the great mage forced him out of Alcide's body.

With the threat over, Sâr Dubnotal looked at the Heap and Lerne. "Thank you both for your assistance." He spoke to the Doctor. "Return to your rightful place." Lerne briefly turned his empty eye sockets toward Emma before climbing back into his grave. As he buried himself back in the ground, the skeletal horror that Sâr Dubnotal had created fell to pieces.

The Heap then walked over to the mystic. The mage placed his hand on the monster's shoulder. "I have spoken to Nicolas. He knows his role to play in the future." The beast looked at me and then fell to pieces.

With all of the monsters that had been a part of the horrific event gone, I asked Sâr Dubnotal. "What of LeBay and Olsen? Were they sent to the afterlife too?"

"No. Their bodies are still alive elsewhere. I sent their consciousness back to those vessels."

My body shivered at this thought. "The two of them still have at least part of the knowledge of how to switch brains and consciousness."

"Indeed, they are a concern, but I do not have the time to devote to them now as my abilities will soon be needed elsewhere."

A thought occurred to me. I turned and grabbed Emma by the shoulders so she was looking into my eyes. "Emma, our lives here are over. Alcide is gone. I can no longer live here. Join me and together we shall track down these two villains. Should they use their dark power, we shall alert the Sâr to help us fight them."

Emma agreed. We traced LeBay and Olsen to the United States. During that time, we renewed our relationship as lovers. While I was madly in love with her, I could never bring myself to ask her to marry me, due to her fickle nature.

We found Olsen first. In a situation eerily similar to what had just occurred, he had moved to America and tried to work with Lerne's formula for combining man and plant. He fell in love with a woman whom his assistant coveted. The man sabotaged the formula and exposed him to it. Olsen's body began taking on plant-like characteristics, very much like the Heap. He used his new form to gain revenge on his assistant but was still rejected by his lover. We informed Sâr Dubnotal of this occurrence and he dealt with Olsen by directing him to some manner of arboreal parliament.

LeBay moved to Rockbridge California. Emma and I moved into a neighboring town and quietly kept an eye on him. For the most part, he has remained quiet. Ten years ago, he purchased a Plymouth Fury that he had taken such a liking to, that he christened Christine. We kept an eye on him to make sure he did not transfer his consciousness into it as Klotz had done.

Sadly, Emma died of cancer roughly a year ago and I have been left on my own. My health has been poor and I fear my time is coming to an end. I still recall Sâr Dubnotal's words to me about finding the right person to whom to pass on Lerne's notes. I also recalled that whoever got these notes could become protectors of Earth's plants, but a danger to humans.

Before me I have two separate letters from a Doctor Ted Sallis and a Doctor Alec Holland. For the first time in my life, I have a feeling that these two men may have some destiny connected to the merging of man and plant.

179

*This is not the first time that our writers have connected the world of Jules Verne and H.P. Lovecraft, but this is certainly one of the most imaginative stories, in which the classic "Steam House" invented by the great French author in 1880 is comprehensively reimagined in an American context...*

## Paul Di Filippo: *The Steam House in Innsmouth*

### *1869*

Never did I, Henri Maucler, bold Parisian globetrotter and explorer, dare to imagine that I would experience an adventure more thrilling than that which obtained when I and several stout comrades traversed the length and breadth of the Indian subcontinent in our miracle conveyance, the Steam House, whilst on the track of that rogue and scoundrel, Nana Sahib, otherwise known as Dandou Pant, instigator of the Sepoy Revolt. Those uncommon exploits will be chronicled in the near future by my good friend and compatriot, the scribe Jules Verne, in an aptly but less-than-ingeniously named volume *The Steam House.* Said exploits culminated in much death and destruction and parting of the ways amongst the legendary troop of comrades who had called the Steam House home for however limited a time. And so with all my brothers-in-arms scattered to the four corners of the globe, and with the miraculous modern vehicle that had enabled our travels lying in smoldering ruins, I rashly forecast that never again would this assemblage reunite and experience anything comparable. I resigned myself to having lived already, at my young age, the apex of my wondrous wanderings.

But, unlike Monsieur Verne, I proved to be no prophet. For only three years later, in 1869, much to my delighted surprise, the entire heroic troupe had miraculously reformed, albeit in a shockingly foreign and unanticipated setting, with the precipitating impulse being the creation of a newer and far grander Steam House, and the securing of an ambitious mission worthy of its instantiation. For, once assembled, our chosen enterprise proved to be even more outré, dangerous and exhilarating than even our pursuit of the Hindoo terrorist.

But prior to launching into a recounting of the rebirth of the Steam House—Steam House II, it might be dubbed—perhaps I may be allowed—very briefly, so as not to trespass overly on the hospitality and patience of my readers, new and old—to offer a précis of our earlier exploits.

Assembled in Calcutta in 1866 were as marvelous a troupe of stout and brave souls as ever graced an argosy. I will immediately discount in all due humility my own presence, for I served mainly as observer, journalist and commentator. But the others can withstand any falsely modest minimizing.

First came Captain Blake Hood, a renowned soldier recuperating on long-term wounded leave, facile with both gun and fists, and always desirous of bagging exotic prey, whether animal or human. His resourceful aide-de-camp manifested in the person of the wry and boisterous Freddy Fox.

Our accepted center of gravity was Colonel Sir Edward Munro, retired, who boasted a constitution stronger than that of many men half his age (he was a venerable forty-seven at the time) and the wisdom of a man double his years. At the outset of our exploits, his wife, Lady Beverly Munro, was among the sadly missing, but later restored to our happy company by a set of circumstances too incredible to synopsize. And of course, ever by the Colonel's side was his bluff and hearty manservant, Sergeant Jake McNeil.

There were also involved several hired men of grand proletarian character, serving as cook, coal-stoker and driver of the Steam House. But these chaps, scattered to the four corners of the globe at journey's end, were not to be found when we reconstituted ourselves, and we had to discover acceptable substitutes, as shall soon be demonstrated.

But I am reserving until this moment any mention of the final figure of our core company, the man who made our whole mission possible, and that is Josiah Banks, Mechanical Engineer par excellence. Banks it was who invented and perfected the Steam House, having accepted the challenge of fashioning a conveyance with the flexibility of a coach, the luxury accoutrements of a railroad train, the buoyancy of a ferry, and the massive indomitability of a battleship.

The main component of the Steam House was the *Behemoth*, a steam engine comparable to that of any rail company stock, but able with its more flexible undercarriage to pursue any trackless road, and also to take to the water when deploying its built-in paddlewheels. As befitted our Hindoo venue, the carapace of the engine was fashioned in the semi-realistic likeness of a mighty steel elephant, many hands high. Behind the Behemoth, securely attached to that motive engine, trailed two small palaces on wheels, in the Hindoo style, each of three stories height. Here were commodious living quarters, plenty of storage space, a well-equipped kitchen, a small but sufficient armory, and facilities for ablutions.

Thus was our party equipped to travel swiftly and in style and ease, all thanks to the technological ingenuity of Engineer Banks.

And travel we did, up and down the Indian countryside, until a mortal battle with our enemies that left our conveyance in flinders, and saw the survivors set aflight like straws in the wind, harking back to their native abodes, with only keen and vivid memories to sustain the legend of the Steam House.

It is at this point in my reminiscences—and I beg just a few more minutes of patience from any of my readers eager to hear of Steam House II—that I must introduce one last personage. He was not an original member of our troupe, but was encountered midway in our peregrinations and played a sizable role—a role which was only to increase in magnitude and centrality during our new forays.

In fact, this fellow, along with Banks, could be said to have actually launched Steam House II into its fantastical new mission.

I refer, as my seasoned readers might have guessed, to Mathias van Guitt, former Professor of Natural History at the Rotterdam Museum, but thereafter turned supplier of exotic beasts to circuses, zoos, sideshows and exhibitory animal reserves across the planet. If I may be so lexically parsimonious as to recycle my perfected initial description of the man, I will do so now.

"Mathias van Guitt, menagerie purveyor, was a spectacled man of about fifty. His smooth face, his twinkling eyes, his turned-up nose, the perpetual stir of his whole person, his exaggerated gestures, suited to each of the sentences which issued from his wide mouth, all combined to make him a perfect type of the old provincial comedian. His language was always composed of the choicest terms, and he was sometimes rather annoying to his interlocutors if they could not keep beyond the radius of his gestures."

And so, with my friends all assembled pictorially before your gaze at last, and with some concept of the marvels of the original Steam House laid out, I can now embark on the astonishing tale of how we all reunited and to what glorious purpose.

The precipitating telegram found me ensconced mid-morning on a fine June day in my Parisian flat on the Left Bank. For the several years that had passed since my Indian foray, I had been making my living as a journalist for *La Presse*, that penny paper whose sometimes louche ways caused much controversy. I was not overly enamored of the job nor of my lowly social status, but was not ambitious enough to throw over a decent income in favor of more speculative pursuits. And besides, the freedom afforded me as a roving reporter suited my tastes. I could spend many an hour over an *apéritif* at Les Deux Magots or The Café de la Paix, and charge it off to research, without arousing the ire of my bosses.

Last night's alcohol-fueled *flâneurisms* had caused me to rise late today, and so I was on hand for the arrival of the messenger boy at my door. He seemed slightly in awe as he handed over the telegram to me. "It's all the way from America," he said. The first trans-Atlantic cable had been laid only a few years before, and such long-distance communications were still novel enough to provoke curiosity and interest.

Still groggy, I made no comment in return, but tipped the sallow-cheeked boy generously. Upon his departure, I tossed the *communiqué* to a side table, since I still had to deal with my post-festivities headache. When I finally felt well enough to read anything, I focused on the sparse words, and a feeling of bewilderment, anticipation, wonder and joy gradually overtook me.

HAVE RECONSTRUCTED THE STEAM HOUSE AND ESTABLISHED A PLAN OF ACTION STOP WOULD BE GRATEFUL FOR YOUR

PARTICIPATION IN THE ENTERPRISE STOP PREPAID TICKETS TO AMERICA AWAITING YOU CUNARD LINES LIVERPOOL STOP YOUR STOUT COMRADE, J. BANKS STOP

This news was almost too fabulous to comprehend. Apparently, Josiah Banks had somehow found the funding and motivation to reconstitute his trackless engine and its equipage, and, even more startlingly, had secured backers who had a use for the vehicle. And he was asking me to be part of the crew! How could this invitation be anything but a life-altering inducement to toss aside all my stale daily rituals? I hesitated not a moment in my decision.

I dressed hastily and went immediately to the offices of *La Presse*, where I boldly tendered my resignation. But Etienne Drouet, my editor, was not quick to accept it, instead embarking on an interrogation of my motives. After hearing my long disquisition akin to that I have placed before my reader here as a preface, he came to the decision that I should keep my position on the paper and serve as foreign correspondent for the duration of the expedition of Steam House II! This was truly the happiest of scenarios! Adventure *and* a paycheck.

Within three days I found myself stepping from the train in Liverpool, carrying only a single valise, and hiring a hansom cab to convey me to the Cunard line offices. There I discovered that the arranged tickets in my name secured me passage on the top-of-the-line Cunard vessel christened *China*—dual engines, three decks, iron construction dating from 1862, luxurious first-class accommodations—and that departure was two days hence. Chafing at the bit as I was, I nonetheless found a hotel room and set out to enjoy the nightlife of Liverpool until departure.

Perhaps I was a little too accomplished at drowning my impatience to leave in a welter of wine, women and song, since on the appointed day, and at nearly the appointed minute of leave-taking, I found myself rushing pell-mell to the docks and, last passenger ashore, racing up a gangplank that was in the very process of being unhinged from the ship!

But make it I did, by the skin of my teeth, and quickly repaired to my cabin, freshening up before essaying any social appearance in the eyes of my fellow passengers.

I entered one of the main saloons with its impressive eight-foot ceiling and ornate furnishings. It seemed as if most of the *China*'s two-hundred-plus first-class travelers had chosen to congregate in this dramatic space. I quickly secured a glass of champagne and, keeping an eye peeled for unmarried women desirous of companionship, began to circulate.

I was halfway into the scrum when I heard a voice at once totally familiar and utterly anticipated.

"And so there I was, halfway across the open plain, when I spotted the rhino getting ready to charge me. I turned to Fox, my man, and calmly requested him to hand me my Sharps fifty-caliber rifle. As the beast bore down on me, I took steady aim, fired, and bagged the monster at a distance of only thirty yards. His dead decelerating body plowed a trench practically to my feet."

I immediately began weaving through the crowd to verify the import of my ears. And my eyes soon attested to the aural evidence. There stood Captain Blake Hood, surrounded by appreciative listeners in all his hearty manliness. However, his costume of formal wear disconcerted me, for I had never before seen him so attired.

I dove upon him, giving him a bit of a start, and then we were embracing warmly. After some mutual surprised splutterings, I ventured to ask what his presence here betokened. He replied with a story identical to mine: the telegram from Banks, and Hood's quick assent and journey to Liverpool. It turned out that Hood had been conveniently back in London for several months, looking to clear up some military paperwork connected with his extended leave.

"And is your man Freddy Fox with you?"

"Yes, of course. He's down in second-class, doubtlessly hoisting a few tankards and swilling down platters of corned beef and cabbage."

"Wouldn't it be something if the Colonel were waiting for us in America?" I suggested. "Then we'd have the whole gang reassembled for whatever exploits await us."

Hard upon my musings came a solemn, pontifical, yet comradely voice, equally resonant with my cherished memories.

"But why should we delay our reunion until arrival on the North American continent, gentlemen, when we can enjoy eight days of pleasure here on this fine ship?"

Hood and I both swung around eagerly, and were met with the welcome sight of a smiling Colonel Sir Edward Munro, looking even more hearty than when last seen—an effect obviously derived from enjoying three years of the restoration of his charming wife, once feared lost. And by his side, there she stood, elegant and sophisticated: Lady Beverly Munro. No one seeing her chic figure now would ever believe that she had once wandered the subcontinent as a bedraggled madwoman dubbed "the Roving Flame."

Hood and I and the Munroes exchanged a flurry of greetings—Lady's Munro's dulcet tones charmed my soul—and we all agreed to retreat to one of the tables set against the saloon's walls, where we could take up our discussion in a more comfortable manner, around a small collation of drinks and food.

One of the first things we ascertained was that the Munroes had received— at their estate in South Shropshire dubbed "Little Switzerland"—a *communiqué* identical to that sent to Hood and myself. (I also was happy to learn that Sergeant Jake McNeil, loyal servant, also currently enjoyed a second-class berth in the *China*'s bowels.) We tossed out various speculations as to what awaited us at the end of our journey, but could come up with nothing conclusive. And so we tabled the matter, and set about enjoying our cruise.

The eight days till Halifax passed joyously. The subsequent short ocean transit to Boston was painless. All six of us disembarked onto the busy, bustling quay as a unified party, but were at a loss as to how to proceed. The telegrams had led us thus far and no further. I think we had all expected to see Banks awaiting us on the dock, but such was not to be.

Yet we should never have underestimated engineer Banks's planning and preparations. For we were hailed—"Munro and company?"—almost instantly by a young, round-faced and ginger-haired fellow dressed in a clean workmanlike manner. He doffed his cloth cap to us, smiled broadly to disclose a few missing teeth, and said, "The name is Wilberforce Phillips, navigator and general dogsbody aboard Steam House II. We have another small journey to make, before your reunion is complete. We'll be taking a vessel of the Fall River Line, the *Old Colony*, down to Providence, where your host awaits. I hope you have not quite lost your sea legs yet!"

Suiting his actions to his words, Phillips soon had us and our luggage aboard the *Old Colony*. The short voyage passed pleasantly—although Phillips refused to share with us any information about Banks's doings.

"The master engineer will spill all in due time."

At last our long passage from the Old World to the New was complete. We stepped onto land at India Point. And there, surrounded by a gawping crowd, stood Steam House II.

The reader will here recall my description of the original Steam House: a massive train engine concealed under the wrought-iron camouflage of a gigantic elephant simulacrum. And behind, attached by subtle and responsive linkages, two pagoda-like domiciles on wheels. So engraved was this image on my brain cells, that I had never considered that Banks, when reconstituting the apparatus, would deviate from the old plans. And yet, strikingly, he had—and what other maneuver, in retrospect, could have been more natural? Here in the New World, brash young America, an elephant and pagodas would have seemed utterly out of place, and even perhaps be construed as an insult to the native culture. And so, Banks had contrived a most fitting appearance for Steam House II.

The engine—and I was to learn that in the past three years, many sophistications of this motive technology had come to pass, rendering Steam House II an even more powerful and formidable contrivance—was cloaked in the image of an American Bison—*Bos bison bison*, to be precise. The enormous metal torso sloped from shoulders (twenty feet high) down to rump. The shaggy and horned head represented a fusion of the arts of metalworker and furrier. The legs were folded into a couchant position, so as to conceal the engine's wheels. (As I would soon learn, this configuration imparted to the engine, when in motion, an uncanny appearance of gliding along the road.)

And what of the trailing domiciles? What else would have consorted so well with the mighty buffalo as two enormous conical teepees, or wigwams, constructed not of fabric, but cunningly bent and varnished wood? Each of them was three stories tall, and featured many windows and balconies at each level.

Plainly, this was an indigenous arrangement that would have pleased the god Manitou himself!

This unprecedented and unanticipated sight had plunged all of us into an amazed silence and fascination, so that we did not immediately spot Engineer Josiah Banks himself. But once I was able to draw my eyes away from the spectacle, I saw Banks the man, grinning broadly, with hands in his trouser pockets. I rushed to greet him, and the rest of the party followed suit.

The clever fellow was just as we had last seen him, vivacious and keen-eyed. His only newness was that he had adopted the style of abundant facial hair made famous by the American General Burnside. After he had accepted our affirmations and congratulations—Fox and McNeil resorted to whistles, war-whoops and mild imprecations—and had made his own protestations of undying friendship in return, Banks explained how this situation had come to be.

"Once the original Steam House had been reduced to shards, and our mission to rescue Lady Munro was complete, I found myself tired of India and longing for my native Scotland. Thence I returned, a divagatory journey of over a year. Upon entering my apartments, I found a wealth of old mail awaiting my inspection. But among the letters was a more-recent missive from an American firm called Darling, Brown and Sharp. The owners—Samuel Darling, Joseph Brown and Lucian Sharp—had heard of my achievements with the Steam House and been impressed. They were writing to offer me employment with their firm. What they detailed—their ultra-modern facilities, their open-minded investment in new techniques and processes, their willingness to give me free rein—was irresistible. And so I hied myself to Providence, and commenced the construction of Steam House II—a task which has filled most of the past two years. You see the result before you."

"Incredible," I said. "Such a rare and fortuitous meeting of talent and resources. The like may never happen again."

The others bestowed similar encomiums. But then the ever-practical Colonel Munro cut to the heart of the matter.

"Impressive as this monster is, Banks, it remains merely an idle toy, if it lacks any goals governing its usage. You spoke of a mission of some sort...?"

"Yes, indeed, Colonel. Not a mere excursion either, but an expedition to acquire something most rare. I will explain all when we return to the factory. Please, step aboard and make yourself at home."

Hood and his man Fox accompanied the Colonel and Lady Munro and McNeil into one of the wigwams, their luggage loaded by some idle stevedores here at this busy India Point transit site. I, however, chose to follow Banks and Phillips into the cab of the engine. Access was obtained through a door in the buffalo's flank. The artificial lighting inside the shell was subdued, and a series of periscopes and a kind of inverted camera obscura provided images of our forward path, and likewise displays to rear and sides. A clever arrangement of hoppers and chutes served to feed coal to the hungry beast. Tucked up inside the shell were the paddlewheels for aquatic travel.

With Banks at the controls and Phillips navigating, we were soon in motion.

"The factory is on South Main Street, just a short distance away."

As we trundled away from the edge of Narraganset Bay, I could admire, through the optics from our secret vantage, the astonished citizenry, the startled horses, and the quaint architecture of this city, my first brush with a New World metropolis. Whilst not a patch on the splendors of Paris, I found nonetheless a definite charm deriving from the colonial ambiance.

True to his word, Banks had us at the Darling, Brown and Sharpe establishment—a sprawling set of brick warehouses and workshops—within just fifteen minutes. I don't think we had traversed much more than a mile, thereby according the pace of a walking man to the mighty engine. As if intuiting my thoughts, Banks said, "Don't worry, Henri—on a straight road and without crowding, we can get our speed up to thirty or forty miles per hour, or above. Enough to outrun any band of brigands on horseback, such as beset the first Steam House in India."

Phillips had parked us neatly next to what seemed the main building, and the three of us left the engine, to find our comrades already disembarked from the wigwams. They formed a celebratory scrum around an unseen figure. Making my way closer, I soon discerned the person at the center of the happy melee. It was none other than Mathias van Guitt, big-game trapper extraordinaire.

The jovial, vociferous Dutchman in his colorful brocaded vest cast off his well-wishers and moved to share his bountiful camaraderie with me. When all the hearty backslapping was finally accomplished, van Guitt assumed a pontifical air, as if preparing to address a stadium of worshippers.

"My good friends, fellow seekers of adventure and glory, not to mention profits—may I announce to you that you see before you the first individual to commission the services of the new Steam House and its creator—at a very reasonable rate, influenced, I have no doubt, by longstanding ties of affection. Indeed, I, Mathias van Guitt, need this marvelous vehicle—and also am desirous of securing the skills that you all possess—to penetrate into a semi-hostile territory and return with a prize and treasure beyond compare, next to which the trapping of tigers and apes will pall into insignificance. Let it be known amongst our select band—but not by the suspicious and ignorant hoi polloi, who might choose to misunderstand or interfere—that van Guitt the Audacious, van Guitt the Fearless, has volunteered to capture one or more of the legendary aquatic Deep Ones of New England, to be delivered to none other than that master showman, Phineas Taylor Barnum!"

187

The lights in the spacious, windowless, walnut-paneled conference room of Darling, Sharp and Brown had been lowered to a mere flicker, lending the scene the air of a séance. The room's chairs had been arrayed in rows—with an aisle down their middle—to face a portable screen. On a table at the rear stood a magic lantern, making the air above it waver with the heat of its lamp. Our company had taken up seats while van Guitt fussed with the projection device, which was aimed down the middle channel at the screen. Eventually he had to give over its operation to Banks. But this surrendering of manual control only allowed him to focus more passion on his speech.

"My fellow celebrants of the Life Afield! I have prepared this small presentation as the quickest and best way of infusing the parameters of our quest into your noble craniums! So without further ado, let us commence. I have arranged the talk in what might seem a topsy-turvy fashion to you, but in a manner which suits my sense of building a foundation before erecting a superstructure. And so I will start with a look at the ultimate backer of our expedition. First slide, please, Josiah....

"Here you see the canny visage of one P. T. Barnum, hitherto known to the wide world as the great showman whose Museum in New York City featured such attractions as the Feejee Mermaid and General Tom Thumb. Next slide, please. Barnum also patronized the arts by sponsoring the tour of Jenny Lind, the Swedish Nightingale. But upon the conflagration last year—slide, please, Josiah—which claimed his Museum, Barnum was at a loss as to what venture he might next undertake. I am happy to report that the great genius of the entertainment world is now holed up productively in the midwestern state of Wisconsin with his new partner, William Cameron Coup, putting together 'P. T. Barnum's Grand Traveling Museum, Menagerie, Caravan & Hippodrome,' a roadshow guaranteed to surpass any such enterprise ever before attempted. To accomplish this miracle, however, Mister Barnum needs freaks and natural wonders never before seen. Apprehending these requisites in my ceaseless quest for clients, I began to cast about for how best to fulfill Barnum's needs. After meticulous research—conducted here at Brown University, and in nearby Massachusetts at Miskatonic University—I found just the thing to ensure the Menagerie's success, and approached Barnum with my proposition. He rapidly assented, and entered into a contract to pay me the princely sum of fifteen hundred English pounds, could I but deliver the promised goods. And that brings me now to the second part of my little lecture. Josiah, if you would be so kind..."

Onto the screen now flashed without warning or preamble a photographic image so bizarre and horrifying, even devoid of Nature's colorations, that the men involuntarily grunted as if belly-punched, and Lady Munro emitted a piercing shriek.

Depicted on the screen was an expanse of water and the rim of a stony beach, with the perspective being that of a photographer placed a bit further inshore from the marge. Standing in the shallow water, only their bare scaly upper halves exposed, were two creatures best described as fish-men. A hideous hybrid of *homo sapiens* and some be-gilled denizen of the deep, the monsters exhibited a menacing calm, as if utterly sure of their right to exist and a kind of ownership of the scene. Their huge jellied eyes and rubbery mouths contributed to a countenance expressive of an alien sentience, at once allied to mankind's, yet utterly other. One gill-man held both his arms by his side, his hands below the waterline. The other individual had one arm upraised—in greeting or admonition, who could say?—revealing a pale paw with webbed digits and talon-like nails.

It took some time for the gruesome reality of these beings to be absorbed by us the audience, and van Guitt allowed us our period of silent reckoning before continuing.

"The creatures you see on the screen represent—in the best judgment of such experts in ichthyology and paleontology as Professor Louis Agassiz, with whom I have been in constant consultation—a species of living fossil, survivors of a distant past. To display one or more of these before the public would make the reputation of any showman. And also crown with laurels the bold souls who captured the beast. And I aim for our troupe to earn that high distinction.

"This, in short, concludes my presentation. But I will certainly accept questions and comments, following which I must ask for your pledges of secrecy and commitment to the project—all contingent on a share of the fee, naturally. Of course, those who so choose may take their leave of the enterprise without prejudice."

At this point Banks extinguished the magic lantern and turned up the whale-oil lamps. I winced at the brightness, then turned my recovering gaze to my comrades.

Banks, with foreknowledge of the mission, was obviously fully onboard. After all, it was his invention that would provide the transportation and protective embrace for our party. Captain Hood and his aide-de-camp Fox were all aglow with the prospect of bagging new trophies. The Captain's quest to slaughter fifty tigers in India paled beside this novel venture. "St. Hubert be my speed!" he exclaimed. "You may count me in, van Guitt. I assume there's a colony of these creatures and that some of them might put up a fight before we capture our specimens. That's where Fox and I will shine."

"Indeed, Captain, the only known colony of these creatures exists in the bay adjacent to the small Massachusetts town of Innsmouth, near Ipswich and Rowley in Essex County. That is to be our hunting grounds. It is only some ninety miles distant from Providence—a short and easy trip for the mighty Steam House. We shall proceed north to Boston, and then aim for the coast."

Now the man we all looked up to, Colonel Munro, spoke, with somber mien. "If I am to accompany you all—and I devoutly desire to do so, for the sake of science and glory, and to add some excitement to a homebody's life that, while congenial, has grown a bit tepid of late—then Lady Munro will be my side. After our long and painful separation, we swore never to be apart again. You know her as a resourceful and brave woman—and in fact she is so self-reliant, she disdains the bevy of maids I would happily employ for her—but she is nonetheless still of the gentler sex. What kind of safety measures are in place to constrain these beasts, if we succeed in capturing them?"

"Ah, my most excellent Colonel, surely you did not think I would neglect so vital an aspect of my plan! You saw firsthand my thoroughness with the savage jungle denizens of India. First, the creatures will be entangled in heavy-duty netting, then cudgeled into submission and manacled. Then, they will be ensconced in their special guest quarters. The lowest level of one of the wigwams—the teepee containing the kitchen and storage rooms, not your personal quarters—features a large water tank for their pleasure, and that tank is the repository for a strong cage of iron bars which may be winched in and out. You'll see its efficacy at the proper time. So you see, nothing will endanger your lovely wife—or any of us."

Now all eyes turned to me, as the last to register my vote. I struck a mock heroic pose. "My editor dispatched me to America to supply reports of local color and human interest. He could hardly have imagined that I would be privy to the story of the century! So long as I have exclusive rights to retail the account of our expedition—when permitted by Mr. Barnum, of course—you may count me fully enrolled."

A round of applause went up then, and Banks brought out a bottle of champagne and glasses for a toast.

Finally van Guitt addressed us all. "I must now introduce the final member of our party. I have hired a local girl to act as our cook. You surely recall how greatly the skills of Monsieur Parazard enhanced our Indian trip, and we could hardly choose to fare less well in a new land. Josiah, please bring in Miss Jenny Arbutus."

Banks left the room and returned with as stunning a lass I had ever laid eyes on. Dressed in a plain gingham skirt enhanced by a fashionable "garibaldi" blouse, our new chef was a redhead with a fiery glint in her eyes and a buxom figure. Jenny Arbutus regarded us all with no slavish false humility, but with a native New England pride and eagerness to please. Her voice was a charming contralto.

"If any of you don't like Yankee vittles, you can scrounge your fare from the countryside. Johnnycakes, cod and baked beans rank high in my repertoire, but I ain't averse to other sensible requests, such as a Delmonco steak or a tray of steaming laplanders—so long as they don't involve frogs' legs, haggis or any other culinary abominations!"

The laughter was general, and I took the occasion to bestow a gallant Gallic kiss on each of Jenny's cheeks, to which she seemed in no ways disdainful.

This trip, I anticipated, would be even more delightful than I had at first imagined.

Our excursion north to Boston proved uneventful, except for the experience of being accompanied by a daily entourage of wild urchins—and one dicey ambush of indeterminate nature. I will detail the first phenomenon lightly, merely to add some naturalistic touches to my portrait of America, but expend more detail upon the latter incident, since in retrospect it foreshadowed consequential events in Innsmouth.

Directly following Mathias van Guitt's presentation, and a fine repast at a local restaurant, all of us spent the night comfortably in our new teepee quarters. Lady and Sir Munro occupied the highest level of one wigwam, with Captain Hood and I sharing the next lower slice, and Fox and McNeil on the most spacious ground level, along with Banks and Phillips; Jenny Arbutus had her sleeping room just off the second-floor kitchen in the adjacent teepee, above the fishmen storage tank, while van Guitt had commandeered the third level of that second domicile, thus placing himself—at least physically, if not metaphorically—on the same plane as the Munroes.

In the morning, Jenny whipped up a splendid breakfast of buckwheat "flapjacks," eggs, bacon and beans, which we enjoyed communally in the teepee dining area. (I made so bold as to offer to give her lessons in making croissants, and she replied with equal verve: "Just so long as you keep your hands out of Jenny's wet dough!") A few last-minute supplies were brought onboard. Then the mighty Behemoth engine was fired up, and we departed downtown Providence, aimed at the famous Boston Post Road that would lead us north. (I chose to ride in the teepee, not in the cloistered, hot and smelly engine cab.). Whilst still within the city limits, a few citizens hailed us and wished us well. But it was only when we transitioned into the countryside and smaller burgs, where the inhabitants were less cosmopolitan, that we attracted any crowds. This was a novel sensation, since the original Steam House in India had tended to affright the natives, rather than allure.

It being the month of June, school was out of session, leaving all the children idle. And they found the Steam House to be an irresistible cynosure of their juvenile attentions. Mobs of them accumulated, whooping and dancing around our cars, only to fall away when we reached the borders of their precincts, passing the baton of attention to their identical peers to the north of their neighborhoods. Some of the little vandals even threw eggs and tomatoes at us, necessitating the closure of our windows. And so, every few hours, when sighting a lake or pond, we had to stop to slosh cleansing buckets of water over our carriages and besmirched bison engine carapace. While I suspected that English juveniles might have behaved in a similar irresponsible manner, I knew for a fact that well-bred French children never would have acted so coarsely.

In any case, we survived these harmless depredations. But with the frequent stops and the necessity to proceed cautiously, lest we squash careless little Johnny or Susie Hayseed, we made an average speed of only five miles per hour. And so we were approaching that Massachusetts landmark known as the Great Blue Hill, some thirty-five miles from our point of origin, around supper-time, making it a reasonable place to call a stop for the day.

Not wishing to impede traffic on the Post Road by our enormous parked presence, we—or, I should say, Banks and Phillips—maneuvered our caravan into a kind of spacious empty half-wild glade, conveniently reached by a short dirt track barely wide enough for our passage. In fact, I could hear the snapping of green branches that marked our progress. But eventually the Steam House was snugly parked, in what might have been some old impound for cattle, its prow aimed for easy departure, thanks to slowly circumnavigating the circum-ference of the glade so as to, once again, line up with the exit.

Almost immediately, delicious smells began to issue from Jenny's kitchen. Banks and Phillips repaired to the washroom to cleanse themselves of the smut of their engineering endeavors. Captain Hood, Fox and McNeil were out on the lawn, avoiding the gathering shadows whilst they played a makeshift game of croquet. I assumed van Guitt in the adjacent teepee was preoccupied with his library of abstruse and scientific books. Above me in my room, I could hear snores—presumably from Sir Munro—and a low gentle contented wordless singing—presumably from Lady Munro. It amazed me that she could have re-gained such a mild and sanguine character after her Hindoo ordeals.

All, in short, seemed idyllic, and I was just changing my cravat for a more lively one which, I hoped, would appeal to Miss Arbutus, when the peace was shattered by gunshots!

I knew not what was transpiring, but I had the sound instincts anyhow to grab my own pistol before rushing down the single flight of stairs that separated me from ground level.

A most horrific sight met my astonished eyes.

Captain Hood and his man Fox stood back to back against a horde of seem-ingly unarmed but extremely violent invaders whose lineaments I could only half-apprehend in the confusion. Hood was using his empty pistol as a club, while Fox deployed his croquet mallet like a truncheon. Stretched out on the ground was the unconscious—I prayed, not dead!—form of Munro's man McNeil.

I let out a spontaneous battle cry that I hoped would unman the attackers, then, from the porch of the wigwam, began to plant my limited bullets where they would do the most good. I swiftly brought down the bodies of three attack-ers. A couple of the survivors, recognizing me as a menace, began to head my way. With my dwindling ammunition, I was on the point of despair. But then came relief!

Banks and Phillips, both naked to the waist from their ablutions, emerged with blazing rifles in hand. At the same time, I heard a window on the third level of the teepee open, accompanied by a blast from Sir Munro's ever-present Boss & Co. shotgun.

192

That renewed assault was enough to send the brutes loping inhumanly back into the woods from whence they had first come.

The three of us on the porch jumped down to solace those on the lawn. Our first concern was the supine form of McNeil. Much to our delight, he proved to be merely unconscious, with no evident wounds. Chafing of the wrists and application of wet cloths soon revived him. We later learned that he had gone down from a glancing roundhouse blow to the skull from one of the attackers—a blow which, we deduced, would have been fatal, had it fully connected. And in fact, McNeil suffered mildly from the effects of a concussion for days afterwards.

Hood and Fox, while sweaty and exhausted, were unharmed.

Having ascertained this good news, we turned our attention to the three corpses on the grass.

The creatures were uncanny, a chimerical mix of humans and some type of great apes. Pale as fungi, their skins were more hirsute than those of mere men, but less so than the pelts of other anthropoids. Their mouths were stuffed with sharp teeth, their long arms left their paws dangling at knee-level, and their bare feet exhibited prehensile toes. Thankfully, their intimate regions were covered with a kind of rude breechclout so familiar to us from our travels in India.

Now we were joined by Jenny and van Guitt. Our cook exhibited no trace of the female vapors, but gazed boldly on the fallen forms, her eyes lingering, I thought, a tad too long, on their nether parts. Van Guitt, it eventuated, had imbibed a few too many drafts of his potent Dutch gin, and fallen asleep before we entered the glade, waking only at the sound of gunfire. But now he forced himself to alertness, and bent down close to the creatures to scrutinize them. Just as he regained his full height, the Munroes arrived, so that our whole company was now assembled on the field of battle.

"Our foes," pronounced the Dutchman, "belong to that Congo River Basin species known as the 'white apes.' Legend has it that they were mysteriously and surreptitiously introduced many decades ago in small numbers into England, thanks to the interventions of the Jermyn family. But I had no idea their kind had reached North America. How I would have liked to capture a living specimen for my patron, Barnum!"

Captain Hood snorted derisively. "You should have gotten down here sooner then, you old reprobate! You could have grappled hand to hand with the brutes as we did, and seen how successful you were!"

Unabashed, van Guitt tsk-tsked, then bent to finger the fur of one of the apes, as if he contemplated skinning them for profit.

Colonel Munro now commandeered the discourse. "The unanswered question is, why did these alien apes attack us? I presume it is not because we trespassed on their tribal lands. Any such enclave of oddness would surely have attracted the attention of the press and the authorities before now, and led to a campaign of extermination. No, I tend to suspect that the apes were imported here by someone tracking our expedition, someone who wished to frustrate our plans, and who then unleashed the assailants upon us."

Banks asked, "Do you think we should immediately resume our course towards Boston and safety?"

"Not at all," said the Colonel. "On the soon-benighted roads, we would make an easy target for another ambush. And even the Behemoth at full throttle could not outsprint these creatures. I suggest that we light a bonfire and keep watch overnight, then depart in the morning. We are as safe here as anywhere."

We all approved of the strategy, and our encampment fell into a smoothly oiled functioning. The white ape corpses were buried, and tables and chairs were set up outside. Guns at the ready, under the stars, we all had a pleasant meal—boiled beef, new potatoes, dandelion greens, biscuits and a dessert of shortcakes and whipped cream—foregathered around the campfire, so as not to leave the sentries—Fox and Phillips took first watch—feeling lonely. McNeil was excused from the roster due to his injuries, but the rest of the men were assigned intervals of wakefulness.

As I was helping Jenny carry dirty dishes into the wigwam, I bandied with her.

"Perhaps you'll bring me a midnight snack, and we could utilize any convenient shadows to get to know one another a little better, my dear, leaving the solo sentry duties for a short time to my comrade in arms."

"Only if you was equipped with the same man-tackle as those hairy critters," Miss Arbutus replied. "Which I can see you ain't."

Although shocked at the boldness of her reply, I was able to make a feeble riposte along the lines of: "The stature of an actor matters not when the actor knows how to perform." But Jenny merely laughed and went inside to clean up.

I could see that more than a florid cravat would be needed to charm this lass.

As we left Boston behind us, the chuffing sounds of the Behemoth by now a familiar diapason, pleasant memories solaced us all, and provided a buffer for the rigors ahead.

Our entry into the "Hub" on the day after the attack was greeted with large enthusiastic crowds blatting on horns and tossing confetti. It turned out that van Guitt, taking a page from the playbook of his patron Barnum, had publicized our arrival in advance. Without mentioning our ultimate goal of visiting Innsmouth and kidnaping some of its aquatic citizens, he had touted our trip as a display of the technological prowess of Darling, Brown and Sharpe. And so the populace received us as the latest representatives of sheer American industrial ingenuity. Banks had to address several learned societies, while the rest of us were given the keys to the city by Mayor Nathaniel B. Shurtleff. Three days passed in sheer hedonism and revelry. But then at last came the time for our departure.

Now, rolling along merrily, we were following a coastal route, the sea often being in sight and the air freshened by oceanic scents, as we headed towards our overnight stop preliminary to Innsmouth herself: Salem. Innsmouth was not much further than that fabled town, and so we could have made the whole journey in a single day. But such a push would have meant we arrived at Innsmouth after dark, and this we did not wish to do, especially after the affair of the apes.

Luckily, we had not been molested again.

Around four in the afternoon, the fabulous Steam House entered the city limits of Salem. Our reception here was allied to the one in Boston, but of a much smaller magnitude. We were all treated to a banquet at the City Hall on Washington Street, replete with stultifying speeches, but also offering a fine Continental repast. I was pleased to sample some familiar and sophisticated French cooking, for although the meals prepared by Miss Arbutus were wholesome and tasty, they did tend towards a certain colonial rudimentariness.

Not wishing to leave the Steam House unguarded, we declined the offer to take guest lodgings elsewhere, and all slept in our accustomed quarters which, by now, had come to seem like home and were in no wise deficient.

Early in the morning we were off, without so much as a single nocturnal visit from any of the town's fabled ghosts and witches.

It was a mere ten or eleven miles from Salem to Innsmouth, and van Guitt used the interval to finally brief us on his exact plan to capture his specimens. All of us—save for Banks and Phillips, who steadfastly continued to drive us forward in the Behemoth—were gathered in the room containing the water tank (still empty) with its inserted cage. The mild jouncing of the wheeled wigwam, smoothed by clever leaf-springs, gave a sense of being on some carnival ride.

"Observe," said van Guitt, while cranking a winch, "how the cage may be lifted from the water tank. When we arrive at the shore, we will remove the cage entirely, and our brawny heroes will muscle it onto a special small platform at the rear of the Behemoth. Then the Behemoth will set to sea, powering out into Innsmouth Harbor and heading towards the notorious Devil's Reef, where the gill-men are known to congregate. We shall lure two or more to the surface, subdue them, confine them behind bars, then return to land. *Et voila*! Mister Barnum will have his unique attractions, and all of us will be considerably richer."

Captain Hood had been massaging his chin in puzzlement, and now spoke. "You say you'll lure and subdue them, making it sound as easy as salting a bird's tail. But how, exactly?"

"The means of attracting the fish-men shall be revealed when we reach Innsmouth. But the trick of subduing them is right here."

Van Guitt picked up a cinched cloth sack that was obviously full of some kind of flour or powder. "This is an extract from the *akia* plant found in the Sandwich Islands. The natives use it to stupefy fish to aid in their capture. It is

195

absolutely harmless to humans, but when sprinkled on the waters it will almost instantly render any finny creature *hors de combat*."

Hood nodded approvingly, and the rest of us assented as well to the plausible ingenuity of the scheme. The meeting concluded, we separated to prepare for our entry to Innsmouth.

Out the windows, I could see that we were passing through a landscape of sand, sedge-grass, and stunted shrubbery, monotonous and dreary in the extreme, with the grey Atlantic off to the east.

And then, after a small ascent, we looked down on Innsmouth.

A seemingly lively and bustling town at this date, whatever its past or future held, it nonetheless seemed to hold implicit in its structures the possibility of immense decadence and decay—just as a shining young beauty may foreshadow the wizened crone she shall become. A kind of future phantom under the skin. The spires of several churches seemed a sign of wholesomeness, however—assuming they were of respectable denominations. The busy harbor area featured many wharves and schooners. Several flourishing mills obtruded, including the famous gold refinery of Captain Marsh. It was a town of wide extent and dense construction, a tangle of chimney-pots, gambrel roofs and peaked gables. There were some large square Georgian houses, too, with hipped roofs, cupolas, and railed "widow's walks."

The town was bisected by the Manuxet River, which ran west to east before dumping into the harbor. Three bridges united the two halves of the town. But I knew, from talking to Banks, that the Steam House would be confined to the southern, closest segment of the town, since the bridges would never bear the weight of the Behemoth.

Now we were among the dwellings and businesses, observing for the first time the citizenry of Innsmouth. Most appeared utterly normal, although they displayed a curious indifference to the phenomenon of a giant mechanized bison pulling two enormous teepees. But here and there, with features half-concealed, I thought to detect beings of odd physiognomy and flopping gait.

I noted by the signage that we were traversing Eliot Street, and this avenue soon debouched into a most curious plaza, formed by the conjunction of no fewer than five other avenues. This town square had the arcane dimensions of some obscure sigil. Carriages and pedestrians came and went, but paid us no heed, as if any visitors to Innsmouth could be of no import to local affairs, "foreigners" unworthy of acknowledgement or contemplation.

The Steam House came to a stop, and we all disembarked. Out of one building, as if awaiting our arrival, stepped a comely and exuberant blond lad, dressed rather dandyishly. He trotted over to us, hand outheld to be severally shaken, while he announced himself.

"Zadok Allen at your command, friends. I assume one of you is Mathias van Guitt...? Ah, very pleased to meet at last, sir. Your correspondence has been most illuminating. I'd like to discuss certain rituals of the Ponape islanders with you at greater length."

"All in due time, my boy. I assume you have the items that we need to complete our mission…?"

"Indeed. I will show you now."

And so saying, the lad took out of his coat pocket a knotted handkerchief. Untying it, he revealed the contents: a dozen small stones, the *ne plus ultra* of ebony, engraved with cryptic runes.

Van Guitt grew excited. "The summoning stones of the Deep Ones, just as you promised."

"Yes, brought back by yours truly from the Caroline Islands, after my last stint aboard the fabled East Indiaman the *Narragansett*, out of Providence. I had taken on the side-task of acquiring these for Professor Freeborn at Miskatonic. But alas, he did not live to receive them."

Admiring the stones, van Guitt said, "The savant's loss was our gain then. I thank you sincerely."

"Thanks are appreciated, naturally. But perhaps you might tender the payment, just as you promised."

"Half now, and half upon their demonstrated efficacy."

"But of course. I will be happy to abide with you until the return of your explorers with the prize tomorrow."

The exchange was made. Then Allen said, "As for the timbers and planks you ordered, they await you on the sands at the end of Water Street. Just follow Waite to Water, turn right, and you can't miss them."

Allen strode off, the rest of us clambered aboard the Steam House, and soon our train was in motion. A short run brought us to where Water Street petered out at the edge of the sea. There the promised lumber was heaped. Banks took over with engineering prowess.

"We must make a wooden roadbed over this short stretch of sands to allow the Behemoth to enter the sea without becoming mired on the beach."

All we males—even the fastidious van Guitt—stripped off our shirts under the July sun and got to work. Again, we received no idle attention or interference from the natives. Although I thought to detect a few observant faces framed in the windows of the nearest houses.

The simple but burdensome construction took us till supper time, and we were earnestly ready for some of Jenny's hearty fare. I fancied she looked at me more admiringly thanks to my demonstration of brute masculine prowess.

We all retired early. Since we had not abandoned our ritual of sentries inaugurated after the ape attack, I was roused at three a.m. for guard duty. But a subsequent return to the arms of Morpheus from six to eight left me feeling completely refreshed.

And now, after so many preliminaries and travel, it was finally time for the assault on Devil's Reef.

Uncoupling the wigwams from the Behemoth was but the work of a minute. Lifting the cage out of the water tank and manhandling it onto the platform at the rear of the big engine took hardly any longer. It was then secured with chains. But subsequent preparations were more elaborate.

First, four special saddles were brought out of storage and emplaced with straps and buckles to the spine of the bison carapace. A ladder that was already affixed to the flank of the bison facilitated access. Van Guitt nominated the riders.

"Captain Hood, Colonel Munro, Mister McNeil and Mister Fox. You four will take up your perches and act as lookouts and snipers, if needs be. Two of you face fore, and two aft."

The marksmen did as they were bidden. I was heartened to think that we would have their protection.

Now van Guitt turned to me. "Henri, you and I will ride in the cab with Josiah and Wilber. It will be our chore to heft the stupefied gill-men out of the water, manacle them and thrust them into the cage."

Seeing Jenny and Lady Munro watching us, I clicked my heels, made an extravagant salute, and said, "Fortune favors the brave, *mon frère*, and you have found your man in me!"

I hoped for at least some batted eyelashes from Jenny, but instead received only her protruded tongue and a squint.

Truth be told, I still at this moment had little faith that this hunt would come to anything, despite van Guitt's magic-lantern lecture and associated folderol, and so I was willing to talk big.

Van Guitt and I entered the engine's cab, and Banks got the Behemoth rolling over the improvised boardwalk. When the snout of the sea-going bison overhung the water, he stopped. He and Wilberforce jumped down and effected a miraculous change in the Behemoth, like stage magicians.

First, a series of concealed overlapping plates were swung out from their niches and angled underneath the engine, forming a. kind of seaworthy hull. Then, two paddlewheels, hidden beneath the bison, were lowered into place on either side of the Behemoth, and hooked into the motive power, which was disengaged from the conventional wheels. Suddenly the Behemoth had become a sea-going craft, but more capably so than its primitive functionality in India.

With the land-wheels unpowered, the four of us had to push the Behemoth into the water. But having foreseen this eventuality, Banks had greased the boardwalk, making our task much easier. Once the bison boat was afloat, we splashed through the shallows and climbed aboard. The paddlewheels began to revolve, a rudder came into play, and we sailed off, a most astonishing sight, I am sure!

I waved to the ladies on the shore, and saw that they had been joined by Zadok Allen, who awaited his payment. I felt momentarily jealous of the gay youth's proximity to Jenny, but soon realized that my return as conquering hero would trump his bumpkin charms. I was further buoyed by their shouted good wishes for success.

As we drew further from land, we entered a moderately busy scene. Various craft came and went. But again, no one deigned to hail us with either cheer or malice.

In a relatively short time we approached the legendary Devil's Reef, discernible by a change in the ocean's hue and by unique wave configurations: a long, black line scarcely rising above the water yet carrying a suggestion of odd latent malignancy.

Banks caused the paddlewheels to cease their rotations and we dropped an anchor to afford us a stable perch.

Van Guitt called up to our snipers, elevated above us for better vantage. "Any sign of interference? No? Very good! Keep your eyes peeled though, boys!"

The Dutch big-game trapper took the mystic stones from his pocket and tossed them hither and yon into the water, murmuring unintelligible words while doing so. He next made ready the bag of *akia* powder. And then we all waited anxiously.

I have seen many paintings of Shakespeare's tragic heroine Ophelia as she lay drowned, with her face just protruding from the water, or even an inch or two below the surface. And it was this morbid image which, unbidden, sprang into my mind as I saw the first of the Deep Ones.

Obeying the magical summons, they yet chose not to emerge from the ocean. Rather, they hovered effortlessly with their horrid upturned visages just below the watery interface, drowned green gargoyle masks. The depiction of their tribe that van Guitt had shown us had failed to convey their utterly disconcerting and abnormal blend of bestial and human. We were encircled by a gallery of bizarre fluid-warped countenances, as if a troupe of mummers all in black had thrust their chalky faces out of the night. I was fascinated, horrified and thrilled. Here indeed was a prize beyond price.

Van Guitt wasted no time, but immediately began strewing the *akia* drug with broad motions.

The faces quickly disappeared, and I feared the drug had had no effect. But no! Once stricken, the monsters were only sinking momentarily before bobbing to the surface again, this time with their whole unseemly comatose lengths stretched out, limbs dangling underwater.

Producing a long-poled billhook from somewhere, van Guitt began fishing. "Henri, Wilber! Grab the ones I choose and pull them aboard! I'll assume the smaller ones are female!"

Matching deeds to words, van Guitt hooked—none too tenderly—a big brute and brought him alongside. Almost falling into the sea ourselves, Wilberforce and I sought a grip under the creature's slippery armpits. Finally we contrived to lift the insensate brute out of the water. He weighed no more than a man his size. Wilberforce quickly clapped manacles on the creature's wrists and ankles, and we dumped him through the cage door.

We repeated this procedure with a smaller, ostensibly female Deep One. Van Guitt eyed the other floating bodies with an avarice denied, then reluctantly gave the order to Banks.

"Josiah, get us to shore!"

The two gill-beings remained unconscious in a heap behind bars, and I wondered how long they would continue that way, and what they would be like when they regained awareness. I shivered, and tested the stoutness of the lock again.

As we neared the beach whence we had departed, I could see that Jenny and Lady Munro had also been busy, per the Dutchman's orders. A small hand pump and a length of hose had served to fill the holding tank with sea water. The women were just uncoupling everything when the prow of the Behemoth ground onto the sand, aligned with the boardwalk.

Van Guitt yelled up to the four marksmen. "Fellows, stay in your saddles until we get the trophies secured, just in case any belligerents should approach!"

Phillips and Banks quickly reversed all the adjustments they had done earlier to make the Behemoth seaworthy, and her wheels engaged the plank road. Within seconds, our mighty engine stood safely on terra firma.

Racing against imagined dire consequences of our actions, we quickly hooked up the wigwams to the Behemoth, then carried the heavy cage and its somnolent occupants inside and emplaced it in the sea-water tank.

I was sore, sweaty and even a bit trembly from this uncanny expedition. But when I received a congratulatory buss from Jenny (she kissed all of us) and a warm handshake from Lady Munro, I felt sufficiently rewarded.

Zadok Allen and van Guitt were concluding their financial transaction. Allen looked a trifle disconcerted.

"I never actually thought you'd bring this off, Mathias. Even though I've lived in Innsmouth all my life, I can't predict how my fellow inhabitants will react. I'd make haste to clear the neighborhood as fast as possible, if I were you."

"This is exactly our intent! All right, you sharpshooters, you may come on down!"

Sir Munro replied, "I think not, Mathias, for I see a mob approaching! Best we remain on duty up here. Now, get her under steam!"

At this mention of a mob, Allen quickly scuttled off.

The thought of a pack of angry citizens—was that their subliminal riot of voices I heard?—converging on us was sufficient spur. We all got onboard the Steam House and, after some little confusion, took what appeared to be a rutted dirt road out of town.

But the unimproved condition of the terrain did not permit the Behemoth to attain her full speed, and soon the mob was upon us. A horde of wild-eyed, howling, almost slavering maniacs, some normal-seeming, some with contorted limbs and warped countenances, they were armed with pistols, rifles, shotguns and even axes and pitchforks. Their wordless ululations struck terror into the heart, more so than any tribe of Hindoo thuggees. Bullets thwacked the wooden teepees and pinged off the engine's sides.

From atop the bison's spine, our four gallant snipers got to work. But for every Innsmouthian they felled, it seemed two sprang up.

Van Guitt and I were inside the domestic wigwam, on the first level. Without explanation, the Dutchman yelled, "Follow me!" He raced to the stairs, up to the second floor, and then to the third, where the Munros lived.

"My lad, you see that ladder on the wall. If you ascend it, and go through the trap door, you should see our salvation. I would make the climb myself, but am too old and fat. Go now!"

I did as he directed. Poking my head through the trap door, I found myself in a tiny conical room constituting the very tip of the teepee. A tiny room indeed, but big enough to host a shiny, oiled, newfangled Gatling gun.

I saw instantly that the top of the room was hinged, and secured now by a single bolt. I slammed the bolt out of its embrace, pitched back the roof, and was exposed to the open air.

They say that journalists acquire a jackdaw's nest of odd knowledge, thanks to interviewing so many diverse people. And I felt an instant gratitude for the assignment that had taken me some months ago to the training grounds of the army of France's Second Empire, where I had received a vivid lesson in the usage of such a weapon.

Canting the gun's multiple barrels towards the ground and our pursuers, I commenced firing.

The resulting slaughter was far from pretty. But it achieved its goal, allowing the Behemoth to find the easy road to Ipswich and outpace any surviving antagonists.

An hour later, once we knew we were safe from all pursuit, we stopped the Steam House, allowing our valiant snipers to descend. All of them had received grazing wounds as badges of honor, but they were quickly patched up. As for myself, I was hailed as the ultimate savior of the day, and received a plethora of kisses from Miss Arbutus, as well as a surreptitious squeezing of my manhood. Truly, to the victor belongs the spoils!

While all of us were still exulting outside in the road at our success, van Guitt ventured into the tank room to survey his captives. But he emerged a broken, ashen-faced man.

We all rushed to his side, but he could not speak. So all of us crowded into the tank room.

The wooden tank was chest high. The taller cage stuck up out of the tank. It was assumed that the gill-creatures could crouch down fully underwater when desired, or stand upright to peer out from behind their bars. Right now, they were not visible, so they must be crouching. Dare we get close enough to peer in? Van Guitt must have done so without harm, so we all did too.

The vat of sea-water was stained with a thin kind of blood, making it hard at first to discern the condition of the captives. But eventually we saw the reality of the situation. Despite being manacled, the brutes had managed to tear out each other's throats with their savage teeth, dying in a mutual suicide pact that was obviously preferable to captivity. A kind of brutish nobility we had not anticipated.

We all went outside to commiserate with the Dutchman, and soon, through our kind words and jollying, he came around to his old boisterous, unconquerable self.

"Oh, well, perhaps it's for the best that the civilized world remains ignorant of these monsters in their midst. I suppose I could interest Phineas in some more common creature. I wonder if I could ever secure a particularly large elephant for him. That might work…"

On that note we all retired to our rooms for a well-deserved rest, prior to supper. The Steam House got underway, its gentle motion conducing to a long nap on my part.

What woke me were some unusually savory odors wafting from Jenny's kitchen. My stomach began to growl, and I was very glad when, with dusk an hour or two away, we pulled off the road and began the familiar setup of outdoor tables and chairs, linens, china, wine glasses and utensils.

All of us were seated when Jenny emerged, aided by McNeil and Fox. The three of them carried huge platters of steaming batter-coated gobbets from which issued that palate-tantalizing fragrance. The platters were ringed with fried potatoes.

"What have we here, Miss Arbutus?" inquired van Guitt. "I don't recognize this item from the larder."

"A good old New England feast of fish and chips. I've sampled it earlier of course, and will swear by its powerfully delicious flavor!"

I studied the meal in growing disbelief. I glanced left and right at the equally stunned faces of my compatriots. Then a wave of sanguine disillusionment and acceptance swept over us all, followed by gales of laughter.

And we heartily tucked in to the feast.

*Brian Gallagher closes the book on his WWI saga featuring Gustave Le Rouge's criminal mastermind & mad surgeon, Doctor Cornelius Kramm, originally penned in 1912-13, and Countess Irina Petrovski, a character played by Silvia Tortosa in the 1972 film,* Horror Express...

## Brian Gallagher: *The Secret Archive of Vienna*

*General Phillipovich barracks, Sarajevo, 6 November 1918*

Captain Nemec aimed his rifle and fired on the approaching French troops. The Frenchmen scattered and retreated. The Captain stopped firing. He was at the gate of the barracks. These Frenchmen—how were they here so far from their lines?—seemed well armed, but his own men, lined up along the walls of the barracks could hold them back. They had the measure of the French.

A man from the French side came forward, waving a white flag. He wore the uniform of a Colonel, and Captain Nemec held his fire. The Frenchman spoke in German. As an officer in the Austro-Hungarian Empire, the Captain knew the language.

"My friend, the war is virtually over. Let us through—we only wish to take what was agreed between your emperor and my government. You know of the materials we mean."

"What agreement?" the Captain said. "The war isn't even over yet."

*What agreement indeed,* Hart thought. There was no agreement; they were here to take certain materials before France's other allies did. The British and Americans already had their people on the way. And he heard that the Russian Bolsheviks were up to something as well.

"Your emperor has agreed to let us take certain items here away for inspection part of the coming ceasefire," Hart said. He had no compunction about lying. In reality he was a senior officer in the *Deuxième Bureau.*[18]

The Captain, and some of his men knew very well what Hart meant by "certain items." The barracks had another purpose—they contained a repository of certain artefacts, items from other worlds and from this one. Weapons and objects of such advanced technology that they could not understand them.

Could the Captain let the French have them?

One of his men shouted something in French to Hart.

Hart responded. "Your man knows French obscenities, I do hope you bring him in line and surrender."

The Captain turned to his Sergeant, "Tell that man to keep quiet!"

"Shut yer trap!" the Sergeant shouted at the private.

---

[18] The French military intelligence service.

The Captain was not amused by the soldier's intervention. It demonstrated a certain breakdown in discipline in the wake of the Austro-Hungarian Empire's defeat in the war. At least, however, the man seemed willing to fight.

And so could he.

"Colonel Hart, I fear I must decline to surrender to you. I have had no instructions to surrender anything to anyone."

"I would urge you to reconsider, Captain," said Hart. He had hoped that he would not have to use his advantage. And now he did. He waved to one of men.

Captain Nemec and his men looked stunned as behind the French troops, the air seemed to shimmer. And then appeared what the Captain recognized as French 75 mm artillery field guns, along with some vehicles.

The Captain knew that artillery would destroy them. It would be suicidal to resist. The French could kill them all and take what they wanted anyway. Perhaps they could destroy the items before surrendering to the French?

As if he could read the Captain's mind, Hart said: "Any movement now from your troops and my artillery start firing directly at you all."

The Captain did not relish sacrificing himself and his men for nothing. That is, assuming that his men would obey such instructions. They were loyal, but even that loyalty would be strained, given their side's defeat and the political situation which was seeing the Empire dissolve. He felt privileged to have served with his men. In whatever came next for the peoples of the Empire, they would be needed at their homes. This war had created so many widows and fatherless children—why create even more for no gain?

"Very well," said the Captain. "You may proceed."

Matters were swiftly dealt with. Hart and his men took the artifacts. Things labeled coming as belonging to "far and distant things" and metallic body parts trom "Planet 10" and various other strange weapons and objects. Hart was delighted. However, there was no documentation. Hart knew that such files existed in Vienna. However, he did not have the resources to take them. Coming to Sarajevo with an invisible convoy from the Dalmatian coast was one thing, but to get to the heart of the Habsburg empire in such a way? No, that was not feasible, and his superiors had forbidden it in any event, fearing it might jeopardize the German surrender negotiations. Further the invisibility device was already starting to wear out—based on the remnants of Saturnian machinery constructed by one his more difficult employees.[19] Once it burned out, that would be the end of it for that technology. However, now Hart had much more to play with—as soon as his scientists could work it all out.[20]

---

[19] See *The Projector of Death* in *Tales of the Shadowmen* Vol. 19.

[20] The captured hoard would add to France's already impressive knowledge and use of such esoteric science. The effects on French society and the world are documented in many books published by Black Coat Press.

Dr. Cornelius Kramm looked around him. He was in a locked room. He sat on one chair, and a couple of feet away was a desk with another chair. US Marshals stood outside. He sighed. He had become complacent. He, the legendary "sculptor of human flesh, had become complacent. He had fled the United States, careful to ensure that the authorities thought him dead. From being one of the Lords—the leading one—of the notorious Red Hand criminal empire, he had eventually come to Europe with a new identity and set himself up as a criminal for hire based in Berne. His cover of Dr. Malbrough had been blown in 1914, but he'd found Berne too congenial to leave and simply changed his name again. That had been a grave mistake.

A man entered. The Doctor would have considered a possible attempt at getting hold of the man and holding him hostage. However, given that he was manacled to his chair, this would not be feasible.

The slightly stocky man sat down on the chair behind the table. He was dressed in civilian clothing, but Dr. Cornelius noted a military bearing.

"My name is Hamilton. Dr. Cornelius Kramm, I am here to inform you that you are to be returned to the United States to face trial for a number of charges in relation to your leadership of the Red Hand criminal organization. Murder, racketeering, torture and much more, including causing a rail crash."

The sculptor of human flesh replied in his best innocent manner, "I am but a simple surgeon. My name is Cerral, I am not this Cornelus Kramm you are after."

"Your attitude will change once you are strapped into the electric chair," Hamilton said.

Dr. Cornelius considered the man for a moment. He could sense something was going on. "I find it odd that I was not simply arrested and handed over to you. Instead, I was kidnapped from my apartment by mysterious Swiss agents and dumped here. Perhaps it would be less embarrassing to the Swiss authorities? However, I have been held here for three days. If I were indeed Dr. Cornelius Kramm, surely, I would already be on my way to the United States?"

The military man started impassively at his prisoner. "You are a man of unique talents and knowledge," he said.

Dr. Cornelius tensed. He could see that there was a way out of his predicament somewhere here and replied. "I am indeed—and my talents are for hire. I am not cheap, however."

Hamilton decided to take things forward. "Dr. Cornelius, we have a proposition for you."

"I like propositions, but who am I dealing with?"

"The Military Intelligence Division of the United States Department of War."

"I see. And your proposition?"

Hamilton leaned back in his chair. "We can easily take you to the United States, ensure a swift trial and execute you shortly after—the public would demand it. However, we think you can serve your country."

Dr. Cornelius smiled. He had more or less forgotten he was a US citizen. "How might I do that? And what would be my reward?" he asked.

"We would like you to confiscate the Vienna Archive."

"The documents, papers and history of esoteric items? All the Austro-Hungarian secrets of an unusual nature. I can do that. However, I have to go immediately—others will no doubt have eyes on it. My reward?"

"You avoid a trial. You work for us as an agent in these matters. The Swiss have frozen your accounts and we have found your other accounts in other countries—we have used various means to discreetly take control of those; indeed we intend to use those funds in the service of our country. We will give you a salary. If you escape us, we will track you down, as we just have, and kill you. No trial."

"You must be desperate," said Dr. Cornelius. "However, you are right to offer me this deal. The old empires have had a near monopoly on alien technologies and strange science. The United States, despite its growing power, has none of this. I, on the other hand, am one of the few Americans who has experience of such matters. Have you considered appropriating the actual artifacts, held in Sarajevo?"

Hamilton looked rueful. "The French got there first."

"Ah, Simon Hart," the sculptor of flesh replied. "He hired me during this war; it does not surprise me he has moved so fast and so brazenly. I have to assume that diplomatic considerations prevent him from doing something similar in Vienna. A few days ago, I received a communication from him—then your Swiss friends swooped. Perhaps he was going to hire me go to Vienna, on some kind of deniable basis, of course, unknown to his superiors, but it seems that perhaps you somehow intercepted that message whilst looking for me."

Hamilton said nothing.

Dr. Cornelius continued. "The Habsburgs also have a facility in Transylvania, a castle that once belonged to one Count Dracula. There they stored their supernatural materials. Are you not interested in that?"

"No," said Hamilton. "Superstitious nonsense. In any event, we understand that Russian Bolsheviks led by the former German spy Von Bork has taken everything. They killed most of the people there to do it."

Dr. Cornelius considered this man to be ignorant—the Bolsheviks knew what they were doing. Still, his own experience of the supernatural was limited, and he much preferred dealing with largely scientific matters. He did not think that the Military Intelligence Division had found all his assets; but very likely they had left some alone in order to catch him should he renege on the deal and try to access them. He had become complacent and had been found. Now, he would make the best of the situation. He would work for Washington for now and bide his time.

"Your terms are acceptable. You have re-awakened my patriotism," he said, beaming. "We of the New World will surpass the Old World in these esoteric matters. Now, if you would release me, I have work to do to secure the archive—unless the likes of the Russians or British have gotten there first."

Warily, the military man called the Marshals to free his newest agent.

*Restaurant Nervosa, Berne, 8 November, evening*

Hamilton was seated at the usual table of the US ambassador to Switzerland, which was in a discreet corner, out of earshot of the other diners.

"You trust this Dr. Cornelius?" asked the Ambassador, taking a drop of some fine wine.

"No, I do not," answered Hamilton. "However, he knows we are likely to simply kill him should he in some way double-cross us or flee."

"I must admit, Major Hamilton, that I am uncomfortable with all this. Dr. Cornelius Kramm should be tried and executed for his crimes, yet we are employing him instead."

The military man sighed inwardly. This diplomat was naïve. "I appreciate the moral concerns. However, our country is far behind our knowledge of the world of the fantastic. We entered this war and now our President is taking a leading role in constructing how world affairs are to be conducted. We cannot let our growing power be undone by some old empire suddenly understanding the secret sciences and knowledge they have locked away. Conceivably, the Germans or the Habsburgs could turn everything around tomorrow if they utilized some alien weapon they have—and our allies, the British and French, may could also pose a problem. And then, there are the Bolsheviks…"

The diplomat nodded his head. He had only recently been told of such things. Alien beings and so on. He was not even sure he believed it.

"I bow to your judgement," he replied. "I am glad that my contacts with the Swiss were of use. When will Dr. Corneilus leave the country?"

"He has already left—we needed to move fast. And your contacts proved invaluable—many thanks."

"Invaluable indeed!" a man said to himself not too far away.

Percy Phelps of the British Directorate of Military Intelligence had to restrain himself from bursting out laughing. One of those contacts was in fact his contact, who had told him of the strange requests from the Americans.

He was at a table in a small room discreetly behind the restaurant's kitchen listening to the two Americans. The table had been bugged for some time given that the US ambassador always liked to sit there. This was facilitated in an arrangement with the restaurant owner involving certain information regarding a mistress not getting to his wife. The information gleaned this evening would be of great interest to his superiors. He doubted anything would be made public—the American were their war allies, after all. However, something useful could be done with the information. He looked at the machine he was using. It was a Detectifone listening device, made and purchased from a company based in New York City.

*The Americans have much to learn about espionage* Phelps thought.


*Castle Schoenbrunn, Vienna, 11 November*


The Countess Irina Petrovski had been summoned to see the Emperor Karl. An armistice had been signed. Germany and her ally, Vienna, had lost the war. The Austro-Hungarian Empire was collapsing—the nationalities were asserting themselves, emboldened by President Wilson's fourteen points. She herself was preparing to leave for her homeland of Poland. Nonetheless, she was still technically a citizen of the Austro-Hungarian Empire and felt that she should answer the summons.

The Emperor was in the Blue Chinese Salon part of the building, known to be particularly sumptuous. She was shown to the Emperor, without any formalities. *A very obvious sign of the times*, she thought.

"Thank you, Countess, for coming at such short notice," the Emperor said. He was standing, dressed in military uniform. He gestured to her to sit, which she did, and he took a seat opposite her. An aide sat a short distance away.

"I believe you are heading for Poland?" he asked.

"That was my plan, given the apparent collapse of everything" she replied. "My efforts for a united Poland under your guidance has come to nothing with our defeat. However, I believe that General Józef Piłsudski will play a strong part in the future of Poland. I intend to help him."

"I am concerned for the fate of all our peoples. I wish your countrymen would consider remaining within the Empire," replied the Emperor.

"My countrymen are happy to have independence without being part of an Empire. I am afraid the simple fact of defeat has not contributed to the credibility of Vienna. And further, your former foreign minister Count von Czernin's deal with Ukraine—and your own unfavorable comments about Poles—have not impressed any Pole, including me."

The aide looked appalled. "You cannot speak to the Emperor like that!" he exclaimed, standing up.

The Emperor waved him back down. "If anyone has earned the right to speak frankly to me," the Emperor said, "it is the Countess."

The Emperor looked awkward. He knew very well of the Countess's strong Polish patriotism. "You must understand that I have had to balance the interests of all my peoples. As you know, I have made efforts to federalize the Empire in recent months. However, I do accept that an independent Poland would be just."

The Countess softened, "I do fear for the future without the Empire. Whatever faults it may have had, it was in a position to protect its peoples. And that included defending them from threats from beyond."

"You have guessed why I have summoned you," the Emperor replied.

"Yes. The raid on our facilities in Sarajevo of our scientific materials, and in Transylvania of our supernatural ones. The French and the Bolsheviks being respectively responsible.

The Emperor nodded. "Yes, and now all that we have left is our archive here in Vienna. The documents contained would be invaluable to the French and the Russians. It would give them a degree of insight into what they have. It is bad enough the French having all that information—but the Bolsheviks!"

"I quite agree," said the Countess. "The Romanovs were our enemy during the war, it is true. However, I knew them personally and they did not deserve their fate. The thought of such unholy things being in their hands disturbs me. I must say that days ago, I approached the *Evidenzbureau*.[21] It was half-deserted. Prince Wilhelm[22] was not even there. Nobody seemed to be in charge, and I had to leave. Later, I heard about the raids."

The Emperor responded to the mention of the Bohemian prince. "I am told he left to return to Bohemia; he believes he will now be crowned King despite the public believing he is dead."

"I am sure Mr. Masaryk[23] will inform him otherwise," said the Countess. "Had he stayed at his post, perhaps we could have organized something to at least save the Sarajevo artefacts. I am aware the supernatural did not come under his authority. With him gone, that was when I started to make plans to return to Poland."

"Countess, I would ask you to put off your journey for one final assignment for the Empire."

"Of course."

"The Secret Archive here in Vienna is being guarded by soldiers. However, reports suggest that their loyalties to the monarchy may not be solid. It is only a matter of time before other forces intervene. Further, I do not trust the new authorities that are emerging either here or in Budapest. I was thinking that you could see to it that the archive is transferred to Germany?"

"Your highness, Germany has been defeated. It is now unstable. The archive could be stolen from them—or misused by whoever takes power—as much as here."

---

[21] The Habsburg Empire's military intelligence service. Formed in 1850, it was the world's first such organization.

[22] Prince Wilhelm, a pretender to the throne of Bohemia, had been given a senior post in the *Evidenzbureau* to keep him content.

[23] Tomáš Garrigue Masaryk, who a few days later became the first President of Czechoslovakia.

"Where else is there?" asked the Habsburg ruler.

"The archive must go to those who will use it appropriately to protect humanity. The French cannot be trusted, as their raids shows. Their man, Simon Hart, is not someone who would use these things responsibly, only for furtherance of French goals. The Bolsheviks, of course, must not have them. Whoever takes possession must be strong enough to keep the information away from Von Bork. I believe my own country has too much to deal with already to take this on. The Americans are too young a country. There is only one realistic option: The British."

"The British!" exclaimed the Emperor. His aide looked as if he was about to faint.

The Emperor continued, "You cannot be serious Countess! They are the ones most responsible for our defeat! Further, have you forgotten their attempts with the French to destroy the city of Pula—which you prevented?"

"Of course not," the Countess responded. "I was not thinking of those responsible for that. I was thinking of my old friends, Professor Saxton and Doctor Wells."

"I know of them—you were involved with them in that... 'Horror Express' incident in Siberia."

"Yes. they were responsible for ensuring the destruction of alien creature that posed a threat to life on this planet. A creature that had murdered my husband, Count Petrovski. That incident convinced me to take a role in combating such evil. In the years afterwards, they have defeated a number of unearthly threats, and I have helped them on occasion. They informally run an independent department for the Brtish government. Working with them, we saved a large part of London from destruction in 1906—at the very time the great Austrian exhibition took place. Many of our fellow citizens were saved."

The Emperor nodded. "Yes, I recall."

The Countess continued, "Let us not be naïve—they will likely use the information for the protection of the British Empire. However, they do have a sense of responsibility—they will help outside of their Empire, as demonstrated in the Prague incident of 1910 where we asked for their expertise against the Jovian incursion. And we do know they have an antipathy towards Simon Hart and his department. Hart worked with other Britons in the Pula incident—primarily the lunatic Lord Burydan, but that had nothing to do with my friends. And we can be sure that once in their hands, they will be secure from Von Bork."

"It seems I have little choice," said the Emperor. "Very well. It will not surprise you to know that later today I announce that I will renounce all participation in the affairs of state. Thus, this will be the last covert order I give as Emperor. Countess Irina Petrovski, I task you with ensuring the Vienna Archive is entrusted to the care of the British."

"I will carry it out."

The Emperor opened an ornate box on the table. He brought out what looked like a key, made of something resembling white marble. "The Vienna Archive facility is not only guarded by loyal troops, but the most sensitive area is defended by what I understand is termed a force-field."

"Ah, yes," said the Countess. "It was left behind by the Jovian incursion. The *Evidenzbureau* could not fathom how it worked. However, I am glad it has been put to good use."

The Countess took the key from the Emperor's hand. "I know how to use this," she said. "I will move immediately. I will need a letter of authority from you. I will also contact Professor Saxton and Doctor Wells—we have not been in touch since the war began, but I have a method of communication.

Soon, she left the building. She went to her vehicle *Elizabeth*—a gift to her from her British friends. The car had served her well during the war, being resistant to bullets and capable of moving over any terrain. They were coy about its origins—it was something they could not quite work out, like so much fantastic technology that fell into the hands of the Empires. And the experts she allowed to look at the vehicle were also non-plussed. It had a communication device, letting her speak to her friends in London, who had a receiver. It had not been used since 1914. She had much to tell them now, including about Lord Burydan. She switched the device on and could hear the ringing tone to London.

*The Vienna Archive, Nottendorfer Gasse*

Dr. Cornelius stood at a short distance from the archive. The evening was drawing in. He had no disguise; he was limiting his face-changing skills at the moment, claiming—falsely—to his new masters that materials were short. He was observing the archive building. It was an *Evidenzbureau* building, but one that did not reflect the splendor of Vienna, and thus did not bring much attention to itself.

*Cleary, someone was thinking sensibly by placing the archive here*, thought Dr. Cornelius. There were a number of soldiers parked around the building. A frontal assault would likely end in failure. He had only a few men in any event, remnants of his old Red Hand organization in Austria, whom he had to hire for this job, and they were not cheap either. *How good of the United States Department of War to provide their wages*, he thought.

A number of guards left the building, ending their shift. Dr. Cornelius observed them—one split off from the others. He nodded in his direction. As if out of nowhere, three men appeared from different directions, all following the guard. They looked as if they were locals, and started singing with bottles in their hand, playing drunk. The guard looked around at them, and then ignored them. They caught up with him.

"Drink! Drink!" they said to the guard and held the bottle under his nose. The soldier looked angry, but then the vapor from the bottle hit. He suddenly

211

looked delirious and grabbed the bottle from the hand of one of the men, pulled away from then and took a swig.

Dr. Cornelius caught up with them, exasperated. "Get the drug away from him!" One of the men took the bottle away from the guard. They took the guard arm in arm, and then singing an Austrian drinking song, they all walked away.

A couple of streets away, they all entered a fashionable-looking house, which was in fact one of the Red Hand organization's old European safe houses. A man in his sixties let him them in. He looked harmless, but in fact he was Dr. Cornelius's former employee, one Tamas Varga, who looked after the house and simply took it over when the Red Hand collapsed. He hired it out to wealthy types who wished to conduct illicit affairs or to have meetings away from prying eyes. It amused him to charge an outraged Dr. Cornelius extra. After all, the criminal mastermind would be conducting rather strange activities during his stay.

Dr. Cornelius and his men bundled their captive into what was a living room, with opulent furniture. Their captive immediately started dancing in the middle of the room, singing *Gott erhalte Franz den Kaiser*.[24]

"Get him into a chair!" snapped Dr. Cornelius. His men did as they were told and slung the unfortunate guard into a chair.

The Doctor noted that the guard—a soldier—appeared to have taken off some of his K&K[25] insignia related to the Habsburgs. He grabbed a chair and sat next to him. The drug he had taken was a special one, a recent concoction by the sculptor of human flesh. It made the subject highly intoxicated and also rendered very suggestible.

"My man," said the Doctor in fluent German, "you appear to have got yourself a bit drunk. We are going to look after you, and we will take you home. First, please, do tell us your name and rank. "

"I am drunk? I don't remember drinking?" replied the guard.

"We found you singing in the street, in these times we can hardly blame you. Now, tell us your name and rank and where you live?"

"I am Corporal Simon Fischer, I'm not bothering with the barracks any-more, I was heading back to my father's house in Favoritenstrasse."

"Please tell us the full address so we can take you there," replied Dr. Cor-nelius.

The soldier did so, and one of the henchmen wrote it down.

"Excellent!" exclaimed the Doctor. "Whilst we await a carriage to take you home, I am curious about your role. I was in the army myself you know," he lied.

"I was an *Evidenzbureau* soldier. We guard the Vienna archive on Notten-dorfer Gasse"

---

[24] *God save Francis the Emperor*, the Imperial anthem of the Habsburg Empire.
[25] Imperial and Royal.

"Really? What is kept there?"

The soldier looked a little scared. "Documents describing terrible things, it is said. The worst is kept on the ground floor, in an invisible safe.

The Doctor looked non-plussed. "Invisible safe?" he asked.

"Yes," the Corporal said. "You can see the cabinets, but you cannot get to them. They're protected by invisible walls. The key was kept by Prince Wilhelm, but he has fled Vienna, and my part of the *Evidenzbureau* has simply disintegrated. We work for Renner now."

Dr. Cornelius nodded. He was aware that the Social Democrats, under the leadership of Karl Renner, had effectively taken over the governance of Austria. What of this invisible safe? It must be a force-field of some alien manufacture. It would present a problem.

"Who has the key now?" asked the Doctor.

"It is rumored the Emperor has it."

The Doctor asked a few more questions about the guards and the layout of the archive building. He then told the young man to sleep, which he did.

"Now, we must take a copy of his face," the Doctor said. "And then, one of you will see that he gets safely home. We cannot have his father go out looking for him and bring unwanted attention. He will sleep, intoxicated, for hours."

Felix Lechner was none too sure about having his face transformed into that of Fischer, if only for a short time. Dr. Cornelius told him that his physique was closer to that of the young guard, and he only had the resources to change his face, not his body. Lechner was uncertain as if that was meant to help persuade him. However, the Doctor offered him a special bonus—in US dollars—that swiftly pushed away his doubts.

Now, he approached the *Evidenzbureau* facility. His cover story was that he had lost the keys to his father's home and wanted to see if they were inside. He was surprised that the guards on the door simply smiled at him and let him just walk through. Discipline was clearly breaking down. Lechner wandered down the main corridor—there were a number of rooms, largely offices, all with filing cabinets. He came to the end of the corridor to which there was a lift. He went in and took it down.

As soon as the door opened, a gunshot rang out and Lechner ducked. He was relieved that the shot appeared not to be aimed at him. He looked down at the corridor before him and about 20 feet away he could see a reinforced door, which was open. He could hear laughter. Lechner cautiously moved down the corridor. This was where Fischer said the "invisible safe" was—what Dr. Cornelius had said was in fact a "force-field."

There were four guards inside, with a machine gun next to them. The room was circular, about 20-feet wide. Hans could see safes and cabinets of varying sizes, all with the K&K insignia on them. Right in front of him on the floor was a rectangular box about 1-foot wide and high. It was glowing a strange color; one he did not think he had seen before.

One of the guards was seemingly knocking a hammer against thin air.

"Simon!" said a Corporal. "Come to try and break in again and get the Emperor's riches? We've had no luck, but Hans here decided to shoot his way in again, almost killing us in the process," he said, pointing to a sheepish guard next to him and then to a hole in the wall where clearly the bullet had landed after ricocheting off the force-field. "Hans is new," he explained.

Lechner laughed and nodded. He then put his hands to the force-field. It was solid, like a strong wall. He started to move around it.

"It's still a square shape," the Corporal said. Lechner affected a coughing fit to cover his different voice and gasped, "Just checking," he replied. He noted that that the safes inside appeared to float on a centimeter of thin air, no doubt the floor of the force-field.

Before he could inspect it further, the sound of machine-gun fire could be heard. "Stay here and kill anyone is who not one of us," the Corporal said to the guard with the machine gun. "The rest of you, with me!"

Lechner also went with them. This sounded like serious trouble, and he had no intention of potentially being trapped underground. Getting out fast was his priority.

The Corporal charged up some stairs rather than using the lift, and they emerged on the ground floor. There was heavy gunfire coming from outside. Lechner held back, allowing the Corporal and the other two men to charge along the corridor towards the exit. *Let them get shot rather than me*, he thought.

The Corporal and his men got to the entrance. Ahead of them on the road outside were the bloodied bodies of four men lying on the floor. To the Corporal's side were the guards who were manning the entrance. "Looks like Red Guards, they tried to storm the building, but hadn't reckoned with old Pichler upstairs with his machine gun."

There was more firing from across the street, a gunman behind a street corner, clearly aiming at the machine gunner. Then, from the same corner ran three men, shouting as they came. The Corporal and his men picked them off easily.

It then went quiet. After a few minutes, some curious civilians started to move on the road, looking at the bodies. A few came from around the corner from where the shots were being fired – almost getting themselves machine-gunned, save for one of the figures being recognized as a guard. The man ran over to the Corporal. "I was in the pub. I heard gunfire. What happened."

The Corporal responded, "We were attacked. You came from where we were fired on. Did you see anything."

The guard nodded. "Yes, a group of armed men ran past me,"

The Corporal motioned to a couple of the men, and they ran across to check, coming back to report the gunmen had indeed gone.

"Given the slogans they were shouting, they appear to be those Bolshevik Red Guards," the Corporal said.

At that moment, a man on horseback appeared. He had a military uniform on—that of a Captain. Unlike the guards at the building, his unform still retained Imperial insignia. He got off his horse.

"Don't you salute an officer?"

"To hell with you. The Empire is finished. We'll be taking no orders from you."

The officer looked at the Corporal. He had experienced much of this of late. He decided to ignore the man's comments rather than threaten him, which he knew would result in nothing more than ridicule, and perhaps even violence.

"What has happened here?" he asked.

The Corporal obliged him with an answer. "Red Guards, trying to steal the riches here. We dealt with them."

Lechner quietly listened. He was sure Dr. Cornelius would want to know why an officer had stopped by. He was aware that the Doctor had someone watching this building at all times.

The officer appears to nod in approval. He reached inside his tunic and gave a piece of paper to the Corporal. "This is a direct order from the Emperor himself," he said.

The Corporal sneered. "I don't care. We work for Renner now," he said.

"Nonetheless, it is a legal order, whatever you might think. Renner is also being told. What will happen is that the Countess Irina Petrovski will soon arrive with the British military. All the men here are to give their complete cooperation."

"We will see what Renner says about that," responded the Corporal, to grunts of approval from the other men. The Captain decided that this would be a good time to leave. He had done as he had been ordered. He mounted his horse and rode off, to jeers from the guards.

Lechner made his excuses and left to report to Dr. Cornelius. However, he was not the only one to leave. One of the men with the Corporal slipped away. *Damn those fools*, the man thought. *What an insane attack! Did they not listen to me when I told them of the machine guns? How did they expect to take the materials from the invisible safe? Revolution will not be achieved in Vienna by such incompetence.* He was also angry that they attacked when he was present, putting him in danger. He would report back to the others on what had happened. Experienced military men were needed, not those such as the dead in the street were little more than local agitators—men who he presumed also did not believe his reports of the invisible safe. He would ignore the useless local comrade in charge and contact Von Bork directly. The spymaster would want to know of the involvement of this Countess.

Dr. Cornelius listened to Lechner's report. "The Countess. Again," he said. Lechner looked puzzled.

"A regular foe," the Doctor explained. "She seems to have cropped up at least once a year during this war. Even at the end of it, she still causes me trouble... The great Habsburg Empire she served now has to give its secrets to the British. However, given her mission, I would hazard a guess that she has some form of key to deactivate the force-field..." He looked over to Varga. "Where might the Countess be in Vienna?" he asked of him.

"Innere Stadt. She is a public figure due to her journalism and her nursing during the war," he replied. "She receives prominent guests. I can send some men to keep watch on her home?"

The Doctor shook his head. "No, we shall go with as many men now as we can. Time is against us. The British are on their way, and these Red Guards may yet cause further trouble."

The man turned to go to gather as many men as he could, when Dr. Cornelius stopped him. "Do you have links with these new authorities?" he asked.

"Indeed, I do," Varga replied. "I have done much business lately with one of his colleagues. "

"Can he delay the British?" he asked.

"For enough money, I am sure, although I suspect not for long. I have heard of a group of British troops heading towards Vienna. A diplomatic mission. it is being said."

"Pay him. I will recompense you later," Dr. Cornelius.

"This involvement of the British, could this be connected with the presence of a British Lord in the city?" asked Varga.

"British Lord?" the Doctor responded, immediately interested.

"A Lord... Buried?"

"Burydan."

"Yes, that's right. He's been seen in various pubs insulting people and waving a gun around."

"What else do you know of his activities?"

"Nothing, bar that. He is liable to get himself killed. He has already been in a number or fights, coming out on top."

Lord Burydan! Dr. Cornelius knew him well and was certain he knew why he was in Vienna. This British Lord was an old enemy. The Doctor was responsible for the man's hideous burns and scars, driving him more insane than he already was. The sculptor of human flesh later removed those scars, in return for this "Peer of the Realm" working for him. The Doctor had told him a lie that the Countess was responsible for his burns. Lord Burydan had served him well— and even enthusiastically. The Doctor had no doubt as to why the Brition was in

Vienna. With the war effectively over, he was here to take his revenge on the Countess.

"Find him and bring him here immediately," he ordered Varga. "Tell him I am here, and I know where to find the Countess. Tell him there is money in it too—and a bonus for you if he is here within the hour."

*The Residence of the Countess Irina Petrovski, Innere Stadt,*
*11 November, early evening*

The Countess looked around her. Some of the most loyal people she had worked with were here. She had told them to go home, but with this final mission they wanted to stay. They seemed to be concerned about, as was she—as if trouble was in the air. She looked outside her window. She could see her old friend Lieutenant Mayr; he was taking a look around the street. He in particular was feeling uneasy. Up to recently, he was a Sergeant, but his services to the state earned him a commission to officer. The Countess had to help persuade him to take the commission, pointing out that the extra wages would help his family and the *Evidenzbureau* needed experienced men like him in authority, no matter how junior. That was a few months ago. His future, along with so many, was now uncertain. With her in the room was Captain Vuljanić, recently promoted from lieutenant, and Kata, an *Evidenzbureau* agent. She had been recruited in Sarajevo and acted as an assistant to the Countess, working as her maid as cover. Kata had ensured that the countess's children were transported safely out of Vienna to relatives.

The Countess's telephone rang. Kata picked it up. "Countess Irina Petrovski's residence" she announced. She handed the receiver to the Countess. "The Emperor's diplomatic adviser," she said. The Countess took the phone and spoke to the adviser. She listened to what he had to say and then said, "See what you can do via diplomatic means. I will try and find out what is going on from this end. Goodbye."

She turned to her friends. "It would appear that Renner's men are blocking the British passage into Vienna. Their reasoning is that whatever agreement has been made with the British has no validity as Renner is in charge. The British force is only around 20 men and their vehicles, they cannot fight their way through and also have orders not to engage anyone in order to prevent any kind of incident—although Renner does not know that."

"Do they apply such logic to the armistice?" asked Kata.

"No. Something is going on. Others, perhaps, are after the archive." The Countess was concerned. The British were being delayed, the archive was in the hands of this man Renner and all she had were her friends here. Still, that had often been enough in the past.

Lieutenant Mayr burst in. "We may be in trouble," he said. "A group of men are approaching,"

217

"We are already here," said a voice behind him.

Everyone in the room saw a man enter, followed by others. He aimed his gun at Mayr's head.

"Greetings, Dr. Cornelius!" said Lord Burydan.

Dr. Cornelius was slightly startled. He and his men were just leaving their safe and boarding a lorry. Varga had brought him. The Briton patted his jacket pocket. "Only just holstered this. Your man could have been anyone, but glad to see he really does work for you," he said slapping the old man on the back hard enough to push him forward.

"I have work for you," said the Doctor, "however, I am curious to know why you are here," he asked.

Lord Burydan beamed, "Why, revenge of course! With the war effectively over, I have been able to move around Europe a bit more. It is past time to settle scores with the Countess. She lives here in Vienna. I see no reason to delay dealing with her. You wouldn't happen to know where she is? I always find getting around these foreign places a bit difficult."

Dr. Cornelius looked at this supposed peer of the British realm whose body he had restored. He knew full well the Briton was not of sound mind.

"Then I have good news for you, Lord Burydan. We are about to embark on a mission to her residence right now. I have something to collect from her. There may be resistance from her minions. Your undoubted skills of violence will come in useful. You will be paid well."

"Excellent," said Lord Burydan. "However, I have a condition—I must be allowed to kill the Countess."

"Of course," said the Doctor, "but only after I have got the item I need from her." Burydan nodded his assent. The Doctor gestured to the Briton to get into the lorry.

At the Countess's residence, It was the archive guard who earlier had left the archive building to report to Von Bork who was holding a gun to Mayr's head. The guard, a Private Brunner, was very pleased with himself. Von Bork, who was controlling this operation from somewhere out of the country. He had told the German spymaster—now a communist—of the incompetence of those in charge of this mission and how he, Private Brunner, could do better with his military experience. Von Bork let him take control. He, a mere private, would help bring the revolution to Vienna.

The Countess knew nothing of this, of course. She just saw some grubby-looking armed men in front of her.

With his gun still aimed directly at Mayr's head, Brunner said: "I will kill this man, if you do not comply with my orders,"

"Who are you?" asked the Countess, sternly.

"Who I am is of no importance, save that I serve the working class!"

*Bolsheviks*, thought the Countess. The Red Guards she had heard of. *Probably working for Von Bork.*

"And what the does the servant of the working class want?" she asked.

"You have the key to the invisible safe. Give it to me, and we will go. If not, your friend gets a bullet in the head."

The Countess went straight over to a desk. "It's in here," she said pointing to a drawer. "I shall of course take it out slowly lest you think I am reaching for a weapon." In fact, she, like all her friends in the room, had small weapons secreted about their person. The Countess slowly took the key the Emperor gave her from the drawer. Mayr's life was more important—they could retrieve the key later. However, she was concerned that these Red Guards may simply try to murder them all, at which point they would draw their weapons, come what may.

"Hold it out," said Brunner. The Countess did as ordered.

Brunner studied the key in her hand. It was clear to all that he had been briefed on how to recognize the key. He held his free hand out. "Very well. Now, put it in my hand—carefully."

With the key handed over, Brunner moved his gun away from Meyr and aimed at the Countess. "I have heard, Countess, that before the war, you were friends with the Romanovs."

"That is the truth," she replied. "The war changed things. Then your people murdered them," she said bitterly. Whatever their faults, the Countess had some respect for them. Their murder at the hands of Lenin's men had a profound effect, convincing her that Bolshevism spelt nothing but horror for humanity.

"Murdered?" Brunner was angry. He had seen much horror fighting in the war. And then a fellow soldier told him of the revolution in Russia, how the workers had taken over and taken the country out of the war. He read the words of Marx and Engels, and became convinced, and decided to devote his life to world revolution. "No, they received justice, as all aristocrats and capitalists will get for starting this war. Including here in Vienna. Starting with you," he said, gun aimed straight at the Countess.

Everyone was thus surprised when Brunner's head appeared to explode. The three men with him looked startled.

Kata was first to collect her senses, grabbing her small pistol in her garter and firing at the nearest Red Guard. The Countess grabbed the key from the floor where Brunner had dropped it.

The surviving Red Guard hid behind a chair, firing in all directions—including at the doorway. Who was out there?

"Everybody out," she shouted, pointing at the stairwell. Her three friends ran down the stairs. She gave covering fire, shooting at the Red Guard, wounding him. She glanced at two men coming through the door—Dr. Cornelius and Lord Burydan, armed. She took a chance and headed for the stairwell.

Dr. Cornelius saw what must be key in her hand—it looked alien—and was about to shoot her, when Lord Burydan knocked the gun out of his hand.

The Countess disappeared down the stairwell, and an Austrian grenade came flying up from it and hit the floor.

Lord Burydan grabbed Dr. Cornelius and shoved him back out of the doorway. The grenade exploded, wrecking the room, but the two men were unharmed.

Exiting from the side of the building, the group of friends ran to *Elizabeth*, which was parked at the front. Two of Dr. Cornelius's henchmen were outside, looking the wrong way. They swung round with their guns, only to be shot down by the two *Evidenzbureau* officers. The four of them got into *Elizabeth* and drove away at speed.

Inside the residence, Dr. Cornelius was furious. "What did you do that for!" he shouted at Lord Burydan.

"I was saving your life, old man," the Briton replied nonchalantly.

"I meant, your preventing me from shooting the Countess."

"Our deal is that I kill her, not you. I was not going to let you cheat me,"

"You could have shot her yourself."

"You were in the way, old man."

Dr. Cornelius glared at him. The Briton was always arrogant. However, previously, his behavior had been tempered by needing the Doctor's serum to maintain his face. As a reward for good work, the Doctor let the man keep his features permanently—a decision he now regretted.

The Doctor silently walked downstairs. Lechner was outside. The henchman gestured to the road. "The Countess's work," he said. Many people were coming out of the other houses to see what the explosions were about.

"We must leave," said the Doctor. "Leave their bodies but get their guns." The three men got into the lorry, with Lechner driving. The Doctor and Lord Burydan got into the back.

"These silencer things of yours are pretty damn good," said Lord Burydan, pointing to his gun with a tube on the end of it, as did the other weapons the men had used. "Those men didn't hear the sound of their own deaths coming—very strange seeing that man's head explode. The Countess is in my debt, although I want to shoot her myself—and make sure she know it's me. She owes me her life. Ironic, no?"

Dr. Cornelius ignored him. He did not have the resources or time to plan things—he had no idea of the residence of the Countess, and not enough men. He had to find out where the Countess had gone.

In *Elizabeth*, the Countess congratulated Captain Vuljanić, "I think that grenade held off Dr. Cornelius and that mad Briton. Well thrown!"

"It is fortunate that you keep a supply of such weapons," he replied.

The Countess, driving, replied "Given the matters we deal with, it is best to be prepared. Although we were still taken too much by surprise. On some level, I still did not believe that my home could come under attack. However, I never thought the Empire would collapse." The cab went silent.

They drove past the Archive, slowing to take a look. There were significantly more men outside the building.

"Let us see what the authorities have to say," the Countess said and drove on.

The authorities were less than helpful. "Countess, quite frankly you have no authority," said the man before her in a government building. "Neither you, the Emperor, let alone the British, have any right to issue orders or take documents. The archive belongs to the people of Austria."

"The archive belongs to all the peoples of the Empire," the Countess retorted angrily. "Only the Emperor has the authority to dispose of it—to the hands of those who will use it responsibly. I demand to see Karl Renner."

"Mr. Renner is busy governing."

"Does he not realize that there are armed groups trying to capture the archive?"

"We repelled the Red Guards. As for Dr. Cornelius, he has only attacked your residence, assuming that is true. Perhaps the police should detain you, to find out what is going on."

The Countess glared at him. "I shall go to the Emperor himself and we will take matters up with the British government. Let me remind you that they have won the war, and your lack of cooperation could well jeopardize the peace."

She turned and walked out. She went straight back to *Elizabeth*, where her friends were waiting.

"We must go to the Emperor at Schloss Eckartsau.[26] He has gone there as Vienna is not safe. Very wise, as we have found out tonight. The Red Guards, Dr. Cornelius and perhaps Renner's men are all targeting us."

The official came out and watched *Elizabeth* drive off. He had been paid well to hold up the British. He suspected that the money had originally come from this Dr. Cornelius. Perhaps the Doctor would pay also for the detail of the conversation he just had.

*Schloss Eckartsau, 13 November. Morning*

The Countess finished her breakfast. She had not slept well. They had arrived at Schloss Eckartsau She had contacted Professor Saxton and Dr. Wells. In the meantime, the Emperor had pursued his diplomatic lines. She looked around the table at her friends. They all looked tired.

---

[26] The hunting lodge of the Habsburgs, east of Vienna.

221

Mayr spoke. "I have to say, I never thought I would be eating at the Emperor's table."

"Pity it's in these circumstances," said Captain Vuljanić. "It does feel like the end, doesn't it? I can't say I am keen on the British taking the archive, given they have been our enemies—especially Lord Burydan. However, better that then the current authorities. Apart from anything else, are they able to stand up to the Red Guards? No, let the British have it. I trust your judgement that your friends Saxton and Wells are honorable men, unlike Lord Burydan."

The Countess looked sympathetic. She knew he was worrying about his wife and their newborn child. "Have you heard from your family?"

"Yes, the Emperor's staff were able to get me news. They are well, in Zagreb. However, the political situation is not good. There is talk of a state of Slovenes, Croat and Serbs, formed from within the Empire. That, I can live with, but this talk of uniting with Serbia... Given that country's role in starting the war, I can only view that with concern. The monarchy's authority is broken, alternatives are not being presented strongly enough."

The Countess nodded, "Yes, I have heard from my friends on the island of Brač. A bust of Franz Joseph in Supetar has found its way to the bottom of the harbor. In Poland, where I have already sent my children, there is turmoil. I shall join them soon. And what of you, Lieutenant Mayr and Kata?"

"I am stuck in Austria with Renner," said Mayr. "I may have to end with fighting with his men if the Red Guards become a serious problem."

"I shall be returning to Sarajevo," said Kata. "The Captain and I may well share the same fate as to who rules us."

"We shall stay in touch," said the Countess. "I have some thoughts on the future, and not just about Poland. I believe..."

She was interrupted as the Emperor Karl strode in. They all stood up.

"Please, sit down," he said. "I have been in touch with Renner's people. It appears the British government have made clear there will be consequences for non-compliance with our agreement. These have not been specified, but Renner has promised that the British will no longer be obstructed. Of course, he claims one of his staff was responsible and that he knew nothing about it. In any event, the handover is scheduled for 18:00."

"We will be there," the Countess said.

Outside Schloss Eckartsau, Dr. Cornelius and his depleted force had appeared in a car. The old man claimed there was no one available to replace the men who had been killed. The Doctor suspected that the man simply didn't want to hire men that would end up dead, damaging his reputation. He would have to make do with Lord Burydan and Lechner—Varga being too old for this. Still, Varga had at least got the information from his contact about the whereabouts of the Countess, even if he had only received the information in the early hours.

They were all dressed in the field grey uniforms of the Austro-Hungarian army. Dr. Cornelius wore the uniform of a Colonel, Lord Burydan as a Major and Lechner as a corporal. For a further fee, Lechner had retained the face of the guard they had kidnapped. That was to keep him quiet—the Doctor did not have time to bring back his old face at the moment.

The car drove slowly to the front of the hunting lodge. There were two guards at the gates. Dr. Cornelius walked up to them, striding purposefully with his hands behind his back. The guards looked at him suspiciously. They had strict orders not to let anyone pass. Yet, this man was clearly a Colonel. The Empire was falling apart, including the army, but these men would treat this officer respectfully. They did not salute, given they were holding rifles, but spoke to the Doctor respectfully. "I am sorry sir; we have orders direct from the Emperor himself – no entry to anyone not expected.

From behind his back, the Doctor brought out a gun with silencer and expertly shot both men dead, swiftly and to the head.

Lord Burydan bounded up. "Headshots! Just like me. Good to see you getting your hands dirty,"

The Doctor ignored him. He did this himself, rather than ordering one of them to do it in order to demonstrate that he was a force to be reckoned with, in case these two—especially the Briton—had any doubt.

Upstairs, the Countess left the breakfast room and headed to her bedroom to collect her things. She was planning for her group to leave early as she could sense the Emperor had much to deal with and she did not want to be in his way.

Dr. Cornelius's group entered the lodge. They walked around unchallenged. There appeared to be few people, no-one challenged them, presuming that as they were inside Schloss Eckartsau, they were supposed be there.

Soon, they came to the breakfast room. The Doctor motioned to his men to keep quiet. The Emperor was speaking. "Captain, take this folder to the Archive when you leave. It contains papers regarding alien interventions in the United States—which we knew about, but the American authorities did not. I had hoped there may be something in there to discuss with President Wilson, perhaps to win him over a little. Looking at them, however, I think it may be counterproductive."

*Interesting*, thought the sculptor of human flesh. He strode in, gun in hand just as the Emperor was putting the papers onto the breakfast table.

"Who the devil are you?" demanded the Emperor.

"As the others here will tell you, I am Dr. Cornelius Kramm. We met in Split.[27] However, I am now wearing my own face. I see the Countess is not here.

---

[27] See *The Projector of Death* in *Tales of the Shadowmen* Vol. 19.

You will be good enough to tell me where she is, or, if you have the force-field key, I will simply take that."

The Doctor had no idea what he would do if he did get the key. However, a somewhat desperate plan was forming in his mind—perhaps poison gas to kill all in the archive, allowing him access? Varga get such weapons—if money did not sway him, torture no doubt would. It was then that he noticed that Lord Burydan was not with him and Lechner.

The Countess emerged from her bedroom, with a bag of belongings in one hand and the key in another. The bag was a bit heavy. It contained her trusty Doppelpistole. She turned around a corridor, and ran straight into Lord Burydan. He raised his gun.

Dr. Cornelius was alarmed. Clearly, Lord Burydan had gone to look for the Countess. He did not care if the Briton killed her, but would he retrieve the key from her?

"Well?" he asked the Emperor.

"The key is none of your affair," said the Emperor, unwisely.

"It very much is," replied Dr. Cornelius. "Shall I kill you all one by one before you tell me where the Countess is?"

"I am here," said the Countess, walking in with her bag.

"The key," the Doctor said simply.

"It's already on its way to Vienna. We are going to be contacted when it arrives—at which point we can order it returned here, or wherever you want, provided you release everyone here."

The Doctor was suspicious but nodded his assent.

"No Lord Burydan?" asked the Countess.

"He is searching for you. Do not concern yourself—you will come to no harm if you cooperate," said the Doctor. In truth, once he had the key, he thought it best to simply let the Briton kill her.

"I take it he is still unaware that you pushed him into the flames of that burning ship in 1914, not me. Perhaps I will tell him that when he appears."

Dr. Cornelius laughed. "He won't believe you. He's insane. He believes you did it. And why not? Remember, technically he and I were on the same side. Why would I do that? Of course, I must confess that it was a moment of revenge for me, which worked out in the end with his working for me."

Dr. Cornelius's knee exploded. The Doctor screamed in agony, collapsing to the floor. He grabbed the tablecloth as went, pulling down some of the breakfast plates on him as well as the Emperor's folder.

Lechner collapsed next to him, dying from a shot to the heart.

Lord Burydan towered over the Doctor. "Insane, am I? You know, I really was on my way here to find the Countess. I was intercepted by a friend in British intelligence. He told me that you had pushed me in the fire, not the Countess—she has friends in London to whom she told this, apparently. He also told me you were working for the Americans, no need to tell me that, but we both are members of the same club. Of course, I had to find out, and he obligingly let me go on my way. I just sent the Countess in here to start a conversation on those events, so I could hear what you would say."

The Captain and Lieutenant grabbed the Emperor and shoved him outside the room. The Countess indicated to Kata that she should go with them.

Through gritted teeth, Dr. Cornelius talked for his life. "Yes, I did. However, you are wealthier than you have ever been, having worked for me. You owe me!"

Lord Burydan laughed and aimed his pistol at his head. "I owe you a bullet," he said.

"Enough!" the commanding voice of the Countess made the Lord turn around. She had retrieved her Doppelpistole from her bag and was now aiming it at him.

"What do you care about him?" the Briton. "He wanted me to kill you in the past."

"I will not let him be killed in cold blood," she replied. "I intend to reveal to the press his presence in Vienna, and to hand him over to the Americans. They will, of course, deny employing him. He will have to be tried for his crimes and executed. Put your gun down."

"By jingo, he could be sent to that electric chair I've heard about! Perhaps I could even attend! Very well! Give him to the Americans," said Lord Burydan placing his gun on the table. Lieutenant Mayr took the gun away.

"It's all working out swimmingly," the Briton continued. "I don't care that you foiled my plan in 1914, Countess. You've lost. Your crappy little Empire is over and the Germans are out for the count. We have much to thank that man Princip for!" The Briton looked down at Dr. Cornelius. "Yes, old man, I have to say I did enjoy some moments working for you, great fun!" Dr. Cornelius, being attended to by Kata, simply glared at him.

"Your fun included to killing my friend in Split," said the Countess. She was recalling how Lord Burydan had shot and killed Captain Marić in Split, a brave man whom she had come to respect.[28]

"Did I? Ah yes, I remember now. You must admit, it was a good shot on my part!"

The Countess still had her Doppelpistole aimed at him. She had had enough of this lunatic. She could feel the anger rise in her.

Lord Burydan saw the look on her face and felt cold fear. "Now, don't do anything hasty, old girl," he said, raising his hands slowly, his face now ashen.

The Countess was shaking with anger, and then she felt a hand on her shoulder.

---

[28] See *The Projector of Death* in *Tales of the Shadowmen* Vol. 19.

"There has been enough death, has there not?" She looked around. The Emperor had come back in and was speaking to her. She regained her composure.

"Quite," she said.

Lord Burydan felt relief, but thought it best to say nothing further.

A short while later, the Countess went to see the Emperor in his office. Aside from the events at Eckartsau, a republic had been declared in Vienna and the Red Guards had mounted a failed attack on Parliament. *Quite a day*, she thought. "Your highness, we are leaving now," she said.

"Good," he replied, getting up from his desk. "Thank you, Countess. I would ask you to stay. I do have some hope that something of the Empire can be saved. However, I know you wish to go to Poland, and I will not make that difficult for you,"

"Thank you," she answered. She doubted that anything could be retrieved, except... "Your highness, my priority is indeed my homeland. However, there will be continuing threats from strange technologies, alien incursions, the supernatural and the likes of Dr. Cornelius. I intend to create a loose network of people across the former empire and Europe, some kind of defense. My friends with me will be part of it, as will others. And there will be close liaison with Professor Saxton and Dr. Wells."

The Emperor looked heartened. "Thank you, Countess. I am glad to hear that. If you need my help for anything, please do not hesitate to ask. Now, I have to prepare for a delegation arriving tomorrow from Hungary."

They made their farewells. She looked back as she left, seeing him seated at his desk, alone. She would never see him again.

*Vienna. 15 November*

The handover with the British went well. Renner's guards had simply melted away upon their arrival. The key worked perfectly, the force-field deactivated and the British soldiers efficiently took the papers.

The Countess and her friends discreetly ensured the key and force-field generator did not go with them. The deal was only for the papers, not the device, which the Countess considered could be of some use to her fledgling network.

Lord Burydan got on board the lorry with the other British troops. He had attempted to take command, but a Sergeant told him to shut up and sit down, giving the Countess some satisfaction. She watched the lorry drive off.

She turned to her friends. "We will meet again, because I have no doubt our specialist experience will be needed. For now, though we are all needed elsewhere."

They made their farewells and went their different ways.

*US Army facility, France. 16 November.*

Dr. Cornelius looked at the stern visage of the US Marshal who stood over him. The Countess had deposited him with trustworthy police. The press had indeed reported on his presence in Vienna—squeezed in amongst the major political news and by various means he had been taken to a US Army unit in France where he had been handed over to this Marshal. His leg had been saved, but he would not walk properly again—or rather until he had access to his own special surgical instruments. Now he was seated in a cell, handcuffed.

"Deal?" the Marshal said. "and you were supposed to steal documents about creatures from another world, strange sciences? You seem to be preparing for an insanity plea. The court will see right through that. You're going to fry."

Dr. Cornelius knew he had failed in his mission. However, he did have one last chance—something to show that he can be useful. "I am sure you have been told to report back whatever I say to your superiors." He was still wearing the army uniform he had at Schloss Eckartsau. He slowly, so as not to alarm the marshal, reached into his tunic—somewhat awkwardly given he was in handcuffs—and pulled out a folder.

They contained the papers the Emperor had consulted regarding the United States and which had fallen to the floor when Lord Burydan had shot him. The police had failed to search him properly, given his injuries and captured state.

"Give this to them," he told the Marshal, handing the folder to him.

*The residence of Dr. Wells, Kensington, London. August 1928*

The Countess pointed to the newspaper on the table in front of her. "The Croatian politician Stjepan Radić has died from his wounds inflicted weeks ago by a gunshot from a Serb politician in Belgrade parliament. I met him during the 'Projector of Death' incident in 1916. He impressed me. The Yugoslav experiment is not going well, like much else in Europe."

Her friends Professor Saxton and Dr. Wells nodded in agreement. They were all seated in Wells' drawing room.

Professor Saxton leant forward, "In Germany, this man Hitler clearly spells trouble. He is clearly ludicrous. How can the Germans take this lunatic seriously?"

"The Versailles treaty has produced the conditions for such men to spew their bile," the Countess said.

Dr. Wells sipped his cup of tea. "And Russia—in the hands of communists. Their man Van Bork is gathering recruits to his supernatural division."

"My friends", the Countess said, "I know I have said this before, but it was a grave mistake for the Austro-Hungarian Empire to be completely dismembered. It was a protector of the small nations. Who knows how Germany may develop in the future, let alone Soviet Russia. Who will defend those nations?"

227

"Poland has its independence," said Dr. Wells. "We know you are pleased about that."

"Yes," the Countess replied. "I am, yet my country faces threats. Just a few years ago, we repelled a Soviet assault. How will the smaller nations fare in the future? We can all see the storm clouds forming."

"At least," said Dr. Wells, "systems are being put into place to deal with extraordinary threats. Within the British Empire, we have organizations and people ready to deal with alien threats and supernatural ones. Your pan-European network, Irina, has been very effective indeed."

The Countess nodded, "Yes, it was something salvaged from the Empire. Had he not died so young, I am sure Emperor Karl would at least have taken comfort from that. However, it will remain run by private citizens—the governments of Europe, I do not trust."

"I trust that does not apply to the British government," said Dr. Wells, smiling.

"Of course not," replied the Countess. "Provided you two remain in complete charge of such matters. I am grateful for your allowing the Vienna archive to be consulted by my people when needed. The governments of Europe and the Americas are setting up their own organizations, all in secret. The coming decades will see many such groups. I can only hope that there will be a high level of cooperation between them."

"Only to a degree," said Professor Saxton, "You won't get much help from the likes of Von Bork—he is likely to cause trouble in the Soviet quest for world revolution or whatever."

Their conversation was interrupted by the doorbell. The butler entered "A Dr. Cerral, sir," he announced to Dr. Wells. "He claims to be looking for an old friend at this address but will not say who."

"Dr. Cerral?" said the Countess. "That's a name of a surgeon of some notoriety—someone with questionable transplant procedures."

"Could he be armed?" Professor Saxton asked the butler.

"Very doubtful, sir. He is a wearing suit, with no apparent bulges indicating a firearm. Nonetheless, I am discreetly armed, and will be outside, should you wish to see him."

"I think we shall see what the fellow wants," said Dr. Wells. "We also have certain concealed defenses in here in any event."

The butler showed Dr. Cerral in. All three friends stood up to greet him.

Dr. Cerral was a thin man with a closely cropped haircut. "I am Dr. Wells, the owner of this residence" said Wells, and these are my friends, Countess Irina Petrovski and Professor Sir Alexander Saxton."

Dr. Cerral looked at them all. "I must apologize to you all; I am looking for an old medical friend, but I appear to have come to the wrong address." He looked at the Countess. "However, I think I recognize you—you are a journalist, are you not?"

*There is something familiar about this man,* the Countess thought. She felt uneasy. "Yes, I occasionally write articles for the European press about Poland," she said, glancing at her friends who understood immediately something was up.

"And you, Dr. Cerral, your name is also familiar."

"Ah" he said. "I am not *that* notorious surgeon," he replied. There was something about the emphasis on the word 'that' which made the Countess tense.

"As I say," said Dr. Cerral, "I was looking for an old friend, to say good-bye. You see, I have been working for an American medical firm since the war, most recently here in London, but my relations with them have broken down somewhat, and I am leaving for new horizons." He smiled at her. "I just wanted to pay my respects to my friend before leaving. I have taken enough of all your time. I apologize again for disturbing you."

With that, he promptly left.

The three friends looked at each other, and all swiftly went outside, only to see a car driving off in the distance. "I have the license plate number," said the butler, who was already outside.

"Please ask the police to try and find the vehicle and the driver. I doubt they will find him, but we must try," said the Countess.

"Use my authority to get them to do so," said Dr. Wells.

They went inside. "Well, Countess, what was that about?" asked Professor Saxton.

"I cannot be certain, but I think that may have been Dr. Cornelius Kramm. There was something in his manner."

"The Americans executed him," said the Professor.

"They said they did, after a brief trial in which he pleaded guilty. Let us re-call that the Americans severely restricted those who could watch the execution. Your countryman Lord Burydan—who himself has hardly paid for his crimes—was most disappointed at not being allowed to see it."

"Why would Dr. Cornelius come here?" asked Dr. Wells.

"Just to make sure I know he is alive—and that I cannot do anything about it. Even if the police catch him, what could we then do? He has changed his face, how could we prove he is Dr. Cornelius, who is legally dead? The Americans would hardly admit to keeping him alive to work for them."

"There seems little we can do then," said the Professor.

"We can alert our networks. Assuming it is indeed Dr. Cornelius, it is best that he is considered a potential active threat—whatever the Americans say.

"Now, what say we go to one of London's finer restaurants?"

Meanwhile. Dr. Cerral drove through the Kensington streets. He was high-ly amused at his little farewell. After a short while, he parked the vehicle and left it—he had stolen it after all. He took out an envelope from inside his suit jacket and briefly checked the contents. Inside were tickets for voyage on a 1st class liner to Bolivia. *New horizons*, he thought.

**John Gallagher:** *Shadowmen* **(illustration)**

*With this story, Martin Gately also completes his latest multi-part saga, one fea-turing Jules Verne's Robur—more precisely, Young Robur, since this is about the early days of the future would-be conqueror and Master of the World. Like Captain Nemo initially, or Arnould Galopin's Doctor Omega, Robur was not given an origin story, not in the 1886 novel, or in its 1904 sequel. This has ena-bled Martin to spin a rich tapestry around this mysterious figure, one that has taken us all over the world and beyond...*

## Martin Gately: *Young Robur and The Masada Pattern*

*That which happened long, long before...*

Over twenty years ago, Grand Pater Platanus founded the Christian reli-gious community of Woodlanders Haven in the forests of Northern California. Those entering the community, and those born within it, were given the names of trees and plants to symbolize their closeness with nature. Then, a devastating forest fire destroyed the Woodlanders Haven compound. Although no one was killed, a number of the inhabitants were very severely burned. They were kept alive by the ministrations of Sister Avellana, the chief nurse.

Grand Pater Platanus determined that God was displeased with the Wood-landers, and sought to introduce stricter and more fundamentalist doctrine which was to be enforced by a new cadre of religious police formed out of the injured but now recovering burns victims; now known as the Eschar—"the Scarred." The Eschar wore white robes and bandages to hide their disfigurement.

The Woodlanders traveled away from California and chanced upon two people during the journey, Professor Oxalis, a naturalist, engineer and former associate of Platanus who had left the community previously on a personal voy-age of scientific discovery. And the young French chef, Tapage, who provision-ally joined the Woodlanders, but refused to relinquish his name. Tapage took on the role of spokesman for the Woodlanders when they had to interact or negoti-ate with outsiders.

In an attempt to divert Oxalis away from his potentially blasphemous re-search, Grand Pater Platanus presented the Professor with the baby son of two of the Eschar to raise as his own. This was the boy, Robur, to whom Oxalis sought to bestow all of his scientific knowledge, and in doing so, fostered in him a de-sire to be a pioneer of powered flight.

Ultimately, a new Woodlanders community was founded deep in the desert of the Arizona Territory, its privacy assured by The Forest of Mirrors—a mirage creating device designed by Oxalis which rendered the small town virtually in-visible from a distance.

*That which has happened more recently...*

Inevitably, the clash between the fundamentalist religion of Platanus and the science of Oxalis resulted in an irresolvable conflict between the two men, and Oxalis was cast out.

But it was Oxalis who had brought the Woodlanders to the desert, and he did so with an ulterior motive. His research had led him to believe that the legendary race of intelligent insects known as the Anu Sinom were a reality, not a myth. He found their hive and lived with them and their Hopi allies while building a prototype flying machine.

Robur was still bereft at the absence of Oxalis when he found the injured Deputy Sheriff Thaddeus Frycollin in the desert and brought him to the Woodlanders Haven to recuperate following his battle with outlaws. His arrival set off a train of events which would culminate in Platanus seeking revenge against Oxalis and causing his death, and Robur and Frycollin traveling fifty years into the future via an energy curtain which resembled an *aurora borealis*.

They eventually returned from that war-torn future with the British airship *Venger* and its crew only to have Frycollin lynched at the hands of the Ku Klux Klan riders in North Carolina.

Meanwhile, Robur's former sweetheart, Artemisia, was sent to the town of Rock Ridge on a special mission by Grand Pater Platanus.

*That which is happening now...*
*Panko Saloon, Rock Ridge, Arizona Territory, 1867*

Artemisia had heard the man crying out in the night, and Dr. Johnson arrive for him. The sick man's room was only just along the landing. The crying out had stopped now, so she presumed the man was dead. It would've been a busy night for the doctor. People would've been dying all over town, one way or another. She had wanted for a long time to join the elect Eschar and thereby be promised a seat at the right hand of God in the Kingdom to come. But the attainment of this ambition had not been easy. It had been degrading to lay with the men who came to the saloon and put down their cash to take their pleasure with her. Had she really only been here for three days? It seemed like months. She thought back to how on the first night she had snuck out just before dawn and put the slow-dissolving poison into the town well. She also thought back to a week ago when her husband, Grand Pater Platanus, had injected her with a syringe, telling her that she would be a carrier, but not a victim, of the disease within her.

She readied the two flasks she had been given. Her stealthy crusade against the sin and godlessness of the outside world was almost over.

With two kicks, Artemisia's bedroom door splintered open. The man who had kicked it in was the Mayor of Rock Ridge and one of Artemisia's last clients. It was obvious that he had dressed hurriedly and not shaved. He looked pale and feverish.

"What have you given me?" he demanded. "What have you given meeee?" he repeated desperately.

His voice was thick and sluggish, as if he had a swollen tongue.

"Everything I touched you with… put inside you… is diseased… suppurating," he pointed at her with an ulcerated index finger which was dripping pus from its end liker a tap with a leaky washer.

"Keep away from me! Don't touch me!" begged Artemisia.

"You're spreading some kind of leprosy," judged the Mayor. "But you won't give it to no one else."

Reaching into his jacket pocket, he pulled out a small Derringer pistol and aimed it at the girl. Artemisia knew that it could not end like this. Her mission for Grand Pater Platanus was not yet complete. She flew at him like a fury, grabbing his wrist with surprising strength and forcing the Derringer away from her. She raked the Mayor's face with the nails of her free hand. Then there was a muffled report as the miniature pistol went off. The bullet had gone upwards through the underside of the Mayor's jaw and then through the already necrotizing tongue he had used to pleasure Artemisia the previous night. The bullet continued to burrow upward through the man's brain, but did not have the power or momentum to burst out of the top of his skull. The Mayor voided his bowels and collapsed.

Artemisia knew that the sound of the shot would bring men running. There was no time to waste. She opened the first of the two flasks of accelerant and poured it over the bedsheets, furniture and the floor. The second flask she poured over herself. She lit one of the special matches Platanus had given her and threw it onto the bed. A second match she held to her oil-soaked nightdress. A blazing conflagration began to devour the room and its occupants, both living and dead. Artemisia knew only joy. There wasn't a scintilla of doubt or regret in her mind. She began her ascent to the Right Hand of God.

After the whole saloon was ablaze, the flames were whipped up by a strong easterly wind. Soon, the entire town was burning.

It was a day and half later when Idaho Jones and Robur rode into the still-smoldering remains of Rock Ridge.

"There was a saloon girl here who said she was from the Woodlanders Haven," explained Jones. "She was carrying some kind of disease—a fatal disease—she gave it to her clients."

"The name of the girl?" asked Robur.

"I think they said her name was Artemisia."

Robur choked back a sob. She had been his first love—his only love. She had left him without revealing why shortly before he and Frycollin had departed the Woodlanders Haven.

"They say she put something in the well too—a poison, but it also turned the water flammable. The more water they used, the worse the fire got," continued Jones.

"This is the doing of Platanus," said Robur. "He is bringing about the final confrontation with the authorities of this World that he has always prophesied."

"You are right. The sheriff has reported the poisoning and arson to the Governor already. The Army will be deployed to locate the Haven."

"And a prolonged, deliberate search by Army scouts would probably find it," confessed Robur. "Ironic that these people drink the beer the Haven produces, but don't know where it is."

"That's another thing," began Jones. "The last consignment of Woodlanders Haven beer was poisoned; a slow poison—thirty men died in agony."

"We have to get to the Haven and depose Platanus before the Army lay siege to it and cause a massacre," concluded Robur.

"I suppose this means just you and me are headed for it?" asked Jones.

"Yes, it is too far to return to the *Venger*'s place of concealment at Meteor Crater and enlist the aid of her crew in this enterprise," said Robur. "We could perhaps find allies amongst the Hopi and the Anu Sinom, but I am reluctant to involve them."

"Is there no one in the Haven we could rely on for help?" queried Jones.

"Maybe just one man, but even that I am not sure of now," said Robur.

Meanwhile, in the brig of the aforementioned airship *Venger*, medicine show confidence trickster and potential future President of the United States of America, Walter Trump had a series of complaints and questions.

"This food is slop! I won't eat it!" he began. "I'm used to the finest meals, the best hotels. You can't hold me prisoner here, I've served my time, and a lot of it in the prison hospital. I'm not a well man. Why are you holding me? What is this place anyway? Is the United States at war with Great Britain? Are you aware I may take legal action against you?"

"I can answer none of your questions at this time," said Tom Turner, neutrally. "Perhaps when Captain Robur returns, he will be able to enlighten you.

In the adjacent cell, Trina Dressard, former agent of the Prussian Empire and part of a conspiracy to subvert American politics and values, and bring about a global war, sat quietly and bided her time. She would not waste her breath on the stoical and iron-willed Turner, but there were others who could perhaps be seduced into helping her escape.

Robur and Idaho Jones rode their horses across the scrubby chaparral grass of the High Desert, and ultimately made camp in the shadow of a large boulder. Idaho Jones insisted on standing guard after they heard the cough-like cry of a mountain lion out in the twilight. He was happy to take the long first watch and let Robur sleep. He knew that the young man was unaccustomed to long horse rides, whereas, in his youth, Jones had been a cowboy on the Skimmerhorn Trail which ran from Texas to Colorado.

By the time Idaho Jones woke Robur, it was almost dawn, the fiery desert dawn of late July which starts a delicate mauve-purple before turning blast furnace orange. Jones settled down on his bedroll and told Robur to awaken him in about an hour. Robur allowed him a little longer than that and even cooked bacon and beans for breakfast, but the pair were soon on their way.

Once they were within about four miles of the Haven, their course intersected a trail which was heading straight for the town. It was the tracks of a light cart or wagon. Robur postulated that it was Tapage's vehicle, which he used to deliver the Haven's beer to local communities. The trail would not be as easy for an Army scout to follow as it perhaps first appeared for Oxalis had placed in the ground a device which scuffed over the tracks and laid a false trail in the wrong direction. It was strange how reliant the Haven was on the scientific and engineering inventions developed by Oxalis, particularly since Platanus so strongly disapproved of science. Oxalis had perhaps been the ultimate polymath, a master rather than a jack of all sciences; equally at home with engineering as with biology. Robur did not doubt that the strange and deadly plague unleashed at Rock Ridge by Artemisia had originally been part of Oxalis' menagerie of weird diseases in his biological laboratory.

The trail scuffing device would've had them believe that the cart turned south towards the great field of boulders where Robur had first encountered Frycollin. But Robur knew better. They carried on towards the blank, empty haze which danced just above the horizon.

"I'm not sure this is right," said Idaho Jones. "There's nothing out there."

"Trust me," smiled Robur. "I lived within that mirage for almost my entire life."

As they got nearer, and still nearer, the efficacy of the "Pepper's Ghost"-style illusion generated by the Forest of Mirrors started to break down. They dismounted and carefully picked their way through the strange array of curved reflectors. In his childhood, Robur had spent countless hours helping Oxalis to keep the mirrors clean and polished, now they had a dusty and neglected look.

"Platanus isn't keeping things maintained," said Robur. "He doesn't care about the community's invisibility anymore."

"Then he wants the confrontation that's coming."

For the first time, Idaho Jones noticed that the soft blurring of the distant vista had dissipated and he was able to see directly ahead the cluster of white stucco buildings and the central campanile. He was about to turn to Robur and say something about the nearness of the Haven when the ground seemed to give way beneath Robur's feet.

He fell in a cascade of sand and loose rock, and his horse fell with him. Yet, this was not some naturally occurring geological disturbance; he was falling into a steel-walled trap, some kind of metal box.

235

Idaho Jones' horse reared up in fright, so he grasped its reins firmly and led it away from the newly-appeared sandy maw to avoid his mount falling in on top of Robur. Jones was about to remove the lariat from his saddle with a view to raising Robur out of the pit when a steel plate slid over the entrance to the hole, trapping his young ally inside.

Jones' assessment was that this was a sensible time to make a withdrawal. It would be of little use if he were captured as well. He remounted and spurred his horse into a trot, allowing it to weave its own way through the great mirrors. Nevertheless, he did feel bad about abandoning Robur. But the best way of getting Robur the Hell out of there was to share his intelligence with the Army. Perhaps the plan for deposing Platanus had always been a forlorn one, or maybe Robur could still pull off some sort of insurrection if he told the general population what Platanus had been up to. Surely, they would not approve of the destruction of Rock Ridge. And then Idaho Jones remembered: this was a community subject to extreme religious thinking and indoctrination. They only had to be told that the inhabitants of Rock Ridge were sinners and they would approve of their fate.

Perhaps it was fortunate that Robur's horse broke its neck in the fall, or he would have been trapped inside the steel cube with the panicked creature and potentially severely trampled. Robur realized almost immediately that he had lost his Royal Naval Air Service issue heavy revolver somewhere in the pit. It had slipped from his holster during the fall. He spread out his fingers and moved them through the sand around him, partly just to pass the time. Of course, the pistol could have been under the horse, which would have been impossible to lift. In any event, he did not find it.

It was difficult to judge the passage of time precisely while entombed in the inky blackness of the pit, but after about half an hour the air became stale and unwholesome. Was this the purpose of the trap, simply to kill intruders by depriving them of air? Such a tactic would not work on a deployment of US cavalrymen. They could not all be trapped in such a fashion.

Then there came the sound of metal grating against stone, and it seemed for a moment as if the pit was bathed in light. In fact, the illumination merely came from an ordinary oil lantern. A small door-aperture had opened, and as his eyes quickly adjusted from total darkness to light, he could make out two figures dressed entirely in white, their faces wrapped in clean white bandages; a man and a woman. Could these be his parents, for they were among the Eschar? The odds were that they were not his parents, the odds were that he would never know either way. He called to them.

"It is I, Robur, apprentice and foster son to Oxalis."

And the call was returned. "Be glad, for this thy brother was dead, and is alive again; and was lost, and is found."

Perhaps Robur had been away too long for he had almost forgotten that the Eschar never truly conversed, they merely quoted biblical verses.

At Fort Courage, Idaho Jones' report on the dangers of approaching the Haven was met with a combination of skepticism and incredulity by Major McIntosh.

"My entire company will be riding on this Haven of yours come first light," assured McIntosh," and I don't suppose it will present any problems my men aren't able to handle."

"I hope you are right," said Idaho Jones. "But this isn't an attack on the encampment of a small group of hostiles. There will be innocent women and children in the community who probably know nothing of the poisonings and arson."

"The information I've received from the Governor is that the population of the Haven may be infected with disease, in which case, they will all be subject to a military quarantine. I've already wired Fort Humboldt to put them on alert in case we need their medical assistance and expertise."

Jones knew that McIntosh was a good man and no fool, but he had difficulty convincing him that any real and substantial danger lay ahead.

Because of his status as a Secret Service Man, Jones was accorded every courtesy and even given a private room at the fort usually reserved for visiting senior officers. He carried his saddlebags into the room and removed an item even Robur did not realize he'd been given custody of. It was something called a radio transmitter and an anachronism in this time period. It had been given to him to use only in the event of an extreme emergency by Tom Turner, First Mate of the *Venger*, who was chagrined at being ordered to stay behind in command of the airship when he felt that his role encompassed keeping Robur out of trouble. Idaho Jones activated the battery pack, put on the headset and waited for the equipment to warm up, just as he had been instructed.

"Raider to *Venger*, Raider to *Venger*... do you hear me?"

"We read you strength 2, Raider," said Tom Turner from the *Venger*'s steering room. "Go ahead."

"Robur has been captured in the vicinity of Woodlanders Haven. I've retreated to Fort Courage. A military expedition will move against the Haven in the morning."

"We can be with you before then and join in the attack," suggested Turner.

"Robur wouldn't want that," said Idaho Jones. "You know his strictest order is that the existence of the *Venger* be kept secret."

"And you know as well as I do that there have already been a few newspaper articles based on eyewitness accounts," said Turner.

"But they weren't widely believed. Most people thought those 'Phantom Airship' reports were just *Prairie Gazette* fillers and hoaxes," said Idaho Jones. "Let's wait and see how the situation looks after the cavalry assault. The commanding officer seems to be a good man."

"Very well. Keep me informed of all developments, Raider. *Venger* out."

Tom Turner descended down the series of ladders which led from the steering room to the sick bay, with a view to visiting the facility's only patient: Seraphina. Turner arrived to see her blood pressure being checked by a medical orderly. He was acutely aware that they had a sick bay without a doctor, the ship's physician having been left behind in Dahomey in 1916. He wondered how she was faring. It seemed unlikely that they would ever return to their own time to find out. The *Venger* had almost been destroyed by its journey through the energy curtain to the nineteenth century, and nothing but death likely awaited them if they did return. It was far better that they placed themselves under the leadership of Captain Robur. Though he did rather wish that the Captain had procured them a new doctor as a crew member rather than a cowboy Secret Service agent and a newspaperman. Idaho Jones was a fierce and resourceful warrior, albeit somewhat baffled by the futuristic engineering technology of the Venger. Gideon Spilitt had proved himself a natural logistics man and record keeping clerk. His journalist's curiosity also meant he had been easy to train up to do some of the simpler engineering jobs.

Nevertheless, it was a doctor they really needed. Of course, they had also been handed a couple of prisoners, Trina Dressard, Idaho Jones' old enemy, and the con man Walter Trump. But with no illness or injury amongst the crew, the sick bay seemed to have been turned over entirely to being a maternity ward for a single patient, the beautiful and regal Dahomey Amazon who was now four and a half months pregnant with the late Deputy Frycollin's child.

"I wouldn't want to cause you any undue distress," said Turner. "But I feel duty-bound to inform you that Captain Robur has been captured by the enemy while approaching the Woodlanders Haven. He was with Idaho Jones, who was unable to effect his rescue."

Turner thought for a moment that she was going to give no reaction at all, that she would internalize it totally or that the capture of Robur meant little to her, but he was wrong. She closed her eyes as if experiencing monumental grief and then said:

"The human race overestimates the virtue of bravery. I can sense that it is a boy-child who grows within my swollen belly, and I tell you this now. I will raise him to be a coward. For it is the cowards who live long and happy lives at home, and brave men who die dreadful and untimely deaths."

Turner couldn't argue with this because in essence it was true, but he hoped she would relent, for though he had only known Frycollin for a short time, he was sure he would not want his son brought up in such a way.

Airman Alistair had been picked by Turner to be the jailer for Trina Dressard and Walter Trump, mainly because he was the oldest man aboard, and as such, Turner felt that he ought to have a certain immunity from the seductive charms of the Prussian agent. But the *Venger*'s first mate was obviously unaware of the ancient adage, "there's no fool like an old fool." At first, Alistair was merely flattered by the young woman's advances, but soon he was quite convinced that she was in love with him, and the feeling was quickly reciprocated. Noisy and therefore hardly clandestine lovemaking took place on the iron cot at the back of the woman's cell. In the adjacent cell, Trump stopped up his ears with torn bits of cloth and fragments of soap to blot out the sounds from next door, tolerating them because Dressard had shared her plans with him.

For old Alistair, there was only one question: How would he and his beloved Trina leave the *Venger* and start a new life together? Surely the airship would not be hidden in the crater for many more days. An opportunity was bound to present itself.

The progress of the line of cavalry had been slow, partly due to the caution of the scouts, and also an over-wariness by Major McIntosh who seemed to be expecting traps and ambushes when they were still miles from their objective. The fierce and merciless sun was high overhead and the familiar protective haze which obscured the Haven was now before them. Idaho Jones looked at the shimmer through his telescope and then answered McIntosh's latest questions.

"No, I've no idea precisely how many traps, but unless you lose a substantial number of men, I would recommend continuing with the attack and freeing them later."

There was nothing else to say so McIntosh ordered a bugler to sound the advance. The discordant notes echoed back off the nearby boulders and the encircling stony hills like the call of some prehistoric leviathan. The Cavalry troop moved forward. Practically every man was a veteran of skirmishes with hostile Indians. They had one other thing in common, a sort of mental image of their adversaries—religious fanatics armed with muskets and hunting rifles, or bladed agricultural implements. But these suppositions were quite wrong.

The column got nearer to the mirage haze. And nearer. There was a clanking sound which reminded Idaho Jones of the working of a windmill or waterwheel, and then the haze illusion vanished completely. The mirrors comprising the fabled Forest of Mirrors had changed alignment. About half of them now pointed up to the sky—to the sun—and the other half directly at the Cavalry column. There was a smell of burning flesh, both human and horse, a charring of uniform fabric, as well as the wood of weapons. The first dozen or so men were incinerated. Half dead horses staggered away, still carrying their smoking, cadaverous riders.

The column had been caught like a line of ants beneath a child's burning glass. Major McIntosh screamed the order to retreat.

"Withdraw! Withdraw!"

Half the remaining men, including Idaho Jones and Major McIntosh, took shelter in the cover provided by the field of boulders. The other half rode away at top speed across open ground, and there was nothing to spare these men the horror of the heat beam. For a second, they were a horde of fiery, galloping ghosts and then little more than smoldering bones. The beam arced relentlessly back and forth, in some places turning the desert sand into beads of glass. Tears streamed down Major McIntosh's face. He had lost more than half of his command in less than a minute, and without even gaining sight of the enemy.

"Robur did not warn us of this," said Idaho Jones. "He obviously knew nothing of it."

"Or he's part of this conspiracy and an enemy of the United States," raged McIntosh.

From their position of concealment, Idaho Jones scanned the terrain with his spyglass.

"There are still injured soldiers moving out there," said the Secret Service Man. "I count at least three."

The Major went to grab the telescope from him, but he held onto it tightly, as if there were more to see.

"I can see heliograph flashes between the Haven belltower and a couple of the other buildings," said Idaho Jones. "Someone up there is giving orders."

"We need to recover the wounded," said McIntosh. "Can you signal the Haven to arrange a truce?"

"Sure, I have a signaling mirror in my saddlebag," began Idaho Jones," but…"

"But nothing," said McIntosh. "Ask for a truce and I'll lead a rescue party of volunteers. I don't expect any man to do something I wouldn't do myself."

"Your valor is not what's at question here, Major," said Idaho Jones. "I'm under your orders and I'll send that message, but we've already seen how merciless they are. I wouldn't trust them any further than I could kick them."

Jones moved clear of the boulders and from a crouched position commenced to send the request to the Haven for a truce in Morse code. And then he waited.

"There's no response," said Idaho Jones, after about five minutes had elapsed.

"Very well," said McIntosh, and with that he and his two volunteers started to make their way across the open sand in a sort of hunched over run.

Jones flashed the message again in case it had been missed or misunderstood the first time.

*Request truce while we recover wounded. No hostilities at this time.*

Again, there was no answering signal directed to him in Morse. Just random flashes between the belltower and some of the other buildings. He put down his rectangular signal mirror and took up his telescope again so he could monitor the progress of the rescue party. They were closing in on the injured men at a sprint now. Jones saw them start to pick up the survivors, and then one of the rescuers put his man back down. Either, it turned out he was a corpse, or he had just expired.

McIntosh and the other trooper began the long walk back. The cavalry man without a burden had been ordered to run back to the cover of the boulders as swiftly as he could. He arrived back at Jones' position within just a minute or two, but McIntosh and the other volunteer, Sergeant Duignan, lagged far behind.

Idaho Jones noticed a shifting, almost a shuffling, in the position of the mirror lenses. He ordered the troopers to open fire on the mirrors; he was unsure if they would take his orders, but they did. It was too late. The withering power of the heat beam lighted on the four men who were out in the open, and turned them to charcoal scarecrows. The troopers' carbine shots ricocheted harmlessly off the mirrors, for they were constructed of steel, not glass.

Jones directed the surviving troopers back to the cover of the boulders. A moment later, a wash of wild, boiling heat rippled over the great stones. But, as long as they stayed in the shadow of the boulders they could not be harmed. And just a few minutes after that, he led the men away at high speed. They rode off, keeping their backs to the boulder field until they passed over the horizon and then headed Northwest. They had lost a lot of good men for the rather meager intelligence that the Haven could not be taken by a standard cavalcade approach.

They had all been naive. He realized now that he needed advice from the greatest tactician he had ever known, Major Steve Clark. Clark's secondment to the Secret Service had ended, and he had returned to the Army. Fortunately, he was nearby.

Robur awoke again and found that his situation had not altered. He lay on some kind of uncomfortable wooden-slatted bed, propped up by hard, lumpy pillows that might as well have been sacks of grain. His wrists were bound comparatively loosely with something that felt like piano wire. Last time he'd been awake, he'd worked on loosening those wires, but had been forced to stop when the pain of the restraints slicing into the top of his wrists had become too extreme. This was his first visit to one of the Eschar's "re-education" chambers, but it was much as the whispers had described it.

At the far end of the room was a wooden frame containing taut white cloth, something like a bedsheet, and this was the back-projected screen used in a continuous magic lantern show of alternating images of Heaven and Hell. During all of his waking hours, a male Eschar sat on a small wooden stool at his side and whispered into his ear in hushed but oddly menacing tones the Ten Commandments and a selection of verses from the Book of Revelations. Robur had heard tell of how this was supposed to snap the minds of transgressors, make them beg for forgiveness, and so on, but, as a deeply religious person, he merely found it to be meditative and highly therapeutic.

For about twenty minutes he had reflected on the Sixth Commandment, "Thou shalt not kill," and he thought of all the people he had killed by ordering the firebombing of the Ku Klux riders picnic. Yet, his conscience was clear. Perhaps he did not exactly consider himself to be an instrument of God's vengeance, but on Judgement Day, he would be happy to justify his actions to the Almighty.

The holy whispering continued. Judgement Day was still far off. His priority should be to escape and reunite with Idaho Jones, but he was in a quandary. Might it be possible for him to subdue the Eschar, depose Platanus and perhaps even install himself as leader of the Woodlanders Haven, before the likely attack by the army? No, it was pure foolishness. He had lost track of time, for all he knew the Haven had already been besieged by the military. His priority had to be escape. He had to know exactly what was going on.

He worked at his wrist bindings again. Suddenly it all seemed easier. Some kind of lubricant was allowing him to slip his hand free. Then he realized this lubricant was his own blood. He struck his Eschar guardian hard in the face. The man fell from the stool and Robur threw himself on top of him. This was no time for squeamishness or second thoughts. He applied his knee to the Eschar's trachea and crushed it. His attempt to escape must not be thwarted. The lives of everyone in the Haven might depend on it.

After a single rattling wheeze, the Eschar was dead. Robur turned and saw that the continuous magic lantern show was still in operation. While he felt he had made little concession to stealth, the female Eschar operating the slideshow had not heard the demise of her counterpart. Robur picked up the wooden stool by one of its legs and held it like a club. He strode to the back of the cloth screen where the woman still labored away to produce the Heaven and Hell slide show. She looked up just as he belted her across the temple with the stool.

Robur returned to the man and started to remove his white robes and bandages. He was going to need a disguise. He unwound the tight white bandages from the man's face. What lay beneath was what he had expected. The epidermis flayed away by the cruel flames of the forest fire all those years ago. The nose gone. The eyelids half-destroyed. The mere vestiges of ears. He knew his parents were lost amongst the Eschar. So, could this be his true father? In his desperation to escape had he snuffed out the life of the one who had sired him? No, he had not. For Oxalis was his only true father. And Platanus had been directly responsible for the death of Oxalis by releasing the lethal worms that had attacked the combined Hopi and Anu Sinom underground settlement.

Robur dressed himself in the male Eschar's garments, and applied the bandages as tightly as he could to his own face, in imitation of the style used by the Eschar. Inevitably, he was reminded of the raiment worn by the Ku Klux Riders. He left the re-education chamber and started looking for the stairs into the Haven proper. To be an Eschar was the perfect disguise: anonymous, entitled to be anywhere, since their job was to observe the populace, and they were not expected to speak.

Robur wended his way towards the Council chamber, which had a religious as well as civic function. Not only was Platanus often found there during the day, the Eschar frequently prayed in the chamber's side chapels. He adopted the slightly arrogant swagger of the typical Eschar, and, arriving at the chamber door, paused to read the noticeboard, which simply indicated *Private audiences with the Grand Pater*. To secrete himself in the chamber for such audiences would be a good way of judging the concerns of the Haven folk.

He entered and took a place in one of the Rosewood pews, assumed an attitude of prayer, and waited to see when Platanus would arrive. He would not have to wait long, within ten minutes Platanus entered with a handful of Eschar, and they approached the altar. On it the Eschar assembled something Robur had never seen before. It was a large set of ceremonial or ornamental scales. But what they placed in the scale's cups, he had seen before. It was two of the glass globes Oxalis had used for the transportation of germs in his disease bestiary. Robur was surprised that Platanus had had the knowledge and skill to maintain the bestiary after Oxalis's departure. He was also aware that the bestiary contained samples and hybrids of the most dangerous diseases on Earth. Ominously, Robur could hear thunder in the distance, a storm was obviously approaching. Platanus had entered carrying a small wooden chest, which he put down next to the altar.

A few minutes later, the Eschar ushered in the first person due a private audience. Robur was both pleased and surprised to see that it was his old friendly rival, Carpinus. His adversary in many of the Haven's chili-eating contests. Robur fondly recalled the last such competition in which he had participated, where Frycollin had declared him to have the digestion of an ostrich. But Carpinus had not sought this audience on a frivolous or trivial matter. His face was streaked with tears and flushed with hot anger. The young man looked as though he had summoned all of his inner strength for this confrontation with the Haven's leader. Robur had the overwhelming urge to comfort him, and regretted that he could not.

Carpinus went to the bowl of sacred oil near the entrance and anointed his own hands and forehead, as was traditional before addressing the Grand Pater.

"What is it, Carpinus?" asked Platanus, "Why do you come here today?"

"You know!" said Carpinus. "You know full well! It is your decision to dissolve all of the marriages in the Haven, and take all the women for yourself, even though the holy ceremony itself says, that what God has brought together no man may put asunder."

"I am no ordinary man," began Platanus, "and these are the End Times, when a Sinful Messiah will bring a benediction of love to all women. Uniquely, my seed may be able to survive the coming Apocalypse, and so must be placed in all women."

Carpinus screamed through the tears, "Sister Myrtle and I have been married for less than a month and already you have taken her abed. It is cruel and unfair; we are in love and I am not allowed to see her."

Robur's mind was numb with what he had heard. There had always been a streak of vengeful cruelty in Platanus, but now he was just insane. A power-drunk despot, devoid of any morality.

"These are matters of no import Carpinus," said Platanus. "The great enemy Satan himself is at our gates in the form of the forces of the federal government. Go to your abode and pray. Pray for your own redemption."

The Eschar dragged Carpinus from the Council chamber. Robur, cold with rage, continued his pretense of prayer, seemingly ignoring what had transpired. He knew there was no action he could take—yet—but it was obvious when the invading forces reached this chamber, Platanus would break open the disease globes. And did even he know what that would mean? Oxalis had abandoned his hybrid germ experiments for fear he was creating a weapon capable of destroying the entire population of the world. In the distance, he could still hear thunder, but now he knew it was artillery fire.

On a rock promontory about a quarter of a mile from the Haven, four US Army cannons under the command of Major Steve Clark continued to direct their fire at the Forest of Mirrors. Most of the steel mirrors were now so much wreckage. The capability of the lenses to be used as a weapon had been destroyed.

The veterans of the first expedition to the Haven had been reinforced with a fresh cavalry regiment. The veterans were out for blood, there were whisperings and murmurings that they would be taking no quarter. A massacre was in the offing. Clark hadn't seen men so riled for years; it reminded him of times when the cavalry had been called in to avenge mass murder by hostiles. He doubted if any of the Haven's men would be taken alive. He would do what he could to save the women and children, just as he would in a hostile's encampment.

While the cannons continued to discharge, a lot of men sat outside their tents, sharpening their sabers. Their weapon of choice for revenge. But this was an enemy Clark had not yet got the measure of. He expected more deadly ruses, he expected mass casualty and death. Where was Jones? He could not see him. This seemed to be a different Jones to the one he had known at the time of the Prussian conspiracy just months before—more secretive. Clark's instincts normally served him well, and his instinct was that Jones' allegiance was elsewhere. Where was the man? Surely even he wouldn't have sought to sneak away and approach the Haven while the artillery barrage was still in effect.

No, Idaho Jones had not left the cavalry camp on the promontory, he just needed a little privacy to operate his radio sending set. The battery pack was almost dead, he perhaps had enough charge for two short messages.

"Raider to *Venger*, Raider to *Venger*."

"We read you, Raider," said Turner "But barely on strength one. Make your message quick before your pack dies."

"Launch and head for the Haven. There's a rock formation with an army camp about a quarter of a mile due south. Land there. I need you in reserve. I don't know how this attack is going to play out."

"Understood and will comply," said Turner, "The closer I am to Robur, the happier I am."

Steve Clark opened up the flap of the tent and drank up the sight of Idaho Jones with the strange electrical device. Clark drew his Colt.

"Talk fast, Idaho," said Clark. "What is this thing? If Trina Dressard has seduced you into working for the Prussians, I'll shoot you where you are."

"It's a wireless telegraph device, not Prussian, but British. I'm working with a British military group who are opposed to the Haven. Their leader is American though, the young guy I told you about, Robur."

"And how did they come to have a mechanism like this?" said Clark, pushing his hat further back on his head.

"Are you sure you want the truth?" asked Jones.

"Since you only ever tell the truth, I guess I'll have to swallow whatever you give me," said Clark.

"The British are from the future, trapped here in their own past. You'll see soon enough. I have just asked them to come here, and they will be arriving in a kind of balloon ship that won't be built for decades."

"You've either taken to telling some tall prairie tales, cowboy," said Clark, "Or the world is a very different place to what I've been imagining."

For perhaps the first time in his life, Robur felt as if he was locked in a total stalemate. There seemed to be no prospect of his grabbing the bestiary germ globes and making off with them. He was stuck in the entrance to the side chapel, trying not to draw too much attention to himself, but if he received a random order from Platanus he would have to at least make a pretense of obeying him. That would likely take him out of the Council chamber. He could still hear sporadic artillery fire, so an invasion of the Haven by the military was presumably some way off.

The door swung open and the next citizen due a private audience entered. Again, Robur had to resist the urge to greet the newcomer. He wanted to embrace his old friend, the French chef Tapage.

"Have you made the necessary preparations?" Platanus asked Tapage.

"Yes, Grand Pater," answered the chef. "The apricot squash has been prepared in sufficient volumes for everyone to drink of it."

"Good, good," said Platanus. He then reached down to the wooden case he had placed by the altar and opened it. "This is Nithon fungus, the final ingredient. Add it to the fruit juice in all of the communal bowls. Leave it to the Eschar to ensure that all drink. The enemy are at our gates. It is time for the Masada Solution. Just as the Jews at the ancient fortress of Masada took their own lives, rather than fall into the hands of the Romans, so must we. A handful of girls and women who carry my seed are to be spared. These are known to the Eschar, and will be sequestered away. In due time, I will be reborn and the pattern will repeat itself."

"It shall be done, Grand Pater," said Tapage, as he took the case of fungus from the patriarch and snapped it shut.

Beneath the tight bandages Robur's mouth hung open. Tapage had always been the least willing of Platanus' acolytes. For him to assist in the killing of a whole population was unthinkable.

Platanus gestured to a pair of the Eschar. "Two of you go with him to monitor and assist."

Robur regretted now his position of semi-concealment in the side chapel. If only he could have gone with Tapage, reasoned with him, but if he had done that he would have left Platanus alone with the germ globes. He now needed to be in two places at once. The situation was at once intolerable and impossible. The Gordian Knot that could not be cut. Robur thought of the "Brides of Platanus" that he had impregnated. Had he used Oxalis' equipment to make them immune to the germ globes' plagues, or would they be carriers of it? And he thought of those who would be drinking Tapage's fruit juice, and then sinking into the black abyss of death. Death and the potential for death enveloped him like a cold fog.

The final supplicant for an audience with the Grand Pater was brought into the room by a remaining Eschar. It was Sister Avellana, the chief nurse of the Woodlanders Haven hospital. The normally composed and intimidating matron had obviously been crying. She made a dismissive and sweeping gesture aimed at the Eschar.

"Get them out of here," she said.

Even Robur quaked slightly. This was not a tone one adopted with the Grand Pater.

"They stay to watch and protect me, even in these final minutes of the history of the Haven."

Platanus' voice was different now, he normally spoke like a hellfire preacher, projecting to the back of the congregation. Now he was quieter and more diminished.

"You went too far when you dissolved the marriages and took the young girls into your bed—casting me out. I can't believe I didn't denounce you then, for I have always known what you are, from when you were first brought into my hospital during the Opium Wars, and to think I pitied you then, Albert."

"Speak not my old, dead name. Speak not of events which have no relevance or meaning. It is the End Times. It is Judgement Day. And you have been found wanting."

Platanus strode forward, faster than Robur had ever seen him move. His arm raised, poised to strike Avellana.

"You are an amoral monster, aside from the other girls, Myrtle, our Myrtle, is pregnant with your child instead of her husband's. Perhaps if the people knew what you truly were, the spell would be broken, and they would string you up."

Platanus struck her brutally across the face and sent her colliding with the pews, which she knocked over like skittles. Robur went to assist her, automatically righting the pews and lifting the desolate and injured woman onto them. Their eyes locked. Robur had understood and been sickened by Platanus' crimes. A flicker of recognition played across Avellana's bloody face. Yes, she had recognized Robur's eyes, for she had delivered him as a baby, and this Eschar disguise was not sufficient to obscure who he really was. And in her eyes a momentary hope was formed, until Platanus' voice started to boom.

"Stand away from her," he said to the anonymous Eschar who had moved to care for Avellana so solicitously.

"They would never have turned on me, their Messiah," said Platanus. "Now it is too late, I bring them salvation and death."

"You're sick and insane," spat Avellana.

Platanus moved forward as if he was going to brutally kick her, but Robur interposed himself. Oddly, Platanus accepted this, after all, the Eschar were the moral arbiters of all behavior even on Judgement Day.

"Not for you, the grace of death. The invaders will find you alive, and I don't doubt that your fate at their hands will be more terrible than it would be in mine."

It was almost an hour later when those invading forces began to arrive in the grounds of the Haven proper. The cavalry had dismounted, and a few soldiers were left in charge of the horses while the others moved forward in a skirmish line, with Steve Clark and Idaho Jones at the head of it.

The pristine idyllic beauty of the stucco buildings and how they were arranged had come as a surprise to Clark, who somehow had been expecting a hovel, or at least somewhere with an outward show of its malignancy. The first of the skirmish line entered a courtyard, the men spread out, making use of the available cover.

In the center of the courtyard was a fountain, and by that a small wooden trough with a large ladle in it. About a dozen men women and children lay apparently dead, their lips blue, and their clothes dyed yellow by the poison from the trough. Their beakers abandoned, some rolling back and forth in the desert breeze. Still suspecting a trap, Idaho Jones moved forward. He pulled the glove from his right hand, and put two fingers to the throat of one of the children.

"There's no discernible pulse, Major."

And these words seem to startle two Eschar from their hiding place behind a courtyard column.

"Halt! Halt!" shouted Clark. They kept running, and he gunned them down without mercy. Clark moved forwards, to examine their bodies.

"These are the ones you told me about—the burned ones?"

"The Eschar, a kind of secret religious police, I should think we are going to run into more of them. The Eschar here would have presided over these murders under Platanus' orders."

"And the only description we have of Platanus is that he looks like some kind of Old Testament prophet?" asked Clark.

"Robur said he looks like Moses, so I guess we will know him when we see him."

Clark gave the signal to move forward, but everywhere they went it was the same. In the public gardens, alleys and private dwellings, they found the Haven to be a necropolis. The population had largely drunk the juice without question, and died from it not far from the bowls in which it was contained. Some had vomited it up, but that had not saved them. Once in a while, they saw evidence that the Eschar had had to force feed someone. Once in a while, they found Eschar who had removed their bandages so they could drink.

"They all killed themselves, rather than be taken by us. What did they think we were going to do to them?"

"Don't give me that, Steve. Your men were all fired up for revenge. What would they be doing if these people were all alive right now. Would they be treated better than a hostile's camp; where they would be killing the men and raping the women?"

Clark gave no answer.

Wherever they searched it was the same. Just death. Becoming more fearless in the absence of an adversary, the invaders dispersed into pairs. Clark and Jones headed to the Council chamber and the adjacent belltower. Jones remembered all too well, the flashing heliograph command signals from the time of the heat beam attack.

Clark tested the heavy oaken double doors to the council chamber, expecting them to be locked or barred, but they started to swing open easily. He stepped through with some confidence, but with his army Colt raised. After all, Jones had told him that all weapons were forbidden in the Woodlanders Haven. Idaho Jones was right behind him, a six-shooter in his hand. Clark was shot twice, just as he cleared the threshold. One slug caught him in the shoulder, and the other clipped his ribs. He fell to the floor and rolled in pain.

"Drop your weapons," said Platanus, "I'm pretty handy with this."

Robur took cover behind the pews, anticipating a prolonged gunfight. He was astonished to see his own Royal Naval Air Service double action revolver in the hands of Platanus, pulled from the Patriarch's robe pocket just a second before.

"I surrender my weapons to no... Wait, you're Platanus? You must be kidding me," said Idaho Jones.

"I remember you, lawman," said Platanus "Though it has been many a long year."

248

Platanus' voice was so different now, oddly relaxed without his stentorian delivery, but Robur could not put his finger on who this new voice reminded him of. He put down his hood and began loosening his bandages, in readiness to reveal his identity.

"I'm fine… I'll survive just keep him covered," said Clark from the floor.

The still bleeding Avellana struggled over to him and began tending his wounds as best she could.

Robur, now the only remaining "Eschar" in the Council chamber, half stood up.

"Idaho, it's Robur, don't let him reach those glass globes, they're plague bombs."

Idaho Jones didn't even turn his head, just nodded to acknowledge Robur, and kept both of his six-shooters trained on the Patriarch.

"Robur the prodigal, and Jones the busybody lawman," said Platanus. "Fitting that you should both be here at the end." He kept his revolver leveled on Jones. "So, it's a standoff, we'll have to see who tires first." With that, he edged slightly in front of the scales and their deadly load. "But I am in a reflective mood, let me tell you the true story of this place and how it came to be. I think it will…"

There were three shots from Clark's Army Colt in quick succession. It had been a long time since Avellana had fired a weapon, but she had not forgotten. Dying, half-falling, half-reaching, Platanus dove for the scales, to grasp or smash the globes; to make sure the world died at the same time he did. Robur and Idaho Jones both rushed forwards. Robur's objective was the great bowl of sacred oil, while Jones sought to catch the falling orbs.

"Look out!" said Robur, as he smothered the globes with several pints of oil just as they broke.

"Suspended in oil, the germs will be less contagious, but we need to burn down this building and get all the soldiers and residents out of the Haven."

"It's too late for me," said Idaho Jones, oddly leveling his pistols at Robur. The Secret Service man showed Robur the back of his right hand. A tiny fleck of smashed glass from one of the globes had broken the skin. The wound was already an angry red, and starting to suppurate.

"Take Clark and the woman and get out of here," said Idaho Jones. He removed his satchel and tossed it to Robur.

"There's a radio set in there. The battery is almost dead, but you should be able to contact the *Venger*; they are nearby. Now get out of here! I don't know how contagious I am. I'll set that fire."

Robur simply said, "I am so sorry, Idaho. I will always remember you." What more could one say to a dying friend?

Robur hoisted Clark over his shoulder, as if he weighed no more than a mannequin, and urged the Haven's head nurse to leave.

"Sister Avellana, we must go now!" shouted Robur, she obeyed, but was little more than a blank faced sleepwalker, deep in shock.

They departed along the straight white corridor, away from the Council chamber and Robur heard Idaho Jones bar the door, there was a pause. Was it really long enough to set a fire? Then he heard the report of a six-shooter. And a wonderful and heroic man was no more.

At the end of the corridor, they passed through a portico and into an open courtyard. Robur saw the trough of juice and the bodies of a dozen people scattered about. Sitting apparently despondent on the edge of the fountain was Tapage.

"Robur!" shouted the chef. "What are you doing here, old friend?"

Robur was white with rage.

"I can only have been sent by God in place of an avenging angel, for I know the dreadful responsibility you bear; I have no weapon but by the Good Lord, I will tear you apart with my bare hands."

He put down the unconscious form of Clark.

"And to think I once thought you the best of men."

"Wait Robur, I beg you," said Tapage. "The fruit juice was a powerful soporific, but not lethal, I did not add the fungus that Platanus gave me. I could not follow such an order. All should recover in time. Some may require medical attention. The main additive was laudanum from Sister Avellana's pharmacy."

Robur looked again at the bodies in the courtyard, and mercifully it seemed to be true. They were starting to come out of the death-like sleep, he could see the shallow rise and fall of their chests. It was some strange, dark miracle, the inverse of a massacre.

Robur embraced Tapage and kissed him, and they wept together. Emerging from her shock, Avellana wept too.

Suddenly Robur was conscious of cautious booted footsteps, still at some distance.

"We're in danger," said Robur "The cavalry men will be suspicious of us. They may even shoot us on sight, but I have an idea." And for the first time in a good while Robur smiled, for he saw some hope.


Airman Alistair arrived back at the brig and relieved the current guard. In his hands, he held a large and conspicuous bundle of cloth. Alistair used his key to open the cell of Trina Dressard.

"My love, we will be landing soon, somewhere in the High Desert. And I must get you down to the winch platform undetected."

"Not just me, darling," said Dressard. "Don't forget that Mr. Trump will need to come with us."

"I have followed your instructions to the letter, and brought him a uniform too," said Alistair, sounding very much as if he wished he was not going to be encumbered with Walter Trump during this escape.

Alistair unlocked Trump's cell too and untied the bundle, passing him a standard airman's uniform, and an air cadet's to Dressard, the smallest outfit available in the stores. Trump kept his voice lowered, but was still ranting about his court case against the Captain of the *Venger* for damages, and how Alistair would be called as a witness.

Trump pulled on his uniform and this reminded him of an event from his past, upon which he elucidated.

"Of course, I could have joined the US Navy, but they told me I actually scored too high on the aptitude tests."

Trina and Trump made up their beds as though they still slept in them. They moved out of the brig as quietly and warily as cats.

Robur, Tapage and Avellana reached the base of the belltower. Robur and the chef carried the semi-conscious Clark between them. They went inside and paused at the bottom of the spiral stairway to rest. Avellana immediately checked and tightened the improvised dressings she had made for Clark's wounds.

"I am going to send a wireless telegraph message for the *Venger* to pick us up, from the top of the campanile tower. That way Clark will get the best possible medical attention. But there is something else I want to try, and if it works, whatever you see, whatever you hear, whatever you do, don't move from the top of the tower."

Tapage and Avellana carried Clark with Robur lagging slightly behind, he was trying to remember which door he needed. For there were a multitude of doors off various landings. It had been a long time since he had been in the "General Address" room. Finally, he located it and the others continued on without him. The General Address room contained a dizzying array of controls, and a group of lenses which could be adjusted to focus on the face of the person making the address.

Robur noticed that a universal power outlet was still illuminated. That meant that somewhere, far below in the caverns beneath the Haven, one of Oxalis' electricity generating turbines was still functioning. Robur removed the wireless pack from Jones' satchel and connected it to the outlet.

"Conqueror to *Venger*. Conqueror to *Venger*. Are you receiving me?" transmitted Robur.

"We read you strength five, Conqueror," said Turner. "We are approaching the promontory near the Haven now."

"*Venger*, divert to the Haven itself and pick up from the top of the belltower. Major Clark, two Haven allies and myself."

"Understood, Conqueror. We will ready the scramble nets."

In the absence of an operating manual, Robur activated the general address system using his best guesses at the engineering principles behind it, and common sense. He warmed up the voice amplifier and triggered the smoke canisters on the roof of the belltower, hoping this wouldn't alarm his allies too much. He activated the magnesium flares within the image projector, also atop the belltower. Before finally focusing the lenses on his face and bringing the voice sensor a little nearer.

"This is Robur," he said, and his voice was so powerfully amplified that it blew in every glass window for five hundred yards. Troopers dropped their weapons to shield their ears with both hands. The cavalry men turned to the belltower to see the image of Robur's face projected in the sky, at the dimensions of about eighty feet from chin to crown of that magnificent head. Robur reduced the volume. Few of the troopers understood that this was a projection. To them it was a theophany, the very face of God.

"I repeat, this is Robur, currently allied with the US military. Major Clark is with me. He is wounded, but the approaching airship will provide medical attention. Do not fire on the airship. Please evacuate the populace of the Haven; they are not dead, but in a death-like sleep. The leader of the Haven has been killed. The people are not responsible for the actions of this Tyrant. Treat them kindly. This is Robur, signing off."

Robur deactivated the General Address system and ascended to the top of the belltower. What he saw in the sky astonished him. It was the green energy curtain which resembled the aurora borealis. Why had it returned to the firmament above the Haven? And why now? It seemed more intensely bright than it had before, almost blinding. It was also lower, scarcely above the belltower's lightning conductor. One more thing, the curtain was more storm-like than it had ever appeared before. It seemed angry.

*Four and a half minutes earlier...*

Trina Dressard, Walter Trump and Airman Alistair made it to the observation gantry. The Venger was anchored to the promontory about eighty feet off the ground. Airman Alistair uncoiled the egress rope ladder, and tossed it over the side. He guided Trina towards the rope, seeking to assist and follow her over. Sensing this opportunity, Trump stepped stealthily up behind Alistair and snatched the heavy revolver from the airman's holster. He then held Alistair at gunpoint.

"You're not going anywhere, old man," said Trump. "Beat it, back up into the ship, or I'll blow your head off."

"Trina? Tell him we're escaping together to start a new life. He doesn't understand," said Alistair.

"I am sorry, Alistair. Do as he says. I don't want you to get hurt."

But inside Alistair's chest was a constriction akin to cardiac arrest. And yet this was not a heart attack: his heart was simply breaking. He dropped to his knees.

Trump paused, and for the first time drank in the vista of the Arizona Territory around him.

"Hey! Wait a minute, I know this place. This is where my brother Albert has his religious community. We should head over there. He was a pretty good con man until he found religion, or maybe that was just another con. Either way, it was a far cry from how we started out, as mentalists at the Dunn & Duffy Combined Circus."

His reverie over, he kicked Alistair to one side and strode to the top of the rope ladder. Trina Dressard had already disappeared over the side.

Trump did not hear the sound of someone descending the main stairway onto the gantry. Finally, the tread of heavy boots striking the deck did make him turn.

"What's going on here?" asked Airman Shanks.

Trump made the mistake of leveling his revolver at Shanks, and was immediately shot for his trouble. The impact sent him barreling over the gunwale, yet bizarrely his body did not fall. Instead, it was struck by a bolt of sickly green lightning. He was born upwards by the lightning higher and higher, his arms and legs still flailing, until he was lost from sight.

Shanks walked past his old comrade Alistair, from just a glance he could tell he was a broken man. He pointed his gun at the lithe figure who was descending the ladder.

"And where do you think you're going?" Shanks looked up. Intense, violent ribbons of energy were oscillating across the sky. The *Venger* was already starting to shudder and shake.

About five minutes later, the *Venger* banked and then came to a full stop adjacent to the Haven's belltower. Shanks, assisted by an almost somnambulist Alistair, dropped the scramble nets. And Avellana, Tapage and Clark made their way onto them. Then Robur jumped high onto the net, and started to scale onto the gantry, he had to see Turner. He did not stop running until he reached the steering room.

"Captain Robur!" shouted Turner, "Thank God you are alive!"

"I've had so many close shaves today, it is indeed God we must thank," agreed Robur.

"I must tell you something of great import that I have just learned," said Turner.

"Yes, yes?" urged Robur.

"Shanks just told me via communication tube that Walter Trump was killed while trying to escape, and that Trump's death summoned the green aurora; does that not seem strange?"

"That makes no sense at all," judged Robur. And then he paused for just a moment to consider further.

"Or perhaps it is the key to understanding everything that has happened in recent months. But right now, my friend, we have other urgent concerns."

"What are they?" asked Turner.

"There's a container holding a virulent disease in the Council chamber, Idaho Jones was going to destroy it, but I think he succumbed before he was able to. We need to blow out a section of the roof and drop in a small incendiary. The building is well constructed, so I am hoping the fire doesn't spread."

Robur relieved the steersmen and took the helm of the *Venger* himself. He brought the ship around and held her in a station keeping position. Turner barked orders to the bombardiers, who were used to conducting bombing raids in more difficult circumstances than this.

Only a few moments later, the precision bombing took place, and the realization dawned in Robur's mind that he would never see the lawman Idaho Jones again. Jones had been cut from the template of the typical western hero; it seemed incredible, unthinkable, that he had not beaten the odds, not found some way out. Robur now rejected such thoughts as childish and formed a wall around his grief. This was not the same as the loss of Frycollin, but he could not allow himself to feel such emotional desolation again.

The green tendril of energy snapped like a whip across the glass of the steering room window, as if trying to break in, snatch Robur and drag him to his doom. Robur took the *Venger* even lower to avoid this strange attack and steered the reverse of the last logged course back towards the promontory. More tendrils played across the surface of the gas envelope, damaging the helium bags, others wreaked havoc with the engines until the craft started to lose altitude and trim.

It was as if the *Venger* itself was part of some invading disease being rejected by the Earth's own defenses. Robur and Turner used every scintilla of skill and knowledge they possessed to keep the *Venger* in the air. They wrestled with the controls like men fighting demons. They even somehow managed to gain a little height as they approached the rocky outcrop, with buoyancy fast fading away and engine power dying. They were in for a jarring impact.

"All hands brace for heavy landing," warned Turner using the intercraft address system.

Robur stood the *Venger* almost on end as it came in, so that the uninhabited tail section took the brunt of the impact, before the craft lowered, almost gently, onto its belly. They would subsequently find out that no one had been injured. Turner looked at Robur with admiration, again he was savior of the crew, if not this time the ship.

"Anchor crews, tether the craft." ordered Turner.

"Mr. Turner. Let's go outside and check the damage," suggested Robur.

The green energy curtain continued to rage overhead like the creation of some angry storm deity. Walking around the fuselage and its deflating gas bags, Robur was forced to the conclusion that it might take weeks or even months to repair the *Venger*. Indeed, it might be easier to simply rebuild her.

Then it really began. More than a dozen blue streaks rocketed skyward from places of concealment on the desert floor. Robur really could not believe his eyes. The things being launched from shafts deep in the rock were very similar to Oxalis' flying machine, the *Storm Petrel*, but with an extended fuselage, presumably for passengers. As each craft made contact with the curtain, it blinked out of this existence, to reappear who knows where? Just as Robur and Frycollin had done.

"What are those things? What's going on?" demanded Turner.

"It's the Anu Sinom—the Ant People," said Robur with tears in his eyes.

"They lost the ability to fly generations ago, but now they have built flying machines based on Oxalis' design, to take them home, or perhaps somewhere quite different."

As the last Anu Sinom craft intersected with the aurora, it faded away and the sky returned to the normal dusky blue of the approaching twilight.

The crew and passengers of the *Venger* gathered on the promontory. Some watched the desert vista; others took shelter in the abandoned US cavalry tents. Robur noted a handful of absences. He guessed Clark was still in the sick bay with Avellana tending to him. Probably a certain Dahomey Amazon was there too. He saw old Alistair cuffed and in the custody of Shanks; he would get the story on that later. Soon the cavalry column would return here too. Robur's plans to keep the *Venger* a permanent secret were dashed, what the future held he did not know.

In the fading light Turner looked the *Venger* up and down.

"Perhaps a hundred days to refit her," he judged.

"Maybe less if we get help from the Hopi engineers," said Robur.

"Then she will rise again like a phoenix," smiled Turner.

"Not a bad name for her, but I have a better one," said Robur. "She will be a bird of ill-omen to all who seek to wage war—an Albatross. And I have some ideas for how to improve her. She is too reliant on gas bags for lift. Once refitted she will have powerful mechanized rotors, along the lines of the aeronef principle."

Robur looked off in the direction of the Haven. The fire in the Council chamber had burnt itself out. The Haven's buildings would survive, but the people being evacuated, now free of the influence of Platanus, would return to normal lives.

After a little while longer, Tom Turner tapped him on the shoulder and pointed to the dark column of returning cavalry which was snaking its way towards them. He wondered what he would say to them. Of course, they would know him from his use of the general address system. Then Robur saw walking behind the cavalry, with the weary tread of refugees, came the inhabitants of the Haven. Some of them staggering a little drunkenly, as they recovered from the soporific poison.

When Robur saw who was leading the cavalry column he nearly dropped to his knees. He fought against that, but could not prevent his vocal cords seiz-

255

ing up until they felt like overtightened piano strings. His hair was standing on end, his eyes starting to bulge. Was this a ghost? Was he the only person who could see it? The figure rode up the slope to the promontory outcrop and reined his mount to a halt.

"I guess you weren't expecting to see me again," he said.

"Idaho Jones?" questioned Robur, his voice a dull rasp. "You should be in quarantine! You could kill us all!"

"Nope, I reckon I'm okay, Robur," said Idaho Jones, though he looked like he was in a lot of pain.

"I cauterized the wound on the back of my hand with a powder burn. You probably heard the shot."

"Heard the shot?" said Robur. "I thought you had killed yourself!"

"I wasn't sure if it had done the job so I searched for more of that oil. I found a stash of it in the side chapel. Maybe I did too good a job."

Idaho Jones slowly pulled his arm out of the improvised sling, revealing his right hand. It was very badly burned, like charred meat. It would be months or years before it was properly healed, and he might never regain full function of it.

"I haven't got a fever, nor any other symptoms. It's not suppurating, so I guess the disease is destroyed."

"Come on, let's get you checked out in sick bay," advised Robur as Idaho Jones dismounted.

Robur led the way to the crippled *Venger*.

"What will you tell your superiors in Washington about all of this?" asked Robur.

"I'll give them some sort of heavily edited version that they might actually be able to swallow. You won't feature much, and as for the *Venger*, nobody really believes in phantom airships."

*Epilogue*

In the following months the *Venger* was refitted and reconfigured to be an aeronef, and formally renamed the *Albatross*. The crew developed a number of hidden bases in the United States and beyond.

In the following five years or so, Robur became concerned, obsessed really, with what the future might hold, since it would be impossible now for Walter Trump to ascend to the presidency. But what about Phil Evans, future Vice President who would reinstitute slavery immediately after becoming President?

Turner recalled that Phil Evans came from Philadelphia, so a plan was hatched for Seraphina to take a job as a housekeeper in the home of Phil Evans' parents, one of the most prominent households in Philadelphia. Subsequently, Seraphina's son, also named Frycollin, took up a place as an apprentice valet to

Uncle Prudent, leading citizen and President of the Weldon Institute in Philadelphia.

About fifteen years later, Norwegian and Swedish astronomical observatories sighted a huge bird or aerial monster in the center of an *aurora borealis*, showering off from its body certain corpuscles which exploded like bombs.

This was of course the *Albatross*. Robur was conducting experiments using synthetic radium bombs to see if the *aurora borealis* could be energized sufficiently to be used as a conduit to other places in space and time. It seemed it could not. And Robur gave up such experiments permanently.

A few months later, Robur determined to make a final judgement on Phil Evans, abducted both him and Uncle Prudent (as well as his spy Thaddeus Frycollin, Jr.) and held them prisoner just as he had Walter Trump all those years before.

Young Frycollin suggested a possible way forward.

"Remember when I was a kid and you and I used to have aerial sleigh rides in a basket hanging out the back of the *Albatross*?" said Frycollin.

"Sure, what of it?" said Robur.

"What if you give me a sleigh ride and I pretend to be terrified, to beg for mercy? In his reaction to this you should be able to judge anything you need to know about Evans' attitudes."

"But why on earth would I put you in the basket in the first place?"

"I'll make a ruckus in my room, lots of noise, you pretend to be annoyed," said Frycollin.

"I wouldn't drag someone behind the Albatross just for making a noise, that's ridiculous." said Robur.

"Aw, come on, ham it up a little, Robur. Pretend you don't even like black folks," said Frycollin.

And so, Phil Evans was appalled at the treatment of Frycollin and intervened on his behalf. While Frycollin was being wound in, Robur took the opportunity to ask Evans directly if he supported slavery. He said vehemently and sincerely that he did not.

That evening, Robur and Frycollin smoked cigars and drank brandy together after having consumed a gourmet meal prepared by Tapage. Robur was in a quandary, Frycollin rather less so.

"From a young age he has been exposed to my mother's strength, character, and love, and maybe that was enough to shape his views for the better. In any event, it's something the Phil Evans of the other reality didn't have the advantage of."

"I certainly can't condemn him to death, they must be released. Or more likely, allowed to escape."

About nine months after the siege of the Haven, Trina Dressard gave birth to a healthy baby boy. Robur issued no harsh punishment to Airman Alistair. He could not find it in his heart to do so when the transgressions had been committed out of love.

Trina Dressard lived aboard the *Albatross* for many years before succumbing to cancer. Her handsome son rose to be a senior helmsman on the airship.

The "Brides of Platanus," including Sister Myrtle, got clean away from the Haven and were never found. Be on your guard then, in case the pattern of the Masada Solution repeats itself.

Gideon Spillit
Airman Third Class (Logistics)

*Jules Verne appears to be especially popular with this year's crop of writers, as new contributor Lex Gil paints a very different picture of Robur than Martin Gately, pitting him in direct conflict with Captain Nemo...*

## Lex Gil: *Masters of the World*

*1890*

"Professor Aronnax."

The tall man meant me, Professor Pierre Aronnax. I have no idea how they'd found me. I never told anyone where I went, whenever it was that I decided to go.

I'm a marine biologist and, due to being good at my profession, years ago I had the most extraordinary voyage, whereby I met that archangel of hatred who called himself "Captain Nemo," a most extraordinary figure, an incredible genius, unlike anyone I'd ever encountered before or since.

Twenty thousand leagues under the sea we went, and I beheld truly incredible things, unlike any I will have the opportunity to witness ever again. Unfortunately, such an extraordinary voyage turned into an ordeal, a symphony of violence and tragedy that lead the Captain and his exquisite machine, the *Nautilus*, into the great Maelstrom, which probably took his life, and those of the men who faithfully served by his side.

I wrote reports and papers, scientific papers, describing in utmost detail the wonders of my journey, but I lost a battle I didn't even know I was fighting. The papers I presented disappeared, my home was broken into, ransacked, left in a chaotic mess. It was a message—which I ignored. I kept writing, submitting my articles to institutes, newspapers, the government—anyone who should listen.

I was ignored—then threatened. More than once. I was told to cease and desist, to never mention my extraordinary voyage ever again.

And so I did. Forced by "circumstances," I submerged myself into my work at the Museum National d'Histoire Naturelle of Paris. The construction of a new gallery of zoology, followed by one of paleontology and comparative autonomy, ended up draining the Museum's budget, and, as the place began to run short on funds, emphasis was set on teaching. My career is now better than ever, as my students listen to my lectures with profound interest.

The negative side of things, besides the lack of funds themselves, is that it lead us on a collision course with our most despicable rival, that unholy and despicable den of iniquity known as the Faculté des Sciences of Paris.

I may have been forced to keep quiet regarding my extraordinary voyage, but I became obsessed with the identity of its architect. I wanted to find out who truly was Nemo, why had such tragedy struck him and made him dedicate his

259

life to fighting the tyrannical terrors perpetrated by surface-dwellers. But no matter how deep I dug, how many stones I turned, I always found the exact same thing: nothing. Always nothing, until I quit out of my own volition. No threats necessary.

And so, I now divide my time between teaching young bright minds with a taste for knowledge, molding them into even brighter minds, so that our world become not so worthy of Nemo's rage.

This section of the Breton shoreline near Saint-Marc-sur-Mer is where I went for silence and solace, to daydream, and I always bring my watercolors with me, although for some reason, I only pretend to paint.

But as soon as I saw the two men walking towards me, I knew that something was about to change. I just didn't know how much, or if it would be for the worst or for the better.

"Yes, that is indeed I. And may I inquire as to who…?"

But the tall man already had his identification out, rudely interrupting me as he held out a wallet containing some kind of badge.

"I'm James West, Secret Service."

"From good old U.S. of A. My name's Artemus Gordon," added the second man, also showing me his badge.

The tall man had managed to interrupt me before I was able to utter a single word. Rude, but effective, I'll have to admit. But I was already calculating that his associate would answer my next question, without the need for me to even ask it. And, indeed, the fellow did not disappoint:

"Want to have a guess as to why we're here on such an urgent matter, that made us cross an ocean simply to talk to you?"

So, the two Americans did like to play games, at least to some extent. Probably as long as they were the ones holding the trump cards.

"Messieurs, I have neither the time, age or patience to engage in such nonsensical games. Still, I'll play along. You're here somehow due to the 'Golden Suns' incidents. I've skimmed through the matter in the papers. Black flags with golden suns, planted on top of landmarks all over the world: the Statue of Liberty, the Great Pyramid of Giza in Egypt, and in my fair country, our own Eiffel Tower. A symbol somewhat similar to that of Captain Nemo's—a black flag emblazoned with a golden N. I was expecting someone from my own government to come first and ask me all kinds of stupid questions. Yes, I met the Captain, who provided me with the most extraordinary voyage of my life, because he was a brilliant man of the sea, and I am a brilliant marine biologist. Matters of the air are of no concern of mine, nor do they pique my interest. The matter does sound like an epic-scaled prank. A bad one. But I do admit that I take solace in knowing that someone had the bravery to go to such trouble. For now, I feel vindicated."

"Are you done, or simply pausing for breath, Professor?" asked West.

I proceeded to march back towards the Hotel de la Plage. I'd thought that my small speech would have been of assistance in venting years of built-up anger, indignation and frustration, but it hadn't. However, what Gordon said next, simply and completely froze me on my tracks:

"He's alive, Professor."

I remained facing forward, my back to the two Secret Service agents. I dared not look back and face him, as I offered my next question:

"Nemo?"

"Nemo."

"But how? The maelstrom…"

"It was a tragedy," West explained. "The *Nautilus* was salvaged by another nation, on the other side of the world. Our government had to send a special team to retrieve him from foreign hands—along with what was left of his ship. It had been nearly destroyed and all his men were gone. Dead. He was the sole survivor. If he'd been bitter and angry before, now, he's a husk for pure anger. We expected to use his vast intellect by improving the conditions of his imprisonment, but he's steadfastly refused to cooperate. We told him about the black flags with the golden suns, and I saw a twinkle in his eye. You excel at your profession, Professor, but we excel at ours, and I can assure you that Nemo knows something. It wasn't just the symbol, but where and how they were placed as well. My government fears that some great evil might be afoot.

"The flags aren't the only uncanny incident. There also have been sightings of other machines. Various ships at sea from different nations have sighted an enormous metal creature. A metal vehicle of similar description has been spotted on American mountain roads, like in the Blue Ridge Mountains. And then, there's the music. Several reports throughout America speak of music coming from nowhere but the sky itself. We've approached the Captain more times than any human can bear, but every time we try to reasonably explain the situation to him, he simply explodes into a barrage of blasphemies, the kind that no gentleman should utter nor should hear. It's impossible to reason with him—unless you can pierce his bitter shell, since you two were friends, right?"

A lesser man would have needed time to digest all that information, but I am no lesser man:

"What kind of music?" I asked.

"What kind of music? How very droll. Professor. Trumpet. Mostly."

"Trumpet? Bah. Not my favorite instrument at all. Are you going to take me to Nemo, since that's obviously why you're here, or will we engage in more battles of wits. Well, poor attempts at it, at least."

"What I read about you didn't mention you being so grumpy, Professor," said Gordon.

"The weight of the years and the disappointments of life have had that effect on many great men, Messieurs."

We traveled by car to Brest, where we embarked on a small boat which reminded me of an ironclad, only smaller and somewhat different, as if the designer of such contraption had taken a note from the *Nautilus*, with the lower half of the machine beneath the surface and its upper half above it. But it was its speed, that was the most impressive. I don't think even the *Nautilus* had been that fast. And that small futuristic boat took us to a normal-sized one, anchored at sea, which I can only describe as discreetly warlike.

I was told that Nemo's prison had been a small island located somewhere off the East coast of America, where he was allowed to roam at will, under tight supervision. In a way, that reminded me of Napoleon, although I suspect Nemo would have detested such comparison. But he had been transported here for our meeting. The irony didn't escape me that they had christened this vessel the *Liberty Bell*.

After boarding the ship, I found myself closely following Agents West and Gordon in a swift march, with three other agents closely flanking us. I had a feeling they were as fiercely loyal as Nemo's crew had been.

I knew that the locked, ominous-looking door at the end of the corridor held Nemo captive. The shorter the distance became, the more I realized how nervous I was regarding our forthcoming encounter. I did not know how the Captain would react upon seeing me again. Would he even remember me? Of course, he would. But since an enormous personal tragedy had led him to become the man I knew, capable of great and terrible things, then how would he react now, when his next family had also been violently and suddenly taken away from him?

My anxiety did not take long to turn into pity for such a bitter soul. But how could he not be bitter? I can't even begin to imagine the torment that such tragedy could do to any man—not to mention, the loss of his precious *Nautilus*. And to be held as a prisoner in such a way… I would indeed be quite surprised by the amount of sanity that he had been able to retain.

And then we stopped. Beyond that armored door was the once great and terrible genius. I truly shuddered at the thought of finally meeting him again, after all these years, after all the things he had been forced to go through.

West opened the door and I stepped through the threshold, an anxious soul, not knowing what else to think.

"Nemo?" I uttered.

He was standing, gazing outside at the calm sea through a porthole. He still maintained the posture of a dignified Captain. How he was still able to do so, I do not know. Perhaps, it was just for the sake of appearances, but I think not.

"Hello, Professor," he said, as he casually turned around to face me. The distance between us felt awkward.

In spite of his dignified posture, there was something definitely fractured in his soul, a burden unseen upon his shoulders. Perhaps grief, perhaps anger, or both, or more, much more. The eyes gave it away mostly. But, somehow, there was also a twinkle in there. That I did notice. Like a man holding a trump card, who wants you to know that he has one during the game.

"I was wondering how long it would take until you showed up, Professor Aronnax," he added.

He took several casual, calm steps towards me. I think I might have shrunk back a little in a reaction of fear, or caution. Although the threat of a smile curled up discreetly in the corner of his mouth, he seemed to try to ignore his own reaction, as he held his outstretched hand for me to shake. Which I did.

"I missed our conversations, Aronnax," he said.

"So did I, Nemo, so did I."

After that brief but heartfelt handshake, he again joined his hands behind his back, keeping his Captain's composure, as if we were in his own ship. Perhaps, in a way, we were, and everybody else just didn't know it.

"So?" said he.

"So," said I. "I wrote about you, you know? A lot. But my papers, my research, my reports, everything kept disappearing or being censored. Until I was threatened, more than once. They even turned my own home upside down when I wasn't there."

"I'm not surprised. Unfortunately."

"I also did research, exhaustively, about you, trying to find out more about why you did what you did. And how you ended up doing it."

Again, he flashed that trump card-smile. There was a certain devilish characteristic to it, and he knew it.

"The one responsible for these flags knows all about it. And he would surely inform you, without a moment's waste, since he always liked to brag."

"You know what this business is all about, then? Strange flags atop monuments around the world? Music from the skies? A vehicle seen at sea that sounds like it could rival the *Nautilus*; another on land, going so fast that it was impossible to properly discern it?"

"First of all, my dear friend," I was actually surprised to hear him say that he considered me his friend, "the *Nautilus* has no rival. And it never will. No matter the ordeals that it is put through, I can always improve on its flaws and weak points. Secondly, the vehicle in the sky, the other in the water, and the one going by land, they're all the same."

I was flabbergasted: "What? The same? But the *Nautilus* was already such a wonder, how can a single machine master all those elements?"

"Trust me, Professor. I know the man who created it. I met him many years ago, in fact. When they told me about the flags, I needed to hear no more. His name is Robur. Once, he and I were brothers."

I was flabbergasted.

"You wanted to know how I ended up becoming Nemo, Captain of the *Nautilus*, whose only home is the sea? Before I was Nemo, I was Dakkar. Before I was a Captain, I was a prince. And before the sea was my home, it was

India. I was always an inventor, a creator of extraordinary things. Either a blessing or a curse, it was one of the characteristics that defined me. I started imagining the *Nautilus* in my mind when I was a child, for I had a great fascination with the sea, due to all the books I'd read about it. When my father sent me to England to perfect my education, on my first great sea voyage, our ship was attacked by a group of sperm whales. Nobody knew why it happened, but it did. I was one of the few survivors. Then, I swore off the sea, and developed a great dread and rage towards it. I focused all my efforts on becoming the best successor to my father's position that I could."

I noticed that Nemo seemed to be humbled by his station as a prince, as if it had been a great burden, a great duty, rather than a monarchic position of power.

"As I became an adult, I met my..."

For the briefest instant, it seemed to me that he would break down in tears, for he was not simply telling me the tragedies of his life, he was reviving them. The amount of pain that such a man had gone through was indeed too much for anyone.

"...I met my wife. We had two beautiful children. I was truly happy. Then the Rebellion happened. I lost my family. All those close to me were gone, due to the arrogance of man, the bloodthirst so typical of humanity. Again, I faced tragedy, and I was once again filled with unbearable rage and anguish. I took all my inventions and used them to exact my revenge, as violently as I could. And violent it was, as I destroyed all those responsible for the death of my family. But in the end, I was left with nothing. I had no family, and as I had killed all their murderers, I had no revenge anymore. I was lost, contemplating ways in which to end my life. I decided that it would be fitting for the sea to do it. I took a small boat, and deep into the horizon of the sea I went, waiting for the end. As it seemed closer than ever, a most magnificent sight came upon me. An ocean liner, the greatest ever built, its grandness without equal, like an immense floating city. The *Great Eastern* was her name..."

As he continued to speak, his tone now became a bit livelier, in the way that men of science, dominated by their thirst for knowledge, can achieve.

"Although it had all the appearances of being the greatest ocean liner ever built, it was much more than that, for it truly was a floating city. It was the work of a man as grand as the *Great Eastern*. His name, I'd rather not utter, but he had great ideas, and the means to bring them to life. And that was exactly what he had done. The *Great Eastern* was home to an enormous group of scientists who, of their own free will, had joined this great patron.

"The world was at our disposal, and we were going to change it, for the better, in the name of freedom and true happiness, where one's gender, race, creed or station was unimportant, for all men would be treated as equal. It would be a world greatly improved by science itself. We all had our inventions, our creations, our ideals. That's where I met the man known as Robur.

"Upon introducing myself to him for the first time, I became Nemo and found a new life. Although we were both cursed with enormous egos, we became the best of friends, our ideas complementing each other. We were like brothers, until..."

I already knew that, yet again, what I was about to hear indicated another abysmal point in Nemo's life.

"...Until one day, our great patron gathered us for a fateful meeting. He disclosed his grand plans for the betterment of the world. It was simply world domination. Those were his true plans. Perhaps he didn't see things as such, but that is as it was. To use our inventions to bend the world to his will. Initially, by a show of sheer force, through devastation and destruction.

"I was greatly disturbed. I felt betrayed. Deeply so. And I wasn't the only one to feel that way. The difference on how to enforce the ideals that we all shared lead to a split in the *Great Eastern*'s population. Those in favor found no other choice but to take the world by force. Those against had had enough bloodshed and wanted no more of it. It led to a civil war of sorts. Robur was in favor of shedding blood. I wasn't. That little war of ours, where the fate of the planet was being decided, unbeknownst to the world, eventually reached its peak. The *Great Eastern* was destroyed. Many lives were lost. Once again, witnessed too many precious souls being taken away. That's when, adrift at sea once more, I found the island that became my base. And where the *Nautilus* of which I had dreamed all my life was born."

Nemo stared at me and I stared back. I needed time to digest all that. Such a life, so full of tragedy and wonder, of epic proportions...

"I... Goodness... I don't quite know what to say...." Was I supposed to say something? Did he expect me to do so? "Goodness," I muttered once more.

"And now, my dear friend, my only friend, I will help you catch Robur, preferably before he conquers the world."

"Preferably, yes." That was good news, at last.

"Under one condition, however, that must be granted by our American friends."

"No."

James West was quite casual in his reply, without a tinge of anger, not a single octave was raised in his voice.

Nemo had wanted his *Nautilus* and his freedom back, giving his word that there would be no more ship attacks, but that was still too much. West's tone was adamant. I had to reason with him:

"But, Monsieur West, the truth is that we need his help. A machine that can master the oceans is already a danger in itself. And we know that this new machine can not only master the oceans, but land and air as well. You have proof of it. Nemo knows this Robur, knows how he thinks. And, unlike Nemo, Robur has nothing less than world conquest in his mind. The flags atop monuments was but a warning. If not with Nemo's help, how else can we defeat him?"

"The problem, Professor, is what the Captain asks in return."

"Is it not a small price to pay for the fate of the world? Is it not just for Nemo to want his life back? After all he went through? All he lost? Or do you think Robur can be defeated with sheer military brute force, without his help? Do you have airships that match the capabilities of Robur's?"

West fell silent.

"Admit it, Monsieur West, you knew he was going to ask for those things before you came to fetch me."

"What if we come upon that Robur character," interjected Artemus Gordon, "and since the two were comrades before, they join forces? What's to stop them then?"

The idea hadn't even crossed my mind. I desperately searched for a proper answer. But then fate intervened.

Another agent burst in, without bothering to knock. (Strock, I believe his name was):

"Agent West, we got a message. The machine was seen, over the British parliament. They say it's enormous, on a biblical level. And it dropped a bomb on Big Ben. They're calling it *The Terror*."

An apt name, I thought, as I visualized in my mind's eye how horrifying it must have been to see such a terrible thing for the first time and bear witness to the destruction of a landmark known throughout the world, one that had withstood the test of time, and history itself.

West stared at me again. There was nothing else that could be done, and we all knew it. Nemo had to help us save the world.

Nemo again had that defiant twinkle in his eyes, which somewhat contradicted his rigid, commanding posture.

He, I, West, Gordon, Strock and the other agents were anxiously waiting for the new *Nautilus* to emerge from beneath the ominously still waters. Well, I was anxious; the others did not look like it. They might as well have been waiting for their lunch. Nemo might have looked as if possessing the coolest resolve, but I suspect that he was even more anxious than I was. It was his creation after all; he knew there would be unapproved changes made by the U.S. government.

Then, it rose. Like a terrible majestic creature of fearsome metal, chilling in size, structure and appearance. Nemo's jaw clenched. His eyes narrowed. His forehead creased into a disapproving frown. He did not like what they had done to his creation. This *Nautilus* was more fierce-looking, more aggressive in design, lined with mouth-drying spikes, like an enormous predator, ready to strike.

"What have you done to my ship?" asked Nemo to no one in particular, voicing the disgrace that had assaulted his soul.

Inside the *Nautilus*, no one would have confused the vessel with anything else other than a military ship. Nemo's jaw remained clenched, his eyes narrow, his brow creased. He was infuriated, and rightly so.

The *Nautilus'* new captain took a step forward, towards Nemo, extending his hand for a shake. Although a man of authoritative posture, but perhaps due to being slightly younger, he was obviously respectful of Nemo, even though the two had never met before.

"Welcome, Captain Nemo. I'm Captain Nicholl."

"I hardly recognize my ship," replied Nemo. "What have you done to it?"

"I understand, Captain, and I truly am sorry. I know that the *Nautilus* now looks like a weapon of war. The damage she suffered was great. We couldn't exactly replicate your work, but our engineers did their best. If it's worth anything, I fought against making her look so... warlike."

There were incredibly long seconds as we held our breaths, wondering what Nemo's reaction would be. He didn't lose his scowl, but he did, at least, extend his hand to shake Nicholl's. And he did seem sincere when he replied:

"Yes. I believe you, Captain Nicholl. Thank you for trying."

Nicholl's body language seemed to relax. "Thank you for not doubting my word," he said. "Now, please, follow me into the war room, where we can discuss our plan of action."

"It has a war room now?" observed Nemo. "Fascinating."

Considering that this *Nautilus* was a grimmer version of his creation, in the hands of another man, one could assume that Nemo's sarcastic response was very much mild.

We followed Nicholl to the war room, as I took note of how all the crew acted with military precision. There was a stricter way of doing things than had been the case with Nemo and his crew.

When I had traveled in the *Nautilus'* previous incarnation, it had been a gift to be a part of such wonderful creation. Being in this new version made me feel oppressed, like I didn't belong there. The previous *Nautilus* had felt like someone's opulently home. The current one felt like a war machine.

In the war room, we gathered around a large rectangular table. My whole body ached for a rest, but I didn't want to lose face, so I remained standing like the rest of them.

Captain Nicholl unrolled a large map and turned to Nemo: "What's our next step, Captain?"

I could not help but notice that Nicholl addressed Nemo as if he was the man in charge, dismissing the Secret Service agents. His attitude was not lost on West and Gordon, but they were smart enough to know when to keep their mouths shut.

Answering Nicholl's question, Nemo pointed to a point on the map, in the middle of an ocean, with nothing else around it but water: "Here," he said.

He then turned to West and removed three envelopes from inside his coat.

"You need to place a black flag with a yellow N on each of the previous monuments where the black flags with the golden sun were found, and with each flag, you must leave one of these envelopes. Then, we'll wait, at the coordinates I just indicated."

"Why that specific point?" asked Nicholl.

"How are we supposed to get those flags up there?" asked West. "And what's in these envelopes?"

"I'm sure a man of your intellectual caliber will have no qualms in finding a way to do so. Regarding the content of the envelopes, they're all the same. It's an invitation from me. It should work."

"An invitation?" asked Gordon.

"For Robur to meet me where the ship where we met, and used to live, sunk."

West had no qualms in ripping open each of the envelopes to verify its contents. He seemed satisfied after reading each identical letter contained within, which quite briefly said: *Meet me where the Great Eastern sunk*; and it was signed: *Your only and truest rival, Nemo.*

There was a certain look of amusement adorning Nemo's face, I believe, upon witnessing West and Gordon's tactics. I think the Captain actually liked the two Secret service agents.

"Satisfied?" asked Nemo.

"Satisfied enough," replied West, as he and Gordon walked out the door, leaving the rest of us under the watchful eye of armed guards.

"We will reach these coordinates soon enough, but once there, how long will we have to wait?" Nicholl asked.

"I don't know."

I could not hold myself anymore.

"Wait for what?" I asked. "That madman Robur just destroyed one of the world's landmarks. What is supposed to happen if we meet that vessel of terror? He clearly has an advantage over us. I'm sorry, Nemo, I know the *Nautilus* is your precious creation, even if it's now unrecognizable, but it is a machine for the seas. Robur possesses one that is its equivalent not only in the seas, but in the air and on land as well. What chance do we have in a direct confrontation? One with such a machine is, quite simply put, the master of the world."

"You should trust this new version of the *Nautilus*, Professor Aronnax," interjected Nicholl. "Its changes might seem barbaric, but they are no less necessary to confront someone like Robur. It is indeed a weapon of war now, and a powerful one at that. The advantage that Robur's machine has over the new *Nautilus* might be impressive, but you shouldn't dismiss our new capabilities either." He then turned to Nemo: "What about you, Captain? Do you trust me to handle your own modified creation?"

"The only men I ever trusted are all dead, but I do believe you when you refer to the *Nautilus*' new capabilities for war. And you seem to be a good Captain—but I have been wrong before."

Days later, with the *Nautilus* at high but controlled speed, as to save energy and resources for the imminent confrontation, we had reached our designated destination. We were somewhere in the Caribbean—that much I knew.

The *Nautilus* divided the time between being fully submerged and, on occasions, breaking halfway through the surface, so that Captain Nicholl and Captain Nemo could survey the area, which was nothing but vast sea—not the tiniest spot of land was visible from where we stood on the deck.

Boredom, not being something that easily mixed with anxiety, played heavily on my nerves. It wasn't like the first time when I had been both prisoner and guest of Nemo. This time, there would surely be a confrontation with a machine even more formidable, its master sounding like an evil version of Nemo himself, for as misguided as the Captain might have been, whatever heinous acts that he might have committed, he was never an evil man—unlike his descriptions of Robur.

Nemo seemed to be less and less sure as days went by, becoming more somber. Then, I heard it. We all did. Just as my level of boredom had reached unbearable heights, I heard the sounds of trumpets coming from the sky above. The music was the antithesis of the situation itself, for it was far too joyful.

We all looked up in the air, searching for its source, but none of us could find it. Then we saw it, for it had found us.

*The Terror.*

An appropriate name to call such a terrible and powerful machine. With the slowness of calm, the great beast of metal descended from the clouds in all its horrific glory.

In many ways similar to the *Nautilus*, the immense man-made creature sported addition features, besides sharing the basic design of Nemo's craft, with it vast batlike wings spread like a predator's, clearly intended to terrify, and a set of wheels underneath, distributed in a way not unlike that of an automobile.

Slowly, taking its time, the *Terror* descended in front of us, just out of the reach of the *Nautilus*' cannons, I suspect, until it landed with far too much grace for such a nehemoth.

And there it stood before us, as if it were mocking us by simply being there, completely still and quiet. Waiting. Taunting us.

Nicholl didn't know exactly what to do. Nemo seemed contempt with simply waiting. West and Gordon were, I suspect, waiting for some kind of violent, sudden action. Stock and the other agents were waiting for orders.

I was, quite simply, overwhelmed. Should I be taking notes? Should I talk to Nemo, ask him what was the next move, as if we were merely playing some kind of sadistic game of chess? Should I be panicking? Should I just let myself faint? Should I even say something? But there were far too many things to be said and asked, and I did not know which one I should say.

The silence was broken by Nicholl, addressing Nemo, He had seen something in the *Terror* through his binoculars, which he lent to Nemo to look for himself.

When Nemo looked through the binoculars, I looked through my own spyglass in the same direction. It took me a few moments to realize that the object of their attention was a dove, which had been released from somewhere within the *Terror*, and was making its way toward us. It was odd. Was it some kind of request for peace? Or one of Robur's violent pranks?

A small smile crept up on the side of Nemo's mouth, as he lowered the binoculars and returned them to Nicholl. It seemed that he was somehow familiar with that initiative from the *Terror*, for he reacted like someone who recognized it.

Moments later, the dove reached us, having decided to land on my shoulder. It was a charming, well-trained little creature, seemingly more than smart enough for what it was. There was a tiny roll of paper attached to its little paw.

Nemo carefully removed it and, just as he was about to unroll it, West snatched it from his hand with expert movement.

As he unrolled the small message himself, the Secret Service agent issued a warning: "Let's not forget who's actually in charge of this operation," he told Nemo. And then to Nicholl: "Agreed? Regardless of the vessel, Gordon and I are still in charge. Not you, Mr. Nicholl, and certainly not Nemo. Understood?"

Nicholl seemed to have something to say, but he held is tongue and simply nodded.

West read the message. He then handed it over to Gordon, who gave it to Nemo, who then passed it to Nicholl, who then handed it over to me. The suspense was cruel, but ended as soon as I was allowed to read it myself, although I admit that my feelings weren't unhurt when Nemo gave it to Nicholl first, rather than to me. The message was as clear as it was brief:

"*I have the Columbiad cannon. Bring no more than yourself and four others or I'll obliterate you. Yours ever unrivaled, Robur*"

"What's the Columbiad cannon?" I asked Nemo.

"A gigantic cannon, devised by the fellows from the Gun Club as a means to reach the Moon. I assume that, despite it being too far for us to see it, it's pointed at us. And it could indeed obliterate us. One thing that Robur is not is a liar. So if he says that he has the Columbiad cannon, then he does. That gun could raze an entire city with a single blast."

Not long later, Nemo, Nicholl, West, Gordon and I, all were heading towards the *Terror* in a tiny rowboat, each taking turns rowing. We all remained silent. My heart was racing again as the *Terror* came ever closer, truly deserving its moniker. The only soothing thing was the lovely little dove that had decided to perch itself on my shoulder for the brief journey, and which stood there, always quiet, always still.

As the other four in that cramped vessel all seemed to maintain brave faces, I tried my best to mimic them.

As we came within reaching distance of that immense hull, being my turn to row, and Nemo making a point of being the one who rowed the most, a small hatch raised itself at the front, dangerously inviting us in. It was barely large enough for us as we kept going, until we were swallowed whole by it.

We kept rowing into the immense structure until we reached a raised platform, where dozens of uniformed guards, bearing the golden sun on a black flag insignia, were waiting for us, silent, still—and armed. Meanwhile, the water was slowly draining itself through a series of small portholes on both sides, returning to the ocean.

As our small boat touched the platform, the guards parted ways, with practiced efficiency, like cogs in a machine. From the corridor formed by the aligned soldiers a man stepped up to the edge of the platform. As he did so, the dove flew from my shoulder and landed on his. The newcomer was of medium height with a geometric build. He carried himself like the only man in charge of anything; he was comparable to an intellectual bull.

The guards returned to their previous positions, closing the corridor. There was nothing but silence and tension for the longest of instances.

"Robur," said Nemo, politely breaking the silence.

Robur gently ran his finger over the neck of the dove on his shoulder. "Nemo," he replied.

"You have been busy," said Nemo.

"So have you," immediately replied Robur. "The difference being that you got caught by lesser men than yourself. I warned you about the perils of being soft."

"So you did," Nemo said somberly.

Robur turned on his heel: "Come," he said.

As soon as he did, the guards parted ways once again, with the same swiftness of timing and cohesion as before. Robur never made any point in pausing or waiting in the slightest.

We stepped out of the boat and onto the platform, following Robur, who walked with a long but calm stride.

Our walk was silent. Our loud and tense steps were emotionally deafening and the only sounds echoing throughout the metal interiors of that most terrible vessel.

Nemo took the lead in our small group, remaining no more than a single step behind Robur. West made a point of rushing up to Nemo, trying to keep at least half a step in front of him. The three of us followed meekly.

Right behind us walked about a dozen armed guards, about half of the amount that had waited for us at the platform. And we encountered many others, besides the ones accompanying us.

Finally, we reached the upper deck. Without chimney, masts, or rigging, it made the sea around us seem as majestic as if we were seeing it for the first time. Both vessels were equally awe-inducing.

Robur stopped. And so did we, and our armed escort. The other men went about their work as if we were not even there.

"Make no mistake," Robur's voice almost boomed. "You are not my guests., you are my prisoners. Behave accordingly, or your lives will be extinguished."

"Where is the Columbiad cannon?" I asked Robur. My mouth was extremely dry. I needed a glass of water, desperately. And, although I meant to ask for one, when I uttered my words, that is the question that came out.

Robur replied to me only with a look of complete and utter disdain. One might even say disgust. When he answered, he did so as if Nemo had been the one who had asked the question:

"Close enough. Certainly within range. I assure you. On Propeller Island."

Nemo's jaw dropped. He took a step towards Robur. All the guards raised their rifles. But the Captain was simply shocked with surprise. He had no intention of harming Robur, who held his guards at bay with a gesture.

"Propeller Island?" Nemo asked.

"Neither you nor I were the only survivors of the *Great Eastern*'s civil war," replied Robur. "I gathered all the other survivors. Those who didn't join me willingly, did so by force. I knew it wouldn't be a good idea to try to find you, but I did keep myself informed of your, er, escapades. Your own brand of justice. A worthy intention, marred by insufficient and unfocused actions. But now, you're here. After all the terrible things you went through., both before and after the *Great Eastern*'s fall, I'm asking you to join me, Brother."

Nemo's eyes narrowed. From what I knew of the Captain of the *Nautilus*, he seemed to be seriously considering the request.

"Why? What for? What is the purpose of all this? I destroyed weapons of war. Men intent on harming others, for the mere sake of war. What about you? You call my actions insufficient and unfocused? What about planting flags on monuments? Are those not simply dangerous pranks? And destroying Big Ben? What's the focus in such terrorist actions? Another destructive prank?"

"No," replied Robur. "But before we go on, it's better for us to leave this place and take you to Propeller Island. Your friends might get unwise ideas." Turning to the steersman, he ordered: "Mr. Hart, take us to the skies."

The steersman nodded. Orders were shouted. Workers changed from one task to another, swift in action. Once, I had noticed a certain sense of family among the *Nautilus* crew members, something that seemed to be missing in the *Terror*'s crew, although the military precision was all there.

Robur pointed at me: "He can come. Professor Aronnax, I presume?"

I nodded, as Nemo looked worriedly at me.

"Perhaps, you will enjoy a fresher breath of air before we gather in my cabin," continued Robur, as the small smile of a sadist crept up from the corner of his mouth. I raised an eyebrow at this. Nemo just looked at me., and then at Robur.

Then the *Terror* picked up speed, cutting through the water faster and faster, traveling in the opposite direction of the *Nautilus*. As the *Terror*'s wings extended to what seemed their full capacity, the vessel simply took off into the air until we were soaring through the skies.

My eyes bulged at this. I had taken a balloon trip or two before, but nothing was comparable to this, with the skies surrounding us. We were now so high that we were piercing through the clouds themselves. Fresher air indeed! I nearly fainted, but I was in such awe that my senses simply didn't allow me to do so.

Nemo, on the other hand, had a reaction unlike I had ever witnessed before. For the first time, there seemed to be fear upon his face. He tried to keep himself stoic, as he most obviously did not enjoy flying, but did not succeed.

Nichol, West and Gordon were quite taken by our surroundings but their reactions, or mine, were unlike Nemo's, the only one of us who felt obviously uncomfortable and out of his element.

Robur roared with laughter. He was loving every minute of his friend's discomfort. That's when I realized that putting his flags atop of monuments had not been mere pranks. They were acts of pure sadism.

Scarce minutes later, Nemo and I were in Robur's cabin. And it was indeed the cabin befitting one commanding such a vessel. Even bigger and more opulent than Nemo's in the *Nautilus*.

The Captain and I took our seats in the two mildly comfortable chairs in front of Robur's desk, while he plopped down in a chair that was obviously quite comfortable and raised slightly higher than ours. He then produced a bottle of some decanted alcoholic beverage from one of the drawers, along with three glasses, and poured a generous dose each.

Robur took brave gulps from his glass, but I was reticent. So I looked at Nemo, who, after taking a whiff of the drink, took a brave sip himself. And then he coughed a little. I took a gulp myself, trying to match Robur's control, but such an action immediately backfired, as I coughed incessantly for the next couple of minutes, almost choking. Surely there was a trick of some kind, for I do not believe that any human being could have acquired a taste for something so revolting.

Robur roared with laughter. Nemo just snickered. Like a reasonably good sport.

"Puts hair on your chest," said Robur.

"Quite," I replied.

"So," said Nemo.

"So," replied Robur.

"Er," was the only word I could muster, more akin to simply being a feeble sound. "Why did you allow me to participate in your reunion with Nemo?" I asked Robur.

"Excellent question. Professor," he replied immediately. "It seems Nemo holds you in high esteem. Interesting people are hard to find. And if Nemo holds you in a minimum of esteem, then you must have such characteristics. Unlike Captain Nicholl and Messrs. West and Gordon."

"You are well-informed," said Nemo.

"You have no idea, Old friend. I have operatives everywhere. After the *Great Eastern*'s civil war, I, along with a few other survivors, were approached by a secret cabal of American billionaires led by one William Boltyn. Incredibly powerful men, among the wealthiest in the entire world. They keep watch on world affairs. They are the ones who financed all this, and more. Much, much more, as you will soon see."

Nemo downed another dose of the nefarious liquid, after having poured it himself: "Get to the point, Robur."

Robur also downed a generous dose of the alcohol himself: "Join me, Nemo. Together, we will be unstoppable. A talent like yours can't go to waste."

"To do what?"

"Return the world to its proper path. The first domino piece to be brought down is the British Empire. By using the Columbiad cannon. The flags I spread all over the world were more than mere pranks. They were warnings. Better yet, threats. And you know that my threats are never empty., don't you, Nemo?"

Nemo's somber look said it all.

"Destroying Big Ben," continued Robur, "was a matter of escalation. A true warning—not a threat. Soon, I shall take action against that most vile empire, and you should be there, standing by my side, as we watch it crumble. We will be the true masters of the world."

Nemo sat still and silent, deep in thought. There was great anger running through his soul, that much was obvious. But as to who or what such anger was directed at, still eluded me.

"You're going to commit genocide," Nemo said surprisingly softly.

"Call it what you will. The British Empire was never above such measures. You know it, you felt it. You had your own life destroyed by it. And this is war. It's already started. They just don't know it yet. Such measures are necessary in war, for there to be peace afterward. My cause is just, you know it, Nemo, like yours was. This is a war for justice, for freedom; a righteous war if there ever was one. Stand with me, brother. Truly. We will be masters of the world."

I saw it in Nemo's face. He was truly pondering Robur's offer. I shouldn't have been surprised, but I was truly shocked.

"Nemo!" I despaired. "You can't seriously be considering this!"

Nemo calmly replied: "But I am, Professor."

I couldn't just stand there and be a part of that: "But…"

"In America," Nemo interrupted, "didn't the North have to go to war with the South, in order for slavery to be abolished?"

"Yes, but…" I replied.

"Was it not necessary?"

"Yes, but…"

"Do you support slavery?"

"Of course not! But…"

"But what, Professor?"

"But…"

"Should good men do nothing while evil prospers? Is the British Empire not responsible for the appropriation of many lands that are not their own? Of resources that are not their own? Of exploiting and oppressing cultures that are not their own? All in the name of expanding their empire? In the name of civilization? When, in fact, it has been nothing but in the name of greed and arrogance. As if the British Empire itself was exempt of savageries. When, in fact, they would never have conquered those peoples if not for their atrocities. And the fair citizens of such Empire live by such actions. Approve of them. Motivate them. Participate in them. Does that sound correct to you, Professor? Does that sound civilized? Robur will do something about it. I can do something about it. But what about you, Professor? What will you do about it? Will you do anything at all about it?"

All the tension fled my body. I did not know what to say. I simply let myself sink in my seat. For some reason, I simply felt ashamed.

Robur roared with laughter. He had the most annoying sense of timing, and none of the proper politeness that any gentleman in such a station should have.

Then, he downed another drink.

Minutes later, I was in a cell, along with Captain Nichol and the two Secret Service agents.

"I knew it!" exclaimed West. "That bastard Nemo has sold us all!"

Captain Nicholl simply looked tired, and disappointed—extremely disappointed.

We hardly traded any words, until several hours had passed. Nicholl assumed night had fallen, for everything felt quieter, almost still, although we were surely still moving, although we did not know if by air, sea or land, for there were no windows in our tiny, cramped cell. The light coming from outside had dimmed. Somehow, that made things only more desperate.

What probably were a few days and nights went by. We were in motion, that much we knew. Hours passed in stillness and mostly quiet. Gordon, Captain Nicholl and I spent our time trading theories of what was happening. Of how Nemo and Robur were going to take down the British Empire. Of how the true captain of the true *Nautilus* had deceived us. In the meantime, we also traded anecdotes to pass the time, to try and better our moods.

Then, we heard two muffled screams outside. We immediately assumed that it had been the guards, and we were immediately intrigued. Seconds later, the door slammed open. And silhouetted in threshold was the unmistakable figure of Captain Nemo.

He tucked away a knife in the back of his belt as he drew a pistol from a waist holster and unslung a rifle from his shoulder. He never broke stride, as he crossed the small corridor towards us, and snapped open the lock with the butt of his rifle, heavy and swift.

We were all flabbergasted, but no less glad to see him, for he was obviously coming to our rescue.

Nemo gave the rifle to Nicholl, the pistol to West, and from each of his shoulders, he drew a pair of pistols, giving one to me and one to Gordon.

"I don't know if you have any experience with firearms, Aronnax, but the principle is basic: point and pull the trigger," he told me.

It was neither time nor place to mention my younger days, reluctantly hunting with my father.

"Follow my lead," he said, already turning on his heel, heading for the door. None of us said anything, as we followed his lead, heading outside with a brisk walk. There were indeed two guards fallen on either side of the doorway.

We kept following Nemo amidst the vast and odd place, where the people were all probably asleep.

At the edge of the perimeter surrounding us were lined a series of large propellers, as tall and as large as buildings. In the middle of what seemed to be an island, was what could only be the largest cannon ever built. An instrument of epic destruction.

The three of us kept running behind Nemo, still following his lead, at a contained but steady pace. We kept our heads low, our shoulders slumped, our noise to a minimum and our attention at its fullest.

We reached a dock, where a smaller, prototype version of the previous *Nautilus* was moored.

"It was meant to carry at least six men, so the five of us will fit just fine," Nemo said, as he opened the hatch and slipped inside. Followed by Captain Nicholl, then me, and finally West and Gordon.

Once inside, there wasn't much that the Secret service agents or I could do, as far as operating the vehicle, which was a very bare bones version of the old *Nautilus*.

After a few minutes of Captain Nemo and Captain Nicholl moving about, we started moving, increasing in velocity.

"What about Robur?" I asked Nemo.

"He won't be a problem," Nemo said with an incredibly somber look—the same look he had after his *Nautilus* had violently destroyed a ship destined for war.

Just then, with Propeller Island becoming distant behind us, it exploded suddenly and vastly, in an immense display of obliterating destruction.

We watched it happen from a porthole window, completely chilled by the level of violence taking place, as smaller, more precise explosions erupted all around that large island, swiping whatever it might have been still left standing.

I gulped. Nemo kept navigating the *Nautilus'* smaller version, taking us away to safety.

*In this tale, Micah Harris takes on a rollercoaster ride that happily mixes espionage and supernatural fiction, cleverly blending element taken from* Twin Peaks, The Prisoner, Kiss Me Deadly *(the film), and others. The hero, Teddy Verano, is (or more accurately was) a popular pulp detective created in the 1930s by French writer Maurice Limat. Interested parties can read a few of his adventures in* Mephista, *published by Black Coat Press. Considering the fact that he didn't age throughout the series, it is more likely that the books written post-WWII feature his son, rather than the original...*

## Micah S. Harris: *The Secret Alchemy of Very Bad Balloons*

*Los Angeles, 1954.*

Fearful lest the darkened beach house would be illuminated by the headlights of his hearse, the driver quickly turned them off. At once, the night was everywhere as he pulled over to the roadside on the California coastal highway.

He put the hearse in park and turned the key, stilling the engine. The sound of the surf rushed to fill the silence. For a few moments, he sat, watching the beach house on stilts for any sign of activity that would indicate his approach had been noticed.

Seeing none, Teddy Verano checked to see his revolver's arm holster was snug beneath his suit's coat, and that another, far more crucial object was similarly secured and hidden upon his person.

This artifact was sheathed in a phylactery. Its contents: the effulgence of broken hearts, tortured souls, and suicidal levels of despair. But it was the desperate fear *of* dying that made the base for this bitter perfume: *eau de larmes*.

He grabbed the unopened vegetable tin from the passenger's seat and stuck it in a coat pocket. Then he picked up from the floorboard the sturdy attaché case, the contents of which were also crucial for his mission, and opened the car door.

He was just standing to his feet when a woman's scream shrilled out of the night, causing the thing in the phylactery to hum like a struck tuning fork.

"Angie...."

He groaned her name, drew his gun and began running along the roadside toward the beach house, attaché case swinging alongside him.

He thought of the receptionist at the athletic club, shot dead behind the counter, whose murderer he had reason to believe was holding Angie in that beach house.

As he neared the raised structure, he ducked and bolted beneath the house, pausing to lean against one of the wooden stilts and catch his breath. There had been no more sounds from inside the house. Only the roar of black ocean hurling froth-fringed wave after wave against the shore

Verano stuck his head out to survey the backyard. Determining that he was, indeed, alone, he scrambled up the backsteps.

He found the back door unlocked, an indication that his enemy inside was either confident that he was perfectly concealed, or was in a major hurry, or both.

He pushed on the door and followed it inward. From the front of the house, he heard what sounded like the effete voice of a professor of mythology and world religions holding forth: "Pandora... Lot's wife... Medusa..."

The Mediterranean mythology references made him wonder if Angie was being addressed, for the Mediterranean was from where Angie Rona hailed. Her mission had brought him here, but now he was here for *her*, too.

And he was going to rescue her *first*.

He raised his gun and began making his way down the narrow hallway. Then he heard the soft whimpering of a woman from behind a door to his right. The distress in her voice again unsettled the phylactery pressed against him.

He tried the knob and found that *this* door *was* locked. Verano holstered his gun, then removed from his coat's inside pocket his small lock-picking kit. He already knew which pick he needed for an inside doorknob. In a few seconds, he had it sprung, his lock kit back in his coat, and his gun back in his hand.

He shoved the door inward, then swept his gun over the room as he surveyed it, prompting a muffled scream from the bound and gagged woman in the dark on the bed before him. Because of the gag, her screams sounded more like lowing, but it was enough to prompt yet another tremble from the phylactery.

She writhed frantically against her bonds as he shoved the door closed behind him and locked it.

"It's all right!" he said, not daring to flick on the light switch at his hand. "It's Teddy, Angie, baby. Your Theodore! Don't worry. I'm going to get you out of here, honey."

In a moment he was over her, gently tucking her head and pushing his fingers into her silky dark hair to untie her gag.

The gag removed, the woman's head fell back onto her pillow. World-weary eyes in a pixie face looked up at him.

"Thanks much," she said, "but who are you and who is Angie?"

### Paris, 1946

That was what Verano had been asking himself for almost a decade.

He had first met her in Paris, not long after the end of the second world war. He was in a café in a bad section of town, staring at the wet ring left by his beer mug on the letter from his father. Verano *père* had written to inform him of his illness that he was determined to fight.

He did not know where the men drinking with him had come from. Veterans like himself, he thought. The acrid whiff of burned gunpowder hung about them. They must have been in the thick of some prolonged battle, he mused, so prolonged that the stench got into their skin.

"You are hurting, my friend," one of the men said, tracing the damp circle on the letter stationary with a fingertip with what looked like soot beneath the nail. The whole hand had been blistered. Somehow, his acrid smell reminded Verano of a fireman's after a fire. "We know pain. Let us take you to pleasure."

"Pleasure?" The word rattled in his throat as a sardonic chuckle as he stared blankly at the letter.

"To Judy," replied the fireman. "There are pleasures in *her* house. Pleasures to make you forget. You come, eh?"

"Get away from him."

Verano looked up with the others at the pure tones of the woman's voice. The sound was like an enormous bell of light had suddenly tolled. At once, the men were scraping their chairs away from his table and withdrawing.

"And tell Judy that *I* am seeing to his wounds. Now, scram, you powder monkeys."

Unlike his uninvited bar friends, that voice and its possessor did not repel but *drew* him. Their acrid scent was replaced by her aroma, that of rain-scented air in springtime.

The perfectly proportioned rondure of the woman's body was impeccably presented in the crisp uniform of one of the WAAF. Brown hair in wavy curls was pulled up beneath her uniform's billed hat. The gaze of her bright, blue eyes felt like beautiful music was looking at him.

Beneath a patrician nose, her full lips parted as the corners of her mouth curled up to reveal even white teeth, bright against her olive complexion. A single smile from her was sufficient to shred like tissue the shroud that had bound his heart.

That lush mouth might belong to an opera singer; little wonder her voice had boomed so powerfully from it. Now it was the melodious whisper of windchimes when she spoke.

"May I join you?"

"You don't really expect me to say no, do you?"

She laughed, the girlish tones touching him like bright, chaste kisses. The years of war that had warped him into manhood and left him bent suddenly fell away, and he felt his soul inside him lift, as it were, its shoulders and stand tall.

And just like that, she became *that* girl for him, the type most men get to experience just once, and that early on in their lives: the one who first awakens a lad to the dizzyingly blithesome inapprehensible, when what happens between a man and a woman is yet a pure and giddy mystery to him.

She thrust out her gloved hand. "Hello. You are?"

"Teddy Verano," he said and shook the offered hand. As she withdrew it, she cocked her head at him, and, with teasing eyes, said, "That's short for Theodore. What a coincidence; I'm Theodora."

He chuckled and shook his head at her. "You are not," he said as he first held the chair for her, then retook his seat opposite.

With a tight-lipped smile, she nodded. "I am. Don't you know what your own name means?"

He creased his brow as he momentarily glanced again at the letter from his father, whom he was named after. Then, he sighed, and looked into her soothing blue eyes. "I do. My father named me, as his father named him, in the happiness of having a son. It means *Gift of God*."

She reached across the table, interlocked her gloved fingers with his own—and immediately triggered a blithesome intake of breath. He had forgotten how, once, just holding a girl's hand could be happiness enough.

"Well, then, I am God's gift to you, tonight, Theodore Verano."

"I believe you!" he said, staring at her olive-complexioned little hand holding his. It felt more like she was cradling his heart.

"Tell me all that troubles you," she said with a quick nod at the letter on the table. "Everything."

He did. They talked about the loss of his mother shortly before the second world war began; about the young men standing beside him on the battlefield, lives snuffed before their bodies hit the ground; about the illness that had stricken his father, and their now-threatened dream of a father-son detective agency.

She more than listened. As he relived each suffering, he recognized the precise pain of which he spoke on her face. As she took in each hurt, he felt it perceptibly less. Without touching him, she was wiping away his tears; tears not upon his face, but upon his heart.

And afterward, while he still felt every loss he had suffered, he also felt something that startled him because he had forgotten what it was like: he felt himself smile.

Then, in the pale light before sunrise, she tapped his hand, slid back her chair, and rose to her feet.

"I have to go."

He frowned. "Why?"

"Cinderella…" she said, her fingers busy adjusting and repining her cap to her hair.

"Eh? I'd think you're more the fairy godmother type."

"…liberty. *Cinderella liberty*, the Yanks call it."

She nodded at the morning taking possession of the quaint, cobblestone street just outside the window. In the dim but ever brightening light, shop owners were emerging from their doors to dash mop water to the sidewalks. A horse clomped by, pulling a milk wagon.

"It is now officially September 23, and *I* am now officially at the end of my leave," she said as she finished adjusting her hat.

Verano shoved back and rose from his chair, smiling. "Ah... I understand. Can I come see you at the air force base? Soon? Pick you up to take you on a proper date?"

She wrinkled her nose at him. "*You* go be with your father now, Theodore Verano. Let him teach you everything you need to become a detective just like him. Whatever happens in regard to his health, you will never regret this time with him."

He stepped closer to her. "But... papa is in Versailles. That is too much distance. I... I want to get to know *you*, Theodora."

She cocked her head at him and sighed, her eyes tender. "I know that you do, Teddy. But right now, it's most important that you become a detective like your papa."

"But you might be reassigned at an any time. Especially now that the war is over. What if you are transferred before..."

Again, she wrinkled her nose at him as she reached out and touched the tip of his with her gloved finger. "Become the detective your father is, and you will develop the skills that will help you find me again."

"But... that will take years."

"I'll be around." She pinched together the tips of her thumb and forefinger and put the oval space between the two to one eye. "Be seeing you, Theodore." She held up a forefinger perpendicular to lips curved in a smile, then flung him a kiss from it.

She was already making her way to the door before he had even seen her turn and go.

"Wait..."

"*If you love me, you will find me out.*"

He gave his head a quick shake. "Your final words to me and they are not even yours—they're Shakespeare's!"

"First folio foiled," she said over her shoulder. Then the door closed behind her.

"Wait, Theodora... Theodora? I don't even know your real name!" he shouted at the closed door, waking the tavern waiter who had been dosing with one side of his head to the bar. Only then did he realize that he had made no effort to stop her leaving... that he wasn't even pursuing her now.

"Hey! Hey!" the waiter yelled at Verano, intercepting him before he could exit. The waiter wagged a thick finger, ready to curl with its fellow digits into a fist, in Verano's face. "I been up all night, at your service, *mon gars*. You owe me a big tip!"

Verano fumbled some crumpled francs from his pocket into the waiter's hand, then darted out the door... to find Theodora long gone.

Though, of course, he knew where to look for her.

"I am sorry, Monsieur Verano, but there is no one named Theodora at this air force base."

"I said she *called* herself Theodora. Let me describe her for you. She was about... uh, five feet, six inches tall. Slim, but well-rounded figure. Curly brown hair... more wavy, but curly, too. Olive complexion. Blue eyes that lit up your soul."

Lieutenant O'Houlihan to whom he was talking leaned over her desk and narrowed her eyes at him, pursed her lips and regarded him sidelong.

"Wait here," she said as she rose and walked out of the room.

He waited at least a full half hour. Finally, O'Houlihan returned with an armed guard who said nothing, but took his place by the door once it was closed behind them.

*What is going on?* Verano thought.

O'Houlihan sat down behind her desk and laid on it a manilla folder that she had brought back. She opened it to reveal a black and white photo of a young woman.

"That's Theodora!" exclaimed Verano. "I mean... that's who said her name was Theodora."

"This is a woman named Angie Rona," replied O'Houlihan.

He could not help himself. He reached out and touched the black and white photo. "I knew she did not give me her real name." He sighed.

"She should not have been able to give you anything, Monsieur Verano."

"Eh?"

"Not recently, anyway."

"What do you mean?"

"Angie Rona was on a plane that went down over the Mediterranean Sea a year ago. The plane and the bodies of her and the pilot were never found."

"Then, she survived."

"So it would seem."

He touched her picture again and sighed. "She told me if I loved her, I would find her out."

"Angie always was the theatrical type."

"Eh?"

"She was quoting to you from *The Merchant of Venice*."

"That's right."

"Angie had studied theater and was pursuing a career in movies before the war."

"Did she ever make any movies?"

"A couple for Alexander Korda... At least, that is what our information on her says."

"I need that information."

"You will have to get it elsewhere."

"But..."

"I'm sorry, Monsieur Verano. I may have said too much already. I suppose that hurt-puppy look in your eyes got to me. There *is* a heart beneath my Irish lass countenance, you see. But the file on Miss Rona, like the one on her plane accident, has been sealed by the government."

"*Which* government?"

"Good day, Monsieur Verano. The soldier will see you out."


Teddy Verano, of course, sought out his mysterious angel as much as he could in the years immediately following their encounter that had mended him on the cusp of autumn, 1946. He had contacted by mail the Alexander Korda studio in London, but was informed there was no record of any actress ever having worked there named either "Angie Rona" or even "Theodora."

Often, he had puzzled over her parting words to him. Of course, they were a clue... but just to her having had a career as an actress? Something always nagged at him that there was more.

But given the constant proximity to his ailing father required to make a detective of him, he could not actively search for her.

As it turned out, someone had been searching for him, too.

How long, he did not know. But one day, his detective skills had become honed enough to let him know that he was being followed.


*Paris, 1953*


The year now was 1953, and Teddy Verano was handling a high-profile divorce case while his father and his old friend Marco worked another. It was clear this would be one of Verano *père*'s final adventures, and Verano *fils* had very much wanted to be at his father's side.

However, locating, and, hopefully, catching in the act their wealthy client's huband and the medium Lionella would go far in ensuring his father's legacy that was the Verano Detective Agency.

Lionella's trail took Verano to a used bookstore called *La Galerie du Zodiaque* located rue Monsieur-le-Prince in Paris' 6th arrondissement. Verano paused as he passed the business, bit his lower lip as he peered into it, then decided to take some time out to pursue his ongoing *personal* investigation.

He stepped off the sidewalk into the store. The frantic tingling of the tiny bell at the top of the door turned the attention of a dark-haired man with an angular face, nattily attired in dark navy-blue tie, matching slacks, and tallow-colored sweater.

He propped upon the ash tray his half-consumed cigarette, a thin ribbon of scented smoke unfurling from its ashy end. "May I help you, Monsieur?" he said, rounding the counter and approaching Verano.

"I hope so. Are you the owner?"

"No, but I used to be," replied the man. "My name is Pierre Véry. I'm always happy to help the current owner when he has a day off. Is there anything in particular that you're looking for?"

"Do you know something of an edition of Shakespeare's plays with foil?" asked Verano.

"Eh? You mean *foliated*?"

"I guess?" Verano tucked his head, put his hand to the back of his neck, red with embarrassment, and gave it a quick rub. "No. I don't even know what that means."

"You're not asking for a 1623 First Folio of Shakespeare's plays? I cannot help you there. Heh! If we had one of those, it would be gone in a flash and my successor would not be selling used books; he'd be in Monte Carlo with a beautiful woman on each arm."

"I see," Verano said, lost as ever as to the significance of Angie's clue. He gave Véry a nod, turned…

"Or perhaps you meant Shakespeare's *foiled* First Folio?"

Verano turned on his heel. "Isn't that what I said the first time?"

With a grin, Véry clucked his tongue. "No. That is a single volume, a botched first pass at Shakespeare's First Folio. It ended up being something like what we call a proof today. It was supposed to be destroyed, but wasn't, and has passed through some very exclusive, very wealthy hands over the three hundred years since. That proof, of course, is rarer than even the corrected published edition. It is currently held in an extremely private collection. But I have seen photostats of the erroneous pages that foiled the printing."

Verano leaned slightly toward Véry, for his detective's instinct had begun to tingle. "What were the nature of these errors?"

Véry picked up his cigarette, and pursed his lips. He blew a ragged aromatic smoke ring, then waved the hand through the air and shrugged.

"There were two marring the text of *The Merchant of Venice*…"

"It *was The Merchant of Venice*? You're sure?"

"Yes, *The Merchant of Venice*. Do you not know it?"

"Yes, yes, I know it. Of course, I know it. It is my favorite. What were the variants?"

Véry took another slow draw on his cigarette, eyeing him curiously. Verano's pulse quickened at the thought that the other was considering not telling him…

Véry sent another ragged smoke ring floating. He looked down as he pressed the crumbling ashy-stub of the cigarette into the tray. He left it there, folded his arms across his chest, and stared at Verano.

"You will recall that the play's heroine. Portia. rules a fairy tale kind of kingdom: caskets, riddles, etc. That's not Venice; it's called Belmont."

"Which means *Beautiful mountain*," Verano said almost reverently.

"Yes," Véry said. Then he chuckled warmly and added, "A copyist's error foiled the folio by calling *The Merchant of Venice*'s Portia 'Miranda,' who is the ingenue from *The Tempest*, and writing Belisland instead of Belmont."

Verano creased his brow. "Why would he mix up the two heroines and mistake an island for a mountain?"

Véry shrugged. "I suppose *The Tempest* was the copyist's favorite?"

"So, there's an island in *The Tempest*?"

"I take it that one is *not* your favorite, eh? Yes, there's an island. The characters are shipwrecked on it. There's a magician already there in exile named Prospero—the former Duke of Milan. He is sort of directing everyone through this scenario, a master manipulator. Machiavellian, but in a good way. By the end, he's back in Milan and Duke again. He takes his daughter Miranda with him, and she is married off to a prince or some such who was one of the shipwrecked. For some reason, the copyist made the error of having Prospero call Miranda 'Portia,' as if this mage who's three steps ahead of everyone else would slip up on his own daughter's name."

"Did Prospero's island have a name?"

"No, Shakespeare never gave it a name. He indicates it's somewhere in the Mediterranean, between the coasts of Europe and North Africa. Could he have been more vague? One wonders what he was hiding, eh?"

Verano arched an eyebrow. "You think Shakespeare was hiding something?"

"The island serves the plot. That is all that is known or needs to be known."

Verano again stared into space. "Belmont. Belisland. Islands *are* mountains... volcanic mountains..."

"They can be."

Verano looked aside and murmured: "Venice is in Italy... Milan is in Italy... *If you love me, you will find me out.* Was she hinting I should look for her in Venice or Milan?"

Véry slightly turned his head. "That depends on whom you're looking for, Portia, or Miranda?"

"I'm looking for someone else. Someone either in Italy or on an uncharted island in the Mediterranean, it's sounds like."

"Funny thing about Mediterranean," Véry said, looking sidelong at him. "Everybody thinks *sea*, but the word literally means *inland*."

Stroking his chin, Verano murmured, "Inland... Mediterranean... *medius* plus *terras*... And *medius* doesn't mean *in*, it means *middle*... I translated that all on my own, by the way."

Véry chuckled. "Very good!"

"Not an island in the sea, then, but a mountain in the middle of Italy? Or one between Milan and Venice?"

Verano slapped a hand down on the counter. "Do you have used encyclopedias here? Anything on Italy with a detailed map?"

Véry nodded, took a moment to take another quick drag off of his cigarette, then slipped into the back. He came back with a thick volume. Verano immediately opened it on the counter and began flipping through it.

"What are you looking for?" asked Véry.

"I'm looking for what is halfway between Milan and Venice... and see if there's a mountain there."

He pulled the encyclopedia page with the map close to his face, checked the scale...

He still had to shake his head, then stared into space as he laid the encyclopedia spread open on the counter.

"So?" Véry asked.

Verano looked at him and pointed. Véry looked at the map on the page.

"The *Corno d'Aquilio* in Verona," Verano said. "That sounds almost like my name. It's as if she were calling to me from the page."

Véry flashed a grin. "A bit too on-the-nose, don't you think? Still, *Verona* does mean *truth*, so it looks like you might find it there. Perhaps the truth that you and your lady are meant to be... or not."

"What do you mean?"

"Both *Romeo and Juliet* and, of course, *Two Gentlemen of Verona* are set where you're heading. One play is a tragedy, the other a comedy."

Verano slowly closed the encyclopedia. "I'm hoping for the happy ending."

"Aren't we all?" said Véry.

As Verano stepped out of the store and onto the street, he noticed a man with greasy hair quickly tucking his head and taking a drag on his cigarette. The man began pacing back and forth in front of a shop, glancing at a nearby public clock, as if he was keeping up with how much time he had left on his work break.

Verano turned his head in the direction he had intended to go and began walking, as though he had taken no particular notice of the man.

He paused a block down to pretend he was window-shopping suits in a Men's Fashion store. In the reflection of the store glass, he saw the man crossing the street behind him. As Verano had expected, he did not approach him, but continued straight, disappearing as he passed the opposite corner.

Verano dashed into a small alley just a few feet away from the clothing store. He flattened himself against the alley wall out of sight of his stalker and waited...

The man bobbed into view, walking faster, trying to recover his mark. He was staring intently ahead...

Verano lashed out, latched down on both his shoulders, yanked him into the alley, and, while the man was too surprised to resist, slung him headfirst against the wall, stunning him.

Verano began dragging him down the alley. The man dug in his heels so that they scraped the cement and slowed their progress. Verano smashed his fist into the man's temple, and he fell to the alley floor in a sprawl.

"Don't...," the man pleaded.

Verano drove the especially-designed steel toe of his shoe into the tender spot just below the man's ribcage, sending him sucking raggedly for air through his grimacing mouth. Afterward, Verano was able to rifle the man's pockets without resistance.

When he had his adversary's weapon and his wallet, he stepped away, leaned against the alley's far wall, and trained the man's .357 Magnum on him.

"Hug the ground like it's your lover, sweetheart. I'm risking no ricochet this close, and I *will* shoot and leave you to bleed out alone in this filth, no problem."

The man stuck out an opened palm and waved it in the air. "I believe... ummf... I be... lieve... yew... ummf..."

With one eye on his stalker, Verano let the gun relax enough for him to start pulling cards from the wallet.

Then, he latched onto one and let the entire wallet fall.

"Norman Nash... *M16*?" Verano's eyes bulged. He had assumed he was being tailed by a thug sent by his wealthy client's husband, or his lover Lionella, the medium herself.

"I... I'm... secret service," Nash gasped. "Don'... t'ink you... you... wanna kill sum 'un on her majesty's se... cret service...."

Verano took fresh aim at him with the man's gun. "I might. That could all depend on what you say and if I believe it. *Talk*. Why are you following me?"

As he drew deep breaths, Nash looked up into the pistol barrels. "You, uh... ummm... remember that fan letter you wrote?"

"What?"

"Korda Studio... London. Askin' 'bout that actress... Angie Rona."

Verano cocked his head. "How do you know about that? Why does M16 know about that, or even care?"

"Angie Rona was in the WAAF..."

"Tell me what I don't know."

"...those women operated radar and wirelesses, analyzed reconnaissance photos..."

Verano clicked back the hammer on the pistol. "I said tell me what I *don't* know."

"Angie was one of those analysts—one with a *very* high security clearance. She disappeared with certain reconnaissance photos, right down to the negatives."

"In a plane that went down in the Mediterranean. I know that, too."

"Then you know as much as M16. So, Teddy... maybe you can fill me in on why you were rendezvousing with her a year after she vanished?"

Verano cocked his head. "You think I was in with her on stealing those photos?"

"Oh, come on, Teddy Bear—you've been cuddled! No one smart enough to be *her* partner in crime would waltz into the base she stole those photos from, asking for her. You're her *dupe*, man! You've met her; seen her; probably made an excuse to touch her. Woman like that, she has no problem getting men to do whatever she wants."

"Shut up! She hasn't tried to make me do anything. If I'm such a disposable dupe to her, why have you been following me for—*how* long?"

"Since you left the American Orly base that day."

"For seven *years*?"

"And we've always known just where to find you since that letter you sent."

He gave his head a quick shake. "So, Angie was never in any movie at the Korda Studio. That Irish lieutenant I talked to lied to me, baited me, so that I'd send a letter, give M16 an address... because you were hoping she'd come to me if I didn't lead you to her, right, Mr. Nash?"

Verano lifted his shoulders, raised the man's Magnum with a bend of his elbow, and said, "Scurry back to your masters, Crumpets, and tell them if I haven't led you to Angie Rona yet, I am not about to now. I have no idea what she is up to. I saw her once, years ago, and never have since. Now, stay on the ground and don't come out of this alley for ten minutes, unless you want to risk taking a bullet."

Nash nodded, his greasy, disheveled hair slicking his forehead. Eyes still trained on the M16 agent, Verano took a step back, then left.

*Verona*

"Goldfinger. Auric Goldfinger."

The maître d' to whom Verano he had slipped a note, was responding to his question, "Who is the man with the lady?"

The lady was Angie. His initial elation upon laying eyes on her for the first time in years had been immediately stunted by the sight of the stocky man with the crewcut hair who sat at the table with her.

At the bandstand, jazz virtuoso Charlie Parker was improvising a sax solo in the middle of *Koko* while the upright bass and snare drum played bottom and the pianist carried the rhythm. Women in strapless and backless gowns sat at small, candlelit tables with men in immaculate white tuxes, like the one Verano wore.

This club was *not* cheap. Neither was the mountain resort of which it was a part on the *Corno d'Aquilio* in the Province of Verona, where he had finally tracked her down.

With eyes narrowed on Angie and this Auric Goldfinger, Verano straightened his black tie and began crossing the darkened club's floor. He continued sizing up his rival as he walked. He was stocky, broad-shouldered, and a bit pudgy, given the crease in the back of his cleanshaven neck.

*Well, Monsieur Doigt d'Or*, he thought, *let us test your mettle.*

Despite the fear that he was too late, that Angie already belonged to another, the sight of her still caused a smile to break out upon Verano's heart. She was more ravishing than ever, every vibrant atom of her freed of the regimented WAAF uniform and running rampant in a sleek evening gown.

That gown was off the shoulder, baring olive complexioned skin from her neck down to opera gloves that that started mid-bicep. Her hair was up. She looked every bit as if a beauty of ancient Rome had plopped down into the cigarette smoke and smooth jazz of this mid-twentieth century nightclub.

With a blithesome grin, Goldfinger was reaching to caress Angie's delicate jawline. She reclined her head to avoid the touch.

"But, baby," Auric Goldfinger was saying, "I only want to protect you. I know the League of Ten Thousand is intent on procuring you, whether you like it or not. They are convinced your talents are essential to restoring their organization to the glory days of Jacques Collin.

"And I've heard the Don of the Marsellus family intends to steal you away and set you up as the Tutelary of his gangster turf in Los Angeles. He means to present you to his son Marcus when the lad grows up. So, you *must* commit yourself to my keeping, my dear. In fact, I won't take no for an answer."

"I'm afraid you're going to have to," Verano said.

Angie looked up, startled. She cocked her head and mouthed "How?", then her lips construed into a smile of bemused relief and gratitude.

Goldfinger turned his head to look up. "Huh?" he said, the chin of his sunburned face resting on a napkin he was using as a bib. "Who are you?"

Angie's smile lifted her cheeks, her eyes bright upon Verano. "He's from out of town, Auric. I told you I was waiting for someone."

Goldfinger looked at her. "You always say you are waiting for someone, Angie."

"Well," she said and wrinkled her nose at Verano just like she had in Paris, "here he is at last."

"Here I am. At last," Verano said and offered her his arm.

Angie rose from the table, took his arm, and they began to walk away while Goldfinger looked on, eyes bulging like a spurned frog prince.

"I can't tell you how good it is to see you," Verano said.

"The same. Walk fast. He has men who will trail us. How are those detective skills you are supposed to have been developing for me? Can you shake any tail he puts on us?"

He grinned. "Watch me."

Verano was not so naïve that he did not suspect Angie might try to shake him again, as soon as he had helped her elude her unwanted pursuer. So, he held onto her gloved arm, even when they were in the cab or on the road. She did not try to disengage.

"I am so glad to see you, Theodore," she said, "and not just because of Auric."

"And I am glad to see you too, Theodora. Or do you prefer Angie?"

She smiled, tightlipped, then looked him in the eyes. "You have done your homework exceedingly well. In fact, you have done everything exceedingly well to have found me. You have rewarded my faith in you, Theodore Verano."

"And what is to be my reward, Angie?" he said, turning his head to survey the road behind, noting one pair of headlights perhaps a little too close.

Her mascaraed eyebrows lifted. "What?"

He held up his hand to silence her as he turned his face back toward the driver. "Hey, my man?"

The driver regarded Verano's reflection in the rearview mirror. "*Si?*"

Verano jerked his thumb at the back window. "We need to lose someone. Think you can do that for an extra 500 lira?"

The driver responded by gassing the pedal, throwing Verano and Angie against the back seat. They looked at each other and laughed.

"Now, what was this about some reward that you were expecting?" she said.

"You were saying how pleased you were that I had followed your clues to find you, as though *you* were the one due satisfaction. But it is *I* who have done all the hard work. To the victor goes the spoils, Angie."

"I think I like *reward* better," she said and frowned, but there was a hint of a grin at the corners of her mouth.

He smiled and lifted the gloved hand of her arm he still held to his lips. "How about *prize*?"

She reached out with the other gloved hand and traced a velvety finger along his jawline. "Even better," she breathed.

"That is my preference as well. I wish you to reward my curiosity. You…," He gave her gown clinging to the contours of her body a blatant look over, "…have very much aroused my curiosity, Angie Rona. There are things about you I yearn to… uncover,' shall we say?"

"Teddy!"

"Chief among them: why did my one informal meeting with you in a Parisian bar suffice to put M16 on my trail for years?"

"What? You do not think they followed you here, do you?"

"Didn't I tell you I know how to lose a tail? Driver!"

The reflection of the man's eyes in the rearview mirror met Verano's, who indicated with a jerk of his head a hotel coming up on the left.

The driver pulled into the parking lot. Verano and Angie climbed out of the back of the cab. Still hooking her gloved arm with his, he passed the driver his lira, then began strolling to the hotel, walking her along with him.

"You have a room here?" she asked.

"We're not going to my room; we're going to your place."

"This isn't where I stay, either."

"I didn't think it was. Listen, I suspect your friend Goldfinger has already bribed every taxi driver servicing that jazz club tonight."

"You mean… the driver you just paid to lose Auric's tail…"

"…Has already been paid much more by Goldfinger to send him or his goons right where he deposited us. From what you told me, and the look I saw in his eyes, he's taking no chances on losing you again, Angie. I actually sympathize with him."

They entered the lobby, walked straight through and out the door onto the other side of the parking lot.

"I have no desire for your friend with the Midas touch to know where I am staying, and certainly not to know where you are."

She grinned. "You are the slick one, Theodore. I am more and more impressed. But Auric is wealthy—and motivated—enough to have paid off every cab driver in town. And I cannot walk to my place. In *these* heels? Out of the question, Teddy! What are you doing?"

"Breaking into this person's car. It will get us where we need to go. No driver involved."

Angie shot a nervous look back at the hotel. "But we can't…"

"Why not?" Verano said as he opened the door. "I know how to hotwire a car, and the petrol tank is full."

She bit her lower lip but could not suppress her smile. "Impressive. But it's still stealing, Theodore."

"The car will be found abandoned and undamaged not far from here. I'll even leave some lira on the front seat to replace the petrol. But, Angie, we got to go. Unless you want your friend Auric to get his hands on you, gold fingers and all."

"No, no!" she said ducking inside. "Let's go."

"To your place?" Verano, who had yet to enter the car said, aiming a mock-imploring look down at her.

"Yes! I'll take you to my place. Just, please, let's get out of here *now*!"

Her place was a flat in a nineteenth century palazzo renovated into apartments that set atop a hilly village street. As she fished her keys from her clutch, Verano held her shoes. Their shedding had been necessitated when, having learned they were in walking distance of their destination, he had left the borrowed car at the bottom of the hill. The walk was preferable to parking it telltale in front of their retreat.

They entered the restored palazzo through a vestibule, climbed a flight of narrow, wooden steps, and then Angie was unlocking the door to which they led. They stepped into cool darkness. She shut the door behind them, then began moving through the room, clicking on a series of lamps.

Verano stood by the door, his eyes still adjusting to the dim light. A door of glass panes opened onto a balcony. He crossed over to it, drawing back the wispy, pale curtain just enough to see where they had just come from. He found everything the same as they had left it; only the Northwind stirred in the street.

"Do you mind if I slip into something more comfortable?" she said and pointed at her bedroom through its open door.

Verano quickly crossed the living room floor, passed her without comment, and entered the bedroom.

"Theodore! That was *not* an invitation. Or are you afraid that Auric's men have somehow discovered my whereabouts and are waiting in my boudoir to carry me back to him?"

"No," he said, one corner of his mouth turned up as he stepped back out of the bedroom, "I wish to be certain there is no door through which you might get away from me again, Angie."

Verano recognized genuine hurt in her eyes prompted by his words.

"Theodore... Teddy," she said, putting her gloved hand to his face, "I understand why you might feel that way, but I have never been running from you, not like I am from Auric... and others. Stop and think. How is it that you were there to rescue me from him? How is it that you are here with me now?"

She poked him in the chest with a gloved forefinger. "Because I gave you clues about how to find me. Don't you think I knew you would go to Orly after our night at the café? That I was risking making myself vulnerable..."

"You mean. to M16."

She nodded. "Them, and, oh, so much more than you can begin to imagine."

*I can begin to*, Verano thought. She did not know that he knew about her faked death at sea, and her theft of that mysterious reconnaissance file with its photos and negatives.

"But I did it because I sensed that *you* were worth the risk, Teddy," she continued. "You needed the proper motivation to get you out of that hole you were in, that was about to reveal new depths to you that, believe me, were horrible beyond comprehension. So, I directed you to focus your attention and affection on your father, and, in the process, claim your proper vocation as a detective. And I gave you clues so that, should my confidence in you be prove to be well-placed, you would find me."

293

He waved his hand through the air. "Yeah, yeah... all that Shakespeare... *If you love me, you will find me out,*" Verano said. "Very well. We have established my feelings for you. Angie, what are yours for me?"

She smiled. "It is different for a woman, Teddy. Let us say that you are still being tested, but now it is *I* who assume the risks. So do you mind if I slip into something more comfortable, something more like my own skin?"

He lifted her gloved hand to his lips then looked up from it, his gaze warm and soft as he stared into her eyes.

"I will only be a moment," she said with a smile, then stepped into her boudoir and closed the door behind her. Teddy listened. There was no sound of a lock clicking or a key turning.

With a sigh, he loosened his tie, walked over to a plush divan and plopped down. A volume of Apuleius' *Metamorphoses* lay there. He picked it up and opened it to where Angie had been reading—in the original Latin—*Psyche et Cupido.* He closed the book, set it back down on the couch, and surveyed his surroundings.

There were green potted plants setting about, all of the indigenous variety. A single framed picture hanging on a wall made him furrow his brow; it was a large black and white photo of an atom bomb cloud. On a set of bookshelves against the opposite wall, there was a small, classically sculpted statue of a robed woman with a finger to her lips. Beside it set a framed photograph.

Verano rose from the couch and walked over to the photograph, curious to see who it was of. To his surprise, the subject was Angie and a group of children, one of whom had an arm in a cast, another resting on a crutch. Angie's long, curling hair was down, and she wore no makeup. She had donned a long-sleeved shirt, her hands were covered by gardeners' gloves, and her legs by a pair of women's trousers. This was a much more down-to-earth presentation of herself than either the pragmatic WAAF uniform or the glamorous evening gown afforded, and the one which Verano found himself preferring.

He picked up the sculpture of the woman with a finger to her lips and looked at the base. There was a label from a shop still stuck there. It read: *The Shop.* He shrugged, put it back in place and walked over to the black and white photo of an atom bomb cloud mounted on the opposite wall. Before he reached it, he noticed some letters on a desk. With a glance at the closed bedroom door, he quickly made his way to it.

Angie had opened a letter, its single page unfolded and laying beside the envelope. It was written in Italian; he was able to make out the opening lines: *Dear Miss Feronia, I do hope this letter reaches you. I wanted to tell you again how much the children enjoyed your...*

Verano wrinkled his brow. Miss Fe*ronia*?' Ronia... Rona... Angie *Rona...* He sighed. "Who are you *really*, love?"

He noticed that she was apparently in the process of some correspondence of her own. A paperweight held down a lavender envelope. Verano lifted the paperweight and examined the stationery. There was no address. The stamp was unlike any he had ever seen: a stylized image of a horse and chariot.

He heard the bedroom doorknob turning. He immediately set the paperweight back down on the envelope and took a couple quick strides in the opposite direction.

Angie had stopped at cracking the door. She whispered through the slight opening: "Theodore... Teddy..."

He turned to the door and grinned. "Why so bashful? Come on out."

"You remember I told you that I would be the one taking risks now?"

"You're in no danger from me, Angie." He beckoned emphatically. "C'mon out, love."

"I *am* making myself vulnerable, Teddy. I am trusting you to keep secret what I am about to reveal about my person. I cannot afford another, er, admirer like Auric."

"C'mon, Angie... Do you seriously think I'm anything like that guy?"

"Promise you won't say anything."

"I promise!"

"Silence is golden, Teddy. You *must* understand that to understand me: silence is golden."

He laughed. "I promised! Come out."

"No. *You* come in."

Verano walked to the boudoir door and opened it completely to see Angie draped on the bed in only a brief nightie, her entire body the color of gold.

He slowly crossed the room. "Angie... what is this? Theatrical paint? Is... is this your kink, Angie?"

He guffawed with relief and slapped his thigh. "And to think, you were starting to scare me. My dear girl, this is absolutely *nothing* as these things go."

"You don't mind?"

"Mind what? That you are so voluptuous?"

"No," she said, grinned, and held a forefinger perpendicular before her lips. "Not voluptuous. *Volupia*."

"Well, I don't care how you pronounce it. In fact, I don't care about talking at all right now, do you?"

"No. Just know that this does not give you any claim to me, Teddy. Even though I am giving you much, you are still being tested. I have the right to issue prohibitions."

"What do you mean? No kissing?"

"Nothing like that. And it's just one prohibition; it's always just one, as these things go. You can take me completely as your lover tonight, on the condition that you spend the night in this room. Do you understand? You are *not* to step beyond my bedroom door once you close it behind you until dawn. Can you do that for me, Teddy?"

He closed the door behind him.

She did not disappoint him as a lover. There was tenderness afterward, too, and he fell asleep in her arms.

She woke him while the morning was still night. She was moving quietly about the bedroom, but the door to the living room was now open. He could see her writing desk straight ahead from where he lay.

He did not speak, but watched her through narrowed eyelids. Later, he would wish he had said something then. Later still, he would admit to himself that it would have made no difference regarding what followed.

She padded on bare feet to her closet from which she produced an over-coat. She slipped it over her nightie. He noticed her long legs were still the color of gold.

*She hasn't taken time to wash her body paint off? And she's going out in the middle of the night, in just a barely-there nightgown under her coat? What has happened since I fell asleep that is so urgent?* His stomach clinched like a fist. *My word, is this her way of getting away from me again?*

If she was so inclined, he was convinced to confront her with it now would only postpone her inevitable escape. Better to be still, let her go, then follow.

Carrying a pair of flats in one hand, she closed the bedroom door behind her. He lay still, holding his breath, listening for the outer door to open and close. When he heard that, he threw back the sheets, tugged on his pants and shoved his shoes on over his bare feet.

He had not forgotten her prohibition and was aware this all might be some sort of test. But he had only promised not to leave the bedroom; if he merely opened the door but did not cross the threshold, he would remain true, and she could not be angry with him.

So, he opened her boudoir door, and found himself completely alone. She had left him. Again.

Unless… she was waiting on the other side of the outer door, waiting to see what he would do…

…Or making her way down the mountain at that very moment, headed somewhere, anywhere, in the whole wide world while he just stood there and let her.

He darted to the outer door and threw it open on the empty stairwell. He trotted down the steps and walked out onto the cobblestone road. Tiled-roof houses rose along the forested mountainside above him.

She was not on the street in front of the palazzo. He heard the chaffing of shoes on sidewalk…

He darted after the sound, paused to peer around the corner…

The street was empty except for a single public garbage bin. He began to slowly walk down the street and paused to lean against the turquoise metal trashcan with the swinging door marked *SCIUPARE.*

He listened; only whispers of wind…

He was about to round the next corner when a thought froze him in his tracks: what if Angie found him here on the street or went back to her flat and found him gone?

*Idiot! She's only wearing an overcoat over a nightie. Of course, she is coming back! You're acting like a desperate, twiddle-pated schoolboy.*

He turned and ran back for her flat.

A car's sudden ignition roared up the hill as headlights flared and taillights glared in the distance like angry, red eyes from the spot where he had left the auto he had borrowed.

Apparently, he had not been the only one between the two of them who knew how to hotwire a car.

"Angie!" he bellowed down the hill, after the speedily receding lights of the car. "Angie! Baby! Don't go! *Angie!*"

His shouting set one dog barking and then another and another. Here and there alongside the hill houselights blinked on. Behind him, a window lifted, a woman began harping at him in Italian. Another window raised and ejected a hot water bottle that smacked his shoulder.

He immediately retreated inside and slumped up the steps. When he found her flat still empty, he began smacking himself upside his head.

*Perhaps that wasn't her taking the car... or even if it was, if she's mad, that doesn't mean she's going to stay mad. It doesn't mean she not coming back, right? This is her place, after all. I should just sit here and wait...*

*...there's no way I'm going to just sit here and wait!*

He went to her desk. Immediately, he noticed the letter she had been writing and the envelope were gone.

*She went out barely dressed in the middle of the night to mail a letter?*

Again, he scurried down the stairs and darted outside to the iron wrought mailbox mounted in her apartment house's front wall.

It was jammed full of letters, so anything Angie had mailed should have been on the top. He pulled out as many as he could and examined each envelope. He found no letter with either her lavender stationary nor that odd stamp with its stylized horse and chariot.

He stared into space, eyes narrowed and brow creased.

If she could have mailed her letter right outside her door, why had she put on an overcoat? Apparently, she did not wish to mail it from her place of residence, perhaps for reasons of privacy. So, was there a public mailbox nearby?

Stuffing the letters back into the palazzo mailbox, he trotted along the roads, looking for one on the street. He found nothing within the distance she could have walked before driving off, no public receptacle at all, except...

*...That trash can just around the corner from her flat?*

He returned to it. With a groan, he lifted it, turned it over, held its swinging door back, and shook...

...and found among the debris a fresh letter, still sealed. He snatched it up and recognized at once the lavender envelope with its horse and chariot stamp!

There was no mailing or returning address, only a series of what reminded him of a cheque's routing numbers. Verano had never seen anything like it.

He scratched his head. Why on earth had she gotten up in the middle of the night to throw away a letter in a public waste basket instead of using the garbage can in her flat?

Was it because she feared he might recover it if she left it in the trash there? But why would she even think he would care to? Nevertheless, her "stay in my room" prohibition could indicate that she did not want him to see what she did with it.

He shook his head. No. She had not been planning to trash the letter. It was stamped and sealed. She must have intended to mail it, but changed her mind at the last minute. He ran his finger over the sealed fold. He needed to steam it open and read what it said.

Outside had become less dark now. *So*, he thought, *another Angie-departure with the coming dawn. Perhaps she is subject to prohibitions as well as issuing them.*

Best to give a thorough sweep to her flat while he could, then remove himself elsewhere before delving into the mystery of her letter. It would not go over well at all if Auric Goldfinger and his thugs managed to trail her to her flat and found only him instead.

And, as good at shaking a tag as he had become, M16 could still be on the way as well.

He took a moment to turn the can upright, toss back as much trash into it as he could, and kick the rest into the gutter. He did not want to leave evidence of the receptacle being searched. In the process, he noticed that, under *SCIUPARE*, someone had written *WASTE* by hand on it.

His first thought was that the translation was redundant since it was clear that the object was a trashcan even to the non-Italian speaker.

But why do that and put an initial after every letter of the translation, too?

Someone had picked up Verano's trail, and he had no idea why.

Of course, he knew it had to do with Angie. But, to his utter incredulity, he discovered he understood her even less than he had before their intimate rendez-vous. And he understood nothing at *all* about her letter which read:

*Bunny,*

*The hares have filled their baskets with eggs. Three eluded us, now we are at risk of Hatchlings.*

*Red rover, red rover! So, I'm sending you right over! A wild hare got up my trail, my own hare hopping mad! He turned to Evello in Angel City. Sober in there—beware. He betrayed his Haprocrates oath for the oeuf. And watch out for Judy—Utukku to you, too!*

*The Miliphen project, almost reversed now, and "now" is "won" spelled backward -wow!*

*Silencio,*

*Ange*

## Paris, 1954

Whoever was following him, he was certain, thought he could lead him or her to Angie. Of course, he could not. But he wished neither Goldfinger, nor M16, nor any of the other shadowy groups who had taken an interest in Angie to get their hands on her letter.

So, he took a most circumspect, and consequently time-consuming, route as he made his way out of north Italy and back to France. He was headed back to Paris, and the only person he knew might be able to give him some insight into Angie.

He was relieved to find Pierre Véry sitting behind the counter at the *Galerie du Zodiaque* bookshop rue Monsieur-le-Prince.

"Ah, there you are, my friend," Véry said. He was again smoking a cigarette and wearing the same sweater and matching tie and slacks that he had been when Verano had last laid eyes on him months earlier.

Verano smiled. "Hello. I am glad to see you're here."

The man blew a ragged smoke ring onto the air, then pointed at him with his cigarette. "And was your ending the one you wished, I hope? The happy *Two Gentlemen of Verona* one?"

"I am afraid I am still unsure of which Act I am even in."

Véry set his cigarette in the tray on the counter, crossed his arms and smiled. "But I take it I have been cast in the current scene being staged?"

Verano nodded. "I suppose you might put it that way."

"Well, then," Véry said, "I will try to play my part well. What can I help you with today?"

"That depends. Do you know as much about stamps as you do about rare books?"

"It depends."

Verano produced the same envelope that he had removed from the public wastebasket in Italy. He opened it and shook out some stamps he had taken from Angie's desk.

He then laid the stamps out in a line on the counter. Véry carefully picked up and brought each one close to his eye. "These... look... different," he said.

Having placed the stamps back on the counter, he reached behind it and withdrew a magnifying glass. Peering through it, he examined each stamp.

"Where did you get these?"

"While I was in Italy."

Véry looked up at Verano. "That is an obviously vague answer. You need to understand that this store does not deal in stolen objects."

Verano's cheeks burned. "Why would you think I stole these stamps? I suspected that they were rare, but why would you think I stole them?"

"These are not mere prizes sought by collectors. These are rare *historical* artifacts. They should be in a museum, but...," Véry sighed and flashed Verano a wry smile, "...I suspect they would be very quickly suppressed."

"Suppressed? By whom?" The detective looked at the stamps on the counter. "And these are freshly minted. How are they in *any* sense historical?"

Véry crossed his arms and regarded Verano. "Can you tell me anything about how you obtained these?"

Verano tucked his head and massaged the back of his neck with one hand. "These may be connected to a... mailbox—of sorts--that I might have turned—*tipped* over."

Véry grinned. "By accident, of course. Tell me about this mailbox."

Verano swallowed. "This will sound strange..."

"Go on."

"The Italian word *sciupare* was stenciled on it in paint, and beneath that, someone had handwritten the word *waste*, but each letter with a period after it. Like it was an acronym."

"It *is* an acronym."

"For what?"

"*We Await Silent Trystero's Empire*. That mailbox belonged to the final stage in Europe of the old Thurn and Taxis postal system which goes back to the Thirty-Year War. In more recent times, it became known as the Trystero postal system—or Tristero—and serves those who dwell in the margins of society. They went out of business here, though there *is* a rumor that Trystero is still active in the States, where they provide an illegal rival to the U.S. Postal system."

Véry pointed at the stamps. "These have no marks identifying them with Trystero. I think, rather, that yet another alternative postal system has appropriated Trystero's abandoned infrastructure. This one is much older and, apparently, still quite active on the continent... and parts unknown."

Verano lifted his eyebrows and slightly inclined his head toward him. "What are you basing that on?"

"To begin with, the fact that you came across these in Italy is not without significance. You noticed the stamps' Mediterranean imagery, of course, but look at this stamp here... See this stylized carriage horse and cart here?"

"Yes, I noticed that."

"This other one has stylized imagery of an ox and cart. The postage for the one with the horse and cart is probably higher, eh? I daresay it gets faster delivery."

Verano looked at him. "Why would you think that?"

Véry picked up his cigarette, blew another ragged smoke ring, then set it back into the tray. "Augustus Caesar, the Roman emperor at the birth of Christ, implemented the first postal system of which we have the best historical records. Under Augustus, the mail was delivered in a chariot with horses. Under one of his successors, Diocletian, another means of delivery—a slower one—was implemented: a cart drawn by oxen instead of horses."

Verano pointed at another stamp. "So, this penny-farthing bicycle signifies yet another later delivery method? A more modern one, replacing the horses and oxen?"

Véry puckered to take another drag off the cigarette, eyes squinting as he looked at Verano. He blew another ragged smoke ring and nodded.

"Like the Thurn and Taxis system, the Caesars' is also now defunct... officially. Done away with in Italy during the fascists' regime, when they established the Ministry of Communications. But, as you point out, *these* stamps are from freshly minted sheets."

"So, it still operates in Europe, like the Trystero in the States," Verano said, "as an alternate postal system, for those who wish to remain, er, peripheral."

The detective gently bit his lower lip and nodded. It all made sense. If anyone operated out of the edges of things, it was Angie Rona.

As Véry concentrated on his cigarette again, Verano regarded his unlikely ally, whose knowledge of the esoteric was quite astonishing. Was he really only a retired bookseller?

"There's something else," Verano said.

"Yes?"

"Before we go any further, I must ask for your confidence first... and also about the stamps."

Véry momentarily knitted his brow. "Of course," he said, returning the cigarette to its tray.

Verano produced a stamp from Angie's desk that he had held back. The image was that of the classical statue on her shelf of a woman with a finger laid perpendicular on her lips. He laid it on the counter beside the other stamps. Véry peered through his magnifying glass at it.

"Ah," he said, "another image of ancient Rome: the goddess Angeronia."

"Did you just say Angie Rona?"

"No, no." Véry shook his head, then enunciated carefully: "An-ge-ron-i-a. The goddess protector of ancient Rome, the goddess of secrets... also called Feronia or Volupia."

Verano stared at him, his jaw slack. Had the man been listening at Angie's bedroom door when he'd called her voluptuous and she had corrected him. She had placed her forefinger to her lips just like that statue and the image on this stamp and said, *Not voluptuous. Volupia.*

"How... how do you know about all that?"

Véry rolled his eyes to indicate the filled shelves surrounding them. "Oh. I read a lot." He winked. "Angeronia is the Roman goddess of silence. Harpocrates was the Greek god of silence. Odd that the Romans didn't just adapt him as they did so many other Greek deities and just change the name. They changed his name *and* gender. Like she came from somewhere else and assumed Haprocrates' authority."

Verano thought of the line Angie had written in her letter to Bunny: *He betrayed the Haprocrates oath. He turned to Evello in Angel City...*

With a tightlipped smile, Verano nodded and reclaimed the stamps. He knew where he needed to go.

"Thank you again for all your help, Monsieur Véry. I would have never gotten this far without you. If you should ever need a detective..."

"I already have my friend Prosper Lepicq, but if I do, I will let you know. Good fortune."

*Sounds as though I'm going to need it,* Verano thought as he exited the bookstore. He was so deep in thought about how to catch the first flight from Paris to Los Angeles that he did not notice the alleyway in which he had his tussle months earlier.

Hands thrust out of that alley, latching onto his shoulders so painfully that his wince made him shrug...

...Then he was pulled backwards, spun around...

To find himself staring into the face of Agent Norman Nash.

"Oh, you are *too* easy," his old adversary said with a grin of glee and derision as he brought his fist into Verano's temple.

As his knees folded and the world went dark, he heard Nash say:

"Regards from Angie!"

*The Village*

Verano had a sense from time-to-time of moving, occasionally stirring to semi-consciousness, followed by a sharp sting to his arm and another relapse into darkness...

Then came the awakening from which he was not rushed back to black. As his eyes fluttered open, he found himself staring at the ceiling of a room, became aware of the comfortable bed beneath him, something that had not accompanied his previous "rest."

"There you are!" a woman's voice said.

"Angie!" he shouted and bolted upright at the waist.

He swung his legs over the side of the bed at the sight of her, but his head became caught in a sudden eddy of vertigo, and he collapsed back onto the mattress.

Immediately, Angie was hovering over him. Her hand, in a lacy wrist-length glove, was delicate and cool on his forehead, like an incarnate Spring

302

breeze. The vertigo faded away at once, and he started to rise again, reaching for her.

Angie gently but firmly lowered him back to the bed as she sat down on it. "Shhhh...," she said. "Still too soon. You've been out for a while, and I'm afraid my associates have not been as gentle as they might have."

"Yeah. I got your *salutation*. Thanks." Verano gingerly pressed his fingertips to his temple and was surprised to find it not as sore as he would have expected. He looked at her quizzically: was *she* the reason his head did not hurt as much as it should?

"Oh, Theodore... I'm so sorry about that."

He craned his head to look beyond her, out the window which he realized was open, and observed the architecture of the skyline. Then, his head falling again onto his pillow, he asked: "Are we in Italy?"

"No. Portmeirion."

He swallowed and moistened his lips. "Where's that?"

"Wales."

"*Wales*?" He lifted himself again at the waist. "I'm in *England*? I was in France the last I knew anything! How long have I been out, Angie?"

"A couple of days, that's all."

"That's all? I've been robbed of two days of my free will—my life!"

"I know. I am sorry, but it was necessary." She leaned in and ran her hand again over his forehead. For the first time, her touch made him flinch.

"Necessary? I trailed you down to be with you, woman! Waited years, worked through your riddles, traveled all the way down from France to Italy, all just in hope of reuniting with you. If you wanted me in England, all your lug had to do was to tell me!"

She lifted her chin and looked at him with hooded eyes. "And you would have voluntarily come with a man you had every reason to expect bore you a grudge?"

Gnawing his lower lip, his cheeks flushed, Verano continued to glare at her, then he collapsed back onto the bed. He threw his arm over his eyes and groaned. "Couldn't you have sent someone else?" His arm fell back alongside him, and he cocked his head at her from his pillow.

She dipped her chin, sighed, and shook her head as she rose to her feet. "No. I could not."

She walked over to the window, which was open. A breeze wafted in, lifting the ends of her long, curly locks as it ruffled the curtains. Verano caught the scent of salt air. She stood before the window, the Tuscanian roofs and a belltower visible behind her.

She frowned. "By necessity, it's a very small, very tight circle that you broke when you stole my letter, Theodore. You were wrong to do it. You promised me..."

Again, he sat up. "C'mon, Angie! I had every reason to suspect you were slipping away from me again like before!"

She stabbed her finger at him. "You had no reason to suspect that. I had just slept with you! I made myself as vulnerable to you as anyone can, and you immediately demonstrated how unworthy of my trust you are!"

"Oh? Perhaps you would have preferred to have bedded down with your friend Auric Goldfinger. Because that was where things were headed, whether you liked it or not, before I showed up."

Her jaw went slack, her face red beneath her olive complexion. "So, I owed you... but you owed me nothing after you got what you wanted?"

He scowled and shook his head at her. "And when exactly did I ever get what I wanted, Angie? I want you. Not just your body for one night. You! I want a life with you."

She cocked her head and peered at him, searching his face.

"The life that you gave back to me," he said, his voice choking. "I want nothing more than to give back to you."

Her expression softened, and, in a moment, she was on her knees by the bed and grasping both his hands in her gloved ones. He lifted hers to his lips, kissed them, then brought them to his chest, refusing to let them go.

"Oh, Teddy," she said. "We were wrong to go about it like we did. There are prohibitions that you broke, that I broke ..."

He cocked his head. "Are you religious or something?"

"Or something. Listen to me: what we did was not just four bare legs in a bed. I'm partially to blame, too, because I wanted it. I should have kept you at bay. That precipitated everything. But, still, it was you, Theodore, who took my letter, so you are the one who has to make it right now."

He reached to embrace her. She rose to her feet.

"Angie, I'll do anything for you, baby."

"Not me, Theodore."

"Well, who, then?"

"Teddy, someone *died* because she did not get my letter."

"What?"

"Because my bunny did not get the information. One of my hares who has betrayed me for a rival organization was able to play on her trust to get her in his power."

Verano's forehead beaded with cold sweat. "He... killed her?"

Angie shook her head. "No." She sighed. "She would have been better off if she had not escaped him, in fact. Oh," she nodded emphatically, "he would have killed her after he had what he wanted, no doubt. But he would just have put her to sleep, far preferable to the underworld hands into which she fell once she slipped free of her original evil, if genteel, captor."

"Angie, I am so sorry. But I had no idea that taking that letter would cost someone her life."

304

"You would have been much sorrier, except for my assurances that you could be trusted to make it right. It was the only thing that has saved yours."

"What?"

Now he did successfully revolve his legs over the bed, sit up, and rise to his feet.

"…That, and because it is a tight, tiny circle, and by stealing my letter, you placed yourself in it. I told them it was best that no one else be brought in. It would take time to find someone else who can be trusted, and there is no time. But your actions have still put you on thin ice… Put us both on thin ice with them."

"With who? What are you talking about, Angie?"

"The people who operate the island."

"The island," he said. "That would be the one where you and that pilot from the Orly base disappeared to?"

She nodded.

"And were the surveillance images you stole of this same island?"

Again, she nodded but said nothing.

"You don't seem surprised that I know all this."

She shrugged. "Nash is my agent, too, yes? A double agent, perhaps even a triple agent. Since I brought him into my fold, he's filled me in on what happened at Orly after I vanished, including your visit. And he let me know all about M16's keeping tabs on you. He has been a valuable resource."

"He's been a pain in the ass—or in the head, as it were. But I suppose he and I are on the same side now, eh? Yours. So, tell me: what is it about this secret island that you chose to operate out of instead of all the other places in the world?"

"What is it about that island, you ask?" she sighed. "That is a long story. It has an illustrious and ancient history."

"Then, begin with that."

"In 407 A.D., toward the end of Rome's occupation of Britain, some of their military elite stationed there were secretly informed ahead of time of the coming recall of their soldiers to defend the Imperial City. This private communication from the then-emperor ordered them to leave Britain ahead of the general withdrawal. But they would not be returning to Rome. They were sent on a secret mission to a Mediterranean island outside the known seafaring routes.

"This select military band was to conquer any indigenous people and establish a hidden retreat for the emperor and his chosen ones. The soldiers did just that. So there, on that secret, solitary island outpost, classical Rome would continue on as a society long after the empire fell."

Verano blinked. He had thought that mystery from Shakespeare's First Foiled Edition had been satisfactory resolved when he'd found Angie at *Corno d'Aquilio*, the inland mountain referred to in her riddle as an island in the Mediterranean. And it had been, but now it seemed there was a double, literal meaning as well.

"Naturally, these hidden exiles would have had an ongoing interest in the outside world," Angie continued, "as would their descendants over the following centuries. To that end, they developed a secret, alternative system of mail based on Rome's ancient one.

"Then, in the 1500s, Machiavelli discovered this secret network and began usurping it for his own intrigues. Uncovering how it functioned ultimately led him to the island. Thus, Italy's atavistic classical civilization collided with its Renaissance heirs."

"And what was the result of the meeting of these two ages of Italy?"

"Oh, the island encountered more than just Italy. Other nations converged on it, too. Machiavelli's spy network was the precursor to our modern international ones. He had already infiltrated England's Court, and others on the continent. That international enclave's power increased after what Machiavelli accomplished on the island."

Verano cocked his head. "And that was…?"

"After taking control of the descendants of ancient Rome, Machiavelli took advantage of the temple that had been built there by the original exiles to the goddess Volupia…" Here, she bit her lower lip, sighed, rolled her eyes, and he knew what she was going to say:

"… also called Angeronia."

In mock surprise, Verano lifted his eyebrows and pointed at her. "So, you have worshippers on that island? No wonder you like it there. It sounds like every woman's dream."

She tucked her head and ducked his question. "You see, as well as being their tutelary goddess whom the Romans had transported to the island, Angeronia was also the goddess of secrets, of confidences kept, and the satisfaction of fulfilled desires when it comes to having achieved one's objective. That is the climactic pleasure that her alternative name Volupia means, not sexual satisfaction, though, the two are obviously easily confused. Machiavelli used that to his advantage in gaining control over both his agents and powerful men of his day."

"You mean," Verano said, "that he seduced important statesmen to come to this island to enjoy some authentic Roman sex rites at the temple of Volupia. He then held this knowledge over them to force them to give up their secrets after they returned to their lives in Christendom?"

She nodded. "Eventually, anyone involved in the espionage network who knew too much to live, but could not be simply killed or allowed to roam free, were exiled to this island. There, they were kept with their minds' contents at hand should their masters desire, well, *information*."

"And so…," Verano said, leaning against the wall, arms crossed over his chest, "…this island more or less continues to serve the same purpose that it has since the sixteenth century."

"It does. Though, of course, its inhabitants now constitute a small if select village. Also, its architecture has undergone a major redesign. To honor Machiavelli, its new buildings are now in a more classic, Mediterranean design. But not all of the original Roman architecture was destroyed. Much of it was built over. Currently, a sophisticated surveillance center is being planned that should be up and functioning early in the next decade. It will be built over, while still preserving, the ancient Temple of Volupia."

He pointed at her. "*Your* temple, eh, Angie-ronia?" he said. "I take it you are the official priestess there?"

"I am their counterpart to... Judy."

He arched an eyebrow. "Judy? What—Judy Garland?"

"I'm sorry. In French, you might call her Juliette, or Judith. Do you remember those men who smelled of gunpowder at the bar the night we met?"

"The Firemen? They wanted to take me to Judy's house..."

"Theodore, you are *never* to go there, if they try again. No matter what they say or do."

"Angie, I have no need for a madame's services, I assure you."

"That's not what her *house* is. Listen. The men who accosted you are her servants—the kind who do *not* put out fires. Along with Judy's Dugpas, they seek to manipulate world events from their Black Lodge. The secret government coalitions on both sides of the Iron Curtain foresaw Judy's intrusion into their affairs and agreed on the necessity of some kind of balance, an ongoing corrective." She bit her lower lip. "So, I was... created."

"You mean your *position* was created."

"That, too."

"What do you mean?"

"I mean that I am *not* my own, Theodore. There are powers, deep powers of state... that found me... found me *dwindling*... alone, forgotten... They rescued me and brought me into their service."

He cocked his head, squinting at her. "Angie... You were an orphan?"

The corners of her mouth lifted, but there was sadness there and in her eyes.

"Yes, I suppose so. A man—a genius—named Quentin Moretus Cassave found me... clothed me with the... identity... of Angie Rona. I took, I guess you could say, much better than most of his earlier experiments."

"Experiments?"

"I misspoke. Say, projects."

"Is this relationship ongoing? Do you work for him? Are you... lovers?"

She lifted her chin. "No. I was more like a daughter to him. It was through him that I met Auric Goldfinger. You see, Cassave was something of an alchemist, and Auric was keen on learning how to turn lead to gold. He sought Cassave out, found him, and saw me. You see... my skin is also the results of Cassave's endeavors."

"That was *you*? You're weren't wearing body makeup?"

"I wear body makeup in public to appear normal."

"My word! This Cassave experiment did that to you?"

She shook her head. "No. He's enabled me to be more myself, actually. Does… does it make a difference to you, Theodore?"

He shrugged and gave his head a quick, little shake. "No. Not at all. It's a bit of a surprise, you will understand, but…" he smiled, "…I love you, Angie. Why would it matter?"

His earnest response triggered a sudden, trembling smile on her own face and caused tears to pool in her eyes. "Theodore… Teddy… I am so sorry…"

"About what? Putting my life in danger?" He grinned large and made a dismissive pass of his hand through the air. "Think nothing of it. Business as usual for the Verano detective agency. I've been threatened by experts."

She shook her head at him, her lips curving up into a smile.

He pointed at her. "But you, young lady… I do not like one bit that I have put you out of favor with this international espionage network. So, tell me what I need to do to make this right. I take it, I am to become your new Peter Cottontail hopping down the bunny trail? So, where is it that I need to go?"

She crossed her arms. "You read my letter. You tell me."

"Los Angeles?"

"Very good, *Monsieur le detective*! And do you remember the framed photo on my flat's wall?"

"The nuclear bomb test at Trinity."

She nodded. "That was when they opened the door to her house and let her out."

He startled. "Her?' You mean Judy?"

She again nodded. "Her and her eggs. The atom bomb experiment was also an experiment in mating the evil that men do with supernatural evil."

"Nuclear physics mixed with black magic? But you're talking about men of science—advanced science."

"The story of western science being completely detached from and dismissing the supernatural is a false narrative, Teddy."

"You're making the most rational, visionary minds of the twentieth century sound positively medieval."

"I wish that they were medieval; there was much more active interest in the occult among intellectuals of the Renaissance than there was in the Middle Ages. The fact is, there has never been a clean break between the scientific community and the occult."

Verano put his hand on the back of his neck and shook his head. "Can you give me some examples?"

"I can. Sir Alfred Russell Wallace, the independent co-theorist of natural selection, and Sir William Crookes, the inventor of modern chemistry, a pioneer in atomic theory—both had a keen interest in necromancy. Right now, there is a

California State University instructor named Jack Parsons whose discoveries in jet propulsion will make space travel a reality. He is also an admirer of Aleister Crowley. This type of techno-occultists, of whom you'll never find an official record, were involved with the project *within* the Manhattan Project: Project Babalon."

Verano sighed. He did not know how much of this to believe, even if Angie did. What he did not doubt was that his interception of Angie's letter had needlessly ended a life. That, and the need to propitiate this powerful coalition of shadow governments into whose disfavor they had fallen.

"So," he said and shoved his hands into his pockets, "from what you've said, I take it the letter I intercepted had information your connection needed to remove one of these *Judy eggs* from circulation?"

"That egg is now a hatchling we're calling BOB."

Verano blinked. "Why not Robert?"

"We named it BOB. The reason will become apparent. What you must focus on right now is containing that Hatchling before anyone else gets hurt. One woman is already dead because of *you*, Theodore!"

She closed her eyes, slightly turned her head, and held up her palm at him. "No. Recriminations are pointless now."

She walked over to a thin attaché case against the wall that he had not noticed before. He pointed at the briefcase as she laid it on the bed.

"Is that supposed to be my bunny basket?"

"No, that's not what this—although, the Hatchling is currently held in a briefcase much like this one. Unfortunately, there is a very real danger of it being released, whether by ignorance or with intent, at any moment. Now, I need you to memorize this combination: 7-7-7," she said as she slid the dials of the attaché case's lock. She opened it.

"Forgive my keen grasp of the obvious, but it's empty," Verano said.

She shut the lid and scrambled the combination. "It won't be." She turned to him and poked him with her forefinger. "You do not open this until the penultimate moment, when you are facing BOB."

"And how will I know which moment is the penultimate one?"

"When the Firemen arrive—the ones who do *not* put out fires. You open it right then, Theodore. Or you will fail. Understood?"

Brow knit, he nodded. "7-7-7. Got it. But...," he nodded at the briefcase on the bed, "...if that isn't to contain the Hatchling, what is it?"

From her pocket, she produced a phylactery, prompting a raised eyebrow on Verano's part. "What's in there?"

She popped it open and shook out what looked like an unused condom.

Verano's smile lifted his cheeks so that he squinted. "Angie, baby..." He opened his arms and moved toward her.

She dodged his embrace. "Calm down, Theodore. How can you even think of that at a time like this? Oh. You're a man. That's how. This is for the Hatchling. Now, watch this."

She opened a drawer in a bureau against the wall and set on top of it an oblong plastic and metal box with a large speaker built into it.

"What's that?"

"An advanced recording mechanism; it's called a cassette tape player."

Verano stepped forward and peered over her shoulder at the machine. Through its small, plastic window, he saw someone had labeled the cassette inside *Experiment IV*.

"Is that jazz?'" he said.

She shook her head. "There's nothing melodious about it. This is a recording from a secret project of the British military, an attempt to learn how to kill with sound."

"Kill with sound? The sound of what?"

"Desperate cries of mothers, agonizing screams of psych ward patients... they recorded it and put it in their machine. When they turned it on, this mélange of aural agony called up an ancient *Uttukku*, one of Judy's ilk, which feeds on pain and suffering. Quite a banquet it had on Her Majesty's ticket," she said as she opened a nearby stocked pantry, and produced a tin and a can opener.

Putting the tin beside the tape recorder, she opened the can.

Verano tilted his head to look at the tin's label. "Cream corn?" he said.

She shook some of the sickeningly yellow goo and slimy kernels onto a forefinger. "For purposes of tack. Watch what I'm doing, Theodore. You'll need to remember. It could save your life and a lot of others."

He knew better than to ask if she was serious as she ran the tip of her cream corn-covered finger, first around the mouth of the round opening of the flat membrane from the phylactery, then inside it. She placed its opening over the tape recorder speaker and brought her thumb down on the chunky *Play* button.

The shrieks that little speaker emitted caused Verano to flinch; they caused the flat membrane to balloon to the size of man's forefinger.

"Angie, what is that?" Verano said as she held the fear-inflated tumor, wiggling violently like a fish, from her pinched thumb and forefinger.

She smiled, and Verano noted the pride in her expression. "This tissue is another creation of my father, Cassave."

She placed the bloated membrane into the phylactery and snapped the lid closed. She handed it to him. "Do not lose this."

He looked at her. "And what exactly am I supposed to do with it?"

"You're going to do what I did just now with the cream corn, but you're going to open the membrane for BOB to go inside. The pain and sorrow I siphoned into it from Experiment IV will draw him in."

"The Hatchling is that small?"

310

"The Hatchling is mutable and not limited like physical bodies in time and space. Now, this is what you need to know before all that. I know you've read my letter, so some things in it are about to be explained to you.

"The Hatchling has been transferred into what looks like a mundane, heavy-duty valise. That valise is now the object of a hunt winding down the underworld corridors of Los Angeles. Be very wary of one Carl Evello, Theodore...."

*...Evello in Angel City...*

"Evello has connections with the U.S. shadow agency whose occult-techs piggybacked their experiment to seed Judy through the atom bomb test. Their operative in L.A. has been working there covertly under his professional capacity as a physician. He betrayed me to join them. His name is Soberin."

*He turned to Evello in Angel City. Sober in there—beware. He betrayed the Haprocrates oath for the oeuf.*

"Doctor Soberin was the one who first held my female agent, my bunny, hostage in Los Angeles. Christina Bailey was her name. She was recaptured by thugs working for Evello. They tortured her to death, but she never gave up the secret."

Verano flinched at the thought of what this Christina must have suffered in the hands of such hardened men and their crude tools of inquisition... pliers, blowtorches... And needlessly, because of him. He shuddered, his cheeks flushed with shame.

"However, she did reach me from a payphone and told me where she had hidden the valise with BOB."

She walked over and shut the window on the Mediterranean skyline, then closed the heavy wooden shudders and walked back over to the pantry.

Verano creased his brow. "So, how am I supposed to know how to find this valise?"

"Christina holds the key. I'm sending you to her."

He blinked. "You said Christina was dead."

"I'm sorry, Teddy," Angie said as she put on the gas mask that she had just taken from the pantry.

He had managed to take one step toward her when a hissing sound brought him to a halt. He turned his head and saw a little cloud billowing through the room's keyhole.

Holding his breath, he turned and bolted for her, hands in claws poised to tear the mask from her face. She turned her head, ducked, and hunched her shoulders, imposing one between them as he grabbed her.

"Teddy! No!" Her voice was muffled. His hands were already dragging down her mask...

She thrust her elbow into his stomach. His mouth gaped open as he doubled over and dropped back onto the bed, breathing in the deep the bluish-white miasma that now filled the room.

311

His mouth curled in a sardonic smile.

*I bet this isn't even Portmeirion,* he thought as he passed out.

## Los Angeles, 1954

He awoke fully dressed in a suit, laid out as though lying in repose.

Different bed. Different room. Different building. Different country. Different continent.

He rose at the waist and rubbed the back of his neck as he examined the room. "Angie...?" he softly groaned.

He swung his already shoed feet over the bedside, found he could stand with no problem, then walked over a slippery rug that ran almost the length of the room to exam himself in the mirror.

"I look like a funeral home director," he mumbled to himself.

He walked over to the window and looked out at the palm trees, their fronds gently swaying above the highway traffic in the bright afternoon light of Southern California.

He turned, looked back at the bed, and saw the attaché case with the dial combination laying flat on it. On the nightstand had been placed the phylactery, a pistol in a shoulder holster... and a can of cream corn.

He took a couple steps toward the objects, and the slip of the rug made him stumble. He noticed the floor gleamed from a recent polish. He stepped off the rug and finished crossing the room to the bed and nightstand.

When he lifted the creamed corn, he saw it had been placed as a paperweight on top of a business card to forestall the latter falling to the floor. Verano brought it to his eyes and immediately saw that he had been on the nose regarding his suit. The card read:

*The Best Way To Go!*

*M&D FUNERAL COACH*

"Well, that explains why I am dressed like a mortician," he mumbled. He turned the card over in his hand. On its back was handwritten the address of a Los Angeles morgue. So, Angie was sending him to see the dead Christina.

Behind the can of corn was a car key. He pocketed it, checked the gun, then re-holstered it and put it on, then gathered up the can and the briefcase. Checking the hallway, he took the stairway to the lobby and entered the hotel parking lot through it.

"Now," he thought, "where is the hearse that goes with this key?"

He was not surprised to find that it was the only hearse in patron parking. His key did unlock the door and fit the ignition. A glance in the rearview mirror revealed a coffin back there, one in which he supposed he was to place Christina's body—and then what?

312

He sighed. He was certain Angie and her masters would know when he had the corpse in his possession. The best way to be contacted by them would be to return to the hotel, park the hearse, and wait in the room they had obtained for him.

He wove through the traffic, bringing the hearse to stop before the morgue. He entered it, a tingling little bell summoned a reticent, balding, spectacled little man. He was holding an icepack to his other hand.

"Yesssss?" he hissed, his face contorted with pain.

Verano produced his card. The mousey man tentatively stepped forward and peered at it.

"I'm here for the body of Christina Bailey."

The mouse bolted for his hole. Verano overtook him, yanking him back from inside his office before he could shut the door.

"Don't hurt me again!" he whined as Verano held him writhing in his grasp.

"I never hurt you the first time."

The little man held up and shook his injured hand, the ice bag having fallen away in his attempt to escape. Verano winced at the sight of his fingers, bruised and swollen like purple sausages.

"The other one did!"

"What other one?"

"The other one who came for the body... for Christina!"

"Evello?"

"I don't know his name!"

"So, *this* guy's got her body?"

"No! He's got the key—that's what you're here for, too, isn't it? That key she swallowed that I found."

"The key's what I want. That's right. Give it to me."

"I don't have it! I can't give it to you; I can't barter for it... That was my mistake with *him*."

"Calm down," Verano said and began gently releasing his grip on the man. "I have no desire to hurt you. Just tell me this: do you know what the key was for? And don't say a lock, or I'll have to reconsider that part about not hurting you."

The little man cowered. "No, no! I've been humbled! Can't you see that? I won't be smart with you. I looked the key over before he ever saw it. There was a letter on it... A stylized letter, like part of a logo. I looked it up. The key belongs to a local health club. It probably goes with a locker there."

"You said you looked this gym up?"

"Yes! In the phone book."

"Look it back up and give me that address. Right now."

He did.

Verano drove the hearse to the health club.

"That was quick!" a man sporting gym shorts, a basketball jersey, and a crewcut said. He was looking at the hearse through the club's window when Verano stepped into the lobby.

Verano cocked his head at him. "What do you mean?"

"I mean, you got here before even the cops did."

Verano's pulse throbbed in his temples. "Why are the police coming here?"

"Huh! Why do you think? Same reason you are. He's back there," the man with the crewcut said and jabbed his forefinger at the counter.

Verano leaned over it... and saw collapsed on the floor the club's late receptionist: a thin, older man, his life leaked out in the scarlet pool in which he lay.

He whirled around to the man with the crewcut. "Where is the locker room?"

The man blinked. "You are the most animated undertaker I've ever seen!"

"Locker rooms!"

The man jerked his thumb over his shoulder. "Through that door."

Verano charged, bumping the man in the passing. He found the locker whose number matched the key... fumbled it in... opened the door...

...and found it empty, except for a slip of paper. On it was a typed note:

*They have BOB; plans have changed; wait for me at your room. Hurry! Ang.*

Again, he shoved the man with the crewcut as he ran through the lobby and out the door.

"Hey!" the man shouted as he watched Verano pull the hearse out onto the street. "Aren't you forgetting something?"

Verano rushed up the stairwell to his hotel room and threw open the door... on Nash, his Magnum ready and leveled at his chest.

"Shut the door, then lose your gun."

Eyes trained on the gun barrel, Verano nodded and did as he was told.

"I'm going to guess that this time, you're not representing Angie," he said as he carefully undid his shoulder holster, "and she had nothing to do with that note I found in the locker sending me back here."

Nash flashed a crooked grin. "Never trust a double-crosser," he said. "Angie made me a better deal than M16; someone else made me a better deal than Angie. Too bad for you." He smiled again... and there was cruelty in it.

He licked his lips. "I don't have to answer to Angie anymore, and I owe you good for that day you busted me up in the alley. I'm still taking pain pills. But I'm waiting to pop my next dose. I want to be sharp while I'm working on you."

314

Verano nodded as he carefully extended his holstered gun to Nash. His enemy shook his head. "Bend down and scoot it across the room to me. And do it slow."

"The holster will snag on the rug before it reaches you; I need to slide it over the smooth wood of the floor. Will you allow me to take one step aside to do this?"

"Do it, but be sure you move slow."

Verano nodded and stepped off the rug on whose other end Nash stood. He bent almost to the knee, then sent his holstered gun easily sliding over the slick floor to his enemy. Keeping his eyes and his own weapon aimed at Verano, Nash bent and reached out with his other hand to pick up the holstered pistol…

Verano seized his end of the rug with both hands, yanked, and sent Nash backwards to the floor. The enemy agent didn't realize what was happening before his head had been knocked hard. Then his breath was thrust out of his lungs as Verano hurled himself on top of him, backhanding the fist that held the pistol, and sending the gun flying across the room. Verano's other fist fell hard upon Nash's nose.

"Where's Angie?" he snarled. "Do Soberin and Evello have her?"

Nash thrust the heel of his hand into Verano's chin. "That… would… be… tell… ing," he grunted as his brawny arm began pushing Verano back.

Verano grabbed him by the hair, yanking and slamming his head repeatedly against the hardwood floor until Nash was so unconscious that Verano was content that he had come as close as possible to putting him in a coma.

He searched him, and found nothing but the bottle of pain pills Nash had mentioned. Verano smiled at the name on the label—G.E. Soberin, M.D.—and at the phone number beneath the prescription.

Recovering his gun and taking Nash's Magnum, he dialed the number. A woman answered. "Dr. G.E. Soberin's answering service. May I help you?"

"I'm one of his patients…," Verano looked at the label and noticed Nash's name, or rather the name he had given Soberin, "…Bond. James Bond. My pain's really bad; I need something more heavy duty than these pain pills the doctor gave me."

"I'm sorry, sir, but Dr. Soberin is at his beach house. You might call him there."

"Yeah, yeah. I'll do that"

The woman gave him the number, then added: "He might be a little surly. He's off duty, and you're the second person to call him at his retreat tonight."

"Thanks for the heads up. You have a good evening."

With a quick glance to confirm Nash was still unconscious, Verano pulled open the drawer of the table on which the phone set. He pulled out the phone book, found three "Soberins," and then the address of the one matching the number he'd been given.

He bound Nash's hands behind his back with his own belt, his legs with a ripped bedsheet, and gagged him with the rag left over. He then deposited him in the bathtub, pulled the shower curtain, pulled the bed up against the door, ripped out the phone's wire from the wall, then locked the door behind him.

Night now lay over southern California.

Within the hour, Verano was nearing Sorin's beach house address. He turned off the hearse headlights before they lit up the insidious doctor's retreat and could warm him that retreat was in danger of being breached.

He made certain of his gun and the phylactery in his pocket against him, and picked up the combination-locked attaché case from the floorboard of the passenger's side of the car.

Just as he exited the car, the sound of a woman's shriek cut through the air.

"Angie...," he groaned.


Except the woman he had found inside the beach house wasn't Angie. Nor did she have any idea who *he* was.

"Are you with Mike?" she asked as he loosened her bonds.

"Who's Mike?" Verano said.

"Mike Hammer. I'm Velda, his secretary. Ah... thank you... Those ropes were chafing something awful. And who are you, again?"

"My name is Teddy Verano. Velda, was that you who screamed?"

"It was. I managed to belt one out before they got that gag on me, in case Mike was nearby."

"Was there another woman being held here with you whom they've removed elsewhere?"

"You mean this Angie you thought was me?'" Velda shook her head as she massaged her wrists. "The only other person in here with me is over there." She indicated with a nod that he should look over his shoulder.

Verano startled and whirled to see a man in a business suit crumpled in a corner, eyes open in an unseeing stare, a knife sticking out of him.

"Who...?"

"Soberin called him the late Mr. Evello."

Verano stared at the knife buried in the corpse almost to the hilt. "He who lives by the sword, eh... or the switchblade in this case. Did Soberin do this to him?" he said as he turned back to Velda.

"No. He seemed to regret his loss. He thought Mike was responsible. That's why he wanted me for leverage; he said he intended on defecting—"

The air cracked with gunfire—a single shot. Velda's eyes went wide.

"Mike!" Velda shrieked the name as her balled fist flew to her mouth.

Verano took her firmly by the shoulders. "If your friend is involved, I will do what I can to help him. But you need to get out of here while you can. The longer you stay here, the more your own life is at risk."

"What if Mike was shot? I won't leave him!"

"I understand your feelings completely. So, if you won't go, lay low. Do *not* follow me. If you can, stay here, and I or your friend Mike will return for you. OK?"

She nodded. He picked up his attaché case and slipped out of the room, closing the door behind him.

As he moved down the hall, he heard a decidedly different male voice from the one before. Instead of effete and professorial, this one sounded like it belonged to a nightclub bouncer or a jock. Verano's pulse quickened; he hoped the speaker was Velda's Mike, and that he had killed Soberin.

Then he heard a woman's voice , confirming the man's identity:

"Kiss me, Mike."

Again, a gun fired—and a heavy thud followed.

Verano crouched, gun cocked and ready. He thought of Velda; if Mike hadn't been shot before, it sounded like he had been now. Verano pinched his lower lip with his front teeth, and, still bent, moved stealthily forward...

Pressing his body against one wall of the hall, he craned his neck forward, pistol raised, and peered into the room...

The woman was flipping back the lid of a valise. Verano knew it had to be the one that contained BOB. He stepped into the room, shouting...

The woman never saw or heard him.

Out of the valise leapt a shaft of light wrapped in a pillar of flame, its color not of this world, perhaps one out of space. It immolated at once the Atom Age Pandora...

...all the while snarling one reverberating, vicious, jagged tone. An accompanying growing whine of a dynamo's building power drowned out the woman's shrieking as she finished torching into a flaming corpse on her feet.

*Why didn't she run for the ocean?* Verano thought, then realized Judy's progeny had seized and held her there, *feeding* on her.

The blinding light flooded the room, and the dynamo-whine was now a roar shaking the beach house atop its stilts. Verano glimpsed a bleeding Mike Hammer staggering to his feet, heard Velma calling for him through the din...

He wanted to help them, but he had to contain BOB while it was still possible. If he did not, there was a danger of Judy's spawn spreading into a sentient holocaust that would consume multiple, innocent lives.

He dashed for the front door, barely avoiding colliding with Mike as he bolted for the back of the house and Velma. Verano's skin felt sunburned beneath his clothes from the Hatchling's heat; his shirt and pants hurt, scraping his sore flesh as he moved.

Verano ran out the door and over the sand, the attaché case in one hand repeatedly bumping his thigh...

...then pulled up short of the transparent figures taking shape out of the fading morning darkness ahead, hooking arms like the little plastic apes from a child's Barrel-Of-Monkeys, to form a line to block him.

His jaw dropped as he recognized among the sooty faces those of the men who had tried to seduce him to Judy's house in Paris almost ten years ago!

Attaché case tucked under his arm, he sprinted to the left and the joined line of phantoms effortlessly slid sideways to cut him off. He ducked to the right, and the line intercepted him again…

Beach house windows were now exploding from the heat, flames erupting and running like jagged, fiery tendrils over the roof. He saw Velma stumbling along with Mike over the sand. The slight woman was struggling to manage his bulk as he staggered from his wound. They were headed toward the surf.

Something like a wave of heat, something the same unearthly color that had immolated the woman, separated from the burning building and now hovered over the beach.

Verano gritted his teeth. His old friends "the powder monkeys," the Firemen who did not put *out* fires, meant to hold him here for BOB…

*You open it right* then, *Theodore. Or you* will *fail.*

The penultimate moment come at last. Verano dropped to his knees with the briefcase, thumbs frantically dialing…

7…7…7…

He threw back the lid…

An ethereal fountain of gold erupted from the attaché case. It rushed over him in a soothing, fragrant salve, taking away the ache of his skin, then rippling out left and right in a transparent golden wall between him and the Firemen that then circled and contained them.

BOB roared with rage, palpably evil, coming for him.

Verano realized he was seeing only the epidermis of the thing, that it had weight and dimension outside the frame of his eye's ability to perceive. Its presence made him feel flat by comparison, like he could only look *across* it, never up and down.

With a pocket knife, he punched a hole in top of the vegetable tin. Then he opened the phylactery and removed the agitating sheath. Dribbling cream corn on one finger, he pried apart the skin's circular opening and gave it a fresh coating… something that suddenly struck him as akin to a hunter spraying animal musk on a decoy.

The ocean breeze carried the scent of the cream corn to BOB. The Hatchling caught the smell and came *roaring*.

Verano planted his feet, stretching the opening of the membrane, holding it before him in the face of the onrushing nightmare…

He stepped aside, arms outstretched like a matador's. The impact knocked the sheath from his hands and hurled him aside a good five feet, sending him on his back into the sand…

…As with a roaring *whoosh* of a vacuum being filled, the Hatchling was sucked into the membrane, billowing the sheath into a ten-foot white ball, raging and roaring, ponderous, yet light as a balloon carried on the wind…

…As it bobbed away.

Verano lifted himself on his elbows and looked after it. The balloon now appeared to be the size of a ping pong ball, its muffled bellowing fading into the distance with it.

"That's *it*?" Verano said to himself, rose to his feet, and began beating the sand from his clothes as he saw that the sun was rising.

Only then did he notice that both the Firemen and the wall of golden light were gone. Growing louder was  the mechanical, hornet-like buzzing accompanied by the weighty slapping of water. He looked to the ocean to see an encroaching squad of men in wetsuits astride jet skis. Two of them were gathering Mike and Velda out of the surf.

He began looking to locate where in the sand he had left the briefcase  and saw one of the men in wetsuits with the now closed attaché under his arm.

Verano ran toward him, waving, and shouting. "Hey! Hey! That's mine!"

"Now, that's not true, Mr. Verano. You know that," the man in the wetsuit said in a pleasantly chiding tone and smiled. "You were merely using it in our service."

Verano cocked his head at him and narrowed his eyes. "Who are you? Why are you here?"

Still smiling, the man replied, "My name's Drake. And if by 'why,' you mean 'how,' then, you summoned us." He held up the briefcase and gave its side a quick pat. "You sent up the flare so that we could locate you at the proper moment. Remember?"

He lowered the case. "If you do mean 'why,' as opposed to 'how,' we're here on the same mission you are. Angie had us in place for mop up once you were done."

He jutted out his hand. "Job well done, sir. The Hatchling is contained."

Verano massaged the back of his neck with one hand. "Not… exactly. I got it into the membrane, but it's still loose. It went…"

He turned to point and was startled to see the large, white ball skidding over the ocean, surrounded and being herded back by a group of men on the jet skis. The rising sun tinged the ball's pale membrane with rosette…

…Or, perhaps, Verano thought, the Hatchling had eaten someone since he last saw it.

He turned back to Drake, whose hand was still extended for him to take.

He didn't.

"You sound like you take orders from Angie," Verano said.

Drake's hand fell to his side. "Didn't you?"

"Yes, but she said she had masters, too."

Drake drew the case up under his arm. "We are all on a leash of *some* kind. Even her."

"Where *is* Angie? Is she all right?"

Drake smiled. "Angeronia cannot help *but* be well, no matter where her location." He patted the attaché case. "She's rather like a cat in that regard; thrives well, even in small spaces."

Now Drake looked out at the ocean, at his fellow agents on jet skis struggling to keep the malicious balloon corralled as they drove it northward. With a furrowed brow, he pointed in their direction. "Looks like my boys need me. That Hatchling may escape us yet. Must dash." He turned and began briskly striding toward the surf, where his jet ski was beached.

Verano trotted after him. "Hold up! Did Angie not have a message for me?"

Drake, attaché case tucked under his arm, was now mounting the jet ski. "Oh, she does, she does…," he said and started up the motor.

"Well, what did she say?"

Drake smiled and saluted Verano by pinching together the tips of his thumb and forefinger and bringing the oval space between to his eye. Over the raucous rumbling of the jet ski, he shouted:

"Be seeing you!"

Then he was plowing waves into the ocean, off with the others herding the nightmare toward the edge of the world.

*Over the years, Travis Hiltz has chronicled the misadventures of various heroes trying to thwart the schemes of a time-meddling Rotwang (from the film* Metrop- olis)*, and this tale is but one more fragment in that vast saga...*

## Travis Hiltz: *The Ghosts of Gascony*

### Gascony, 1650

Dusk was approaching, as Porthos steered his road-weary horse towards the tavern. It was a humble, rustic, one story structure, sagging with its years of service.

He was a large man, made of equal quantities muscle and fat. His clothes, though covered with the dust of the road, were of fine quality, if not of current fashion.

Removing his wide-brimmed hat, he used it to dust himself off. A ragged, barefoot stable boy came jogging out, and skidded to a halt. He peered up at the new arrival.

"Close your mouth, lad," Porthos admonished, absently brushing at his sleeve. "Unless it is open because you are offering to care for my horse or rec- ommend the fare and drink of this tavern. Otherwise, you'll catch flies."

"Uh...," The boy replied, originally impressed by the size and build of the traveler and now slightly confused by his speech.

With a slight chuckle, Porthos, handed the reins to the lad. He felt a tug on his sleeve.

"Careful, lad, that's Portuguese silk."

The boy cocked his head, indicating the musketeer should follow him. Puzzled, Porthos returned his hat to his head and followed, as the stable boy lead his horse around the back of the tavern.

"Where are we going?" he asked, in as quiet a tone as he could muster. He felt something clandestine was occurring, but was just baffled as to what that thing was.

"Come with me," the boy replied, in a nervous hush.

"Why...?"

"He said to look for the giant with a beard and a hat." the boy replied, looking pointedly upwards at the tall musketeer, his need of a shave and his hat.

Feeling a touch self-conscious, Porthos, removed his hat again, and ran a hand through his hair.

He had come to Gascony to join his comrade, D'Artagnan, at the latter's family castle. He could think of no one else that might wish to rendezvous with him, beside his friend, and was quite puzzled how D'Artagnan could have known that his fool horse would take the wrong road and he'd end up at this rustic hovel.

Shrugging his broad shoulders, Porthos plodded along, too tired and hungry to question further.

The barn behind the tavern was, if anything, even more worn and rundown. If time had weighed heavy on the tavern, it had mistakenly sat upon the barn. Its thatched roof was sagging, and its walls seemed to be struggling to stay straight and upright.

Porthos frowned, concerned that if the cooking was on the same level as the carpentry, his stay was not going to be enjoyable.

He ducked to enter the building, and, after watching the young peasant stabling his horse, the musketeer peered around the shadowy interior. He saw no one else, but spotted a comfortable looking haybale on which to rest, while he waited.

He was brushing dust off his hat and adjusting the plume, when he felt the knife pressed against his throat.

"Who sent you?" a hushed voice asked. "What have you done with Isaac?"

"I had heard much of Gascon hospitality," Porthos sighed. "I must speak to D'Artagnan about his countrymen."

He moved as though to replace his hat and instead swatted his assailant. Sputtering, the knife-wielder stumbled backwards. Porthos turned, grabbed the other by the bel,t and yanked the slim figure up and over.

Balanced on the burly musketeer's knee, pinned by a one-armed bearhug, his assailant dropped the knife and struggled to get free. With his free hand, Porthos patted down his attacker, in search of other weapons or some clue to who his new acquaintance was. Reaching under the attacker's tunic, the musketeer suddenly made a startling discovery.

"My apologizes, Mademoiselle!" Porthos stammered, getting to his feet and dropping the young woman to the dirt floor.

He shuffled his feet, and attempted to straighten up his clothing, appearing like an overly large schoolboy confronted by a stern teacher. He offered a gloved hand to her, keeping his gaze averted.

"Aren't you a modest soul!" she said, accepting the offered hand, which dwarfed and enveloped her own. She got to her feet.

She was slim and petite. Her attire, all repurposed men's wear, was various shades of blue. The outfit had seen some wear and tear. She retrieved her own hat, a near shapeless thing with a grey plume, and stood, hands on slim hips, gazing up at her new acquaintance.

Despite the differences in their heights, she had the air of being the figure of authority in this encounter.

"Do you have a name, my modest mountain?" she asked, with an arched eyebrow.

"Yes... uh... Baron du Vallon de Bracieux de Pierrefonds, at your service, Mademoiselle," he mumbled, with a faint, awkward bow.

"Well, that's a mouthful," she replied, taking a step back and stroking her chin, thoughtfully. "I'm generally less formal with the men who grope me..."

"Porthos," he added, avoiding her flirty gaze.

"And you may call me Orlando," she said, reaching out and patting his muscular arm with her slim, gloved hand. "Please, sit. I promise you; I have no intention of screaming for someone to come and protect my innocence. That ship, as they say, sailed long ago and crashed upon a reef."

Orlando perched on a bale of hay and patted the one next to her. The musketeer, feeling increasingly confused and awkward, joined her.

"I think we have stumbled across each other," the young woman continued, "and are speaking at cross purposes. You seem a gallant sort. Let's sift through this misunderstanding."

Still unsure, Porthos merely nodded.

"Now, why don't I begin," Orlando said, with a disarming smile, and an offered wineskin. "Much like my choice of dress, I live an unorthodox life, as you might have guessed. It is a... very, very long story, which I won't bore you with. The reason I'm in this this charming locale is, I'm on an errand for the... hmmm, we'll come back to that... I was supposed to meet a friend here, and while Isaac is a bit taller than you, there is enough of a passing resemblance for the stable boy to make an honest mistake. You see...?"

Orlando gave a brief smile and a "and there you have it" shrug. Porthos gave a noncommittal nod. He found this strange vagabond of a girl charming, and perplexing. With his fellow musketeers, he had generally been content to trust their judgement and go along with whatever course of action they devised. On his own, he tended to make what seemed to him perfectly reasonable decisions. Many was the time, he would later discover, others did not see the obvious logic of his actions. It was quite puzzling and lead to him to, on rare occasions, doubt his choices.

This was such a moment. He missed his comrades Athos and Aramis. He felt he could trust their counsel. Without even his loyal servant, Mousqueton, to use as a sounding board, he felt adrift. Orlando seemed very self-assured and clear in her purpose, but Porthos was unsure if letting a woman be in charge was a wise course. Taking orders from the Queen was one thing...

"Are you listening?" Orlando asked, peering curiously at her new friend. "Are you falling asleep?"

Portos shook his massive head, took the offered wineskin and came close to draining it, before he handed it back. He nodded his thanks, as he wiped his mouth on the back of his hand.

"I have a comrade in the musketeers," he said, haltingly. "He is a Gascon and invited me to visit his family estate. I'd grown weary and bored over a dispute with one of my neighbors, and so set out."

"And got lost and ended up here, as I was waiting for Isaac," Orlando muttered thoughtfully.

"I?" Porthos rumbled, stroking his mustache. "Lost? I have an uncanny sense of direction! It was that dunderhead, Mousqueton, and that sloth of a horse that got lost. I was the unfortunate victim of their bumbling." He shook his head and helped himself to the wineskin, warming to his subject. "You could drop me in the most remote, barren of lands, blindfolded," he continued, "and I would find my way home. Unfortunately, I nodded off, and placed too much trust in that nag!"

"Yes, yes, who hasn't fallen prey to a treacherous horse," Orlando replied, with mock sympathy, as she took the wineskin back and took a swig to rival that of the massive musketeer's before getting back to her feet. "I do apologize for the misunderstanding. I'll find the stable boy and we can set you upon your way..."

"Now, wait!" Porthos interrupted, also standing up. " I feel I have, er, slightly wronged you and should make amends. You are, no matter how clandestinely, a young maiden..."

"Truly, I am neither of those things," Orlando said, attempting to steer Porthos away from any more long speeches.

"...in need of assistance, and I," Porthos continued, unabashed and barely pausing for breath, "as a musketeer and a gentleman, would be a rogue of the lowest order if I ignored that fact!"

"I am sorry," Orlando said. "What are you saying?"

"You are bereft of your companion. I shall accompany you until this bearded giant of yours arrives, or your task is complete."

He placed one hand upon the hilt of his sword, the other he held out to his new acquaintance.

Orlando's dainty hand was swallowed in the musketeer's. Her pale forehead wrinkled in puzzlement. Several heartbeats of thought resulted in a smooth forehead and an impish smile crossed her lips.

"Yes, yes," she drawled. "I think your keen mind and strong sword arm might be just the thing to ensure success, of my... um... quest... well, errand."

With a final shake, she disengaged her hand from Porthos' and turned, heading for the barn door.

"Come along, my mountain!" she called over her shoulder.

"Where?"

"I'm not eating dinner in a barn," Orlando explained, airily. "And I am expecting one more arrival."

The room was large, low-ceilinged; the wood darkened by years of cook fire smoke. Seated at a corner table, his back to the wall, and a wide swath of empty space between him and the rest of the tavern's patrons, sat Orlando's other acquaintance.

The years were etched onto his dour face. His white hair hung to his shoulders. Despite his obvious age, he sat ramrod straight; his dark eyes held a spark that marked him as a lion amongst lambs. He wore the plain, black garments of a puritan, the only difference being the brace of pistols and scabbard at his belt. Like his garments, they showed no ornamentation.

Propped against the tavern wall, by his right arm, was a wooden staff. It was decorated with hieroglyphs and the carved head of a cat.

Orlando went directly to his table and pulled over a stool.

Porthos leaned against the bar, relaxing a bit, as he contemplated the tavern's dinner offerings.

"Who is your friend?" the Puritan asked, with the barest movement of his lips or eyes. "Does he bring word of the Wandering Jew?"

"No, he does not. Events have gotten... interesting," Orlando explained, helping herself to the mug on the table. She pulled a face, upon realizing it was only water.

"Talk sense, changeling," the man muttered.

"There's been no sign or word of Isaac," Orlando replied, losing her glib manner. "If I was of a suspicious nature, I'd suspect he was being deliberately kept from meeting us, but knowing Isaac, he could just have been distracted by a hundred other things. Which means, it is just you and I, Solomon. A strong sword arm and a tendency not to overthink matters could serve us well."

She casually gestured, gaining Porthos attention, and much like the proverbial China shop bull, the large musketeer made his way across the room to join them.

The stool groaned and creaked under his girth, as he arranged his bowl of stew, mug of wine, hunk of bread and eating utensils on the small table. Once his meal was arranged to his satisfaction, he raised his mug.

"To your health and the success of our undertaking," he exclaimed, before draining the mug and waving the buxom serving wench over for a refill.

"Now, what might our undertaking be?" he asked, dipping a hunk of bread in his stew. "How can we help you, Monsieur...?"

"Firstly, by lowering your voice," the Puritan replied.

"He's rude, but Solomon has a point," Orlando nodded, as she helped herself to Porthos' wine. "There are political undertones to our undertaking."

"I am known for my discretion," Porthos rumbled, through a mouthful of bread. "Though, I really have no head for politics."

"As you know, Gascony shares a border with Spain..." Orlando began, quietly.

"Spaniards!" Porthos said, frowning. "A troublesome people. Which is a shame, as I do appreciate their wine and women..."

"Pay attention, my mountain," Orlando chided, gently, reaching up to give Porthos' beard a quick tug. "There have been... incidents of a mysterious nature. Both France and Spain are suspicious of each other, so it is doubtful they could work together to investigate them without exacerbating the whole thing. Everyone aware of these incidents would prefer not to go to war over a ghost story."

"Ghosts?" Porthos asked.

"We'll get to that," Orlando continued. "It was decided it'd be wiser if matters were handled by... free agents, shall we say."

"You are both British," Porthos said.

"Well spotted," Orlando said, with a patronizing smile. "I have, on occasion, been employed as a courier for the Crown, while this gentleman, Solomon Kane, has a very pronounced sense of justice...."

The Puritan's frown deepened, and his hand moved to the hilt of his sword. Orlando paused to glance at her somber companion, and judged he did not appreciate her frivolous tone.

"Kane" Porthos mused, oblivious to the tension between his tablemates. "I have heard that name..."

"I had put out word," Orlando continued, hoping her narrative would not be derailed by either Kane's temper or Porthos' contemplative nature. "Isaac and Solomon agreed to join me."

"What is it that we face?" Porthos asked, eagerly.

"Ghosts?"Porthos mused to himself, once they were on their horses and on their way.

His horse lagged a bit behind the other two. He sounded more thoughtful, than skeptical. His two new traveling companions rode ahead of him.

"I am sure you are bursting to chide me," Orlando said, quietly, glancing back at their new acquaintance.

"No."

"Really?"

"Lord protect me, but I can see your reasoning," the dour adventurer said, his voice low, his gaze straight ahead, his ornate staff across his lap. "Our cause is just, but we are stepping into a potentially explosive political quagmire, and neither of us is known for, er, our diplomatic skills. Having a French musketeer at our side may smooth our path."

"Very good," Orlando nodded, with a smile. "It doesn't hurt that he's a renowned swordsman and built like an oak." They both glanced back at Porthos, still deep in thought. "I admit, he's no Wandering Jew," Orlando shrugged. "But what do they say about beggars and choosers...?"

"We have not been followed," Kane said. "So, whatever we face is ahead of us."

"Most likely," Orlando replied, thoughtfully. "Hard to sift through the tales and discover what is the truth and what is rumor."

"Whatever is happening is no mere subterfuge by a would-be political schemer," added Kane, one hand brushing the runes carved into his staff. "Something... unnatural is in the air."

Orlando lifted her head and gave a sniff. "Yes, it's out there," she nodded, running the tip of her tongue across her upper lip. "I can taste it on the wind. It's... not what I was expecting... smells... almost familiar?"

They rode along in silence for several moments. Kane seemed willing to wait as Orlando pursued her thoughts. She frowned and shrugged.

"It's gone," she concluded. "Too many memories, from too many lifetimes, for one delicate, attractive head to hold, I suppose..."

Kane's frown deepened, as any reference Orlando made to her immortality or ability to change sex caused him to bristle.

While Solomon Kane and Orlando had been occasional, reluctant allies, the Puritan warrior had always harbored the belief that there would come a day that he would be forced to treat Orlando like any other supernatural creature and put his one-time comrade to the sword.

Despite his dedication to his crusade against the wicked forces and creatures that lurked in the ungodly fringes of the world, there were rare instances where he encountered beings who challenged his view, his belief that all such things were evil.

Orlando was frivolous, reckless, and too interested in the pleasures of the flesh, but at the same time, she ...or occasionally he, was a reliable companion. Some small corner of his mind was unsettled at the idea of having to cut Orlando down.

Such thoughts invariably led him to also ponder his own unsure placement in the natural order. Whether through the possession of the ancient *juju* staff, once gifted to him by an African shaman, or decades of exposure to various mystical forces, he had lived long, perhaps too long. Had he become the kind of being he had spent so many years hunting? His flesh and blood had been gifted with energy, vitality and years beyond human ken, but what of his immortal soul?

"Is my attempting to plan strategy interrupting your brooding?" Orlando asked.

"I was pondering the future," the Puritan replied quietly, his eyes straight ahead.

"I suppose, if I reach your advanced years, I'd want to start contemplating my sins too," Orlando mused, dryly. "I would hope that if one of my comrades in arms would pay attention, you would be the one. I suppose that leaves... Where is he going?"

Both riders pulled their horses to a halt and glanced back to see Porthos steering his weary steed towards the side of the dirt road.

"Excuse me?" Orlando called. "My dear Baron, where are you going?"

Porthos halted his horse and dismounted, approaching his fellow travelers, before speaking.

"Be discreet," he chided them, unaware that even hushed, his own voice tended to be booming. "I have said, my holiday in Gascony is a quiet affair."

"Yes, and so far," Orlando mused, "you have been the pinnacle of subtle discretion. My question still stands."

"Which question was that?" Porthos asked, absently, as he glanced about while fanning himself with his hat.

"Where were you going?" Kane asked, in the barely patient tone one uses with an exasperating child.

"There's a track between the trees," Porthos explained, patiently, as though it was perfectly obvious. "You can glimpse a barn from here."

He nodded, as though his point was made, only to notice that his companions were still looking at him expectantly.

"It's growing dark, and I am growing tired," Porthos explained. "And as I have made plain, that horse of mine is a poor navigator. I fear if I were to nod off, the wretched beast would have me in Athens by dawn."

He clamped his hat back on his head and returned to his horse.

"Well," Kane said, dismounting and slinging his staff over his shoulder. "The dunderhead has a point. We have all been on the road for days. Those of us that must deal with... mortal frailty could use some rest."

He took hold of his horse's bridle and followed after the musketeer. Orlando shrugged, sighed, and nudged her horse to join the others.

The barn was grey with age. One corner of the roof was sagging, but its interior was relatively dry and rat-free.

Porthos found a heap of dried straw and sprawled, his saddle bags a makeshift pillow. Solomon Kane perched on an overturned wooden bucket, his back against the wall, his cat-headed staff propped up next to him, as though both were standing guard.

Orlando strolled around the building, taking in the windows and dodgy section of roof, before making herself a nest of straw and wrapping up in her cloak. Despite her disdain for her companion's decision, she soon found her eyelids growing a bit heavy.

"Tell me more about these ghosts," Porthos' voice drifted across the barn like a thrown rock.

"Of course," Orlando sighed, sitting up. "The first rumors of spectral sightings were about a month or so ago. Nothing unusual; dead relatives walking the land; French and Spanish soldiers and knights from bygone times patrolling the roads and lurking in mountain passes. Quite dramatic."

"Interesting," Porthos murmured in drowsy thought. "I would be reluctant to fight women, children or grandsires, but it would be a worthy story if I were to pit my blade against the warriors of a past age... My friends would scarcely believe such a thing!"

"We do not walk this path in order to obtain tales to entertain drunkards and trollops," Kane said, grimly, crossing his arms.

"Speak for yourself," Orlando smiled, wiggling in search of a more comfortable seat upon the dirt floor. "So far, the ghosts have been fairly benign. People are frightened, and no one has been attacked, but it has, as would be expected, made both the French and the Spanish suspicious of each other... What's that noise...?"

"Your audience," Kane said, pulling his own plain, black cloak tighter about him.

Orlando got to her feet. Porthos was sprawled in the hay, his hat over his face, snoring like a cannon.

"Sweet dreams, my mountain."

The sky was dark, with only a few, obstinate stars, forcing their way through the clouds. Porthos shifted, brushed aside his hat, and slowly sat up.

Nature was calling, and the over-sized musketeer fumbled with his sword belt and untangled himself from his cloak as he sleepily trudged across the stable, and then through the yard toward a convenient bush.

His business attended to, Porthos blinked away his grogginess and paused to adjust his sleep-rumpled clothing. Upon looking up, he was startled to see three people standing in the stable yard, looking at him. Two men and a woman, all dressed in the drab clothes of peasant farmers. One of the men had a small hay bale slung over his shoulder; the other held a rough walking staff. They had startled looks, seemingly as surprised to see Porthos as he was at their appearance.

The trio seemed as mundane and plain as any of the workers of Porthos' own estate, except for the fact that they were translucent. He could see the trees behind them clearly. They also seemed to have a faint glow, no brighter than moonlight.

"Um... good evening," Porthos called. "Or perhaps 'good morn'... Hard to judge when it's this cloudy."

He moved to doff his hat, gallantly, only to realize he had left it behind.

"I do not mean to impose. We had no idea someone owned the barn. We'd be more than happy to pay for having a roof over our heads... and perhaps some breakfast?"

He patted at his clothes, before coming up with a coin. He held it up, offering it to the trio.

The ghostly peasants recoiled slightly at the coin. The men moved as if to protect the woman. Instinctively, Porthos' hand went to the hilt of his sword. He then felt a hand on his arm.

"Wait," Solomon Kane said, in a quiet, firm voice. "These phantoms will not be dispelled by a blade."

329

The Puritan stepped in front of Porthos and held out his cat-headed staff. It seemed almost to hum, like a violin string, as he waved it slowly, back and forth. The carved recesses that served as the cat totem's eyes glinted faintly, as though reflecting the dim starlight of the Gascon night sky.

The frown creases about his face deepened, and Solomon Kane placed one hand upon his own sword hilt. "Something is wrong here," he said, puzzled.

The trio of ghosts moved tentatively toward the two swordsmen, growing fuzzy around the edges and more transparent with each step.

"Back, phantoms!" Porthos commanded, stepping forward, his sword drawn. "You seem to be the spirits of decent, hardworking folk, but that will not spare you from my blade!"

Almost within reach of the duo, the ghosts merely dissipated. Both men felt an odd tingling, as if a brief static charge had passed through them.

Porthos sheathed his sword and smoothed out his mustache.

"Curious," he rumbled, thoughtfully. 'Do ghosts often act like that? I bow to your experience, as I am a novice to such things."

"No, this was... different," the Puritan replied, speaking directly to the bedraggled musketeer, as one would to a peer, rather than to one who is tolerated. "There is something about these apparitions that I do not understand."

"In the stories I was told," Porthos mused, using his fingers to comb his hair. "I was led to believe ghosts were vengeful, angry things... Sometimes sad women... This lot seemed quite... dull... Whoever has heard of ghosts performing chores?"

He began to pace, while he pondered, giving the appearance of a restless bear. Solomon Kane stood, straight and stiff, his arms crossed, his staff tucked, like a cane, under one arm, giving the impression that both man and figurehead, were interested in Porthos' thoughts.

Kane was granite-faced to all outward appearances, stoic to the point of boredom. Yet, he took in every word Porthos uttered, adding it to his own thoughts.

"What in the world are you two up to?" a sleep-rumpled Orlando asked, joining them, her sword, a Japanese katana, held lazily in one hand, its blade nearly dragged in the dirt.

"There were ghosts," Porthos replied, gesturing to where they had been, while sounding like a child caught by a stern parent.

Orlando looked at the two swordsmen, while sheathing her sword and continuing to adjust her clothing. When she glanced at Kane, he merely nodded in response to her unasked question.

Orlando ran her tongue over her teeth, while she absently glanced around the barnyard. "There's something wrong about all this," she muttered. "I can taste it in the air."

The trio stood, wrapped in their own thoughts.

"These ghosts are not just rumor and tall tales," Kane intoned.

"No, they are not," Orlando nodded, crossing her arms in thought.

Porthos peered out at the slowly lightening horizon. "What are our plans for breakfast?" he asked, glancing at his companions. "There are scant resources here. Is there somewhere along the road we might stop?"

They saw to their horses and were soon back on the road. They rode through the day. Fields and farms soon gave way to rocky hills.

Like the landscape, the ghosts they saw also changed. At first, they caught glimpses of spectral farmers and peasants. Soon, they were replaced by shepherds and bandits.

The ghosts continued about their mundane tasks. There were occasional bursts of human drama and surprise. A translucent wolf stalked an equally ghostly boy and his flock.

At one point, Kane and Orlando had to restrain Porthos from racing off to protect a phantom damsel being pursued by a phantasmic enraged suiter with a dagger.

"How are you faring, my mountain?" Orlando asked, coming alongside Porthos. "This, I would imagine, is not the restful holiday in Gascony you envisioned?"

"I am... unsure of my words," he replied ,scratching at his beard in thought. "My years as a musketeer have not been uneventful, but nothing prepared me for... this..." He gestured with a gloved hand at a group of ghostly, ragged children, as they joyfully chased a scrawny dog across the dirt road and into the tall grass. "What can one say?" he continued. "If my three comrades were here, they could articulate the thoughts that swirl about my head. I am known more for my sword arm and my impeccable dress."

"No doubt," Orlando replied dryly. "We appreciate your skills and reassuring company."

"It is a little... disorienting, I suppose," the musketeer continued. "I have never spent much time in spiritual contemplation. Generally, I leave that to Aramis.... But, to see the spirits of the dead with my own eyes! None of them seem particularly vengeful though."

"No, they have been most benign and even a bit dull," Orlando nodded. "Curious that so many should appear, only to go about their previous lives."

"And very few seem to have taken notice of our presence," Solomon Kane added.

"I can see how so many ghosts would frighten away the locals," Orlando mused. "But, if none of them are attacking, or even taking notice of the living, what is behind it all? A manifestation of this size does not just happen. Someone or something had to summon them."

"By design or by accident, then becomes the question," Kane said.

"A question for the morning," Porthos said. "Night is drawing in and I do not trust those clouds."

"True," Orlando frowned, glancing about. "Even if the storm passes us by, I do not relish navigating these, for lack of a better term, roads, in the dark. We need shelter and maybe a wild hare. Our larder is quite barren."

"There is a side trail," Kane said, pointing off to the right. "It leads to a small clearing with a bit of an overhang. We could shelter there for the night."

The ground was rocky, but the surrounding hillside gave the clearing a bit of shelter. Porthos was content to guard the makeshift camp and tend the small campfire, while Kane and Orlando scouted around, in search of a better path through the mountains, grass and boughs for bedding, and something for dinner.

Once they had accomplished all three chores, they returned to the clearing to find Porthos, his back against the rockface, his hands clasped across his stomach and his chin on his chest.

Solomon Kane. frowning in disapproval, sat on a stone, across the fire from the musketeer and began to skin and gut the rabbit he had caught.

"So, now that we have proven to our satisfaction that the ghosts are real, and not rumor or political trickery, what do we do?" Orlando asked, dropping a bundle of grass bedding, and brushing off her hands. "I confess, I find myself puzzled." She folded her cloak, into a cushion, sat down and tugged off her boots.

Kane looked up from his work, his face wooden. A briefly raised grey eyebrow encouraged her to continue speaking.

"This feels... unplanned," Orlando continued, flexing her aching toes. "A summoning this large must have had a human agent behind it, but this has all the earmarks of a novice: something has gotten out of control here."

"And it is causing political unrest," Kane said, not looking up from his preparations for dinner. He now had the rabbit on a skewer, over the fire.

"But upon both sides," Orlando countered. "It may give certain statesmen an excuse to push towards war, but the whole thing still feels clumsy. I can't imagine it's anything more than an accidental side effect."

"There is a trail that connects with a better road, through the mountains," Kane said. "Perhaps if you escort our musketeer towards the massing French forces, we may learn more."

"And you?" Orlando asked.

"Someone should keep an eye on the Spanish."

"You also want to keep turning the skewer," Porthos said, not opening his eyes. "Don't want to scorch the rabbit."

The trio awoke in a foggy pre-dawn, broke camp and made their way in the dim light in search of the promised mountain road.

As they ascended, the ground grew rocky and desolate. Reaching the road, they paused to rest the horses and take the lay of the land. The clouds were huddling together, so the approaching sunrise was dim and uninviting.

"I do not like the looks of that storm," Orlando muttered.

Kane had dismounted and leaned on his staff; his fierce, grey eyes gazed upon the clouds with disapproval.

Porthos rubbed his unshaven chin as he steered his horse down the narrow path and onto the mountain road. He dismounted and squeezed the last few drops out of the wineskin, while he waited for his companions.

The road snaked through the mountain, curving back down to the farmlands, as well as up towards the craggy peaks.

Porthos glanced about, noticing several game trails branching off into the undergrowth and amongst the rocks.

"Well, this is a bit better," Orlando said, looking with approval at the hard packed dirt road and picturesque view of Gascony below. "Though, this is likely the way both sides will move their troops."

Solomon Kane peered at the ground, poking at the faint remains of some footprints with the end of his staff. "Some may have already gone this way," he said, straightening up.

"We need to look for shelter," Porthos said, taking a few steps forward, holding his reins, loosely in his hand. "Those clouds are darkening quite fast. Even the ghosts have gone to get out of the rain."

The other two glanced around, uneasily.

"He is right," Orlando said. "As we moved into the mountains, the ghosts have become fewer. We have not seen one since we got up here... Curious..."

Solomon Kane, idlily dragging his staff in the dirt, walked slowly along until he came alongside Orlando. "Something is moving," he said, his face expressionless. He glanced about, as though there was nothing of interest to see. Kane made a vague gesture, showing Orlando where to look.

As the mountain road curved, there was dense undergrowth and a scattering of thin trees. There was movement there that couldn't be explained away by the wind.

Orlando glanced away, acting as though she was taken in by the view. "Animals?" she asked, under her breath.

Kane shook his head faintly. "They are using the trails," the dour puritan said, matter-of -factly. "It may be a frightened shepherd or a bandit..."

He stopped mid-sentence, as two bulky, metal forms emerged from the underbrush.

"Well," Orlando mused, her hand moving to the hilt of her sword. "I know it will seem out of character if I am the one advising caution..."

"Ho, good sir knights!" Porthos called, dropping his wineskin, drawing his rapier and approaching the two new arrivals. "Hold and state your allegiance!"

He strode up to the armored duo, his sword held casually, but his posture indicated he could bring it into play at any second.

The musketeer paused, an eyebrow raised in curiosity. He did not recognize the style of the newcomers' armor and they sported no design or emblems. They even lacked sword belts.

The armors were bulky. There was no sign that the helmets were a separate piece. Their face plates sported two circles for eyes and a thin slit of a mouth. Their boots were blocky, and Solomon Kane realized they were the source of the odd footprints. Their gauntlets did not have fingers, but resembled large crab claws.

The odd pair moved slowly, lumbering along almost like sleepwalkers, more than soldiers on the trail. They trudged to within a yard or two of Porthos and then halted, as though they were equally confused by this encounter.

"From where do you hail?" Porthos asked. "What king do you serve?"

The armored duo continued to stare blankly at the musketeer.

"I do not wish to be rude," Porthos continued, needing to fill the empty space in the conversation. "But I am upon a mission and cannot allow you to proceed until I have ascertained your intent. My apologies in advance if I have besmirched your good character."

Standing back, Solomon Kane stood, statue still, while Orlando took up a casual stance, her Japanese Katanna resting lightly upon her slim shoulder. Her body language indicated someone watching a mildly interesting stage play.

The armored figures clanked and made vague humming sounds, but otherwise made no response to Porthos interrogation.

"I must warn you," Porthos said, sternly, as though addressing errant children. "If you will not speak in your own defense, I will be forced to treat you as foe, and, much as I am loath to brag, my foes do not fare well."

His rapier moved through the air, with a sharp *swish*, and then he took up an *En Garde* stance.

Slowly, one of the armored figures raised an arm and opened its claw-like hand. In the center of its palm was a metal disk. A thin arc of lightning shot out, and when it touched Porthos' sword, the metal sparked and the burly musketeers' whole body shook.

He wrenched his sword loose, and promptly landed flat on his back in the dirt.

His companions sprang forward. Kane stood before his fallen companion, his staff held out, as he stood on guard. Orlando ran at the duo.

Formulating a plan to fend off these malignant ghosts, Orlando was caught completely off guard, when her sword drew sparks when it came in contact with one of the metal forms. She stumbled, turned, and threw a punch at the other.

There was a loud clanging sound, and Orlando stepped back, wincing and shaking her injured hand. She switched hands, and swung her sword wildly, in the hope of driving the two back. Her blade drew sparks, but there was little force behind her attack, as she had expected the duo to be as gossamer thin as the ghostly peasants they'd encountered.

Orlando was unsure if she should be attempting to dispatch these armored foes, or just drive them back, until she and Kane had a chance to make sense of things.

The two clunky, blank-faced knights backed away. They stood, heads together, silently pondering their options. Then, they ponderously turned and shuffled off, down a side trail.

"Well, that was unexpected," Orlando breathed, blowing on her bruised knuckles. "Are the ghosts manifesting as solid beings, or have we stumbled into a new complication?"

Kane strode forward, his staff held out, pointing to where the mysterious knights had stood. "I do not understand this," he muttered. "It does not make sense."

Orlando nodded, while tracing idlily in the dirt with the point of her sword. "There is something here," she muttered. "I have accumulated too many memories to sort through, over the centuries..."

"Did we win?" Porthos mumbled, struggling to sit up. "I hope you dealt with whichever one of the miscreants struck me from behind."

Kane saw to the horses, while Orlando sheathed her sword and helped the musketeer back to his feet.

"Plans have changed," she explained, dusting him off, while he swayed slightly and fumbled to sheath his rapier. "Those knights were not in the least ghostly."

"They bore no ornamentation that I could identify," Porthos muttered, adjusting his disheveled clothing. "So, someone is clandestinely summoning these ghosts, after all?"

"I think we have to concede that point," Orlando nodded. "But it leaves us at a loose end, as there is nothing about those knights that tells us which power might be behind things... Or even if we are dealing with some third group we had not even considered."

"You are complicating matters," Kane said, squinting into the surrounding foliage. "They do not move fast, and they leave an obvious trail. We will have to leave the horses."

"Good," Porthos said, patting the ancient Puritan's shoulder as he strode past him. "We will hunt the villains to their lair!"

He tromped up the mountain road until he spotted the side trails and poked at the undergrowth with his sword. Kane glanced over at Orlando. He did not speak, but she felt the full effect of his chiding her for inviting the musketeer along. She merely shrugged back, before tethering the horses, near a good-sized patch of grass.

Portos pushed aside some of the brambly shrubs. Solomon Kane and Orlando joined him in studying the ground. Amongst the gravel and stone, were more blocky footprints.

335

"Do ghosts leave footprints?" Porthos asked.

"No," Orlando said. "Monsters do. As do men."

"Which are we dealing with?" Kane asked, thoughtfully.

Swords drawn; the trio moved down the trail. It was a narrow snake of dirt and stone, widened by the armored duo, so along with footprints there was a great deal of broken branches and trodden grass to indicate the path they should follow. While Porthos wished to take the lead, Orlando felt there should be an attempt at stealth, and convinced him to bring up the rear.

The path wound its way up the mountain; it would occasionally branch off, but nearly all of them petered out, and they would backtrack to the main trail. One side trail brought them to a narrow stretch. It would have been overly generous to describe as a clearing. The three of them, standing shoulder to shoulder, barely fit, and it fronted upon a steep incline of rock.

"There are footprints," Orlando muttered. "But there's really nowhere to go."

"No handholds," Porthos added, thoughtfully peering upwards. "Climbing would be quite difficult."

Kane stood, silently peering at the stone wall. He rested his staff against the rock, pulled off one of his gloves and ran his fingers along the surface of the stone incline.

Pressing his fingers into a recess in the rocky surface, a section of wall slid away, revealing a cave that tunneled back into the mountain.

"Curious," Porthos said, stooping slightly, as he stepped into the cave.

Thin veins of luminescence ran along the ceiling. Porthos brushed his fingers along one strand. "Feels like wire," he muttered.

The tunnel widened gradually, as it went. There was a hum in the air and a distant sound that gave Orlando the thought that someone was mining.

"There's an odor in the air," Kane said. "Reminds me of an alchemist's den."

The tunnel opened up, forming a chamber, like an enormous, overturned bowl. Several of the armored figures lumbered about, moving boxes and strange metal devices. At the far end of the cave sat a featureless, grey cube, the size of a peasants' hut.

The whole place had the makeshift feel of an army camp, littered with bizarre items and figures, that felt like approximations of the familiar. As if it had been built by a child, who had to use whatever toys he had to create the scenario in its imagination.

The trio stood, struggling with their mixed feelings: confusion, and a slight feeling of awe, so they were unaware of two other armored creatures, stationed in alcoves on either side of the entranceway.

One caught Porthos in a bearhug that pinned his arms to his sides. The other grabbed Orlando and Kane, each by an arm, clamping down hard enough that the combination of surprise and pain, caused them to drop sword and staff.

"Don't struggle," Orlando said, out of the corner of her mouth, as she was dragged past Porthos.

Kane scowled at the loss of his staff, but went along, as he too surmised, they were on the verge of receiving some answers.

Making a token struggle, the trio were forcibly escorted across the chamber, closer to the mysterious, grey structure. Amongst the sounds of machinery, they could hear voices.

Coming around the back corner of the cube, was an elderly man and a young woman. The man walked with a pronounced limp. His white hair, flared around his head, like neglected shrubbery. He was clad in a heavy overcoat, over multiple layers of brown and grey. One hand was clad in a glove that was such a tight fit, it could have been painted on.

"Oh, our clever hunters!" he rasped in a heavy German accent. "We do not appreciate unwelcome visitors."

He leaned on the young girl's arm. She had an ethereal quality, like a painting come to life. Her gossamer dress was unseasonably light. She moved with a dancers' grace, and her features, while pleasing to the eye, had a still quality about them, again suggesting a portrait of a young woman.

The old man peered at the trio, accusingly, as he hobbled nearer.

"I should have known that you would eventually track me down here, Omega!" he said, in a sullen snarl. "You could not stand to see me... Wait!"

He looked closer at Solomon Kane, pushing the Puritan's hat back, so his face was no longer in shadow.

"You're not... I don't know you," he said accusingly.

"Nor I you," Kane replied, pulling his hat back in place. "But there is the stench of unnatural arts about this place."

The old man, glanced upwards at Porthos, who looked back with equal curiosity. Their captor dismissed the large musketeer with a vague gesture. He then halted before Orlando.

"You," he muttered, darkly. "You, I know."

"Do you?" Orlando asked. "I am sorry, I don't recall meeting you before."

"Don't be foolish. It hasn't happened yet."

"Ah, I'm notorious for arriving early," Orlando nodded, despite her circumstances finding herself more amused than concerned over this strange old man and his metal soldiers.

"Still a frivolous popinjay," he grunted, with a disapproving shake of his head.

"Well, good to know," Orlando said.

"So, you are a warlock?" Porthos asked, puzzled. "Or perhaps, an alchemist? I am afraid I do not know the proper terms..."

337

"Warlock?" the old man snapped, turning back to Porthos. "I am Rotwang! The finest mind of my era! Master of robotics! I do not play with herbs and spells. I bend the flow of history to my will!"

"Oh, dear," Orlando muttered. "Time travel. I knew there was something in the air that felt familiar."

"Attend me, Hélène," Rotwang said, reaching out to the young woman. "These fools are nothing more than a distraction. Have the Volkites detain them until we are finished."

Supported by the vague dancer, he hobbled away from his captives.

"I truly do not understand what is happening," Porthos said, showing no sign he was bothered by the armored man holding him, as he was too distracted by events.

"For once, we are in agreement," Kane muttered.

"Rotwang is not a mystic," Orlando explained, struggling to tug her arm free, with no success. "He is more of an alchemist, or a scientist. They are almost as much trouble as wizards."

"You've met this Rotwang before?" Kane asked, his posture and tone giving the impression he considered being held captive by a large, armored figure no more than an inconvenience. He was focused on the conversation.

"No, but apparently I will in the future," Orlando explained, tapping at the Volkite's arm. There was a whirl of machinery. "You see... This is the tricky bit. Almost makes me miss Omega. He's better at this sort of thing. Time moves like a river. We move, as the current pushes us, or we are on the shore, watching the river flow by. Some people can travel back and forth on the river, go against the current and go ashore wherever they like."

Porthos merely nodded, accepting the information. He was not an imbecile, but neither was he a deep thinker. He tended to trust those around him to do the thinking, and he did what was required to deal with a given situation.

"Most are merely travelers or dabblers in history. Rotwang seems to fall into the other category: those that meddle, threatening history itself, or too deluded or egomaniacal to realize the damage they are causing."

"His metal... constructs... there does not appear to be any men within this armor... they are mining," Kane said. "Perhaps he needs some mineral or substance in order to continue his traveling?"

"But why does he need ghosts?" Porthos asked, moving his arm in order to scratch his chin, and then remembering his arms were pinned to his sides.

"I don't think he's doing that intentionally," Orlando explained, feeling distinctly uncomfortable in her role as fount of wisdom for the group. "Like when you drop a stone into a pond; if you travel in time, you cause ripples. That's what I think the ghosts are."

"This ragged alchemist is causing a war by accident?" Kane asked.

Orlando shrugged, then grimaced, as the Volkite tightened its grip, thinking she was attempting to escape.

"So, if we stop him, the ghosts will go away and tensions between France and Spain will settle down?" Porthos suggested.

"Likely," Orlando replied, looking about.

"Well, then we must stop him," he said simply.

"Yes, about that..."Orlando said, attempting to move her trapped arm.

After several minutes of thought, Porthos leaned forward, as if taking a deep bow. As he did, he arched his back, rolled his shoulders, and lifted up the Volkite holding him, until its feet no longer touched the ground.

Teeth gritted and his face turning red with the exertion, Porthos took several halting steps and then allowed himself to stumble backwards, so that the metal creature slammed against the stone wall.

He managed to step back and slam back against the stone two more times, before he sank to his knees. When he did, the Volkite tumbled off his back, emitting a wheezing, grinding noise. Its back was a mass of dents and scraps.

While Porthos was struggling with his captor, Solomon Kane reached into his belt, drew one of his flintlock pistols, turned slightly and stuck it in the Volkite's eye, before pulling the trigger. It loosened its grip on the two adventurers as it staggered backwards, a whisp of smoke drifting out from the jagged hole where its eye had been.

"Am I the only one who hadn't formulated an escape plan?" Orlando asked, rubbing her sore arm, before moving to help Porthos back to his feet. The large musketeer accepted the hand thankfully, before straightening and dusting himself off.

"What next?" Porthos asked, looking around.

Kane moved to retrieve their scattered weapons, leaning on his staff, while tucking the swords under his arm.

"That grey block?" he asked, handing his companions their blades.

"Probably how he travels through time," Orlando admitted. "Those... um... wires and pipes, most likely... gather fuel and... I don't know, but if we cut those, it will either stop him, or possibly force him to flee else...when."

"I will deal with the guards," Porthos said, giving his rapier a swish and tossing his hat aside, before marching off. Kane glanced up, from reloading his pistol, and looked a question at Orlando.

"Have you a plan now, changeling?" he asked.

"I do not have any answers," she replied. "I barely have questions."

"Then, let me see what I can do," Kane said.

He tossed her one of his flintlocks, before moving closer to the blocky structure. The Puritan found a sandy patch in the cave floor and stuck the wooden *juju* staff into the dirt. He pulled off his gloves and rested his hands upon the carved headpiece. He closed his eyes and lowered his head, until his brow nearly rested upon his gnarled hands. He might be praying or napping, for all Orlando knew.

"There is an energy here," he murmured. "It is being used for evil. I must see it. I must know."

Orlando stood by, waiting, and ready to defend him.

After several moments, she began to grow antsy, as the remaining Volkites were too occupied with Porthos.

"I'm not letting him have all the fun," she announced, running across the stone chamber.

Unnoticed by her, the hieroglyphs carved down the length of the staff began to glow, with a faint blueish light.

Porthos' shoulder blocked one of the clunky mechanical creatures aside, swung a punch square into the flat, blank face of another and bounded past a third to reach the makeshift collection of metal contraptions, wires and chunks of luminescent blue crystal.

A flurry of swordplay kept them at bay, while the musketeer pondered what to do now that he'd managed to reach his destination. A solid kick sent bits and pieces flying and its hum became a discordant growl.

Feeling metal claws grabbing at his shoulders, Porthos spun, and with his back to the stone wall, fought them off. His rapier was unable to do more than scratch their metal plating.

Orlando leapt and with a wild, downswing, severed one of the Volkites' arms. A side slash stabbed through a second's torso, only for Orlando to then be unable to pull her blade free. She let go of the sword and, pulling out the borrowed flintlock, shot her remaining metal opponent in the knee.

The Volkite toppled like a felled tree, into the other one, and the two performed a bizarre dance, struggling to stay upright. They failed and collapsed in a loud heap, trailing wisps of smoke.

Orlando planted a heel on the fallen Volkite's head and pulled her sword loose. Looking up, she watched Porthos jab his rapier through the mouth of his opponent, grab the Volkite by its blocky head and slam it against the collection of machinery, damaging both.

"Well, that's seen to," Orlando said, with a satisfied smile. "What is that noise?"

Almost drowning out the sounds of the damaged Volkites, was a persistent hum, one that you could feel in one's bones. It sent a tremor through the entire cavern, throwing a rain of dirt and stone down upon the trio.

The grey block structure didn't exactly shake, but for a brief second, it seemed to blur. A door-shaped panel in its blank surface slid aside and Rotwang and Hélène rushed out.

"What have you done?" Rotwang raged, wild-eyed, his odd, gloved hand gripping the edge of the doorway.

"Us?" Orlando asked, glancing from the fallen Volkites to the shattered machinery.

Hélène flowed out of the cube, and danced around Orlando, her eyes wide, her expression blank. She turned back to face Rotwang.

"If they are not interfering with the time cube, who is?" Rotwang snapped, in response to a conversation, only he seemed able to hear.

Everyone turned towards Solomon Kane, who had not moved from where he had planted his ancient staff. Both the carvings and the figurehead's eyes were glowing brightly, and the old man's body trembled.

"Solomon?" Orlando breathed. "What are you up to?"

Kane took a deep breath, raised his head and opened his eyes. All about him, blue light, flowed like water. He wondered if he was standing at the bottom of the ocean, or perhaps on a cloud floating through a clear, spring morning.

He was equally shocked to look down upon his hands and see the gnarled, wrinkled skin, like ancient leather, traced with veins, was gone. They were now the hands of a younger man. A younger Solomon Kane. The hair that drooped past his eyes was no longer stringy and white, but rich ebony.

"What have I done?" he asked, puzzled.

"I was rather wandering that myself," a voice replied.

Standing before him was an old man, dressed all in black. His collar-length white hair was swept back, except for one rebellious lock, and his face was wrinkled and careworn.

"You must be... Omega?" Kane said.

"Doctor," the old man said. "Doctor Omega, if you please. Have we met?"

"Perhaps. I am not sure... Maybe in a dream. Or maybe it hasn't happened yet. I have been told such things are possible."

Doctor Omega nodded, as if what Kane had said was so straightforward that it required no response. He tugged at a ribbon, attached to his lapel and drew out a monocle. He seemed to have forgotten the Puritan wanderer, in his interest in the wooden staff Kane held.

"Now, that's interesting." Doctor Omega muttered, excitedly to himself. "Never thought I'd lay eyes on one of the... My, my, good to know life can still surprise you!"

He straightened up, smiling to himself and twirling his monocle ribbon.

"Well, you have stirred up something, haven't you?" he chuckled.

"Have I?" Kane asked, brow furrowed in puzzlement.

"Oh, dear, yes. Poked your stick into the pond and stirred up the silt and sleeping fish, as it were." Omega nodded. "But, you haven't the faintest idea what I'm talking about, or what you have hold of."

"My staff? It was given to me by..."

"Someone who wanted to see it stir up trouble in the world," the white-haired savant interrupted. "Well, I'm quite busy at the moment, so I can't stand

341

around for whatever story you might want to tell. Who is it you're tangling with, hmmm? Hopefully not Morlocks?"

"He calls himself 'Rotwang," Kane said.

"Oh, dear. Well, he does keep causing this kind of havoc," Omega said, with a slight, sad frown. "You'll have to deal with him. Here's what we'll do..."

He reached out a hand and placed it on top of Kane's. The staff trembled in his grasp, and the hieroglyphs, as well as the stone in Doctor Omega's ring, shifted and glowed with a greenish light.

Omega closed his eyes and muttered under his breath something that sounded equal parts mathematical equation and lullaby.

"That should do it," the Doctor said, pulling his hands away. "Now, things are going to happen quickly, so you need to wake up and get away from... whatever Rotwang is up to. On your way."

He snapped his fingers, quickly and sharply, mere inches from Kane's face, and when the Puritan adventurer opened his eyes, he'd returned to the cavern and his tired, ancient body.

The stone chamber trembled, the air was thick with dust and grit, and his companions were on the other side of the room, standing over the remains of the Volkites, while receiving a harsh lecture from Rotwang.

The large, grey block went in and out of focus, like an image reflected on the surface of a pond and all the scattered shards of crystal now glowed with the same green light from his vision... dream... whatever it had been.

"Orlando! Porthos! To me!" Kane shouted, drawing his flintlock, as he realized he was also drawing the attention of the few remaining Volkites and the blank-featured girl with the wide eyes.

Trusting their comrade, and feeling that the cavern was no longer a safe place to remain, they pushed past Rotwang's metal minions and ran to the Puritan's side, then followed him back the way they had entered.

Kane's pace slacked, and his breathing grew labored. He began to stumble. Porthos sheathed his sword and threw his new friends arm over his broad shoulder, until Kane was no longer sure his boots touched the ground.

Orlando snatched the pistol out of his hand and fired over her shoulder at their lumbering pursuers.

Rotwang's ranting grew harsher and more frantic, as the trembling in the walls and the glow of the crystals increased.

The trio struggled to keep their feet, as the tunnel shook. There was a roar, behind them, like a massive wave, crashing against a beach, and a blast of gritty wind struck, sending them tumbling out of the hidden tunnel and into the brambly undergrowth. The mountain itself seemed to shake, and the air was filled with a strained moaning-growling sound.

Orlando staggered to her feet, spitting out grass, and wiping dirt from her face, with the back of her gloved hand.

"Anyone still alive?" she called, wading through the brush .

Porthos' path was easy to track, and she soon arrived at the small clearing he had made on impact.

"I feel I must still live," he muttered, sitting up and blinking in the sunlight. "As I sincerely doubt death hurts this much. I wish we still had some wine."

Holding Porthos by one muscular arm, Orlando helped him to his feet, and steered him in the direction she believed Kane had fallen. They found his staff, stuck into the trail, as though waiting, expectantly, for its owner. Kane was sitting up, looking bruised and frail.

"How fare you, Solomon Kane?" Porthos asked, crouching down, concerned for his new comrade.

"I live," the Puritan replied. "I merely feel the weight of my many years and the miles I have trod across this wide earth. Perhaps it is time I returned home to rest, and leave these strange secret undertakings to others."

"Yes, find a comfortable chair, a full flagon of wine, and leave this sort of thing to the youngsters," Orlando nodded, as she and Porthos helped the Puritan to his feet and to his staff.

Both men gave her a puzzled glance, but for very different reasons.

They were all pleasantly surprised to find the horses still there, having fed and rested to their hearts' contents, while their owners were galivanting about.

"It has been an adventure, my friends," Porthos said, patting his steed's flank. "But I fear both my good friend, D'Artagnan, and my addle-headed servant will be worried over my lateness. So I should be on my way. If you would care to join me, I plan to stop at the nearest inn or manor house that I find, drink my fill, and restock for my journey."

Kane mounted, nodding his assent.

"Lead on," Orlando said, with a hearty smile. "I must attend one last, brief task and then will rejoin you. I, too, have a powerful thirst and would be amiss to not reward the efforts of my noble comrades."

Unsure what that entailed and to which of them, or both, she was speaking, the swordsmen gave the flirtatious immortal, and then each other, sideways glances and unsure words of farewell, before heading back down the mountain road.

"Come along," Orlando called, once the pair were past the bend in the road and out of sight. "You're wasting daylight, playing shy."

From behind a tree, emerged a ghost, but this one was familiar to Orlando. It was a translucent child, a young girl dressed in fashion, several decades out of date.

"Well, better late than never, I suppose," Orlando said. "Where's Isaac?"

"My father is making his way," the ghost child replied, with a slight frown. "We have been quite busy."

"You've been busy, Lotte? I've postponed a war, shooed away a malicious time traveler, missed breakfast, and have a potential rendezvous with two swordsmen and a serving wench."

Realizing the unearthly child had no idea what she was talking about, Orlando merely smiled, patted Lotte upon the head. and fished something out of her belt.

It was a small shard of crystal from the cave, flickering with a faint light that flowed from blue to green.

"Here, little one. A shiny bauble for your father to add to his collection. I'm going to join my friends. If he can, have Isaac meet me at the tavern. If he cannot, let him know I'm next off to catch a ship to Venice. I have been informed by an acquaintance of mine that there is something lurking in the canals..."

*Riley Hogan, a new contributor, made it just in the nick of time with a story fea-turing a dramatic crossover between Harry Dickson and Seabury Quinn's for-midable sleuth, Jules de Grandin...*

## Riley Hogan: *The Epicurean Slaughters*

### London, June 1935

The curtain rose on the second act of *Platée*. Lord Horace Chiltern stared at the dancers. He enjoyed one of the finest balcony seats in the Royal Opera House—the perks of donating to the London Opera Company.

Chiltern was thin with hollowed cheeks and gray hair. His sunken green eyes were captivated by the performance. He looked like a college professor in an ill-fitting tuxedo. The aristocrat strained his ears. He thought he'd heard something. Somehow, over the orchestra, he heard a voice. He got up and approached the door. It was singing. A soft voice from the aisle.

Chiltern felt drawn to that voice. The singing grew louder as he opened the door. He stepped into the empty aisle and walked toward the melody.

Tom Wills woke to rapping on his bedroom door. Through bleary eyes he saw pitch darkness through his window. The young man stumbled out of bed toward his dresser.

"It's work," called his employer.

"Right-ho, guv," he replied.

Tom had the distinction of serving Harry Dickson, the so-called "American Sherlock Holmes." During his time in the famous detective's employment, he had experienced adventures he could scarcely comprehend. In a haze, he strug-gled to dress in a well-worn dark suit. He splashed his face with water. In the bathroom, he glanced at a mirror to see a youth with disheveled brown hair.

He almost threw himself on the landing to meet Harry Dickson. The detec-tive wore a navy-blue suit with a brown trench coat.

"Good man," Dickson said with a kind smile.

"What time is it, guv?" asked Tom.

"A little after two in the morning," replied the detective.

Tom followed his boss outside and into the muggy London night. A police cab waited across the street under a gas lamp. Both men filed into the backseat. The cab sped away before either man had time to settle into their seats.

"What's the trouble, guv?" asked Tom.

"Lord Horace Chiltern was slain at the opera," replied Dickson.

"That nob who runs all the charities?"

"Correct."

345

The policeman at the wheel drove like a madman. Dickson and Tom lurched with every sharp turn. The young man winced as the car rocketed past a lorry. *Scotland Yard must be desperate for Dickson's services*, he thought.

"It'll be a short drive," the driver pleasantly announced.

"That's what I'm afraid of," muttered Dickson.

Without a care in the world, the driver careened through red lights. He triggered his siren. A couple of times, the detective had to remind the man to keep his eyes on the road. Soon, the car mercifully stopped in front of the Royal Opera House.

The palatial neo-classical building resembled an ancient temple more than a theater. Dickson and his assistant had to struggle past a few reporters that had managed to come despite the early hour. At the door, the police welcomed the two men. Every man in Scotland Yard knew Harry Dickson.

They were quickly admitted inside. They stepped into a lobby with glass display cases of various opera costumes. A mob of policemen congregated near the colossal marble stairs at the center of the lobby.

"Mr. Dickson! Thank you for coming so fast!"

Dickson turned to see his old friend, Superintendent Samuel Goodfield standing near a group of uniformed officers. The police detective was a frequent ally in his investigations. Goodfield had maintained an athletic physique in his middle age. His brown hair was now streaked with white.

Dickson and Goodfield exchanged greetings; then the three friends began to climb up to the crime scene. Tom felt a sense of dread as he hiked up the alabaster steps.

"When was Lord Chiltern murdered?"

"Shortly before midnight," reported Goodfield.

They reached the top of the stairs: a landing flanked by opposite corridors. Tom was delighted to see that it displayed a view of the amphitheater. He swept his eyes over the row seats before the sprawling stage. All the red balconies were trimmed with gold laces.

"Did my man tell you how he died?" the superintendent inquired.

Dickson shook his head. "I barely had time to get dressed."

"The crime scene is this way," Goodfield gestured to the left hallway. "I hope you two have strong stomachs."

Dickson feigned searching his pockets. "Tom, I think I left my tobacco pouch in the car. Could you go check?" The detective knew that his young assistant could tolerate gore, but there was no point in shocking him needlessly.

"Alright," said Tom turning away, but not fooled. Still, he was grateful for a respectable exit.

The two detectives walked down the left corridor, past doors to balcony seats. Dickson smelled carrion before he saw the crime scene. A pale constable admitted them into what looked like a slaughterhouse. Blood coated the once stately walls. Entrails rested on the scarlet carpet.

Lord Horace Chiltern's remains festered in the center of the hallway. He had been bisected above the waist. His upper half lay face up, staring off into the unknown. Shredded bowels spilled out of his belly. A pool of bile could be seen near his legs. Dickson stared at the lower half of the corpse. The torso was lined with unevenly splintered bones

The detective was careful not to step in any soggy patches of blood. He gave no sign of being perturbed by the gore. He appeared more like a schoolboy studying a book. His eyes swept over the remains. The legs had not been cleanly severed from the torso. The groin was a mess of unevenly fragmented bones. Intestines trailed from the trunk, green bile smearing much of the tissue.

The Lord's evening jacket had been ripped in various sections. Dickson caught sight of a ring on the left index finger. It was engraved with an epsilon symbol. He stood up, his examination complete

"I've seen enough," he said.

Both men left the crime scene. The constable guarding Chiltern's body felt sorry to be left alone again. From the top of the stairs, Dickson saw that the police presence had been increased.

"Any witnesses?" he asked as they hiked downstairs.

"None," replied Goodfield shaking his head.

"Did anyone hear anything?"

"No one reported anything, except for the opera. *Platée* is a thunderous work. Chiltern's cries would likely have been drowned out by the percussion instruments."

The two detectives rejoined the police in the lobby. Dickson soon lost sight of Goodfield in the crowd. The uniformed men seemed too terrified to approach the scene, but too intrigued to leave. He found Tom staring at a display of Venetian festival costumes.

"What did you see, guv?" asked the young man.

"A man torn in half," replied Dickson, somer.

Tom whistled. "Blimey."

"Mr. Dickson?"

The detective turned to see that Goodfield had returned with a stranger in tow. The newcomer was powerfully built with blond hair and a curved mustache. He wore a charcoal-hued American-style suit complete with a Windsor knot.

"This is Doctor Jules de Grandin," Goodfield said, gesturing toward his guest. "He's agreed to consult on this case."

"Doctor de Grandin... I've heard of you," Dickson said, as the two men shook hands. "This is my assistant, Tom Wills."

"*Splendide!*" De Grandin replied, smiling warmly.

The Frenchman had a reputation as a brilliant medical mind. One of the foremost physicians of his generation, he practiced criminology much like the late Joseph Bell, though his reputation was not as spotless. Some derided De

Grandin as a kook who wasted his time chasing phantoms. In the eyes of some in the medical establishment, he had thrown away a brilliant career to hunt things that went bump in the night.

"What do you make of the horror upstairs?" asked Harry.

"I shouldn't say anything before the coroner's examination," the Frenchman replied with some feigned modesty.

"Make a guess," suggested Goodfield gruffly.

"It looks as if someone seized his lordship's person and tore him in two."

"Impossible. No human could have done such a thing!" Tom exclaimed.

"Who is to say that the killer is human?" De Grandin' blues eyes sparkled with excitement.

Dickson groaned. "Surely, you can't be suggesting that the murderer is some kind of boogieman?"

De Grandin groomed his mustache. "Then what is your theory?"

"Lord Chiltern was likely cut in half with some kind of blade," ventured the detective. "It was rumored that Damascus steel could slice through bone in one stroke."

De Grandin meditated on the idea. "A blade wouldn't have spattered the body all over the room, however."

Goodfield cleared his throat and said, "We must pay a visit to Lady Chiltern."

Dickson and Tom joined De Grandin in the third car of a police convoy destined for Kensington. Dickson and De Grandin bonded over mutual interests. They had similar theories about the notorious Fantômas.

It was a little after five in the morning by the time they arrived at the Chiltern townhouse. A gaggle of reporters already besieged the front door. Goodfield, Dickson, De Grandin and Wills were admitted by means of a servant's entrance. They followed a valet from the kitchen to the door of the drawing room. The valet rapped gently on maple.

"Enter," came a soft voice.

They entered a parlor with pale blue wallpaper and baroque furniture. Lady Julia Chiltern wore a black dress with her gray hair arranged in a *chignon*. Dickson studied her faded beauty. To look at the noblewoman was much like hearing echoes of a silenced symphony.

"I am sorry for your loss, Lady Chiltern," he said.

"*Toutes mes condoléances*," added De Grandin.

Lady Spencer was the opposite of what Tom had expected. This demure creature seemed more like a librarian than an aristocrat. She only nodded in acknowledgement of their condolences.

Superintendent Goodfield launched his questioning. "Did your husband have any enemies that you knew of?" he inquired.

"No." Her thin lips formed a weak smile. "Horace thoroughly segregated his work and home lives."

348

Goodfield ground his teeth. "Please state what happened on the date of the murder."

Lady Chiltern recounted that she and her husband had risen before noon. The couple had breakfasted on the terrace with their sons. Horace had surprised his wife with tickets for *Platée* at the Royal Opera House. However, she was feeling unwell and had bidden her husband to go alone.

"I went to bed and woke up a widow," she concluded with a sigh. "That is everything."

Tom and Harry looked at each other. Nothing to do now but return to Baker Street.

Lord Algernon Lorton followed a trail into Kew Gardens Conservatory. The London institution offered a greenhouse to anyone with a halfpenny. Morning light shone through the conservatory's glass canopy.

Lorton wore a military surplus greatcoat over his navy-blue suit. His brown hair was crowned with a homburg hat. A pencil mustache distinguished his sharp face. He made a beeline for the southwest corner of the greenhouse. He joined a blond lady near palm trees. The couple embraced and passionately kissed. For the first time in a week he felt alive, free.

"Algie, a week without you is hell," said the woman.

"Actually, Doris, that's what I came to talk about," Lorton said, breaking the kiss.

"What are you saying?"

"It's over." Somehow Lorton was able to meet her gaze.

"You can't..." She began to speak before her words faded into babbling. Her eyes became inflamed with pain and shock.

"Try to understand! Friends have told me that my wife has hired a private detective!"

"So?" Doris asked defiantly. Her tears flowed.

"If she learns about us, I'm finished!"

"You're nothing but a kept man!" Doris spat.

Lorton's ears burned at her words. He had married for money, and his wife had married him for his title. He would be ruined if she discovered his infidelity.

"You said you loved me, that we'd run off together!" Doris wailed, gesturing as she spoke.

"Men say a lot of things when women and wine mix." He would need much wine tonight to numb the rot in his heart.

Doris tore a locket from her neck. "You gave me this on our night in Paris!" She threw it to the ground. "Keep it. She probably paid for it anyway!"

Doris stormed off. Lorton felt relieved and wounded to see her leave. If given the choice between wealth or love, he would always choose the former. Now, he had to wait. It would be unwise to be seen leaving with his former mistress.

Lorton stared off into the brush. He saw a shape through the greenery. At first, he thought it was a hedge. Then he realized it was a person. Terror inflamed his nerves. Perhaps a detective? He was about to run when suddenly singing reached his ears:

*Tell tale Tit,*
*Your tongue shall be slit;*
*And all the dogs in the town*
*Shall have a little bit.*

Lorton became equal parts perplexed and afraid. Finally anger roused his soul. It was only one man and the conservatory was nearly empty. He parted the bushes to expose the unknown individual and came face to face with the last person he ever expected to see. The recognition nearly caused his heart to stop.

*Tell tale tit...*

Dickson and Tom breakfasted on poached eggs and Earl Gray tea. Mrs. Crown, the detective's housekeeper, interrupted the meal:

"Visitor for you, Mr. Dickson!"

"Who?"

"French gentleman, blond," she giggled girlishly, "ever so handsome."

Dickson stood up and wiped crumbs from his mouth. "Send him in at once."

Jules de Grandin walked into the dining room to make an announcement. "There's been another one."

"Come again?" Tom asked, dumbfounded.

"Another British aristocrat has been murdered"

"We must leave at once," said Dickson, getting up and grabbing his coat.

"Are you armed?" De Grandin gestured to a bulge near his ribs.

Dickson and Tom loaded and packed .38 caliber revolvers. De Grandin guided his friends to a waiting cab. The Frenchman loathed British taxis for resembling hearses. It was one of countless dismal details about life in the UK.

"Tell me everything" Dickson demanded as the cab sped off.

"*Naturellement!* Less than two hours ago, the police discovered the body of one Lord Lorton."

"How was he killed?"

"Cut in half," De Grandin replied

Kew Gardens was located in Richmond. The borough was less than ten miles from Baker Street. Dickson and De Grandin spent the short journey sharing theories about the murders. Tom could barely follow the lightning exchange of scenarios.

The taxi deposited the three men at Kew Gardens. It was surreal to step into a forest after a commute through a metropolis. De Grandin led his friends along a gravel path to the conservatory. The greenhouse was occupied by a small army of policemen.

They were quickly admitted inside. Tom gawked at what appeared to be a crystal palace containing a jungle.

"Sorry to get you up so early again," said Superintendent Goodfield stepping out from behind the ferns.

"Always happy to assist Scotland Yard," replied De Grandin with a humble smile.

The Superintendent took them to the crime scene. Policemen circled around the corpse. Dickson stepped into the crowd to witness a familiar sight. Lord Lorton's blood had drained onto the ground, leaving a deep stain. All present felt that the garden had been forever defiled.

The Lord had been cleaved in two above the navel. His face was locked in a death scream. The arms lay stretched out as if reaching for something. Ribs jutted out. The rest of the body lay diagonal to the upper half. His legs were still attached to a truncated stomach.

Dickson made a discovery that chilled him to the marrow. Lorton's cufflinks bore the same epsilon symbol as the engraving on Chiltern's ring! Thinking fast, he grabbed one of the cufflinks. He then slowly stood up from the body and motioned for Tom to join him.

"Tom, take a taxi to the British Library and Fleet Street," said the detective holding out some money. "Try to find anything connecting Chiltern to Lorton then return to Baker Street and wait for me there."

"Right-ho guv," said Tom, accepting the banknotes. He hurried for the exit He was an excellent researcher, able to tirelessly scan through newspaper archives for hours.

Dickson then turned to De Grandin. "I need to show you something."

"*Quoi?*"

The detective produced Lorton's cufflink. "I took this off the body."

De Grandin whistled, "You tampered with evidence."

"Note the engraving," said Dickson, ignoring the remark.

De Grandin's eyes narrowed as he studied the cufflink. "So?" he asked.

"I saw a ring on Lord Chiltern's body with that exact same design."

"*Incroyable!*" The Frenchman paused. "But useless in Court."

Dickson smiled. "We need to talk to the widow again."


Back in Kensington, Lady Chiltern received her two guests. It felt strange to see a Frenchman and an American working together. Dickson and De Grandin enjoyed tea in her drawing room.

"Your Ladyship, did your husband know Lord Algernon Lorton?" Dickson asked after pleasantries had been exchanged.

The widow threw up her hands. "Mr. Dickson, I only met a precious few of my husband's friends. I cannot remember any of their names." She bit her lip. "As I told you, he kept his home life and social life separate."

De Grandin sighed. Suddenly, inspiration struck; a plan formed in his mind. He began coughing as if deathly sick. The Frenchman fumbled with his cup and let it spill all over his suit.

"*Mon Dieu!*" he exclaimed. "I am such an oaf."

"You poor dear," Lady Chiltern said, concerned for her guest. "The lavatory is down the hall."

De Grandin sheepishly left the room while Dickson sputtered apologies. He stepped into an empty hallway with green carpeting and five doors. The first entrance opened to the maid's quarters. De Grandin opened another door to the lavatory. Frustrated, he tried the door at the end of the hall only to find himself in the study.

The Frenchman almost ran to the desk in the center of the oak-paneled room. It was covered with unopened letters. He began to sort through a stack of correspondence. He did not recognize any of the names on the envelopes. How much longer before Lady Chiltern sent a maid to check on him?

Without thinking, he grabbed a stash of letters. He scanned one after another, his hands rapidly shuffling paper. Only minutes remained before someone would check on what was taking him so long to tend to a stain. Suddenly, something caught his eye.

A nearly frenzied De Grandin exited the study. He forced the paper into his pocket. Halfway down the hall, the Frenchman removed his jacket and cradled it in his arms. He stopped a minute to collect himself.

Harry Dickson and Lady Chiltern looked up to see De Grandin enter the room. He was disheveled with the stained coat draped over his arms.

"*Désolé, Madame!* My clumsiness will be the death of me."

"I should hope not, Monsieur de Grandin," murmured Lady Chiltern.

"Please forgive us, Your Ladyship, we're leaving," said Dickson as he rose from his chair.

"Do come again," the noblewoman warmly replied.

With a bell, Lady Chiltern summoned a maid. The servant guided Dickson and De Grandin back to the front door. It was almost noon when two detectives stepped out of the house.

"That woman is a saint," said Dickson on the sidewalk.

"*En effet,*" Jules concurred.

Dickson hailed a taxi while De Grandin wrung tea from his jacket. He then handed a letter to his friend. "From the Chiltern study. I hope my act with the tea was convincing."

Inside the taxi, Dickson's initial frown of disapproval faded when he caught sight of the envelope. The letter had been sent to Lord Chiltern by Lord Lorton.

"So Chiltern and Lorton knew each other!" he exclaimed.

"*Certainement!* This is a clear connection between two victims."

"Baker Street, guv'nors," the driver called.

"We must ask Goodfied to investigate Chiltern's friends," Dickson said as he paid the fare.

The two detectives disembarked from the taxi. Inside 221B, De Grandin and Dickson were greeted by Tom Wills. The young man appeared pleased with himself.

"Do any of you gentlemen know a Cecil Arnheim?"

Dickson and De Grandin looked at each other.

"Not personally," Dickson replied.

Tom launched into a detailed report. He had researched high society columns of various newspapers and found an article about Lord Chiltern and one Sir Cecil Arnheim. The article featured a photo of both men at a charity luncheon for crippled children from immigrants' families.

"Excellent work!" Dickson exclaimed. "It all fits."

"What do you mean, guv?"

"Lord Chiltern knew Lord Lorton," said Dickson.

"*C'est vrai!*" De Grandin added. "I found a letter between the two."

"So Arnheim's life could be in danger too," Dickson's eyes narrowed.

Tom waved a sheet of paper. "I have his address."

The three men looked at each other for a moment, then rushed outside.

Sir Cecil Arnheim was a renowned entomologist who had discovered heretofore unknown insect species. He lived in a relatively modest flat in Marylebone. Dickson rang the doorbell, flanked by Tom Wills and Jules de Grandin.

A portly valet answered the door, "Who may I say is calling?"

"Harry Dickson. Your master's life may be in danger."

The valet's face lit up: a celebrity guest! "Right this way gentlemen."

The valet led them into a dimly-lit study. Sir Cecil Arnheim sat at a desk studying specimens under a magnifying glass. He was overweight with red hair, much like that of an Irishman. His jowls hung heavy about his lower face.

"How do you do?" he said, without looking up from work.

"My name is…" began Dickson.

"I know who you are," Arnheim interrupted with a tired smile. "The American Sherlock Holmes."

"Yes. These are my friends Jules de Grandin and Tom Wills."

"And what can I do for you, gentlemen?" Arnheim asked, still studying his rare butterfly.

"Did you know Lord Horace Spencer and Lord Algernon Lorton?" De Grandin asked.

Arnheim frowned at the Frenchman's accent. "We were acquainted through charity work."

"Then your life is in danger," explained Dickson.

Arnheim laughed, "What rot!"

Tom spoke up, "You need police protection!"

Arnheim sighed. "The only thing I need is to catch a train."

"We will have to accompany you," De Grandin stated.

"Or Superintendent Goodfield can have a word with you," threatened Dickson.

Arnheim bit his lip. "Fine, you may accompany me."

A taxi conveyed four men to London Bridge station where they boarded an overnight train for Edinburgh. The interior appeared untouched since Queen Victoria's diamond jubilee. Arnheim welcomed his bodyguards into his reserved compartment.

Dickson and De Grandin scrutinized entry point into the maple-paneled compartment. Arnheim and Tom settled into navy-blue seats. The Frenchman was vaguely disgusted by the lime-green ceiling. Then the locomotive launched into action forcing everyone to sit down.

The four travelers settled in for the journey. Tom became entranced by the view from the windows. Dickson reviewed his notes on the murders. Arnheim struggled to pretend that he was alone, and that the presence of his "protectors" didn't annoy him. De Grandin read a newspaper which he had purchased at the station.

The murders of Lords Chiltern and Lorton dominated the front page. Tory pundits theorized that they were the work of some Bolshevik madman determined to inflict his own reign of terror. A masterful robbery had been executed by the Vampires gang, who had stolen the Pink Panther, a priceless diamond.

Arnheim suddenly rose to his feet. "You gentlemen are welcome to join me in the dining car for supper."

De Grandin, Dickson and Tom followed him down claustrophobic corridors. In the dining car, a narrow aisle separated rows of tables stationed near oblong windows. The men selected a corner table that would allow the detectives to watch the exits and most passengers.

The menu provoked De Grandin's visible disgust. Tom was nervous about what to order in such a posh setting. Dickson's appetite always declined during his investigations, so he only wanted a spartan meal. Eventually, they ordered steak, salmon, sardolive sandwich, and clam broth.

Arnheim looked away from the window. He'd heard some unnatural sound. Was it the train? It sounded like singing. The melody seemed to come from everywhere and nowhere at once. He stared at his uninvited guests who ate as if nothing was amiss. How could they not have heard the sound?

"Excuse me," he said, getting up, drawn to the singing.

His guardians paid no mind as Arnheim walked away from the table. No doubt, he was only going to the lavatory. The entomologist moved towards the south of the dining car.

A waiter in a white uniform arrived with a food cart. The small man distributed four meals among the detectives' table. Dickson took slow bites of his sandwich, careful to make it last. De Grandin sliced into his steak, too well cooked. Tom fished for clams in his soup.

"Sir Cecil is missing some good food," the young man observed between bites.

Dickson and De Grandin exchanged a glance. At once, they leaped up from the table. The entomologist had been far too long! Tom followed the two of them as they hurried south after the missing man.

"I never should have let him leave alone!" Dickson hissed as he ran for the next car.

"Focus on the matter at hand!" De Grandin said. His countenance betrayed no sign of stress.

They entered the next car to find it deserted by passengers, who'd all gone to supper. Sir Cecil Arnheim was standing near a window with his back to them.

"Sir Cecil!" exclaimed Dickson. "It was grossly reckless to wander off like that."

Arnheim ignored him. "Can't you hear it?" he asked.

"Hear what?" De Grandin asked. At the moment he only heard the locomotive.

"The song—so sweet," said Arnheim, staring off in the distance.

Dickson clamped a hand on Arnheim's shoulder. "Your food is getting cold."

The entomologist spun about, as if emerging from a trance. "Quite right.," he said, facing his bodyguards.

"*Tell tale tit*," came a voice from the southern end of the car.

A small figure stepped into the car from behind Hesketh. It appeared to be a little boy. Dickson saw that he was dressed in rags, yet couldn't make out his face in the dim light.

"Are you lost, mate?" Tom called.

The boy stepped into the light. He had golden blond hair with a baby face. All four men became awestruck as they saw his eyes, which were pure black! There was no trace of any white. Anyone who looked into his eyes stared into the void.

Terror distorted Cecil's face. He half-collapsed into a fit of spineless panic. His jowls shook as he sobbed. It appeared that his will had left him.

"It can't be," he hissed.

The child leaped at the men. He tackled Arnheim down to the ground. The entomologist blindly groped at his tormentor's shirt. His quivering hand tore away the dirty cloth. Tom almost threw up. De Grandin stopped in his tracks. The boy's arm was a mess of exposed bone and pale flesh.

Dickson was the first to come to his senses and to Arnheim's aid. He grabbed at the boy, causing him to turn. De Grandin found himself staring into pure black eyes. In a frenzy of motion, the inhuman child struck the Frenchman, who collapsed to the floor, then freed himself from Dickson's grip.

The boy then returned to his prey. Arnheim tried to crawl away, but to no avail. His attacker struck him in the face. The punch nearly knocked the entomologist unconscious. The detectives stared in awe as the blond youth launched a battery of blows at his victim.

Dickson drew his revolver. Through an act of sheer will, he fought back every instinct telling him that this was a child to be protected, every feeling telling him to drop the gun, as he took aim at Arnheim's monstrous assailant.

They recoiled at the deafening sound of the gunshot. The child became motionless with a hole through his shoulder. But they couldn't see blood or any sign that he had suffered damage. The boy ignored them and continued to face Arnheim.

"Do you remember me?" His voice was like howling wind.

"You… are… Igor Samsa…"

A punch silenced the entomologist. Then, the boy lifted his prey into the air and walked south. De Grandin reached for his revolver, but changed his mind out of fear of hitting Arnheim.

The boy approached the doorway and struck a hole in the wall. Another blow from his pale fist demolished the wall to create a crude door. With his prisoner in hand. the abomination jumped out for the next car.

De Grandin and Dickson ran toward the boy's exit. They saw him climbing a ladder with one hand and Arnheim in the other. The roof was a perfect place to vivisect his victim in peace.

De Grandin left through the regular exit. Dickson waited for the boy to reach the roof. He then leaped into space, easily clearing the distance between the two cars. His steely fingers locked onto the railing.

Tom watched his boss mount the ladder. He climbed two rungs at a time to reach the top. Then, carefully, he stepped onto the roof. Fierce wind almost forced the detective off the train. Fortunately, the roof was equipped with rungs intended for workers.

Dickson struggled to see in twilight. The boy and his captive were a car away. Igor held Arnheim suspended by the throat. With precious time left to act, Dickson raced toward them. It was vital to stay in the middle of the car in order to avoid slipping and falling off the train. Arnheim wailed as he was thrown down onto the roof.

Dickson jumped onto the boy's car and yelled, "Stop!"

The boy turned towards Dickson. A chill wind whipped his blond hair. His angelic face was a terrifying sight. His black eyes narrowed in annoyance. Dickson drew his revolver again, merely causing the boy to smile. Inhuman laughter erupted from his pale mouth.

"I can't die."

Somehow Dickson heard every word over the wind. He took careful aim at Arnheim. "But he can," he said.

The child's face collapsed. His dark eyes widened. It was unearthly to see such an abomination display fear. If Dickson shot Arnheim, that would deny the boy the satisfaction of killing him. And it would be an act of mercy towards Sir Cecil.

"Ahhrrg." Igor Samsa gnashed his dark yellow teeth.

He was not unlike a caged tiger. He paced across the roof, looking for weakness. If he attacked Dickson, then the detective would fire off the gun.

Dickson was so focused he almost failed to notice De Grandin across from him. The Frenchman clung to a ladder. He threw himself onto the car behind the boy, balanced on the roof's edge. At the sound of a body landing on the metal surface, the boy snarled and turned.

With a bestial grunt, Igor Samsa leaped at Jules de Grandin. Dickson opened fire, but missed. De Grandin executed a savate kick that struck his enemy in mid-air, knocking him back. The boy fell down between the train cars.

All men shared an instinctive disgust as the train jolted from running over the golden-haired youth.

De Grandin turned to see the rear of the train. The locomotive had left behind the pitiful remains of a child's body. But the body began to move. The detectives witnessed it crawl off the tracks. They caught sight of a small figure limping into the brush before the locomotive turned a corner.

It was obvious they had to leave. It was almost pitch-dark and one slip meant death. The three men began to climb down the nearest ladder. They eventually returned to the passenger car where Tom was waiting.

"You're alive!" he exclaimed.

Congratulations were exchanged by all. Arnheim set about groveling like a court jester. "I owe you gentlemen my life," he said, extending his hand.

Dickson smiled and reached out, but instead of accepting the handshake. he grabbed the entomologist by the wrist. Arnheim sputtered as his ring finger was exposed. The jewelry bore an epsilon symbol.

"What does this mean?" Dickson barked.

"It's just a Greek symbol," Arnheim stammered.

De Grandin stepped forward, "Chiltern and Lorton all bore that sign." He slapped Arnheim across the face, more to stun than wound. "Explain."

The entomologist broke down. He had seen too much to maintain the lie. "It's the symbol of the Epicurean Society," he sobbed.

Dickson glanced at his comrades, then faced Arnheim. "What is that? Some fraternity?"

"You could call it that," Arnheim answered bitterly. "Some old friends of mine formed a society dedicated to pleasure."

"What manner of pleasure?" De Grandin inquired.

"It was just a drinking club at first. Just a means for gentlemen to throw secret parties."

"No one has ever been murdered over a drinking club," snarled Dickson.

"Chiltern changed the club. He started hiring women for us to enjoy…"

"Ladies of the evening?" Dickson asked.

"Er, no, from his charities for wayward women."

Dickson felt his anger rising.

"But the club soon tired of these women," Arnheim continued, his eyes shut in shame. "He then began to procure children."

Tom was now of half-a-mind to throw the posh bastard off the train. De Grandin recoiled from a man who was more inhuman than some of his earlier opponents.

"Horace would hold parties at his estate. He would bring children taken from the immigrants' population—Czechs, Poles, Rumanians... No one would miss them." He described how the children were raped by the members, each "party" becoming more savage.

Dickson's heart was now inflamed with murderous rage. Somehow, he resisted the urge to draw his revolver. "Go on," he said.

"One night, Chiltern brought a special lad, blond-haired, from Prague."

"The same boy we saw tonight," De Grandin said.

Arnheim shook his head, "Impossible. That boy died."

"How?" De Grandin felt more beast than man.

"Lorton choked him to death, but it was an accident," Arnheim explained. "I examined the body and helped dump it in a refuse pit."

De Grandin looked at Arnheim. "You and your friends horribly murdered that boy."

Arnheim tried to talk, but his words died in his throat.

"And you didn't bury him in consecrated ground, you only dumped him like garbage."

"What are you saying, Mister Grandin?" Tom asked.

"He's a revenant," the Frenchman declared.

He explained that in Eastern Europe, the people believed that the dead who had been horribly wronged often returned to seek revenge, especially if they were denied proper burial. "To this day. millions of Eastern Europeans believe that faulty burial of a body can spawn a revenant," he concluded.

"In truth, the boy made no attempt to kill us," Dickson noted, "because that was not his purpose."

"That thing will keep coming until he is avenged," De Grandin continued. Then, turning towards Arnheim, he added, "You only have a reprieve. A short time to rest before it reappears."

Arnheim sprang to his feet. "You must protect me!"

"*Absolument pas!*" De Grandin curtly replied.

Dickson's eyes narrowed. "There's only one way to save your life, Sir Cecil…"

Days later, at a police safe house, Sir Cecil Arnheim's solicitor reviewed his deal with the Crown prosecutor. He had confessed to monstrous acts against children in return for a lighter sentence.

"In exchange for your testimony against the other members of the club, you will be subject to a lifetime house arrest in rotating safe houses," the solicitor explained. For Arnheim, it amounted to free police bodyguards.

"Can you provide enough evidence?" the prosecutor asked. "If not, the deal is off and you'll go to the gallows."

"I will give you everything."

Arnheim kept his word. He turned over an oak chest to the authorities. Police opened it to find images from Hell. Photos of children suffering obscene abuse at the hands of the Epicureans. Paintings, sketches of torture victims. Some officers required sick leave after seeing photos of Chiltern and Lorton committing acts depraved beyond imagination.

Acting on Arnheim's information, the police uncovered similar boxes in the homes of the surviving Epicureans. One man kept souvenirs of his evil acts barely hidden in his library. Ten men were arrested on charges of obscenity and rape. All came from the highest social orders.

The murders of Chiltern and Lorton remained officially unsolved. Scotland Yard officials couldn't care less. There was no pressure to solve the homicides. Now the police reveled in the acclaim they received for bringing the deviants to justice.

"It's the scandal of the century, guv," Tom Wills declared as he discarded a newspaper.

"I should have thrown Arnheim off the train," said Dickson brooding over his morning tea. He felt violated for having risked his life to protect the man.

"If you had done that, a lot of evil men would be free right now," replied Tom. "Arnheim is set to testify and put them away."

"You have a visitor, Mr. Dickson!" Mrs. Crown sang as she admitted Jules de Grandin.

"Jules! Damn good to see you!" exclaimed Dickson.

"I wanted to say my goodbyes. Soon I'll be returning to New Jersey via steamer ship."

The men shook hands. Peril creates a bond among survivors.

Tom asked, "Do you expect further violence?"

De Grandin shook his head, "I don't think so. The little boy has been avenged. He has found the peace denied him in life. He can rest now."

*Leo Saint-Clair a.k.a. The Nyctalope, gained his strange powers and artificial heart in 1898. In the early 1900s, when this story takes place, Jean de La Hire, his "biographer," stated that he had various adventures in Central Africa and Tibet. At one point, he met Koynos and had an affair with German agent Wanda Stielman. His father, Jean, passed away in 1901 or thereabout. His first, full-blown adventure,* The Nyctalope on Mars, *took place in 1911...*

## Matthew Ilseman: *The Nyctalope at the Earth's Core*

### The Early 1900s

They found the bodies lying mutilated in the dark. The caverns of the inner earth had hid them well. Jan Bjelke, the expedition's guide, held an electric torch over one of the mangled corpses. It was impossible to tell which member of the expedition it was. The only way they knew it even was a member of the expedition, and not an inhabitant of Pellucidar, was the torn remains of its clothes and the compass in its hand.

"Now we know what happened to the previous expedition," Bjelke said.

Leo Saint-Clair, who did not need torches to see in the dark, studied the body. He then looked around. He counted six corpses. All horribly mangled.

"Not all of them," said the Nyctalope. "There were more members of the expedition. From what I see, they were headed back to the surface when they were attacked. I believe the others might be still alive."

"Aye," said John Rutherford. The Scotsman held an air rifle at the ready. Leo thought he looked like he was expecting something to jump out of the dark. He might not have been wrong.

"I suppose that we should bury the corpses?" said Bjelke. The big Dane looked physically ill.

"Yes," said Leo.

"Then what?" asked Rutherford.

"The only thing we can do," Leo replied, "is go forward into the dark." He picked up a book lying next to a body. It was a journal of the expedition. "This might give us a clue about what happened," he added.

The Lidenbrock Society existed for one purpose: to explore the inner earth known by its primitive inhabitants as Pellucidar. Ever since Otto Lidenbrock had made his famous expedition, there had been great interest in the scientific community in what lay below the surface of the earth. There had also been interest by the Powers-that-be in colonization.

Since no one could agree who should get to colonize the inner earth first, the Society had been formed for the benefit of all humanity. A base camp of explorers from many nations had been set up at the core. Every couple of years, the explorers would return to the surface to unveil their findings to the scientific community. When they did not return as scheduled, the Lidenbrock Society sought out the Nyctalope.

"You are perfect candidate for the job," said Dr. Abner Perry, the current head of the society. "Aside from your powers of night vision, you have experience with dangerous situations."

"I don't know if I'm the best choice," Leo replied. "I'm still relatively inexperienced."

They sat in the posh meeting room of the Society located in a brownstone building in Manhattan. A giant map of Pellucidar hung on the wall. Leo knew that most of it was pure speculation since most of the inner earth was still unexplored.

"Well, you have been to Africa and Tibet, two of the most perilous, unexplored regions on Earth—and you did avenge your father's death not too long ago."

"Yes, though I'm surprised you know so much about me."

"We have resources," said Perry. "We keep an eye on those who might be useful for our explorations. Anyway, you will not be going alone. You will go with Jan Bjelke and Professor Rutherford. They both have experience down there."

"I've heard those names before."

"Mr. Bjelke is the nephew of Hans Bjelke, who went with Lidenbrock on his first expedition. He will serve as a scout and guide. Mr. Rutherford is a relative of Dr. Challenger, the discoverer of the Maple White Land."

"Perhaps they should lead the expedition?" suggested Leo.

"Rutherford will be in charge of most of the planning, but I want you for a special job."

"You want me to find out why you have not heard from the previous expedition?" asked the Nyctalope.

"Exactly!" said Dr. Perry. "They might have been attacked by the natives. I spent some time on the American frontier. There were horrible mistakes made dealing with the indigenous population that led to a lot of bloodshed on both sides. I had wanted to avoid that, but it may not have been possible."

Leo nodded. He thought awhile, then he said, "I'll go."

They traveled on in the caverns lit only by the newly-invented electric torches they carried. Time passed and eventually they reached the earth's core. They emerged from an eternal night into an eternal noon.

Leo looked around. What he saw took his breath away. They had emerged on a grassy plain. The lands of the inner earth curved up in the distance. In the distance, a herd of woolly mammoths grazed.

Bjelke and Rutherford had been here before, but even they seemed struck by wonder. It was Rutherford who recovered first. "The camp should not be far from here," he stated.

As they walked, Leo kept glancing at the herd of mammoths. Part of him expected the hairy beasts to charge. From behind one of the beasts, a giant in skins appeared. He saw the three and held up his fist. Bjelke and Rutherford did the same. The giant turned and went back to gazing at his herd.

As they entered the camp, people came out to stare at them. Most were members of the expedition. Others were natives of the inner earth. They stared at the newcomers. Leo did not think he sensed any hostility.

A Russian came up to them, "Bjelke, Rutherford, what are you doing here?"

"Making sure you're still alive, Trukhanov," said Rutherford.

"Of course, we're alive," replied the latter. He looked at Leo. Then turned back to Rutherford. "Didn't Clairancy make it to the surface? We've made some exciting discoveries."

"I am afraid that Clairancy and the rest are dead."

They told them what they had found. The Russian was quiet for a while. Then he said, "Do you have any idea what killed them?"

"No."

"Anything unusual found with them?"

"Like what?"

"Anything. Something that might indicate how or why they were killed."

"No," said Leo. "We were hoping you might have some idea about that."

"I don't," replied Trukhanov. "I suppose that some creature could have followed them into the caves. Or perhaps there is some as-yet-unknown monster who inhabits these caves..."

"What?"

"When we were last there, we heard something. Something strange."

"What?"

"It sounded like a child crying."

"Did anyone else hear it?""

Yes, but we don't know what it was. We didn't try to find out because we didn't want to get lost."

"So you do think there might be *something* in the caves."

"Yes. Something crying in the dark."

Night did not come. It never came in Pellucidar. Leo, not at all certain of the time, had tried to sleep. He had lain in one of the cabins half-awake for what he estimated was an hour before rising. He had heard that living in the inner earth took some getting used to. He wondered if he ever would. He wanted to go back to the caves, both to try to find out what had killed the expedition, and because he realized that he preferred eternal dark to eternal light.

362

He flipped through the journal he had found. He started at the end hoping to find some clue, but it talked about nothing of importance. He came to a passage at the beginning. It said: *We are not alone in the caves. Something is following us. We do not know what.*

Leo continued reading. It was mostly a daily description of the expedition. Eventually, he came to a place where several pages had been torn out. The next page described their arrival at the base camp.

Leo got up and left the cabin. The sun was still in the same place. In the sky, a flock of prehistoric winged reptiles flew: Pterodactyls or Pteradons.

Rutherford was outside watching them. He came over to Leo who told him about the missing pages.

"What do you think happened to them?" the Scotsman asked the Nyctalope.

"I don't know," replied Leo. "I suspect something happened that someone did not want recorded. It may have to do with the massacre, but I can't be sure."

"Any ideas what was responsible for that?"

"No, but I think they were ambushed by something in the caves. What that is, I don't know."

"Hum," replied Rutherford. "What do you think of Trukhanov?"

"I don't know. I heard he was a highly respected biologist."

"I've known him on and off over the years. He seems to be different. As if he were hiding something."

"Like what?"

"I don't know."

The next day, they interviewed everyone. No one seemed to know anything. The expedition members vouched for each other. They all said their relations with the natives had always been friendly. Leo had begun to suspect that whatever had killed the expedition dwelt in the caverns.

There was nothing left but to go back into the dark.

Leo, along with Rutherford and Bjelke, descended back into the tunnels. Igor Trukhanov had decided to go with them. They all carried specialized air rifles. These guns had been invented by a German engineer. They were somewhat infamous for having been used by the notorious Colonel Sebastian Moran during an attempt on the life of Sherlock Holmes. They had been chosen because they made less noise than a regular gun. They kept them ready as they walked through the tunnels.

It did not seem long until they heard something. It sounded like the cries of a young child. It froze them in their tracks. A chill went through Leo's body. The party looked around as if expecting to see something. Even with his night vision, Leo could see nothing dangerous.

"Is that the sound you heard before?" Leo asked Trukhanov.

In the light of the torches, the Russian nodded.

"Quiet," said Rutherford. "We don't want anything to know we're here."

"What do you suppose it is?" whispered Bjelke.

"I don't know," said Leo. "It may be nothing. Some trick of sound. Or it may be what we're looking for."

"It seems to come from one of the other tunnels," said Bjelke. "Should we investigate?"

"No!" said Trukhanov. "I mean, we could get lost. We should go to where the bodies were found. There, we can piece together what happened."

Leo remained silent for a while. Then he said, "All right, but let's watch out."

Eventually, they came to where they had found the corpses. The ground of the tunnels had been too hard to dig, so they had constructed rude cairns for the deceased. It seemed fitting since they were already buried beneath the earth.

Leo noticed that something had changed in Trukhanov's countenance. He looked around expectantly, then frowned.

"You did not mark the graves?" the Russian said.

"No," replied Leo. "The corpses were so mangled we could not determine who was who.

"Did anyone have a large satchel?"

"No."

"Then where could it be?"

"Where could what be?" replied Leo.

"Clairancy carried a large brown satchel. It had plant specimens in it."

"We found a journal," said Bjelke.

"We need to find that satchel," said Trukhanov.

Leo wondered what the Russian was actually looking for. He doubted it was just plant specimens.

"There are several tunnels off the main way," said Trukhanov. "We should search them."

"Now you want to search them?" asked Leo. "Earlier, you were afraid of getting lost."

"We have to find the satchel," replied the Russian. "There are four of us and four tunnels. Perhaps we should split up?"

"Don't be foolish," said Leo. "There is strength in numbers. Whatever killed Reynolds and the others may still be out there."

"Aye," agreed Rutherford.

"Maybe groups of two?" suggested Trukhanov. "We won't be alone and we could still search more rapidly."

"I don't like it," said Leo.

"I think we should do it," said Bjelke.

"Why?"

"We need to find out what killed them," replied the Dane looking at the cairns. "Exploring the other tunnels might give us an answer. Besides, whatever it is killed all six of them. There are four of us. I don't think our numbers will keep us safe."

"That really reassures me," said Leo.

"I am really sorry," continued Bjelke, "but it's true. What we need more than anything is to find out what we are up against. We will split up and search in two tunnels then come back in say an hour."

"I still don't like it," said Leo.

"It's your call," said Rutherford.

"All right, but we return in an hour," said Leo. "If you find anything living, turn back at once. Rutherford will come with me. Bjelke, you go with Trukhanov."

The Russian headed into a tunnel. Bjelke made to follow after him. Leo caught his arm.

"Be careful," said Leo. "I don't trust him."

Bjelke traveled with Trukhanov for the better part of the hour. The Russian carried the torch in front of them. Bjelke carried an air rifle at the ready. Trukhanov' own rifle was strapped to his back.

The tunnel was dark and featureless. If Bjelke had not been so scared, he would have been bored. He half expected something to leap out of the darkness.

"Does the dark frighten you?" asked Trukhanov.

"No," Bjelke lied. Truth was, he had been afraid of the dark since he was a kid. He considered it childish, but under these circumstances, he was not sure anymore. He just kept his hands on his rifle and his eyes on the dark in front of him.

Eventually, they came to another cairn. This one smaller than the ones used to bury the dead. Trukhanov began moving the rocks. He found a satchel. It bulged with something.

"So he was going to hide it and keep it for himself," muttered the Russian.

"Let me see that," said Bjelke.

"Why?"

"I want see it," said the Dane. He pointed his gun at the Russian. "I don't want to shoot you, but I have to know what you're hiding. Give me your gun."

Trukhanov shrugged, then unstrung his rifle and handed to Bjelke.

The Dane leaned the rifles against the cave wall. He then opened the satchel. What he saw took his breath away.

It was a ruby—larger than any he had ever seen. He knew now what Trukhanov was hiding. Everything found in Pellucidar was to be turned over to the Lindenbrock Society, but the Russian had wanted the wealth for himself. Clairancy was probably his partner in a scheme to smuggle it back to the surface.

But Bjelke hadn't seen Trukhanov pick up a rock from the floor. The Russian swung it down against his head.

Bjelke never saw anything again.


Leo and Rutherford walked through the tunnels. Only the torch in Rutherford's hand lit the way. Every once in a while, they heard what sounded like the cries of a child.

"What do you think that is?" said Rutherford.

"I don't know," Leo replied. "It could be anything. Wind. An underground river. Or some unknown creature."

"That reminds me of something," said Rutherford. "A story I heard from one of the natives last time I was here. About creatures they called the Unseen Ones. They supposedly dwelt within the earth—that is to say, in these caverns."

"What about them?"

"They are said to be invisible and cannot be killed. They apparently eat anything, including people. Of course, the natives are superstitious. They also talk about something called a Mahar that can control a person's mind."

Leo shivered. This was a bad discussion for the place they were in. Still, there might be some truth to the legends. Pellucidar was still largely unexplored.

As they walked, the crying grew louder. They seemed to be heading toward it. Leo kept his rifle at the ready.

"It looks like as if we're going to find out what's making that noise," said Rutherford.

The cries grew louder and louder. The tunnel twisted. Eventually, they came to an opening. By then, the cries where just short of a cacophony.

"Do we continue?" asked Rutherford.

"Yes," replied Leo.

They went through the opening. It led to a cavern large enough to hold a city. It was lit by a strange greenish light that did not seem to come from anywhere. Rutherford spotted great structures like buildings carved into the cavern walls. The cries were much louder.

"A city," said Rutherford. "An empty city..."

Leo stared and did not reply.

"There doesn't seem to be any inhabitants."

Leo turned to look at Rutherford. He said, "What are you talking about? They're everywhere!"

"What?"

"The creatures. The spiders."

"I don't see anything but a cavern."

Then Leo remembered what Rutherford had just said about the Unseen Ones. They were invisible to him. Only his enhanced night vision allowed him to see them.

Creatures like giant spiders covered the cavern. They were translucent like ghosts. Along with the eight legs of the spider, they had arms and hands like a man. What was most horrible were their faces—faces like that of children.

At first, the creatures seemed unaware of the two men, but then, one saw them and let out a cry. The child-like faces turned and looked at the intruders.

"There are creatures here," said Leo. "I think they are invisible to you, but I can see them."

One of the creatures started their way. Leo raised his air rifle. He hesitated. Part of him wondered if they were truly hostile. Then he remembered what Rutherford said about the Unseen Ones eating people. He fired.

The bullet ricocheted off the creature as if it had been made of stone. Leo fired two more times, but to no avail. The creature just came forward while continuing to make its cry. The others turned to follow.

"I believe you," said Rutherford. "What do we do?"

"We run," said Leo.

They turned and ran. The creatures followed after them.

Trukhanov waited outside of the tunnel, his rifle ready. He had placed his torch on the ground at the opening. He had then taken up a position a few meters away. He planned to shoot Saint-Clair and Rutherford as they walked into the light. He was not a particularly good shot, but he didn't think that he could miss at this range.

After he killed them, the jewel would be his, and his alone. The money he would get for it would be enough to help start looking for more gems. There had to be others. With them, he could become the richest man in the world.

As he waited, he heard the cries. He didn't know what they were. If some sort of creature came with the two men, he would shoot it too.

He licked his lips and waited.

They ran in the darkness, Leo ahead, Rutherford behind. The Scotsman had dropped the torch in fright and now clung to the Nyctalope's sleeve so that he wouldn't become lost. Leo, for his part, navigated the tunnel.

Up ahead, he could see a light. He ran towards it. Soon, he could see a torch lying on the ground. Neither of them stopped to pick it up when they exited the tunnel. There was a cracking sound. A bullet whizzed by him, sounding like a derange bee. It struck Rutherford in the shoulder. The Scotsman screamed and fell.

Leo saw this and turned. Another bullet whizzed by. He dropped to the ground and rolled out of the torch light. He could see Trukhanov lying prone, rifle in hand. Only the dark kept the Russian from firing at him.

He turned to see Rutherford stagger up. Trukhanov fired again and a bullet struck Rutherford in the side. Leo crawled over to where the Scorsman lay and pulled him out of the light. More bullets whizzed by.

"What was that?" asked Rutherford, clutching his shoulder.

"Trukhanov is firing at us."

"Bloody Russian," cursed the Scotsman. "What does he think he is doing?"

"Presumably, he is trying to kill us."

"Why?"

"I don't know."

Leo looked at the tunnel they had just exited. He expected to see the horrible creatures emerging from it, but saw nothing. They had apparently outdistanced them. Unfortunately, he could still hear their cries. It would not be long until they caught up.

"I know you're here," Trukhanov shouted. "I will make it quick."

Leo didn't reply. They were stuck between a murderer and a horde of unknown monsters. He unslung his rifle. Trukahnov, at least, he knew he could kill. It took everything in him not to fire wildly at the Russian. Still, with his night vision, he had an advantage. Trukhanov, for his part, was literally shooting in the dark.

Leo aimed the rifle. The gun cracked. The bullet hit the Russian in the torso. He curled up, putting his hands on the wound to stop the bleeding.

Leo checked Rutherford, who was still alive and conscious, but was losing a lot of blood. He stood up. Then he pulled the Scotsman up.

"Lean on my shoulder," Leo said.

They staggered to where Trukhanov lied. He wasn't dead, but in too much pain to shoot again. He clutched his stomach. There was a smell of feces around him indicating that the bullet had hit the bowels. Blood gushed forth from the wound.

"You shot me!" he said, accusingly.

"You shot first," growled Rutherford.

The cries of the Unseen Ones had grown even louder in the meantime.

"We have to get out of here," said Leo. "They are coming. Quickly, Trukhanov, why did you shoot at us?"

"The jewel," he said. "I wanted the jewel all to myself. It's mine."

For the first time, Leo noticed the satchel. It was open and he could see the jewel glowing red.

The cries of the creatures grew even louder. The Nyctalope closed the satchel, slung it over his shoulder, and looked at the Russian.

"You can't leave me," said Trukhanov.

"I am sorry, but I can't take both of you."

They exited the tunnel, leaving the Russian behind. A spider creature appeared. Leo knew that Trukhanov couldn't see his death coming. He and Rutherford continued to stagger away.

The creature sprang upon the wounded Russian. Its little girl's head bit down on him. Trukhanov screamed.

He kept screaming as Leo turned his back and left.

Leo and Rutherford made it back to the core. The fact that the creatures had stopped to feed on Trukhanov had allowed them enough time to get away.

When they got to camp, Leo bandaged Rutherford and managed to stop the blood flow. It was a miracle that the Scotsman hadn't died of blood loss. Even so, he passed out.

Leo told the expedition's second in command, a Frenchman named Jacques de Mésange, what had happened. De Mésange shook his head.

"You said something about a jewel?" he asked.

"I think he meant this," said Leo getting the satchel. He opened it. The red jewel shone.

De Mésange stared at it. Then he shook his head again. "That's undoubtedly valuable, but it isn't worth a human life."

"No," said Leo. "And it was more than one human life. We haven't seen Bjelke, but I imagined that Trukhanov killed him."

"The things men do out of greed."

Leo nodded. He closed the satchel and went to hide it in his cabin.

For three days, Leo and Rutherford recuperated at the camp. The Nyctalope kept inside mostly. The eternal sunlight of the core bothered him. He couldn't sleep. Even though Trukhanov had tried to murder them, he felt guilty for abandoning him to such horrors. He told Rutherford how he felt.

"He brought it on himself," replied the Scotsman bluntly.

"I should have at least put a bullet in his head so he wouldn't have been eaten alive."

"Perhaps, but we had to get away."

Rutherford was in bad shape. He began to smell of rot. Leo had checked the wounds and was horrified to see signs of gangrene.

"I'm not going to make it am I, laddie?" asked the Scotsman.

"You could still recover."

"No," said Rutherford. "I will not."

Leo did not reply.

"Have I ever told you about my wife?"

"No," said Leo.

"Before I came here, she had a dream. She said she saw me die at the Earth's core. I never really believed in things like that, but it looks like it's coming true."

"We don't know that yet," replied Leo.

"We know," said the Scotsman. "I can feel death coming."

Again, Leo did not reply.

The Nyctalope left the cabin. Storm clouds gathered blocking out the sun. Lightning flashed. A few rain drops fell. Thunder cracked.

369

For Leo, the storm was a welcome break. The sun had seemed to beat down on him. It was his enhanced night vision that made it so unbearable. If he had been normal, he might have been able to bear it. He couldn't wait to get back to the surface.

The natives, on the other hand, did not deal well with the lack of light. They were nowhere to be seen. Even the other researchers had gone into their cabins.

Standing in the doorway of his own cabin, Leo felt something was wrong, but he was not sure what. They had gotten away from the Unseen Ones, but it didn't seem over. Then, there was the jewel. Trukhanov had murdered for it. He wondered how it fit in with everything else.

Thunder cracked again. The ground trembled. Leo wondered if they were having an earthquake on top of the storm. The trembling of the earth came at irregular intervals. It also seemed to get stronger each time. A cold hand gripped his artificial heart.

He returned to Rutherford's cabin. The ground trembled and, this time, began to crack. The cracks spread across the camp. Then the ground under the Scotsman's cabin caved in.

Leo ran to the crater. He looked down, hoping against hope that Rutherford had somehow survived. What he saw horrified him. One of the Unseen Ones was crawling out of the great hole. Rutherford was alive, but in the hands of the creature. It dragged the Scotsman down into the dark. Leo heard the man's screams.

Drawn by the screams, a crowd had gathered around the crater. The cries of the creatures came up out of the dark. Leo shouted to them to run, but it was useless. They couldn't see the monsters,

Another of the creatures came out of the hole, followed yet another. On its spindly legs it climbed out of the crater and, with its hands, grabbed a native near its edge. The face, so much like that of a child, bit into the native.

Leo had always been a brave man, but now he was struck by the horror. For a moment, he just stood there. Then, he got a hold of himself. In the midst of tall he horror, his unconscious mind told him what to do. He ran back to his cabin where he'd hid the jewel. He grabbed the satchel, and ran back to the crater.

Outside, some of the onlookers, seeing the native being devoured by an unseen creature, had started to run. Others just stood there, staring in incomprehension. One had fainted.

Leo ran to the edge of the crater. He opened the satchel and took out the gem. It glowed like a small reddish star. He laid it on the ground before the crater.

"It is yours," Leo said. "You can have it back."

There was no way the creatures could understand his French, but he felt he had to try to make his intent known.

For a moment, the Unseen Ones stared at him. Then the largest came up to jewel and scooped it up. It turned back and descended into the hole. The others followed.

They descended back into the dark.

Leo Saint-Clair once again sat in the posh meeting room of the Lindenbrock Society. He had just finished telling his story to Dr. Abner Perry and wondered if the scientist even believed him. Still, the survivors of the expedition had backed him up.

"And only you could see these creatures?" said Perry.

"I know it sounds..."

The doctor raised his hand. "I believe you. The others could not see the creatures, but what they said backed up your story. It must have been your special sight that allowed you to see them."

"Very likely, yes."

"And they were after that jewel? You think Trukhanov stole it from them?"

"Yes. Iin Tibet, I've heard of legends about an ancient ruby called the Heart of Ahriman... "

Dr. Perry sighed, "I'd hoped we would do better inside the earth than outside. I thought that by allowing only scientists on the expedition, we might avoid the tragedies that often happened on new frontiers. Unfortunately, it seems they can be just as greedy and foolish as anyone."

"I suppose so," said Leo. "Wisdom and knowledge are not the same things."

"Apparently," said Perry. "I'm going to propose that we make no more expeditions in the near future. We'll close off the entrance to the core. That will prevent more tragedies."

"Perhaps," said Leo. "Perhaps not."

"What do you mean?"

"Someone may find another entrance. Or open the old one. People will mine metals and drill for oil."

"Perhaps."

"That's not the bad part," said Leo. "The Unseen Ones are still there. They know of us now. They may be waiting down there in the dark. Or they may come up on their own someday."

Abner Perry didn't respond, or say anything. He just looked down.

They both pondered what more horrors lay down beneath their feet.

*Rick Lai's jigsaw puzzle of a vast historical saga of the various branches of the Black Coats acquires here a new (and final) piece in this convoluted tale of murder and betrayal, where we meet an altogether different cast of characters borrowed from a variety of spaghetti westerns...*

# Rick Lai: *Executioners Also Die*

*Texas, 1895-96*

I, Jezebel Garvin, the daughter of Glenn Garvin, am a murderess, Over the last four years, I have slain more than a dozen people. Quite an accomplishment for a woman only 26 years-old. My first two victims currently reside in the cemetery shared by the neighboring towns of Silver Creek and Burton City. I was thoroughly justified in killing both of them.

Shortly after the end of the Civil War, my grandfather, Tom Garvin (1817-1872), and Ken Kluster (1828-1872) became equal partners in an investment firm called Garvin-Kluster Partners. The company funded new construction to rapidly expand Siver Creek, a Texas mining town. On the verge of financial ruin, the city's fortunes suddenly turned around when a new silver deposit was discovered in 1866. Garvin-Kluster Partners owned nearly every business in town, including the silver mine, the bank and the saloon. In 1870, Tom was convicted of illegally selling guns to the anti-Juarez rebels in Mexico, and was subsequently sentenced to four years of hard labor. My grandfather's incarceration enabled Ken, illegally, to seize control of our family's assets. Two years later, Tom escaped from a federal prison. Ken had the bank issued a $5000 bounty for him.

That's how Luther Ringo, a bounty hunter, came to work for Ken, and eventually fatally shot Tom. However, Ringo never reached Silver Creek with Tom's body. My father Glenn (1844-1895), Tom's son, intercepted him and gained possession of Tom's body. Glenn then delivered his own father's body to the authorities, collected the bounty, and this proved Tom's demise. He freely admitted that it had been Ringo who'd slain my grandfather, but when asked about the man's whereabouts, he never gave an adequate answer, so everyone assumed that Ringo had been buried in an unmarked grave somewhere, but since one can't prove murder without a corpse, the matter was left open.

As a boy, Glenn had been woefully neglected by his father. Supposedly, Tom had once told his wife and son that he was taking a brief trip to the store to buy tobacco, and then then disappeared for five years. Glenn didn't know what his father did for a living. It wasn't until he saw his face in a "Wanted Dead or Alive" poster that he learned of Tom's activities in Silver Creek.

Prior to his demise, my grandfather had given his son a colorful nickname. When learning how to ride a horse, Glenn's spurs had made annoying "jingles-jangles" noises. So, Glenn was nicknamed "Jangles" by Tom. Some journalists have confused Glenn "Jangles" Garvin with Ignaz ''Django'' Djanko, the Croatian-American gunfighter known to use a machine gun.

Glenn then went on to argue that he'd inherited half of the Garvin-Kluster company upon his father's death. Subsequent events have become shrouded in mystery. The Silver Creek Bank was robbed. Glenn and Ken accused each other. Glenn eventually recovered the stolen cash, but Ken disappeared. Glenn was hailed as a hero while Ken was declared a wanted fugitive from justice. Now, as the sole owner of the company, Glenn had the bank issue a $5000 bounty for Ken Kluster, dead or alive.

Ken's disappearance became somehow linked to the unsolved murder of his second wife. In 1844, Louise Lupin, Ken's first wife, had died giving birth to their son, Jeffrey. In 1868, Ken remarried, wedding the treacherous Jessica Texar, who had been a ruthless Confederate spy during the Civil War. But he didn't know that she was still secretly married to a Doctor Theodore Marley of Boston. Her deception was exposed, however, when the latter came to Silver Creek. On the night of Ken's disappearance, Jessica was found fatally stabbed in alleyway. It was assumed by everyone that Ken had killed Jessica.

My father had a wicked sense of humor. He defied public convention by naming me after the most evil queen in the Bible—Jezebel. Jeffrey Kluster had a similar iconoclastic sense of humor. He named his daughter after the most evil Empress of the Roman Empie—Messalina. Little was known about her mother—Jeff's wife. Her maiden name was listed as Belinda Bordon on Messalina's 1867 birth certificate. She apparently died shortly before her husband perished.

The orphaned Messalina was adopted by her great-uncle, Fergus Lupin, who owned a casino in Burton City, a few miles north of Silver Creek. During 1885-1893, she supported herself by working as a school teacher. In 1894, she was hired by Penny Bannington, a wealthy heiress ln her late thirties, to be her personal secretary. Penny was at the time romancing Buron City's wealthiest man, Issachar Coffran, who had inherited a fortune while only in his twenties and owned nearly every business in town, including the local newspaper, *The Clarion*. But after Coffran complimented Messalina on her beauty, Penny fired her. Developing a fanatical attraction for Messalina, Issachar married her and made her the newspaper's new editor. There, the girl soon decided to turn it into her own instrument of vengeance.

Penny Bannington was known for raising money for raising money for the Salvation Army. Messalina wrote an article accusing her of diverting all the contributions to a secret bank account. While she had posed as a member of the Salvation Army since 1877, that organization could not find her name listed on any of her rolls. Convicted of fraud, Penny was arrested, but managed to escape from the Burton City jail before she could be transported to a federal prison. She hasn't been seen since her escape.

In the spring of 1895, Messalina penned an article attacking my family, suggesting that my father had murdered her grandfather, and even her grandfather. A loyal son, my father made regular visits to Tom Garvin's grave. After my mother's death in 1893, these trips transpired on an almost daily basis. After the article appeared, he went to El Paso to secure the services of a noted libel attorney to sue *The Clarion*. But in my absence, all hell broke loose in Burton City.

There was no train station in Silver Creek, but we were visited by a hooded woman on horseback. Dressed in the clothes of an 18th-century highwayman, including a cape and a wide brimmed hat, she was armed with two colt revolvers rather than flintlock pistols. Calling herself "Maud Allinghame," this female bandit ordered the stagecoach passengers to remove their valuables and drop then into a sack held by the driver, Jedediah Delay. After the sack had been s returned to her, she shot Jedediah and all the coach's horses, before riding away. Luckily, the stranded passengers were able to walk back to Silver Creek.

The next night, the masked woman broke into the Burton City Bank, opened the safe with dynamite, and stole all the money inside. The next day, *The Clarion* printed an editorial calling for the formation of a vigilante posse to apprehend her. Messalina traced the origin of the name "Maud Allinghame" to an 1855 poem by Frank E. Smedley. The title character was an Englis noblewoman who committed nightly robberies as a masked rider. The editor voiced the suspicion that the current "Maud Allinghame" might also be a prominent member of society. But a few nights later, the Highwaywoman threw a firebomb into the empty offices of *The Clarion*. However, the fiery blaze was quickly extinguished, resulting only minor property damage.

Hysteria swept through both Burton City and Silver Creek. The Vigilante Posse evolved into the "Daylight Legion," a *de facto* private army controlled by the Coffrans. The sheriffs of both towns agreed to legally deputize the Legionnaires. Messalina then made a suggestion. Since the Civil War, there had been numerous instances of bandits hiding their stolen loot in graveyards. She recommended that that the two lawmen together inspect the graves in the towns' shared cemetery. They did so and discovered that the soil around my mother's grave seemed to have recently been tampered with. Digging down, they found three satchels containing the money stolen from the bank.

After the money had been counted—ascertaining that all the bank money had recovered—the two lawmen decided to search the grave adjacent to my mother's—my grandfather's. There, they found another body resting atop Tom Garvin's coffin—that of Ken Kluster! Riddled with three bullets, his remains had been hidden there for more than twenty years.

When my father returned from El Paso, he found the Silver Creek sheriff, Bill Norton, waiting for him. Arrested for the murder of Ken Kluster, my father went straight to the Silver Creek jail. I was unable to visit him during his imprisonment. Two hours before his arrest, Nathaniel Cassidy Jr., the Burton City sheriff, had come to the luxuriant ranch once inhabited by Ken and Jessica Kluster, nut which had been my home since childhood.

Armed with a search warrant, Cassidy examined every nook and cranny of the ranch. To my utter surprise, he discovered a hidden wall panel in the basement. Inside that secret closet was the costume worn by the Highwaywoman. Charged with murder, robbery and arson, I, too, was destined for a jail cell!

A trio of deputized Legionnaires, two men and a woman, had assisted Cassidy in his search. They all wore a uniform consisting of an orange tunic, black pants, boots, and a belt with a holstered gun. The woman's tunic was a darker hue of orange than those worn by her associates. This difference indicated that she outranked them. Her short brown hair barely touched her shoulders. The hazel eyes of her cherubic face were largely obscured by glasses with thick lenses.

"I am Troop Leader Amula Cronin of the Daylight Legion," she introduced herself. "Sheriff Cassidy has entrusted me and my two fellow Legionnaires with transporting you to the Burton City Jail. Regulations require that handcuffs be placed on your wrists."

Nodding to her two subordinates, she watched as they manacled my hands and shoved me into a prison wagon. Through the bars, she smiled at me.

"You and I have a special bond. Jezebel; you are probably destined to be my first."

"Your first what?"

"My first execution. My father recently retired as the hangman for the County. I succeeded him as public executioner. I'm probably the first hangwoman in history, and I'm only 21."

Arriving at Burton City, I was forced to wait for half an hour in the prison wagon before my cell was ready. With no explanation for the delay, the Legionnaires pulled me out and hustled me into the Sheriff's Office. From there, we passed through a door which led to a two pairs of jail cells facing each other, each with iron bars, a hinged door, and a barred window at the back. I was pushed into the first cell on the left. An extended curtain was strung across the middle of the cell. While her male subordinates gripped my arms, Amula removed the handcuffs. After locking one handcuff around an iron bar, she placed the other on my right wrist.

"We will be back momentarily," she announced. Without bothering to shut the cell's door, the Legionnaires abruptly left. I was curious about what was hidden behind the curtain. With my right arm shackled to the bars, I could only use my left. However, the curtain remained beyond the reach of my free hand. I futilely stretched my body in a vain attempt to touch it.

"One moment, Daughter of Jangles," said a female voice with a French accent. "There is no need for you to strain yourself." The speaker occupied the cell diagonally opposite mine. Nearly six feet-tall, she was a buxom blonde whose short hair was stacked up in a bouffant. Her tightfitting dress was a provocative mockery of a housemaid's uniform.

"You're wondering if I have been arrested for public indecency? Rest assured that is not the case. I am Colette Mordaunt, former Can-Can dancer and Savate instructor of at Montour Academy of Fencing and Boxing. Throughout the music halls of Europe, I have starred in a burlesque entitled *The Clueless Housemaid*. I wore this costume during my act. While on their honeymoon in Paris, the Coffrans saw me perform in a Montmartre cabaret. Monsieur Coffran convinced his wife to hire me as her personal bodyguard. I am not a prisoner. My inappropriate clothes are merely intended to serve as a distraction..."

Colette pulled the rope. The curtain slid open sideways from right to left. Facing me was a female photographer standing behind a camera mounted on a tripod. Resting in the palm of her right hand was the activation button attached by wires to the camera. Her left hand held the T-shaped lamp loaded with flash powder. A blinding flash caused me to close my eyes as she took my picture. She had curly blonde hair cut short in the Roman style and wore a red dress with a red necktie. Her blue eyes stared at me with an intensity that sent chills down my spine.

"Considering the long animosity between our two families, it's surprising that we haven't met before. I am Messalina Coffran. Colette is busy moving my equipment back to *The Clarion*'s offices which you unsuccessfully tried to burn to the ground. I'm printing a special edition with the front page displaying a picture of you in jail under the caption *Highwaywoman Captured*. I'll send you a free copy once it's published."

"This is a frame-up! You planted that bandit costume in my home!"

"What an imagination! Did I also plant the stolen money in your mother's grave?"

"Yes! And I'll make you pay for that desecration!"

Rapidly pushing my left arm through the bars, I tried to grab my tormentor, but to my chagrin, Messalina stood just a few inches beyond my reach.

"So far, Jezebel, you have proven yourself to be an extremely poor antagonist. Therefore, I have left you a gift on the floor of your cell. Hopefully, it will teach you the fundamentals of strategy."

I picked up a book from the floor. It was Julius Caesar's *Commentaries on the Gallic Wars*.

Messalina's eyes sparkled triumphantly. "You really should study Caesar's concept of how to divide and conquer your foes."

Rejoining Messalina, Colette was now wearing a coat to cover her scandalous maid's costume. "The camera has been returned to *The Clarion*'s offices," she reported. "The photograph is being developed. Is Madame ready to depart?"

"As soon as Jezebel has commented on my gift."

"Sweet Messalina, your gift shall cause your immediate downfall," I promised.

Messalina never replied because *Commentaries on the Gallic Wars* slammed into her forehead after I threw it through the bars of my cell. Her eyelids flickered briefly before collapsing into Colette's arms.

"All-Mother!" moaned Colette as she gently placed her unconscious mistress on the ground. She then swiftly rose to her full height. Extending her hand between the bars of my cell, she quickly grabbed me by the throat. Caught in a grip of steel, I could barely breathe.

"Mademoiselle Garvin, no one harms Madame Coffran. I easily crush your windpipe, but you are slated to pay the law. The Hangman's Daughter shall have the pleasure of extinguishing your existence."

Colette withdrew her fingers from my neck. Gasping for breath, I fell backward. Lying on the floor, I embraced the temporary oblivion in the land of dreams.

When I eventually awoke, Messalina and Collette were long gone,

My father and I were imprisoned in separate locations, but we had a few allies we could use against the Coffrans. First, there was my mother's kid brother, William "Billy" Skelton. When my father had arrived in Silver Creek, Billy had been 12 years-old. Now, he was 35. "Uncle Billy," as I called him, managed the Garvin-Kluster Bank. He was also engaged to a remarkable woman.

Born in 1866, Louella Burbank was the daughter of Gilbert Burbank of Jacksonville, Florida. In the 1880s, she'd been among the first American women to graduate from law school. Moving to Paris in 1891, she'd joined the team of lawyers assembled to represent American investors in the defunct Panama Canal company. During the Civil War, the Burbanks had fought on the Union side. They then had become embroiled in a deadly feud with the Texars. Jessica Texas, as I have said, had been married to both Doc Marley and Ken Kluster. Her two brothers had worked as Confederate saboteurs. Working secretly with Belle Boyd, the famous Confederate spy, Jessica had nearly changed the course of the war. She had almost secured Gatling Guns for the Confederacy. Jessica and Belle had often confused the Union authorities by impersonating each other. Louella Burbank thought that a biography of Jessica Texar had the potential of becoming another best-selling book.

Returning to the United States in 1894, she'd traveled to Silver Creek to research Jessica's final years. When her *Queen of the Gun Runners* had been published in early 1895, it had become extremely popular. While in Silver Creek, she'd met my Uncle Billy. They were currently planning their wedding. My uncle asserted that Louella and I got along so well because we were both feisty redheads. Louella had started a legal in Texas practice with offices in both Silver Creek and Burton City. She had many prominent clients, including my father.

My third ally was my best friend, Glenda Gordon. She was the daughter of Fred "One Sleeve" Gordon, Uncle Billy's predecessor as bank manager. When my mother had become Mrs. Garvin, she'd summoned Branwen Skelton, her cousin from Lost Knob. Texas, to take over the management of the Silver Creek saloon. Fred had fallen instantly in love with Branwen, and their subsequent marriage had led to Glenda's birth in 1874.

Glenda and I had been "tomboys" in our youth. We both could shoot and ride horses as well as any man. She wore her black hair in a mullet style. While I have abandoned the pants of my "tomboy" days for a skirt years ago, Glenda still wore pants. She was also extremely resilient. She'd survived an outbreak of tuberculosis that had killed both her parents. Orphaned at the age of 18, she'd declined an offer to live with me and my father. Not only did she continue to live in a room on the bar's second floor, but she'd become the saloon's new manager as well. That job was not an easy one. Unruly patrons had to be ex-pelled. Glenda had to employ bouncers or become a bouncer herself. She chose the latter. Barney Maguire, the heavyweight boxer, once visited Silver Creek for a series of exhibition bouts. Glenda had romanced him into training her in the fine art of fisticuffs. For a slender woman of average height, her fists packed tremendous power. I once saw her break the nose of a man twice her size.

While I was being thrown in jail in the Burton City jail, my three potential allies were reacting to my father's arrest in Silver Creek. While my uncle and his fiancée remained there to deal with the authorities, Glenda rode to Burton City to see me. Her face was overcome with tears as she spoke to me through the bars.

"Jez, I'm sorry. I should have come here earlier. Forgive me!"

"Glenda, there's nothing to forgive."

"Maybe you should ask for *my* forgiveness," interrupted Amula Cronin. According to the Sheriff's regulation, all conversations between a prisoner and a visitor must had to be listened to by either the sheriff or a deputy. The only ex-ception was the prisoner's lawyer. Amula had been listening to our conversation from the beginning.

"Ask for forgiveness?" said Glenda. "I just met you."

"No, we were both about 13 when we met. Amula isn't my true first name. My real name is Thelma Cronin."

"That name still means nothing to me"

"You called me Stinkpot!"

"Ah, I remember you now! You were that nasty girl who made fun of me because I have pointed ears. My retort was that you stunk like a chamber pot. The other girls then nicknamed you Stinkpot—"n apt punishment for insulting me. |

"I wasn't trying to insult you. I was a shy and awkward girl, whose wid-owed father had recently moved to Silver Creek. I had no friends. By contrast, you were one of the most popular girls at school. You'd just changed your hairstyle to a mullet, and everyone was complimenting you on your new look. I only said that your hair style revealed your beautiful ears, which are slightly pointed, like the ears of the pixies from the fairy tales."

"You may have intended to compliment me," conceded Glenda, "but your clumsy words sounded like an insult to me. You earned my retort."

"Your retort was no ordinary insult! I'd been called names before—'Four-Eyes,' 'Moon-Face,' 'Bookworm,' and the likes. I'd shrugged all of them off, but 'Stinkpot' struck at my humanity. You were comparing me to manure. As more echoed your abuse throughout the school, life became a living hell for me. I decided to kill myself. I couldn't use my father's guns because he kept them locked in a closet. Since he was the County's hangman, there was plenty of rope. Placing a noose around my neck and securing it on a clothes' hook, I stood on a chair. Before I could leap into oblivion, my father walked in and stopped me. He tearfully hugged me as I told him what had driven me to suicide. I never returned to the Silver Creek school. We moved to Burton City, and my father enrolled me there.

"Later, he convinced the County to allow me to be his apprentice. He believed that life could only be enjoyed by people who understood the finality of death. When I reached 18, my favorite teacher gave me an unusual birthday gift, a copy of Ambrose Bierce's *The Monk and the Hangman's Daughter*. Set in Germany, its heroine is ostracized for being the offspring of the town's executioner. After reading it, I changed my name to Amula."

Glenda yawned before commenting. "Let me guess, Amula is the name of the Hangman's Daughter in the book."

"No, Benedicta is the name of the Hangman's offspring. Amula is the woman who persecutes her for stealing her lover. I identified myself with the persecutor in the novel because she had a justifiable grievance and sought to punish those responsible. I have an outstanding grievance against you."

"And what do you intend to do about it?"

"Absolutely nothing. Your cousin and her father are already destined for my gallows. It's only matter of time before you do something stupid that will be equally rewarded with death. For example, you must really want to slap my face."

"You bet I am!" answered Glenda. "Actually, I want to blacken both your eyes, but you're wearing glasses, so I'll settle for a face slap."

"Don't do it, Glenda!" I exclaimed. "Aluma's a deputized officer. If you assault her, she can shoot you. She has a gun. You don't."

Aluma's hand hovered menacingly over her holstered revolver. "Don't worry, Jezebel. Your cousin hasn't the guts to slap me.'

With lighting speed, Glenda right hand slapped Amula's left cheek. So powerful was the slap that it caused Amula to topple forward. Lying on her stomach, it took a few minutes for the Hangman's Daughter to regain her strength and lift herself off the floor. But during that time, Glenda had already left the jail.

The next day, Louella Burbank, acting as ma my defense attorney, visited me in jail. She was also my father's attorney. Since both Silver Creek and Burton City shared the same County prosecutor and circuit judge, it had been decided to hold my father's trial in Silver Creek, and then mine in Burton City.

Before discussing my case, Louella updated me about my father's situation. Her information shocked me. My father was going to plead guilty! He confessed to killing Ken Kluster as well as Luther Ringo. He'd made this decision in order to secure my inheritance. So he had fraudulently denied Ken Kluster's descendants of their 50% interest in Garvin-Kluster Partners. Not only was Messalina entitled to that 50%, but she was in an excellent position to claim the entire company as compensation for the income she had been denied for years by my father's fraud.

In exchange for my father's confession, Messalina agreed to split the company along the following lines: I would get the silver mine while Messalina got the hacienda, The bank, the saloon and the other businesses were split down the middle. The current managers would all remain in place. I thought my father has secured this *proviso* to protect Uncle Billy and Glenda. If Messalina and I disagreed on a business decision, the dispute would be solved by a competition acceptable to both partners. Choices ranged from a poker game to a brutal bare-knuckle boxing match.

With respect to my own case, my defense rested on the fact that Glenda and I were holding a bridal party for Louella at a Silver Creek restaurant when the Highwaywoman had killed the stagecoach driver. I had no alibi for the nights of the bank's robbery and the newspaper's firebombing. I'd been home alone and asleep when those crimes had occurred. The County Prosecutor claimed to have evidence that would break my bridal shower alibi. It apparently involved testimony by Jedediah Delay's widow, Sonia, who was being held in protective custody in the Silver Creek Sheriff Office,

We discussed the curious phraseology that had been used by Messalina's French maid.

"*Pay the Law* is French criminal slang for framing someone for a crime he didn't commit," explained Louella. "I never heard of an All-Mother, but the All-Father was the leader of a legendary gang of outlaws called the Black Coats."

Louella showed me some reviews of the recently published *Queen of the Gun Runners*. Most praised the book for presenting a fair and impartial portrayal of both sides in the Civil War, but others criticized it for glossing over the evils of slavery. The positive reviews included one written in *The Clarion* by Messalina herself, who commended Louella for treating the Kluster family fairly.

I did not see my father again until the day of his execution. Sheriff Cassidy allowed me to be transported from Burton City to Silver Creek by a deputized female Legionnaire. It couldn't be the vile Amula because she would be performing her part as executioner. The role of my watchdog fell to the latest recruit to the Daylight Legion, Colette Mordaunt.

"Daughter of Jangles," she quipped, "I hope this orange uniform doesn't make me look fat."

"Your belt could be tightened slightly Let me adjust it for you." My right wrist was handcuffed to Colette's left. I reached over with my left hand towards her belt only to have my fingers swatted aside by her right hand. "Imbecile! Did you really imagine that you could grab my gun and rescue your father?"

The gallows had been erected right outside the Sheriff's Office. Standing near the noose was the executioner, Amula Cronin in her Legionnaire uniform. Members of the Daylight Legion composed a majority of the crowd. I spied Uncle Billy, Louella and Glenda at the feet of the gallows. They were all dressed in attire generally worn at a funeral The large crowd prevented me from getting any closer.

Escorted by Bill Norton, the Sheriff of Silver Creek, my father had left his jail cell. With his hands tied behind his back, Glen Garvin mounted the stairs that led to oblivion. Amula first put a black hood over my father's head. After placing the noose firmly around his neck, she then pulled the lever that released the trap door beneath his feet. Dropping to my knees, I screamed at the sky in agony.

When my father's neck snapped, the crowd applauded. Public executions in American towns can devolve into obscene celebrations of death. Such was the case that day in Silver Creek. Hoisted on the shoulder of two muscular Legionnaires, Amula was carried triumphantly through the swinging doors that formed the entrance to the Saloon. Colette and I were returning to the prison van when a thin man accosted us.

"Colette, I need to talk to the prisoner. My condolences on your loss, Miss Garvin. I am Issachar Coffran. I sincerely regret my intrusion on your mourning, but your presence is required by Sheriff Norton."

Issachar, Collette and I walked into the saloon. Among the crowd were Glenda, Louella, Uncle Billy, Messalina and Amula. During my father's execution, Glenda had worn a dress normally reserved for funerals. In the immediate aftermath of my father's hanging, she had returned to her quarters on the saloon's second floor to swap her mourning clothes for the shirt and pants she normally wore as manager of the saloon.

Sheriff Norton summarized the situation. "Miss Garvin, there is a dispute concerning the saloon. The Legionnaires want Troop Leader Cronin to sing some songs while standing on the bar. Mrs. Coffran, your partner, has granted her permission. However, Miss Gordon, the manager, insists that Troop Leader Cronin's serenade can't proceed unless your permission is also secured." Norton moved his head closer. "The crowd is getting very angry," he whispered. "If you support Glenda, a full-scale riot will erupt."

I decided to embark on a bold strategy. "Messalina, I invoke the competition clause of our recent partnership agreement."

"We must first agree on an arbiter," replied Messalina. "I propose your attorney, Louella Burbank. Her recent book proves that she can act with impartiality towards my family."

"Messalina, I accept your choice of arbiter. I yield to Louella."

"Ladies and gentlemen," said Louella, "the issue of whether Amula Cronin will be permitted to sing will be decided by a competition between the two dissenting co-owners. If Messalina Coffran wins, Amula will sing. If Jezebel Garvin wins, she won't. As Miss Garvin issued the challenge, Mrs. Coffran will choose the method of competition. Shall I list the choices?"

I was overwhelmed to finally have the opportunity to strike at Messalina, so I said, "I accept the competition, whatever the method."

"I, Trooper Collette Mordaunt of the Daylight Legion, object to this," interjected Colette. "My orders from Sheriff Cassidy are to keep the Daughter of Jangles handcuffed to me at all times. Therefore, it is impossible for her to compete fairly and she should appoint a surrogate to fight in her place."

"If she gets to pick a surrogate, then I should be entitled to one as well," objected Messalina.

"So you shall," decreed Louella. "Are there any further objections? No? Therefore, the combatants shall be surrogates chosen by the dissenting co-owners of this saloon. Mrs. Coffran, choose your surrogate."

"I choose she who has the power to overcome any obstacle. She is the first woman executioner in the United States of America. I choose Amula Cronin."

"Very well. Mrs. Garvin, choose your surrogate."

"I choose my cousin, Glenda Gordon."

"Now that our champions have been chosen, Jezebel, perhaps you would like to increase the stake of this bout?" asked Messalina.

"I fear that your greed will get better the of you, Messalina," I replied. " What do you have in mind?"

"My fifty percent of the saloon against yours."

"Agreed, but why stop there? Let's add my fifty percent of the bank against yours."

"I accept. Louella, please inform our patrons of the revised wager," said Messalina, grinning mischievously. "You're becoming just as reckless as your uncle."

"Uncle Billy? What are you talking about?"

"He ran up a considerable gambling debt at Lupin's Golden Circle, the casino owned by my uncle. Fortunately, he recently paid it back in full."

My eyes scanned the room looking for my uncle. He was placing a bet on the fight with Issachar.

Louella had the bartenders and barmaids pull back chairs and tables to give the combatants room to fight.

"I have an issue with this brawl!" shouted Sheriff Norton. "Amula's wearing glasses! A punch to the face could blind her for life!"

"I'm willing to take that risk!" said Amula.

"Don't worry, Sheriff," added Glenda, "I'll end this fight with one punch to her jaw."

"OK then!" replied the Sheriff. "Amula, it's your funeral"

Amula smiled grimly, "No, it's Glenda."

"Let the fight begin!" yelled Louella.

Glenda swung at Amula and missed. The Hangman's Daughter may have had a glass jaw, but she also had the legs of a ballerina. Amula expertly dodged Glenda's blows, then successfully counterattacked with a series of Savate kicks. The first two landed on Glenda's stomach. The third slammed into my cousin's face.

Falling backwards, Glenda slammed into the floor. She was barely conscious when her right arm was seized by Amula. Lifted her feet, my cousin was pushed through the swinging doors of the saloon.

Amula sang:

*"My blows made you eat dust.*

*"I made your life a wreck.*

*"My noose yearns for your neck.*

*"You have nowhere to run.*

*"Let us have some more fun,*

*"When all is said and done,*

*"We need to fight with guns."*

"Stop right there, Hangman's Daughter!" shouted Glenda when she heard the lyrics. She was wearing a belt with a holstered revolver. Normally she had kept her gun belt locked in a desk drawer. Forced to vacate her apartment, she had probably put it on without much thought. "No more games, Amula! Let's end this now!"

"I concur. Draw!"

Both women went for their guns, Glenda pulled the trigger first, but her gun clicked on an empty bullet chamber. Amula's bullet pierced Glenda's heart ending her life,

Examining Glenda's gun, Sheriff Norton found no bullets inside. He concluded that Glenda had forgotten to load her revolver, but I knew someone working for Messalina must have removed the bullets. The sheriff ordered the saloon shut down for the night. Colette escorted me back to the prison van. I was too overcome by grief to offer any resistance.

The next day, I had an unpleasant visit from the woman who had killed both my father and my cousin. Amula smiled sadistically at me. There was another female Legionnaire with her. She was a brunette with long dark hair. She held a very large sketch book and a pencil.

"I'm here to inform you of two recent developments, First, neither Trooper Colette Mordaunt nor myself will be your escort when you leave this jail. That duty will be taken by Trooper Juanita Brown. Besides being a member of the Daylight Legion, she is also the principal sketch artist for *The Clarion*. Second, your lawyer, Miss Burbank,, will be arriving two hours late for your consultation. She is overwhelmed by the burden of planning three funerals."

"Three? My father, Glenda and who else?"

"Your uncle. Last night, he committed suicide by shooting himself in the head."

Several hours later, Louella arrived to see me. I knew all about Billy's debt. He'd intended to pay the casino back with funds embezzled from the bank. Unfortunately, he still had the money on him when the bout between Glenda and Amula was announced. He'd bet it all on Glenda in a wager with Issachar.

Louella shed a tear. "If only Billy had told me about the embezzlement, then I wouldn't have agreed to Messalina's request for an audit the next day. Everything I told you was in the note he wrote before emdimg his lifer."

Louella used the deaths of my relatives to postpone my trial for a few days. During that interval, a bizarre stranger rode into Burton City. It was a woman with a mass of shaggy black hair. Her pale complexion resembled a corpse's. She wore a black shirt and pants. In addition to a holstered six-shooter, she was armed with an 1892 repeating rifle that was capable of firing 12 rounds. The most striking thing about her was that her right eye was missing. Instead of wearing an eye patch, she had a glass eye lodged in the socket. Furthermore, that artificial eye was not made to resemble a human eye. Its pupil had a vertical slit like the eye of a reptile. Unlike her normal eye, the glass eye remained stationary and did not move from side to side.

When the woman rode into Burton City, she held the reins of a second horse trailing slightly behind her own. Draped over that horse was a blanket upon which was slumped a dead woman with her arms extended. The deceased was a blonde in her late thirties. She was dressed in a Salvation Army uniform.

While walking to the Sheriff's Office, Louella had seen the strange newcomer arrive. Rushing to my cell, she described her and speculated about her identity. "That woman is talking to Sheriff Cassidy. She must be a bounty hunter. I recognized the dead woman. It's Penny Bannington. There was a $10,000 bounty on her head."

The next day, I learned the stranger's identity. Sheriff  Cassidy always gave me his copy of *The Clarion* after he had finished reading it. There was a sarcastic obituary for Penny Bannington in it. She was depicted as "a Robin Hood who stole from the poor and gave to herself." More importantly, the newspaper published an interview with Penny's slayer, conducted by Messalina.

The bounty hunter had identified herself as Lizzie Ringo, Luther Ringo's daughter.

Lizzie had found Penny hiding in the Mexican border town of San Miguel. When Penny had begun her masquerade as a Salvation Army member in 1877, she'd established a phony Soup Kitchen in San Miguel to serve as a future hideout. Lizzie had confronted Penny, and the wanted fugitive fll on her knees and begged to be taken alive. When Lizzie agreed to spare her life, the treacherous Penny pulled out a derringer out of her sleeve. Before Penny could fire, Lizzie's Winchester had sent five bullets into her body.

Lizzie's father had slain my grandfather and then had been slain by my father. When asked if she held a grudge against my family, Lizzie acknowledged that she did. However, it was not for killing Luther. She felt a son deserves the right to slay his father's killer. Lizzie was incensed by my father's failure to reveal where Luther had been buried. She wanted to leave flowers on her father's final resting place. While regretting not being able to attend my father's execution, Lizzie had every intention of attending mine.

Juanita Brown proved to be less of an annoyance than Amula or Collette. She was the daughter of John Obadiah Brown, am outlaw of the 1870s, and Carma Vasquez, a Mexican artist. When monitoring my conversations with visitors, she maintained a discrete silence and drew a sketch of the visitor.

On the day before my trial was scheduled to begin, Louella arrived with a burly man in his sixties. Wearing an expensive suit, he carried an ornate cane. Juanita normally would leave when Louella came since I was permitted to confer with my lawyer in private. Juanita argued that she had to listen in, since this man wasn't my lawyer.

The man with the cane pulled a letter out of his coat pocket and showed it to Juanita. "This letter signed by the County Prosecutor, Ezekial Bingham, reveals that Miss Garvin now has two lawyers, Miss Burbank and myself, Dr. Theodore Marley."

Marley had been Jessica Texar's first husband. He was quite an accomplished man with degrees in both medicine and law. Popularly known as "Doc," he had been a friend of my father. Despite that fact, we had never met until today. From colorful stories that my father had told me, I knew that his cane was a deadly weapon. A hidden switch in the handle released a retractable knife-like blade from its bottom tip.

Louella explained the situation. "Prosecutor Bingham informed me that he planned to call me as a witness for the prosecution. This decision makes it impossible for me to defend you properly. Therefore, another attorney must present the defense I have prepared. I immediately thought of Doc Marley,"

"Jezebel, the last time I was in Silver Creek, I acted as a witness at your parents' wedding. For the last 23 years, I have been living in the Mexican state of Sonora. I didn't want to return to Silver Creek. This place has too many painful memories."

Doc was alluding to Jessica. They had married just before the Civil War had broken out. They'd found themselves fighting on opposing sides. Doc served in the Union army, while Jessica joined the Confederate Secret Service. Louella's book treated Doc sympathetically and absolved him of any role in her death.


My trial lasted a week. During that ordeal, my enemies sat together gleefully in the courthouse. Besides Messalina, Amula, Colette and Juanita, who was constantly adding new pictures to her sketchbook, there was the creepy Lizzie Ringo.

Prosecutor Bingham's case rested on the stolen bank money found in my mother's grave, and the highwaywoman costume discovered in my former home (now occupied by Messalina). My defense consisted of my unbreakable alibi for the afternoon when the coach driver, Jedediah Delay, had been murdered.

It took two witnesses for Bingham to place my alibi in a radically different context. The first witness was Louella. After allowing her to testify that I had attended the bridal shower with scores of potential witnesses, Bingham shifted his questions to Louella's recent book.

"Did Jezebel Garvin read *Queen of the Gun Runners*, Miss Burbank?"

"Yes. In fact, she even did me the favor of proofreading it prior to publication."

"Does your book discus a concept called the 'Captain Jackson Ruse?'"

"Yes."

"What is the 'Captain Jackson Ruse?'"

"The 'Captain Jackson Ruse' is a stratagem by which two people agree to share a common identity to confuse their enemies."

"How did Jessica Texar employ the 'Captain Jackson Ruse?'"

"During the Civil War, Jessica served in the Confederate Secret Service alongside another woman, Belle Boyd. Jessica would often impersonate her in order to mislead the Union authorities pursuing the real Belle."

"Who originated the 'Captain Jackson Ruse?'"

"Captain Jerry Jackson, a seventeenth century English highwayman. Wearing men's clothes, his mistress, Barbara Worth, would impersonate him.

"Miss Burbank, did your book mention all those historical facts?"

"Yes."

"Did your book also mention Barbara Worth's marital status?"

"No. She was married. Worth was her maiden name."

"What was her husband's name?"

"Sir Ralph Skelton. Barbara was more commonly known as Lady Skelton."

"Why was the surname Skelton never mentioned in your book?"

"Because I loved a man whose last name was Skelton and I didn't want to offend him or his family."

"Are you referring to the late William 'Billy' Skelton, the uncle of the defendant?"

"Yes. The maiden name of Jezebel Garvin's mother was Skelton, Lucy Skelton."

It was obvious what Bingham's strategy was. He was going to argue that there were two Highwaywomen working as partners. My mythical partner would be Jedediah Delay's killer, and I would be credited with the bank robbery and the firebombing.

Bingham's next witness was even more dramatic. She was Sonia Delay, the coach driver's widow. A slender woman with blonde hair, she couldn't have been more than 21 years-old; She revealed that her surname was an alias. She and her husband were the notorious bank robbers, Sonny and Jed Trigardo. Wanted for numerous crimes in both the United States and Mexico, they had tried to establish new identities in Silver Creek and retire from a life of crime. Buying a home on the outskirts of the town, they'd changed their surname to Delay ("Trigardo" being the Spanish word for "delay"), and Jed had gotten a job as a coach driver.

Sonny claimed that she and Jed were awakened one night by two female masked intruders, both wearing the Highwaywoman costume. The mysterious visitors had revealed that knew the married couple's true identities. They wanted to hire Jed to use his knowledge of munitions to make an explosive device capable of opening the safe in the Burton City bank. Jed had agreed to do the work. Two nights later, the women returned to pick up the bomb and pay Jed. Jed was drunk that night and pulled off one of the women's masks. The other woman punched  him in the jaw, and the masked duo fled into the night.

"When Sheriff Norton came to inform me of Jed's murder, I confessed everything to him. Afraid that the Highwaywoman might seek my death, Norton hid me at his house with his wife and son. Even though I'm wanted for murder and robbery, I told Norton the truth. If the gallows are my destiny, so be it. I don't want to live in a world without Jed. I just want to see those two highwaywomen brought to justice."

"What did the unmasked woman look like?"

"She had a thin face with long black hair. and wore square spectacles like Ben Franklin's. They were tinted blue. She looked nothing like Jezebel Garvin."

"Could Jezebel be the other highwaywoman?"

"Objection!" exclaimed Doc.

"Sustained!" ruled the judge.

"I have no more questions," stated Bingham. "The prosecution rests."

Louella was visibly upset by the testimony which Bingham had forced her to give, but Doc argued that it only provided the prosecution with speculation. The real damage was caused by Sonia's testimony which proved the existence of two highwaywomen. Nevertheless, Bingham had damaged the murder charge against me. He was accepting my alibi, and attributing the murder to an un-named confederate still at large. The judge had no choice but to accept Doc's motion to dismiss the murder charge.

Unfortunately, the jury found me guilty of bank robbery and murder, and I was sentenced to twenty years in prison. Awaiting transportation to the State Penitentiary at Huntsville, I was amused to see a "Wanted" poster for Maud Al-linghame with a picture drawn by Juanita Brown. It depicted a woman with black hair and spectacles.

*Roman Leary returns to* Tales of the Shadowmen *with a story featuring the Nyctalope which forms a perfect bookend to his tale "The Heart of a Man" published in our Volume 5...*

## Roman Leary: *The Legacy of a Man*

*What, then, are we to make of this man? Was he a patriot or a traitor? A misunderstood hero or a cynical opportunist? The question has become academic. If, as some believe, he still walks the Earth, he has outlived everyone who loved or hated him, and survived only to become an obscure relic of a bygone age. This, perhaps, is the ultimate fate of the Nyctalope; not to be condemned by history, but to be forgotten by it.*

Laura Simons
*Destroying Angels: Mystery Men of Europe 1900-1950*
Chapel Hill Press, 2005

*Phuket, 2007*

His table at the small outdoor restaurant was directly adjacent to the beach. He was savoring a papaya salad and enjoying the evening breeze when he noticed the immortal at the bar. She was a tall Teutonic blonde, her slender frame draped in a simple black dress that provided a sharp contrast to her pale complexion. Her ice-blue eyes gazed out over the modest eatery to the wine-dark ocean beyond as if it all belonged to her alone. Although he did not know her name, he recognized her immediately. He never forgot a face, and he could vividly recall the first and only time he beheld this woman's beautiful countenance. He had seen her across the room at a jazz club in Montmartre. He had tried to speak to her on that memorable night, but she somehow disappeared before he could make her acquaintance. He'd made some discreet inquiries, but no one he talked to knew anything about her. He had been disappointed, but fate, that most fickle of all his mistresses, had brought them together once more. The time had come for a proper introduction.

*And it only took seventy-three years*, he thought with a wry smile.

It did not occur to him that he might be mistaken, nor did the impossibility of this woman's youth and vitality give him pause. His own long, long life had been marked by countless impossibilities, not the least of which was his own survival.

He finished his salad and was gesturing for the check when there was a flash at the corner of his eye. He turned to find a girl, maybe ten years-old, grinning at him and holding a Polaroid camera. The camera ejected a picture that she grabbed and gently waved in the air.

He smiled and said in Thai: "I didn't know they still made those things."

The girl's eyes widened in surprise. "It belonged to my papa," she said. "You are handsome, like a movie star, and this will be a good picture. I'll sell it to you for a hundred *baht*."

He laughed. "For someone as handsome as me? Surely I'm worth more than that." He reached into his pocket and produced a five-hundred *baht* note, the equivalent of about fifteen dollars.

"You're very nice," she said, handing him the photo. "I'll give you one more for free."

The flash went off again as he rose from the table. He had noted the approach of his waiter, and he could see the man was frowning deeply. "You can keep that one," he said to the little girl. "Something to remember me by."

The child looked disappointed. "OK," she said, "but will you at least tell me your name?"

"My name is Leo," he said. "Once upon a time I was called the Nyctalope, and I was more famous than any movie star."

"Really? Why did they call you that?"

"Because I can see in the dark," he said with a wink. "What's your name?"

"I'm Malai," she said brightly. She pointed at the waiter, who was now at Leo's elbow. "That's Khin," she said. "He thinks I'm a pest."

Khin, a somber young fellow with a refined manner, passed Leo his check. "I'm sorry for this disturbance," the waiter said. He looked at the child and said, not unkindly: "Please, you've been told about this. Run along before the manager sees you."

"She hasn't bothered me," Leo said, handing the waiter some folded bills.

"See?" Malai said to Khin. "He's nice, not like you."

Khin sighed. "I am the nicest person you know; you just don't realize it. Come back in twenty minutes and I'll walk you home."

"Can we take the long way this time?"

"Yes," Khin said, "we can take the long way."

Malai laughed and, after a final wave at Leo, turned and ran down the beach.

Leo turned to Khin. "How well do you know her?"

"Very well," the waiter said. "She's my sister. We live across the bridge on Kho Sirey."

"She's very charming. Your parents should be proud of both of you."

Khin smiled sadly. "They were."

There was an awkward silence, and Leo thought that Khin might be chiding himself for being overly familiar with a *farang* customer. He held up the photo he'd bought and considered his likeness. He was looking at a man who might be in his early middle-age, trim and athletic in his linen beach suit, a comical look of surprise softening his otherwise chiseled features. He smiled. "Your sister was right," he said. "It is a good picture. Tell her I will always keep it, and think of her whenever I look at it."

"She'll like that," Khin said.

They wished each other a pleasant evening and Leo made his way toward the bar.

She glanced at her watch in irritation and pretended to sip at her drink. She considered impunctuality, even in a minor assignation, to be a sign of disrespect. Worse, her solitude at this tawdry bar was inviting unwanted attention. If her date did not arrive soon, she would have to start fending off advances from some of these pathetic...

"Excuse me, but have we met?"

With a small chuckle, she turned to face the speaker. His overture was so trite and clichéd that it was actually amusing. She was about to dismiss him with a contemptuous rebuff, but a glance into his strange yellow eyes brought her up short.

"You recognize me," he said. It was not a question.

"Indeed, I do," she said, "but I don't think we've ever met, Monsieur Saint-Clair."

"I saw you at *Le Grand Ecart* one evening in the spring of '34."

A smile pulled at the corner of her mouth. "So long ago? I must have made a powerful impression."

"Indelible," he said, "and you're just as beautiful now as you were that night. In fact, you haven't aged a day."

"The secret is in my liquid diet," she said, and her lip curled to reveal an elongated, razor-sharp canine. "What about you? You're remarkably fit for a centenarian."

He shrugged. "The unexpected side effect of a life-saving operation."

"Ah, yes, the famous artificial heart powered by magnets. Is it a fountain of youth as well?"

"It's a little more complicated than that."

"Please, don't bore me with details. I'm more interested in what you're doing here. I can't believe you've been hunting for me all these years."

He smiled. "A mere coincidence, I assure you. My hunting days are over."

"Is that so?"

"It is. I'm afraid I've grown rather indolent in my old age. These days, I live on my boat, traveling the world, chasing the sun..."

"Righting wrongs?"

He slowly shook his head. "I recently read something about myself. The author called me a *relic of a bygone age*. I think she was right. I'm just trying to enjoy whatever time is left to me."

She stared at him, weighing his words. She leaned in close. "You say that," she whispered, "but I look into those magnificent eyes and I see the soul of a warrior, a knight in search of a dragon to slay." She reached up and caressed his cheek. "I consider this, and I ask myself: Am I to be the dragon?"

He took her cold hand and gently pushed it away. "I mean you no harm," he said softly. "I just want to talk."

She leaned back. "To talk? Then, I will tell you something. At any moment, I am expecting a lovely woman to appear. She is late, which annoys me, but I will forgive her. We will go for a stroll down the beach, very romantic, which will end at her seaside villa. Once there, I will draw her into my arms, whisper into her ear, and take her to heights of ecstasy that she has never dreamed of."

She lifted her drink, swirled it, then set it back down.

"Tomorrow," she continued, "the woman will awaken in her bed alone. She will feel weak and listless, and there will be a soreness at her neck, but she will attribute these things to her activities the night before. She will yearn to see me again, perhaps even weep over my absence, but her grief will be in vain. Time will pass, and she will find it more and more difficult to remember my face, even my name, until the day I fade completely from her mind, and it will be as if I never existed."

"I remembered you," he said.

"That's because we never kissed," she said. "I have told you what is about to happen. I will ask you plainly: Are you going to interfere?"

"No."

"That is good," she said. "It would pain me to kill you."

He laughed. "Are you so certain of that outcome?"

She considered it. "I don't know," she said at length. "I would prefer not to find out. There are so few of us relics left. Why should there be one less?"

There was a silence between them, and she felt a peculiar longing to abandon her rendezvous, to spend the rest of the evening with this ghost from the past. Perhaps they could go out on his boat and reminisce beneath the stars. When was the last time she had passed a night with someone who knew exactly what she was? Someone who understood her true nature, and would not judge?

Then Thalia appeared at the entrance of the restaurant and the moment passed. The statuesque brunette spotted her and began to approach with a confident, catlike grace.

"I believe your date is here," Saint-Clair said.

She rose from her chair and impulsively kissed him on the cheek. "Until next time, Monsieur le Nyctalope," she whispered.

"Until next time, Madame...?"

"Countess," she said with a smile. "Countess Carmilla Karnstein."

Thalia sidled up and possessively linked arms with her. "Sorry I'm late," the brunette said. She gave Saint-Clair a look of frank appraisal. "Is this a friend of yours?"

"An old acquaintance. We were just saying goodbye."

Carmilla felt the Nyctalope's eyes upon her the entire time she was walking away.

Vargas crouched in the darkness, fighting sleep. The sultry air, the lapping of the night-tide, and the absence of even a single ray of moonlight all combined to lull him into an almost hypnotic state. He should have been tense, electric with nervous energy, but he had felt strangely relaxed the entire evening. He was so confident in his skills and equipment that he simply couldn't imagine any outcome but total success for the operation. Even the relative inexperience of his team didn't bother him.

He glanced at his compatriots. There were three others hidden with him in the gazebo, almost invisible in their black tactical gear. They had assured their privacy by announcing a tsunami drill that cleared the residents for a quarter-mile stretch of coast. It wouldn't take long for the civilians to realize they had been duped, but Vargas and his men only needed about thirty minutes. Later, when it was discovered that nothing had been damaged or stolen, the whole thing would be dismissed as an idiotic prank and quickly forgotten.

"They're coming," Foley whispered. He was the youngest of the team. He was staring down the beach with a pair of night vision binoculars.

Vargas was instantly alert. He lifted his air rifle and gazed through the Starlight scope. He settled the crosshairs on the vampire's neck and waited for her to walk into range.

"I wonder why there are no lights on in any of the houses," Carmilla mused. It was a casual observation. She didn't care, in fact, but the words seemed to strike a chord with Thalia. The brunette's pulse immediately picked up, and Carmilla suddenly detected a sour scent of fear.

"What does it matter?" Thalia said lightly, trying and failing to mask the tension in her voice. She stepped away from Carmilla and seductively tugged at her shoulder straps. "Unless you want me right now, and you were hoping for an audience. Is that it? Personally, I like a cozy bed, but this is exciting, too."

Carmilla's eyes narrowed. "What is this about?" she asked, her voice low and dangerous.

There was a *pfft* sound from a nearby gazebo and a dart appeared in Carmilla's throat. Eyes blazing and fangs bared, she snatched the offending projectile from her neck and lunged at the perfidious bitch who had led her into this clumsy trap... and she fell flat on her face.

*What the devil?*

Her limbs were sluggish and unresponsive, and she felt a consuming lethargy that seemed to be clawing her into unconsciousness. She managed to turn to her side and watched as a group of what appeared to be soldiers approached and surrounded her prone form. The tallest, a Latin fellow with a neatly trimmed beard approached Thalia and placed a hand on her shoulder.

393

"That was close," Thalia said with a grin.

"Are you alright?" the man asked.

"Thanks to you, Vargas," she replied. "I'll see to it that you get a bonus."

Vargas looked down and his eyes met Carmilla's. "Looks like she's not completely out," he said. He knelt and smiled. He reached into a pocket and produced a syringe filled with what looked like crude oil. "Wondering what I hit you with?" he asked, wiggling the syringe in front of her. "It's called Daybreak, something my old employers cooked up. It tricks you suckheads into thinking the sun's about to rise, and out you go. Looks like you need a little more than I anticipated..."

He was about to plunge the needle into her when one of the other men said: "Civilians."

Vargas frowned and rose to his feet. With a supreme effort, Carmilla turned her head and saw a man and a child, a little girl, walking toward them. They approached hand in hand, clearly oblivious to the danger that lay before them in the inky darkness.

"What do we do?" a soldier whispered.

Vargas did not reply. He handed Thalia the syringe, then drew a knife and quickly advanced on the unsuspecting pair. He fell on them without a word, knocking the child to the ground and stabbing the man several times in the torso. The girl screamed. There was a pair of bright flashes, as if from a camera, and Vargas cursed loudly. He violently brought down his foot and Carmilla heard a crunching of plastic. Then he did something to the girl and her cries abruptly stopped.

Vargas returned breathing heavily, the child draped over his shoulder. He passed her to one of the other men and then grinned at Thalia. "Tell Hubert that's my bonus," he said. "Let's wrap this up and get to the boat."

Carmilla tried to speak, but all that came out was an animal growl.

"Oh, shut up and take your medicine," Vargas said, lowering the syringe.

Khin felt the life ebbing out of him as he stared up into the sky. How long had it been since he was attacked? Minutes? Hours? He knew he was doomed, but he fought to hold on, to get moving, to live. He had to survive for Malai's sake, if only long enough to tell someone what had happened, what he had heard...

*Who am I fooling?* he thought. *I don't even have the strength to turn over. How could this have happened? What did we do to deserve this?*

"Please," he whispered to the void. "If my mother was right and there is a God... Please hear me... I don't care if I die... but please help Malai... I'm begging you..."

He closed his eyes and tears streamed down his cheeks. Then he opened them, and there was someone there; a vaguely familiar face in the darkness, and within the face a pair of faintly luminescent yellow eyes.

"Hold on," the stranger said in Thai. "I'm going to help you."

The man from the restaurant? Yes, it had to be. Malai said his name was...

"Leo?"

The eyes widened slightly. "Yes," the man said, and he gently lifted Khin from the sand. "Where is your sister?"

"Kidnapped... along with someone else, a blonde woman. I saw her earlier. I think... I think you talked to her at the bar..."

Khin felt himself slipping into unconsciousness, or perhaps death. He struggled against it, drifting in and out of waking agony and blissful oblivion. He was aware of being carried to a nearby house. He felt a shudder and heard a crash as Leo kicked in a door. He felt the hard surface of a table beneath him. He heard the bang and rattle of cabinets and drawers being hastily searched...

"Talk to me," Leo said. "Tell me everything you remember."

Khin talked. He gasped as he felt the cold, biting sting of wounds being cleansed.

"You're doing well," Leo said. "Malai took pictures, you say? I suppose it's too much to hope for that..."

"I have one," Khin rasped. "He took the other, smashed the camera, but he missed one."

Trembling, Khin reached into his waistband and produced the wrinkled, bloodied photo. Leo took it. He stared at it intently. "I know this man," he said, pocketing the picture.

"Are you sure?" Khin said.

"I never forget a face. Tell me more."

Khin continued to speak. He used every breath he could take to share every detail, every impression. There were four of them. There was another woman there as well. The man who took Malai was friendly with her. He said something about a bonus...

Khin winced through the prolonged, tugging pain of improvised sutures.

"Hubert?" Leo said. "You're sure he used that name?"

Khin was sure. They were going to talk to Hubert...

"And he said something about a boat?"

Khin felt the comforting tightness of expertly applied bandages. What were they talking about? A boat? Yes, they took Malai and the blonde woman. They were going to wrap it up and get to the boat...

There was darkness. Khin heard the murmuring of a one-sided conversation. There was an indeterminate passage of time, during which a strong, comforting hand never left his shoulder.

Sirens... Flashing lights...

"Can you hear me?" Leo asked.

Khin gave a small nod.

"The paramedics are outside. I am going to leave before they see me. Do not give them my name. Do you understand?"

"Yes," Khin whispered.

"Good. Your injuries are serious, but you are a fighter. You will survive this."

"Malai…"

"You will see her again."

The hope that rose in Khin was almost painful. "What I told you… It's enough for the police?"

"It was enough for me," Leo said as he slipped away. "I'm going to get her back, and I'm going to rain hellfire on the men who took her."

Khin believed him.


Leo typed the codes for the satellite link into his laptop and waited impatiently for access to be granted. As soon as he was in, he made a video call to a number he knew by heart. He may have outlived everyone who loved or hated him, but there were still people who owed him favors, and one of them should just now be sitting down at her desk.

Sure enough, a window opened almost immediately and the bewildered face of a sixty-something woman appeared. Her iron-gray hair framed a face that was deeply lined by age and worry, but was still attractive, especially to someone who had known her in the full bloom of her youth.

"Leo?" she said in a voice made husky by years of smoking.

"Hello, Françoise," Leo said. "I hope I haven't caught you at a bad moment."

"Well, there's a meeting of the Brigade, but… I'm just so surprised that… Wait, are you on a boat?"

"Yes, in my yacht, the *Sylvie*. I'm docked at the Royal Phuket Marina."

"What on Earth are you calling me for? It's been, what, nine years?"

"Ten, actually. I wish we could catch up, but time is short and I need your help."

"Help with what?"

"Is the *Brigade des Maléfices* running any operations in Thailand?"

"What? No! Why are you even asking me that?"

"A little over an hour ago, a four-man team executed a Code Varney in the middle of a private beach. The target was a vampire named Carmilla Karnstein. The operation had all the marks of one of your 'asset recruitments,' except for the fact that they kidnapped a child and almost killed a civilian in the process."

Françoise's expression darkened. "OK, now you're insulting me. You know that none of my people would ever be that sloppy."

Leo held up the photo he had taken from Khin. "Not even Tommy Vargas?"

Françoise took a deep breath and slowly exhaled. "He's been off the team for two years. It came to our attention that he had some… unacceptable proclivities. We were going to bring him in for a talk, but he disappeared and went off the grid completely."

"Did these *unacceptable proclivities* involve young girls?"

"What makes you say that?"

"Vargas told someone that the child was going to be his bonus."

Françoise grimaced. "All right," she said. "Tell me what you need."

"I think Vargas is working for someone named Hubert. Does that mean anything to you?"

Françoise tilted her head. "You say you're in Phuket?"

"That's correct."

"It's him," Françoise murmured. "Has to be." She tapped on some keys and a picture appeared in a new window on Leo's screen. It was of a smiling middle-aged couple at some black-tie affair. The man was big and bluff and handsome, his looks only slightly marred by the arrogant smirk on his clean-shaven face. The woman was Carmilla's date from the restaurant.

"I know her," Leo said. "I'm certain she was working with Vargas."

"Then your mystery is solved," Françoise said. "That's Thalia Tomasis, the heiress to a Greek shipping empire. The man is her longtime boyfriend, Hubert de Mauvouloir. He's a billionaire who owns about fifty different software companies around the world."

"Why he would be interested in capturing a vampire?"

"God only knows. The man's a degenerate, a pimp for the elite. He owns a twelve-acre island about ten kilometers southeast from where you are now. The whole place is a glorified brothel for wealthy perverts and pedophiles."

"Vargas said they had to get to a boat…"

Françoise tapped some more keys and the picture of the couple was replaced by an overhead shot of a small island paradise. She floated a cursor over the picture to give Leo a virtual tour. "Here at the northernmost point is a floating pier. This is the main point of entry for Mauvouloir's staff and guests, although he does have a helipad over here behind the main house. That's his private residence."

"And the other two houses?" Leo asked.

The cursor moved clockwise. "This is the guest house. Basically, a small hotel. Eighteen rooms, gymnasium, even an indoor pool."

"Impressive," Leo said.

"Nothing but the best for the scum of the Earth," Françoise replied. She moved the cursor to the third villa. "This is the servant's quarters, but it's mainly a luxury bunkhouse for the security staff. Mauvouloir's little praetorian guard is made up of men who share his kinks. That's how he ensures their loyalty and discretion. Tommy was a natural fit."

"What about the domestics?"

"They ferry over from the mainland. He doesn't like civilians present on nights and weekends."

"What's his power source?"

"Solar, very eco-friendly, but he does have backup generators fueled by propane. You can see the tanks here and here."

"What about that structure on the eastern peninsula?"

"The cube?" Françoise said, circling it with the cursor. "I'm not sure. Mauvouloir has claimed it's a 'meditation room,' but that's just ridiculous. It sits at the highest point on the island and commands a magnificent view, but it has no windows. Also, you can't really see it from this angle, but that's a statue of Baal on the roof. Draw your own conclusions."

Leo said: "Françoise, it's clear that you've been gathering intel on this man for quite a while, and you obviously despise him…"

"So why haven't I taken him off the board?"

Leo nodded.

"I've tried," Françoise said, "but Hubert de Mauvouloir is untouchable. He's bought or blackmailed almost everyone who has set foot on that island, and a lot of powerful people have been in that guest house."

"People who can protect him even from you?"

"Even from me."

There was a silence, and something seemed to pass between them. Then Françoise Cordier smiled and said: "I still think of Morocco, from time to time."

"I do as well," Leo said. "I have to go now."

"I know. Check your email when you sign off. I'm sending you some things you may find interesting. And Leo?"

"Yes?"

"Good luck."


Leo anchored the *Sylvie* about a kilometer from the shore of Mauvouloir's island. The moonless night made the yacht invisible from the coast, although the darkness was day to his own extraordinary eyes.

He stepped below deck and removed an artfully concealed panel to reveal his private armory. As he surveyed the inventory, he thought of Carmilla and smiled. The vampire was right; he wasn't quite the lazy retiree he pretended to be.

He selected his trusty Browning and fitted it with a silencer of his own design. It wouldn't completely suppress the sound of a shot, but it would reduce the report to little more than a soft thump. This was for the quiet part of the campaign.

Then he chose an M249 machine gun—more commonly and aptly referred to as a SAW—and grabbed three ammo drums filled with two hundred rounds each. This was for the noisy part.

He complemented these with an eclectic selection of explosive and incendiary devices that he loaded into a rucksack he had carried into combat on five continents.

He loaded himself and his gear into a Zodiac and set out from the yacht's tender launch onto the warm and gentle Pacific current. The battery-powered outboard engine purred quietly as it propelled him to the southwestern shore of the island. This, according to the data Françoise had emailed him, was the weakest point in Mauvouloir's security; a steep and rocky bit of coastline that was subject to only a few perfunctory patrols on the night watch. After the Zodiac was safely moored, he was going to head east for the cubic structure which he had come to think of as 'the temple.' It was clearly the focal point of the estate, and that was where he planned to start.

He felt well-prepared, but he had only the vaguest outlines of a real plan. This did not bother him. His objectives were clear, and he would do what was necessary to achieve them. As a virtuoso in the art of mayhem, he was perfectly comfortable with improvisation.

Carmilla awoke to find herself manacled to a Saint Andrew's cross. Her dress was torn and damp with salt water, and she could still feel sand on the bottom of her feet. She immediately strained against the bonds, but they were resistant even to her formidable strength. Snarling in frustration, she lifted her eyes and surveyed her dimly-lit surroundings.

The cross was mounted in a large circle of tile with, ominously, a drain at the center. The circle was surrounded by plush, burgundy carpet and ornate furnishings that would have been at home in a Christie's catalogue. The light gray walls were decked from floor to ceiling with instruments of torture and mutilation. It was like an abattoir crossed with a Victorian bordello. The effect was both unsettling and unbearably gauche.

A door opened and Vargas appeared, still dressed in his tactical gear. He looked at Carmilla, then turned back to the door and said: "She's awake."

A moment later, the treacherous Thalia walked in followed by a tall, muscular man wearing a loud Hawaiian shirt and a pair of loose-fitting shorts. He was smoking a foul-smelling cigar clenched in a repulsive, self-satisfied grin. He removed the cigar from his mouth and said: "Hello, Countess Karnstein."

"You must be Hubert?" Carmilla said.

"That's Baron Hubert de Mauvouloir to you," he said, and he stepped forward and pressed the burning tip of the cigar against Carmilla's neck. She cried out in surprise as much as pain, and the short chains at her wrists and ankles rattled as she writhed in impotent fury.

Mauvouloir moved back and watched in amazement as the burn in Carmilla's flesh instantly began to heal. "Incredible," he said.

Vargas said: "Told you so."

Mauvouloir turned to him. "That you did. Well done, my man."

"My pleasure," Vargas said. "Speaking of which, I think I'll go claim my reward, if you don't mind."

Mauvouloir glanced at his watch. "Actually," he said, "you need to get on monitor duty. I'm sure Tyler is ready for a break."

Vargas didn't bother to hide his anger. "What the hell are you talking about? I just delivered you…"

"Watch your mouth," Mauvouloir said. His tone was mild, almost genial, but Vargas reacted as if he had been slapped. "You've earned your bonus, and I won't keep it from you, but I didn't give you permission to claim any extras on your errand, and I certainly didn't say you could kill anybody. You need to take a little time to reflect on the value of self-discipline. Besides, I'm doing you a favor. You'll enjoy it more after you've built up some anticipation."

Vargas clearly wanted to argue, but he decided against it. "Yes, sir," he muttered through clenched teeth, and he walked out the door.

Leo had avoided the guards, cameras, and motion detectors with childish ease. Mauvouloir's security measures were actually quite good, but they were no match for a soldier with perfect night vision and a century of experience. He had circled the island swiftly and quietly, leaving more than a few surprises along the way. When he was about a hundred meters from the temple, one of the large oak doors opened and out stepped Tommy Vargas.

Leo, shrouded in darkness, watched in perfect stillness as Vargas marched away down one of the illuminated paths that crisscrossed the estate. Keeping the man in sight, Leo stealthily fell into step behind him.

"What do you want from me?" Carmilla asked.

"Haven't you guessed?" Mauvouloir exclaimed. He gestured at the walls and the terrible devices that covered them. "You're my new plaything!"

Carmilla had guessed, but she couldn't accept it. She said: "I will not allow this."

Thalia laughed. "Allow?" she said. "You're priceless."

Mauvouloir shared her amusement. "*Ma chère*," he said to Carmilla, "your days of allowing anything are over. You belong to me, now. In fact—and you should take this as a compliment—I officially consider you my most prized possession."

"How so?"

"Are you kidding? You're a dream come true! The thing is, I've been getting a little jaded lately, a little bored. So, when Vargas told me he had spotted an honest-to-goodness vampire on Phuket, and he explained that he knew how get her for me, I was *very* intrigued. This was something new. Something *unique*."

Thalia added: "When he pointed you out to me, I couldn't believe how luscious you were. I volunteered to be the bait. I just couldn't wait to get close to you."

"I'm flattered," Carmilla said.

Mauvouloir stepped over to a nearby wall and took down a flogger. It was a serious implement, with tiny bits of metal at the tips of the leather thongs. He twirled it playfully about. A wistful, dreamy look came into his eyes.

"I can do *anything* to you," he continued, almost to himself, "and you'll always recover. Every night we can start all over again."

"You're perfect," Thalia said, practically salivating. "You're a toy that never breaks."

Carmilla wondered how many "toys" had been broken in this room by these two sadists. She was an unapologetic predator, but she had never reveled in cruelty the way these people did. They were monsters.

"Well," Mauvouloir said, seeming to emerge from his reverie, "I'm famished. I believe I'll go to the house for tapas." He passed the flogger to Thalia. "Want to keep our guest company?"

"I'd love to," Thalia said.

They kissed, and Carmilla rolled her eyes with disgust.

"I don't think she likes us," Thalia said with an insipid giggle.

Mauvouloir leered at Carmilla. "Thalia's going to warm you up a little," he said. "When I get back, it'll be party time."

Carmilla spat at him, but he was too far away to hit.

"That's good," he said. "It wouldn't be fun if you didn't fight. Just know this, before I am through, you will beg to be my slave."

"Just know this," Carmilla said, "before I am through, you will beg for death."

Mauvouloir laughed and walked out of the room.

It was a short walk from the temple to the guest house. Vargas entered a side door, and a few moments later another guard emerged. As the man walked away toward a waiting row of golf carts, Leo stepped up, caught the door with the barrel of the SAW, and quietly slipped in. Immediately to his right was an open door that revealed a large, well-appointed office dominated by a bank of high-definition monitors. Vargas, his back to the door as he poured a cup of coffee, observed them with great interest. They revealed scenes from all over the island, including inside the rooms of the guest house. Leo took these in at a glance, and was sickened.

Intellectually, he had known what he was going to find on this island. He was prepared for it. However, being confronted with the objective reality of it was like a physical blow. There were nine children—the oldest no more than twelve—in as many rooms. One of them was Malai. She sat alone in the center of a large bed, visibly weeping. Of the other kids, four of them, along with Holland's *guests*, were mercifully asleep. The others were not.

The ones that were not…

Leo set down the machine gun, drew his Browning, and stepped into the room. He leveled the silenced pistol at Vargas' head, and said: "Hello, Tommy."

401

Vargas froze and slowly turned. To his credit, he kept his composure, but he was plainly stunned by the sight of the man before him. "Saint-Clair? What the hell are you doing here?"

"Where's Carmilla?"

"The suckhead? She's in the Black Room with Mauvouloir and his psycho girlfriend."

"The Black Room?" Leo said. "Is that where you just came from?"

Vargas nodded.

Leo gestured at the monitors. "No cameras in the Black Room?"

"Mauvouloir doesn't like being filmed."

"Do these people?"

Vargas shrugged. "They don't know. They'll find out later, when it's convenient. Then Mauvouloir will own them."

"He won't own anything after tonight. Give me the master key."

"What makes you think I have one?"

"You're in here, so you've got monitor duty. You're the first responder if something goes wrong in one of those rooms. Now, give me the damn key."

Vargas pulled a card from his pocket, flipped it through the air, and Leo neatly caught it.

"What now?" Vargas asked.

Leo shot him between the eyes.

Malai had nearly cried herself to sleep when the door opened and a man stepped into the room. She was about to scream when she recognized her new friend.

"Hello, Malai," Leo said. "I've come to get you out of here."

Her terror and fatigue disappeared in a wave of exultant joy. She ran to him and held him and never, ever wanted to let him go.

"Take it easy," he said, returning her embrace. "You're going to be safe now."

"I thought you were that man," she gasped. "The man who killed Khin. He said he was going to have some fun with me. I think he wanted to hurt me."

"Khin is alive," Leo said, "and that man is never going to hurt anyone again."

Malai's mind was reeling. She felt as if she had snatched from the jaws of a ravenous monster and handed a winning lottery ticket. Then she thought of something. "Listen," she said, "I think there are some other kids here. I heard someone crying…"

"You're right," Leo said. "There are some other children. We're going to take them with us. Will you help me?"

Malai nodded.

"Excellent."

Leo took her into the hall and whispered some instructions in her ear. Then he drew a pistol with a very long barrel and swiped a key card in the door of the next room over. He stepped inside and Malai heard a soft *thump,* like someone hitting a pillow. A moment later, Leo stepped out with a little girl about the same age as Malai. She had a blanket over her shoulders and she looked drowsy and dazed, but when Malai smiled at her she smiled back. Then Leo went to the next room and the process was repeated.

Soon, Malai was surrounded by boys and girls, some of them sleepy and confused, others frightened, others quietly weeping. She tried to comfort them all, and it seemed to help, even with the ones who couldn't understand Thai.

No grown-ups came out of the rooms Leo entered, but she did hear some of their voices. Her English was limited, but she knew enough to understand the few words she could make out before they were cut off by the pillow sound.

"What's the meaning of this?"

*Thump.*

"Wait, I have money!"

*Thump.*

"Don't you know who I am?"

*Thump. Thump. Thump.*


Carmilla hung limply from her chains. Her dress was in tatters, and blood dripped to the tiles from her lacerated flesh. Her long blonde hair fell over her face, obscuring her features.

"What's wrong with you?" Thalia gasped, breathless from her exertions. She waved the flogger in frustration. "You're supposed to be healing faster! That's what makes it *interesting!*"

Carmilla murmured something indistinct.

"What was that?"

Again, the hoarse, barely audible mumbling.

Thalia grabbed a handful of Carmilla's hair. She lifted her head and glared at her with utter contempt. The once imperious and defiant vampire now looked completely broken and exhausted. Her skin was waxy and jaundiced, and the smeared mascara around her closed eyes gave her an absurd, almost raccoon-like appearance.

Sneering with disdain, Thalia leaned in close. "I'll ask you again," she said through clenched teeth. "What did you say?"

Carmilla opened her eyes. "I said," she whispered, "*I just need something to drink.*"

She snatched both of her hands through the manacles around her wrists. There was a spray of blood as the steel bracelets stripped away her flesh and made ragged red ruins of her hands. She threw her arms around Thalia and pulled her into an inescapable embrace.

Leo commandeered one of the golf carts to transport himself and the kids away from the guest-house. He had checked the monitors to make sure the guards on the night watch were safely scattered around the island, so their short drive received no unwanted attention. It felt surreal and a little ridiculous, as if they were enjoying a midnight jaunt in a silly little car, but the occasional whimpers of fear and lingering pain from the children annihilated any humor he might have found in the situation.

He stopped the cart in front of the temple, told Malai to keep the kids together, and tried the door. To his surprise, it opened without a sound to reveal a roomy vestibule outfitted with some luxurious chairs and a wet bar. He drew the Browning and crossed the room toward another set of doors. Passing through these, he found himself in what was apparently an opulent torture chamber.

The smell of blood hung thick in the air, and there was a woman's body lying at the foot of a Saint Andrew's cross. He could tell by the dark hair that it was Thalia Tomasis. Even from where he was standing, it was clear that she was dead. Her corpse was little more than a desiccated husk. He looked around the room.

"Countess?" he whispered.

"Good evening, Monsieur le Nyctalope," said a voice directly at his ear.

He turned and there she was, smiling with what seemed like genuine pleasure. Her dress was hanging on by threads, but she practically radiated power and danger. She looked like a Nordic goddess.

"Is this a rescue?" she said.

"Yes," he said, "for you, and some others."

"Others?"

He told her about the children.

"Barbarism," she spat.

"Will you help me?"

"What would you have me do?"

"I have a Zodiac moored southwest of here. Can you get the children there safely?"

"Of course."

"Excellent. You can find the boat by…"

Carmilla waved a hand. "Don't bother. I have your scent."

He wasn't sure what to say to that.

"I will do this," she said, "but there is something I want in return."

"Yes?"

She told him, and he found the terms acceptable. They quickly made a plan.

They stepped outside and Leo explained to the kids that the "nice lady" was going to take them to a boat and they should wait for him there.

"But what if the guards catch us?" a little boy asked.

"Then I will kill them," the *nice lady* said, and the boy seemed to like that answer.

Leo retrieved the SAW from the back of the golf cart. It was time for the noisy part.

"Saint-Clair," Carmilla said as they were parting ways. "A question, if I may?"

"Certainly."

"Had it not been for the child, would you still have come for me?"

Leo smiled. "There are so few of us relics left," he said. "Why should there be one less?"

Mauvouloir was in his kitchen savoring a glass of Chateau Lafite 1787 when the lights went out. He wasn't alarmed. This was far from unheard of. He waited ten seconds for the generators to kick in.

Thirty seconds later, the generators had not kicked in.

Frowning, he pulled a small radio from his waistband and pressed a switch. "Vargas," he said, "any idea what's going on with the power?"

Static.

He turned a small knob. "Foley, can you hear me?"

"Yes, sir. Something seems to be wrong with the generators."

"No kidding. Grab a couple of guys and get over to the guest house. I think something's going on over there."

"Roger that."

A few minutes went by. Holland left the kitchen and stepped outside into the tropical night. A warm breeze tousled his neatly coiffed hair. He walked around the house toward the helipad and considered the Augusta 109 he had parked there. He wondered if he should start it up.

"Mr. Holland?"

"Yes?"

"We're at the guest house. Something isn't right. The side door's wide open. We're checking the monitor station... Damn! Vargas is dead! Wait, what the hell? Is that a claymore?"

Static, coupled with a muffled explosion from the direction of the guest house.

Holland turned the knob on his radio. "Chapman! Stevens! Miller! Get your teams together! We're under attack"

A click, then a sleepy voice: "Chapman, here. I'm sorry sir, what did you..."

A series of explosions, one after another, coming from every part of the estate. A few seconds of silence, then a pair of thunderous, earth-shaking eruptions. A ball of fire rose into the air that briefly illuminated the entire island in a red-orange glow.

*Those were the propane tanks*, Mauvouloir thought. He turned to the Augusta, and it blew up, too. The force of the detonation knocked him flat on his back, but he was otherwise unhurt. He forced himself to his feet, grabbed the radio, and started to run.

His only hope now was to get to the pier. The *Shibari* was too much for him to pilot on his own, but the *Justine* was perfect; a fast-moving Sealine sports cruiser that could get him to safety until he figured out what had happened here.

*But what if the boats are burning, too?*

He dismissed the thought. One problem at a time.

*What about Thalia?*

Thalia was a big girl. She could look out for herself.

He did not give a single thought to his guards, his guests, or his captives.

His radio crackled. "This is Stevens. I'm approaching from the southwest. It looks like all three villas are on fire! Can anyone tell me what the hell is going on?"

"This is Miller. I'm on the east side of the bunkhouse with what's left of Bravo and Charlie teams. We've lost at least four guys and…"

A roar of machine gun fire.

Miller again: "Shots fired! Shots fired! At least one gunman, maybe more! I need anyone available to get over here right now!"

Holland pushed himself to run faster. He was suddenly very grateful for all those hours on the treadmill.

"This is Foley! Chapman's down! We're being cut to pieces over here!"

More machine gun fire. Mauvouloir thought they could hear it in Bangkok. He went off the path into the trees. It would slow him down, but he didn't trust the walkways. What if they had been booby-trapped? What if there more raiders waiting in ambush?

A crackle, then the voice of Stevens: "Hey, I think I just saw a woman and some kids… Wait a minute, is that the blonde Vargas brought in earlier?"

Mauvouloir paused in his flight and lifted the radio. "Stevens," he wheezed, "listen to me. Do not approach that woman. Get to the bunkhouse and help Tyler. I will…" He paused, then decided on a strategic lie. "I'll meet you guys at the Black Room. I'm headed there now."

Static.

"Stevens?"

Static.

"Tyler?"

A crackle, then a deep voice with a slight French accent: "The Black Room is gone, Monsieur de Mauvouloir. I blew it to pieces."

"Who are you?"

"I'm a destroying angel."

Mauvouloir resumed his headlong flight. In his panic, he tripped and fell, badly twisting an ankle in the process. Ignoring the pain, he struggled back to his feet and hobbled through the pitch-dark undergrowth.

After a few minutes that felt like an eternity, he emerged from the trees and thanked a god he had never believed in when he saw the pier intact and the boats safely bobbing at their moorings. He was seized by a sudden terror that this was a trap; that he would start the Sealine and be consumed in an explosion. He stood there, paralyzed by fear and indecision.

The destroying angel spoke from the radio: "Where are you hiding, Mauvouloir?"

Mauvouloir ran for it. He had to take the chance.

"You're only delaying the inevitable."

He was on the surf, completely exposed. He traced a messy serpentine pattern in the sand.

"You can't escape what's coming."

He was on the pier, his sandaled feet slapping against the boards.

"You can't escape justice."

Mauvouloir was on the Sealine. He was in agony. His heart was about to burst. He wanted to collapse, but he pushed himself to rush through the undocking, casting off the lines, starting the engines...

He closed his eyes.

The twin diesel sterndrives rumbled to life, and the *Justine* did not blow up.

"You can't escape me."

"Oh, yeah?" he muttered. "Just watch me."

He was away from the pier, safely in the open water, pushing the Volvo engines for all they were worth. He looked back, and he was temporarily blinded by the explosion of the pier, and the *Shibari* with it. A thirty-million-dollar yacht, gone in the blink of an eye. It was horrifying and spectacular and it made him laugh because he had gotten away again, just like always. He really was untouchable.

He pointed the boat north and activated the autopilot. Soon, he would chart a course for a Bangkok marina and start working the radio, but for now he just wanted to sit down, have a drink, and start planning his revenge.

Wincing in pain from his ankle, he left the helm and limped down into the salon. He flipped on a light, and found himself looking into the ice-blue eyes of Carmilla Karnstein.

"It's party time," she said.

Soon, he began to beg for death.

Eventually, she gave it to him.

Malai emerged from below deck and joined Leo at the helm of the *Sylvie.*

"How are they doing?" he asked.

"Good, but they're still scared."

"Why?"

"They don't know you. I told them they could trust you, but they don't feel safe. At least not yet. Where are you going to take them?"

He hadn't really thought about it. He had been so focused on the job at hand that consideration of what came next had been easy to push away.

"I know people," he said, "and I have money. I can arrange for them to get the help that they need, get them back to their homes."

"What if they don't have homes to go back to?"

That was an unpleasant thought. He had delivered these children from a living hell, but what was to become of them now?

*I'm just one man*, he thought, *and not a very good one, some would say. What more can I realistically do?*

He looked down at Malai. She stared up at him, waiting for an answer.

"I have an idea," he said.

### Epilogue: Phuket, 2024

Niran stood at the door of the great house, and she was afraid. It was so big and so gorgeous that she couldn't help thinking it might hide some dark secret; a gingerbread house with a witch inside.

"Goodness," Mrs. Chaiya said with a chuckle. "Are you trying to break some bones?"

Niran loosened her grip on the older woman's hand. "I'm sorry."

"There's no need to apologize, and you don't have to be scared. These are very good people. I've known them for a long time. They've helped a lot of children like you."

"But I want to stay with you."

"Oh, don't worry. You will see plenty of me. I'm here a lot."

The door opened, and there was the most beautiful woman Niran had ever seen. Her smile was like a sunny morning. Niran knew that awful things could hide behind pretty faces, but she didn't think this was a mask. *Not a witch*, she thought. *This is a princess.*

"Davika, how are you?" the princess said to Mrs. Chaiya. "And you must be Niran. Please, come in."

They went inside, and the princess gave her milk and fresh-baked cookies while she spoke to Mrs. Chaiya in hushed tones. Grown-ups, even the best ones, did that a lot around her. After a little while, Mrs. Chaiya gave her a hug and promised to come back soon. Niran wanted to make Mrs. Chaiya proud, so she did not let herself cry.

When Mrs. Chaiya was gone, the princess sat down beside Niran and took one of the cookies from the plate. "Aren't these delicious?" she said. "After we finish our little snack, I'll take you upstairs and show you your room. Then we'll sit down and I'll explain the house rules. Don't worry, there's only a few and they're easy to follow. Later, I'll introduce you to the other children."

"How many other kids live here?" Niran asked.

"Right now, eleven. You'll like them. They're all very friendly."

"Where are they now?"

"My brother took them for a trip to the beach. They'll be back in a couple of hours."

"Have they…" Niran hesitated. "Have they all been…"

"It's all right," the princess said, and her voice was so warm that Niran thought she could go to sleep in it. "They've all had experiences like yours. They'll understand."

For a little while they sat in friendly silence, enjoying the cookies. When the last one was gone, the princess said: "OK, ready for the tour?"

"Sure," Niran said. "Can I ask you something first?"

"Of course. What would you like to know?"

Niran pointed at something mounted on the opposite wall. It was a very small photo in a very large frame with a light mounted above it. The picture, slightly blurred, showed a handsome man in a white beach suit rising from a table at a restaurant. He was smiling in a way that was kind of friendly, and kind of sad. Niran thought he looked lonely.

"Who is he?" Niran asked.

"That's Leo," the princess said. "Once upon a time he was called the Nyctalope."

"Why was he called that?"

"Because he could see in the dark," the princess said. She made a sweeping gesture that seemed to take in the whole house. "He started all of this, and made sure there would always be enough money to keep it going. When I was a little girl, not much older than you are now, he saved my life."

Niran was impressed. "He did?"

"Yes, he did. The very night I took that picture, in fact."

Niran studied the photo. It was probably a trick of the light, but the man's eyes almost seemed to glow. "What was he like?" she asked.

The princess stood up and gently took Niran's hand. "That man was a hero," she said with a smile. "Never forget his name."

*This rather unique crossover by Sean Lee Levin brings into the Shadowmen universe* Filibus, *a 1915 Italian silent adventure film directed by Mario Roncoroni and written by future science fiction author Giovanni Bertinetti. It features Valeria Creti as the title character, a mysterious air pirate who makes daring heists with her technologically advanced airship. Brazilian writer Pedro Nava described it as a film "of major importance," praising the gender fluidity and mythic aspects of the character, as well as its innovative use of science fiction motifs.*

## Sean Lee Levin: *The Vampire and the Air Pirate*

*Paris, 1918*

*IRMA VEP STRIKES AGAIN!*
*ELSTIR'S* POPULUS (FALL) *STOLEN FROM LOUVRE*
*IN DARING DAYLIGHT ROBBERY*

So read the headline of the morning edition of *Le Mondial*. Only a few nights ago, the member of the infamous gang known as *Les Vampires* had reappeared alive and well after seemingly being shot dead by Jane Brémontier, the fiancée and later wife of *Mondial* reporter Philippe Guérande, who along with his colleague Oscar Mazamette had warred against Vep and her confederates two years before. Now the *femme fatale* menaced respectable society once more, plundering and killing daily with impunity.

In the offices of *Le Mondial*, Guérande and Mazamette were discussing their old foe's latest crime.

"Since that she-devil rose from the grave, she's been bolder than ever, Mazamette. Something must be done," Guérande, a handsome young man with a part in his black hair, said.

"You know, I agree with you, Philippe, but what can we do?" asked Mazamette, a balding man with a large nose and a mustache. "Unlike last time, the police have asked us not to get involved. 'Meddling journalists overcomplicating things,' remember? Not that we did so badly before, even if it took me far too long to realize I was on the wrong side."

Guérande put a hand on his friend's shoulder. "My dear Mazamette, you have long since redeemed yourself for your association with that band of fiends. You saved my life, and I will never forget it." He was silent for a moment, then resumed, "Tonight should bring another crime. If she gets off scot-free, then I say we should go after her, police be damned."

The following evening, on the Rue Maule, a shapely figure, clad in a black body stocking, walked on tiptoes across the roof of a townhouse. Were anyone else nearby, she would be recognizable as the very same Irma Vep who the two journalists had discussed hours before.

*This should be no trouble*, she thought with a smile. *M. Papopulos and his daughter are at the theater, leaving their most valuable possession in a safe: a Fei Tsui jade necklace worth eighty thousand dollars. God, it feels good to be back in the game. That silly little girl of Guérande's never knew I was wearing a bulletproof vest under my clothing. Nor did either of them or that bumbling turncoat Mazamette know that I was able to seduce the mortician into swapping myself with the body of a vagrant woman disfigured by vitriol. Now that I've built up the suspense, and Lupin and that madman Fantômas are both missing in action, I can stalk the night without competition once more.*

Unfurling a grappling hook, she descended to the topmost window of the townhouse, and used a glass cutter to make a hole in the window. Reaching in and opening it, she climbed through and entered. The safe was right where the maid she had bribed said it would be. It was a Dale safe, but she was an old hand at cracking even a barrier as effective at that, and quickly got it open, extracting the necklace. The necklace was stunning to behold, with sixty beads of six intricate carats each. She turned to the window and saw a rope ladder. *Now what the hell is this?* Irma thought.

A person of indeterminate gender came down the ladder, his or her features obscured by a cap and black domino mask. Her voice revealed that she was female, not to mention Italian, as she said, "So you're the legendary Irma Vep I've heard so much about since I came to this country. A pleasure, my lovely friend."

"And you are?" Irma said, adopting an air of indifference to hide her wariness.

"I've used many names. Two of them were even French, the Baroness Troixmonde and the Count de la Brive. But my real name, more than the one I was born with, is Filibus. Now hand over that necklace, so I don't have to snuff out your life."

Filibus! Irma had heard that name before. Four years ago, she had terrorized Sicily, acting as a pirate from an advanced airship. She had dueled with a detective named Kutt-Hendy and romanced his sister Leonora as the Count de la Brive. "Over my dead body," she replied.

"Believe me, that can be arranged. Would you care to come up to my airship to discuss the matter?"

Irma looked out the window and upward. The rope ladder Filibus was astride descended from an almost boat-like ship floating many feet above the townhouse. "Love to," she finally answered.

"Quite a vessel," Irma remarked as they climbed aboard. Filibus' all-male crew, all masked like their employer, were manning the engines and navigating. "Maybe not on the level of one of Robur's, but still impressive."

"I am a great admirer of *Signor* Robur's designs," Filibus replied with a smile. "Before we begin, perhaps you're wondering what I'm doing in France instead of my homeland?"

"The thought had crossed my mind."

"I would be more than happy to answer. After the incident with Kutt-Hendy and the delightful Leonora, I was able to escape with my loot from the International Bank. Unfortunately, Kutt-Hendy turned out to be far more competent than I gave him credit for. Working with a relative of his, a private investigator named Kutt Hardy who fancied himself a better detective than Sherlock Holmes, if you can believe it, as well as a police inspector named Silvio Montalbano, he thwarted my attempt to plunder the wealth of Don Ciccio, a Mafia boss in the town of Corleone. The mob put out a contract on me, and I thought it would be healthier to lay low. However, I got bored after three years of inactivity, and decided to resume my old ways in a new country. I've always been fascinated by French culture, so I decided Paris would be my new home."

"You do know there are do-gooders here as well, yes? Judex, the Nyctalope..."

Filibus waved her hand contemptuously. "Bah, men! They haven't the advantages we do, my dear Irma. Ténébras and the like couldn't possibly hold a candle to you, and Kutt-Hendy and friends just barely stopped me in Corleone. I've read with great fascination the stories of your exploits. It was quite stimulating, in more ways than one."

Irma realized suddenly that Filibus' seduction of Leonora Kutt-Hendy had been more than just a ploy. "Thanks, but you're not my type. Just because I call myself a vampire doesn't mean I share the proclivities of a Mircalla Karnstein."

"Well, you certainly share her fondness for anagrams. Still, that is a pity. Your outfit is very flattering. If you hadn't gone after the same necklace as myself, I would have gladly considered you for an *inamorata* and accomplice."

"This isn't your night, is it? You're not getting the necklace or me."

"In the case of the former," Filibus smiled, "I'm not giving up without a fight. You may choose the weapons."

Irma snorted. "I can beat you with my own two hands."

"I admire your confidence, however misplaced." Pointing to the door of a cylindrical chamber, Filibus said, "We can fight in here, without the crew disturbing us, or vice versa. I would not want to perish in a fiery wreck."

"I don't think any of us want that," Irma replied as they entered the chamber. She placed the necklace on a table. "Enough talk. Let's get down to business."

Filibus nodded, then let loose a vicious kick aimed at Irma's midsection. The athletic Frenchwoman spun out of the way, then aimed her left fist at her

Italian counterpart's face. Filibus brought her own right hand, palm open, up in a chopping motion, striking Irma's hand out of the way.

Irma clutched her hand in pain. "You know Asian combat arts, I see. Impressive, but I prefer the straightforward route every time."

Filibus laughed. "Your country's foot-fighting method, Savate, isn't much different. I learned it from a mercenary named René Batroc. He bragged about his son, little Georges, and how he couldn't wait until he was older, so he could teach it to him."

"I've heard of this Batroc. *Le Sauteur*, they call him. He supposedly dresses in purple and orange clothing. Not very subtle for a hitman. Black is much more suited to nocturnal killing."

Irma gave Filibus a vicious backhand with her uninjured appendage. Filibus, in turn, struck her in the solar plexus. Irma grunted with pain, but soon recovered. She grabbed Filibus' ankle and tossed her to the floor. "Give up?"

"You're even more amazing than I thought, my dear Irma. The fight is over, but I'm not giving up the prize." Filibus crossed to the table where the necklace was and seized it. Irma ran forward and attempted to grab it out of her hands. In their struggles, they knocked the door open and spilled out. By this point, they were above the Seine. The crew of the airship looked agog at the two women's struggles.

"Stay focused, you fools! Do you want us all to perish?" Filibus shouted. She held the necklace above her head with one hand as she held back Irma with the other. Unfortunately, while her men had regained their composure, even an advanced airship can encounter turbulence. The ship lurched, and Filibus was thrown backward several feet. The necklace fell from her hand into the water below.

"*Cazzo!*" Filibus cursed. "I don't have the proper diving equipment to recover the necklace. All of that for nothing..."

"Yes, it did turn out to be rather pointless," Irma said sardonically. "Why don't you drop me off somewhere, and we can both get on with our lives? At least, if we stay out of each other's ways, because I assure you that if I see you again, only one of us will survive."

"Likewise," Filibus nodded. "Very well. The next rooftop we fly over, I will deposit you. I won't soon forget this evening, I promise you."

Proving good as her word for one of the few times in her life, Filibus set Irma free. Neither said a word as Irma used a grappling hook to cross from roof to roof as she made her way back to her hideout and Filibus' ship rose back into the heavens, its captain already planning future plunder.

The following morning, Guérande and Mazamette interviewed M. Papopulos. "The necklace was a forgery, *messieurs*. Such a valuable item would doubtless be the target of thieves, so I placed the false one in a safe, while I hid the other someplace less discreet, but also less obvious. You will understand if I do not tell you where."

"Of course," Guérande nodded. "I admire your ingenuity, but I think it best to keep it under wraps. Irma and this woman Filibus may seek reprisal against you and your wife if they learn the truth."

"I appreciate that, sir. Now if you'll excuse me, I must write to a friend of mine in America, Lewin Lockridge Grayle. He has expressed an interest in buying the necklace from my daughter Zia and I, and I am only too happy to oblige."

"Well," Mazamette smiled, "hopefully no further thefts will be attempted on this remarkable piece of jewelry, either now or in the years to come."

*David Vineyard has monopolized the writing of stories featuring an elderly Arsène Lupin; the challenge here was to pen the very opposite, the earliest possible tale starring the famous Gentleman-Burglar. Also, I had been wanting to flesh out the* Société Secrète des Aventuriers *(a concept originated by Randy) in a manner similar to Isaac Asimov's* Black Widowers, *and further, find a way to include Charles Rabou's wonderful* "Cabinet Noir" *in the Shadowmen universe (4 volumes translated by Nina Cooper available from Black Coat Press). Mission accomplished!*

# Jean-Marc Lofficier: *A Scepter in a Child's Hand*

> *'Tis much when scepters are in children's hands*
> *Henry VI* – Act IV – Scene I

*Paris, 1924/1875*

That evening, Arsène Lupin had invited a few friends to have dinner with him at the headquarters of the *Société Secrète des Aventuriers* in the third arrondissement of Paris. It was the week before Christmas and the Chef, Athanase Pamplemousse, had promised a *festin* to rival no other.

Those who had responded to Lupin's invitation were Joseph Rouletabille, Francis Ardan, Rose L'Ange (a.k.a. The Phantom Angel), Hareton Ironcastle, Léo Saint-Clair (a.k.a. The Nyctalope), Jacques de Trémeuse (a.k.a. Judex) and the Sâr Dubnotal. All were in a good mood, the food was indeed excellent, the wines no less so, and thus, the evening passed splendidly, until the after-dinner conversation, which turned, as was often the case at such events, to the more obscure corners of each guest's notorious career.

After Francis Ardan had told the company about the unusual dangers he had faced in his youth in the bizarre city of Inramonda, the discussion naturally turned to everyone's earliest exploits. The most colorful tales were those of Rose L'Ange, who told them how she had once outwitted Rumpelstiltskin as a young girl, and the Sâr Dubnotal's, although to be fair, no one quite understood where the city of Kadath actually was.

At that point, Lupin took a puff on his Cuban cigar and said, "Thanks to my biographer, Maurice, most people assume that my first exploit was stealing the Queen's Necklace at age six, but that's not quite correct. My very first adventure took place long before that."

"Long before you were six?" interjected the Nyctalope. "That's impossible."

"Where our friend Lupin is concerned, the word *impossible* rarely applies," observed Rouletabille, with a wry smile.

"Go on, Arsène. I'd love to hear that story," said Ironcastle, puffing on his briar pipe.

"It really is a very simple story, the only merit of which is that it is true," said Lupin. "Where should I begin?... I think it is best to start with the aftermath of the Paris Commune. In the first days of June 1871, so-called regular justice replaced the random massacres of the Communards by the troops of the Versailles army. The Government established councils of war, which sat for the next four years. The human toll is still the subject of some debate, but journalist Prosper-Olivier Lissagaray, a former Communard himself, estimated that the number of people summarily executed during that period is somewhere between 17,000 and 20,000."

Here Lupin marked a pause, perhaps to let that frightening number sink in.

"In 1873, as some of you may already know, my mother, Henriette d'Andrésy had wed my father, Théophraste Lupin, despite her family's strong opposition to her marrying a penniless teacher of gymnastics, fencing and boxing—and a former communard to boot. They were forced to live in Paris in what might kindly be labeled a hovel, where I was born a year later.

"Around that time, my mother discovered that my father was, shall we say, less than law-abiding, and she left him. Rejected by her family, she had to take menial jobs to survive, but she always strived to remain decent and honest."

"What happened to your father?" asked Doc Ardan, curious.

"Oh, he left for America," replied Lupin in a tone that discouraged anyone from asking further questions about Théophraste, "—just before my mother was arrested."

Whether planned or not, this surprising revelation produced an effect amongst the audience.

"Arrested? But for what reason?" asked Judex.

"I'm coming to that," said Lupin, somewhat curtly. "She was taken to the women's prison in Versailles, where she was visited by one Jérôme Clampin, who was at the time the head of the *Cabinet Noir*, a position he had inherited from Vidocq."

Lupin marked another pause, obviously assuming his guests would recognize the names he had just mentioned, but their blank stares told him that he had been mistaken.

"You must excuse us, Monsieur Lupin," said the Sâr Dubnotal, "but most of us here have little knowledge of the, er, skullduggery that you are so familiar with. You will have to explain."

Lupin sighed, and continued.

"In his youth, Clampin was better known as Pistolet. He was recruited by Vidocq—you know who Vidocq is, at least?—(general assent from the audience) and became a rising star in the Sûreté. He was one of the very few agents capable of keeping the Black Coats in check time and again. He eventually inherited the position of head of the *Cabinet Noir*, a Secret Bureau of spies whose job it is to protect the State from anarchists and their ilk."

"I know of the *Cabinet Noir*," said Rouletabille, who had occasionally worked for the Deuxième Bureau. "They have a rather sinister reputation."

"I met the Marquis de Lupiano once," noted the Sâr Dubnotal *à propos* of nothing and not explaining his remark further.

"So this Clampin paid a visit to your mother in her cell?" said Judex. "Did she tell you the story?"

"Yes," replied Lupin. "As I was ten months-old at the time, I would have had no personal recollection of it, of course. Let me tell you how the encounter went.

" 'Are you Madame Henriette Lupin, *née* d'Andrésy?' asked Clampin coldly.

" '*Oui, Monsieur.*'

" 'My bureau has come into possession of three letters written by and to the notorious anarchist Louise Michel. Here they are. Do you recognize them?'

"She looked at the papers Clampin showed her.

" 'Yes, this one is by my husband. It is his signature. But what does this mean?'

" 'It means, Madame, that your husband has been charged with corresponding with the enemies of our Nation, and the Law holds you to be his accomplice, unless, of course, you can help us apprehend him.'

" 'But I don't know where is. I'm innocent,' exclaimed my poor mother, understandably very frightened.

" 'That is most unfortunate,' Clampin replied. 'In that case, you will probably be sentenced to penal transportation to New Caledonia—like the woman Michel.' Then, he turned to the officer who had accompanied him and added, 'Hulet, tomorrow, you will take Madame Lupin to the Central Prison at Auberive where she will wait for her sentence of deportation.'

"He spoke in a matter-of-fact manner, seemingly unmoved by any human emotion. He was as cold and merciless as the blade of the guillotine itself, and indeed, my mother understood at that moment that she was truly lost. In her case, transportation was all too likely to turn into a death sentence.

"With an involuntary movement of fear, she hugged more tightly to her chest the baby she was holding in her arms..."

"The baby? You?" asked the Phantom Angel, genuinely moved.

"Yes, me. When the men from the Sûreté had come to arrest her, my mother had had no choice but to take me with her, as Victoire, our nurse, was absent at the time.

"The child was cheerfully kicking his little legs, unaware of the grim circumstances around him. My mother cast a last sad glance through the window of her cell, as if she was already saying good-bye to the land of her birth.

" '*Bien, Monsieur,*" she said, resigned. 'If that is to be my fate...'

"Clampin was about to say something, most likely quoting the Law or perhaps merely expressing an insincere regret of some kind, but he was prevented from doing so by the baby who had suddenly grabbed his whiskers. Boldly curious rather than afraid at the sight of this fearsome visitor, the child then burst into a series of giggles which were as pure an expression of joy as only God could fathom.

"My mother trembled; she desperately tried to silence me, somehow afraid that my laughter might offend these somber and serious officials, but she failed, as I continued to giggle, trying to reach the shiny buttons that decorated the policeman's coats with my little hands.

"Despite remaining outwardly emotionless, Clampin's face paled.

" 'Is this your child?' he asked.

" '*Oui, Monsieur.*'

" 'How old is he?'

" 'Ten months Monsieur.'

" 'Hum. He's strong for his age,' Clampin remarked as I again tried to pull on his whiskers. 'Do you have a nurse?'

" 'Normally, yes, Monsieur, but she's had to return home to Normandy because her mother has been taken sick.'

" 'I see. So you're the child's only provider?'

" '*Oui, Monsieur.*'

"Clampin bit his lips, thinking. My mother's tears were running down her cheeks, silently. And I, the baby, continued giggling unrepressedly. Then, he turned to the officer and said:

" 'All things considered, Hulet, I have decided to release Madame Lupin. She was obviously unaware of her husband's nefarious activities. The Nation has nothing to gain by sending her to rot in New Caledonia. Release her.'

"My mother fell to her knees, thanked God and, with all her strength, kissed the child who had just saved her."

"That is a beautiful story," said the Phantom Angel, barely repressing a tear.

"And my first and greatest exploit," concluded Lupin.

*Our Australian contributor, David McDonald, offers here his own take on two of the most archetypal fictional figures of the French Revolution: Baroness Orczy's* Scarlet Pimpernel *and Alexandre Dumas'* Chevalier de Maison-Rouge. *Set in Paris during the Reign of Terror, that novel follows the adventures of a brave young man named Maurice Lindey who unwittingly implicates himself in a Royalist plot hatched by the mysterious Knight of Maison-Rouge to rescue Marie Antoinette from prison. Dumas based his story on a real-life attempt by the Marquis Alexandre Gonsse de Rougeville...*

## David McDonald: *Scarlet Petals, Crimson Flames*

*Normandy, 1793*

The smell of smoke hung in the air, stinging at the eyes of the company of young men picking their way through streets littered with debris. But Maurice Lindey was grateful for the pain, as it helped conceal the tears that welled in his eyes despite his best efforts. He wept for his home, the greatest city in the world, the City of Lights. For Paris burned.

While the worst of the fires that had raced through the city in the wake of riot after riot had been extinguished, the flames that concerned Maurice were those that burned in the hearts of his countrymen and women. Paris was like the mountain forests of his childhood at the height of summer, one spark away from a conflagration that would consume everything in its path. He feared that, in the end, nothing of the country he loved, that he had dedicated his life in the service of, would remain—only its ashes.

Maurice used the heel of the hand that was not clenched around the hilt of his sword to dash away a fresh batch of tears before they could betray his inner turmoil to his companions. It was not that he feared their judgement or mockery—they all had been through too much for that. They'd followed him from the day he had been first through the window of the Louvre during the Expedition to Versailles, to the blood and fire of the Battle of Jemappes, and everything in between.

No, there was no one who had seen him throw himself before the cannon of Loyalist infantryman in order to prevent the shedding of innocent blood, or watched him go blade to blade with grim Swiss Guardsmen while musket balls and cannon shot sliced through the air around him, who would question his courage. And, as many had discovered, anyone who had not seen such for themselves and thought to doubt his honor would find they risked paying the price with their blood on the edge of any one of the hundred blades of the Company of Thermopyles.

It was for their sake, the men who had given him their loyalty and love, as unworthy of it as he often felt, that he sought to maintain the illusion of perfect composure that he wore like a suit of armor against the dangers of a world gone mad. He no longer knew how to protect his nation, but he would pay any price for the sake of protecting his men.

He gazed around at the two dozen men flanking him as they stalked their way down the hushed Parisian streets. Like him, each of his men kept their fist curled around the hilt of their weapons, eyes flickering constantly as they scanned for danger. Steely gazes followed the furtive shadows that moved in the darkened entrances of alleyways, or checked rooftops and windows, most bordered by jagged points of broken glass, for the tell-tale silhouettes of snipers. Maurice did not believe that there would be anyone bold enough to take on a group of well-armed soldiers, but he had not survived this long by taking chances. And, in a Paris still spasming from the violence of the overthrowing of the despotic monarchy, and breathing the atmosphere of terror birthed by the growing pains of the new regime, who knew what madness was possible?

He also worried that the unwise and unobservant might not possess the perceptiveness to look past the youthful faces of his men, none older than his two and half decades, and many younger, and would miss the unblinking gaze of eyes more suited to much older men and the air of danger that usually surrounded veterans twice their age. Maurice knew that he himself had been dismissed many times as a young dandy, and that the curling chestnut hair that fell halfway to broad, muscular shoulders and the piercing blue eyes that in better days had crowned a glorious smile were now more burden than gift in a world where making men obey mattered far more than making young women swoon.

Maurice was thankful that at least the clothing that passed for a company uniform showed signs of hard use, with their faded blue jackets free of the garish decorations of parade units and bearing the patches and marks of field service. Maurice sighed as a flash of color out of the corner of his eye reminded him that the drab costumes of his men only served to throw that jarring contrast into sharper relief, and he wondered what unfriendly eyes might be making of the sight of the popinjay beside him.

As if feeling the weight of eyes upon him, the man to Maurice's right sniffed ostentatiously, and raised a scented pomade to his nostrils as pained by the smells around him.

"I say, old chap, I can't say that like what you've done with the place since I last visited," he drawled in a refined accent that set Maurice's teeth on edge. "Frightfully... how shall I put this? Pungent."

Quick as a viper, Maurice's left hand flashed out, clamping down on the sword hand of the man to his left before he could draw more than a half inch of gleaming steel.

"Peace, Gaston," Maurice said, catching the eye of his second in command. "These English aristocrats have delicate nostrils. This Comte probably doesn't have much experience with good, honest odors... though perhaps he will one day get more used to the smell of burning privilege."

A ripple of laughter moved through the nearby men, and Maurice felt the whipcord muscles of Gaston's forearm relax beneath his grip. He stole a look at the Englishman, waiting for an angry response, but was surprised to see his fatuous grin hadn't changed. Did the man not realize he was being made sport of?

"Comte? Oh, you are too kind, old fellow. I'm far less important than that, merely a common-as-muck baronet." He winked conspiratorially at Maurice. "Sir Percy Blakeney, baronet, to be precise." He paused, and scratched under his powdered wig uncomfortably. "But, of course, you Frenchies aren't that big on titles and the like, what?"

Maurice shook his head. He still hadn't decided whether the English envoy was a sign of the decadence of a corrupt monarchy, an elaborate joke, or a calculated insult directed against the new regime. Surely, the English couldn't have seriously thought this man was their best choice for delicate negotiations with the *Comité de Salut Public*? Not for the first time, Maurice took in the spectacle before him, shaking his head in wonder.

Sir Percy at least cut a fine physical figure; he was even taller than Maurice and his shoulders perhaps a tad wider. But, unlike the Frenchman, Blakeney did not have the upright carriage and graceful stride of a swordsman. Instead, he had the slightly hunched-over look of a man who spent more time focused on a wine list than in the training yard, and he affected a way of gesticulating as he talked and walked that seemed so exaggerated to be almost effeminate.

His unprepossessing impression was underlined by his garish appearance. Instead of dressing for a journey through a foreign and unfriendly city, he looked as if he was on his way to one of the balls the aristocrats had once held every night while the poor of Paris starved outside their gates. The bright red of his silken jacket, tight breeches, and fine woolen hose was broken only by the spotless white of elaborate lace at neck and wrists. The man may as well have been wearing a target on his back the way he stood out amongst the rest of the men, like a scarlet flower against drab weeds.

Maurice shook his head at the unflattering comparison, pushing it to the back of his mind. It didn't matter what he thought of the man, his orders were to see him safely to a ship, and back to his country with the contracts he carried. As much as he wished it wasn't true, he knew that the new government needed to keep the lines of trade open and the goods they needed so badly flowing in. Those who had been part of the Glorious Revolution knew better than anyone the dangers of a hungry populace.

An eruption of furious epithets yanked Maurice from his reveries, and he cursed himself for allowing himself to become distracted. His eyes widened at the sight of an angry Gaston waving a dagger under Blakeney's upturned nose.

"What is the meaning of this, Gaston?" he demanded, moving quickly to get between the men.

"This, this *andouille*, he is *bête comme ses pieds,*" Gaston spat. "He wasn't watching where he was going and tripped, and nearly knocked me over. Clumsy oaf!"

Maurice barely caught the end of Gaston's words as something over the man's shoulder captured his attention.

"Gaston, I believe you may owe Sir Percy an apology."

Gaston's stream of invective cut off suddenly as he registered Maurice's use of the Englishman's title, and he gasped as his eyes followed his commander's pointing finger. There, buried almost to its flights in the crumbling mortar and still thrumming slightly from the impact, was a crossbow bolt.

Maurice reached out and plucked the piece of blue fabric that was pinned against the bricks. Gaston took it from him with fingers that trembled slightly as he held it against the perfectly matching hole in his Red Phrygian cap.

"I think this Englishman may have just saved your life," Maurice said, his tine impassive. He stared at Blakeney as Gaston stomped off, muttering, trying to make sense of what had just happened.

Sir Percy gave him a vacuous grin.

"Well, that was a happy accident, what? Couldn't have managed something like that if I'd tried!"

He chortled merrily as he turned away, leaving Maurice to wonder whether he had imagined that brief flash of calculation in suddenly clear eyes before they had clouded over with a simpleton's expression once more.

Despite the heat pouring from the blazing fireplace that dominated the inn's common room, Maurice felt a chill run down his spine as he met the fanatical gaze of the man seated across the table from him. Despite the man's huge hands and sunken knuckles, and the unshaven stubble that covered coarse features, Maurice knew only a fool would dismiss him as just another street tough. Burning eyes gleamed with intelligence, glaring with an impression of missing absolutely nothing, and Maurice knew that underestimating this man would be the last mistake he ever made.

"Greetings, Citizen," the man said. "What is your business at the docks, and in such company?"

Maurice took a deep breath, knowing that the only possible pathway to safety through the maze in which he found himself was to show no fear, and to give an inch was to doom himself and his men. He grinned suddenly—he had always preferred offense to defense.

"My business is the business of the Revolution, *Citizen,*" he snapped. "And my name, as some of us still have enough manners to introduce ourselves, is Maurice Lindey, first soldier of the Company of Thermopyles."

The was a rustle around the walls of the room as a number of men took a step towards the table, fingering cudgels at their belts and muttering angrily at Maurice's tone. Like their leader, they were dressed in long white and red striped trousers and short white jackets. At a minute gesture of his hand from the man they came to a halt, before moving back to their positions. If he was angered by Maurice's words, or impressed, he gave nothing away, his expression remaining as unchanging as stone.

"Well, Citizen Lindey, I am Georges Lemaître." Now his face did change, a slight sneer twisting his lip. "But, I am simply one soldier amongst many of the *Enragés*. We do not need titles... nor do they impress us."

Maurice fought to keep his shock from showing. The *Enragés* were amongst the fiercest defenders of the Revolution, but even amongst them Lemaître had made a name for himself for his zeal in rooting out enemies of the state. Some said that his methods, however noble their motives, went too far but, if so, they said it quietly and only when absolutely sure of their audience.

Something must have shown in his expression, though, because Lemaître's sneer became a smile.

"I see my name is not unfamiliar to you, Citizen. Likewise, your reputation proceeds you". Suddenly, too quick for even Maurice's swordsman's reflexes to follow, he was leaning halfway across the table, and where Maurice had thought his eyes had blazed before, now they were unbanked furnaces. "Some may praise your deeds in the name of the Revolution, but they are fools. You are no better than the aristos we cast down with your sense of gallantry and your so-called heroics. I see the softness that lies rotting beneath the revolutionary façade. Do you think I haven't heard of your actions at the Bastille, or when Capet lost his head?"

Maurice forced himself to match the man stare for stare,

"I will not be questioned by a man like you," he spat. "You have no right to judge me, and I say that I am a true son of the Revolution, and doing its work. Interfere at your peril".

"I don't need to judge you. You are judged by the company you keep. Judged and found guilty". He gestured at Blakeney, who was held between two of the *Enragés*, but, despite a blackened eye, still looked as unworried as he had before they had walked through the inn door and into a trap. "What possible excuse could you have for accompanying this reactionary *ci-devant*? Look at him? He is everything we must destroy, root and branch!"

Casually, as if keeping his hand from shaking was not taking every ounce of effort he could summon, Maurice slid a piece of paper across the table.

"In the name of the Revolution we both love I will forget what you have said. I am not some scion of the *ancien régime* who feels a need to fight duels over matters of honor". He bared his teeth a Lemaître in what was more a snarl than a grin. "But, before you continue I suggest you check the seal at the bottom of the letter."

With an impatient sigh, Lemaître glanced down... and froze. For the first time, Maurice saw uncertainty fill his eyes, and he nervously licked his lips.

"This... this can't be", Lemaître muttered. "Why would Robespierre give you this?'

And the sound of the name a fearful murmur rippled through the room, and the men around the walls flashed each other worried looks.

Sensing his advantage, Maurice leaned forward and snatched back the letter.

"Do you really think the 'why' is any of your concern, Citizen? I certainly did not ask Citizen Robespierre the purpose of his orders, I simply endeavor to make sure they are carried out. I would advise you to do the same."

Lemaître gestured at the men holding Blakeney, and they immediately released him and stepped back. Blakeney cursed as his legs gave way and he thumped to the ground.

"I say, that was hardly sporting!" He looked around at the hostile faces and wisely bit back whatever he was going to say next.

Lemaître stood abruptly, and waved his hand angrily towards the door.

"So be it. Go, and take your parcel with you. Your men are outside, and safe, you may join them." He gave Maurice one final look of loathing. "But, do not think this is the end of the matter. Your time, and that of those of all those who stand in the way of the new France, will come."

Before Maurice could move the was a commotion at the inn's entrance. The doors flew open and two more *Enragés* entered dragging a struggling figure between them. Dwarfed between the two hulking men, the hooded captive seemed almost childlike until one noticed the way that its cloak clung to ample curves that were anything but. Maurice stiffened in his seat as the captive's hood fell back, revealing the face of perhaps the most beautiful young woman Maurice had ever seen. Raven black tresses framed a delicate face, while sapphire blue eyes blazed with anger... and terror.

"And what is this, Raoul?" Lemaître asked, his voice dangerously soft.

The smaller of the two men, still a head taller than Maurice, stepped slightly forward.

"We found her trying to get aboard one of the ships bound for England, Citizen." He laughed nastily. "Should have seen the fuss she made when we stopped her. Henri nearly lost an eye before we got this wildcat settled down."

As his companion stepped closer, nearly knocking his head on the lantern that hung almost seven feet above the ground, the play of light revealed four deep parallel furrows across his face. Just missing his eye, they were still oozing blood and already inflamed.

"Can't wait to teach her a proper lesson," he muttered angrily. Raoul winked at him, and leered at the woman.

Lemaître ignored the byplay. "What is your name, woman?" he snapped.

The woman, no, girl almost, Maurice saw, simply glared at him, refusing to speak. Maurice could not help but admire her spirit as he realized that, frightened as she was, there was more defiance than fear in her eyes.

"One way or another we will discover your identity," Lemaître said. "Rest assured you will receive the justice you deserve. You have nothing to fear from the Revolution if you are not its enemy."

At that, the woman straightened up, and gave Lemaître a look of withering contempt.

"Justice! What would you know of justice?" she spat. "I know what is in store for me and it is not justice. But I will not hide any longer."

Taking a deep breath, she looked around the room, and then her voice, firm and free of any trembling, rang out.

"I am Aline de Kercadiou, Comtesse de Gavrillac."

"Condemned out of your own mouth," Lemaître said. "I hereby arrest you in the name of the Revolution. You will be held here overnight, before being taken before the *Comité de Salut Public* tomorrow for judgement".

"You know what will happen to her, don't you, old chap?"

Maurice started in surprise at the sound of the voice in his ear. In the confusion, Blakeney had appeared at his shoulder without him even realizing.

"It is for the *Comité de Salut Public* to decide her fate, not for the likes of me," Maurice ground out. He did not like the idea, but it was not his decision.

"I mean tonight," Blakeney said softly, all diffidence gone from his voice. "Did you see the way those men looked at her? Is that the justice of the Glorious Revolution? Is that the new France you are trying to build?"

With a sickening feeling in his stomach, Maurice could only shake his head. He knew Blakeney was right.

"Lemaître!" Maurice called across the room. "Will you order your men to ensure she is safe until her trial?"

Lemaître stopped halfway to the stairs and turned back.

"Lindey, as I told you before... I am just one soldier among many. We do not give orders, we obey our consciences." He sounded almost regretful. "The woman is safe from me, but if others choose to seek vengeance, then that is a matter for their own souls".

"For a revolutionary you argue like a Jesuit." Lemaître's face convulsed with rage, but before he could respond, Maurice continued. "But, in that case, you should have no objection if my conscience compels me to stand guard outside her door tonight. I believe in the Revolution, but we did not rise against injustice simply to replace it.'

"So be it," Lemaître said, visibly mastering his rage. "But you will send your men to see this English aristo safely to his ship. I will not let your softness endanger the cause of the Revolution... so, if you stay, you will stay alone. And, don't think that your letter will protect you. Robespierre only commanded your mission be fulfilled, whatever happens now will be on your head alone."

Maurice leaned wearily against the door to the Comtesse's room, trying to judge the hour of the night. It seemed like hours since Lemaître had departed angrily, leaving him with the key and a bound and gagged captive. He had made the mistake of removing her gag, only to discover that, in her eyes, he was no different than the *Enragés* who had captured her. He had only been able to endure a few minutes of her venomous condemnation before he had replaced the gag and bundled her into the room, locking the door behind her with a sigh of relief.

Since then, he had tried to think of anything beside the accusations she had hurled out to him. But as the night dragged on it became harder to hold on to his belief in the justice of sending her to face the *Comité de Salut Public*. Was he any better than the men who simply wanted vengeance simply because he called it a different name? He had to believe so, or else... no, he wouldn't think it. Round and round his mind his thoughts chased themselves as the night slowly passed. It came as a relief when he heard the sound of heavy footfalls approaching along the corridor.

It came as no surprise to see the two men who had captured the Comtesse coming towards him, but Maurice was taken aback afresh by the sheer size of them. Raoul would have been considered huge by any standards, but Henri was an ogre of a man. Hands the size of hams dangled almost down beside his knees, knuckles cracking as he clenched them into gargantuan fists. Beside him, Raoul smirked as he whacked an oak cudgel almost as thick as Maurice's arm into a meaty palm. So completely did their looming presence dominate the senses that Maurice nearly missed the third man completely.

Darting around his companions, he seemed almost childlike in comparison, short and lean, with a rat-like face screwed up in rage. Almost faster than the eye could follow, his hands disappeared behind his back, whipping back into view as silver blurs flashed towards Maurice. Only the reflexes honed by a dozen desperate fights for survival saved him from dying there and then and without conscious thought, his sword rasped from its scabbard, carving an arc of steel before his eyes. With two sharp reports of metal upon metal, the daggers careened away from his blade, one burying itself in the door frame beside him, the other passing so close to Raoul it left a flap of cloth hanging from his shoulder and a trickle of blood running down his arm.

Raoul's mouth dropped open in surprise before he collected his wits again.

"No one is that fast, Antoine! He won't get that lucky twice!"

Antoine needed no encouragement. Before Maurice could brace himself, the smaller man was upon him, two new knives appearing in his hands as if by magic. Despite the advantage in reach his sword gave Maurice, he found himself hard-pressed to keep the knifeman's steel at a distance, his hand darting in and out like hummingbirds seeking a flower. With his back to the door and the corridor walls protecting his flanks, Maurice whirled his sword in furious circles of glittering silver, but Antoine was still able to pink his flesh three times in as many seconds. It was only a matter of time before he would be able to draw enough blood to slow Maurice down for the *coup de grace*, even if the swords-man could maintain his energy-sapping defense.

Knowing the desperate straits he had found himself in, Maurice took a deep breath and braced himself in anticipation of the pain he knew would be coming. At Antoine's next lunge, Maurice dropped his guard, and saw the smaller man's eyes light up with glee as he seized his chance. Following through with his attack, Antoine buried his blade into the meat of Maurice's upper arm only for the knife to catch in his opponent's flesh.

Antoine was only caught off guard for a moment, but that moment was enough for Maurice to whip his word across his body, taking Antoine's hand off at the wrist. Forgetting the blade in his right hand, Antoine sank to his knees with a scream of agony, only for Maurice to bring his sword back in a reverse cut with all his power. Slowly, Antoine toppled over, his head rolling back down the corridor to end up almost at Raoul's feet, empty eyes staring up at him ac-cusingly.

Raoul looked down in disbelief, then screamed in rage.

"You are a dead man! You will envy her by the time we finish with you."

Maurice said nothing, but simply began binding his wound with a piece of cloth cut from his shirt. His arm pulsed with agony with every heartbeat, and he knew that it was only a matter of time before he went into shock. He'd gotten lucky with his first opponent, but his left hand was now almost useless, and he still had two more to face. For a moment, Maurice felt despair, and he waited for them to attack and finish him off. Then, with a jolt of excitement he realized what was holding them back. The corridor was too narrow for two such big men to come at him side by side.

Slightly delirious with pain, Maurice laughed mockingly.

"Who's next? Don't tell me you are scared to face me!"

With a furious cry, Raoul was suddenly charging down the corridor to-wards Maurice, cudgel raised over his head. A look of astonishment crossed his features as, instead of waiting for him, Maurice launched himself forwards as if returning his charge. Bringing his cudgel whistling around with every ounce of power he had, the bigger man aimed at the place Maurice's head would be, only for the swordsman to drop to his knees just before the two men came together. Sliding between Raoul's legs, he brought his sword up over his head, dragging the razor-sharp edge along the massive artery on the inside of those tree trunk thighs.

Blood jetted from the wound as Raoul's momentum kept him staggering forward, sending him crashing headfirst into the oaken door, and making the whole inn shiver with the impact. A big hand clutched at the door handle as he tried to pull himself to his feet, but the loss of blood and the blow to his head were already taking their toll and he sunk back to the ground.

Maurice saw none of this, his attention focused on the other direction as he slid a few paces further down the corridor. He was trying to use the leverage of his sword to make his way to his feet when he suddenly found himself hurtling backwards, his head ringing and lights flashing before his eyes. Coming to a stop crumpled up against the wall, his cheek pressed to rough wood, he tried to make sense of what had just happened. The only thing he had ever experienced like it had been when an Austrian cannonball had landed mere yards away from him, sending him and a dozen soldiers flying, but his dazed mind could not make sense of how the *Enragés* could have managed to get a piece of artillery into the inn.

Suddenly, the world came back into focus, and he realized what had happened...just in time to recognize the massive shadow filling his vision. Henri wrapped his hand around Maurice's throat, fingers the size of sausages able to completely span his neck, and with a grunt of effort lifted him from the floor. Holding him up with one arm, the giant merely stared at him for a moment, then with a convulsion of slab-like muscles threw Maurice down the corridor. Groaning, Maurice tried to lever himself up, but his battered body fell back to the floor as he screamed in pain. He could only watch as Henri slowly walked towards him, craning his neck to look up as the man mountain came to a halt standing over him.

For a moment, Henri simply stood there, then lifted a giant boot, its shadow filling Maurice's vision. He closed his eyes, unable to do anything but wait for the final blow.

"Go on! Just do it," he yelled in defiance, steeling himself for death.

The bigger man's only reply was a puzzled grunt, and Maurice opened his eyes. For a moment, he was unable to make sense of the image before him. There was a strange bulge in Henri's shirt, just over his heart, a red stain spreading in a widening circle. As Maurice watched in disbelief, a shining point of metal appeared from the stain's center, steel glimmering wetly in the light as more and more was revealed. Suddenly, it withdrew and Henri's eyes rolled back into his head, and he fell to the floor.

As Henri crashed to the ground, Maurice's eyes fixed on the figure now revealed to be standing there. Dressed all in black, the only splashes of color to be seen were a cluster of red flowers embroidered around the borders of the mask that covered half its face.

"I say, old chap, you look like you've been in the wars."

Maurice started with shock. He knew that voice! It was Blakeney's English drawl, but stripped of all its foppish affectations, with an undercurrent of steel. Even his body language was completely different, gone was the stoop and he moved with a feline grace that spoke of a truly dangerous man.

"You!" Maurice gasped. "What are you doing here?"

"Couldn't leave the fair maiden in durance vile, now, could I?" Blakeney said. "Just wouldn't be cricket."

Maurice ignored the nonsense comment and tried to focus.

428

"You're him, aren't you?" he forced out. "They seek him here, they seek him there..."

"You Frenchies seek me everywhere," Blakeney finished. "That's right, I'm that damned elusive Pimpernel."

"So, what now? You finished the job they started, then take the Comtesse?"

"Well, I do plan on taking the Comtesse to England with me, but as for the rest, I don't think so." Percy winked at him. "Wouldn't be sporting after all the effort you put in keeping her safe, what?"

Maurice tried to think through the pain, and make sense of what Blakeney was saying.

"But your secret?" he managed to gasp out.

"I don't think that will be a problem. You see, I asked your men about you on the way to my ship, about what happened at the Bastille. You fought your own men to stop the slaughter of innocent prisoners." Blakeney's voice had lost any trace of humor. "I don't think that the man who would do that would betray the man who saved his life... and helped him protect an innocent woman.

"You can't know that," Maurice said. "We are enemies fighting for different sides."

Blakeney looked at him silently for a moment.

"You're right," he said finally. "I can't know that. But I have faith that a man who seeks to protect the innocent, who refused to rejoice at the death of a King he despised, won't always be my enemy."

He leaned forward, tightening the bandage around Maurice's arm and gently checking for any other wounds.

"Until then, you'll live," he said. "And maybe one day you will change your mind about what justice really is. If you do, seek out another man in red. I will make sure he knows who you are."

Blakeney straightened up frowning.

"But for that to happen we need to make sure you don't pay the price for the Comtesse's escape," he said, pulling out a scarlet blossom and dropping it onto Maurice's chest. "I really am sorry for that next part, old chap!"

"Wait... what?"

The last thing Maurice saw was the masked man's bootheel, and then everything went black.

*The murky world of post-war espionage always provides a good background for our stories. In this tale, Rod McFadyen features Bob Morane, the hero of a popular and long-running adventure series of novels which began in 1953 by Belgian writer Henri Vernes, who recently passed away...*

## Rod McFadyen: *Shadows of the Past*

*Paris, 1953*

It was a sun-drenched afternoon outside the café *Les Deux Magots*, on the Place Saint-Germain-des-Prés, in the heart of the 6th arrondissement of Paris. The bistro boasted a spacious and elegant interior, but on such a day, the two dozen small tables on the tiled patio out front were more popular. Covered by a large, green-trimmed awning which wrapped around the corner of the building, the outdoor setting was still intimate. The "magots" in the name were Chinese figurines in front of what was originally a novelty store before it was converted into a café almost 70 years ago. Since then, it had become a cultural institution, hosting Sartre, Picasso and Hemingway among other famous writers and artists.

Bob Morane sat at a table to one side and sipped their famous hot chocolate. The small chair looked like it could barely accommodate his tall and athletic frame, but he gave no indication he was uncomfortable. His dark hair and grey eyes were very striking, and the small scar on his cheek did not detract from his handsome features. A decorated pilot during World War II—less than a decade ago, but which seemed like a lifetime—Morane was now an explorer and adventurer which often gave him material for the freelance reporting he did for the magazine *Reflets*.

"You're looking well, Commandant Morane." A lean, mustachioed man had appeared out of nowhere and slid into the chair across from Morane.

"You as well, Monsieur Mathis," Morane responded. "How is business?"

"Unusually hectic these days," Mathis replied.

René Mathis was an agent of the S.D.E.CE. the French secret service. Morane had worked with him before on a couple of missions when the service needed someone outside their agency with his particular skill set.

"I guess you're about to ask me for a professional favor?" Morane said quietly so as not to be overheard by any of the patrons at the other tables.

Mathis frowned. "Can't I merely call up an acquaintance to enjoy a fine afternoon in companionable reverie?" he asked.

Morane looked at him with a questioning eyebrow. Mathis sighed.

"Finish your chocolate and let's go for a walk."

They were silent as they strolled along busy Rue Bonaparte and turned onto the Promenade Marceline Loridan-Ivens, a wide cobblestone walkway beside the Seine.

"What do you know about a man called Le Chiffre?" Mathis asked when they were out of earshot from any potential eavesdroppers.

"Not very much," Morane replied. "I recall he's an activist with one of the workers' union, but he's somewhat of a mystery beyond that."

"He's very much a mystery," Mathis said, leaning up against a railing and looking down at the river. "The man has no origin, no history, no background. He first appeared at the Dachau displaced persons camp after the war. He claims to have no memory of anything before then, not even his name or nationality. He took to calling himself Le Chiffre—the Cypher—because he considers himself only a number on a passport. He settled in Paris and is now the paymaster of the Alsatian Workmen's Union. He's extremely intelligent, enjoys the good life, is an expert gambler but we know nothing else about him... except for one more thing."

Mathis paused as a young couple strolled past but they seemed much more interested in each other. Morane guessed he was struggling to determine how much of his world he could reveal to someone outside the service.

Deciding that Morane was trustworthy enough, and that he needed to be trusted as well, he continued. "He operates on behalf of our counterparts in the Kremlin."

"A spy. I can see why he's of interest to you."

Mathis nodded. "Le Chiffre is also of interest to Britain's MI6 and we've jointly been monitoring him for some time. We recently discovered he's taken union money and invested it in some risky enterprises, hoping to pocket any profits before replacing the money. Those enterprises turned out to be extremely risky and he lost all of it. He's desperate to replace it before his masters in Moscow find out. They're not known for their forgiving attitude."

"It looks like you have an opportunity to turn him," Morane surmised.

Mathis nodded again. "He needs a lot of money and quickly. He won't try anything illegal, like robbery or blackmail, because that would draw scrutiny from the regular police, which he needs to avoid. Based on his psychological profile and some of his past activities, we figure he'll attempt to replace the money with casino winnings. He's made money that way before. We're coordinating an operation with MI6 to thwart that. They have an agent available who is himself = an adept gambler. If we can cut off that avenue, defection to our side will be his only alternative to prevent his untimely disappearance."

"You have everything in hand it seems. Where do I come in?" Morane asked.

"Something that may be nothing," Mathis said with a frown. "We've tapped his phone, of course, and since yesterday, Le Chiffre has been making calls, trying to find out the location of one Antoinette Vague."

Morane jogged his memory but came up blank. "Should I know that name?"

"I'd be surprised if you did. She's a clerk for a glassmaker's shop in Toulouse. Unmarried. Her father died fighting in the war; her mother passed away two years ago from an illness. No brothers or sisters. She is not wealthy and doesn't own any property other than the family home. We haven't found anything particularly notable about her."

"Not that it's a common name, but how do you know that she's the Antoinette Vague he's looking for?"

"Timing. Her name appeared in an obituary in a provincial newspaper last week. Not her obituary, I might add, but her uncle's, Henri Leblanc. Leblanc recently died in prison from cancer. The obituary mentioned Mademoiselle Vague as his last living relative. We presume Le Chiffre came across it somewhere and now wants to find her. We have no idea for what reason."

"Perhaps it's not her but her connection to someone else that he's interested in. Nothing notable about the parents either?" Mathis shook his head. "Why was her uncle in prison?"

Mathis' voice took on a dark tone when he answered, "He was a member of the Vichy regime."

To most in France, the Vichy regime was another term for *Nazi collaborator*, a governing body of French citizens controlling the lower half of the occupied country on behalf of Germany during the war. It was a shameful chapter of France's history and, after the war, the members of the regime were put on trial and either executed or given long prison sentences.

Mathis leaned against the railing, looking into the water below again. "My superiors think it's strange that he's looking for her, but they believe that an investigation would distract from our current operation. They won't authorize any resources to look into it. It may be nothing, but it's certainly a coincidence that it's happening now."

"And you hate coincidences," Morane added.

Mathis hesitated and turned to face Morane. "I need a favor."

Morane grinned. "*Quelle surprise.*"

Mathis at least had the decency to look abashed. "I'm asking you to look into this Antoinette Vague as an outside consultant, shall we say. There can't be any hint of involvement from our agency, which might otherwise alert the Soviets before we have a chance to act. Will you help?"

"I believe you already knew the answer before you asked the question," Morane said.

Mathis visibly relaxed. "You'll be acting alone, but so will Le Chiffre. He can't involve his side without risking exposure. Still, don't underestimate him. It may take him a little longer to track her down, but I have no doubt he will find her. He may have a trusted man or two, but he'll need to keep things small and quiet."

"Hopefully he won't hire an outside consultant, too," Morane added with a chuckle.

Toulouse was founded as an outpost of the Roman empire and has had a storied history since then. It was very French, but the influx of Spaniards and Italians fleeing fascist regimes of their countries in the 1920s and 30s combined to give the city a unique culture and cuisine. Morane was not there to sightsee, however.

He parked his car in front of the address provided by Mathis. The street was cobble-stoned, tree-lined and quiet, and the house was a quaint bungalow. The exterior could do with a fresh coat of paint, but the small garden at the side of the house was well-tended. He went through the wrought iron gate and knocked on the front door. A pretty blonde, perhaps twenty, wearing a navy-blue skirt and white blouse, opened it and regarded him closely through intelligent blue eyes.

"*Oui*?"

"*Bonjour*, Mademoiselle," Morane said to her. "My name is Robert Morane. I work for *Reflets* magazine. Are you Mademoiselle Antoinette Vague?"

"I am," she replied in a soft voice. "Why would you want to speak to me?"

Morane had given a lot of thought on the drive to Toulouse as to how he wanted to approach the situation. He suspected that Henri Leblanc was the key somehow, but he had no idea what to look for and no idea how to direct his questions. He'd decided to keep things as open-ended as possible and honest.

"I'm writing a retrospective on the families of some members of the Vichy regime." Well, relatively honest.

"I see. My uncle," she said, impassively.

"Yes," Morane replied. "My condolences, by the way."

She shrugged. "We weren't close."

She continued to apprise him and finally came to a decision. "I'm just about to head to market. You can ask your questions while I shop. And you will carry my bags."

She did not wait for him to respond but grabbed her purse and closed the door, walking past him without waiting to see if he followed. Bemused, Morane trailed behind her, oblivious to a dark panel van parked in the street in front of the neighbor's house.

"I last saw my uncle when I was eight," Antoinette said, examining some fruit at a produce stall. "My father was a carpenter but joined the French army when the invasion became certain. He died in a mortar attack when the Nazis advanced through Belgium. My mother took it hard. Her brother, my uncle, was not a very good example for me, and she cut off all contact with him when he joined the Vichy administration." She selected some apples and held the bag out to Morane, which he took without comment.

"What did your uncle do before?" Morane asked.

"Uncle Henri got a geology degree from the Sorbonne. He was the first in our family to get a university degree and they were all very proud of him. He was employed by various mining companies, mainly working in the Pyrenees mountains along the Spanish border." She handed him small bags of asparagus and potatoes and stuffed two baguettes in with the apples.

"How did he get involved in Vichy?"

Antoinette sighed, motioning to a nearby bench by a small grassy area in the market square. They sat down and she lit a cigarette, offering one to him which he declined.

"From what I understand, the mining business was already tight on the Spanish side of things with Franco in power before the war. It came to a stop when Hitler's troops rolled into France. With no work, he had to move in with us. He did odd jobs when he could but we depended on mother doing laundry and cleaning to support us." She took a long drag of her cigarette, her mind a decade in the past.

"I've read that some who joined the Vichy government justified it as preserving the French way of life as much as possible under Nazi rule. For others, it was a chance to obtain personal power. Or just a regular paycheck. I don't know about my uncle's reasons as she forbade me to talk to him." Her hand trembled slightly as she ground out the cigarette on the arm of the bench.

"My mother worked her hands to the bone. Losing my childhood during the war was bad enough but I had to grow up fast when she became sick. I took typing and shorthand courses because I did not want that fate for me. Now I'm alone, and stuck here, in the same town that my mother lived in her entire life. I've never been anywhere else."

"You seem to be a very capable, very self-assured young lady," Morane said.

"With no prospects of any kind," she replied.

They stood and shopped a bit more and then made their way back to the bungalow, Morane burdened by numerous grocery bags. He still had no inkling as to why she would be of interest to Le Chiffre.

When they got to the front door, it was ajar.

Morane quietly put the bags down on the front stoop and peered in cautiously. There was no one there but a small desk in the foyer had obviously been rifled through, papers scattered on the floor. He motioned for Antoinette to stay outside, but she followed him in. They saw a chunky malacca cane leaning against the wall inside the front door.

The front room to the left was empty, with books and more papers strewn about. The door to the right==a bathroom or bedroom perhaps—was closed. Morane looked through the open doors first. He crept down the short hallway and peeked in an empty kitchen. Then, he heard a muffled yelp behind him. He turned and saw a stocky man, who must have quietly come from the room to the right, grab Antoinette around the neck, dragging her backwards out the front door. She struggled uselessly. Morane lunged forward, but a tall grey-faced man sprang out of the same room between them and brought him up short.

"Grab him too," the stocky man shouted, shoving Antoinette into the rear of the black panel van.

The tall man confidently took a step towards Morane. He made a feint with his left hand and then swung with his right. Morane blocked it as he ducked and sent an uppercut to the man's jaw. His punch was blocked as well, and the man took a step back, measuring Morane now. He stepped forward once more and directed a roundhouse kick to the side of Morane's head. Morane countered with another block, swung his arm to catch the leg, and then gave a vicious elbow to the man's knee, eliciting a grunt of pain from him as he fell.

Before Morane could press his advantage, he was hit in the head with the cane from the stocky man who'd come back into the house. Morane dropped to one knee and struggled to remain conscious. The cane swung again and he slipped into darkness.

The men picked up his body and dumped it into the back of the van, slamming the rear door shut. They climbed in and sped off.

When Morane came to, he found his wrists and ankles tied to a chair in a dusty, dimly lit room. He shook his head to clear his vision fully and saw Antoinette similarly restrained in another chair beside him, still unconscious. The smell of chloroform lingered in his nostrils. He gave a couple of strong tugs at his ropes but they held firm. The chair was sturdy and unyielding. He looked around the fair-sized room. Other than the chairs they were tied in, the only other piece of furniture was a simple table. He noticed his wallet sitting on the table. Obviously, he'd been searched when unconscious. There was broken glass and debris scattered around the wooden floor. There was a door, closed, and a window, broken and covered with tar paper held in place by two nailed boards. There were enough holes in the paper to allow light to stream in, but it was a fading light as evening was obviously approaching. He could not hear traffic or the typical sounds of town so he assumed they were somewhere in the countryside.

Antoinette slowly awakened. "Where are we?"

Before Morane could answer, the door opened and three men walked in. He recognized the tall man he fought and the stocky man with the cane as their kidnappers. He felt a small measure of satisfaction as the tall man was limping slightly from the blow to his knee. He carried an unlit kerosene lantern and put it on the table, taking a moment to scowl at Morane.

The third man was well-dressed, clean-shaven, pale and below average height but he held himself with the confidence of a larger man. He dusted off a spot on the corner of the table and sat down on it, lighting the lantern with a match.

"I hope Basil and Kratt were not too rough on you," he said, nodding to the kidnappers, his voice soft and even. "I need you able to answer my questions. I

435

will introduce myself. My name is Le Chiffre."

He picked up the wallet and sifted through the contents, ignoring the money. He held up the press identification for *Reflets*. "Humph, a journalist. No telling what he knows. You did well to take him too," he said to his men. He tossed everything aside, turning back to Antoinette.

"Explanations are in order. It's a matter of history that the Nazis looted France of many of its treasures during the war. Artwork, statues, books, jewels... Thousands of artifacts were taken from museums, libraries, homes. Goering was especially enthusiastic about collecting. In the last years of the war, these riches were transported to Austria and hidden in salt mines, where the Nazis hoped to recover them in the future. However, the Allies found the mines and seized control of them at the end of the war. But here is something that history does not know. Not everything was sent to Austria.

"I find the Nazis a fascinating subject," he continued. "Germany, a country left devastated after World War I, rises from the ashes to threaten all of Europe a mere twenty years later. The archives I've read describe men who are certainly flawed, but they let nothing stand in the way of their accumulation of power. I like to think I can identify with them.

"Some time ago, I came across a water-damaged journal in a box of records recovered from a chalet occupied by the Nazis. The journal was kept by a *Hauptmann* Kruger, a member of Goering's staff. It took painstaking effort to piece together his notes. He was a coordinator of the truck convoy taking the stolen treasure to Austria. Apparently, he did not believe in putting all the eggs in one basket.

"Without Goering's knowledge, he secretly diverted part of those treasures in the other direction, west. The journal mentioned a geologist in the Vichy government who was familiar with hiding places in the mines near the Spanish border, one Henri Leblanc." The smile on Le Chiffre's face was devoid of all warmth.

"Like Goering, Kruger was convicted at the Nuremberg trials and, also like Goering, he committed suicide before he could be hanged. Your uncle would have been the last living person to know where those treasures are but he was inaccessible. Now, even that source is lost to me."

He leaned in close to Antoinette, the false smile fading. "Your uncle must have left journals, notes, letters... Something that reveals where that hiding place is. Where are they?"

"He left nothing," she replied defiantly.

"He must have!" Le Chiffre straightened up slowly and looked down at her. He suddenly backhanded her across the face. Morane strained against his bonds, but they held.

"I really don't have a lot of time," Le Chiffre said, leaning in again, his face inches from hers. "Perhaps a trade, Mademoiselle. The whereabouts of your uncle's papers in exchange for a promise not to torture you. And him." He motioned to Morane.

"I will give you a little time to consider my offer. A very little." He turned and walked towards the door, his two henchmen falling in behind him.

"How's the knee?" Morane asked the tall man before he reached the door. "I guess you won't be kicking anyone in the head with that leg for a while." He put on the smuggest grin he could manage and then braced himself.

The man snarled and then lunged forward, whipping his leg around and kicking Morane in the side of the head, tipping the chair over on its side. Morane rolled his head slightly to counter the full force of the kick, but allow enough contact so the momentum would cause the chair to tip over sideways. As it was, he felt that kick all the way down his spine, the crash to the floor exacerbating the shock.

"Basil!" exclaimed Le Chiffre. "You can play later! Pick him up." He righted Morane's chair roughly. Morane managed to conceal the piece of glass from the floor in the palm of his hand. They left.

Morane rolled his head, trying to shake the cobwebs free. He managed to shift the shard of glass in his hand and started sawing at the rope holding his wrist in place. It was awkward and he winced as the shard also cut into his hand.

"Did you know about these men?" Antoinette asked. "It seems a bit too much of a coincidence." She flinched a bit as her lip started to swell.

"I can't tell you how, but I knew he was looking for you; I just didn't know why," Morane said, continuing to work the edge of the glass into the rope. "I didn't realize the lengths he would go. I'm sorry. My only priority now is to get you to safety."

"I... I don't know what to tell them," she said softly. "Anything my uncle left behind, my mother burned."

Morane freed his wrist and quickly began working on the other one. It went faster as he was now able to apply more leverage. When the second wrist was freed, he discarded the shard and began working on the knots at his ankles. The cut on his hand stung as he untied them. Free, he stood and shook the circulation back into his limbs. Quietly, he moved the chair to the door and set it under the doorknob. He hurried back to Antoinette and began to work her knots.

The doorknob rattled, followed by shouting from the other room and banging on the door. Morane redoubled his efforts, managing to free her one arm and leg before the old door collapsed.

Basil stumbled into the room, but tripped over the chair and jostled the table. The lamp smashed to the floor and the kerosene soaked the debris on the floor, immediately starting it on fire.

Kratt stood in the doorway and raised his cane towards Morane. Morane earlier suspected it was a sword cane, based on its impractical size and heft. The way he held it though...

Not a sword. A concealed gun!

There was a sudden loud roar as some nearby tar paper erupted in flame, startling Kratt. The cane wavered and a muffled shot hissed past Morane's face.

Morane rolled and hefted the table, half on fire, towards the men, forcing them back out of the room as the fire spread to the door frame. He glimpsed Le Chiffre in the outer room, his face twisted in rage. He saw them run out of the front door of the house as the dried wood of the wall became engulfed in flames.

He turned to Antoinette who'd slumped back in her chair, pain on her face as blood seeped from a wound in her shoulder from the wild shot. Morane desperately clawed at the ropes on the remaining arm and leg.

Finally freeing her, he stood her up and guided her to the window as fire climbed to the ceiling. He ripped a board free and pulled down the tar paper. He lifted her out first and then dove out of the window, just as the roof collapsed. They scrambled away from the house into the tall grass. In the background, they heard the van speeding away.

Morane tore a piece from his shirt and pressed it on the wound to stop the bleeding. She gritted her teeth, letting out a small whimper.

"You can't go back home right now," Morane said. "Matters should resolve themselves soon, but it's not safe for you there."

"I have nowhere else to go," Antoinette said.

Morane thought a bit. "I have some contacts in Paris that might have an opening for a self-assured woman with secretarial skills," Morane said. "You survived this; it won't kill you to experience what else the world has to offer," he added with a grin.

Le Chiffre, dressed meticulously in a dark double-breasted suit, walked through the front entrance of the Casino Royale. The smell of smoke still seemed to linger in his nostrils from the debacle two days ago. He closed his eyes briefly, calming himself and preparing himself mentally. He then made his way to the baccarat table.

"There's your quarry," Mathis said to the man beside him, observing from the bar. "Good luck."

Bond grinned, finished his vodka martini, and made his way to the same table.

*Harry Dickson is now well-known to our readers. Only two women in the entire series seem to have broken through the American detective's tough emotional armor and touched his heart: the notorious Georgette Cuvelier, a.k.a. The Spider, and Minerva Campbell, an avenging character who appeared in #114,* Le Châtiment des Foyle *(The Punishment of the Foyles) (1934), and whose grave our hero visits at the start of this story...*

## Nigel Malcolm: *Sow the Wind*

*December 1945*

The rain clouds and the dampness in the air made the town colder and darker than it would otherwise have been at three o'clock in the afternoon. Harry Dickson kept his umbrella over him as he walked into the churchyard.

The rain was more like fine spray, and the umbrella was almost useless against it, but Dickson did not want to be recognized, even though he knew that there was probably no one around here who could identify him. And even if they did, would they really care? He doubted any professional criminals would be following him anymore. After what Europe had been through recently, everyone was tired of all the death and damage that had been meted out over the last six years.

A service was taking place inside the church. The lights were on, illuminating a stained-glass window, as well as the plain glass windows round the side of the building. Clearly, a bomb had exploded nearby, causing the damage to the windows that had been there before, and the church could not afford stained-glass replacements. Nobody had any money anymore.

Could that mean a bomb had exploded in the graveyard? Dickson's pace quickened as he walked around the side of the church to the gravestones located there.

Fortunately, no. Everything was more or less as he remembered it. Including the grave he had come to visit.

He stopped for a moment and folded down his umbrella. He fumbled with it, as well as the bunch of flowers he had brought with him. He did not want the flowers to get damaged because he had handled them clumsily. If anyone had been tailing him, he felt that he must be giving the appearance of a shambling middle-aged man.

Organ music and a congregation's singing drifted through the air. The carol sounded familiar, but it was not anything he had heard since school chapel. *Once in Royal David's City.* Something like that.

Now feeling better composed, Dickson approached the grave he had come to visit.

439

*Minerva Campbell.*
*Rest in peace.*

"Hello again," he said, laying the flowers in front of the headstone. "Sorry I haven't been able to visit over the past few years. I've been very busy."

He remained silent for a moment.

"So has the entire continent. It is astonishing how far people will go to find ways to kill other people," he added. "You'd have thought I would be completely used to it by now—especially after the War. And yet, I can still be surprised at humanity's capacity for inhumanity. You should have seen what I saw only a couple of weeks ago…"

*East Berlin, two weeks prior*

The convoy of Soviet troops moved north-east, away from the ruins of Germany's capital city into a countryside that seemed incongruous by contrast.

In one of the cars, Harry Dickson looked out at the greenery.

"If we look at the countryside, it is almost as if war never happened," said Lieutenant Dimitri Klebb who was sat opposite the investigator, between two subordinate officers.

"I know it happened," said Dickson without looking away.

Klebb nodded wisely.

"Yes, but at least nature hasn't been affected by wars of men," he said.

Professor Bernard Quatermass was sitting in the same car, blowing into an unlit pipe.

"Not out here perhaps, though I shudder to think how the natural world might be affected by radiation in the aftermath of an atomic bomb," he said.

"Admittedly, we know little about the effects of atomic radiation," said Klebb, "but I can say this, Professor: Nature always finds a way."

Quatermass seemed mildly taken aback, and amused, by this response from the army lieutenant. Dickson looked round at him with an air of approval in his eyes. He liked this young officer. He was sharp, observant, and when his superior officers weren't around, precocious. Klebb was also well educated—he had taken a degree in Botany before being drafted into the army.

Klebb, knowing that he was the most senior of the three soldiers in the car, continued to explain himself to the two British specialists in his care: "Given time, nature will evolve and adapt. Man has to work hard to keep nature at bay."

"Some might argue that man has already mastered nature through agriculture, and prospered as a result," said Quatermass.

Klebb smiled—an unusual thing to see a Russian doing.

"Perhaps," he said, "but under certain circumstances, nature can take over once more. Man's biggest advantage is that he is faster, that is all."

"Oh, nonsense! Man is also cleverer!" said Quatermass.

The car pulled over into the enclosure. It followed two other trucks and another staff car.

"Perhaps," said Klebb.

The five passengers got out of their car. The Nazis' secret base, half an hour's drive from Berlin, had been captured by Soviet forces and was now under their investigation. There were a few temporary huts and a concrete structure further away which must have served as a port for vehicles landing and taking off vertically. In the opposite direction, close to the underground entrance, were some glass houses filled with plants and trees. Even from this distance, they looked like they had been collected from exotic locations.

Dickson took all of this in, and then looked behind him at the rural surroundings. Soon Klebb was standing there with him.

"Something wrong, Mr. Dickson?"

The detective looked round at him.

"Wouldn't one normally hear birds singing out here?"

Klebb looked at the fields beyond. "Yes, one would," he replied.

"You're a keen observer of nature, Klebb. Would you say that birds and other creatures have a sense for when something evil is nearby?"

"Yes. Absolutely. Even I can sense it," replied the officer, looking at the glass houses.

Dickson noticed Klebb stiffen and stand to attention. Captain Kronsteen, the group leader, strode up to them.

"The site is safe and secure, Mr. Dickson," said the young captain. "We will now go into the underground tunnels."

Dickson nodded.

They walked towards the entrance. Quatermass was already there, surrounded by troops, two of whom were using Geiger counters.

Several soldiers managed to force open the metal door that sealed off the entrance, and the party cautiously walked down the steps into the subterranean network of tunnels.

As they walked, Dickson could sense something very nasty about this place. He had spent his entire career—and invested his entire identity—in his skill for using his five senses to reason out the environment around him, without any problematical sixth sense. Yet, there was no other way to explain it. An intuitive feeling told him that something evil had happened here and lingered on. *It is all in the mind,* he thought. *Try to ignore it.*

The group walked through the tunnels. They passed a few bicycles that were stacked up against a concrete wall. If bikes were needed to get around this network, then clearly it was much larger than the group had initially expected.

They walked past a room that Dickson quickly glanced into with his flashlight. It was an office of some sort. He would look through it more thoroughly later after exploring the rest of this complex.

He continued onwards with Quatermass and the others stepping deeper into the complex, until they came into a large room. The beams of the party's flashlights danced around this space. Flashing over two large smooth objects, one in the center of the room, and another in the far right corner. There was a small cluster of furniture in the other corner.

Then one of the soldiers must have found a power generator and got it working because the complex's lights came on overhead.

In the middle of the room, on a raised platform, was a bell-shaped flying saucer. In the corner, there was a second saucer.

The two British investigators stood there, taking in this sight. Inwardly shuddering as they remembered saucers appearing out of thin air and crashing over London during the war.

Quatermass was the first to speak.

"I wondered what I'd feel when I saw one of those again."

"So did I, Professor," said Dickson.

There was a hole in the side of the craft, as though something had burst out from inside. Twisting the metal and warping the swastika painted on the outer hull.

Quatermass seemed to brace himself and walk up to the saucer on the raised platform. Some of the Russians were using Geiger counters to see if it was radioactive.

Klebb was far enough away from his commanding officer, and near enough to Dickson, to lean over to him and ask a question.

"Is there really a risk of radiation?"

"Not really. The saucers that came to London and survived the journey were not powered by any atomic technology. This is just a precaution," the detective answered.

Across the room, Quatermass looked round at the others. "The craft is safe. I'm going in," he said.

The rocket scientist cautiously went up to the hole in the side of the craft and peered in.

Dickson walked over to join him. Klebb and Captain Kronsteen reluctantly followed on behind, stepping through the crowd of soldiers who were redundantly pointing guns at the craft.

Quatermass ran his fingers carefully along the ragged edges of the hole.

"This was created by something inside trying in order to get out," he said, tapping on the surface around the rupture. "The warp flight process altered the structure of the materials. The aluminum might have been reshaped shortly after it came out of the warp field." He examined it further. "Yes, yes, when it came out of warp, its structure was weak enough to burst on contact with the environment it arrived in."

The Professor borrowed a flashlight from a nearby soldier and shone it inside the craft. It was completely empty.

"It might be possible that whoever or whatever was inside combusted, but I would still find it difficult to believe they would combust with such force they would cause this much damage. Even if the atomic structure of the metal has been temporarily altered," he said.

Dickson looked around at the rest of this hangar-sized room. The second flying saucer looked intact. Either its test flight had been successful, or it had not been tested. He also saw a few sticks of office furniture in the other corner, including a makeshift wooden noticeboard. He walked up and examined the sheets of paper pinned on it.

"These charts indicate they intended *Kraft 6* for a flight upwards. Far upwards," he said, before realizing the full significance. "Into space."

Captain Kronsteen and Quatermass joined him and studied the charts.

"Yes. I think it is a planned space flight," said Kronsteen.

Quatermass looked at the board, then glanced back at the damaged saucer.

"Yes, I agree. Of course, that explains it," he said, before turning to his rapt audience. "That saucer is *Kraft 6*. It must have gone into outer space. Outside the Earth's atmosphere. Now, it might have ruptured because the structure of the metal was altered in warp drive, causing the air to escape. Alternatively, the craft's structure just couldn't cope with the conditions of outer space. We don't really know for certain what's up there."

His audience was surprised. "Hopefully, one day we will be able to go up there and find out," added Quatermass, smiling to himself.

Captain Kronsteen spoke. "The Germans' V2 rockets were the first to travel beyond the Earth's atmosphere. They did not seem to be affected by being in outer space."

"That could be because the V2s weren't above the atmosphere for long enough," replied Quatermass, rubbing his chin, before adding: "No, I think you are absolutely right, Captain. Yes, I'm inclined to think that the saucer's structural integrity was damaged by the warp drive process. But what an intriguing possibility. I wonder if the Germans would have traveled to the Moon in these? Or Venus? Or Mars? There might be some proof around here somewhere. I'd like to find out."

Then Kronsteen interjected: "Well, if we find any evidence, we must find it in the next few hours. Our mission is to secure this site. Let's proceed with that."

He strode off, giving out orders to the rest of his men.

"I'll look through that office we passed. There may be some useful information there," said Dickson.

"And I'll examine the two saucers," said Quatermass.

Over the next hour or so, the squad scouted and searched above and below the site. Meanwhile, Dickson went to that little office and riffled through the filing cabinets, searching for documents of interest, discarding some and stuffing others into the kit bag he had brought with him.

443

He occasionally looked up through the office's open door and saw soldiers carrying various pieces of equipment back and forth. Well, he and Quatermass were in Russian occupied territory. He knew it had not been easy for Control to negotiate their inclusion in this party with their Soviet counterparts. They had no jurisdiction here. They were only really allowed here for a few hours, on Captain Kronsteen's sufferance, to complete their investigation. Could Soviet scientists use this technology? Yes, they could, as much as British, American, and French scientists would if they got their hands on it. Dickson was not sure if this would really be of benefit to the nations of the world. However, he would take what he could and deliver a report as comprehensive as possible to Control. At least, they would know what to watch out for.

Suddenly, a soldier's scream echoed through the tunnels. Dickson almost dropped the documents in his hands. He then heard shouting and footsteps. The shouting became shrill.

It sounded genuine, though he knew it could be a ruse. He also knew that all sorts of evil could have happened in this place, and he may have to leave it quickly. He hurriedly stuffed the papers he had accumulated into his kit bag, slung it onto his shoulder, and then left the office to see what was causing the commotion.

Dickson strode down the corridor, and turned right towards the entrance, which was crowded with troops. He tried to see through the crowd. Some soldiers stood aside and let him through.

In front he saw Quatermass, Kronsteen, and Klebb.

"I don't believe it!" said Quatermass, almost rasping.

In front of them was a large plant. It stood on top of the body of a soldier who was now clearly dead.

"It's still moving!" shouted Klebb.

The plant lashed out some sort of long thin tongue at another soldier. The man screamed in agony and collapsed. Several soldiers started firing at the thing, in panic—without any effect.

"Retreat!" shouted Kronsteen.

The surviving Russians all scurried backwards, almost carrying Dickson with them.

As they turned left back round the corner, Kronsteen shouted at his men to barricade the corridor with any furniture they could find.

Further up the corridor, Dickson, Quatermass and Klebb regrouped.

"Was that thing—some kind of plant? I didn't see it properly," said Dickson.

"Yes," answered Klebb, "It was a plant of some kind."

"But I saw it moving.... *Walking*," said Quatermass.

Klebb nodded: "Yes," he said.

Quatermass seemed very resilient to this turn of events. He composed himself and started to theorize, a quality Dickson had noticed the rocket scientist was preternaturally good at doing.

"Some kind of plant-animal hybrid perhaps?" Quatermass asked.

"I would say that it is completely a plant. Even though it is capable of movement," said Klebb.

"It seemed to kill the soldiers with that... 'stinger' coming out of its head," said Dickson. "Am I correct?"

The other two nodded their agreement.

"There are at least two other soldiers, near the entrance. Those poor wretches died screaming in pain. At least, they died quickly."

Dickson put a hand on Quatermass's arm for a moment. Then he started theorizing too.

"I do not think that that plant can have been developed by the Germans. They may have found them, or something similar, elsewhere."

Klebb glanced round to check no one else could hear him, and leaned closer to the two British investigators.

"We have had intelligence that the German scientists had discovered them. Probably from somewhere hotter and drier. We do not know if they have been engineered by the Germans, but it is possible," he said.

"It makes me wonder what else they have lying around here," said Quatermass, looking further down the tunnel that seemed to go on for miles.

Captain Kronsteen marched up to them. Klebb stood to attention.

"What are you all doing here? Just chatting?" he asked, sternly.

"We were assessing the situation to work out what that plant thing is, and how to deal with it," said Dickson, partly to prevent Klebb from getting into trouble with his superior officer.

"It is hostile and deadly. That's what it is," said Kronsteen.

The Captain turned to the Lieutenant and snapped some orders in Russian. Klebb presumably said "Yes sir", saluted, and scurried over to the barricade to help the others.

Dickson was aware he and Quatermass weren't supposed to know what had been said. The detective had been taught ancient Greek at school, which helped him to work out what was often said around him in Russian. But his lessons had been a very long time ago, and most of the time he could only guess without complete certainty.

"Captain, if that creature is unaffected by bullets, what about fire?" Dickson said to Kronsteen.

The Captain thought about this for a moment. "You are right. Fire might be our only option."

He quickly returned to the barricades and shouted some orders to the troops. Several soldiers moved to new positions. Some stood by to open up the barricade, while Klebb looked round to find something to use as a flaming torch.

Shouting statements to his fellow soldiers about what he was trying to do, Klebb made his way back to the office Dickson had been going through shortly before. The lieutenant saw a wooden chair. He broke it so that only the chair's back and its hind legs were left. He then scrunched up some papers around the tips of the legs and bound it on with some tape he found.

He came back out into the corridor where Kronsteen, Dickson and Quatermass were waiting.

"Do any of you have a light?" said Klebb.

"I do," said Quatermass, taking out a box of matches. "We'd better get to the barricade first."

They hurried back to the barricade, where the troops had cleared out of the way. Quatermass lit the double torch.

Some men pulled away the barricade and Klebb waved and jabbed the fire at the monstrous plant. It hissed and juddered angrily before moving backwards.

Slowly, over long minutes, the thing moved out of the underground faculty. Still rasping aggressively, with its stinger occasionally sticking out and in again, like a lizard's tongue.

Eventually, it was out in the open, in bright natural light, under metal grey skies, Klebb still driving it out in front, with Kronsteen, Quatermass, Dickson, and some of the soldiers following several meters behind. The plant was retreating to the glass house.

The party were all shocked to see four other plants like this, moving across from the glass house. Klebb most of all. Those plants were smaller, clearly in earlier stages of development. They were moving slowly and the smallest one was probably about chest height, but these smaller plants seemed somehow more freakish and frightening.

The stinger lashed out at Klebb's hand while he was distracted. He screamed in pain and dropped the torch, collapsing onto the ground. Another man quickly ran up and picked it up, continuing to wave the plant back. Then throwing the torch at it, causing it to catch fire.

Klebb lay there, first clutching his left hand, and then trying with supreme effort to get something out from inside his tunic.

Kronsteen had sprung into action, shouting orders to the rest of the men in Russian, sounding harsher that usual in order to snap them out of their stunned hesitation. They started to run to the vehicles they'd come in.

Quatermass went over to Klebb's body.

"What's going on? Aren't you going to give this man some medical attention? Where's your medical officer?"

Kronsteen looked round at him and Dickson.

"It is too late for Lieutenant Klebb. A pity. He would have had a great career in Military Intelligence. But we have to go now."

Kronsteen looked around at the plants. The large one was burning and dead. The smaller ones seemed to be keeping back. So he drew his revolver and pointed it at Dickson, who grimly accepted this new situation. Quatermass was appalled. Kronsteen continued.

"I am sorry, gentlemen, but I, too, have my orders. You will both stay here. Oh, and your bag, Mr. Dickson. Give it to me, please."

Dickson slowly took the kit bag off his shoulder and put it on the ground, as Kronsteen gestured with his gun.

Behind him, most of the convoy had already filed onto the trucks and the engines were revving up. One by one, they sped away. Kronsteen quickly picked up the kit bag full of papers.

"Thank you. It was a pleasure to know you—both of you," he said, before saluting and turning to stride back to his waiting car. The engine was clearly already running.

Quatermass knelt down by Klebb's corpse. There was an envelope in the young man's hand. He picked it up and realized it was actually two sealed envelopes—letters with addresses on them in Cyrillic.

"Professor," said Dickson, "I've just realized... The orders Kronsteen gave... He's set off a bomb. We're supposed to die in the blast."

Quatermass stood looking at Klebb's body, taking this is.

"He's set off a bomb, Quatermass!" said Dickson again.

"Right," said Quatermass, stuffing the two letters into his inside coat pocket. "It must be where the flying saucers are."

He hurried back into the tunnels, pausing only to grab a bicycle. Dickson followed him, becoming more aware that the rocket scientist was younger than him.

When he caught up with Quatermass in the main saucer workshop, he saw his colleague kneeling over a large device, fiddling with it in a way only an expert would.

"Is it a nuclear device?" Dickson asked, slightly out of breath.

"No," said Quatermass without looking up. "But it's the most powerful conventional bomb not to be. It could blow us both up, and those plants outside. No wonder the army left so quickly."

He flicked a switch and the bomb's countdown stopped.

"Why didn't I notice we came with this thing?" said Quatermass.

"Well, I didn't know either, and I pride myself on my observational powers. They deliberately hid the fact from us. And it wasn't as if we were in a position to ask too many questions."

He stood there in silence. Quatermass continued kneeling there in silence. He rubbed his face again.

"Although it might be best if I reset it to go off in, let's say, two hours. That should take care of all this technology and those plant-things outside. And give us enough time to get away."

447

"Yes, I agree," said Dickson. "Set it for one hour. We'll leave on these bicycles and get far enough away in time—assuming the bomb isn't supposed to reach as far as Berlin."

"Very well," said Quatermass, before carefully reattaching a wire, altering the timer, and flicking the switch back on.

"It's set. Let's go," he said, getting up, walking over to where Dickson was holding their bikes for them. They both peddled out of this big room.

They both dismounted when they reached the tunnel entrance. Walking and wheeling the bikes over the grass, looking out for the plant creatures. They were nearby, but not close enough to pose a threat to the two men.

When they had got to the nearby lane, they both remounted their bikes and peddled, with varying degrees of confidence, in the direction the motorcade had come from.


They reached the outskirts of Berlin just in time to hear the explosion in the distance. They watched in silence as the smoke rose into the air. The local inhabitants in the rumble-strewn streets around them murmured to each other. Clearly, this explosion triggered memories of the trauma from only a few months before.

The two men stood there in silence, watching the explosion and hearing the anxiety of the general public around them. Then, with unspoken agreement, they continued to ride on for a few more miles until they finally dismounted and left their bikes propped up against a wall two streets away from Checkpoint Charlie.

As they walked this last stretch of their journey back to the West, Quatermass saw a mailbox and was reminded of Klebb's letters. He pulled them out of his pocket and showed them to Dickson.

"Klebb really wanted someone to post these letters. Can you tell where they're addressed to?"

Dickson looked at the envelopes.

"One is addressed to his parents. The other is the name of a woman. Presumably his sweetheart. You may as well post them. I can't see there being any harm in it. At least, we will have done something for poor old Klebb," replied the detective.

Quatermass posted the letters and they trudged on to Checkpoint Charlie and West Berlin.


"I'll never understand why so many lives have to be wasted like this," said Dickson to Minerva's grave. "You would have thought that peace was an easier option than conflict, wouldn't you."

He looked around. The graveyard was getting dark, and he wanted to get home, away from this damp cold.

"Anyway, hopefully I'll have more mundane things to tell you about next year. Merry Christmas." He tipped his hat, turned, and walked away.

*This story requires a lengthier introduction. First, let's sort out the facts from the fiction. There was a French publisher named Bernard Grasset (1881-1955) in the 1930s; his sisters and associates did turn against him and tried to steal his company by portraying his various eccentricities as a form of madness; the matter came to court and Grasset won; also, he did publish Hitler's* Principes d'Action *(a collection of early speeches) in 1936—but he bravely refused to publish* Mein Kampf *in 1942, and also published noted antifa writers such as Ernst Glaser and Ernst Erich Noth. After the War, Grasset was arrested in September 1944 and imprisoned, but released a few weeks later due to his poor health. The Publishers' Union decided to ban him for life from publishing, along with several others, including the Nyctalope's creator, Jean de La Hire. Anecdotally, Grasset's right-hand man, Louis Brun, portrayed in this story, was murdered by his wife because of his many infidelities. Xavier Mauméjean has transplanted this bizarre tale from the annals of French publishing into a surreal universe where the scientists from* Radio-Terror *(a novel available from Black Coat Press) and other Golden Age SF characters are behind an epidemic of madness caused by that world's very own version of Hitler, the figure imagined by Charlie Chaplin...*

## Xavier Mauméjean: *The Recerebration Machine*

*"The public is used to the incredible... When one witnesses a new miracle every day, one quickly becomes jaded, and one stops paying attention..."*
Eugène Thébault – Radio-Terror.

*Paris, 1933*

In the early afternoon of September 20, 1933, the weather in Paris was superb; passersby strolled the boulevards, enjoying the last glories of summer.

Two men had just left the Office of Scientific Research on the Avenue des Champs-Élysées. One was short and slender, with stooped shoulders, graying hair and a pointed beard trimmed into an old-fashioned style; his name was Mazelier, and he was a well-known scientist. The other was a tall, gentleman who looked younger that his forty-two years, and who was carrying a large, black trunk. His name was Gribal and he was Mazelier's assistant. Both men had just left their workshop and were headed to Number 61, rue des Saints-Pères.

Paris was mostly quiet, and only a few explosions could occasionally be heard in the distance. *Ethernity*, from which the Plague originated, or the "hyperworlds" as the poet Paul Valéry had dubbed them, appeared to be peaceful for the moment.

The Plague had appeared in Paris at the turn of the century, at first unnoticed by its inhabitants, in the way that a degenerative disease sets in subtly and progresses in a barely noticeable fashion. Ultimately, everyone had fallen prey to it, because everyone had an imagination. Before the Plague, people tended to remember things the way they had experienced them. Occasionally, someone might indulge in a small error, such as remembering the location of one's favorite café on Boulevard Raspail as being located on Garges-les-Gonesse or erasing the memory of an irritating old uncle from one's memory of a family banquet. But that was as far as it went.

However, once infected by the Plague, which had come from these "hyperworlds," a man's imagination became unbound. It seized upon the contents of the brain and created images in improbable combinations, distorting and twisting the actual memories and total fantasies, without the victims even realizing that it had happened. Indeed, the Plague might have even gone unnoticed if these mental aberrations hadn't actually impacted everyone in their daily lives, turning every Parisian into an uncontrolled reservoir of fantasy. All it took was for a single person to speak, whether in a café, in their own home or even at the National Assembly, for his illusions to spread, multiply, and be completely taken at face value.

Newspaper vendors, sidewalk merchants, knife sharpeners, window glaziers, florists, mattress salesmen, bus conductors, gas workers, men handing out leaflets, dumpster divers who could turn trash into treasure, even astrologers and fortune-tellers, pulling the days' predictions out of their bags of tricks, had all become carriers of the epidemic.

"By just using the telephone or the telegraph, from one person to the next, in the course of the day, causes everyone to end up contaminated," Mazelier had diagnosed.

This had been closely studied as early as in 1909 by the great Maurice Renard in his celebrated essay "Of Scientific Marvels and Their Role in the Understanding of the Plague Affecting Our Imagination." In it, the famous author and scholar had spoken of the "scenic development of the paradox," the "acting paraphrase of the metaphor," and even contemplated the "implementation of imaginary solutions." The booklet had become an instant bestseller, as everyone wanted to understand what was happening. The writer had even lent his name to a coveted literary prize; but, as the years passed, Parisians learned to live with the Plague, and the Maurice-Renard Award was finally canceled in 1932.

Since the beginning of the year, however, something new, subtle, and evil, had wafted through the streets of the French capital. It had started exactly on January 30, Professor Mazelier believed, and he even had an idea about what it was, but still lacked evidence. His intuition, backed up by subtle calculations, had indicated that the "waves" that were poisoning the Parisian atmosphere came from the state of Tomainia. Their malevolent effect had become more ap-

450

parent on the 8th of the month with their sinister attack on the ceremonies celebrating Alfred Jarry's birth.

Until then, on every such day, the legendary Doctor Faustroll and his assistants, the eccentric Palotins once linked with the King of Poland, had been satisfied to merely mark the occasion with crude pranks, such as purging the sewers with *merdre* pumps in order to smear national monuments, or by taking part in the *Tour de France* in order to restage the Passion in an uphill bicycle race. Civil, military and religious authorities were shocked, but the public approved. Sometimes, it takes very little to amuse the masses.

Since the beginning of the month, however, the Palotins had been transformed into living bombs. These colorful rabbit-headed beings, eating through a hinge and peeing through a tap, who breathed by means of a curved tube, were now blowing themselves up in public places by simply willing it. Thus, they had destroyed the brasserie of La Coupole, the Café d'Harcourt, and the famous White Russian restaurant *Au Poisson d'Or*, killing several genuine and fake princes and dukes.

This, and the creeping miasma coming from Tomainia, explained why Professor Mazelier and Engineer Gribal were on the move that day.

As they reached the Rue des Saints-Pères, Gribal found himself daydreaming in front of an antique shop. *Here's a chest of drawers that would please Madame*, he mused, *and would look great in our apartment on the Rue Boissy-d'Anglas.* But their fourteen-year-old son, Roger, would end up damaging it, and their eighteen-year-old daughter, Paulette, had no use for such bourgeois comforts. At any rate, it was certainly beyond the means of a mere engineer, even one employed by the Office of Scientific Research.

"We've arrived, my dear Gribal," said Mazelier.

They stood before Number 61, facing a dilapidated, dirty and ugly *porte cochère*. Master and student passed beneath the archway and announced themselves to an elderly man wearing a black skullcap and lustrous sleeves, seated behind a grilled window. Gribal noticed that the concierge was using a Sergent-Major pen to address large, thick envelopes to be used for sending review copies of books. The Engineer made a throat-clearing rumble that quickly degenerated into a cough, forcing the concierge to reluctantly look up from his task.

"Yes, what do you want?" asked the old man.

"Professor Mazelier and Engineer Gribal to see Monsieur Grasset."

"Is he expecting you?"

"Yes; I believe he is."

The old man reminded Gribal of Père Bibent, the surly concierge at the Office of Scientific Research. Just then, a clerk wearing in a long gray frock came out of the shipping department. The concierge hailed him from behind his counter:

"Monsieur Muller, these people are here to see the boss. Take them to Monsieur Brun."

451

"It's upstairs to the left," said the clerk.

Mazelier and Gribal followed him, climbing a dirty, dark, narrow staircase. The air was thick with damp plaster and paper dust. The clerk stopped in front of a door bearing a sign reading *Director's Office*. He knocked, and the door opened immediately, as if someone had been waiting for them to arrive. *A theatrical effect worthy of a Boulevard play* thought Gribal.

"It's all right, Monsieur Muller. You can leave us now."

The man who greeted them was tall and massive with thinning blond hair; he had the sanguine cordiality of a southerner. His name was Louis Brun, and he was Bernard Grasset's oldest associate. They had met one afternoon in March 1907 on the Boulevard Saint-Germain. As they were both poor, they had shared a room on the Rue Cujas and there, decided to found a publishing house. Time had since turned their hopes into success.

Louis Brun was quick to welcome the two visitors.

"Weren't we supposed to meet Monsieur Grasset?" exclaimed Mazelier.

"Before you do, I'd like to tell you a couple of things…"

Gribal put down the black trunk that he had been carrying. It was obvious that it was hard for Louis Brun to speak, but when he began, everything gushed out of him in a torrent—a flood of concerns breaking through the dikes of propriety:

"Since September of last year, Monsieur Grasset has been missing. Or, rather, he literally disappears for months at a time! He's allegedly going to a spa. But without him as our captain, our boat is adrift, and will soon begin taking on water. I proposed to our Board of Directors that we should temporarily remove him from power, reinstating him only when he feels back to himself. But Grasset reacted by sending a registered letter to our bank asking them to cancel my ability to sign on our accounts. Since then, no one has been able to run our company! Worse yet, he sent a sixty-seven-page letter to former President Alexandre Millerand and several other personalities complaining that his family and associates were trying to dispossess him of his business! Now, they want to send him to a psychiatric clinic located on the Rue de la Glacière, where they'll put him in a straitjacket!"

"At least he won't go to Palavas-les-Flots!" said Gribal.

Louis Brun nodded, looking downcast.

"It's unfortunate to lose one's mind to such an extent. It's a sad thing to say this about a good friend, but I think he's gone bananas."

Professor Mazelier had listened with attention to Louis Brun's account. Methodically, he sought to clarify certain points.

"What are his symptoms?" he asked.

"He faints in the street, and when he's in the office, he spends hours on the phone crying, screaming and moaning," answered Monsieur Brun.

"I see… A highly emotional character, is he?"

"Grasset may be egocentric and stubborn, but he's been gifted with a subtle intelligence, always on the lookout for new talent! He's a visionary, and he'll leave his mark on our business, as others leave descendants!"

"If he gets the chance," Mazelier replied gloomily. "Is he taking any medication?"

"Too much!" lamented Louis Brun. "He's a hypochondriac, and a heavy drinker."

Mazelier and Gribal looked at each other.

"I called you last night," continued the Director, "after Monsieur Grasset collapsed at Lipp's. I was, myself, in the middle of dinner. It's bad for business to drop your face in a plate of soup in front of everyone!"

The Professor gestured to the Engineer to pick up the black trunk.

"There isn't a minute to lose," said Mazelier. "I must see the patient!"

Through an adjoining door, Louis Brun ushered them into Monsieur Grasset's office. At first glance, one might be struck by its austerity. The walls, with their opaque windows, were bare, except for a mediocre engraving of Marly, next to a filing cabinet with index cards of the authors, a glass cabinet with empty shelves, and an open safe containing nothing. On the mantelpiece was a painted wooden bust of a woman, her hair unfurled. The carpet, worn down to its threads, traced a sad path to the main desk, which was cluttered with a jumble of inkwells, penholders, ashtrays filled to the brim, and stacks of proofs scribbled on in large red pencil notes—the same kind of pen used by carpenters.

Bernard Grasset sat slumped behind it, his head lying on his ash-streaked forearms, resting on a leather blotter. A tiny amount of smoke rose from the cigarette holder that was planted in the corner of his mouth.

"Sir, you have a visitor," ventured Louis Brun.

He tried three more times to elicit a response, to no avail.

When the master of the house finally sat up, Mazelier and Gribal exchanged surprised glances. With his long brown locks tucked to one side and his moustache trimmed neatly to a small brush on his upper lip, they found themselves face to face with an almost perfect doppelgänger for Adenoïd Hynkel, Tomainia's gesticulating chancellor, elected on January 30 and now dictator.

"It can't be a coincidence," Mazelier muttered.

Overcoming his surprise, the Professor urged the Engineer to open the black trunk. Carefully, Gribal pulled out various components which, when assembled, formed a device consisting of a polished copper sphere surrounded by two rings bearing cursors, a dial with pointer, triode lamps, a rheostat, a capacitor and a transformer.

"Voilà!" said Gribal, as if presenting a music-hall act.

"What's all this?" inquired Louis Brun.

"A recerebration machine," answered Mazelier.

"Really?" said the Director, intimidated by the science behind it.

Sensing that his audience wanted to know more, the Professor continued his explanation:

"This machine was originally developed by Doctor Faustroll for the purpose of brainwashing..."

"The Doctor who...?" ventured Louis Brun.

"The same," interrupted Mazelier. "We don't know much about Doctor Faustroll. He claims to come from Circassia, where he was born in 1898, but always gives his age as sixty-three. He is known to have translated Ibicrates of Chios, the Geometer, and Sophrotatos the Armenian. Faustroll sent two letters to Lord Kelvin, discussing his calculations as to the surface of God, which the eminent British physicist considered to be delusional. But the fact remains that Doctor Faustroll is a genius."

"He sounds like a mad scientist!" exclaimed Louis Brun.

"Perhaps, my good sir," replied the Professor, "but a genius all the same. For genius, like rain, falls at random."

These strong words elicited silence. Mazelier finally continued:

"Back to the machine. I have reversed its effects with the assistance of my faithful Gribal, in order to treat nervous illnesses. All you have to do is apply these electrodes to the patient's head and subject him to a wave therapy that will cure the mental disorder."

Louis Brun glanced sadly at Monsieur Grasset.

"That would be wonderful, because, as you can see, he's sullen, apathetic... He acts as if he is drugged!"

It was time to act. Professor Mazelier launched into his preparatory exercises. He inhaled for a long time, then exhaled, several times, rubbing his palms until he felt energy flowing between his hands. Finally, he beckoned to Gribal, who immediately stood to attention.

"Playtime is over! Let's begin!"

With a broad sweep of his forearm, the Engineer swept away the clutter on the desk. He then grabbed Monsieur Grasset and slammed him onto the piece of furniture, while Mazelier loosened the hapless publisher's shirt collar and stuck a fountain pen between his teeth.

"That's so he doesn't swallow his tongue," he explained to Louis Brun.

Gribal attached electrodes to Grasset's temples.

"The machine is ready," he told the Professor.

Mazelier turned a knob, and immediately Grasset's body jerked with spasms.

"You don't want to put a strain on him," said Louis Brun.

The dial's needle oscillated, and Mazelier increased the flow of current. Grasset arched his back, ready to break.

"Aren't you worried he'll blow the circuit breaker?"

Keeping an eye on the triode lamps and the gyration of the sphere, Mazelier replied:

"This step is crucial. We need to induce a positive form of epilepsy in the subject, in order to restore his condition through successive shocks."

"The transformer is almost overloaded," said Gribal.

"We must continue," replied the Professor.

The air was now filled with the smell of ozone, mingling with a whiff of roasted pig. The needle on the dial was gyrating madly.

"Look at his eyes!" Mazelier suddenly exclaimed.

Initially oyster gray, Grasset's eyes had now turned blue and increased in brilliance. The publisher made a strangled gurgle and spat out the pen.

"P... poor..."

"Yes?"

"P... poor... Brun."

The Director's eyes filled with tears.

"Ah, my dear old friend, you are back with us at last!"

Monsieur Grasset smoothed his hair; his lips stretched into an ugly grimace. Then, speaking at first in a calm, nasal voice, he gradually began to shout:

"Yes, poor Brun who, for twenty-six years, has been calling me his friend while stabbing me in the back! A check forger, a handwriting trafficker! A scoundrel, who made a fortune selling rare editions, including five copies of *Swann's Way* printed on Japanese rice paper! A thief of first editions, all for the sake of a few luxuries in La Baule! Not to mention the fact that you've never been able to find a single talented writer, you nincompoop!"

Looking impassive, his tall stature making him resemble the statue of the Commander in *Don Juan*, Louis Brun turned to the Professor.

"Gentlemen, Monsieur Grasset appears to have recovered beyond all expectations. He can now resume his functions at the helm of his publishing house. We'll send a check to the Office of Scientific Research.

"Very well, then we'll leave you to catch up on things."

After packing the machine back into the trunk and going back out to the Rue des Saints-Pères, Gribal turned to Mazelier:

"A rather strange affair, Professor. Do you think it's a case of remote mind control, initiated by the dictator Hynkel?"

"God only knows, my good Gribal. Perhaps that tyrant is indeed trying to manipulate a French publisher into spreading his propaganda. But we can also assume that the Plague in Paris is caused by a simple effect of mimicry."

"It's true that their expressions of anger are perfectly identical," agreed the Engineer.

"In any case, we're not taking the Orient-Express to travel to Tomainia to put Adenoïd Hynkel on notice."

In the distance they heard the sound of an explosion, probably the echo of an attack perpetrated by the Palotins. Engineer Gribal smiled with confidence.

"Thanks to you, science has once again triumphed, Professor!"

The old scientist laughed dryly.

"Well, as you say, I've won! But to what extent? Having lived a long time, nothing surprises me any longer. That's why I have a feeling that the future probably holds many more surprises in store for us. Why not a xenobiotic invasion from Outer Space, alien life forms feeding on electricity, causing a world-wide blackout? Or, quite simply, a malignant radio source that would engender terror?"

"Then, we'd best be prepared."

"It's the best and only thing we can do, until tomorrow comes."

*Translated by Jean-Marc & Randy Lofficier.*

*I won't spoil this one with any prefatory comments, so just enjoy Bill Maynard's and his daughter's clever little tale of malice and snares…*

## William Patrick Maynard & Anna Victoria Maynard: *Malice and Snares*

San Francisco, 2023

"*Hello.*"

Sidney Thomas was conscious of blinking twice in the enveloping darkness. Did he hear a voice just now?

"*Hello.*"

The voice had not come from the darkness that surrounded him, but from somewhere within.

"Who's there?"

His own halting voice registered fear. He had not expected to find himself in total darkness. He had not expected to be able to hear, much less speak while submerged in the tank.

"*I am.*"

Somehow this answer was not reassuring. A voice inside his head he did not recognize was speaking to him. He consciously shut his eyes and tried to remind himself of the fact that he was floating in a sensory deprivation tank, but the knowledge of his physical state was separate from what he was experiencing. Sidney Thomas was elsewhere in total darkness and there was now a voice inside his head.

"*Why don't you use your legs?*"

The rage came in quick crimson strokes that seared across Sidney Thomas's mind.

"If you're inside my head, you know damn well that my legs are useless, dead."

"*Maybe out there, but not inside here. I'll show you.*"

There was a mocking tone to the voice, but suddenly, Sidney was aware of his body for the first time in the total darkness. He was aware of his legs for the first time since the accident had robbed him of their use. Yet here he was lifting them one after the other, feeling stiff muscles and tendons working after all these years of deadening numbness.

"*There. Nice, isn't it?*"

The mocking voice continued.

"No, no it isn't. I'm just a puppet. There's someone else inside my head moving my body or convincing my mind that I have a body to move. Is this death? Unending torture in total darkness while you play with what's left of my mind?"

*"I've wondered that myself. I've been in the darkness for so very long. Just my mind and no one else until you came along. For the longest time I wondered if I were God, but it felt too much like a prison for that. If nothing else, God, I am quite certain, is free."*

Sidney Thomas bent over and felt his legs with his hands. He commanded his body now...or at least he thought he did. Perhaps the voice in his head was sharing control with him the same way one handed over control of a presentation to another participant in an online meeting.

"This makes no sense. I'm alone in an isolation tank. How can you be inside my head?"

There followed a few seconds of silence as if the disembodied voice were choosing the next words carefully.

*"Physically, I am not with you inside your tank. Physically, I no longer exist. If indeed, I ever truly existed. I have inhabited many bodies through the centuries... so many bodies. They used to call me a phantom... a spirit of the times, but now I am alone... until you came along."*

The silence that followed this statement was somehow more terrifying than the words that were spoken. Sidney began to conclude that he was mad. He jumped with fright a few minutes later when the voice in his head unexpectedly resumed speaking.

*"When and where are we? Last time... it's been so long, but I slipped back to the 1870s... I should think. Was it Mexico? No, it was California. I'm still in California now, aren't I? You're not a Spaniard, not a Frenchman, nor a South African."*

"I... I'm an American. My family were English. Canadian English, not England proper. No one ever makes that distinction the way that they do with French Canadian. I don't know why I am telling you now. You are correct, we are in California. San Francisco to be precise. The year is 2023."

Sidney didn't know why he was treating any of this seriously. If he stopped being afraid of a voice in the dark, it was all quite laughable. He was conscious of his body and having a dialogue with himself while floating in an isolation tank. He had two voices co-existing within his mind. This must be the sensory deprivation at work. Perhaps this was the heightened dream state he was hoping to achieve. There shouldn't be another voice talking nonsense to him. If it was him, why did it feel like a stranger within his mind?

*"San Francisco, you say. How very interesting. I should like to see the sun again... to feel its hated warmth on my skin. I should like to be free again."*

There was another long stretch of silence. Only this time, Sidney felt self-conscious as if his mind had been laid bare and an intruder was rifling through his memories as if they were a set of files. He shivered involuntarily at the thought of a stranger looking him over from the inside out.

"I'm a scientist, a metaphysician to be precise. My name is Sidney Thomas. I had an accident many years ago that left me paralyzed from the waist down... That's why I'm in this isolation tank. That probably doesn't make sense to you. I had better explain.

"I have a theory, you see. Well, it's not just my theory... many people have suggested it... that the dream state can be controlled through sensory deprivation. If we can isolate our consciousness so that it exists only in the subconscious state, then we can free our minds from the limitations of the physical world. Time is a function of matter, you see. The controlled dream state could travel lanes in our past and alter the road we took, the choice we made. Waking from this dream state, if carefully controlled, the sleeper could find they have successfully altered their past, present, and future in what we perceive to be reality. Achieving virtual time travel via the controlled dreaming of one's own past."

*"How very fascinating. Pray continue, Dr. Thomas."*

"I had a wife... she left me. She said there were three people in our marriage... the two of us and my work. She said that she couldn't stay in a marriage with a husband who placed his job before his wife. It turned out that she was telling the truth for once. There was a literal third person in our marriage from the start, but I was too blind to see.

"She justified her infidelity so that her conscience was clear and she could maintain that she was a good person who suffered being married to a workaholic and had no choice but to go outside her marriage for comfort and attention. All those years together, she just needed me to believe whatever lies she fed me to protect herself from accepting the truth... that she was a ruthless, calculating, adulterous hypocrite.

"She married him shortly after our divorce. As always, I was the last to know. Despite her betrayal, I knew we could work out our differences if she would just give me time. I was racing to the courthouse to try to stop them when I had my accident. I never even saw the other car that broadsided me. It was a hit and run. They never found the driver.

"I was left crippled physically the same way she crippled me emotionally when I learned the truth of her betrayals through the years. Had she had stabbed me in the chest with a bloody dagger a dozen times and left me bleeding to death in the gutter, it would have seemed merciful by comparison. How can people be so cruel? How can they say their vows and not mean them? Love isn't supposed to be a lie."

Sidney paused. He had never articulated the tragedies of his life before. It didn't feel cathartic. There was no release in unburdening. He imagined what the voice in his head must think of him. Any God sitting in judgement over him would have to agree that Sidney Thomas had been a fool and every fool gets what's coming to them. Always, he felt trapped between his fantasy of love and the inevitable reality of deception.

*"Women, my friend, they are nothing new. Men always think we want them, but we don't understand the first thing about them. They can be callous and self-serving. Men are just a means to an end to them. The insensitive sex was never worth dying for. The sooner you recognize the truth of that statement, the better off you will be.*

*"Now let us talk of this project of yours to control your dream state. You seek to change your past, yes? To prevent your accident... this is only natural. I can help you. Together, our minds will provide the strength of will for you to succeed... to persevere. You and I together will be unstoppable. Think of it, Dr. Thomas. Let me in completely. Give me your very soul."*

Sidney Thomas smiled in the total darkness. He thought of it and felt unstoppable already.

The water.

He was suddenly aware of the warm, chemical-fueled water. It was everywhere. Surrounding his entire body as he floated in the isolation tank. The water stung his eyes.

His eyes.

He blinked and was aware that it stung even more. Moving his arms like oars, he pushed himself up. There was a splash and his head was free of the water. He coughed and sputtered and spit the strange-tasting water from his mouth. His eyes still stung and his ears felt like he was buried under concrete six miles beneath the ground.

The voice in his head was gone. He was back and aware of the isolation tank and his surroundings. Perhaps it had all been some sort of strange dream. That's when he realized his legs were still working. He laughed. He laughed until he wept. He was moving with something approximating coordination of all four limbs. He climbed out of the tank. The room was empty. He grabbed the big cotton towel and began drying himself. He felt independent and in control for the first time in years...possibly ever. He was awash in the feeling of warmth and life where he had felt so useless and cold for so long. He realized he had done it. He had achieved the controlled dream state. He was consciously reliving his past with all his knowledge of the present at his command.

As he finished dressing, he felt a pair of car keys in his pocket. He couldn't explain it until he took them out and held them in his hand. They were his keys from all those years ago. It was as if this weren't a dream and he had traveled back in time with all the clarity of reality. Hurriedly, he padded down the steps. The feeling of elation to be walking again drove any thought of how strangely empty the building was from his mind. As he pushed through the set of heavy double doors and down the front steps to Post Street, he saw it parked by the curb.

His restored 1956 Fairlane Victoria in all its sweeping splendor. The rounded headlamps, the wraparound windshield, the rectangular vent windows, the six-cylinder engine. His beloved Crown Vic. Fiesta Red over Colonial White. He loved that car so much and here she was... his again at last. He could walk, he had the car, now he just needed to reclaim his wife.

He loved her. She had to know that. He just couldn't express his love the way that other men could. Now he would make everything right. Behind the wheel of his Crown Vic, he would get to the courthouse on time. He would stop her from making that terrible mistake. He would prevent his tragic accident. He would have everything back when he finally awoke and emerged from the tank a second time... his life, his purpose, his legs, his wife.

Sidney put the keys in the lock and once seated behind the wheel, he turned the ignition and listened to the engine roar. His head hurt like the devil for some reason. Groaning, he pressed his palm against his forehead, eyes squeezed shut as they still stung from the chemical water and the sudden transition from plunging up from the depths of darkness into the dazzling sunlight of his past.

As he put the Crown Vic into drive and accelerated, he scanned the buildings along Post Street. Everything was as he remembered it all those years ago. Weaving in and out of traffic, he grumbled under his breath, his eyes darting from one lane to the next. He had to be on time. He was nearing Union Street. It wasn't long until the courthouse. He couldn't get this wrong this time. His very life depended upon it. He was determined to stop two lovers from righting their wrong and legitimizing their affair. He was determined to right his own wrong and save both their souls.

And then it happened.

He had a strange sense of clouded thoughts suddenly clearing.

He saw a second Crown Vic just ahead in the far lane. The same year, the same color as his. The realization dawned that he was seeing his past self. Momentarily, he thought he had to beat him, he had to get there first and avert a double tragedy. He put his foot down on the accelerator and quickly cut across the lanes.

That's when he remembered.

This was exactly the way it happened the day of his accident. He had blocked the memory all these years. The seeming impossibility of his psychological trauma was too great to accept. He remembered driving in his car, the same car he was now seeing just in front of him in the next lane. He remembered glancing in his rearview mirror and being startled by the sight of another vintage 1956 Fairlane Victoria identical to his own. The Crown Vic shot forward, he recalled glancing over and seeing the driver glancing at him at the same time. He barely registered the shock of seeing his own face staring back at him from the next lane as if he were driving against a mirrored wall. Involuntarily, he cut the wheel sharp and...

It happened again... just as it had that tragic day. The same vehicle and driver co-existing twice in the same space collided and merged back into one.

Sidney Thomas felt his stomach drop as heated metal twisted and burned. The Crown Victoria began to somersault through the air. He was thrown from the driver's seat as his own car came down hard on his twisted and crumpled form. The pain was impossible to bear a second time. As he lost consciousness and awoke, Sidney thought, "I can't believe it. I did it to myself."

Time had stopped.

The still form of Sidney Thomas was floating in the darkness of the deprivation tank. His eyes shot open. His lips twisted in a sick mockery of a smile. Strong arms reached upward as he took a deep breath and floated to the surface of the tank. Purposefully, he pulled his dripping body up out of the tank and let his head hang down as he hungrily filled his lungs with the oxygen it had been denied for so long.

"No, Dr. Thomas, you didn't do it to yourself," he sneered. "We did it together."

Climbing free from the isolation tank, he tested the strength of his new body and looked at his outstretched hands, flexing his fingers before reaching for the white cotton towel to dry himself. A grim smile played across a stern face newly alive with a dark intelligence.

"Sidney Thomas had to die so that Fantômas may live again."

*In this ambitious and thought-provoking tale, Jess Nevins lets us peek behind the curtain of the pulps of the 1920s and 30s—not just American ones, but also French and Germa ones. The one, in particular, which anchors the tale is* Mira culas, *a 1921 tale, by Gabriel Bernard (published under the pseudonym of H. de Volta) which is part Gustave Le Rouge for its mad scientists and crazy inventions, and part* Fantômas *for its larger-than-like characters...*

## Jess Nevins: *The Fall of Scientific City*

*Part One: Zohra Sips* Atay *and Listens to the Young*
*Ash-hadu an la ilaha illa Allah, Wa ash-hadu anna Muhammadan Rasulu-Allah.*
*Rajab, 1426 (2005 AD), The city-nation of Arrëm.*

At night I sit in Bilal's café late at one of the outdoor tables and listen to the students argue. It is something of a pastime for me now; when I passed one hundred years on this planet, a good night's sleep and I became divorced, and even past midnight my body refuses to yield to unconsciousness. It is an unfortunate byproduct of our life-extension and rejuvenation treatments, the doctors say, but it usually lasts for only a few years, and by the time I'm one hundred and ten I'll be sleeping soundly through the night.

This is something which the doctors say to cheer those of us past our hundredth year. It is true that sometimes the sleeplessness only lasts for a few years, but all of us know someone in their two-hundreds who hasn't slept through the night in a century or more. At least the doctors know enough to prevent those unfortunates from going insane.

I remind myself of that often these days.

So, when the moon is high and midnight is fled, I go to Bilal's café, which happens to be across the street from the apartment granted to me by the Arrëm Council for services rendered to the nation. I would go there even if I didn't like Bilal—who wants to travel across the city late at night?—but Bilal is a veteran of the Revolution like me, and we are friendly acquaintants of long standing.

I sip my *atay*, sweetened by Bilal himself to a nicety—he knows how I like it—and I listen to the students and their constant arguments and contentious discussions. Oh, do the students love to argue! Maliki Islam versus the syncretic Amazigh religion. Arrëm's history as uninfluenced by the world versus Arrëm as the spider at the center of the great African web of nations. Imazghan color theory versus Bambara color theory. Tasikisikit versus Agabas versus Raï versus Algerian techno-hip-hop. Everything under the sun, and many things above it.

I cannot help but compare the students' constant wrangling with the discussions we had when I was their age. We did not have all-night cafés in which to argue, nor an ever-flowing supply of *atay* and *khatfee* to drink while we argued. And we had more important things to discuss: the ouster of the French, and how to bring it about. Oh, the debates between the use of force versus peaceful overthrow from within the colonial system were intense, but everyone was working toward expelling the French from our lands. The debate was merely over methods, not results. But these students have grown up knowing colonialism only as an abstract idea belonging to history, and so they have the liberty and the time to bicker over irrelevancies.

I never intervene or let these young men and women and *ger* know I am listening to them. I sip my *atay* and smile benignly and sit with my back to them. As the arguments rage, I look up. The stars and the moon shine down brightly through the dome over the city, and I enjoy tracing the shapes in the stars that I learned in my childhood. Arrëm is a city that knows no sleep, and so there are always lights on: in the steel and granite towers that loom over the city, on the ramps and walkways and aerial tunnels that connect the towers, on the monorails and airships crossing overhead, inside the city and out, on the fronts of the cafés and markets open to the night customers. Even at night the painted designs on the streets glow in blue, black, red, and green. I have not traveled abroad since the Revolution, but I cannot imagine there is another city that looks as itself as Arrëm. Wakanda, perhaps, but nowhere else.

I smile, thinking of how it was for us in my youth. None of this was here, but we had the dunes, and the green riverways of the Aïr mountains, and they were all good in our eyes. But all is different now, completely so. These bickering children have no idea how good they have it.

I shrug. Let the young think I am just another centenarian, long-since retired and now only a statistic. That I played my role during the Revolution and was the power behind the Arrëm Council for all the long the decades of my adult life—why, those can be my secrets. The students likely would not care. They are young, and history is only a debating topic for them, and old women like me are symbols of the past and not of Arrëm's glorious present and future.

Those are the tracks my thoughts usually run upon, and after one or two hours of quarrelling the students leave and I return home and try again to sleep. Tonight is different, though, and without warning the students' arguments turn to the Revolution, and without meaning to, I listen very closely.

The students are arguing about the causes of the Revolution, one side swearing it was historically determined and inevitable, the other passionately arguing that it was the result of random good luck on our part. Both sides ignore those of us who made the Revolution come true and dismiss us as men and women and *ger* who did not know what we were doing.

I keep my temper even and my face composed until a young Imazghan man barely older than my youngest grandson begins insisting that the forces we faced during the Revolution were not so formidable after all, and that the true heroes of Arrëm were the men and women who governed us after the Revolution and made us the power of the continent that we are.

I cannot stay silent in the face of such nonsense, and so I turn to look at him. I say, "You—youngster. What would you know of our enemies during the Revolution?"

He can barely look at me for all the contempt he has for me. "I've taken several courses in it and written a thesis on it, old baggage, believe me—"

I confess to placing my mug down on my table rather heavily and letting the sudden harsh noise silence him. I say, "And the histories and secondary sources you read for these courses, how many of us did they interview? Or did they all depend themselves on histories written twenty years or more after the fact?"

The young man begins to object, but he is silenced by one of his debating partners, a Badawi who looks at me questioningly, and, perhaps with a little respect. She says, "Ma'am, you said, 'us.' Were you there?"

I shouldn't say anything. I should leave them to their benighted palaver. I should go home. Secrets are for staying secret, mine more than most.

But I cannot. I cannot resist the temptation to teach these youngsters the truth. I have kept it hidden for so long, and it hangs heavily on me, and suddenly I cannot keep silent any longer.

I say to the young woman, "Oh, yes." I roll up the left sleeve of my shirt and let the students see the faded blue tattoos there. Their reaction is gratifying; there are so few of us left now with the markings against the evil eye of the French, and fewer—or so I thought—who would recognize them. These students, however, did. I say, "I'm one of the last who was."

The young Imazghan I'd interrupted scoffs. "Anyone can get tattoos, hag. But what would an *old woman* like you know about the great acts of history, the alliances we won and the revolutions we funded? I—"

"Old woman" sets me off in ways that "old baggage" had not, and to my later shame I fish the pendant I always wear out from under my shirt. I show the young students the medal on the pendant, the medal made for the "Heroes of the Revolution."

The first to understand what I was showing them was a pretty young Hausa woman with a thoughtful expression and deep blue eyes. "Brothers, wait. Ma'am, is—is that pendant—I recognize it. There's one in the Museum. Did you actually fight in the Revolution itself?"

I admit to smiling with open pride at her question, may I be forgiven for it. "Fight in it? Young lady, I *led* the fighting!"

Another young Imazghan woman with a face that belonged in the desert, carrying a rifle and riding a camel pell-mell toward her enemy, exclaims, "You—you're Tamenokalt! Guys—don't you remember what Professor Tidjani Alou called her? "The Queen of the Revolution!'"

That gets their attention, and their regard is more respectful after that.

I bow my head to them and put away the medal. I am beginning to feel foolish; I have said too much, given away a secret that should stay secret. All

465

those years behind the scenes, completely unknown to outsiders, and now I flaunt my identity at the slightest temptation. Shame, Zohra, shame!

A third woman of obvious mixed European and Imazghan parentage, asks, "Tamenokalt, will you settle an argument for us? You were there, you will know better than any book. Isn't that right, *Atbir?*"

Atbir, the Imazghan boy who baited me and insulted me, glowers at me from his chair but says nothing.

I say, "If I can. I am old now and have forgotten much about the Revolution." Which is a bald-faced lie, but it allows me to omit and conceal those facts that it would not do to reveal.

She says, "Was the Revolution historically predetermined, or was it just random good luck?" She shoots a sniffy look at the other young men and women with her, as if to say, "Finally we'll get an answer, and you can argue about something else!"

I sip my *atay* for a moment, wondering if I should respond honestly, then say, "Neither. There was nothing about the Revolution that was predetermined by history—we did that, young lady, your grandparents and great-grandparents, when the time was right. I don't remember seeing history fighting in the streets against the French. We fought, not history. And there wasn't anything random about it, either. We had been waiting for an opportunity for several years, and the Americans finally provided one."

The Hausa with the blue eyes looks surprised and says, "Americans? I'm sorry, I don't remember that from my courses or readings."

Atbir, finally interested in what I am saying, sits up. "What did the Americans do?" He is eager to hear something bad about the Americans. I cannot blame him; none of us are fond of the Americans and their "interventions," and any new thing that can be used to justify our distrust and hatred of them will be of prime interest to eager young lions like Atbir. The government may officially be allies with the United States, but the people of Arrëm? *Never.* Our memories are long; we remember Patrice Lumumba and Rafael Trujillo and Achmed Sukarno even if our leaders pretend not to.

I nod slowly. My desire to answer goes against the habits of a lifetime of keeping secrets, and I suspect that the Council would frown on me saying something awful about the Americans. (Even here in Arrëm the American dollar speaks loudly, and their funding for their "War on Terror" is a welcome addition to the city's annual budget.) But, I argue with myself, who could it hurt, really? What happened at the Revolution was so long ago for these young students that whatever I could say will seem like the doings of a novel rather than of history. And I can remove the delicate parts and those facts which the Council would rather be kept private.

Yes, that should be acceptable to the Council, I tell myself.

I lie.

I tell the students, "Very well, then. I will tell you of the Revolution. I have not told this story since Issouf Ag Ghaly interviewed me for his *History of Arrëm*, and that was forty years ago, so forgive me if my story is faltering, at times—I haven't thought about the Revolution as something linear in decades. But there is something about the Revolution that you should have been taught and were not. I will tell you it now.

"Order yourselves another round of sweetened *atay* from Bilal, and one for me, please, and then I will begin."

### Part Two: Zohra Remembers

I don't know what you've been told about the time before the Revolution, but this, all of this, was different. All of this wasn't here, and I don't mean just Arrëm, I mean the entire mountain we sit upon and all his brothers. In those years, when I grew up, Talak and especially the "Aïr Mountains" were just dunes and tall hills that the Imazghan rode through on our traditional routes. We were travelers, then, and our French masters let us ride where we would, as long as our chieftains knelt before the French colonial authorities.

It was not an agreeable arrangement, for most of us were the sons and daughters of blacksmiths and jewelers and leatherworkers, and no one among us wanted to be thought of as slaves to the French. It was most disagreeable, but as long as the nobility abided by their agreements with the French, none of us were willing to take any extreme measures against them. In truth, it was our pride that was most injured by the French occupation—this is not to speak of the massacres that took place when they invaded our territories, they are *not* forgotten by us—but then, what business did the French have to claim ownership of our desert to begin with? We were the Free People; we needed no colonial masters, nor wanted any, and only gave in to the French when they demonstrated that their rifles were better than our longswords. No, after our submission to them they may not have hurt us much, but even what little there was too much. Ongoing indignity can be a painful wound all on its own.

But then came the cataclysm. We were camping close to here one night, along the small riverways of the mountains, when the earth began to shake so violently that everything was knocked flat—tents, people, camels—and no one could make it to their feet. There were awful lights in the sky, and the sounds of explosions and screaming and what sounded like the sky itself being torn open. Some of us thought that the djinn and *kel asuf* were at war. I myself, who had visited Algiers and seen the French airplanes in their neat rows, thought that perhaps the French were at war with the Germans again.

Then the ground beneath us jumped. We were thrown five feet in the air, and landed to a deafening grinding sound of stone against stone. And then the dirt around us exploded, spewing rock and earth in all directions. Surging up from beneath the surface of the earth were massive, flat-topped stone columns, hundreds of feet across. They shot upwards and kept going, only stopping when they were true mountains, flat-topped *massifs* ten thousand feet high in the air.

As we learned later, the earthquake and the sudden appearance of the mountains were the result of the final battle between an insane German scientist named Walther Spurtzheim and the Frenchman Daniel Dorteuil, who you will know better as "Miraculas."

Ah! Now you hear a name you recognize. Now I truly have your attention.

Yes, it was Miraculas, the evil djinn, the man of a thousand infernal creations, the archenemy. Did they teach anything of his past before he founded "Scientific-City" here?

Miraculas was a diabolically brilliant man. He spent a decade on his island, Goël, far out from the Bay of Tunis, doing little but inventing. He would occasionally leave the island to travel or to fight the enemies of France, but always it was back to Goël for him. Ah, the infamous *genius* of the man. The bones of what you see all about you here in Arrëm were born on Goël. The man had few rivals when it came to pure technological inventiveness. The fibrillator gun, the anti-gravity engine, the delta ray projector, the universal translator? All his. He was fecund with ideas, and brilliant at making them a reality, even if he was a French patriot.

*And how do I know all this? Why, I saw it. The students need never know this, but some years after the Revolution, during the second world war of the colonizers, an American Constellation transport plane crashed not far from here. Inside this plane were two American scientists by the names of Cosgrove and Lundgren—shhh, those names are not to be spoken aloud, ever; the Americans would be furious if they knew the fates of the two of them and their invention, their so-called "Experiment Nine Ninety-Nine." We used it to build the chrono-viewer whose use I oversaw for fifty years, and which has been the key to Arrëm's survival and prosperity—the chrono-viewer that allows us to look backwards to any point in time, to see and hear what happened regardless of how far back in time and space we are watching and listening. When I was first put in charge of the chrono-viewer, I used it to spy on Miraculas and to see how he built his creations. I learned much and taught it all to the techno-artisans of the Arrëm, and they in turn duplicated and sometimes improved upon Miraculas' inventions.*

*But all of this is not to be spoken of to any save the current mistress of the chrono-viewer and the Arrëm Council. The students do not need to know how I came to learn all that I tell them of. Just as well. Information security is paltry in these fallen times, and the students could not be trusted to keep what they I tell them to themselves.*

Miraculas had an archenemy, as you know: the German, Walther Spurtzheim. He had been Miraculas' assistant at Goël, but they fell out—Spurtzheim courted Miraculas' daughter Suzanne, which Miraculas would not allow, and Miraculas threw Spurtzheim off of Goël and forbade him from returning.

Spurtzheim, driven mad by romantic frustration and ruined pride, kidnapped Suzanne and fled. Miraculas pursued and chased him around the Earth and many miles underneath it and up into the solar system and then back to Earth and the lost island known as "Atlantis" before finally running him to ground here in the Aïr Mountains. In their final battle, Spurtzheim set off a device which resulted in the great cataclysm and in the Aïr Mountains gaining much taller members.

Perhaps you know some of this. Years ago, at the University it was taught as a part of our history, but now we have so much more history and, I think, people are less curious about how Arrëm came to be. No? Yes?

I see.

After the great cataclysm, Miraculas had a choice: return to Goël and resume his isolation or end his solitary life and embrace the world. This was Hijri 1339—1921 for the French; their economy was only slowly recovering from their war with the Germans, and the French leader, Aristide Briand, and his Cabinet wanted—no, *craved*—the technology that Miraculas had invented, so that France could again reclaim its position atop the elite of the world.

Miraculas chose the middle way between the two extremes, and founded a kind of Goël, "Scientific-City," here atop Ahennaka, the tallest of the new tabletop mountains in the Aïr. He brought duplicates of all his best technology and machinery from Goël to Scientific-City, along with all of his advisors. He invited other geniuses like himself to join him. His intention was to build the wonder of the world, a technological utopia like nothing known to humanity since Hukuru Zimbabwe.

He allowed the French authorities to believe that because Scientific-City was within the boundaries of French North Africa, therefore it was a French colony. This was either a sardonic joke on Miraculas' part or simply a deception designed to let him do what he wanted there. Whatever his reason, Miraculas' deception guaranteed that the French authorities would treat him and Scientific-City lightly and send only a colonial administrator to oversee it.

In the privacy of his vast complex of laboratories, the ones we allow only the most cunning and inventive of the University's graduates to use, Miraculas began creating further miracles. Thinking machines, wireless energy transmission, a network of wireless video and sound communications similar to but better than the Internet—it seemed for a long while that not a week would go by without some brilliant new creation from Miraculas' labs. With his prisoner Dr. Flax and his cadre of genius assistants, Miraculas created the intellect-enhancing treatments which are now given to all the children of Arrëm. Flax and Miraculas created the weather-control satellites that have brought so much rain to this region and allowed for a true garden of Heaven to spring up around the city.

With the Argentine Ortiz and the Italian Sivel, Miraculas created the biobots we use for farming. With the American Edison, he created the homunculi who form our army. With the American Joe West, he created the omega ray transmitter which powers our rocketships and our orbital platform. With the

Frenchmen Fringe, he created the longevity and rejuvenation treatments which keep us vital and active up to our third century. With the Irishman Sweeney, he designed and built so much of the wondrous architecture of the city—the topless towers, the eternal flames, the auto-walkways and the riverwalk, the caverns of a thousand views and the spiral staircase.

Miraculas and his assistants created a marvel of a city. I know that you all have grown up here, and that its wonders must have faded for you under constant exposure to them, but as someone born to the desert sands, I must tell you that this is a city that only dreams could make. Even the fabled Baghdad of Haroun al Raschid could not have compared to it.

Once Miraculas telegraphed the colonial powers about the existence of Scientific-City, Europeans came in droves to visit. Many chose to stay. Mostly British and Germans, but also Italians, Japanese, French of course, and the Dutch. Within weeks of completion Scientific-City held 30,000 or more outsiders.

What did we do about it? The Imazghan surrendered, begrudgingly, knowing that we could not fight the French colonial forces *and* Miraculas and his assistants *and* their inventions *and* the 30,000. And for several years there was... from the point of view of Miraculas and the French, there was a miraculous peace and harmony in their new technological utopia.

From our point of view, it was several years of waiting, and secretly buying what arms we could with what money we had and stealing the occasional trifle that Miraculas or one of his other inventors let slip and forgot about. We had waited many years to throw off the yoke of the French; we could wait more. We knew that their vaunted technology would eventually fail, somehow, and then French would leave and we would be masters of the sands as before.

They were difficult years, to be sure. The French wanted us to settle in a shanty town of huts around the base of Ahennaka. They detested our traditional practices, especially our traveling the trading routes, and tried all they could to discourage them. With so much trade going to Scientific-City, our traditional trading partners began to ignore us and sell food and drink and cloth and camels to the occupiers at exorbitant prices, leaving us too poor to partake. We had to go farther and farther, over the hottest parts of the desert, to replenish our stores. And the colonial powers, who had alliances with Scientific-City, chose to ignore us, to treat us as slaves, to call us "*bougnoles*" and "*ratons*"—words you've never heard, thankfully.

We were hungry all the time, and constantly harassed by the French colonial forces. But we grew lean and hard and increasingly ready for any kind of revolt or uprising against the French. Scientific-City was on our land, and we did not invite its construction here or welcome it. We did not know the phrase "exploitative settler colonialism" then, but we knew its reality. And all we had to see were our children at night, crying with hunger, and think about the well-fed French, to know that we were being treated evilly, and that (since the French were never going to leave of their own volition) we would have to expel them from the City, and soon, even if we all had to die to do so.

As it turned out, of course, we only had to wait four years to see the fall of Scientific-City.

Are you interested in the true story of the Revolution? Good. Gather close.

*Part Three: Zohra describes a night in Jack Wright's life*

On September 30, 1925, the night after Jack Wright's fiftieth birthday, he received a phone call from the White House asking him to meet with certain government officials the following evening in Washington.

This in itself was not unusual. As both a world-famous explorer and one of the government's most effective covert agents, Wright was often asked to sit in on evening meetings in the White House and in the State, War, and Navy Building. The meetings usually led to missions which benefited both the country and Wright personally.

As Wright discovered when he walked into the fifth-floor conference room, however, this meeting was not the usual sort of briefing he customarily received from government policymakers. Attending this meeting were President Coolidge, Secretary of State Kellogg, Secretary of War Davis, Asst. Secretary Phee from State's Division of African Affairs, Mr. Yardley from MI-8, the "Black Chamber" of military intelligence, and two men Wright didn't know.

Secretary Kellogg opened the meeting. Wright had found him to be open, frank, and honest, all qualities that made him the polar opposite of President Coolidge, and Kellogg had always dealt fairly with Wright. Kellogg said, "Mr. Wright, thank you for coming. I believe you know most of the individuals in the room. The gentleman opposite you is Mr. Bradley Drake, of MI-8 and a specialist in African affairs; the gentleman next to him is Philip Strange, currently a field operative of MI-8 and formerly, during the war, an aerial agent of G-2."

Wright nodded a "hello" at both. Wright was a capable judge of men and could immediately see that both Drake and Strange were experienced operatives in the British style, of the type who would commit murder or sacrifice an ally if it meant achieving a mission goal. The government officials in the room largely fancied themselves hard men; Drake and Strange were the real thing. Wright respected that, as he, too, was a man made hard by both by intent and circumstance—one could not kill large numbers of men, as Wright had, most recently in putting paid to the Mexican rebel Pancho Villa, without acquiring a hard shell, one would go mad otherwise—and he preferred to work with men like Drake and Strange rather than the newer, softer recruits that were being churned out by the government training programs.

Kellogg said, "Now, the following is a state secret, Mr. Wright. I know we can depend on you not to spread it about. You've carried out numerous missions for America overseas, for which we're all grateful. And you've no doubt seen

471

first-hand the current situation in Africa: the colonies of Great Britain and the European powers being used to funnel raw material and gold and silver and precious stones back to the home countries. Africa is one great untapped resource, and the United Kingdom and all of Europe are tapping it in place of the natives, who haven't the wits to do so. And you are no doubt aware that as an imperial power our portfolio of colonial properties lies in a handful of islands in the Pacific, not Africa, and that in point of fact the United States is, compared to Great Britain and the European countries, the loser in the scramble for Africa. Would you agree, Mr. Wright?"

Wright nodded gravely. "I would, Mister Secretary." That the United States had no colonies in Africa or South America was despite Wright's best doings; for over thirty years he'd been active around the world, finding lost races and lost cities and making them ripe for American colonization. He'd found the descendants of Vikings in a hidden valley in the Arctic, the descendants of the Aztecs in a hidden city in Mexico, another hidden city in the outback of Australia. He'd even found Atlantis, or something claiming to be. In all those places he'd pacified the natives and left the cities ready for claiming by American troops. He'd also taken the valuables he discovered in each city, but he thought of that as his fee for bringing the light of Christian civilization into such benighted locations. Wright nursed grudges toward several presidents' failures to carry the light forward and make those cities actually Christian, but those were old feelings easily repressed.

Kellogg said, "It's been brought to our attention that there's a new African location, in the depths of the Sahara in French North Africa, which would be quite profitable for the United States to colonize."

"The French will object to that, surely."

"Not if we strike first and fast and fully occupy the site. The French will object, of course, but in our view—" Kellogg nodded at President Coolidge, "— they will be too preoccupied with their current financial problems and the various colonial rebellions they are already dealing with to make too much of a fuss about the loss of this particular location. They will object to the League of Nations, of course, and I expect the other League countries will support them, but when the metal meets the grinding stone, the League will yield to reality. Prime Minister Painlevé and whoever succeeds him are too concerned with making sure there's not a sequel to the late war to cause another one."

Wright frowned. This seemed to him a logical, reasonable deduction, and therefore he distrusted it in principle. Nations all too often *didn't* act reasonably or logically, and when it came to colonies, new or old, the imperial powers let pride drive them. To Wright it sounded like Kellogg and Coolidge had talked themselves into the position they preferred—that they were mistaking what they wanted to happen with what would happen.

Wright thought, *On the other hand, I won't be the one trying to adminis-trate and defend whatever this new colony is. All I'll have to do is overthrow its leadership.* Wright was good at that.

After due consideration and a mental inventory of his active airships, Wright said, "Very well. What is this location? And what part am I to play in its conquest?"

Kellogg smiled a touch too eagerly. "Very good! We knew we could de-pend upon you. The location is in the Aïr Mountains of the Talak Desert; its name is 'Scientific-City.' From what we know, it is some sort of a scientific au-tocracy. It was founded by a Frenchman named 'Miraculas,' back in '21. He's the current ruler of the city; although, it is officially a French colony. Of Miracu-las we know little, apart from his obviously astonishing scientific acumen—the man churns out inventions like other men pass water. About the City, Mr. Strange can tell you more; he's back from a covert visit there. Mr. Strange?"

Strange cleared his throat, then spoke in a hoarse voice, one obviously worn out by years of shouting. "Scientific City is as the Secretary described. Population is between twenty and thirty thousand, both French and British as well as the native Tuaregs, other Berber tribesmen, and a large smattering of other Europeans and Asians. The city is well-watered, very well-sited for de-fense against attacks by the locals and too far up a mountain for a ground attack to succeed. Moreover, it has a protective dome over it which functions both de-fensively and as a barrier against the Saharan weather. The white population is very satisfied with Miraculas as a ruler, and there's no discord between the Tua-regs and the whites in the City. The level of technology in the City is beyond anything in Europe or the Americas, short of Wrightstown, Readestown, and a few other locations."

Wright nodded and smiled with false modesty at the mention of the town he'd helped turn into a scientific wonder. He was rightfully proud of his handi-work there, and warmly approved of Strange mentioning it as a rival to this "Scientific City."

Strange said, "Everything is advanced there: city transportation, airships, city defenses, buildings—*everything*. Every citizen has an automated servant to serve them; every home has equipment we could only dream of—automatic chefs, visual radio sets, powerful and efficient air conditioners, automatic shop-ping devices, and so on. The weapons of the city are astonishing; focused light beams, sonic commanders, death rays, self-piloted and weapon-bearing mini-zeppelins which can fight on their own, invisible bludgeoners, and so on. The City is… remarkable, Mr. Wright, simply amazing."

Wright frowned again. "Not so easy to conquer, then? And what can you tell us of this Miraculas?" The mission was sounding less and less easy. Of late he'd begun to feel he was too old for the more vigorous missions that the gov-ernment might assign to him, and Strange's words about Scientific City were making him feel exhausted. *Am I up to this?* he wondered.

Strange said, "I was unable to discover anything regarding Miraculas. The whites of the City respect and admire him, but we can't confirm their wilder stories about him. He has a reputation as an adventurer and explorer in addition to being an inventor, but the stories I was told about him were too fanciful to be taken seriously. He established Scientific City in 1921 after some sort of clash with a rival scientist. Been running the city ever since.

"As for being easy to conquer, Miraculas, or whoever designed the city's defenses, made them formidable, but with one exception. Their defenses were built with the expectation that they would be attacked by armed forces at our current level of technology—not what you can bring to bear, Mr. Wright. That's a significant flaw we can exploit."

Wright slowly nodded. "Ah. I see now. Yes, that does seem to be the case. But—surely you don't think I can topple Scientific City's leadership by myself. I can certainly find Miraculas and remove him from the game board, but from the sound of it that won't actually do much to reduce the City's current defensive capabilities."

Kellogg smiled. "No, that won't. But the troops you'll be carrying can do that. What's the capacity of your current largest airship, Mr. Wright? How many people can you carry?"

Wright gave it a moment's thought. "Just troops and personal equipment—no artillery or anything like that?"

"No. You'll be inserting the troops inside the city, not laying siege to it."

Wright said, "Weight won't be the issue; the problem will be finding room. But if I completely cleared the *Liberty* of all superfluous equipment, I could fit a 1,000-person battalion inside it."

Kellogg, President Coolidge, and Secretary of War Davis frowned and exchanged concerned looks. Wright said, "How many people did you intend me to bring?"

Davis spoke up for the first time. "We estimate that no less than three regiments—3,000 men—will be needed to take the City."

Wright shrugged, "I've more than enough active 'ships that can carry that many men. Between the *Liberty*, the *Freedom,* and the *Deliverance*, we can transport three regiments with ease and safety."

Yardley spoke, reminding Wright of a voice he'd once heard in the subways of Boston, the voice of something half-dead but still ravenous. "Three pilots are two too many. Too much potential for wagging tongues."

Wright bridled at the implication but kept his calm. "My people will remain quiet. But, if you prefer, I can control the *Freedom* and the *Deliverance* via radio from the *Liberty*. Only my groundcrew need be involved."

Yardley nodded, curtly.

Kellogg said, "The plan is for a predawn strike on Sunday morning on the 11th of October. For many of its citizens Scientific-City is an opportunity for unlimited decadence, and a great majority of them will be sleeping off their indulgences of the previous evening. There should be no one anticipating you. Make a high-speed approach and drop bombs or fire air-torpedoes or do whatever you need to do to destroy the dome over the city. Land in the central plaza of the city, unload the troops, then elevate and provide supporting fire for our troops. Does this sound achievable to you?"

Wright said, "Yes," his mind already whirling with ways he could improve the plan and increase the chances of his survival.

"Excellent."

Wright returned home to Wrightstown humming the *Deus Irae* and contemplating how best he could profit from Scientific-City's fall.

*Part Four: Zohra tells the stories*
*"The Fall of Scientific-City" and "The Rise of Arrëm"*

We had no idea what was coming, I assure you. When it happened—yes, it was the early morning of 22-Rabi al-awwal-1344, the very day of the Revolution—we were, nearly all of us, asleep in our tents at the base of Ahennaka. It was still dark, and very cold, and silent but for the night creatures of the desert, when the attack began. The engines of the Americans' airships were muffled, so that all that was audible was a humming sound overheard, soft enough not to wake the people below.

The hum woke me, however; I have always been a light sleeper, and I was guarding a cache of rifles stolen from Miraculas' labs and anticipating a French raid on us, so that even the quiet hum of the Americans' airships jolted me awake.

I sat up, groggily, reflexively reaching for my rifle. Then the first of the explosions came. It was *loud*, and quite violent, and unlike anything I'd heard before, and it came from far overhead. To be honest, my first thought was that Miraculas' police robots had found one of our hiding places in the city and were attacking it, but the second explosion disabused me of that notion, for it shook us, ten thousand feet below the city. That explosion blew open the dome and threw shrapnel in every direction and was far too powerful for Miraculas' police robots to have created. It had to have been created by something or someone else.

By the time the third explosion occurred every single Imazghan was out of our tents, rifles and swords in hand, looking up into the sky and at the city far overhead. We were in position to see the lights of the airships glaring down at the city, and to see the shards and pieces of the city's dome falling to the ground all around us. Then came the distant crackling drumbeat of gunfire, many smaller explosions, and roar of voices from many throats.

It did not take me long to realize what was happening: the city was under attack and the dome was destroyed. I knew this was our long-delayed opportunity; we could capitalize on what the airships were doing and finally kill Miraculas and seize the city. The others were slower in recognizing that our time had at last come. So, I fired my rifle once, to catch everyone's attention, and then I shouted at them to follow me, and I began the long run up the mountain road to the city. Yes, I did that, even though the men should have been the ones to lead the charge. For some, the chieftains' sons and others of the nobility, their pride was injured by a woman leading the attack on the city.

But those men were outnumbered by the many hundreds of men and women and *ger* who shouted their approval at me and followed me up the road that wound around Ahennaka to the City's entrance.

Those of us with the weapons stolen from Miraculas' laboratories led the way; the others, with only the Berthier rifles and Lebel revolvers at hand, or even just their swords, followed. When we reached the elevators halfway up Ahennaka we found them abandoned, the guards having fled at the sound of our approach. I gave more orders, because no one else would: our best fighters into the elevators, and everyone else to continue running up the road around Ahennaka. This earned me more resentment from the sons of nobility, but more respect from the people.

When we reached the city, we found it in chaos. Clouds of smoke everywhere. Many buildings were burning, and some had been flattened or blown apart by the Americans' bombs. The sounds of the city were deafening: explosions, gunfire, loud hums and crackles from the ray weapons carried by the Americans and the city's guards, screams and cries from the terrified, the wounded, and the dying. The Americans had destroyed the city's power plants, and in the darkness could be seen flashes from the weapons and a glare from the many fires created by the Americans. There were ugly smells of blood and gore on the winds. It was truly like the Jahannam of al-Furqah and al-Waqi'ah.

The streets were choked with people running from the firefights or toward them—thousands of Europeans rushing to what they thought would be safety in the city or trying to reach the city's exits. I had no time for them; they were colonists, and impediments to what we were trying to do. Was that cold? Heartless? Coldness was what the moment required of me just then, believe me.

The elevators had emptied out into the gardens at the center of the city. I had thought I knew these gardens as well as I knew the waters of Fachi. But just then I was confused, distracted by the constant screams and explosions and unable to see through the low-hanging clouds of smoke and the fires all around us. I knew I had only moments before the men and women behind me would begin to pile up and start shouting questions at me. I didn't know in which direction Miraculas' tower lay, I didn't know where the outer entrances to the city were, I didn't know where anything was just then. So, I made a quick decision and shouted, "This way," to those around me, and charged toward the sounds of the nearest firefight.

That's why they gave me the title "Tamenokalt," you know, as if I were Tin Hinan born again. They thought I led us into battle out of a surfeit of courage and a desire to slay all the men of Scientific-City and cause the Revolution. My actual reason was to find a way clear of the gardens so I could orient myself and then head toward Miraculas' tower. But, afterwards, it was more convenient to describe me as the "Battle Queen" than to tell the truth, so I allowed them to do it. Hence my title and my reputation, such as it is.

Oh—the time. I've gone on too long already. I apologize. I will be brief, so you can go back to your beds and be rested for your classes tomorrow.

We fought Miraculas' forces. We fought the Americans, although we thought they were Germans. We endured firefights and ambushes and house-to-house fighting. We fought at long range and hand-to-hand. We lost many people to death or injury, and those of us who emerged unscathed from the gauntlet were in a red rage and soaked in blood and sweat and panting from the effort. My memory of what happened became hazy and dim almost immediately afterward; I saw and did things my mind decided to hide from me for my own good. But when we finally reached Miraculas' tower, we were reduced by half, and I and the men who appointed themselves my bodyguard were streaked with blood, ours and others, as if we had tattooed ourselves crimson.

We fought our way up the stairwells and hallways of Miraculas' tower and onto the top floors. It was our revolution, you understand, there was no room for mercy just then toward our colonial masters and their guards and soldiers. Miraculas had not thought to make his personal labs and sleeping quarters better guarded than the rest of his tower, so there were no surprises waiting for us there. Those we found there, we killed. I may have killed Miraculas himself; I am not entirely sure, there were too many guns going off at the same time. The others thought me responsible, but I am not certain of it. Be it as it may, Miraculas was dead when the battle was over, and we were the victors.

We had only a short while to recover and to begin searching for Miraculas' personal weapons and equipment—we thought he must have saved his best for himself—when the American troops entered the base of the tower.

We learned later that the surprise of their attack had been complete; their bombing of the city's dome was unopposed. They destroyed the anti-aircraft guns and safely landed their men, and that proved to be the weight that balanced the battle in the favor of the Americans. Their weapons were not as good as the ones the city's soldiers carried, but the Americans had three thousand battle-hardened soldiers armed with the best technology Jack Wright and other American government weapons-makers could provide, and their numbers proved to be the key to victory.

Outside the tower, the Americans were fighting the city's defenders and the Imazghan in a series of desperate close-range firefights. Inside the tower, five hundred of the Americans' best troops were storming up the stairs, intent on taking Miraculas prisoner and seizing his personal laboratories and all the technology in them.

We had left only a few of our people on the lower levels; most of us were on the top three levels of the tower. When word arrived that the foreign whites that we'd been fighting were coming for us, everyone turned expectantly toward me, waiting for orders.

The ruin around me and the many holes in the wall reminded me of a notion I'd had years ago about destroying Miraculas' tower. So, I gave the order to gather up the most destructive of Miraculas' weapons and to follow me down the stairs to the 95$^{th}$ floor of the tower.

I've often wondered if I would have changed my orders if I'd known our opponents were Americans. But I always reach the same conclusion: I would not. The Americans were there to conquer Scientific-City and become our new colonial masters. They meant to oppress us as much as the French ever had. They were our enemy, and they deserved to die. No, my knowing who they were would not have changed anything.

We were on the 95$^{th}$ floor when the Americans reached the top three floors of the tower, having bypassed our floor. No doubt the Americans found many corpses, French and Imazghan, and the ruination caused by close quarters fighting. The Americans likely began looting the jumble of technology we left behind. I imagine that Jack Wright, leading the troops from the front as was his way, would have given orders to send some of his men back to the ground floor to secure the tower.

I gave the Americans two minutes after bypassing us, and then gave the order to fire our new weapons, the heat- and force-beam rifles and sonic projectors we'd looted, at the north- and east-facing walls of the tower. When Miraculas' guards had used them against us, they had cut through our bodies like a knife through blood. When used against the walls and ceilings and support beams of Miraculas' tower, they were only slightly less effective.

Our fire destroyed the north and east walls of the tower, forcing the floors above us to begin to collapse and then to tip to the side. We continued firing until the weapons began to overheat and malfunction and everything supporting the floors above us was gone and they beginning to fully collapse—and then, as I had suspected would happen, most of the four floors above us broke free of the building and slid off of it, falling to the ground hundreds of feet below and taking everybody on those floors with them.

Who was on those floors? The Americans, on the top three floors, along with the Europeans who lived in the tower. They had nothing to do with Miraculas; they were civilians who merely lived in his tower. They died in the fall alongside the American troops.

Could the deaths of the civilians have been avoided? Perhaps. But it was the fight of our lives, the Revolution we'd dreamed of for years, and I had neither the inclination nor the time to think about those Europeans. They may not have patrolled the streets with the City's police, they may not have been enriched by the drain of the area's natural resources, the Europeans may not have harmed the Imazghan personally, but they benefited from our oppression. They were not innocents, and their hands were not clean. I have never wept for their deaths or felt guilty that I gave the order to kill them, and I never shall. I don't expect you to understand that. Perhaps if you are ever in the position I was in, you shall. Until then, best to withhold your judgment.

That was the end of the Americans and the end of the Revolution. Oh, there were still pockets of fighting, clutches of Miraculas' men and groups of Americans fighting each other or us, but when word got out that Miraculas was slain and Jack Wright had been pitched off a building, the enthusiasm for battle left the whites, and they dropped their weapons and surrendered.

I am not surprised you have not been taught this in your history classes, even at the university level. We are officially allies with the Americans, now, and the history books used at schools have been written to reflect that. It would be inconvenient for the American involvement in the Revolution to be common knowledge among us.

What happened next, I expect you have been taught about. The rebuilding of the city and its renaming to "Arrëm." (No more French, no more whites in the city, no more white in our blood or water.) The opposition of the European co-lonial powers and America to Arrëm, an African city-nation led by Africans and only Africans and in possession of highly advanced weapons and transportation technology. The Europeans and Americans would have done to us what the French did to Haiti, except that they knew their military would be no match for our own, especially once Wakanda broke its isolation to send military advisors and trainers to us.

As we rebuilt and read Miraculas' files and spoke with our Wakandan brothers and sisters, we learned much about the world and its true powers, the individuals who like Miraculas changed history all by themselves—the Black Panthers and Mack Wans and Bara. We learned about the conspiracies and in-ternational criminals or revolutionaries who these whites opposed and often op-pressed. We wasted little time in contacting certain of these men and women and *ger*, especially those who ruled their own city-nations as Miraculas had ruled Scientific-City, and we made alliances with those city-nations. Charlemagne Sale-Trou's Haïti-sous-la-Mer, Meztli Xocoyotzin's Cuahuitl Itzimpazoliuhca, Mboya Kapinga's Science City, Saigō Takamori's Tessha Okoku, Professeur Mephisto's Métropole Électrique, Khünbish's Xanadu—Arrëm made common cause with all of them, and formed a confederation with them that sustained us all until the end of the second Colonizer World War. After that, well, we had enough technology, and skill with it, that we no longer needed anyone else, and could survive, and thrive, quite well on our own.

Me? Why, I became a valued advisor to the Arrëm Council for a short time, and then became the librarian and archivist for the government. I held that role for more than fifty years and retired only ten years ago.

*And that is a lie they will find palatable, I believe. The work I did with the chrono-viewer, the assassinations I foiled, the inventions I spied upon and took notes on for Arrëm's own techno-artisans, my career in counter-intelligence— these callow youths have no need to know any of that. If any of them ever decide to join Arrëm's intelligence bureaus, they will be shocked to find my name and portrait in the room where the heroes of the city are lionized. Until then, though, let me be only a librarian to them.*

And now, I think, I have spoken enough, and you have learned enough, and should be on your way back to your rooms. Bilal has been giving me a look for some time now; I believe he would like to return home as well. Farewell, then, students, and remember: revolution then, revolution now, revolution forever!

*As its title indicates, Chris Nigro's story concludes a series of tales that brought together the Phantom of the Opera, various versions of Frankenstein, the Unholy Three, and more...*

## Christofer Nigro: *Full Circle*

*An isolated ice cave, Siberia, early 1937*

The dreaded "Monster of Frankenstein," who preferred the self-chosen patronym of Gouroull, sat huddled in the cavern which he had dug out of a huge mound of ice with his own superhumanly strong hands. It was the most secluded location he had ever visited, a mostly barren and frozen wasteland, all but uninhabitable to humans. This allowed his intelligent but alien thoughts to focus upon a specific line of contemplation for as long as required, with little likelihood of interruption. These ruminations, largely incomprehensible to humans, were primarily centered on the goals and failures he had endured during his long and utterly vile existence.

More specifically, his thoughts fixated upon his endeavors to acquire a mate to bear him children, and to have his monstrous features altered to make him appear like a normal human. The most prominent of those failures had come from seeking the supernatural assistance of Grigori Yefimovich Rasputin, the arcane science of Dr. Herbert West, and the ancient holistic techniques of Wou Ling.[29]

What did the Monster, an evil being of fearsome power and fiendish lusts, glean from such inner scrutiny? Who did he blame for such errors of effort? What might he seek or do differently in his next attempts?

Should he, in fact, continue with this plan, or try another avenue, perhaps even attempt to impregnate more of the readily available human women? After all, the product of at least one such violation yielded a most... interesting result. Even if that progeny had, in fact, nearly orchestrated Gouroull's destruction.

The interior of the cave had no fire to warm the Monster's gray flesh, as the cold meant nothing to him. Accordingly, he was covered by no thick animal skin or thermal outfit of the kind one would expect to find on the few human explorers brave—or foolish—enough to visit such a landscape.

To the contrary, Gouroull was garbed in nothing more than a dark-colored raiment of tattered cloth and thick boots specially tailored to fit his oversized

---

[29] See *The Spells of Frankenstein*; *The Quest of Frankenstein* & "The Blood of Frankenstein" from *Tales of the Shadowmen #10* by Frank Schildiner, all published by Black Coat Press; and *Frankenstein Prowls* by Jean-Claude Carrière for the full details.

feet. The Monster's scar-covered skin, bearing the consistency of soft stone, was entirely indifferent to the temperatures that sunk well below zero within the cavern.

His makeshift domain, likewise, had no discarded animal bones or hides, for the creation of Frankenstein needed no culinary sustenance or hydration to survive. And unlike common humanity, who easily tired, and whose minds depended upon many hours of slumber each day to provide recuperation of energy and a steady supply of dreams to keep them sane, Gouroull's inhuman physiology and alien psyche required little of either.

Hence, a large portion of his "free" time was not caught up in satiating such mortal prerequisites. Instead, when not reading books authored (mostly) by people to absorb whatever tidbits of knowledge might prove useful to him, it was instead spent on lengthy moments of quiet, unfathomable ruminations.

This was what Gouroull was doing when the unlikelihood of being interrupted by humans was unexpectedly breached.

The Monster's uncanny hearing picked up the sounds of thick boots treading through piles of snow towards the cavern. His iridescent yellow eyes peered towards the entrance of the cave to see what he immediately identified as Nazi soldiers stepping in front of the six-foot high entrance. They were heavily dressed, as all humans had to be in such conditions, and they showed no outward sign of suffering from the intense cold.

Gouroull instantly realized that if these soldiers had been ordered to track him there, then the reason must have been one of immense importance to their masters. And also of the utmost discretion, which Siberia could provide like almost no other place on Earth. The man who was clearly the commander of the troop peered into the cavern and locked eyes with the monstrous creation of Frankenstein. He barely trembled, even when the alert Monster stood up to his full towering height in preparation for dealing with these heavily armed interlopers

"Be at ease, Herr Gouroull," the Colonel said in a distinct Teutonic accent. "Yes, you can only be him, so there is no point in claiming to be anyone else. Please do hear us out before any act of hostility, which we will meet with a degree of firepower that may prove fatal, even to one such as you."

Frankenstein's creation kept his inhuman eyes locked on the Colonel with an unwavering gaze while nodding a quick assent. He also opened his mouth to release an audible rumble and expose his array of razor-sharp teeth to make it clear that his anger at the interruption of his solitude was not to be taken lightly. Each of the soldiers, save for their commander, winced and raised their firearms.

"*Danke, mein freund,*" the commander said while making a waving gesture for his troop to lower their weapons while remaining alert. "I am Colonel Ernst Vogel, and I come to you representing the glorious Third Reich. As to our business here, there is no need to ask how we managed to locate you in his misbegotten land. The intelligence resources of the *Vaterland* are vast and can pierce any secret, not to mention locate anyone we need to find. And that intelligence has uncovered much information about your bloody journeys across the globe over the past several decades in search of a partner to share your desires, or a change in your... unusual appearance."

Gouroull again released a low rumbling sound.

"Yes, *Der Führer* knows all about you, along with the illustrious Germanic lineage that spawned you and others like you. Our science is as remarkable as our intelligence, and it is these resources that we offer you in exchange for your services to the Reich."

The response from the gray-skinned monstrosity was a sinister squinting glare, along with the utterance of a single word: "Talk."

"*Danke*. The *Vaterland* currently has a descendant of your *pater* Victor Frankenstein in its employ. He is named Basil Frankenstein, and he has convinced the *Führer* that his brilliance and knowledge of the esoteric surgical and alchemical sciences rival that of the one who brought life to you. This means he can create a lady of your... species for you, as well as 'fixing' your appearance. He is located in Switzerland, and we shall take you to meet him and discuss this matter... if you agree to serve us."

The mysteriously taciturn Monster again uttered a single word in response: "What?"

"*Der Führer* has learned of an object that he wishes to procure for use by our military. It has been mentioned in the Bible and various arcane sources, and is known as the Spear of Destiny. Have you come across it in your own readings?"

Gouroull nodded his ascent.

"Well, it has been discovered to be located among a cache of discarded relics within the Archeological Crypt at Notre-Dame Cathedral in Paris. We wish your first mission for the *Vaterland* to act as a bodyguard for a unit we will send to acquire the object. Your presence will be to ensure that nothing thwarts our efforts. Do you agree?"

It required a mere two seconds of mental analysis before the Monster's alien psyche weighed all considerations and came to an answer. "Yes."

"*Wunderbar! Der Führer* will be pleased... and our resources are now yours, much as yours are ours!"

*The Archeological Crypt at Notre-Dame, the following night*

Colonel Vogel stood addressing a small unit of his solders when Gouroull, now clad in a concealing dark outfit that included a hood, provided for him by the Nazis to make it easier to move about incognito in the darkness, entered the chamber.

"*Was zum Teufel!*" Vogel shouted at the Monster as he joined the group with a surprising degree of quiet for one so huge. "Where have you been, *dummkopf?* We have been waiting here for hours now, while you have been off gallivanting about in the Paris streets doing God only knows what..."

Vogel was abruptly cut off when Gouroull seized him by the throat and lifted him into the air like a rag doll. As the Colonel choked and gasped while futilely attempting to wrest the Monster's hard gray fingers from his neck, Gouroull displayed his razor-sharp teeth while waving the bulky index finger of his free hand at the Nazi in a common disciplinary gesture.

The other soldiers swiftly drew and pointed Lugers at the offspring of Frankenstein, but the gagging Vogel frantically gestured with his right arm for them to cease. He knew that even such a fusillade fired in unison from close range would not likely finish Gouroull before the Monster could kill him.

"At... ease, men," Vogel gasped out. "And also you, *Freund* Gouroull. Please... forgive my harsh tone. It shall not... be repeated."

A loud thud was heard a second later when the Monster opened his hand and allowed Vogel to fall on the hard floor. The Colonel pulled himself to his feet while rubbing the painful dark bruises on his neck, trying to act as nonchalant as possible in front of his men.

*This horrid beast shall receive his comeuppance once we find the Spear,* Vogel silently reassured himself. *Der Führer will doubtlessly balk at having such an abomination in our midst a second longer than we require. He will then use the power of the weapon to obliterate this putrid monstrosity, along with all the mongrel races spawned by nature's mistakes.*

Vogel cleared out his aching throat before beginning his spiel. "Now, all attend! This is the plan for Thursday evening, when civilian visitors will be cleared out early. Within this room is a hidden passageway leading to the Crypt." He pointed to a large diagram taped to the wall. "This map acquired by our informants will bring us to a special archival section for objects not yet on display.

"Sequestered amongst them will be a case holding the item we're seeking. We believe it has been 'hidden in plain sight,' as the *Amerikaners* like to put it. We are to take it, eliminate any guards that may attempt to obstruct us, and spirit the item back to the *Vaterland*."

As each of those present, including Gouroull, had their attention focused on Vogel's instructions, none of them noticed the glassy eyes of one of the small figurines on a nearby puppet & doll display table across the room flicker for a moment. This particular miniature moved his plastic features in response to what was occurring.

*Oh, the master will want to know of this!* Cochinelle thought. *I must get to his chambers beneath the Opera and tell him. And I must separate myself from this collection of figurines as furtively as possible. For if the monstrous*

*Gouroull recognizes me as I do him, he shall move the very heavens to reach me and rip me to pieces.*[30]

Luckily for the little artificial man, Gouroull maintained such intense concentration on every detail of the Nazi Colonel's words that he failed to notice the imp's silent departure through a small hidden hatch behind the puppet exhibit.

*Beneath the Opera, less than an hour later*

"I must say, Erik, that I am displeased at leaving Jeanne-Marie with those nuns," complained the miniscule but deadly Jacques Courbé as he paced back and forth on the expensive throw rug that decorated the Phantom of the Opera's lavish subterranean lair. "I think it is always best that she remain in my care. I trust no one else to keep her safe!"

The mini-man could easily be mistaken for a regal wind-up doll in his distinctive courtier garb, replete with a size-tailored scabbard containing a miniature but razor-sharp sword adorned with a golden hilt. His movements were quick and insect-like, his voice as shrill as a toddler's while containing an air of undeniable menace that belied its comical sound. At his side lay the ever-watchful St. Eustache, the former circus performer's loyal and lethal wolf-dog hybrid.

"Safe?" came the throaty mocking voice of Quasimodo, whose massive, distorted body sat atop a heavy oaken shelf a few meters distant. "What you really mean, little man, is 'on a leash.' *Your* leash, to be precise."

"Be silent, you humped hooligan!" Jacques retorted with a high-pitched screech. "As if Jeanne-Marie would fare any better in your malformed hands!"

The canine growled a warning at the modern-day descendant of the famous Hunchback of Notre-Dame, which he often did during the frequent clashes between the small and humongous man whom fate had brought together with the Phantom as part of his new Unholy Three.

"I would treat her like a princess!" Quasimodo rejoined while ignoring the threat of the massive dog. "Not as my slave!"

"She would be loath to suffer being touched by you!" Jacques shouted back. "Something she will never have to endure for as long as I live!"

"You speak as if she counts the minutes between your conjugal visits to her at the nunnery," the Hunchback spat back. "Rather, I believe the lady cherishes each moment you are *away* from her, all the while praying that you do not return from our latest assignment."

---

[30] See this author's short story "Patricide" from *Tales of the Shadowmen #8* for the first meeting between Gouroull and Cochinelle... and also the Monster's first meeting with the Phantom of the Opera.

"Shut your grotesque face before I slice off your tongue!" the tiny man exclaimed while drawing his small but sharpened blade as St. Eustache stood up and snarled viciously at his master's antagonist.

Quasimodo responded by grasping a heavy glass vase off an adjoining shelf and lifting it over his head as a makeshift bludgeon. "Call off that infernal mutt and put that sword away before I smash you with this and choke the dog by shoving you down its throat."

The latest impending battle between those two was interrupted when the owner of these quarters and undisputed leader of the team leapt between the two in a swift and graceful fashion that would have been the envy of any Olympic athlete.

"*Pardieu!*" Erik shouted. "Must you two always disrupt the sanctity of my home with your incessant bickering over that woman? Need I continue to remind you that we are friends, united by what we share in common with each other but not the rest of this world?"

Jacques slowly sheathed his sword while gently patting St. Eustache on his gray-furred neck as a request to heel. At the same time, the Hunchback returned the vase to its spot on the shelf as he leapt down from the heavy cabinet in a movement whose agility belied his own distorted bulk.

"Quasimodo," the Phantom continued, "I am growing weary of your needling Jacques over this issue. Jeanne-Marie is his wife and is therefore off-limits to you in every way conceivable. For now, those ladies of the night I hire to service you must suffice to satisfy your needs."

"You mean, the ones he kills or maims with his 'loving' embraces," Jacques mumbled.

"What did you say, you mere particle of a man?" Quasimodo said as he stepped forward and raised his massive fist.

"Step back, you ugly gargoyle!" Jacques replied as he drew his sword again. St. Eustache growled at the Hunchback while baring his fearsome fangs as his fur stood up on his shaggy back.

"I said, enough of this, and I meant it!" Erik bellowed. "Defy my orders again and I may forget the friendship I hold with you two!"

The Phantom's mellifluous but chilly voice took on a truly disturbing resonance when his temper was frayed. Both the freakish men that shared his home backed away accordingly.

"*Mes excuses,*" his two house guests said in concert.

"Now, Jacques, allow me to remind you that your precious paramour is under the finest care, while also subject to the tightest of leashes," the Phantom firmly stated. It is easier for her to be kept out of trouble there than taking her on missions with us, particularly after you ceased trusting her under the watch of my *daroga*."

"I could see the way the Persian looked at her," Jacques stated, "so I make no apology for that."

"Then you must put your faith in the nuns," Erik insisted. "You need not be concerned with Jeanne-Marie being looked at in that manner there, at least."

"Are you certain of that?" the Hunchback interjected. "For, I have heard…"

"Be silent, Quasimodo," the Phantom said firmly. "My point being, Jacques, that you need not worry about your dearest wife being pawed by some miscreant at that convent. No males are allowed there, save briefly for special business and only under the tightest of scrutiny. And Jeanne-Marie is kept in her room with the door bolted and the window barred at all times. Only you among all the men in this world are permitted to visit her there, and only because you are married to her."

"That harpy in a habit demanded I produce a marriage license as proof on my first visit!" Jacques sputtered.

Erik laughed. "Ah, that is the Mother Superior for you. A cautious one as I said, *non?*"

Jacques folded his arms as he was forced to accede. "Perhaps she is, but…"

The tiny man was startled when a small hatch in the side of the wall opened and another man, almost as tiny as himself, skittered into the room.

For a moment, this mini-intruder found himself face-to-face—in fact, nearly eye-to-eye—with Jacques. As the two exchanged bewildered glares, the little man in the costly courtier uniform noticed that his counterpart was not human… that is, not truly flesh and blood. Dressed in a simple smock-like garment, he resembled a male dwarf in general size and shape, but his skin had an unmistakable plastic look about it. His eyes appeared to be composed of shiny glass, and the dark red thatch of hair on his head resembled the synthetic mop one sees on a child's doll.

"*Mon dieu!*" Jacques exclaimed. "What is… this?"

Before anything else could be said, St. Eustache leapt onto the scene and wildly seized Cochinelle in his powerful jaws, shaking the little synthetic man about.

"Help me, master!" the animated doll shouted.

"Jacques, tell the dog to drop him," Erik commanded. "He is one of my underlings! And he would not have come here by way of that hatch if it were not a matter of great urgency!"

The dwarf assassin patted the vicious canine several times on his fluffy neck while yelling, "Heel, St. Eustache! *Heel!* Release that… thing!"

St. Eustache immediately did so, and much to Jacques's surprise, the only part of the little person that was shredded was his garment. There was no sign of blood or dangling internal organs. Nevertheless, Cochinelle was shaken to the core of his artificial life, and he skittered behind the Phantom where he knew he would be safe.

Quasimodo was equally intrigued by the sight, and he sauntered over to where Cochinelle cowered. "Erik, what in the name of holiness is that? Is it… a doll? I would think it was a relative of Jacques if not for its artificial appearance."

"Shut up," was the sword-wielding dwarf's reply.

"This is Cochinelle, one of my chief spies," the Phantom clarified. "A remarkable piece of work, is he not? He was constructed by the mechanical genius of Spalanzani over a century ago. He was of much more limited behavior at the time, and used as a servant for performing basic tasks and could only utter simple sentences, save for singing certain tunes. That changed when I was able to enhance his artificial neural capacity several years ago due to technology brought back from the future by Dr. Omega. Ah, some of the machinery I was able to acquire courtesy of that source."

"Master, master!" Cochinelle muttered frantically, "I come with grim tidings! Gouroull has returned to Paris! And he is in the employ of the Nazis who plan to steal some item hidden in the Archeological Crypt below Notre-Dame this coming Thursday!"

Erik's bright yellow eyes widened beneath his mask. He grabbed Cochinelle by the front of his torn vestment and lifted him into the air mere inches from his covered face. "What? Are you certain it was *him?*"

"Would I dare risk mentioning such news if I was not certain of its veracity, master?"

The Phantom calmed down and released his synthetic minion. "No. You would not. I am just irate, as I hoped I had managed to rid the world of the brute whose demonic loins brought me into this life."[31]

"*Quoi?*" Jacques exclaimed.

"This is an... aspect of my horrific past that I have been loath to reveal to anyone," Erik mumbled.

Quasimodo stepped forward and replied in a surprisingly gentle tone. "Erik... we are your friends. And you're the only one that the two of us ever possessed. Moreover, our pasts were as unsavory as your own. You may confide anything to us."

"*Oui,*" Jacques said. "For once, this one and I are in agreement, *mon ami.*"

"Gouroull is a monstrosity in a grotesque semblance of human form," the Phantom explained. "He is the creation of that madman, Victor Frankenstein. At one point long ago, the Monster attacked and despoiled a simple peasant woman named Rosemary. Nine months later, she died after giving birth to... me. The final sight she beheld was the unspeakable horror that she brought into the world as a consequence of her horrid violation.

"I discovered the truth of my genesis over two decades past and sought to destroy Gouroull once and for all, avenging both myself and my poor hapless

---

[31] See J.-M. & Randy Lofficier's *His Father's Eyes* in the Black Coat Press edition of *Phantom of the Opera.*

mother while sparing the world of enduring the birth of more like me. I failed, and nearly lost my own misbegotten life in the process."[32]

The Phantom then turned away and sobbed.

"*Mon Dieu,*" Jacques muttered in his comical voice.

"Erik," Quasimodo said in a tender version of his usual raspy tone. "We are at your side, as always. What shall we do with this information your... doll spy provided you? Shall we kill the Monster for good this time?"

Turning his masked visage toward his only true friends, Erik's response was quick and to the point. "Yes! We *will* kill that abomination. Along with those Nazi fools for daring to employ him for what is undoubtably the retrieval of an item that will make that madman Hitler even more powerful. However, speaking from experience, Goroull may be too formidable for even the three of us. We require help on this mission, and it is time for me to take it out of storage."

"Storage?" was Jacques's query.

"Follow me, you two," the Phantom murmured. "Cochinelle, you return to spy on these Nazis as quietly as you can and provide me with updates as necessary."

"*Oui,* master," the artificial little man replied as he scampered back through the hatch.

Quasimodo and Jacques followed Erik into a section of the Catacombs they had never seen before. Within that forbidden realm, they saw many strange sights, including the remains of what appeared to be a large organ with massive tuning forks attached to it and a large metallic pod-like structure.

The trio stopped before a huge iron cauldron-like structure with a thick translucent window covered by frost. Quasimodo wiped some of the cold dew off the front of the glass to get a better look at what was inside. And what he saw caused his disfigured face to take on a startled expression.

"Erik, what are these...?"

"What you see," the Phantom replied, "are two other *magnumculi,* man-made monsters created through alchemical means in days past; one by the mystic Zametti Pretorius, and the other by Charles von Frankenstein. Both were destroyed in separate incidents, but subsequently reconstituted by the insane Ludwig von Frankenstein in the German town of Darmstadt near the turn of the century. They were thusly christened Zam and Charles by Ludwig's wife, Julianne. Through an elaborate set of circumstances, they ended up frozen like this. In that state they came into my possession, and I kept them here until they were truly needed. They are too unpredictable to routinely use as underlings.[33]

---

[32] For Erik's ill-fated attempt to kill Goroull, see this author's short story "Patricide" from *Tales of the Shadowmen #8.*

[33] The revival of these two Monsters by Ludwig von Frankenstein is detailed in this author's short story "Bad Alchemy" from *Tales of the Shadowmen #13.*

"I doubt either of them could defeat Gouroull one-to-one, but the two of them together, backed up by us and the element of surprise, may very well prevail. And I have the means to both quickly awaken them and maintain temporary control of their actions."

As Erik departed this section of the Catacombs, Quasimodo lagged behind so he could speak to his diminutive ally privately.

"Jacques," he said, "please do forgive me for allowing my feelings for Jeanne-Marie to come between the two of us. If not for that, we could have become great friends, and I hope that is still possible."

"Thank you for being sorry that you allowed this to happen," Jacques replied with a combination of sympathy and acidity. "If you should ever get past these feelings and accept things as they are, then we may indeed become friends—as we should. And then, we need no longer be concerned that one of us may someday end up killing the other. Jeanne-Marie may not love me, but she will never love you either. Think on that for a bit."

The doll-like man then walked off with St. Eustache at his side, leaving a saddened Quasimodo behind to ponder those words for a few minutes.

*Beneath Notre-Dame, Thursday evening*

"These tunnels are really dark at night," Fritz, one of the soldiers under Colonel Vogel's command, grumbled. "I swear I can't see ten feet in front of me even with these flashlights."

"Stop your complaining," another soldier, Georg, said. "You always complain about every little hardship. Are you certain you want to live the life of a soldier?"

"Shut up, Georg!" Fritz rebutted. "You would need to be the Nyctalope himself to get through these tunnels safely, and I am not he!"

"That will be enough, both of you!" Colonel Vogel shouted at the bickering men.

The officer was quite correct, which is why the Monster of Frankenstein led the way down that shadowy path with his preternatural eyesight. He wasn't concerned about serving the Third Reich, as he planned to kill the *Führer* soon after he came through with his side of the bargain. After all, the Nazi commander-in-chief could prove to be a dangerous rival to Gouroull if he continued to acquire more power, and this could not be tolerated.

"Damn it, now this flashlight isn't working," was Fritz's next complaint.

"Do you ever stop with your childish whining?" queried Otto, a third member of the unit.

Fritz proved unable to provide one of his usual *réparties* due to the loop of a Punjab lasso snaking down from a rafter and tightly encircling his throat. The man was swiftly pulled upwards onto the beam in total silence, the life choked out of him within seconds.

490

Colonel Vogel turned around. "Fritz, I warned you to stop your whining before, and I meant it..."

The Colonel could not help but notice that there was nothing but thin air where the soldier had stood mere moments ago. "Fritz, where are you?"

Just then, a panel opened on the left side of the tunnel, and a bulky arm clothed in a brown garment wrapped around Georg's throat from behind, quickly breaking his windpipe while dragging him into the doorway.

"*Vast ist?*" Vogel shouted.

Gouroull glared into the darkness behind him and sniffed the air. What his olfactory senses captured was something familiar, but only encountered once before. "Him."

"Who?" Vogel demanded to know.

The Colonel was startled when a throwing blade suddenly whisked through the air and embedded itself in Otto's esophagus. The soldier opened his mouth and let out a series of gasping sounds before falling to the cold floor.

"He was referring to me, *Herr Colonel*," came the Phantom's voice as his cloaked figure stepped out of the shadows.

"Die, *schweinehund!*" Vogel bellowed as he drew his Luger.

But Erik threw a small object to the floor even faster than the Colonel could pull the trigger, and it produced a cloud of quickly expanding gray smoke that completely obscured his lithe form. Vogel's lead salvo passed through the cloud while appearing to hit nothing.

"*Meine Güte!*" the Nazi hollered in abject frustration. "Where the hell is he?"

"Here!" answered the Phantom's voice as his arm sprung from a hidden passage to the left and stabbed Gunther, the Colonel's aide, directly in the heart. The man yelled "*Ach!*" before falling to the floor dead.

"Open fire!" shouted Vogel.

His two remaining soldiers, Klaus and Felix, instantly did as ordered, but their bullets could not penetrate the thick wooden hatch after it had quickly slid shut.

"Cease fire!" Vogel barked. "Do not waste ammo. That door is too thick for our bullets." The Colonel turned towards Frankenstein's creation. "Gouroull! Smash through that panel! You're our only hope to get to that man."

But the Monster merely glared at the closed hatch, his ghastly features unreadable to human eyes.

"Gouroull, did you hear me? I need you to..."

That was when a panel opened on the opposite side of the wall and St. Eustache rushed out to sink his fearsome fangs into the wrist of Felix's gun hand. The soldier let off a single shot that merely deflected off the floor as the snarling animal crushed his carpal bones and dragged the screaming German to the ground.

"*Gott im Himmel!*" bellowed Vogel. "Open fire on that animal!"

491

Klaus's attempt to do so was savagely interrupted when Jacques leapt off the canine's shaggy back and sliced the soldier's four main fingers off with a single swish of his mini-sword. The German screamed as his Luger fell to the ground alongside his severed digitals.

"Klaus, step aside!" shouted Vogel. "I cannot target the dog with you in the way!"

But Klaus was in shock and could only stand still watching as blood spewed from the fleshy stumps like scarlet water from a row of spigots This provided Jacques ample time to thrust his small but razor-sharp sword into the soldier's groin, puncturing the major artery directly behind the man's testicles. The miniature killer's limited strength was more than compensated by his speed and savage lust for murder.

Klaus dropped to his knees as the bulk of his body's blood supply seeped out of his mid-section. Jacques's frenzy was still not sated, however, and he finished the Nazi off by jumping up and slicing open his throat with a blurry-quick swipe of his sword.

The combatant's fall afforded Vogel the chance to take his shot. The bullet was diverted from its target, however, when Quasimodo's bulky fist hit him on the head from behind. The Colonel collapsed to the ground from the powerful blow without a sound.

In the meantime, as the growling St. Eustache continued to tear into Felix, Jacques leapt on the soldier's chest and stabbed him repeatedly on his neck, throat, and eyes. The tiny assassin ended the fracas by biting off the soldier's nose and contemptuously spitting the mutilated wade of cartilage on his victim's chest.

Throughout the massacre, Gouroull stood indifferent, continuing to fix his inhuman gaze on the Phantom. Erik glared back with eyes that were similarly yellow. Both understood that this would be the final confrontation between father and son, the inevitable coming full circle at last.

Having completed their share of the bloody carnage, Jacques and Quasimodo stood just behind the Phantom, awaiting the expected order to attack the Monster.

"*Bonjour, Père,*" was the Phantom's calm salutation.

Gouroull grumbled an even more simple response: "Son."

"I am quite proud of this passageway to the bowels of Notre-Dame," Erik boasted. "I was contracted by parties I shall not mention to design it. Little were they aware that I included all of these… extras that would work to my advantage in situations such as this. That being said, I have two truly kindred souls accompanying me here today that are eager to make your acquaintance. Zam and Charles, step forth and meet Gouroull."

The Monster's wan eyes opened wide with surprise as two beings very similar to him stepped out from one of the hidden panels directly behind the Phantom. The duo matched Gouroull in being just over eight feet in height with grayish-white skin and dressed in simple garments resembling a monk's robes with thick-soled sandals specially tailored to their size. Zam's facial features were grotesquely skeletal in a manner more reminiscent of the Phantom's unmasked visage, but like Gouroull, he had a thick flowing mane of lustrous black hair. In contrast, Charles's face was more Neanderthal-like with an unruly orange-brown shock on his head.

Erik continued the introductions. "Gouroull, allow me to present to you Zam and Charles, who, like you, are the products of human alchemy. Their might is therefore comparable to your own, as you shall now discover." The Phantom held up a strange onyx-colored rock. "Zam, Charles... kill Gouroull. Tear him to wretched pieces!"

The two man-made titans did as ordered, compelled to obey Erik due to his possession of the fragment of obsidian mineral containing the essence of the Genie of the Black Rock used by Zametti to create his monstrous *magnumculus*.

The twin Monsters rushed Gouroull, their combined strength smashing him into one of the thick walls of the passageway. The strong wood partially yielded in response. Zam and Charles began pummeling their target mercilessly, quickly causing Gouroull's pale face to swell up as black ichor dripped from his nostrils and mouth.

Frankenstein's deadliest creation was not to be undone, however. Zam's skull-like visage  was slammed by an unexpected haymaker from Gouroull, which cracked several of his yellow teeth and sent him back against, and part of the way through, the wall on the other side of the passage. Charles was undaunted and kept up the pounding. But when Gouroull's own bulky left arm managed to deflect one of his foe's jackhammer blows, he struck back with a punch that sent Charles off his feet and sprawling across the floor.

"Are you certain they are fully under your control, Erik?" the concerned Jacques queried near the Phantom's feet.

"They are not," Erik admitted. "This rock needs to be wielded by an expert in the hermetic arts for full effect, but my will should be sufficient to spur those two on for at least a few minutes more."

"Even those two together may take longer than that to defeat the likes of Gouroull, especially if their own will is not truly in this fight," Quasimodo added.

Erik agreed and focused his concentration into the rock to hasten matters. "Hit him *harder,* boys! Rip him to his filthy component parts!"

Zam recovered from being made part of the wall and rushed his kindred adversary, slamming into Gouroull with the force of a rampaging ox. This sent the Monster partly through another section of the wall. Stunned, he was then beset by a series of blows that Zam delivered to his rib cage. The pain of feeling his sternum fractured prompted Gouroull into delivering an uppercut to his foe's chin that caused him to spit onyx-hued blood as it cracked his jaw and sent him to the floor.

The beating that Gouroull was inflicting upon Zam was cut short when Charles's massive arm ensnared the former's throat from behind, pulling him off his ersatz sibling with strength that could crush a gorilla. Frankenstein's Creature began suffering the clear sensation that his trachea was about to be crushed. He had faced a few foes as strong as he was in the past—Hezekiah Whateley and The Creeper came to mind[34] – but never two at once, so this was a battle that would take some effort to win.

"Strike him, Zam!" Charles shouted. "Hit him now, while I have him!"

Acting in both rage and desperation to free himself before Zam could re-enter the battle, Gouroull sunk his razor-sharp teeth into the undead flesh of his opponent's arm. The chalk white epidermis was pierced, and black-colored, foul-tasting fluid oozed from the wound.

"Arrgh! Strike him quickly, Zam! Before this fiend bites right through my arm!"

"I am coming, Charles!" Zam cried as he struggled to his feet.

But Gouroull focused all his incredible strength into moving backwards, his alchemically-enhanced musculature sending them clear through the already damaged wall behind them into the small hidden room beyond. This move stunned Charles, who had taken the brunt of it, and Gouroull quickly took the offensive by punching his stunned opponent with his full strength. This sent Charles crashing through the far wall of the small space… and down a chasm that seemed to lead at least a few hundred feet downwards.

All that could be heard was Charles's hideous scream that became increasingly distant before fading out.

"This is not good," Erik muttered. "Jacques! Quasimodo! Run to the artifact storage room at the end of this passage and find the crate containing the Spear!"

The Phantom then held up the rock again, pouring as much of his will into it as he could muster. "Zam! Avenge your brother while I accompany the others!"

The enraged Zam leapt at Gouroull who ducked the move with amazing speed and threw a retaliatory punch that sent his fellow monster to his knees. He then struck Zam several more times before his opponent could react, knocking him to the floor unmoving with a pool of obsidian-colored fluid streaming from his mouth and nasal passages. Gouroull then turned to follow the Phantom and his cohorts to intercept their attempt to acquire the Spear of Destiny.

"Erik, I think it is in this crate!" Jacques hollered while pointing to a box with a rectangular shape.

"Quasimodo, help me open it!" the Phantom demanded.

---

[34] See *The Spells of Frankenstein* and *The Quest of Frankenstein* by Frank Schildiner, Black Coat Press.

The combined strength of the two was sufficient to rip off the nailed top of the crate in a few seconds. Within it lay a spear of classic medieval design.

"This must be it!" the Hunchback excitedly decreed. "It defies the ravages of time, for it looks as if it were newly minted!"

"That is because it *is* newly minted, *idiot!*" Erik lamented. "This spear is a fake! I recognize its craftmanship. The Nazis were duped."

The trio turned to see Gouroull standing behind them with a look of disgruntled fury on his hideous countenance.

"Did you hear that, *mon père?*" Erik said with a smirk. "You and your Nazi bosses were played for fools. All their mission succeeded in accomplishing was bringing you into my clutches again. Let us settle up for the final time!"

The Phantom drew a broadsword from a hidden sheath in his cloak. He pressed a button on its hilt with a flick of his thumb, causing the blade to emit a loud humming noise as the sharpened metal started vibrating.

"This vibratory feature enhances the cutting power of the steel blade tenfold," Erik explained. "Let us see how well even your stone-like flesh fares against it."

Erik charged Gouroull and executed a brutal slash with the sword. The Monster was stunned to see that it sliced his stomach open. It would have disemboweled him had he not moved backwards at the last possible moment. The Creature ignored the pain from his bleeding gut to duck the next vicious swing from Erik.

The Phantom attacked relentlessly, slashing wildly, with Gouroull's great speed and reflexes barely evading the enhanced sword. The brutal abdominal wound began noticeably healing, so Erik knew he would have to cut the Monster limb from limb to have a hope of fully dispatching him.

Erik managed another swipe that sliced into the skin of Gouroull's left arm, causing him to grunt in agony as more of his dark life-fluid was spilled. But while the Phantom was still off-balance, Gouroull moved forward and slammed the palm of his hand into his offspring's chest. This sent the assassin flying backwards several meters until he slammed into a statue of David. Despite his pain, the Phantom forced himself to roll aside a mere second before the heavy sculpture would have crushed him to death as it fell crashing to the floor.

"Erik is injured!" Quasimodo shrieked. "We must enter the fray and buy him time!"

"St. Eustache... attack!" Jacques commanded.

The wolf-dog hybrid cunningly sunk his powerful jaws into the blade wound just inflicted on Gouroull's arm. Simultaneously, the canine's dwarf master leapt onto the Creature's face punctured one of Gouroull's yellow eyes with a single thrust of his tiny but razor-sharp blade.

As St. Eustache's mouth burned from the rancid ichor that passed for Gouroull's blood, the canine yelped in pain as he fled to dilute the vile fluid by drinking the water in a nearby fountain display. The Monster then swatted Jacques off his face as a person would a fly.

Quasimodo leapt off a nearby column of crates to land on Gouroull's back, tightly wrapping his legs around his adversary's neck for support. He began pounding on the Monster's skull repeatedly with his spade-like hands. This rattled Gouroull but was not sufficient to take him to the floor. Frankenstein's creation reached back, grabbed his foe, and effortlessly flung his 400-pound body clear across the room to slam into and (ironically) shatter a statue of Adonis.

Gouroull then looked out his one good eye to see Erik rushing back towards him with his vibro-sword back in hand. The Monster jumped back to evade the first slash, but it still sliced the side of his neck, resulting in a gaping wound that spurted more dark ichor. However, the Phantom's speed was hampered by three cracked ribs, and his next swing fell short as Gouroull caught his wrist on the downswing.

The Monster twisted the master assassin's hand, snapping the ulna and causing him to drop the blade. Gouroull next grabbed his offspring by the throat and slammed him down against the floor while raising his other fist in preparation for delivering a killing blow.

However, Erik quickly reached into his cloak and pulled out a small object in the shape and size of a pen. With a blur of motion, he shoved the implement up one of the Monster's nostrils.

"Have a care, Gouroull," a wheezing Erik explained. "This item will dispense a tiny explosive with compressed air, exerting enough force to pierce even your nasal membrane to fix itself in the brain. It will immediately explode inside your skull, ending your putrid existence."

Gouroull grumbled in frustration and paused, contemplating his next move.

"So," the Phantom continued, "it would seem we are in what the Americans might call a 'Mexican stand-off.' I urge you to go ahead with your intended blow while I depress the firing mechanism. Let us die simultaneously! It is a true act of poetic justice that we end each other in this fashion!"

"Erik, do not let him kill you!" the now-recovered Hunchback shouted from a few meters away. "You may hate your existence, but you matter to us! You are the only friend Jacques and I have ever had. We value you!"

"He speaks the truth, *mon ami,*" Jacques concurred as he joined his far larger ally on the back of St. Eustache. "You have become the best assassin in the world and have given us a life. We do not want to see you lose your own."

The Phantom pondered their words, as did Gouroull. The Monster's alien mind evidently could not process gentler emotions such as love, but he could experience a form of pride. And in his own twisted way, he was proud of his son for becoming the best there was in dispensing carnage on the mortal race they both detested.

Erik looked up at Gouroull's monstrous features, noticing that his skewered eye was already partly healed. "Well, are you going to kill me, Monster?"

"No," Gouroull replied while releasing his grip.

Despite his injuries, the Phantom forced himself back to his feet. "Let there be an end to our animosity, Gouroull. Perhaps we both serve some purpose in this world, even if no human mind can possibly fathom how evil can have a place in the scheme of things. But do not *ever* return to France. Stay out of my domain and I will not attempt to kill you again. Is that understood?"

"Yes," Gouroull replied in a noncommittal tone.

The Monster then turned and left the passageway, having decided to leave France, at least for now. He knew the nation of Belgium was right beside it, and he resolved to go there next, as it was as good a location any other to continue his latest quest.

"Erik, we must get you to a doctor," Jacques pleaded.

"One moment," the Phantom said. He winced as he forcefully twisted the fractured bone in his wrist back into place. "There... it is properly set. Now it only requires a cast to be placed around it."

At that moment, Zam stumbled into the chamber, completely free of the Black Rock fragment's influence. But instead of hostility, he only expressed sorrow to those standing before him.

"I have lost everything," the sobbing Monster said. "First, my father, who never did anything but use me. Then his wife Julianne, whom I thought loved me, but only gave me betrayal. I may have detested Charles, but he was all the family I had left, and now he is lost to me too. And after reviving me... *you* used me as well. Is this what the twisted parody of my life is always destined to be?"

Zam fell to the floor weeping profusely. "*Please* kill me. I will not try to stop you."

"Erik, will you use the sword to behead him?" Quasimodo asked.

"No," was the Phantom's reply.

Erik walked up to the crying monster and gently placed a hand on his bulky shoulder. "Zam, you are free to come with us if you so choose. I shall not exploit you again."

The Unholy Three then began leaving the museum beneath Notre-Dame Cathedral. Zam stood up and followed them, thus turning Erik's trio of deadly misfits into a quartet.

*A few hours earlier, at the Cour des Miracles*

A nude, traumatized young woman lay trembling in the alley, ignoring the curious rats that scampered about her. For she had become a victim of something far more horrifying than even the biggest and filthiest of rodents. Her present state was the result of the purpose behind Gouroull "gallivanting around Paris," as Colonel Vogel had put it. That purpose was fulfilled with the mutant fetus now growing within the violated lady's womb. The resulting offspring would become a concern for Erik, and the rest of the world, many years later.

*Jules Verne's* The Secret of Wilhelm Storitz *was written around 1897, but not published until 1910—it was the last book sent by Verne to his publisher Louis-Jules Hetzel. The earlier editions of the novel were rewritten by Verne's son, Michel. In it, Myra, the heroine, turned invisible by Storitz, becomes visible again after giving birth to her son and the happy couple moves to Paris, where her husband Marc finds work as a painter. In 2011, a new edition was published, based on Verne's original handwritten manuscript. In it, poor Myra is fated to remain invisible forever and there is no happy ending. This romantic drama is the basis of John Peel's latest yarn...*

# John Peel: *A Singular Haunting*

*London, 1910*

My friend Carnacki has the splendid habit of throwing a dinner party approximately once a month, and he invites me and four or five mutual good friends along. He's something of an epicure, so you can always guarantee a splendid meal and superb wines. That alone would make the evening most rewarding, but the meal is, if you will pardon the expression, a mere appetizer for what then follows. We retreat to his well-stocked library and a glass of refined brandy—he leaves a full decanter for anyone wishing a refresher—and then he tells us of his latest case. No, he is not a lawyer, or even a consulting detective.

Carnacki is a ghost hunter.

His cases are always fascinating—and sometimes even terrifying. He does not always discover ghosts, of course. Fairly often, there are purely natural explanations for observed phenomenon, and quite often they involve fraud, impersonation and other criminal matters. But Carnacki is careful, and undertakes investigation only when the circumstances suggest something intriguing. As a result, whatever tales he tells us, and whatever the outcome, they never fail to engross and entertain. This last occasion was no exception.

I was invited to a house in a suburb of London (Carnacki began his tale). For reasons that will become clear, I would rather not be more specific. It was in a genteel street, one of Georgian houses all well-maintained, each with their privacy provided by substantial walls. I had my cab let me off at the top of the street so that I might examine the neighborhood as I approached my destination. It was clear that this was a well-established set of residences, and that whoever dwelt within certainly possessed good incomes. The houses were all in fine shape, and their gardens and driveways neatly maintained, undoubtedly by a staff of gardeners. The area spoke to me of money, but not of great age. It was not the sort of setting one would expect to discover a ghost frequenting, and yet the letter I had received urging me to this meeting spoke most urgently of being haunted. The tone of the missive suggested a man almost at the limits of his endurance.

This dichotomy intrigued me. As always, though, I intended to keep an open mind.

I reached my target and stood at the gates, surveying the house. It was substantially identical to its fellows—three stories tall, and signs of a lower floor to house the kitchen and storage. It was well-maintained and looked most peaceful. The gardens were neatly laid out, though they showed slight signs of recent neglect. I walked carefully up the pathway to the door and rang the bell.

After a short pause, it was opened by a footman. That was curious in such a house, I should have expected a butler. It was certainly large enough to warrant such. I gave my name, and was invited in. The hallway was tidy, and contained a few small items of decoration and a rather large and ugly umbrella stand. Beyond, there were several doors leading off the hallway, and, at the end, a staircase leading to the first floor. Patches of colored lights indicated the presence of stained glass further up and out of sight.

The footman opened a door to a small room close to the entrance, obviously a waiting room. "If you would wait here, sir," he said, "I will inform the master of your arrival." He took my hat, can and overcoat as he left on his mission. I was left alone, so I glanced about the room. There were several formal chairs, two small tables with lace coverings and a large bookcase along the far wall. There was a portrait of a somber-looking middle-aged man over the fireplace, and one of an equally rigid woman on the wall facing it. From the clothing styles, I estimated that the paintings were at least fifty years-old, so clearly not of the man I was here to meet. I strode to the bookcase and examined the volumes there. Again, the books appeared to date back at least half a century, if not more. There was not a single more recent title to my view in the brief time I had before the door crashed open again. I expected the footman again, but this was instead clearly the man who had invited me here.

He was middle-aged also, but obviously unrelated to either portrait subject. Instead of the bluff Englishness of those faces, he had a thin, Continental face, with a rather Roman nose and slicked-back hair—currently disheveled slightly. His clothes were expensive, but looked as if they might have been slept in. He wore no jacket, but a heavy dressing gown instead. His feet were slippered and not shod.

"Carnacki!" he exclaimed. "By Heavens, I am glad to see you!" His voice was urgent, and there was a distinct hint of a French accent, judging by the stresses on certain sounds. I could not judge more accurately than that. He crossed the broom swiftly, and held out a hand, grasping mine and shaking it heartily. He held my elbow with his left hand as he did so.

"Mr. Roger Danglars?" I assumed.

He nodded. "Perhaps now I shall be able to get some peace," he said. "I am so glad to make your acquaintance. Your name was suggested to me by..." and he named a man I had helped out with a curious affair some eighteen months earlier. "He assures me that you are both discrete and effective."

"I certainly try to be," I assured him. "Your note suggested some urgency to this call, but provided me with no details."

He paused. "To be truthful," he admitted, "I did start another note before that one, one in which I attempted to explain my predicament." He hung his head slightly. "But, as I wrote it, I felt more than a little foolish writing matters down. I was afraid you would read it and think *here is a man who is deranged.* You understand?"

"I do indeed," I agreed.

"I thought it better for you to see my face and hear my voice when I told my story—that it would make it easier for you to judge whether I am sane or crazed. Mere words would not be enough—you would have to *see*."

"That was a wise decision," I agreed. I gestured at the chairs. "Perhaps we should sit, and you can tell me your problem?"

"Of course." Once we were seated, he looked at me nervously. "Forgive me. I am still apprehensive that you may consider me a crazed person. What I have witnessed..." He shook his head. "Should *you* tell *me* such a tale, I would frankly not believe you, you understand?"

"Indeed," I assured him. "But in this matter, I have the advantage over you, for I have seen many things that you would surely find unbelievable. That is in the nature of my profession, you must understand."

"Ah, yes. I can see that it might be so.' He took a deep breath and shuddered. "In which case, I shall proceed. I am being haunted, nightly, by some unseen being that delights in tormenting me."

Now that he had begun to tell his tale, I leaned forward attentively. You must understand that I do not necessarily believe what I am told. Over the years, many people have attempted to dupe me for various reasons, so I am cautious in accepting any tale as the truth. But I have become, perhaps, a cynical observer of human nature. I take everything I hear with a considerable amount of skepticism, and I listen and study as much the person who tells me a tale as I do to the tale itself. And, as he spoke, I came to firmly believe that Danglars was telling me the truth. Ah, no—not *the truth*, as such, but the truth as he perceived it. He was in no way attempting to deceive me. So—on to what he said!

"Every evening, I am... well, visited, by some sort of being. I have never seen it directly, only observed the effects of its presence. At first, it was simply curious things—a glass I left on a table would, when I sought it, be on the mantelpiece. Or a book I had removed from a bookcase to read would somehow be returned to the case. Small matters, almost inconsequential, but disturbing, you understand? Things that were more puzzling or irritating than alarming. And I ascribed them to perhaps my distraction. I am a financier by avocation, and have weighty monetary matters constantly upon my mind, you see? Things that might make me momentary forgetful of my actions, matters that occupied my thoughts that might lead me to becoming distracted and forgetful in small things."

Such did seem to be a logical possibility. "Did anyone else ever witness these occurrences? Your footman, perhaps?" I inquired. I did not add that it might be that any such observer might actually be the *cause* of these events.

He shook his head. "No. And no one else has witnessed any of the more disturbing events, either. I am invariably alone when they occur."

That ruled out one of the more obvious possibilities, then, that a servant might be playing tricks on him for some unknown reason. "And in which room do these events happen?"

He gave a sort of strangled laugh. "In *any* room, Mr. Carnacki." He gestured. "In here. Or my private chambers. In the hallway... The place does not matter—only that I should be alone."

"You are a financier. Do you have rooms in the City?"

"Yes, of course. I work there every day."

"*Every* day?" I queried.

"Yes. My hours are from ten until four daily, including Sundays." He gave a slight shrug. "I am not a religious man, and I have never been frightened of the supernatural. Well, not since my childhood, at any rate. I am a banker—one and one invariably add up to two. No otherworldly phenomena can possibly make it three or four. I do not submit to the whims of some mythical deity that convention calls upon me to accept. And I have never accepted, like the credulous masses, the existence of spirits, or angels, demons or ghosts." He halted.

"Except..." I prompted.

"Except," he said, with some kind of desperation, "that there appears to be no logical alternative explanation for what is happening to me! Books do not continue to lay where I place them, they fly into my face as if to attack me! My cup rises in the air and shatters against a wall. If I attempt a glass of wine, some unseen force throws it into my face. And..." His voice broke off again.

"And?"

"I hear laughter. Sometimes in the same room as me, sometimes in one close by. Laughter! And without any obvious source or reason!"

'Can you tell whose voice it might be?"

"It is a woman's laughter, Mr. Carnacki. And there is no one living here in the house but myself."

"That is untrue, Mr. Danglars," I admonished him firmly. "There is the footman who let me in, for example. And in a house of this size, I would expect there to be other servants."

"Oh, the servants—yes. But I am otherwise alone. I have neither wife, children, friends or family living with me."

"I do not wish to appear rude, but is there any reason for that?"

He gave a shrug. "I am a foreigner in a country strange to me, and have not lived here long enough to have formed social ties."

"And yet, you speak exceptionally good English," I observed.

He made a negligent gesture. "It is of little matter," he said dismissively. "My German and French are likewise impeccable, and my Italian is reasonably decent. As a financier, I need to speak with my clients and my colleagues without the possibility of being misunderstood. Much money may be lost if there should be miscommunication. So I have learned my languages with care."

"An admirable achievement," I said in congratulations.

Again, he dismissed it. "It is what I require to conduct my business. And my business is my life, you must understand."

"So," I said, "to return to the servants. You have many?"

He gave a slight shake of his head. "I have but three."

"Three?" That certainly surprised me. "For a house of this size?"

He sighed. "Most of it, I do not use. Only a handful of rooms. The rest remain empty, and therefore need no upkeep. I require only a man, a maid and a cook."

"Forgive me for asking, but why then take such a large house if you do not need it?"

"These cursed Britons," he snapped. "They are such snobs, especially where their money is concerned. They will not trust a man who does not have what they consider to be a good address. His skills in finance mean nothing compared to a fine dwelling. So—good, I have the correct address, even if it is surplus to my requirements."

"I see." And I did, I can assure you. I was dealing with a man for whom everything was superficial beyond the making of money. "And do you know the history of this house?"

"History?" He looked at me blankly. "Why should I wish to know that? It is here only to serve my needs. I do not need any stories."

"Most hauntings," I explained, "are tied to a place and not to a person. The spirits of the departed stay where they once lived—and died."

Danglars scowled. "You believe I may have leased a ghost along with the house, then?"

"I do not know. That is something I shall have to determine. But if there are spectral occurrences linked to this place, then that would give me a basis from which to work." I considered the matter. "These... events only happen at night?"

"How should I know?" he growled. "I am never here during the day, as I have already told you." As it was early afternoon, I merely raised an eyebrow and he caught my implied question. "Except for today, obviously, when I had to make time to meet with you."

"I understand. Very well, then. I shall need to speak with your servants, to begin with."

He eyed me again. "You think they might be involved in this for some reason? If they are, by God, I'll sack the lot of them!"

I made a quick gesture to calm him down. "I suspect nothing of anyone as of yet. I merely need to discover what they know of these events. And they may be able to shed some light on the background to this house."

"Very well," he said, his temper under control once more. "You'd better speak with the maid first, as she goes home soon. The cook is busy preparing my dinner, of course." I noted that he made no mention of my dining with him. "My man remains overnight, so he is available whenever you wish." He rang the bell, and the footman appeared quite swiftly. "Tell the maid she's wanted here." The man nodded and disappeared again.

"Perhaps I could speak to her alone," I suggested. "If it is not inconvenient."

"Whatever you like," he agreed. "I shall be in my study if you require me again." There was a tap at the door, and a young girl entered and curtsied politely. "This gentleman wants to speak to you," he said brusquely, and then marched out of the room.

The girl turned to look at me, a hint of suspicion and hesitation on her face. I could only imagine what she thought of this business, and attempted to set her at her ease. "My name is Carnacki," I informed her. "And you are…?"

"Ruby," she replied, cautiously. She looked to be about nineteen or twenty years-old. She was neither beautiful nor ugly, merely an average-looking personage. She had wary eyes, though, suggesting an active mind.

"Well, Ruby, I am here to investigate… disturbances in this house."

"Nothing to do with me," she said promptly. "I know me duties, and I carry them out."

"I'm sure you do," I agreed. "And I don't mean to suggest otherwise. Now, I understand that you are a day girl? That you go home shortly?"

"Right you are, sir," she replied. "I won't stay in this house at night."

Ah! That sounded promising. "You are perhaps afraid of ghosts?"

"Ghosts?" She snorted. "I don't give a fig about ghosts. I won't stay in a house at night with a single gentleman who might imagine his money is buying something that it ain't." She glanced at me sharply. "If you understands my meaning. I'm a good girl, I am."

Oh well… "Quite," I agreed. "You sound like a very sensible and proper young woman. You don't believe in ghosts, then?"

She gave a small shrug. "If they leaves me alone, I'll leave them alone. I don't believe nor disbelieve. I just does me job and minds me business."

"Then you know nothing of any strange happenings in this house?" I asked her.

She seemed to have become quite comfortable with me now she'd made herself clear. "Oh, there's always strange happenings in any house," she said. "But they're nothing to do with me, as I tells Mrs. Mullins."

"Mrs. Mullins?"

"The cook."

Ah. "She thinks otherwise, though?"

"She up and outright accuses me of stealing food! As if I'd do that. Chance'd be a fine thing. Like I tells her, I'm here when she's here, and I minds me place. When could I possibly steal a sausage? And where would I hide it? Skinny as a rake, I am, and if I was hiding any pork chops about me person, it'd stick out like a sore thumb, wouldn't it? I tells her it's more likely that stuck-up Henry who's filching stuff, but will she believe me? Fawns all over him, she does. As if he'd give her the time of day, much less a tumble."

"Henry?" I asked.

"Him what answers the door," she explained. "Henry."

The relationships of servants is always a vexing issue for any homeowner. There is a rigid hierarchy, usually overseen and enforced by the butler. But in this house, there was no butler, and I could see that there was a certain amount of jousting going on between the three of them.

This became even more apparent when I spoke next with Henry. He was stiff and reluctant to answer even the simplest question until I decided to ask him if he thought the maid and cook were honest.

His angular face became even sharper. "Is that what this is about?" he asked. "Is someone here suspected of stealing?"

I didn't disabuse him of the notion. "Please, just answer my question: do you think that the two women are trustworthy?"

"I wouldn't call that Ruby a woman," he said, somewhat sourly. "Barely more than a child, if you ask me, and acts like one still."

"In what ways?"

"Well, she has an uppity attitude for a junior maid. Thinks very highly of herself, she does." He was a lot more open now he felt he could air his opinions. "I'd not be surprised if she wasn't setting her eyes on the master. She doesn't have much use for cook or myself."

"But as to her honesty?" I prompted.

"To the best of my knowledge, she's straight enough," he answered. "I've not heard of anything going missing." His eyes narrowed. "Has the master said something?"

I slipped away from the issue. "Have you noticed anything strange occur in the house?"

"Strange? How do you mean?"

"Unexpected and unexplained events."

He looked puzzled. "It's a decent enough place," he said. "I worked worse. The master's a foreigner, of course, with foreigner's ways, but when you get used to them, he's decent enough."

"What sort of ways?" I asked.

"Well…" He was obviously considering how far he could go without getting himself into trouble. "Just little things, you understand. Like him throwing his sherry glass against the wall." He looked apologetic. "Like I said, it's a foreign thing, isn't it? Not what an Englishman would do."

I smiled, as if sharing a joke. "He really does that?"

"Well, he did the other night. I heard him, and went in to see if there was a problem. He told me he'd thrown his drink at the wall, and to just clean it up."

It turned out that Danglars had made similar excuses for books falling off shelves, or vases overturning. Henry ascribed all such events to "foreignness." He made no mention of ghosts. I asked him if he knew anything of the history of the house—who had originally owned it, for example.

"No, sir," he answered. "I was merely engaged to be manservant here. I'd never been near the place before that. The agency told me nothing, and we don't see the neighbors to talk to."

"Where do you go on your day off?" I asked him. "Is there a local you visit, for example?" I asked that because there's nothing like a pub to discover the gossip.

"I don't think there's a pub around here," he said. "And my time's off is my own business. Though I will own there's a girl I have my eye on."

"Ruby?" I suggested, rather naughtily.

"Her?" He actually looked astonished for once. And his accent slipped momentarily. "She's nowt but a lass." Then he caught himself, and the posh accent returned. "She's really not my type."

I had to wait a little while to be able to talk to Mrs. Mullins. Apparently, Danglars had his dinner promptly at six, so the cook and Henry were occupied during that time. I used my freedom to look quietly about the house. It was in very good structural shape, with no damp or other issues. Danglars had all of his rooms on the ground floor, having turned an old receiving room into his bedroom. I knew that neither woman stayed in the house—Ruby had already left for the day, and Mrs. Mullins would depart about eight, after cleaning the kitchen and readying for tomorrow's breakfast making. She would return promptly at 8 in the a.m.

I mounted the stairs and looked at the first floor. It was furnished in a nondescript, semi-genteel fashion. There were tables in the hall, presumably meant to hold vases filled with flowers, but now left bare. There were pictures on the walls, but they were all prints and not originals. I peeked into one room—clearly a bedroom—to see that the curtains were drawn, the furniture nondescript but in good shape. There was a cover on the bed, but no linens or towels. Though not in use, the rooms were tidy.

The third floor was barer, with the walls simply painted and lacking event prints on the walls. The rooms were simply for storage or for non-existent servants. One would obviously be used by Henry—the only other person who remained overnight in the house—but it seemed unnecessarily intrusive to check. I saw no evidence of anything unusual. There were no cold spots, as sometimes accompanied hauntings, but that told me nothing. I should need my equipment to know for certain if there were supernatural energies at work.

By the time my rather cursory examination was complete, dinner was over and Mrs. Mullins was available to talk to. She seemed a trifle flustered as she went about her tidying and then preparations for the morning. She was due to take her leave at eight, and she was quite firm about doing precisely that. She was a slightly overweight woman whose age hovered about the fifty mark. She had a very preoccupied air, but considering her duties, this came as no real surprise.

"I know nothing," she replied when I asked about the history of the house. "What do I care? I'm just hired to cook, and that's what I do." She gave me a pointed look. "I minds my own business and hopes other people minds theirs."

"Do you mean Henry and Ruby?" I asked her. "Don't you get along with them?"

"I don't need to get along with them," she said. "They do their work, and I do mine. We're not required to be friends. Between you, me and the lamppost, I wouldn't have hired either of them, but that's not on me, is it? That's the master's decision, and he's the one that has to live with it."

"What's wrong with them?"

"Nothing—as long as they stay out of my way and my work."

"And do they?" I wondered.

"For the most part," she replied.

"You are talking about the missing food?" I guessed.

She scowled. "So, you've heard about that? Is that why the master's brought you in? To look out the thief?"

I considered correcting her, but then decided that I might learn more by letting her vent. "I am not at liberty to say. How much food are we talking about?"

She paused. "Honestly? Very little. But that's not the point, is it? It's a matter of trust. If there's a thief in the house, then how can there be trust? That's why I mind my own business and advises everyone else to do the same."

"You think that Ruby might be the culprit?" I suggested.

"That girl? Aye, it's likely. She denies it, but then she would, wouldn't she?"

"But why would she do anything so obvious as steal from the place where she works?"

"You're a bit of the innocent, aren't you?" Mrs. Mullins shook her head. "Servants do it so's they can sell the food and earn a little bit extra of the ready, don't they?" It didn't seem to occur to her that this also gave her the equal chance of being the thief, and she could be accusing Ruby to cover her own depredations.

"Does Mr. Danglars pay so poorly, then?" I asked.

"I'm not complaining!" she said promptly. "It's a decent enough living wage. But there's always them that wants more, isn't there?"

That was true enough. "But what about Henry?"

"Him? Steal? Fat chance. He don't do any more work than he has to. Stuck-up snob that he is." She lowered her voice, confidentially. "Thinks he's the butler, he does, and he's no more than a footman really. I can't abide a man who puts on airs."

By this time, she'd finished her preparations for the morrow and informed me firmly that it was her time to leave, and she'd best be off. I watched her depart thoughtfully. One thing that I was certain of was that none of the servants were playing tricks of any sort on their master. Aside from the lack of a reason for them to do so, it was clear that the three of them were more at odds with one another than they were with Danglars. Unless one or more of them was a greater actor than Henry Irving, I knew I should have to look in a different direction to solve Danglars's problem.

There was nothing more that I could do without the aid of my instruments, and so I went to the receiving room to inform him of the fact. As I approached the door, however, there was a loud crash from inside the room, followed by what was obviously a spate of cursing in Hungarian.

I threw open the door immediately. Danglars was standing by the fireplace, an unlit cigar in his right hand and a dark expression on his face. There was a smear of water on the wall beside him, and a vase of flowers shattered on the floor at his feet. I recalled seeing this vase on a table by the doorway earlier.

"What has happened?" I asked.

"Isn't it obvious?" he roared. "These flowers were flung at my head as I bent to light my cigar." I saw a spill on the hearth that he had clearly been using in his left hand to get himself a light from the fire.

"Did you see who flung them?" I asked, urgently.

"Do *you* see anyone else in here with me?" he demanded. "Because I certainly cannot."

He was quite correct: he had been utterly alone when I had flung open the door. The vase must have been flung by some unseen force. Danglars appeared more angered than shaken, even though it must have been very disturbing.

If, of course, it had occurred as he claimed. It wasn't beyond possibility that he might have flung the vase himself, after setting the stage so that he would appear to be the victim. I could not rule out this possibility. After all, he had informed me that these events only took place when he was quite alone. Yet, I could not see what he would have to gain from such a course of action. Why *pretend* to be haunted, and then call me in to assist him? It didn't appear to be very logical.

Of course, the human mind is a strange instrument, and when it malfunctions the results can be most bizarre. Was it possible that his mind was disturbed—say, as a result of business pressures—and he was haunting himself as a result? I did not know, but I could determine the answer.

And then I noticed the faint odor of violets—pleasant, but fleeting. I glanced at the shattered vase, but that had contained only roses and carnations. The scent was mild, but quite certain. Where had it emanated from?

I started to bend to examine the broken vase, but Danglars made a cutting motion. "Leave it. I'll have the girl clean it away in the morning."

"Very well," I agreed, straightening again. "There is nothing more I can do this evening. I shall return tomorrow with my instrumentation, and make a thorough check of the house for any alien energies."

I took my leave of Danglars and went to the exterior door. Then I paused.

Where was Henry? It was his task to see me out, and yet he had not appeared, even after the shattering of the vase…

I returned home to two things: a late dinner and a good deal of thinking. I was not sure there was even a reason for me to investigate the house. It felt… *wrong*. A haunting that only one person was ever aware of? That was unprecedented. Though no two ghostly experiences were alike, they did tend to have common factors. The main one is that a haunting is of a *place* and not a person. If there was a manifestation, anyone present could see it. Yet none of the three servants were even aware of a possible ghost. Only Danglars.

Now, it is true that some people are more sensitive to psychic energy than others. It was remotely possible that only Danglars in that house was attuned to supernatural occurrences, but since it was producing physical effects such as the vase shattering, the servants might not be able to perceive the motivating force, but they should certainly be able to witness the resulting effect. And yet the main topic of interest to them seemed to be the trifling one of missing food! It made no sense to me.

And I had to confess to myself that I did not like Danglars. Partially, it was his rudeness in not offering me food and drink while he indulged himself, but it was mostly because of his attitude. Greed appeared to me to be his motivating factor. His willingness to conform to the outward appearances of class and wealth whilst in reality acting very cheaply was also a mark against him. I wouldn't go quite so far as to call him a fake, but he was clearly a poser. But because his interests were so centered upon money, I found it difficult to believe that he might have any psychic abilities of his own. It was not impossible, of course, merely unlikely.

As for the servants… Well, they were an odd mixture. All three appeared to be good at their jobs, but they evidently didn't get along with one another, and nor did they have much affection for their fellow toilers. There was no requirement that they should be friends, of course, but they all seemed to verge instead on hostility. Probably as a result of their master's attitudes, of course. They did not appear to care for him overmuch.

Still, my client's domestic arrangements were none of my business, and the haunting was. I prepared my equipment for the morning before retiring for the night.

I returned to the puzzling house early the following day to set up my apparatus. From what Danglars had told me, it appeared that the reception room was the site of the major disturbances, undoubtedly simply because it was where he spent the majority of his time whilst he was home. Here I set up my electric pentacle.

As I have mentioned in the past, magic may commonly be considered by the uninitiated as something beyond our understanding, but it is really nothing of the kind. It is merely a form of energy, but one unrecognized and not investigated or described by Science. And any form of energy leaves traces when it is employed, and so I have evolved over time various instruments that can detect, measure and record magical manifestations. My electric pentacle is primary amongst those instruments. I laid it out on the carpet in the room and once it was complete, I set it in operation. I was not particularly surprised when it registered nothing. It was always possible that it was simply that the energies manifested last evening in the destruction of the vase had simply faded into virtually nothingness, but if the room was a focus of a haunting, I should have expected some residual energies to be detected. There was nothing.

So. The room itself, then, was unlikely to be the center of the occurrences. The next possibility was that it was Danglars himself who was the (perhaps unwitting) cause. As he had not yet had his breakfast, he was still in the house, and I persuaded him to stand within the pentacle after assuring him of its perfect safety. Incidentally, I was again not invited to share food with him. I had expected no less, and eaten well before setting out for the house, but, again, it showed his lack of civility and breeding. He wasn't pleased with this minor disruption of his schedule, but he could hardly refuse to submit to testing.

I again drew a blank; there was no evidence of psychic energies about his person at all. He went off to his breakfast, grumbling, and I sat to consider my findings, or, rather, the lack of them. Nothing in the room, and nothing from Danglars. The obvious conclusion, then, was that there was nothing of the supernatural at all about this problem. And that suggested trickery was the cause. As the events only happened when Danglars was alone, there was the clear possibility that he was responsible. And yet... I could think of no reason why he should do such a thing. If he *were* somehow responsible, then it would surely be because he was attempting to hoodwink someone. Me? It seemed unlikely. What possible motivation could he have to fool me? He acted as though he found me an inconvenience, not a target. And the only other people around he might be attempting to defraud were the servants, and why should he want to do so? Besides, they seemed to be completely unaware of any possibility of ghosts or the supernatural. If he was attempting to delude them for any bizarre reason I could not yet fathom, he was clearly doing a terrible job of it.

That left, to my mind, only a single possible option: that someone outside the staff was somehow producing the effects. But how could anyone enter the house unseen and undetected? In older houses, many of them had what are colloquially called "priest holes." During times of religious persecution—mainly the Tudor era, with its deep suspicions about Roman Catholics—priests were often considered enemy agents of Catholic countries, and therefore banned from England. But many of the older families remained Catholics and were in need of such priests. If those ministers were discovered, they might be imprisoned or even killed, so a method of hiding them from discovery was necessary. So tunnels were built to enable escape, and the entrances cunningly disguised. Now the house I was in was Georgian, built two centuries after these events, but it was always possible that secret passages or hidden doors might exist at the whim of the builder. In detective fiction, such items are a necessity!

And so, once Danglars had left for his offices, I began my own work for the day, measuring rooms and halls, and the thicknesses of walls, in order to determine if there might be some secret byways. The servants found my actions most amusing, and offered a selection of what they considered amusing "helpful" advice. Ruby proved to be particularly adept at this. I merely smiled politely and continued with my work.

And I found absolutely nothing untoward. There were neither secret passages nor hidden compartments to be discovered anywhere on the ground floor. Still, I was certain that I must be on the correct track. There had to be some outside agency at work, and one that did not include any elements of the supernatural. And yet, I had exhausted all logical possibilities.

Which left me with only a single course of action: to consider *illogical* possibilities.

There had to be some other person in the house who was producing the supposedly ghostly events, and yet to somehow remain unseen and undetected. No, not *quite* undetected—I had distinctly smelled the scent of violets when no such flowers were present. And there was that odd business of missing food. Perhaps sufficient to feed another unknown inhabitant of the house? Someone who hid during the day to appear only in the evenings to bedevil Danglars alone. Where could they hide during the day? The first and second floors were not in use, save for Henry's room on the uppermost floor, so there were numerous spaces.

It was merely a matter of checking. And the third door I tried on the first floor proved to be the one. It was a bedroom like the abandoned one I had seen earlier, but this one had obviously been occupied. There was a coverlet on the bed that showed evidence of being slept on, and there was the faint but quite distinct odor of violets. But there was no one in evidence at the moment. But I was convinced that I had uncovered my culprit.

But what to do about it?

I returned to the reception room and fell into deep thought. I glanced routinely at my electric pentagram, but it was still showing nothing. It was in this room, though—the only room that Danglars habitually frequented—that the unusual events occurred. However it was that they were managed, it was here that I should have to set my trap. I had a few hours to ruminate, and I evolved a plan. I merely had to convince Danglars to cooperate.

As I knew he was a creature of strict habit, I could await him outside the front door as he returned home precisely on schedule. He appeared surprised to see me. Thankfully, the rain that had loomed most of the day still held off for the time being, and I could speak to him without the chance of being overheard by the occupants of the house.

"Are you still determined to discover the cause of these bizarre attacks upon you?" I asked him.

"Of course," he replied, firmly.

"Then I must ask you to take a chance of another assault tonight," I said. "It is most likely to occur, but I do not believe it will be overly severe."

"I can endure another if I must," he growled. "Do you think you can uncover the culprit?"

"I am certain of it," I promised him. "All that I require you to do is to cry out when attacked, in case I hear nothing, and then stand perfectly still until I enter the room. Then you must rush to the door and out of the room, closing the door swiftly and firmly behind you. Do not attempt to re-enter the room until I summon you."

"And you will uncover the perpetrator?"

"I believe I shall."

"Then I agree," he said.

"I shall join you in the reception room before dinner, and then remove myself after you have finished your meal. You will then enter the room alone. I suggest that you summon Henry to bring you a post-prandial glass. After that, you will be alone until you cry out."

"I admit that I do not understand this, Carnacki, and yet I will do as you request."

"Excellent." I gestured to the door. "Shall we enter now?"

Everything proceeded as I had anticipated—including him excluding me from dinner—and I remained in the reception room while he dined. My electric pentagram still detected nothing, and nor did I. I had checked the flowers in the vase earlier; Ruby had assured me that there were no violets, and she was correct. At the moment, I could detect no scent of them either.

Danglars entered the room after he had finished eating, brandishing a half-smoked cigar. I nodded politely to him and left. A moment later, he rang the bell and Henry answered it. There was a brief period of conversation, and then Henry left the room. I took my station outside the door.

As I had hoped, there was a faint trace of violets.

I did not have to wait for a signal from the financier. It was barely moments later that I heard a crashing sound, and a cry of pain. I opened the doors carefully and slipped into the room. Danglars was standing there, with three of four books on the floor about him. Blood was flowing from a cut in his forehead, above the left eye, where one of the volumes had evidently caught him a glancing blow. It probably looked worse than it was, but I was taking no chances.

"That wound needs attention," I snapped. "Leave! Now!"

He still had the wits to obey me, and rushed out. I slammed the door and locked it before turning back to face the empty room. Or, perhaps, not so empty if my theory was correct. It was certainly wild and speculative, but the only one that fitted the facts.

"I know that you are in here," I said into the emptiness. "And also that I cannot see you. But here you are and here you will remain until we have had a conversation." There was no reply; the person with me was hoping I would assume I had made a foolish error. But there was that faint scent of violets... I took a small container from my pocket. "This is full of talcum powder," I explained. "If I scatter it about, some is bound to settle on you and reveal your location. I'd rather not do this, as I am certain that Ruby would be quite upset if she had to clean it up. And I am fairly certain that you wouldn't enjoy the experience of being coated in this powder." I unscrewed the lid.

There was a very audible sigh from nowhere, and a voice spoke. "Very well, Mr. Carnacki. I concede that you have discovered me." It was a very pleasant woman's voice, even though there was no evidence of her presence. "What do you plan to do with me?"

"Talk," I replied. "After that—we shall see. I confess that I am intrigued to find myself—well, "face to face" might be the wrong expression—in the company of an invisible woman. I am honestly intrigued as to how this came about, and why you are bedeviling Mr. Danglars."

"Because the man is a devil, Mr. Carnacki! Who would better deserve it?"

I gestured to the chairs. "Perhaps we could sit down to discuss the matter?" I suggested. "It seems impolite to require a lady to remain standing."

"Very well," she agreed. There was the faintest of rustling from her unseen garments, and then I saw a slight depression in one of the chairs. I took the other, facing where she ought to be. "What is it that you wish to know?"

"If you would be so kind," I suggested, "I should appreciate knowing your name."

"Certainly, Mr. Carnacki. It is Myra Vidal, of Paris."

"Ah," I said. "I thought I detected a foreign accent, though your English is very fine."

"I practice often," she replied.

"And you know Danglars from Paris?" I suggested.

"Oh, yes, Mr. Carnacki, I most certainly do."

"And clearly not amicably," I observed. "Why, then, have you followed him all the way to London?"

"To destroy him before he destroys far more worthy souls. The man is a fiend, Mr. Canacki, without morality or a conscience. He claims to be a financier, but he is in fact a thief and a charlatan. In the name of investment, he takes money from the unwary and leaves them broken and destitute. Yet it is all done legally enough that the courts find him repulsive, but cannot convict him of a single crime."

Matters were becoming less clouded. "So you have sought him out to punish him yourself," I concluded. "He has injured you personally?"

"Not I, or my husband, Marc—we had become well aware of his terrible behavior. But a very dear friend of ours was lured by Danglars into one of his schemes. He invested a considerable amount of money in the fund—money he could not afford to lose—and lost, Danglars, of course, had withdrawn his own money—with considerable interest—before the fund collapsed, costing our friend and others all that they had invested." There was a catch in her voice. "Our friend killed himself as a result of the loss, and I vowed that Danglars should pay. Since the courts could do nothing, I determined that I myself would be the instrument of vengeance."

"And so you tracked him here to this house in London and set about a scheme to convince him that he was being haunted. Because of his avarice, there were convenient empty rooms for you to lodge in, and your... gift enabled you to steal the food that you required." It all added together neatly. "But *why* haunt him?"

"I wished to make him think he was either haunted or else going insane. Perhaps, in the end, he would shoot himself to escape."

I nodded. "Forgive me for suggesting it, but had it never occurred to you that you might perform the deed yourself? You could shoot him down on a crowded street in broad daylight and easily escape. After all, no one could see you, or testify against you."

There was another deep sigh. "Do not think that this idea had escaped me, Mr. Carnacki," she said, emotionally. "The thought of bringing this odious being to his end tempted me greatly—and still does. But I am not a murderer, and in my saner moments I know that I could never do this."

"You are to be commended, Madame Vidal," I said.

"Now that you know all," she asked, hesitantly, "what do you aim to do?"

"But I do not know all," I replied. "I do not know how you came to be in this most unusual state."

"It is the result of the actions of another evil man," she explained. "One Wilhelm Storitz. He was an inventor and a devil himself. He, too, had an obsession, but it was not with money—it was with me. He kidnapped me and used his instrumentations to turn me and my clothing into this state of invisibility. He

513

perished shortly afterwards and, at first, Marc and I thought that there would be little hope that I would ever be restored to my former visibility.

"However, and miraculously, I became visible again after giving birth to my son. Then, we moved to Paris, where Marc continued his job as a painter. There, I met a man named Joe Rollon who revealed to me that I still had the gift of invisibility and taught me to master it."

"You have suffered much, madame," I said, sympathetically. "I wish it were in my power to aid you, but I do not think any of my own tinkerings would be of use in restoring you."

"It is kind of you to even consider it," she said, with some warmth. "But what of Danglars?"

I considered the matter. "He has hired me to relieve him of the forces that bewilder and bedevil him," I stated. "As he is my client, I am bound to bow to his wishes."

"You will expose me, then?" she asked, bitterness evident in her voice. "Well, I cannot prevent you. Nor do I wish you any harm, Mr. Carnacki. Do as you feel you must."

I nodded, and crossed to the door. I saw Henry in the hallway, and asked him to send his master in to see me. I waited with Mrs. Vidal in silence. I couldn't be sure of her thoughts, but they were most likely filled with despair and loss. I wished I could console her, but that was not possible.

Danglars came tramping to the room. He had a bandage over the wound on his forehead and a severe scowl on his face. "Have you discovered the cause of my troubles?" he demanded.

"I believe I have," I informed him. There was a faint gasp from the apparently unoccupied chair. "You yourself."

His scowl deepened. "You think I am making this up?" he growled.

"Not consciously, no," I replied. "But I can definitely confirm that there is no supernatural agency causing these events." He seemed to calm a little. "You say you speak German fluently. Have you heard of a *poltergeist*?"

"A *noisy ghost*?" He was confused. "Of course. But you just said that there is nothing supernatural in what is happening to me."

"I do not mean that there is a poltergeist involved," I explained. "It is merely an analogy. A poltergeist is almost invariably associated with a teen going through puberty and with associated emotional stresses. Somehow, this causes events like yours around the young people involved—items flying of their own accord, items shaking or falling, that sort of thing."

"But there are no young people about me," he objected. "Unless Ruby..."

"It has nothing to do with Ruby," I said. "You have seized upon the wrong portion of my comments. What is possible in your case is that you are undergoing severe stress, and that these stresses are causing the events. I do not say that this is so, merely that it is possible." Danglars was, after all, my client, and it would be wrong to lie to him. Misleading him, was, however, within my mental gymnastics. "I know that you are a financier, and that sometimes such persons may be skating on the edge of ethical ice. I do not know, but is it possible that you are acting in less than ethical manner in certain cases? And that these cases are causing a conflict in your emotional being? And that this conflict is causing stresses that result in these apparently supernatural events to occur about you?"

His face darkened. "What are you accusing me of?"

"I? Nothing. I know nothing of your affairs. But what I suggest is that *you* may be accusing yourself in your subconscious mind, and that perhaps this is affecting items about you, and even attacks upon yourself." I indicated the bandage on his forehead.

He was looking far less certain now. "What can you do to prevent these attacks?"

"I can do nothing," I informed him. "Only you can do so. Examine your actions and your motives in your business dealings. If there are any... improprieties therein, you would need to change them."

"And you feel that this... self-examination will work?"

"I am convinced that if you do this, then these events will dissipate, and you will be free of ongoing attacks." This was true, for I felt that Madame Vidal would cease her tricks if he repented.

Danglars scowled again. "It seems to me that you are saying that I can provide my own cure."

"Quite correct," I agreed.

"Then it also seems to me that I have no reason to pay your fee," he answered. He gestured at my electric pentacle. "Pack up your toys and get out."

Somehow, this did not surprise me in the least. "As you wish. But bear in mind what I have told you about examining your motives. If you decide that you have wronged me, simply mail me a check. If I receive one, I shall be assured that you have taken my advice to heart."

It was a matter of less than an hour to gather my equipment and for Henry to hail me a cab. As I was leaving the house, I felt a gentle kiss on my cheek from invisible lips, and a whisper of "Thank you" in my ear.

I considered myself fully paid.

Carnacki ceased his tale at this point, and took a sip from his sherry. Then he reached for an envelope on his mantle. "This check arrived this morning."

*After Captain Nemo, Phileas Fogg, the "star" of* Around the World in 80 Days, *is probably the most famous of all of Jules Verne's heroes, Neil Penswick offers here a rather unusual take on this character—short and yet full of unsuspected perspectives...*

## Neil Penswick: *115,200 Seconds*

I stood in front of the door.

I didn't need to knock. He'd be waiting for me.

He was a stickler for time.

He hated anyone arriving early or late. I once said to him that he was "exact," but his response was "I am precise."

Saville Row was remarkably empty. If he knew what I was thinking—and I sometimes thought that he could read my mind—he would have interrupted me and said that "there is nothing remarkable about Mayfair being empty in October."

I glanced at my pocket watch. A minute after eleven thirty-five.

Where was he? I stepped back and looked at the old Georgian House.

White walls, polished wooden door, and immaculately clean windows. His manservant kept the house in perfect condition.

Even the number 7 fixed to the door sparkled.

I put my carpetbag down. I was not as young as when I first met him. I laughed to myself as I could imagine him raising his eyebrows and pointing out to me that this was a tautology. I pressed my face against the window and tried to see if there were any signs of activity.

Was he unwell?

Again, I looked down the street towards Burlington Gardens. There was no one around. Hold on, there was a man standing outside one of the haberdashers. Was that his manservant? No, he's walking away.

It was 11:38. It was inconceivable that he could not be here. He had invited me to be here at this time.

Should I knock? If it was anyone else but him, I would have done.

By 11:45, I was deeply concerned. It was only ten minutes but if you've ever met him, you'd know.

A woman was walking up the street. Dressed all in black. And that looks to be a child with her. Also in black. By God, that thing doesn't look normal. The size of it. And the way it was walking. The woman looked towards me, and I could swear she nodded. They carried on walking away from me down Saville Row.

I've tried to remember if they made any sound.

It all seemed silent. Completely.

When did I first meet him?

I was eight years-old.

I'd fallen out of a tree. An apple tree. I was lying on the grass, aching but laughing. How could I be so stupid?! Stop laughing! It hurts too much. And then I saw him.

Tall, top hat, sideburns, and a moustache. Obviously, I thought he was tall because I was lying on the ground, looking up.

It was damp in the air. I remember the thick mist.

"You've proven Newton's law of universal gravitation. That which goes up, must come down!"

He never did ask how I was. But he held out his hand and pulled me up.

"That does look fun!" He took off his jacket and removed his hat.

We then spent some hours climbing that tree. He stuffed his pockets full of apples then climbed down and handed them to me.

My memory must be wrong here. Have I really known him for thirty years? He never seems to look any different. Mind you he always wears the same clothes. Always trims his hair in exactly the same way.

"Find some vinegar and brown paper," he muttered to me.

He was departing.

"Thanks," I said.

"Never thank anyone—you don't know what they will have to do. In the future.'

He walked away.

"What's your name?" I shouted. In those days, I thought that names were important and an exchange of them gave a mysterious power.

He stopped for a moment as if he was trying to remember his name. He looked around at the murkiness surrounding us.

"Fogg…" he said, walking away. "…Phileas Fogg."

He disappeared into the mist.


I entered through the servant's entrance.

The door wasn't locked. Or if it was, a gentle push resolved the matter.

The house was empty.

Of people anyway.

Of living people.

I had been at 7 Saville Row before.

The manservant had shown me around.

I remembered so well the house. The marquetry floor of the entrance hall, the mezzanine level which moved around the house, and the circular gallery with the blue glass dome supported by red Ionic pillars.

It was mathematically exact. It was a house that was never in a hurry and was always ready.

There were no distractions.

There was no library and no books.

There were no ornaments apart from two clocks. Two electric clocks. In the manservant's room and in Fogg's bedroom. Ticking in unison.

And there was the safe which Fogg had described to me as fireproof and burglar proof.

I searched the house from cellar to attic. There was no-one.

There was little presence of Fogg in the house. He had no personal possessions.

Even his wardrobe never varied. Each trouser, waistcoat and undergarment had a number attached. I picked up a register where he detailed when he'd last worn each item of clothing. I assumed he was wearing a set of clothes and there was another which he would have sent out for cleaning. Otherwise, his clothes were all there.

His manservant's room was sparser. There were electric bells and tubes for when Fogg needed to contact him. There was the ticking clock. And that was it. No clothes or ornaments. In fact, no sign of life.

Apart from the light being on. Someone had left the light on.

Hydrogen powered the lighting and heating throughout the house.

Was there some meaning to the light remaining on? I checked my watch— it was 01:05.

I then noticed something interesting. The electric clock on the mantelpiece was ticking but was reading a different time. It was 04:40.

I picked the clock up. It was ticking. Slightly too fast.

I then went back upstairs and to Fogg's room. The clock was ticking. Loudly. But it was reading 06:10.

The clocks were wrong.

Of course, later, I began to believe that it was my own watch that was wrong. And then, even later, that it was time outside the house which was wrong.

This was the house of the man who was a working machine.

When did I next meet him?

I was much older. About fifteen. And I was at school. I had learnt little, and I was regularly thrashed to beat the ignorance out of me. Beating the Devil out of me, the headmaster said. That, of course, just made me more determined to do what I wanted.

To Hell with you! To Hell with you all!

I was standing in the corner of the classroom having been banished, from my desk, for talking back to the teacher. Or hitting another pupil. It might have been the time that I gave my teacher a bloody nose.

From the corner of the room, I could see out of the window. Just. And I saw him. Fogg. Dressed exactly like I'd last seen him. Still youthful. He was handing money to the headmaster who was animated and gesticulating. Shaking his head. Red about the face. There was a determined pause and then they shook hands.

Fogg smiled. And then he looked up. I didn't think he could possibly see me. His smile broadened. He was staring at me! He waved and turned.

I could never be certain that I'd even seen him.

But from then on, the school changed. I was taught on my own. Only two lessons – how to read and write.

My late parents never had the opportunities. I couldn't even read their names on the gravestone I visited every Sunday. To pay my respects, I told the parson. But it was to remember the good times. Before I went to the workhouse, spent long hours doing manual labor and occasionally going to the school room.

I don't know why Fogg did it. But he made me learn to read and write.

I didn't know what o'clock it was. There were three chronometers in the house, and they all said a different time.

I thought I'd wait for him. I owed him that. He'd invited me to be here. The least I could do was wait for him.

In the pantry there were apples, eggs, and some preserved foods. I ate and then drank water to my fill. I didn't like the taste of this city food—cleaned to take the taste all out.

But that was the way Fogg lived. Everything had to be cooked for him. Well-done, broiled, within an inch of its life. He'd said to me that his insides were sensitive, and he had to be careful.

He did, though, favor sherry, port, and spiced claret. All with fresh ice from the lakes.

I took a bottle of wine to the manservant's room. Out of respect I couldn't stay in Fogg's room. I pulled the cork out with my teeth and poured the wine down my throat. We used to do that on the boats. Straight down the throat. Fresh and warm.

I lay on the bed, laughing.

Thinking of where he could be.

And fell asleep.

It was the noises which woke me up.

Coming from the speaking tubes which connected the rooms to the mezzanine and then to the first floor.

There was a hissing. Like steam rushing down the pipes.

I think it was that which woke me.

And then a clanging. Bell-like. Rhythmic.

I closed my eyes and fell back asleep.

After breakfast, I had a wash. Looking in the mirror, I seemed to have a few days of stubble. I only had a clean shave yesterday.

I checked the pipes in the manservant's room, on the mezzanine and in Fogg's room. I couldn't see anything untoward but the time on the clocks seemed to have drifted even further apart.

From the mezzanine I could see down the street. Still empty. There was the dark silhouette of a man outside a haberdashers. He turned and went in.

A little later there was that woman again with the thing that resembled a child. She must have an appointment and walk the same way every day. With that thing.

I used to work on the ships. From when I was a lad. I moved up to third and then second officer. First of all, on the three masted sailing ships. You felt one with the air, and the sea and the sky. And then working on the SS *Great Western*. Wooden hull. Four steam boilers. I travelled across the Atlantic. I journeyed around the Capes where the demons of hell screamed for you. That all changed when they opened the new Suez Canal when we had scheduled commercial and then passenger ships.

For me, not for the better. I missed the excitement. It wasn't for me being polite and friendly to aristos and toffs and their women folk as they travelled the world. They only knew how to get richer.

Some hoity-toity woman accusing me stealing from her. I know she'd lost the lot gambling. Her husband had me sacked.

In the end I lost a lot of jobs for cussing and fighting and drinking.

My last job was on the HMS *Gannet*. A warship. Beautiful white, wooden rigging. Sailed like it was riding the breath of God. We were an anti-slavery ship. Patrolling the Pacific around Chile, Bolivia, and Peru.

I met Fogg again in Panama City. Perhaps ten years ago. Maybe twenty years.

It was a coincidence.

I had gone to the less salubrious part of the city. Not that there was much decent about the rest of that place in those days. For some months, I'd been at sea, and I wanted to… well you know. I enjoyed a smoke and was gently rocking, in my own world. And then I saw him. Those clothes. And that voice. You think he's English, don't you? But he's not. Sometimes his emphasis gives him away. An odd biting at certain words. Sometimes it's the wrong word he picks—that sounds like the word he wants. You can see beneath his eyes that he's thinking. Grasping for a thought to slow down.

"Fogg!" I shouted. I wasn't certain that he wasn't an hallucination.

"Oh hello," he replied. He beamed as he clasped my hand.

He took me to a drinking establishment. Expensive. An expatriate bar.

Full of those wanderers from the U.S. and the Guerra del salitre. Officials, bureaucrats, and those that would never be accepted back into their own country.

We had a bottle of rum. Probably more than one. He was so interested in catching up with me. I just moaned about the bloody rich people whilst he asked about the many places he said he wanted to visit.

One oddity…

…there was a family.

A father, a mother, and two small children. Pale and haunting. They were obviously escaping something. Lots of people were.

Fogg was staring at the children. There was a tear.

"I'm sorry. So sorry," he muttered.

I didn't think much about it at the time.


The next night I was woken again.

It was the whispers.

It was the second night they started.

I couldn't tell what they were saying.

No, that's wrong. They weren't voices. Not then.

They were more sounds.

It was only later that they began to sound that they were in a language.

When there were occasional sounds that I could understand.


The next day, and the day after passed.

I began to look forward to seeing those people move outside.

The shapes anyway.

I checked with my watch. They weren't at the same time every day.


And then it changed.

The woman in black didn't walk past. She stopped and approached the house. She moved very slowly and stared through the window. She pushed her face against the glass. Her features were distorted like she only had one eye.

As she rubbed her face against the glass, she then seemed to have multiple eyes.

She seemed to have a long tongue.

Something fell.

There was something moving up the outside wall. Her 'child' was crawling up the wall.

Trying to get in.

The house was silent apart from the scratching.

It was trying to find a way in.

I was just standing there.

But she didn't seem to see me.

More days passed and Fogg still hadn't arrived.

I had searched the house, repeatedly.

And there was no indication of where he was.

Of course, there was one place that I hadn't searched.

And I didn't want to.

The safe.

But the voices were telling me that's what I had to do.


I had started to hallucinate.

I saw someone walking around the house and tidying up after me. Cleaning my plates, knives, and mugs.

It looked like his manservant.

But when I approached him, he stopped still.

He moved his eyes, bent his head. But stopped walking around.

I talked to him but got no reply.

"Forster," I directly addressed him.

But nothing.

And after a while I didn't notice him anymore.


The last time I saw Fogg was at the Saville Road house.

After I finished in the merchant navy, he invited me to visit. For one day.

We drunk grog—rum diluted with water, with a slice of lemon.

I told him about my travels and the exotic delights of the Far Eastern cities of Bombay, Singapore, and Yokohama.

Despite having met him in Panama City, he never struck me as a traveller. His questions were all about where the better people stayed, how they looked after their money and what they did if they got into trouble.

"Just seem to be an Englishman Abroad," I said. "And be confident that you have a right to be there."

"That's worked in many worlds for me," he said.

He asked if I had found the love of my life and whether I had children.

I never told him.

Perhaps my life would have ended differently if I had.

Towards the end of my stay, he took me to his room. And he opened the safe.

There were papers, cash, and much gold.

It felt a little uncomfortable as he offered me some moneys to help set me up in my life.

I declined. He had already done so much for me.

I asked about his future.

"I'll do anything for my children," he smiled.

"You make it sound like they've been kidnapped," I said to him.

"Something like that. I have to do what I can to send money."

He clasped my hands tightly. "If anything changes for you, do tell me."

And that was the last time I ever spoke to him.

Some years past.

I grew older, working on the land. I lived not too far from where I'd grown up so could visit my parents' gravestone.

The importance of family.

And then I received the invite to go to his house.

At 7 Saville Row, at 11:35 on Wednesday 2 October 1872.

I've lost that invite.

I had it with me.

I used to read it on the bed to see if I'd got something wrong. In the date, or the time, or the location.

It may have slipped down the side of the bed. Or the manservant Forster not realizing its value had destroyed it.

It was the only evidence that I'd ever met Phileas Fogg.

Weeks had passed. Possibly even months.

Staying in the house reminded me of the long sea journeys. At times the house screeched and screamed like a giant engine powering the universe.

Whilst I felt comfortable in the house, though, I'd never got used to the voices.

They were demonic and malicious demanding "more." Sometimes the words echoed—"they'll be punished," "they'll die"—around the empty dwelling.

I had tried to leave.

Many times.

But the house wouldn't let me.

The electric chronometers continued ticking. All out of sequence. The one in my room ran too slow. The one upstairs ran too fast. I stopped winding my pocket watch as the sound of the three discordant time pieces drove me further insane.

I knew Fogg trusted me. So, I resisted opening the safe. I knew the combination as I'd watched him open it.

Eventually though, I knew it was what I had to do.

I was not going to take anything that didn't belong to me. I was not going to read any private papers.

But I needed to find if there was information in there which told me of the whereabouts of Phileas Fogg.

The shapes outside had got closer. I'd seen the silhouette of the man move towards the house. He, the woman, and the thing tried for several hours every day to get into the house. Knocking on the doors and windows as the thing tried to find a way in.

Most recently I'd heard them shouting over the slowness of time.

I couldn't tell what they were saying. One time, it sounded like "Interstitial police... don't!"

I opened the safe. There were hundreds of pounds in cash.

And there was a train ticket.

A train ticket to Edinburgh, made out in my name—James Strand—for December 17, 1872.

This is where I was going to find Phileas Fogg. 76 days after we'd arranged to meet!

That night I lay down beneath the dome, staring into the night sky. Even though I was an accustomed sailor, I didn't recognize the stars and the galaxies. The colors were spectacular with blazing worlds and dark holes ripping into the skein of the universe. And with shooting stars plunging past planets where other civilizations lived and died. The dreams and nightmares of alien races.

And that's the end of my story.

The house allowed me to leave.

Not that it was a house. It must have been some sort of scientific craft that travelled into the seas of dreams and nightmares of far races.

I walked through the streets of London, the capital of the Empire.

There were many people milling around and traveling.

They barely noticed they were passing the statues of the great explorers, generals, and leaders of the age.

The train brought me to Edinburgh.

And that's where I was arrested for the bank robbery. The police said that I had a long history as a troublemaker. And there were similar crimes where I had apparently just walked into banks and confidently walked out with thousands of pounds. They said that there were other crimes I had committed in America and across the world. And they could show that I'd been there at those times.

They didn't believe a word I said.

That was when they had shown me the newspapers and I discovered that Phileas Fogg was a national hero.

That he'd been on the point of being arrested as the police suspected that it was he who had committed all of the crimes.

It was during the trial at the Edinburgh assizes that it was revealed that I had two children of my own. The papers featured me on the front pages for weeks before I was sentenced to what was the rest of my life in prison.

Returning to my prison cell, following my sentence, I found a handwritten note. Unsigned.

"I didn't know. I am sorry. So sorry. I am coming for you."

I ripped the note apart.

I'd had enough and wanted to be left alone.

*Despite their huge popularity, Fantômas and the Vampires were too anarchistic for the bourgeois sensibilities of the times. A critic wrote about Louis Feuillade: "That a man of talent, an artist, the director of most of the great films which have been the success and glory of Gaumont, starts again to deal with this unhealthy genre, which is obsolete and condemned by all people of taste, remains for me a real problem." So, in order to show that he was not always glorifying villains, Feuillade hired his friend writer Arthur Bernède and, together, they decided to create Judex, the first costumed vigilante in history...*

## Anthony Perconti: *Judgment Knight*

*Manhattan, February 19th, 1939.*

Julie Ziegler closed the door behind him and locked it with a key produced from his coat pocket. The alley behind the Billiard Parlor was dimly lit; the biting February wind blew days-old newspapers and other debris around the man's feet. He started his way down the alley, pulling his collar up against the cold and tugging at the brim of his pancake. A smaller shadow detached itself from the greater gloom and blocked his path.

"Hello, Julie." the voice said.

It belonged to a tall, rangy man, dressed head to toe in black. He wore a slouch hat that hid his features, along with an opera cape over his long coat.

"Ah, *Monsieur le Juge*, I am glad to see you." Ziegler replied. He handed a folded note to the man in black. "There is the location, as promised. A tenement house out in Queens. It belongs to one of Yard's boys. I didn't get the building number, unfortunately."

"No matter, Julie. I'll find the place. How is Rebecca doing?"

"She is well, thank you. She is working as a seamstress, over at Binders."

"Send her my best," the man in black said. Then, "They don't suspect you, do they?"

"Those pig-headed *idyotn*? Heh." Ziegler shook his head. "No, no. As far as they are concerned, I'm just good old Julie. A harmless *nebbish*."

"Good, Julie. Well done. This is for you." The man in black passed over a fat wad of bills to Ziegler. "She'll be sleeping soundly in her own bed this time tomorrow."

Ziegler gave the man in black a hard smile and nodded. "God willing, *Monsieur*. Yard and the majority of his bully boys will be attending the rally tomorrow night. The rumor going around is that Fritz Kuhn landed that priest from the radio, Coughlin, to make an appearance as well. Feh," Ziegler spat, "birds of a wretched feather."

526

"I'll give Yard this; his alibis will be airtight. The whole of Madison Square Garden will see him licking Kuhn's boots." The shadowy figure said.

"But to use a child as a bargaining chip?" Ziegler's face showed contempt.

"Aaron Dumont-Warren will pay the ransom to get his daughter back. He is an honorable man. Yard knows it. Seventy-five thousand dollars is quite a windfall for the American Bund."

"The pogroms never end..." Ziegler stared off into the middle distance. "Even wealth can't protect us from persecution."

"These men only understand one language. Fortunately for Ruth Dumont-Warren, I, too, am fluent in their tongue."

"Although Yard and most of his men will be at the Garden, you can be sure he'll leave a few formidable hands to guard the girl. And armed at that," Ziegler said.

The shadowy figure let forth a sinister chuckle. "Oh, you know me. I wouldn't have it any other way, Julie."

The other man nodded his approval. "Good luck to you, then. Oh, and *Monsieur*? One more thing."

"*Oui*?"

"When you rescue that Dumont-Warren girl tomorrow? Make those child-stealers hurt, eh?"

The dark shape gave a nod of approval and disappeared back into the gloom.

*February 20th, 1939*

The man was seated at a stout oak desk. He wore black jodhpurs, riding boots and a black wool turtleneck. Jacques de Trémeuse's hawkish features were intently focused on the task at hand. He was methodically disassembling a pair of Steyr automatics. When the pistols were broken down before him, he began cleaning and oiling the weapons. He took his time with the process, because he was careful and meticulous. It was a ritual that he always engaged in, just prior to going on a mission. The Zen-like focus cleared his mind of all other distractions and centered him. The present moment was the only thing that existed. In the background, the Philco conveyed the day's top stories:

*This is WOR. And here is today's news. The investigation continues on the whereabouts of Ruth Dumont-Warren, the daughter of French philanthropists Aaron and Miriam Dumont-Warren. A ransom note was recovered from the Dumont-Warren home on Friday the seventeenth. Commissioner Kirkpatrick of the New York Police Department states...*

He reassembled the first pistol and repeated the process on its twin.

*Mayor La Guardia's comment on the Pro American Rally is as follows..."If we are for free speech, we have to be for free speech for everybody and that includes Nazis." The rally will be held later tonight at Madison Square Garden. This evening's weather calls for...*

Once the second pistol was cleaned and reassembled, De Trémeuse began feeding cartridges into the magazines. He slotted the magazines into the grips and placed the loaded pistols on the desk before him.

He stared at the Steyrs for a moment, lost in thought. *Fifty-six years-old. Twenty-six years now, performing my sacred duty to* Domine Lustitiae. *Is it time to put down my tools of war? I'm in a foreign land, with little to no resources at my disposal. Am I too old for this? Let the younger generation take up the cause of Justice? Like that Allard fellow, who can just waltz right in and cloud their thuggish minds, or Doc Ardan, with his team of specialists. Or God forbid, that Spider lunatic...*

Judex reached for the twin automatics and replaced them in their holsters. He wrapped the shoulder straps around the weapons and secured them in a drawer at his desk. He opened a second drawer and took out a leather pouch. The contents *clinked* at the touch. He rose from the desk and snapped off the Philco as he went past.

At the door, he pulled on a knee length black leather coat, fastened his opera cape and took up his slouch hat. He selected a silver handled, cherry-bark oak cane from the umbrella stand, felt its heft and walked out into the night.

The squat brick building was situated on a block of ramshackle row houses and vacant, weedy lots in Queens. Twenty years passed its prime, it presented a façade of peeling paint, chipped mortar and cracked bricks. Walter was seated on the front stoop, having a smoke. The sense of boredom was evident on his cold, red face.

Up the block shambled an old vagrant, the stains and rips visible on his threadbare pea-coat even from a distance. As the old man approached, Walter could make out that his face consisted of a patchy beard shot with gray and he was missing most of his teeth. The few he had remaining were a nicotine stained brown. The old-timer shuffled up to Walter's perch and pulled a crinkled pack of Pall Malls from a pocket.

"Gotta' light, champ?"

Walter sparked the Zippo to life. "Here ya go rummy. Now beat it!" Suddenly, he felt the cold, razored edge of fourteen inches of Toledo steel press against his throat. In place of the old man, now stood the black-clad vigilante, Judex. The business end of a sword cane in hand, ready to end his life. The length of the cane-sheath was tucked in the vigilante's left armpit. With his free hand, he casually took a drag from the lit cigarette.

"What floor is the girl on?" asked Judex.

"Th-th-the little Jew kids on the third floor. L-l-last door on the left." Walter's voice was shaky with fear.

"How many did Yard leave behind to stand guard? Including yourself."

"Th-there's eight of us. I swear to God. Please. Please. Don't kill me, OK?"

"I want you to deliver a message to Kuhn and the rest of your Nazi compatriots. Tell them that Judex is the author of their woes. Tell them it is time to face justice."

"I'll tell them. I promise. C-c-can I leave now?"

"Leave? Heh-heh. You won't be walking for a good long while, I'm afraid." The hardwood sheath smashed into Walter's temple.

*Boom!* The front door of the building crashed inward. A battered and bruised Walter went hurtling through the air. He landed with a hard *thump* on the floor. Startled by the commotion, Will and Mike ran over to investigate.

"What the hell, Walt? What's with all the-oh shit!" Mike said, glancing at the battered man at his feet.

"The cops! The plan's fucked," Will yelled. He pulled a revolver from his waist and fired a warning shot at the ground, alerting the rest of the gang.

"Hello, the house," a booming voice rang out. "This is your only warning. Release the girl into my custody and no will else will get hurt. You have my word on it. However, if you decide not to take heed, you will face the judgement of Judex."

"Ha! And just throw away our big payday? No way in hell, mystery man. You want her? Come in and get her," Mike said.

"So be it, then. No quarter is asked and none shall be given."

Judex charged into the entryway, vaulting over the prone body on the ground. In mid-leap, a span of steel flashed, separating Will's gun hand from its wrist. Crimson sprayed in a torrent, drenching Mike. Will let forth with an inarticulate yelp, before having his throat slashed by the blade's back swipe.

Mike pulled his pistol and popped a shot off at the vigilante, sending his wide brimmed hat sailing out the door. A close call. Judex knocked the revolver from Mike's grasp with a fierce strike from the cane. The man in black wielded the weapon in an icepick grip, blade pointing down, along his right forearm. He swiped up and back down, opening up Mike's chest and abdomen. Three bodies littered the floor, in a widening pool of red. The vigilante raced up the stairs.

Judex dived into a forward roll as he breached the second floor. A volley of hot lead sped past, above him. He dug into his coat pockets and launched a double fistful of sharpened pennies at the shooters. The copper razors hit home in a torrent of surprised curses and shouts. He leapt to his feet and shifted forward in an offensive martial stance. Eric and Hank were preoccupied in pulling sharpened coins from faces, arms, hands and torsos. Judex waded into the pair, moving in close, inside each man's reach. He slashed a bloody figure eight about him. The Toledo blade dripped red from the two gunmen. Judex ascended to the top floor.

Paul was built along the lines of his Germanic ancestors. Blond, well over six feet in height, and heavily muscled, he launched a terrific horizontal blow at the vigilante with his Louisville Slugger. Judex caught, then parried the shot with the cherry-bark sheath. The force of the impact radiating up his left arm. He stepped forward and launched a Savate front kick at the larger man's solar plexus. The big man doubled over and let out a rushing *whoosh* of air, the bat falling from his hands. Judex delivered a savage knee strike to the man's chin. A muffled *crack* issued from Paul's neck as he fell back. Judex stomped the man's neck as he flowed past.

Reno cracked off a shot at the shadowy figure advancing towards him. In a blur of motion, Judex swiped the blade from his right hip, to just above his left ear. Sparks and a metallic *ping* issued from the steel. Reno was momentarily dumbfounded-his mind unable to register the fact that Judex deflected his bullet with a simple sword-cane. In one fluid motion, the man in black hurled the Toledo steel through Reno's left eye and deep into his brain.

Dan was holed up in the room with Ruth Dumont-Warren. The dark-haired twelve years-old was seated on a sofa, still dressed in her school clothes. Her ankles were bound and a blindfold concealed her eyes. Dan could hear the cacophony of gunshots and screams coming from outside the apartment. He had his revolver trained on the girl's head, when he heard footsteps in the hallway approaching. Dan's heart was jackhammering and his breath caught in his chest. The footsteps stopped directly at the apartment door. The doorknob rattle-turned a few times, but no luck-he had locked the door when the gunfire started. Dan pointed the pistol at the door and fired three shots into it.

"Why, Danny? Why?"

"Who's there?" Dan shouted.

"Why, Danny? Why? Why did you shoot me?" The elderly voice croaked.

Dan was overtaken by a growing sense of dread. No, it couldn't be. It was impossible! She had been dead for five years. That couldn't be the voice of his mother!

"You're a terrible boy, Danny! A terrible, terrible little boy!"

"Stop it! You're not my mother!" Dan fired two more rounds at the door.

"Stop! Please! Stop!"

*Boom!* The apartment door slammed inward with an incredible force. A black shape filled the entrance. Its eyes smoldered with an infernal light.

"I've got one bullet left. You make a move and the kid gets it, I swear to God!" Dan backed towards the girl.

"And you will follow her from this mortal coil an instant later. Of this you can be sure. Put the gun down. You don't want to die here, do you?"

"I mean it! Now back up. Me and the girl are going to walk on out of here. Get up kid!" Dan pointed the pistol at Ruth. "You try and follow us and..."

A flash of copper streaked through the room. A razored coin embedded itself in the gunman's wrist, the revolver clattered harmlessly to the floor. Dan let out a surprised scream, trying to staunch the flow of blood.

Judex closed the distance and connected with a flurry of elbows and hammer fists to the man's head. Dan's jaw shattered with an audible *snap*, an instant prior to collapsing in a heap on the ground.

Judex walked over to the sofa.

"I'm sorry you had to hear that." He cut the bonds from Ruth's legs and removed her blindfold. A tender, fatherly smile spread across his face.

"Hello brave *Mademoiselle*. I mean you no harm."

"Did my father send you? Are you going to take me home?"

"In a manner of speaking, yes, he did. And yes, you will be going home. Very soon. Did those men hurt you?"

"No, *Monsieur* Judex. They kept me blindfolded and my feet tied so I wouldn't try to escape. They gave me food to eat and water to drink."

Judex chuckled. "You are very observant, *Mademoiselle*. A very intelligent young lady."

"Papa and Mama always talk of your exploits. I've read about them too, in *Le Matin*."

"Come. Let us be off." Police sirens wailed in the distance. *It wouldn't do, to be discovered in an apartment building full of dead men*, Judex mused.

"Yes, *Monsieur*. Let's go home."

### February 21st, 1939

Jonas Yard climbed the landing to his apartment on the fourth floor. Anger welled up inside him. All those plans, all that preparation, gone to shit. The Dumont-Warren girl was gone, along with the promise of that ransom money. Fritz Kuhn would tear him a new asshole in the morning, he was sure of it. Still though, he fared better than his crew. Those poor bastards Walter and Dan looked as though they got hit by a truck. At least, those two were still breathing. He unlocked the door and stepped inside. He flicked on the light switch—nothing. He toggled the switch a few more times, with the same result. The apartment was as dark as a tomb.

"Goddammit! Is nothing going my way tonight?" Yard threw his jacket on the sofa, dropped his keys and wallet onto the battered coffee table and plopped down, with an audible sigh.

As if by magic, a man-shaped shadow materialized before him. The figure was darker than the surrounding gloom, like the void shaped into the form of a human being. Smoldering eyes on the terrible figure's visage pierced the darkness.

"JONAS YARD, IT IS TIME TO FACE JUDGMENT!"

Those eyes drew nearer. Yard let out an involuntary scream. He felt an iron grip about his neck as he slipped into unconsciousness.

Police Commissioner Stanley Kirkpatrick entered his kitchen in his bathrobe and pajamas. For insurance purposes, he had his 1911 Colt in hand. Just in case.

"Dick? Is that you?"

"Commissioner, if I ever become as bloodthirsty and deranged as that Wentworth fellow, you have my express permission to put me down like a rabid dog."

Judex was seated at Commissioner Kirkpatrick's kitchen table, casually smoking a cigarette, like a pensioner on a Sunday afternoon idyll on the Champs-Elysees.

"Heh. Very funny. A bit far afield from your usual hunting grounds aren't we, *Monsieur Judex*?" Wentworth grabbed the pack off the table and lit one for himself.

"The Dumont-Warren family are French citizens, Commissioner. I always take care of our own."

"Is that what this is about? My men are this close to finding that girl," he pinched his index finger and thumb together. "Detectives are working around the clock. We'll have her back with her mother and father by day's end."

Judex took a drag and blew smoke through his nose.

"I've saved you the trouble. Ruth was admitted to Bellevue late last night. She was unharmed, yet shaken up from the ordeal, naturally." The man in black crushed the cigarette in the ashtray.

"The resilience of the young, eh, Commissioner? Time will ease her pain."

Kirkpatrick just sat there-at a loss for words. "You... You've rescued her?"

Judex ignored the comment. He dug into his coat and placed a New York City Police Department badge on the table between them.

"I found this last night. It belonged to one of Yard's men. One Officer Paul Mueller."

"Belonged?"

"I'm afraid so. Strictly a matter of self-defense. Kill or be killed and all that."

Commissioner Kirkpatrick stared daggers at the vigilante. He pointed the Colt at him. "You're under..."

"Nazis, Kirkpatrick! On your police force! On your watch!" Judex pointed an accusatory finger at the man.

After a moment, Kirkpatrick put the pistol down on the table and gave a defeated sigh.

"The apartment building is on Egan Avenue in Queens. Officers were dispatched last night, due to the sounds of gunfire. A shoddy three-level affair. It is owned by one of Jonas Yard's gang, Freddy something or other... Rump or Dump. I'd take him in for questioning, if I were in your shoes." The vigilante stood and made his way towards the door.

"Beware. The enemy is within. Put your house in order, Commissioner."
The door slammed shut in the vigilante's wake like the crack of doom.

"That is fantastic news, Aaron! Thank Heavens that she is safe. How is
Miriam holding up? Yes... yes. To be expected. What's that? Oh, in the
Spring... Middle of April, or so. Early May at the latest. Once my business is
settled here, I'll be returning to France. Yes, yes... I'll see you in Paris then, my
friend! *Au revoir*."

Jacques de Trémeuse cradled the telephone receiver. He made his way to
the Philco and switched the knob to the "on" position.

*...Doctors at Bellevue Hospital report that Ruth Dumont-Warren is in sta-*
*ble condition and expected to make a full recovery. In related news, American*
*Bund associate Jonas Yard was found dead in his apartment this morning. The*
*coroner's office reports that the cause of death was a self-inflicted wound. Offi-*
*cials say that a suicide note was found at the scene. This is WOR. Now sit back*
*and relax with the smooth sounds of Glenn Miller's* Moonlight Serenade...

A devilish gleam twinkled in Judex's eyes and his lips curved in a knowing
smile.

*The indomitable Passepartout, Phileas Fogg's sidekick, is a character that always deserved more "coverage" than what he received from Verne, and Dennis Power has more than ably filled in these blanks in* Tales of the Shadowmen. *As for the time-traveling Monsieur Ming, a.k.a. the Yellow Shadow from the* Bob Morane *novels, he has the ability to resurrect himself by transferring his consciousness into a clone body each time he dies. ...*

## Dennis E. Power: *The School of Hard Knocks*

> *I've been an itinerant singer, a circus-rider,*
> *when I used to vault like Leotard,*
> *and dance on a rope like Blondin.*
> *Then I got to be a professor of gymnastics,*
> *so as to make better use of my talents...*
> Jean Passepartout to Phileas Fogg,
> *Around the World in Eighty Days.*

*Paris, 1862*

Flesh pounded against marble tile in loud, echoing smacks, making the hallway sound more like a butcher's market than a school for young gentlemen.

The muffled, choking sobs that accompanied the meaty thuds seemed more ominous in the unnatural silence. Moments before, the fight had been cheered and cat-called by a ring of boys surrounding the two pugilists. However, when young Monsieur d'Etraille had won the fight, but refused to stop pummeling and punishing his opponent, repeatedly slamming his face into the marble, everyone quieted, frozen by a combination of fear and fascination at the uncontrolled rage gripping the teenager.

So thick and so unmoving was the ring of boys that their teachers had a hard time breaking through the human barrier. One of the younger teachers chose a different tactic than barreling through the crowd. Vaulting into a handspring, he somersaulted in the air and arced over the heads of the crowd and then used the shoulders of one of the taller boys to somersault once more. He landed on his feet next to the two young combatants.

Jean Passepartout firmly grasped the shoulders of young Jacques d'Etraille and pulled him away from the boy he seemed determined to kill. Pushed backwards, Jacques looked momentarily stunned. He gazed at his blood-smeared fingers as Passepartout bent down to examine the other boy. The young man gave out an incoherent scream and launched himself at the teacher. As Passepartout was bending over, Jacques's fingers latched around his neck, fingers digging into his windpipe. Passepartout reached behind and boxed his attacker's ears.

534

Jacques growled and put more strength into choking his teacher Passepartout's vision went reddish black and a roaring sounded in his ears. He elbowed the pupil in the stomach, then kicked out in a *fouette* sweep, knocking the boy's legs out from under him. He then put him in a double headlock and called for someone to see to the other boy.

Passepartout had an impulse to break Jacques d'Etraille's arms when he saw the other boy being carried away. His pummeled and battered face looked like raw meat; his nose had been pounded into a shapeless lump; his teeth were broken and red stained.

One might expect that young men in their adolescence removed from the modifying influence of their mothers, shut away from the charms of young ladies, and forced into the constant company of similarly high-spirited youths, would at times become argumentative and combative, breaking out in the occasional bout of fisticuffs. So it had been at the Lycée Napoleon until recently.

Lately, however, there had been an unusual upswing in outbreaks of violence between the students, oftentimes over the slightest of excuses. The fighting was not confined to the adolescent boys either; in a few cases, some of the pre-teen boys had attacked a teacher or a classmate.

This was Jean Passepartout's first term as an instructor at the Lycée Napoleon –or at any Lycée for that matter. He had not attended one himself as a youth and so often felt like a fish out of water in the academic arena. He sometimes regretted following his mentor Chevalier Dupin's advice to enter this respectable profession. In the five months since he had been an instructor, he had learned that academics tore into one another worse than hungry hyenas, and that circus monkeys were often better behaved than many young men, especially those of the upper social strata.

The day after he broke up the fight, Passepartout was summoned to the Censor's office before starting his classes.

Censor Severin was a thin, dour-faced man in his late forties who always peered through his *pince-nez* with disdain, at least towards Passepartout. He started to sit in the chair before Severin's desk but stopped at the Censor's freezing glare. So he stood before Severin as if he were a child ready to get a scolding, which for some reason, he felt was the case.

"Firstly," Censor Severin said with a hint of disappointment, "the Baron d'Etraille does not wish your discharge or any criminal charges aligned against you for manhandling his youngest son. Had it been his heir, you might not have been so fortunate." Severin's dark eyes narrowed and a glimmer of a smile played about his lips as he continued, "Monsieur Passepartout, you are no doubt aware of the wave of violence sweeping through our Lycée. We have had twenty fights and ten unprovoked attacks against students or teachers. Still worse, we have had four suicides, including one last night. An overview of each incident has turned up troubling but, in my opinion, not unexpected information."

Severin's cold blue eyes flickered across Passepartout with disdain. "The common factor between these students and their violence is your class, Monsieur Passepartout."

This information came as a blow to Passepartout, leaving him speechless.

Severin smiled slightly at his discomfort and continued, "As you know, I have not hidden my feelings about letting a person with a dubious background and few academic credentials teach at this prestigious institution. It is especially troubling since we have impressionable young men of the finer sort. I suppose some might say you should be commended for passing the necessary tests without formal education. However, the Lycée Napoleon is more than just a forum for knowledge; it teaches social skills and manners, and enables our young men to take their rightful place in the social hierarchy. Our instructors should be role models for our students. This was why, despite your powerful patron, I opposed your appointment. Your background was, simply, a cipher."

Severin's sour look turned smug and his pursed lips quirked into a fleeting smile. "At least, until recently. However, an anonymous source has enlightened us about your antecedents. No wonder you wished them to remain mysterious. You were with a circus for several years—not a respectable profession, I am certain you will agree. Considering your upbringing, you were never going to be respectable. You were a foundling, and therefore most likely a bastard. Unfortunately, one cannot ban someone from our profession because of their birth status."

Anger rising, Passepartout leaned forward and moved his face within inches of Severin's face, taking the Censor aback. "How is it, Monsieur, that the circumstances of my birth have anything to do with the misbehavior of the children?"

Censor Severin met Passepartout's anger with his own. "They sense it, Monsieur, they sense it. Your illegitimacy is a blot on respectable society and its unmistakable mark brings disharmony into their lives. Disharmony brings discontent. Adding fuel to the fire is the street brawling you teach as part of your gymnastics classes. This, I believe, is the key to the increased violence in our halls."

"Savate is simply a fighting discipline, just like fencing!"

"Yes, well... gentlemen use swords; low-class thugs use their fists and feet. Henceforth, this so-called discipline will be struck from your curriculum and you will substitute other forms of gymnastics. As a consequence, since this was listed as one of your specialties, and you no longer will be teaching it, your salary will be accordingly reduced." Censor Severin flashed Passepartout a malicious smile and concluded, "Good day, Monsieur Passepartout."

With this dismissal, the Censor turned away and went back to sorting the piles of papers on his desk.

"It is not quite true that my class is all that the boys have in common, Monsieur Severin," said Passepartout.

Annoyed that the teacher had not left when dismissed, Severin looked up from his papers with a scowl.

Passepartout continued, "I have kept track of the incidents and the boys in question. I know that they all also had European History, Oriental Studies, and Latin in common."

A small hollow laugh escaped from Severin. "Now. now, Monsieur Passepartout, you are grasping at straws. Certainly, you cannot believe that studying history or a foreign language filled these boys with such rage. We have had these subjects for years without any incidents; your gutter thrashing is new this year, as are these bouts of madness. *Ipso facto*, your class is most certainly the cause. But please continue to argue with me, as I would dearly love to have you dismissed for insubordination."

Seeing that his cause was lost, Passepartout made a gracious retreat by bidding Censor Severin a good day.

A few hours later, Passepartout was tidying up the gymnasium after at the end of the day, when a shadow loomed over him. It was Herr Doktor Krogh, a thickly built bull of a man. He was the instructor for European studies which included history and European languages. He was also the fencing instructor.

Krogh strode up to Passepartout and struck his face on both cheeks with a leather glove. Stunned and outraged by this unprovoked attack, Passepartout responded with a jab powerful enough to send Krogh reeling back with a bloody nose. Shocked and choking with renewed fury, the German challenged Passepartout to a duel for having impugned his honor. He issued this challenge while pinching his nostrils to staunch the flood of blood from his nose, giving his accented voice a high nasal quality.

Passepartout's chuckles at his current condition made Krogh all the more infuriated. Except for a gleaming white *schlager* scar, his face burned almost as red as the blood splattering his white shirt. He demanded that Passepartout meet him in the gymnasium that evening for satisfaction. The infuriated German then spun on his heel with mechanical precision and strode off.

Passepartout's first thought was to ignore the so-called challenge, not out of cowardice, but because he gave two snaps about Krogh's opinion of him. He assumed that, whatever Krogh's imagined slight was, it would blow over in a few days. However, when he realized that he, as the challenged party, would have the choice of weapons, he smiled. This would be a chance to prove that savate was a martial art, and not simply brawling.

Word spread and when it came time for the sparring match, which everyone realized was a duel in disguise, the walls of the gymnasium were lined with onlookers. Even Censor Severin was there, no doubt to see Passepartout humiliated. Passepartout grinned and bowed; Severin looked away in disgust. Since this was an affair of "honor," the senior staff was inclined to allow it to happen, as long as it did not get out of hand. Many of Passepartout's fellow instructors considered him to be something of an upstart and looked for him to get some comeuppance.

Dressed in his leather fencing gear, Krogh looked askance at Passepartout who came garbed in his *maillot*, the garment made famous by Monsieur Leotard.

"Your seconds, Monsieur?" the German asked with forced politeness. Passepartout noted that a slight redness was the only sign of his earlier jab at Krogh's nose.

"I have none," replied Passepartout.

Krogh shrugged with a frown and motioned his seconds to come forward. They were the geography instructor and the Classics instructor, both of whom disliked Passepartout. The former held a saber, the latter an épée.

"Choose your weapon, Monsieur," Krogh commanded.

"Neither," Passepartout waved them away.

Startled, Krogh frowned and then a slightly worried look came into his face. "Certainly, you do not mean to use pistols?"

Passepartout understood Krogh's sudden worry. He feared that Passepartout was an expert shot due to his experiences in the circus. Word of his previous life had spread just as rapidly as the rumor of the duel. However, much of the gossip had erroneously pegged him as a clown. True, he had on occasion acted as one, but he was foremost an aerialist and equestrian. Krogh was afraid that Passepartout would have an unfair advantage over him with pistols, yet he was not above using his expertise with the sword on Passepartout.

Smiling slightly, Passepartout shook his head.

Krogh laughed with a dismissive snort. "What do you propose to use then, your lying tongue?"

Passepartout held up his fists and said, "These," kicking out his feet he added, "And these!"

"You may wish to fight like a common guttersnipe, but I do not," said the German.

Passepartout asked, "Oh, then Monsieur, do you concede?" with an insolent grin hoping to goad Krogh into fighting him.

Krogh angrily retorted he would do no such thing and proceeded to insult Passepartout's background and manhood. Passepartout listened to the tirade with aplomb and then made a few pointed remarks about Krogh needing to hide behind steel, and his cowardly insistence on fighting against a man without fencing experience. He ended his exchange with a *fouetté* kick that brushed the tip of his sabot against Krogh's sore nose.

As Passepartout had hoped, the taunting kick had sufficed to make Krogh enraged. He swung his muscled arms at Passepartout in great wind-raising but ineffectual blows. Passepartout dodged the powerful but artless punches, and responded with scientific precision. Kicks and punches to the biceps and elbows numbed and deadened Krogh's arms. He then danced about working on the

German's lower back, thighs, and calves, intending to have the big man fall to the ground without having landed a single blow on Passepartout.

Passepartout half-turned when he heard a skittering sound on the floor behind him. Something heavy struck his foot, cutting into his heel and knocking him off balance. He fell and nearly landed on a saber blade resting against his foot. To avoid falling on the sword, he grabbed its hilt to push it aside.

Krogh triumphantly cried, "Oh, so now you have chosen the saber!"

He snatched the saber from the geography instructor and swung it at the fallen Passepartout's head. A cry went up from the audience at this example of bad sportsmanship. Krogh was so infuriated from his humiliation that his only thought was to kill his antagonist.

Passepartout raised the saber in time to block Krogh's cut. Then, he lashed out with a hard *chassé* kick to the German's knee, throwing him off balance enough for him to slide away and roll back to his feet. The deep cut in his heel still made standing an agony. He hoped the tendon had not been severed.

Despite his injured foot, Passepartout met Krogh's next lunge with a parry and a riposte. Krogh retreated and lunged again, Passepartout responded with a stop thrust and a riposte that became an ensnaring envelopment. The swords encircled one another in a shrill clashing and scraping of metal that ended with the German's sword twisting out of his hand. Krogh was shocked at how easily Passepartout had disarmed him.

"As you can see, Monsieur, I fully know how to fence, but I think that dueling with swords is stupid, barbaric, and uncivilized. Foolish young men kill or maim themselves in the name of being a gentleman. Truthfully, they act no better than a pair of *gamins* in a knife fight, the only difference being the pretense of gentility—and longer blades."

Passepartout stepped back to wait for Krogh's bow of submission. The German, however, snapped up his fallen blade and slashed at Passepartout's unprotected midsection. A parry prime blocked the ignominious blow and a follow-up moulinet swept both the saber and Krogh away from Passepartout. The Frenchman held the sword at his side as he jump-skipped into a chasse lateral that slammed his heel into Krogh's right elbow. The bone crack reverberated through the gymnasium like a gunshot.

As his sword clattered from his numb hand, Krogh lifted his flapping arm and shouted "*l'ennemi est ici*," as his eyes rolled and he slumped to the ground in a faint.

At Doktor Krogh's collapse, the room erupted into a riot. Despite his injured foot, Passepartout waded into the crowd pulling fighting students apart. It took several minutes before he, the other instructors and several of the older boys helped stop the impromptu brawl.

Passepartout caught Severin glaring at him, assigning him the blame for this new outbreak of violence.

Although he had bound his foot, it still bled, but Passepartout allowed the injured students to see the school physician before him.

The Lycée Napoleon's infirmary consisted of an examination room, a small surgery room, a small ward of six beds, and one private room. Doktor Krogh rested in the infirmary, having suffered a profound shock at the snapping of his elbow. Passepartout thought to call upon him and demonstrate that he held no grievance. As he neared the open door of Krogh's room, he heard a fierce whispering between his antagonist and another person, conducted in German.

"...my informant has been reliable so far, and says that he is an agent of Dupin's." Passepartout recognized the voice as that of Krogh.

"Perhaps, but he seemed unaware that anything was amiss. At least, his suspicion did not fall upon you until you were foolish enough to challenge him to a duel." Passepartout did not recognize the second voice.

"He named our classes in his conversation with Severin. Certainly, that cannot be a coincidence."

"He was just blaming us in an attempt to save his job, you *dummkopf*! He had no idea that anything was going on. For your sake, he'd better not become suspicious of me."

"You forget yourself, Chinaman, I am your superior," Krogh laughed, "in so many ways."

The second voice chuckled, "Prussian arrogance at its finest. I choose to work with you and your Herr Bismarck because it suits my purposes, but never for a moment think that I, Ming Tai Tsu, am *your* underling. By destabilizing France at this critical period, both our goals will be met. A weakened and de-moralized France will be a plum ripe for the picking by Germany. And with France occupied, it will not get a chance to consolidate its hold on Cochin China, which suits my purposes."

"I may ask that I be awarded Cochin China and then you would be my coolie!" Krogh's laugh turned into a sharp scream as Passepartout heard a couple of loud snaps.

"The superior man fainted from a small bit of pain! Let me re-pack your cast for you. It is a good thing that your plaster was not yet dried. Unfortunately, the new breaks to your radius, ulna, and humerus were not set so they will heal crookedly. For the rest of your life, you will experience pain radiating up and down your arm, so it will feel as if it had been ripped from its socket."

Hearing a rustle near the doorway, Passepartout stepped back and hid in the shadows. A tall Asian man stepped out of Krogh's room, wiping his hands on a handkerchief.

Monsieur Ming, as he was known at the school, taught Oriental history at the Lycée Napoléon and, oddly enough, theology. When Passepartout had first heard that one of the instructors was Oriental, he had immediately thought of someone out of the illustrations of *The Travels of Marco Polo*. Ming, however, dressed as a clergyman. His shaven head and clerical collar however did set him apart.

According to what he had told his fellow teachers, he was nominally a French citizen, hailing from the newly-acquired province of Cochin China. An outspoken Francophile, he claimed to have been educated by French Episcopalian missionaries and had been inspired to take up the collar and teach. He had seized the opportunity to teach in Paris to help the home country understand its new colony. He had convinced the Director that, by teaching at the Lycée, he could teach France's youth and best prepare them on how to administer their new territory, and so, bring harmony between France and its colony.

When Passepartout had first heard this, he had thought it a lot of blather, but after meeting Monsieur Ming in person, he had understood the sound logic behind it. Now, having heard the conversation between Ming and Krogh, Passepartout forced himself to use some of the logical mental exercises taught to him by Chevalier Dupin and the eccentric Rocambole. According to the latter, these exercises were used by an ancient race in Tibet to reroute the brain's electrical flow.

Suddenly, Ming stopped in mid-stride and looked straight at the spot where Passepartout was hiding. The Frenchman could feel the man's strange luminous yellow eyes fasten on him as if he were not hidden. He held his breath for a few seconds. Frowning, Ming left the room.

Sharp, bone-cracking pain suddenly slammed into Passepartout's head. He knew the pain was a sign he should continue to investigate. Ming had used some form of insidious mesmerism on him.

Retiring to his room, Passepartout worked on the exercises through the night. He used Rocambole's technique to probe the section of his mind where he had located Ming's handiwork, but had not been able to touch it. The area was protected by a mental block imprinted with the image of Ming's face. The vibrant amber eyes blinded like limelight. Passepartout's mental fingers stopped short of it as if blocked by an impenetrable glass. Although he strove to grasp the image, Passepartout's probes slipped away as if this area of his consciousness was composed of oiled glass.

Poking this area of his brain had also set off a trap set by Ming. Passepartout's worst memories and worst fears flooded his consciousness. Wandering lost in the streets of Paris after running away from the foundling home. Being shut into a dark underground room with thousands of squiggling monsters. Discovering a clown hanging off of the tightwire. Plummeting to a certain death after his trapeze wire had snapped. Having his horse shot out from under as he performed in the ring.

This last memory was particularly painful since it was so recent. Passepartout had ridden Bayard since he had been a colt. It had been its death that prompted him to leave the circus.

Rather than debilitating Passepartout, these memories emboldened him because they reminded him why he was called Passepartout. He passed everywhere, a living skeleton key; no cage could hold, no trap could contain him. Even when death seemed certain, he had escaped the Grim Reaper's scythe. On his own, he had escaped from the room of poisoned worms, discovered the clown's killer, stopped his plummet from the sky, and avenged his horse's death.

Gradually, his agile mental fingers found the hidden catch in the psychic glass. He shoved aside the image of Ming and worked on the implanted commands, stripping away the horrific memories like peeling layer after layer of thin paper off of a package. The effort left him drained with a residual headache.

As Passepartout rubbed his head, he grinned thinking that the Chevalier Dupin would have said that he had such a hard time with the exercises because he did not use his mind often enough. Passepartout was a man of action, and he made no apologies for it. Dupin gloried in ratiocination and had, in Passepartout's opinion, an unfortunate tendency to dismiss as lazy or unintelligent those who preferred more direct methods.

The next morning, his head ached as if he'd imbibed too much wine. So he asked his students to review their repertoire of exercises. As per Severin's command, he replaced his savate class with another gymnasium class. Passepartout had hoped that, by exposing the young men to an alternative method of fighting, they would take it up and do away with the asinine practice of sticking holes in each other at the slightest offense.

When his classes were done, Passepartout decided to call on Ming. Since an imperial decree had forbidden philosophy to be taught, Ming had set up an extracurricular club for its discussion. Passepartout decided to interrupt the latest meeting to see what truly transpired in these sessions.

When he reached the classroom, he found it was locked, but he easily picked the lock and opened the door a crack.

Passepartout could not believe his eyes. He had expected that, being a foreigner, Ming might be a bit unorthodox in his instruction technique, but having the students sit in the dark watching a magic lantern show while Ming lectured in a droning monotone was far beyond his expectations.

A brilliant light rapidly pulsed, blinding and burning the eyes in a regular, hypnotic rhythm. As the unintelligible droning continued, Passepartout found his attention drawn to the images of the magic lantern show. The pictures changed rapidly through some means Passepartout could not fathom, but they left an imprint on his mind.

The images had little to nothing to do with Annam, or even Asia in general. They were photos of the Imperial family and other aristocrats, photographs, and drawings of soldiers killed in battle, of duels, of Parisian landmarks, of animals fighting, and of executions. The pulsing light made the images eerie and yet compelling. Superimposed upon these images was a pair of gigantic yellow eyes burning and boring into the mind and soul. Ming was using some sort of insidious mesmerism on the children.

Although exposed to this for only a moment, Passepartout immediately felt uneasy. Nervous tension coursed through him, coupled with an impulse to commit violence. He pushed into the room thinking to dispel the bizarre lesson, however the full force of the flickering lights, the droning, lulling voice, and the amber eyes stopped him. He fell into one of the chairs and an odd lethargy gripped him as he sank into a deep golden light.

His brain and mind became immersed in a deep, comforting warmth, drowning him, dissolving him, and filling him with Ming's words. He squeezed his eyes shut and tried to ignore the sibilant whispers; he strove to regain his senses. His mind felt as if it were weighted with chains as it struggled to swim up through a viscous fluid.

Sudden clarity almost stunned Passepartout as his mind was suddenly freed of the enchantment. He pushed upwards from the school desk with shaking hands and quivering arms. He kept his eyes closed and charged up the aisle at Ming, intending to headbutt him. But his foot caught something and he sprawled forward. Startled, his eyes flew open to see the familiar, grinning face of a young teen. Movement caught the corner of the eye and he turned slightly. An open hand flashed down at him, the edge slamming into the side of his neck. Once again, blinding golden light flooded his vision, this time followed by darkness.

Two stinging slaps woke Passepartout. Monsieur Ming stood before him supporting him with a hand clamped on his shoulder. The Frenchman's feet lurched a bit and his knees wobbled as he supported his weight. They were in the gymnasium. "Now, Monsieur Passepartout, if you will look behind you, you shall see the fruits of my philosophy and you shall reap the rewards of opposing my will," said Ming.

Groggily, Passepartout turned around and was confronted by a semicircle of sharp thin blades centered on his vitals. Six of the students held épées in the *en garde* position.

"Strike deep my children!" Ming cried.

The six blades lunged forward and cold metal slid into warm, yielding flesh. But Ming's shout of triumph transformed in mid-note into a surprised, agonized screech as he felt the six swords skewering his gut. A sudden blurring crossed his vision. Suddenly, he felt Passepartout's presence behind him. He breathed, "Who taught you—Pai Mei?"

Faced by the swords, Passepartout had immediately lunged upwards from the floor in a backtuck that not only enabled him to avoid the swords' lunge, but had flipped over Ming, making the Oriental Studies teacher the unwitting target of the same swords.

Almost in concert, the swords ripped out of Ming with such brutal force that the initial stabbing seemed almost pleasant in comparison. As the Oriental Studies teacher slumped to the floor, Passepartout ran for the pommel horse. On his heels were the mesmerized young assassins. Unlike what happened in the old romances, these enchanted victims had not regained their senses when the "wizard" had become distracted or injured. Rather, they soldiered on with their last command until forcibly stopped.

Reaching the pommel horse, Passepartout vaulted onto it and then sprang towards the *Ringeschwebel*. Grasping the stirrup-shaped rings that hung from the ceiling, he swiveled his legs and torso up away from the threatening blades. He swung on the rings, gaining momentum, lunging, twisting, flipping, and oscillating to avoid the slashes and thrusts of the six swords. After a few moments, the six young swordsmen became scattered and started running around the gymnasium floor, attempting to keep up with Passepartout.

With deep regret, Passepartout counter-attacked, swinging down among his attackers to knock the swords out of their hands, or, if necessary, to knock them out. After a few moments of rapid swings, flashing metal, and meaty impacts, he had struck the six youths twenty times, but only received three minor flesh wounds to his face, hand, and chest, and a stab wound in his calf. All of the young men had received bruises to their arms, shoulders, and heads. Four of them eventually awakened from their hypnotic spell because it had worn off, or their injuries shocked them out of it. Passepartout broke the hands of the two who remained mesmerized with well-placed kicks. The pain was enough for one of the boys to awaken, but the last one picked up the sword in his left hand and awkwardly lunged at Passepartout.

The gym teacher dropped to the floor, avoided an off-balance thrust, and disarmed the boy. Tossing aside the sword, he gave the still-mesmerized youth hard, cracking slaps to both cheeks. The eyes flickered and the boy burst into tears. Passepartout told the boys to report to the school infirmary, then turned towards Ming.

A wide, wet crimson smear trailed across the gymnasium floor like a bloody snail's track. Ming had half crawled, half dragged his profusely bleeding body towards the rear door of the gymnasium. With his back propped up against the door, he sat, attempting to staunch the flow of blood with his jacket and pressure from his hands.

"Monsieur Passepartout, the door is locked," shouted one of the boys.

"Wait there, young sirs, I will be with you presently," the gym teacher replied.

Ming's odd amber eyes stared up at Passepartout, their normal hypnotic luminescence dulled by pain and lassitude.

"You are more than you appear, Monsieur Passepartout. I remembered you too late. Several lifetimes of memories tend to fog some details. I know the course of the future and know what it will mean for my lands to become a French colony. I had hoped to prevent it by using terror as a weapon."

He sneered, "It was such a beautiful plan. Your upper classes move about with impunity, so young aristocrats can gain access to power without suspicion. This is a knife pointed at your soft, pastry-filled bellies. If you will not control your children, someone else shall. A boy of ten suddenly stabs his father's friend, the cabinet minister, as they eat dinner... Another boy on his first hunt suddenly shoots his father's friends from the Bourse... Another young aristocrat being introduced to the Emperor wears a hidden waistcoat of dynamite... Such glorious chaos it would have been, had it not been for your interference... and a few unforeseen complications.

"I agreed to work with the Prussians because I knew of their territorial ambitions. Once I had weakened and demoralized France with my programmed children, Prussia would have invaded. In exchange, Annam and the surrounding regions would have been given autonomy and protection by Prussia."

Ming laughed slightly at Passepartout's horrified expression.

"It wasn't only students who received the treatment. After all, pawns must be directed. Another layer of imprinting was placed upon certain young impressionable and malleable instructors. One of these was coded to be a trigger, a man who could one day, without his knowledge, bring down France."

"Who? Who is it?" Passepartout demanded, shaking the dying man.

As his head bobbed from the force of Passepartout's shakes Ming's lambent amber eyes twinkled with humor as their light began fading. "Who, Monsieur *Passepartout*, who might be the key?"

Passepartout then realized why it had been so hard for him to undo Ming's mesmerism. A fierce grin flitted across his lips, "Ah, but this key has turned, Monsieur Ming."

The other's dying eyes flared with an amber rage that faded just as quickly as it arose. A small smile played on his lips. "So you hope, Monsieur, so you hope... Until we meet again, *au revoir*." As life fled, the smirk remained.

Passepartout unlocked the gymnasium door and told the children to return to their rooms. After he'd informed Severin of Ming's death, the Censor immediately sent for the police to have Passepartout arrested. But the teacher had also sent a message through the normal byzantine channels known only to Chevalier Dupin.

The Chevalier took personal charge of the case. After some persuasion by one of his agents, Doktor Krogh revealed the names of the students and teachers whom Ming had mesmerized. When Krogh was carried out to his new residence—a jail cell—he had gained another broken arm, two broken legs, a broken nose, and was missing most of his teeth.

Officially, the school was shut down for a two-week holiday while replacements were found for the three teachers who had been "taken ill," two of whom died soon after. The Chevalier and his friend Police Inspector Paul Picard did what they could to remove Monsieur Ming's mesmeric conditioning, but the boys would have to be watched closely for the rest of their lives.

While Passepartout was packing his belongings into a leather valise. a twelve-year-old boy with the composure of an adult walked into his room and threw himself down on his bed. Watching the teacher pack his case, he flicked open a cigarette case, tapped one on it, lit it, and smoked, flicking ashes on the bed.

Passepartout finally broke the silence. "Why, Théophraste?"

"Why what? Why did I come to see you leave?" With a saucy grin, the youth shrugged, "Because it pleases me to see you packing!"

"I meant, why to all of it? Why did you set Severin against me? Why did you tell Krogh and Ming about me? But most of all, why did you work with them in this horrible scheme of theirs?"

"I could not help myself. Ming had hypnotized me," Théophraste answered with a slight smile.

Passepartout gave the boy a cold look. "You may have fooled your father because he doesn't want to know the truth—even the most astute of men have their blind spots.—but I know whatever you did, you did of your own free will."

Théophraste blew a plume of smoke at Passepartout and gave him a sour look. "You gave Victor Rougon higher marks than I, although I am the far better athlete."

"Yes, you are a gifted athlete and could excel at any sport. However, you are lazy and do just enough to get by. Victor, on the other hand, strives with all his heart. That is the difference. In life, we must work hard to achieve what we wish. Learn this young and you will succeed."

"Spoken like a true peasant," Théophraste sniffed. "The truth is that breeding counts far more than accomplishment. I should have gotten the high marks, not only because of my superior abilities but because I deserve them by right of birth. Victor is but a merchant's son."

Passepartout shook his head and gave Théophraste a grim smile. "Let's be honest, my friend, poisoning my name with Monsieur Severin and taking up with Doktor Krogh was about much more than my giving you low marks in gymnasium class."

Théophraste blew smoke and watched it drift in a cloud to hover in front of Passepartout's face. The youngster's facade of charm evaporated, twisting into a mask of hatred. His eyes grew cold as a serpent's yet burned with an implacable loathing.

"All my life my father has praised your name. Jean this! Jean that! He lauds your accomplishments and takes pride in your achievements. The very way he speaks your name is an affront to me! Listening in on his conversations, I learned all about you and the work you do for him. He is so *pleased* with the man you have become..."

Théophraste mouth twisted into a sneer of disgust. "It's almost as if... as if he were a father talking about his son. Considering your origins." He made the word sound like something dragged out of a sewer. "One has to wonder if that indeed might not be the case. Certainly, you must have wondered as well?"

Passepartout gave Théophraste a small smile. "The thought has on occasion passed through my mind." His brow furrowed in puzzlement, he tried to fathom the young man's antipathy. "This, then, is why you hate me—because we might be brothers?"

"Never that!" spat Thérophraste, throwing the smoking cigarette butt to the floor. As Passepartout rubbed it out with his foot, the boy jumped up from the bed and stood over the teacher as if he wished to strike him. Indeed, his hand curled into a fist that he shook in front of Passepartout's face.

As he glared down at his teacher, Théophraste Dupin yelled, "Always, always will you be a bastard, never a brother! Whether or not you are my father's get, you are a rival for my father's affections." Forestalling Passepartout's protest, he continued. "Whether you seek it or not, whether you wish or not, there it is." Théophraste then took a breath and calmed himself. "Remember, Jean the bastard, Jean the clown, that I am the true, legitimate son of Chevalier Dupin, and shall always be so."

He strode towards the door and turned around. His handsome young face was once again a façade of charm and civility. "You see, I get quite enough of you at home, so having to endure your company at school was simply unbearable. So I whispered a few pertinent facts about you into old Severin's ears. As for working with Ming and Krogh, Ming was fascinated when I turned out to be resistant to his treatment. Krogh wanted to dispose of me. I convinced them that I could help them, and did so for money—and because it was fun." Théophraste leaned against Passepartout's doorframe and lit another cigarette, tossing the match at Passepartout's foot.

His cheery smile transformed into an evil grin as he laughed. "They never did realize that it was me who caused their little experiment to go awry. That it was me, using the mesmerism I picked up from Ming, who instigated the uncontrollable violent behavior in some of their subjects."

This news stunned Passepartout, not only for the sheer evil that it embodied, but because it meant that Théophraste possessed enough skilled guile to carry out such deception, and the sheer intellectual ability to surpass Ming's mesmeric abilities. Passepartout should have guessed at the boy's intellect, given his heritage, however well he had made efforts to conceal it, but the source of his immorality was hard to fathom.

His horrified shock pleased Théophraste who gave him an ironic bow.

"Why would you do such a thing?" Passepartout asked, still a bit stunned by the revelation.

Théophraste watched the cigarette's smoke trail and shrugged. "I enjoyed watching those fools beat on each other like drunken sailors." Eyes glittering with amusement, he motioned towards Passepartout's case with a wave. "So it's off to another school I suppose. What's the old saw? Those who can't do, teach; those who can't teach, teach gym." He chuckled at his own wit as he stubbed his cigarette on the doorframe. Then he gave the teacher a malicious smirk, "Let me know where you're going next so I can give the Censor of that school a rousing recommendation."

"One reason I wanted to teach was because I thought I'd missed something by not attending school," Passepartout said, closing the leather straps on his valise. "I have discovered since that I hadn't missed much. By and large, students do not want to learn, and teachers care more about advancement than they do about teaching. So I've decided to leave the profession.""

"So I guess it is back to being a clown, then?" Théophraste snickered.

Passepartout let the remark pass. "No, I wanted to teach because I wanted to help people. I don't feel that I was doing enough by simply teaching gymnastics. So I have enlisted in the corps of the Sapeurs-Pompiers."

"Well, in that case, I'll try to stay out of burning buildings," Théophraste laughed. "You'd no doubt leave me behind if you were my rescuer."

Passepartout had held his anger and disgust at bay so far, but could do so no longer and snapped, "No, my young Monsieur, I would not hesitate to rescue anyone; not even you." Calming, he added, "perhaps I am a fool, but I still believe you can be saved, Théo."

Théophraste laughed heartily at that. He shouted at Passepartout's back, "You may no longer be a clown, Jean the bastard, but you are still a fool!"

Passepartout shook his head sadly and continued walking. Although Chevalier Dupin could not or refused to see it, young Théophraste was already far down a bad path.

*Pete Rawlik & Sal Ciano contribute here a lovely and very well executed Love-craftian pastiche. As for the Great Old One Khagnon Faugn, his name is a variation on that of the elephantine Chaugnar Faugn from Frank Belknap Long's* Horror in the Hills. *The lore tells us that Chaugnar and his five brothers once lived in an inaccessible cave in the Pyrenees Mountains, served by the Miri Nigri, humanoids that he had created. They received human sacrifices from the people of Pompelo, until the Romans wiped them out. Chaugnar and his brothers then destroyed Pompelo and moved to Asia to await the "white acolyte" who would bring him back to civilization. When Chaugnar reawakened in NYC in the 1930s, so did his brothers in the Pyrenees...*

## Pete Rawlik & Sal Ciano: *The Deposition of Randolph Carter*

*When, on a memorable joint furlough, the learned young Creole had taken the wistful Boston dreamer to Bayonne, in the south of France, and had shown him certain terrible secrets in the nighted and immemorial crypts that burrow beneath that brooding, eon-weighted city, the friendship was forever sealed.*
Through the Gates of the Silver Key

*Bayonne, 1915*

I appreciate your time, Inspector. I know that this is not your jurisdiction, but... well, you see, I've tried to explain things to the local authorities, and—unfortunately—my French is not as refined as it should be. I appreciate the fact that you have allowed me to repeat my statement in English, and I assure you that what I tell you is exactly what I told your fellow countrymen, even if it was spoken falteringly. I also appreciate the situation I find myself in, so I want to impress upon you once more: no matter how strange my tale may seem, it all happened as I tell it and I am not one who is prone to exaggeration. The events I am about to relate happened exactly as I say.

My name is Randolph Carter, of Boston in the American state of Massachusetts. I am a decorated member of the French Foreign Legion, holding the rank of Caporal, as was my friend Etienne-Laurent de Marigny. We came here to Bayonne on furlough, to visit his ancestral family seat. I urge you to call our commanding officer; he will confirm these facts, my character, and that I am prone neither to flights of the imagination, or morbid jokes. I have and will continue to tell you the truth. There is no point in lying to you. If I am unclear on any detail, it is because of the very nature of the events that unfolded and caused me to flee through the streets of Bayonne and into the arms of a member of the *gendarmerie*.

De Marigny and I were friends, comrades in arms in this terrible war with the Hun. I will not deny that we shared a fascination with certain facets of the strange that haunt our world. I myself have all my life suffered from a malady of premonitions, a peculiar sense of *déjà vu*, and an overwhelming dread of future events that I seem to have unnatural memories of. Even now, in this place, saying these things, it seems both to be a remembrance of something from my past, and an echo of something from my future. Against all odds, de Marigny shared the same kind of dread. He thought himself akin to Oedipus and was concerned that he—like the tragic Greek figure—could not avoid the foul destiny that awaited him, and that indeed every step he took to counter his fate only worked to cement it in place. He, in his very soul, knew that something terrible awaited him, and there was absolutely no way he could not avoid it.

Though my outlook on the future's dark tidings was similar to de Marigny's, it was not nearly so theatrical. I suffer from premonitions, and they were particularly prevalent when I was younger. There was an incident on my uncle's estate in Arkham, and then another when my father was stationed in Warsaw. Little things really, just an odd habit of reminiscing about events and places and things that I hadn't encountered yet or had not happened yet.

Once, a family friend mentioned the village of Belloy-en-Santerre, and I felt such a complete sense of dread that I turned pale and nearly passed out. It was as if that place meant something to me, that it was somehow important, and yet I had never heard of it before that day. I had to do research in the library just to find out where it was. Some of these premonitions have taken years to understand, but of all of them, the only one I have left, the only premonition that has not resolved itself, has been my dread of Belloy-en-Santerre. I think that this place will be the death of me, but I have come to accept it. I have found comfort in the writings of Al-Fuḍayl ibn ʿIyāḍ, and his tale, *When Death Comes to Baghdad*.

I shall take that look of disbelief to mean that you may not be familiar with the story, your comrades weren't, so I will explain it again. A merchant is in the marketplace in Baghdad when he bumps into a figure that he recognizes as the embodiment of death. Death looks at him and calls him by his name. The merchant flees and, in an attempt to outwit death, travels as fast as he can to the distant city of Samarra. That night sitting in a café in Samara, Death joins the merchant for tea. The merchant asks Death, why did you call my name in the marketplace in Baghdad? Death apologizes and says that he was very surprised by the man's presence in Baghdad, because he knew he had an appointment later, to collect the merchant's soul in Samarra.

De Marigny knew the story and understood how I had conflated it with my own fear of Belloy-en-Santerre, but he questioned the point of the premonition. He wondered what the purpose of such premonitions could be. He even cited Charles Dickens' *A Christmas Carol* as an example. What purpose do these glimpses of the future serve, he postulated, if not to provide the opportunity to right wrongs, to correct the courses of our very lives? I countered that our lives might be meaningless, that at the cosmic scale we might be little more than dust, but he rejected such notions. He suggested that human life, as a whole and individually, must hold some purpose, even if it was beyond our understanding. My dread, he was sure, was entirely misplaced and he further postulated that my true destiny might lay in the town of Belloy-en-Santerre. It was the great debate of our lives, and I suppose it set us on the path to this fateful night.

I will not deny that we were intoxicated. We had spent the day exploring Saint-Esprit, the Jewish District that was founded at the end of the Fifteenth Century when the Alhambra Decree had driven Sephardic refugees out of Spain. My friend had found a book, written in an ancient Yiddish script, that he swore was somehow related to the history of his own varied lineage. I, on the other hand, had indulged in the fine pastries and chocolates that the district was known for and ended the day at a café overlooking the harbor, sipping a local vintage. I was admiring my sketches of the *Cimetière juif* of Bayonne, while de Marigny labored over a passage in his newly acquired book. He was quite well versed in the languages of the Levant, but this dialect was rather ancient and was giving him some difficulty. It was not until late in the evening that he suddenly had an epiphany and snapped the book shut in triumph.

Not long after, I found myself armed with an unlit lantern and trailing behind de Marigny as he used his lantern's hood to discreetly consult his book and an ancient map of the city as we made our way to the ancient and decrepit quay downstream of where the river Nive met the Ardour. The lack of light was twofold, de Marigny said when he told me to wait to light my lantern, his hooded lantern would attract less attention if there were guards, and the more fuel we had to light our way, the better. As we walked, he told me of the place's history.

"It was here that the engineers had worked to change the course of the river, digging great pits, and installing huge culverts to shift the flow. That's all well and good, but in doing so they covered up whole histories and that, Carter, is why we are here. Now help me find an old pipe, should be large enough to accommodate a person."

We searched a bit and quickly found the long-abandoned pipe we sought and the rusted grate, with centuries of caked on filth, that covered the opening. With little trouble we tore off a corrupted piece of grating and entered the pipe. Once inside, we paused as I lit my lantern, and he unhooded his. I was shocked when de Marigny produced his pistol and proceeded to check to make sure that the gun was loaded and functional. I suggested that such lethal precautions were unnecessary, but de Marigny suggested otherwise, proffering rumors of rodents of unusual size. I scoffed, but de Marigny offered sound wisdom concerning having a gun and not needing it, versus needing a gun and not having one. I acknowledged his wisdom, but then wondered aloud, to myself as much as he, why he had not suggested that I bring my sidearm as well.

His sneer gleamed in the lamplight, "Because my friend, even after all this time, you are a terrible shot. You are just as likely to shoot me as any monster we might encounter."

I wanted to say something clever in response but could not. He had spoken the truth; I was terrible with a gun. Etienne was my opposite on the range and made for a rather decent marksman. He had once even been a candidate for sniper training. Before I could figure out an appropriate and scathing retort, we arrived at our destination.

We did not pause to consider the situation; into the sewer we strode. It was an aged thing, several hundred years old, which one could tell by the occasional stamping on some of the collapsing bricks. The water around our feet was shallow, but festered with the foul life that forever seems to flourish in such dark and foreboding places. A green-grey scum floated on the surface and coated the walls, supported I supposed by the humidity of the place. Insects flitted back and forth in the thin light of our lanterns, and all around us crawled centipedes, worms, and other vermiform creatures. I saw no snakes, but frogs, toads, newts, and other batrachian beasts were in abundance, fed I suppose by the myriad lesser things that eked out existence in the dark and foreboding tunnel. As we traveled deeper, such creatures became fewer, but those we did see seemed to grow larger, and curiously paler.

After an hour of walking, we spied in the dimness what we first thought to be a small pile of bricks that had fallen from the masonry above, but as we grew closer it reared up and hopped away, revealing itself to be not rubble but a toad the size of a small dog. I found myself nauseous as my mind writhed in revulsion, not at its size but its translucence. The beast's skin was absent of any sort of pigmentation at all and was instead revoltingly transparent, and readily revealed the inner muscles, bones, and organs within. I was completely transfixed in my revulsion and wanted to linger; for something about the creature's circulatory system fascinated me, and then I realized what it was that had caught my attention: the veins themselves were translucent and I could see the blood as it was pulled to and from the heart in response to the toad's sudden fright and consequent flight. I'd never dreamed I'd see a heart pump blood before and the way the blood flowed as it reacted in fright to our noisy arrival was incredible to behold, but de Marigny would not have it and he urged us ever forward.

As I have said before, even then, so deep within the bowels beneath the city, I had no clue as to where my friend was leading me. Every so often he would pause, consult his treasured book and the crumbling map, and then nod and once more trounce forward. In honesty, I do not think he knew where we were going, not exactly, but he was clearly of the opinion that it was somewhere of some great import. And so, I followed my friend through that fetid tunnel, no matter where it went, comforted only by the faith that I had in my friend.

It was in the second hour of our descent that the masonry suddenly changed and took on an older cast. These bricks were cruder and mixed with roughly hewn rocks. Again, a few bore identifiable marks. I still thought them French, but de Marigny pointed out the tell-tale signs of Roman graffiti, particularly one that he said bore the mark of a Roman centurion, Crismus Bonus. "He plotted to overthrow Julius Caesar," mentioned de Marigny. "These ruins tunnels are much older than those documented above, concurrent with the early occupation of the area by Rome." He ran his hand over the faded carved rock revealing even more markings as the dust came away. "Yes, yes! These document the destruction of the pagans at Pompelo, and their escape up the coast. This is exactly what we are looking for!"

While I found the history of the tunnels intriguing, I was beginning to feel a bit foolish. Was de Marigny planning to rob some forgotten and lost grave? I demanded de Marigny explain himself, which he did as we continued our march through the dimly lit aqueduct. "When the Romans arrived in the region, they found it inhabited by a number of tribes, and a variety of faiths. One particularly abhorrent group had settlements on both sides of the Pyrenees, and worshipped a group of monstrous deities they called the Six, or the Six brothers. What exactly made this faith more abhorrent than all the others was never clear, but the Roman drove them relentlessly out of the region now occupied by modern day Pamplona with fire and steel. Legend has it that they took the living idol of their god and fled to Asia, leaving the other five brothers hidden—sleeping or dead, depending on your translation—in cave-like temples around and inside the mountains, tended by their cults in secret. This book suggests that one such temple is here, beneath the streets of Bayonne."

"But what does that have to do with your ancestry my friend?"

He snorted, "Nothing, my friend. I knew of your fascination with your own lineage and thought it a ruse strong enough to convince you to pursue this adventure with me." He must have seen the sour look on my face. "Do not be upset my friend, we needed an adventure! Something to take our minds off of the war, and this, despite the darkness—this is a grand adventure." I could not argue with him.

It was not long before the Roman architecture gave way to a more natural structure, a cave carved by geological processes over ages unfathomable to men. It was through this crack in the earth itself that de Marigny and I descended, contorting our bodies to slip through the misshapen cavern that cut ever deeper into the chthonic world below. The rock and stones of the crevice clawed at us, cut at our flesh, and bruised our muscles and bones, but still we persisted in our quest to travel ever down, ever down into that dim-lit world. We had left any pretense of the human world behind, there was no brickwork, no masonry, no carved stairs, or any handholds. Even the dampness that had once infused the very air was gone. The presence of my friend was my only tether to the human world, and I was his.

Then suddenly we were through the crack in the earth and stumbling happily into a small chamber with a passage leading off into the distance. I thought it to be just another deformation in the rock and voted to turn back rather than face a longer tunnel filled with the same awfulness I'd just felt de Marigny grew excited at the sight of the deformation though. He called me over to him and pointed out that the markings on the walls where the passageway been purposefully enlarged. "This is it Carter, we are at the threshold of the temple itself!"

And then we took those fateful steps out of that chamber and into the cavernous temple cave beyond. It was an awe-inspiring sight: roughly dome shaped, and easily two perhaps even three stories in height at the center. The walls were encrusted with mica, and the glittering nature of that mineral seemed to reflect back our lamplight a thousand-fold. Where once we had slunk about in molasses thick darkness, here we were granted a room bathed in light. There were scattered about the room various objects that indicated that this space was once occupied by men. There were crude tables and stools, all made out of wood that had long since decayed into uselessness. There were also tatters of cloth and leather, of various workmanship. Some seemed to be Roman, others were of more primitive construct. Against one wall there were stacked a number of swords, axes and spears, some of such beauty and craftsmanship that they would be the prize of any museum. But it was the object in the middle of the room that was truly the most remarkable.

It was an idol easily twice the height of a man, and carved from some sort of black stone, with an almost crystalline tint to it. Its titanically thick legs were crossed and ended in blunt, pachyderm feet. Its two great arms rested upon those legs, the hands splayed upright, and in those Brobdingnagian claws rested two carved orbs, one of alabaster, and the other of amethyst. Above these appendages, were two more limbs that were crossed against the chest. The gargantuan thing was topped by a massive, carved skull from which jutted three elephantine faces that each ended with a thick and curling proboscis, tipped with a crystalline dagger. Great ornate ears sat headdress-like atop the head, and two crystal and ivory tusks grew from under the faces and protruded from under either side of the face in the center. It sat there eyeless, and terrible, and silent; unseen and undisturbed for centuries until we—de Marigny and I—had stumbled into its cavernous temple.

"Behold, Randolph Carter," de Marigny announced, "the third of the Six Brothers, the thing men once worshipped under the name Khagnon Faugn, the watcher in time!"

There was this strange look in his eye, a mania I suppose. It frightened me, and I took a step back into the entryway. "Etienne, we should leave this place."

"Nonsense Carter, I didn't come all this way to stop now, on the verge of the threshold." And then he opened the book, and began reciting words that I could not understand, and nor did I want to. For as he spoke those words, they took on a life of their own. The words continued to echo through the air over and over, each syllable repeating and layering itself over the one that came before until the air took on a kind of electric hum, and I felt my hair stand on end.

And here, Sir, at last is where we come to the truly unbelievable part. The words filled the air until I could almost feel their weight pressing me against the wall of the chamber. I could not bear their terrible, crushing embrace and I did the only thing a prudent and sane person would do in such a situation. I ran. I ran as fast as I could because those words had stirred up something long asleep, I did not want to be there when it woke. I did not want it to see me. As I fled, I heard a sharp cracking sound, and I paused briefly in the hallway leading back to the antechamber and looked back to see if my friend still lived. The last image I have of Etienne-Laurent de Marigny is of him rising up into the air and those great, colossal, bestial arms opening to welcome him! It sounds mad, I know. But I swear it happened. I do not know what happened next or what kind of embrace it turned out to be.

I turned and ran, first through the antechamber and then up into the crack in the earth. I climbed wildly and madly, and I did not even pause when my lantern shattered. It didn't matter, there was only one way to go, and that was up and out. I didn't need light for that.

Then I heard his voice, as if he were standing right beside me. "Carter, it is wondrous, incredible, illuminating!"

I didn't want to answer, but how could I not? "What is it?"

"I can see all of eternity spread out before me, like a stream flowing down a mountain into the sea. It is infinite, and yet fleeting. Eternal but finite. I look forward and see the future, I look back and see the past. I concentrate on the here and the now, and I see the complex interplay of... of everything. I see the connections that bind individuals to each other and the world around them. I see how men impact other men, how the flights of birds in Africa generate hurricanes in the Caribbean. I see the light from a star dead for untold eons fall on the lamina of a piece of grass to become energy for the plant, and I watch the energy transfer from grass into a cow and then into a child. I see the connections."

I scrambled up the cleft and into the cave. But no matter how fast or how far I ran, I could still hear my friend's voice as he continued to narrate his ascension into some new state of consciousness.

"I can see you, Carter. Not now but then, the future you, months from now, at Belloy-en-Santerre, and years ago, in Arkham. I can see you, billions of years in the past, and millions of years in the future. You are a constant, did you know that? You exist throughout space time. You are unique, an enduring tangible in a fluid universe."

My heart was pounding in my head as I stumbled through the Roman conduit, careening from one side of the passageway to the other, pushing myself forward when all I wanted to do was fall to my knees in despair, and let the filth rush over me and dissolve me into waste and bone.

But all the while there was de Marigny, chattering in my head. But now there was something wrong in his voice. There was still wonder, but it was laced with something else, something that I thought was doubt, or perhaps fear. "It is you, Carter; it has always been you. The pen moves, it writes, and having written moves on, but the focus is eternally on you. The rest of us, we are nothing, fleeting sands in the winds of time, eddies in the tides of creation. We come into being, we play our part, and then we dissolve back into nothingness. I can feel it already."

My hand brushed the wall of the tunnel, and I felt the smooth surface of centuries old masonry. I must have been fleeing for hours to come so far. My legs were burning from exhaustion. There was a wound in my side, and it ached fiercely as I struggled to recall when I had received it and failed. When I rested, I could hear the fat toads and newts that inhabited this dark and dismal realm as they struggled to avoid my presence. And yet even then, so far from that chamber, I could hear the faint and terrified voice of my friend.

"It is nearly finished. The angels of angles are coming for me. I've seen too much, learned too much, travelled up and down the timestream too many times. The vertex jackals howl my name. I can flee, but where, no, when can one hide? Run, Carter, run! I will distract them. You're losing time. Why do they hate you so?"

He screamed in agony and fear, a shriek wrought of the very essence of the universe. It caught me, like a wave it carried me forward, accelerating down the tunnel. It was his gift to me, a parting chance at survival against whatever it was we woke up down there. Hellish things I think, but not in the traditional sense. A legion of intricacies, of connection, of things our minds were not yet ready to comprehend. Can you imagine it, knowing your place in the universe is inconsequential, to be naught but a roadblock for a friend? While I cannot express gratitude enough for his sacrifice, his end was truly a terrible fate, and I would not be surprised if de Marigny was driven mad at the end. The last thing I heard him say (though I am not sure he even said it, it was perhaps a dying echo of his mind's last thought) was, "*Pulvis et umbra sumus.*" My Latin is a bit rusty, but I managed to translate that bit, and it says: we are but dust and shadows.

And there it is, my dear Inspector Maigret, my tale, as it were. After that, I ran screaming from the quay into the streets and into the arms of one of your local gendarmes. They cleaned me up, fed me and filled me with coffee, and then had me tell my story.

They listened, as intently as I suppose they could. They took notes, made some inquiries concerning this and that, but—unlike you—all the time they seemed to be on the verge of laughter, as if this was some joke I was telling, and it was I alone that did not understand the punchline. I asked—no, I demanded—that they explain themselves to me, and it was then they told me what it was that made them smile. The words they said drove me mad, and I leapt across the table and assaulted one of the officers. That is when they restrained me, and wrapped me up in this straight jacket, and confined me to this hospital. That was a few days ago, and I have since calmed down. I asked for you so that I could tell my tale again, to repeat my truths and now I come to the end, de Marigny is dead, and I barely escaped with my own life. I have told you the truth; the whole and insane truth, and I appreciate you not mocking me or my tale. Now, I need you to help me. Please.

I know that next week, when my furlough is over, I will be forced to rejoin the Legion, and deal with those words that drove me to assault a man of the law. But tell me Inspector, was he just joking? It can't be true; I know it can't. I heard him die, heard the cosmic winds blow him to ashes through the stream of time. So, I know without a shadow of doubt that it cannot be true, so please— tell me the truth. I can bear it; I can bear the truth. So, tell me: What did the gendarme mean when he said those words to me, in his thick English? Those impossible words that still rattle around in my brain, and I confess to a feverish flush of panic even as I think of them now, and I wish I was just hearing things…that his accent threw me off, but I know the truth! I know what he said, and now tell me, please, is there any truth to his words? You know what he said, right before… before I punched him… he said:

"YOU FOOL, ETIENNE-LAURENT DE MARIGNY STILL LIVES!"

*This is a truly wonderful sequel to* Malpertuis, *a 1943 novel by the great Belgian author Jean Ray. Malpertuis is a crumbling, ancient house where a dying warlock (Cassave) has trapped the ancient gods of Olympus inside the "skins" of seemingly ordinary mortals. It was made into a film in 1971 by Belgian director Harry Kümel, starring Orson Welles as Cassave, and Susan Hampshire as Euryale. Now, return to Malpertuis with..*

# Josh Reynolds: *House of Malice*

*Ghent, 1911*

A black motor car prowled along silent streets. Houses slept in the moonlight, and a grey drizzle lent a slick silver sheen to the town. The light cast by isolated lampposts was dim and pallid, diffused by the rain.

The car passed through beams of moonlight like a tiger between the trees. Its motor made only the barest rumble to disturb the stultifying silence that clung to the town like a shroud. The buildings that rose to either side of the vehicle were archaic remnants, crumbling beneath the twin sieges of time and neglect. A few new structures stood out, notable only by their clean lines and unstained brick.

Doors were shut and shutters closed as the motor car passed by; a pointed disinvitation, its passenger thought. No succor here for the weary pilgrim, and no room at the inn. The man who called himself Severus el Tebib, but was known far and wide by a certain class of person as Sâr Dubnotal, the Great Psychagogue, leaned back in his seat and smiled. Not in pleasure, so much as grim satisfaction.

"Is this the place, Master?" the driver asked, glancing back at his passenger. In contrast to his master, he had the soft skin and beardless face of an adolescent, though his pale eyes were no less magnetic than Sâr Dubnotal's dark ones. "Have we found it at last?"

Sâr Dubnotal cleared his throat. "I believe so, Rudolph. Can you not sense the evil that taints the air here? It has a potency that speaks to age." He leaned forward, tawny eyes shimmering with a hunter's gleam. He was dressed finely, his dark overcoat contrasting sharply with the pure white turban that adorned his noble head. "We are close. I can feel the weight of it pressing against my soul. Awful things have happened here; a grand guignol of cosmic proportion." He pointed. "There—the entrance to the Rue du Vieux Chantier."

"Are you certain we should continue, Master?" Rudolph asked as he made the indicated turn. "Perhaps this place should be left with its secrets. It might be better for us all if it were to simply be forgotten."

"No. Such places do not stay forgotten. Not for long. Eventually someone would seek it out, even as our larcenous friend did, and I fear they would not be content to take only a statue. No, Rudolph... It and all that it contains must be sealed away by one who knows how. Ah—there. Malpertuis, in all its defiled glory."

The street was crowded with tall and sinister buildings, but Malpertuis was taller and more sinister than any of them. As he climbed out of the motor car, Sâr Dubnotal studied it with the eye of one who had visited his fair share of unpleasant places.

It presented a face consisting of enormous pillared balconies, high wide steps flanked by stone banisters, high turrets and barred, shuttered windows. Chimneys, long since cold and crumbling, surmounted its roof like the tines of a pagan crown. Child-eating serpents and tarasques coiled in monstrous frenzy across its studded doors. To Sâr Dubnotal's psychical senses, this place echoed with an eternity of soundless screaming; a whiff of the abnatural, as his associate Carnacki might have described it.

This fetid aura contrasted sharply with the placid chapel that crouched at the far end of the street like a sentry. A sense of serenity and peace rose from that place, but it was a serenity leavened with sadness. Then, given the blight it set itself against, perhaps sadness was to be expected.

Rudolph shivered. His pale features were almost white. "This place... it stinks of evil. I wish we had brought Naini," he added, referring to Sâr Dubnotal's gigantic manservant.

"I fear physical strength is of little use in places such as this. Some matters cannot be settled by mere force of arms." Sâr Dubnotal gestured. "The statue, please."

Rudolph dutifully went to the boot of the vehicle and extracted a cloth-swaddled bundle. It was both heavy and not, in a peculiar fashion. Sâr Dubnotal carefully unwrapped the item and studied it with a practiced eye. "The boundary god," he murmured, as he turned his gaze back to the house. "Returned at last to its threshold."

Sâr Dubnotal had secured the statue, and the story of its theft, from the very man who had stolen it. The thief had claimed no evil intent; Sâr Dubnotal did not doubt that he believed it. He had paid the man more than fairly, and sent him on his way. Now he'd come to the house to see it for himself.

"Is this where you hid yourself after your great sin, Cassave?" Sâr Dubnotal asked aloud. There was no reply; perhaps that was for the best. The house was like a wounded animal—no, a dying one. Its master was gone, its inhabitants—save one—departed or dead. The magic which had gone into its creation was fading. Soon, it would fall to ruin, or perhaps simply collapse in on itself and vanish from mortal sight.

But until then, it still held a trove of secrets and Sâr Dubnotal had come to learn them. Such knowledge, as was still contained in the house, was a dangerous thing. In the wrong hands it could lead to great wrongdoing; in fact, it already had. Cassave had been a notorious magus, worse in his way than menaces like Haddo, Crowley or Thorne. That he was dead now meant little. The evil he'd done outlived him. But Sâr Dubnotal would see it put right. It was his duty, if not his privilege.

He glanced at Rudolph. "Wait here, my friend. What lies within is not for your eyes, I fear. Only one who is steeped in the ancient wisdoms can traverse such borderlands safely." Rudolph frowned at this, but didn't argue. He had seen too much in their years together to doubt his mentor's words.

Sâr Dubnotal started up the steps. The serpentine shapes that marked the doors seemed to twist and writhe as he approached them. He could hear their hisses, and the rasping of their scales. They whispered malign warnings to him in an antediluvian tongue, telling him to flee the house of Malpertuis –the house of malice.

At his gesture, the guardian spirits fell silent and still. Once, they might have resisted. But they were weak now; fading from the world. It was all they could do to keep the house intact and unnoticed by passers-by. He had barely touched the handle when the doors practically flung themselves open with the resigned sigh of rusty hinges.

Sâr Dubnotal paused, studying the darkness within. It was placid; patient. Malpertuis was not evil in the same way as 50 Berkeley Square in London, or Belasco House, in Maine, or even that strange, foul house in Ireland he had so recently visited in the company of John Silence and Thomas Carnacki. Its evil was akin to the smell escaping from a putrefying corpse. Pervasive, rather than predatory. Malpertuis did not lurk or loom. It *seeped.*

Steeling himself, he stepped inside. The doors creaked shut behind him. He glanced at them, and then at the foyer. The darkness had taken on a hostile weight now, as if in entering the house he'd woken something up. The great entrance hall stretched away from him, into an infinity of shadow. The pedestal where the statue had once sat was positioned at the midpoint, like a silent sentry. Nooks lined the hall, displaying a legion of stone grotesquerie. He fancied he could hear them hissing in welcome to their long-absent fellow—or maybe their jailer.

A staircase with a stout and massive banister rail stood to his left, rising up and away. A mirror on the right reflected it, in the dim light that sifted through the shuttered windows. There was movement there, in the reflected shadows. Like the twitch of a curtain to reveal a glimpse of someone or something hiding behind it.

Sâr Dubnotal could feel eyes on him as he set the boundary god back upon the dusty pedestal from whence it had been taken so many months before. He stepped back, and waited for his host to greet him. Cassave was dead, but the thief's story had made clear that someone—something—was still residing here.

Finally, a soft voice said, "A strange sort of thief, to return what was stolen."

Sâr Dubnotal studied the mirror. Something was approaching down the steps. A shape at once monstrous and slight, as if it could not decide which it should be. "I am not the one who took it, though I paid well for the privilege of bringing it back to its proper place." He gave the statue an affectionate, if somewhat disrespectful, pat.

In the mirror, the newcomer continued their descent. A claw of gleaming steel slid down the banister rail. Two vast wings spread in the gloom, rustling like leather curtains. Sâr Dubnotal watched without horror or dismay, instead noting with slight amusement that for once the ancient scholars appeared to be correct in their description of the being in question. It—she—paused, and two orbs of green flame burst to life.

Even reflected, the gaze of a gorgon was unpleasant. Sâr Dubnotal had come prepared; there were many charms about his person. His tiepin was made from a splinter of Pridwen, the fabled shield of King Arthur; and his cuff-links had been carved from samples of a certain meteorite that had set the skies of Yorkshire ablaze little over a century previous. Even so, he could not prevent himself from flinching slightly.

She laughed softly and he knew she had seen his moment of weakness. "You are wise to be frightened of me, sir. Even the gods feared me, once."

Sâr Dubnotal straightened and looked directly into the mirror. "So they did. But I am not frightened; wary, yes. But I do not think I have reason to worry. Indeed, you are the very person I have come hoping to see." Deliberately, he turned from the mirror to face her. Just for an instant, he felt the full potency of that infernal gaze and knew in the pit of his soul that his precautions were not so effective as he'd assumed. Then, the moment passed and the green fire dwindled and vanished.

He felt the air quiver, as if something had moved through it very quickly, then, a moment later, a young woman with fiery red hair descended the last few steps. She wore a dress that was thirty years out of fashion, and had a silk blindfold wrapped about her eyes. "Have you then?" she asked. "And to what do I owe such a visit?"

"Salvation," Sâr Dubnotal said, simply. "Freedom."

She smiled slightly. "You would free me, then? Are you a magus, sir?"

Sâr Dubnotal bowed low. "Some men know me as the Great Psychagogue. Others call me Severus el Tebib." He paused. "Cassave might have known me as..."

"Sâr Dubnotal," she said, nodding. "He cursed your name often. It provided me with great amusement. Few men could unsettle him in such a fashion."

"I am proud to be in such company, if so."

"You were not his friend, then?"

561

"Once," he admitted. "In my ill-spent youth. But not for many years. I chose the righteous path, and Cassave... chose another." He felt a flicker of sadness as he said it. He had not thought of the man in years, though he had foiled more than one scheme in the past to find traces of Cassave at its heart.

"Yes. I can feel it in you. You chose the light, and he, the dark."

"Prosaically put, but yes. I suppose so." He frowned and clasped his hands before him. "You know who I am. Might I have your name?"

"You know me, man," she said, with a slight smile.

"I do, but I would have your name regardless."

Her smile widened to something on the cusp of a grimace. "I am Euryale, the Bellowing One. She of the Iron Tresses and Brass Claws. Sister of Medusa. Lover of Jean-Jacques Grandsire." Her expression faded to neutrality. "Last custodian of Malpertuis."

"A pleasure to make your acquaintance, dear lady," Sâr Dubnotal said. And it was, for here, before him, was nothing less than a living piece of antiquity. A being older than the oldest empires of man. He could only imagine what sights she had borne witness to, what wonders and horrors lurked in her memory. The thought all but left him speechless.

"There is a sentiment that few share," she said, with a hint of amusement. "Even Cassave feared me. And for good reason... his spells held no power over me. Nor, I must warn you, will yours, if that is your intent." She tugged at the edge of her blindfold meaningfully.

Sâr Dubnotal shook his head. "No. I prefer conversation to compulsion."

Euryale laughed. "A rare magus indeed. Very well. Would you have coffee?" She indicated a doorway he had not noticed earlier, for the gloom. "It is one of the few pleasures left to me, and I take every opportunity to indulge myself."

The kitchen of Malpertuis was gloomy and crowded with the detritus of forgotten feasts. A great oaken table occupied its heart, and it was here that Sâr Dubnotal sat while his hostess busied herself making coffee. She hummed softly, a melody he thought he recognized but could not place. Finally, the coffee was ready and they drank in silence, until she said, "You came to free me. Why?"

He hesitated, trying to think how best to explain himself. "I know some of what Cassave was up to. What he... intended. I know too that his designs were thwarted, but that you and the other... victims of his scheming were left trapped here, still bound by the geas he imposed on you."

"They are all dead, save one or two," she said, simply.

Sâr Dubnotal nodded. That, too, he'd had from the thief. But he had not quite been able to bring himself to believe it. Even diminished they had still been gods, after all. "You know this for certain?"

"What I look upon dies." She gestured absently. "You may see what is left of them, if you wish. I have not touched their remains, save to sweep up the loose pieces."

"Why kill them?" he asked, though he thought he knew the answer.

"It was time. With the death of Cassave, they were beginning to recall themselves. In time, they might have become dangerous."

"Unlike yourself," Sâr Dubnotal said, with a thin smile.

She sniffed. "Unlike the others, save one, I came here of my own will. Cassave's plan was of no interest to me... until I met Jean-Jacques." She sighed sorrowfully and plucked at her blindfold. "I thought to spare him the adversity that awaited him, but I could not. I am strong, but even I am not the equal of fate."

Sâr Dubnotal nodded. "And now you watch over this place. Why?"

"Someone must."

"You could leave." He paused, then said, "I have heard rumors of another of your kind. A certain Professor Meister of Leipzig University recounted to me a strange occurrence at Castle Borski last year..." He trailed off. She shook her head slowly.

"There were more gorgons in the world than we three, for Athena was not one to let a good curse go to waste. But my sisters are gone to that far country that even the gods dread." Her hands curled into fists. He sighed softly. A long life promised many opportunities for grief. He knew that only too well himself.

"Oh, how I wish she had been among those Cassave shanghaied... I should have liked to have looked upon the face of our tormentor one last time." She took a deep breath but whatever she'd been about to say was interrupted by a sudden, wild scream echoing down from somewhere far above.

Sâr Dubnotal was on his feet in an instant, eyes wide. "What was that?"

"Lampernisse."

Sâr Dubnotal looked at her in puzzlement. The thief had mentioned the odd giant and his obsession with colors and lights. Even as he made to ask the obvious question, a second cry followed the first. But it was a more bestial sound than its predecessor; there was no pain in it, only a savage glee. "And that?" he demanded.

Euryale looked up. "The Eagle. It torments Lampernisse, as it always has. It holds him captive, far above us."

"You did not turn him to stone with the others?"

She shook her head. "No. He did me no harm, and in truth he was—is—the best of them. If his mind were not broken, he might well set this place to rights. He was wise in his time. Wise enough to untangle the spells that Cassave bound him with. I think that is why Cassave hurt him so... and why he allowed the Eagle to hunt its prey. He could not risk his plans being undone by one such as that."

563

Sâr Dubnotal frowned as the cry of the Eagle came again, echoing down through the black bones of Malpertuis. "Monstrous," he murmured. Euryale nodded.

"I have tried to surprise and kill it on the rare occasions it shows its beak downstairs, but it is too swift, even for me. I think it nests in the attic, but even I dare not set foot up there alone. If it were to come to it, I am not certain I would be victorious, and then the house would be left undefended." She paused. "But with help, I might succeed."

Sâr Dubnotal paused, finger tapping his tiepin. Euryale's smile turned sly, and he almost laughed. She did know something of him, after all. "And what do I receive in return for helping you with this quest?"

"Cassave's library. All his secrets, still hidden in the heart of this place. Many have come searching for them. But I think you may prove worthy of them. With them in your hands, I might safely depart this place."

Sâr Dubnotal bowed his head. "High praise indeed." Before his death, Cassave had assembled one of the finest collections of arcane lore in Europe. That sort of knowledge was too dangerous to leave lying about unprotected. But more than that, he could not leave any creature to suffer such agonies as were hinted at by the sounds echoing down from above. Decision made, he knocked back the dregs of his coffee. "Fine. Let us see this Eagle's eyrie."

Euryale led him back to the foyer and up—up and farther upwards, past all reason. They climbed endless stairs, some as broad and grand as temple avenues, others so crooked and narrow as to be all but impassable. The house breathed around them, panting in what might have been fear—or eagerness. Around him, dim corridors containing various rooms stretched out and away in a manner that made little internal sense.

Sâr Dubnotal grew uneasy; he felt as if he had left one world and were entering another. Malpertuis was a borderland of sorts, built atop the remains of something far older. Without Cassave here, it was changing, becoming less coherent. It was at once too large and too small, as if it were convulsing in some incremental fashion.

"It grows, you know," Euryale said, absently stroking a balustrade. "Not the outside, but the interior. It was always bigger on the inside, but now it is unfettered by Cassave's will. It spreads like rot through all that it touches."

"Growing and dying at the same time," Sâr Dubnotal said, somewhat wistfully. "A part of me would love nothing more than to study such a thing…"

"You would not be the first. Others have come here since Cassave's passing, seeking to exploit the strangeness of this place. Nikola… Manzeppi… Haddo; all found themselves disappointed when I refused to guide them through this Tartarean labyrinth, or give way to their blandishments."

Sâr Dubnotal, who had crossed swords with the diabolical Count Manzeppi on more than one occasion, could not help but smile at the thought of his disappointment. If she had resisted Nikola as well, then he'd been correct in his estimation of Euryale's capabilities. "You were wise to refuse them. Cassave was bad enough; if someone like Nikola learned such secrets as are contained within this place, I shudder to think what might happen."

"They were nothing compared to Cassave. He stole fire from the gods and used it to build this place. It cannot be snuffed or stirred by mortal hands; instead, it must burn itself out. Only then will the husk collapse and the world forget."

Sâr Dubnotal nodded, though he did not entirely agree. Malpertuis was not unique; men had used the ineffable for their own utilitarian ends for centuries. There were houses like Malpertuis in every major city in the world; the Shandor Building in New York, for instance. Places where time and space bent to the will of man, often to no good end.

"There," Euryale said, breaking him from his reverie. Above them, a trapdoor was set into the low ceiling above the landing. It was no simple hatch of wood, but a door such as might have adorned some ancient church; perhaps it had. One of Cassave's little jokes.

Sâr Dubnotal made to push it open, but Euryale stopped him. "It will be dangerous. Cassave forbade the others from entering the attic."

"Why?"

She shrugged. "A magician has his reasons. Old Eisengott theorized that the attic was the place where effable and ineffable were joined in Malpertuis. Like the sticky strand connecting a wasp's nest to a door."

Sâr Dubnotal chuckled. "A good description. If so, it will be the most dangerous room in the house. Are you certain you wish to accompany me?"

She nodded firmly. "I am. I must. Lampernisse has suffered enough for any man or god. Let this be the end of it."

Sâr Dubnotal heaved the trapdoor open and it fell away with a dull boom. He couldn't help but flinch at the sound, for it echoed like thunder. Then he was up and standing in a vaulted space made of uncountable recessed polyhedra, picked out by the dull light seeping in through the line of large dormer windows. At first glance, it seemed empty; devoid of the usual *bric-à-brac* one might find in the attic of an old house.

He paused. Something was wrong; the proportions of the attic were askew somehow, in a way that defied his senses and gave him a persistent feeling of vertigo. The windows were too large, too far up, more like those of a cathedral than a storage space. Beams rose like distant mountains, stretching up into an infinite darkness. Were those stars he saw, gleaming coolly in the black? And what was that light that shone through the windows? Not quite the grey of the wet day outside, but something colder, as if they looked out upon Hyperborea rather than an innocuous town.

He shivered. The emptiness extended back and away, a rolling wasteland of board and dust, interrupted only by the occasional oddment—a shrouded pile of something; a crooked curio cabinet, draped in cobwebs. Hills and valleys of wood and cloth that were no less wild than those of the Black Forest. A thin sound at the edge of his hearing caught his attention and he looked up.

Innumerable nets of some strange woven material hung from the overhead beams, drifting languidly in the chill air. As he watched them, he fancied he saw lights flicker among them, and tiny shapes race across bridges of leather and lace. He took a step towards the closest of them, and heard a tinny wail, like that of some miniscule shofar.

"Leave them be," Euryale said, from behind him.

He turned to see her lowering the trapdoor back into place. "What are they?"

"Homunculi. Cassave made them to keep house, but they proved too aggressive. He banished them to the attic. I suspect that is one of the reasons he forbade the others from entering." She stamped on the trapdoor, making sure it was flush. "It would not do to frighten them. They can be vicious, in sufficient numbers, and I would hate to kill them."

"How many did he make?" Sâr Dubnotal asked, watching the lights flicker among the nets—houses, he realized. Or maybe watch-posts. They had borrowed trash and forgotten things and made themselves homes in the eaves of the attic. Somewhere above him, in the gloom, he fancied there might even be some vast city of little borrowers, writ in miniature.

Euryale waved the question aside. "Five, I think. But they are fecund mites, and industrious. I have no doubt that they have long since spread far from this place. Every house in this town probably has an infestation by now." She pointed towards the far end of the attic. "There—the Eagle's perch. Do you see it?"

Sâr Dubnotal peered in the direction she indicated, but at first saw nothing, save more shadows. But the longer he looked, the more those shadows resolved themselves into strange geometries—an assemblage of shapes, one atop the next, overflowing from a corner of the attic. A cold wind ripped down from the spot, and a sudden cry pierced the quiet. The agonized sound bounced from beam to board, swelling to fill the impossible space before fading into the distance.

"Quickly," Euryale said. "It is at its work, and will be distracted. Follow me."

Sâr Dubnotal followed her across the attic, and felt the weight of the place settle upon him. He had traversed higher planes and lower ones in his time, but this was something else again=--a nowhere spot. The cold he felt originated not in the grave, but from the void. He glanced at one of the windows and saw not the turrets and rooftops of the town, but only nothingness... a wet mist that roiled as if something moved through it.

He murmured a prayer to the Elder Gods as the space shrank and expanded around them without rhyme or reason. Cramped one moment, and too large the next. The floorboards flexed beneath their feet, but did not creak. Flashes of light pierced the cracks and crevices and he could feel a dull vibration, as of rushing water, vibrating up from below. He imagined that at any moment, the attic might simply give way and disperse like smoke, revealing the awfulness of what lurked beyond.

Euryale could feel it as well, he thought. She led him along a circuitous route towards the far end of the attic, moving warily, like a cat that sensed the presence of a larger animal. Her mortal guise shimmered and snapped at the edges, threatening to dissolve into static. He wondered if she, being a creature of the abnatural, felt the oddness of this place more keenly than himself. She paused, behind a looming cabinet that appeared made for giants rather than men, and waved him to silence.

She pointed, and he saw a frame of wood erected in the shadows in the corner of the attic. It rose like a torturer's rack, and a long-limbed shape was stretched across its surface, wrists and ankles bound by rags of fabric. A man, he thought – no, a giant. But not a natural one; rather, a contorted, pitiable figure with hyper-extended limbs and a starveling torso, too large for the attic. Too large for the world. It was as if the poor soul were being stretched past the point of physical cohesion.

The giant's wild-haired head was thrown back in an attitude of pain, and an expression of utmost horror was stamped on his wide features. A great, shuddering groan slipped from his lips and thrummed in the pit of Sâr Dubnotal's stomach, like the tolling of a broken bell. "Lampernisse," Euryale whispered, and there was pity in her voice.

"Who bound him so?" Sâr Dubnotal asked.

"The Eagle. Who else?"

He glanced at her, but instead of replying, she gripped his shoulders. "There. It is coming back! Quiet now! *Watch*."

Sâr Dubnotal heard it before he saw it. He hunkered back as another blast of icy wind raced through the attic and nearly bowled him over. He could feel the beating of the Eagle's wings against the air, but could see only the shadow of them, blotting out the windows. It was perched above Lampernisse, in the crossbeams of the roof. It shrieked and darted down to strike the helpless giant, coming into sight at last.

The Eagle was not a true bird, but rather the essence of the term. It was all the things an eagle might be imagined to be; grasping metallic claws, each large enough to scoop up a man; feathers that gleamed like shields arrayed in formation; a beak like the prow of a raiding vessel, cruelly hooked and as sharp as the bite of an axe. But these elements did not coalesce into the expected shape – rather they seemed to exist independent of one another; a whirling tempest that settled on Lampernisse's torso and began to dig.

"It is not a beast at all," he muttered, half to himself. The creature was not wholly present; rather, it seemed to exist simultaneously in other dimensions, as if their world were too fragile to encompass such malevolence. Was it a physical manifestation at all, or only a thing of spirit? His question was answered a moment later as Lampernisse groaned in pain as his flesh parted with a wet snap, and the eagle's beak plunged into the raw redness within.

Sâr Dubnotal closed his eyes, unable to bear witness to such torment. "I recognize its sort if not the thing itself. It is a thing of a higher realm; a predatory Saiitii manifestation from the Outer Circle, bound to this shape by the will of another..." he continued, softly, trying to distract himself from the grisly sounds coming from the corner of the attic.

"Zeus," Euryale said, clutching his arm. He could not tell whether she was disgusted by what she saw, or simply worried about the eagle noticing them. "Zeus called forth the Eagle to punish Prometheus and not even Cassave's magic could gainsay it for long."

"Hercules slew it," Sâr Dubnotal said, slowly stripping off his coat. The cold could be endured; he wanted the freedom to move, if it became necessary. Euryale shook her head.

"No. He drove it away. The legends do not say how."

"They rarely do, I find. Very well, we shall improvise. First, we must get the beast's attention. I will draw it away. You free Lampernisse. Then, it will be up to you to strike the killing blow."

"If I can," she said, doubtfully.

"You slew the Furies, surely an oversized pigeon is no great threat." He tossed aside his coat as he spoke. At her nod, he strode towards the monster and its victim, rolling up his sleeves as he went. This was not the first time he had encountered something dredged up from the Outer Darkness. Mostly, they were small things; easily banished once they were properly identified. But this one had a firm hold on the world, helped, perhaps, by some rite of Cassave's. It would require more inventive means.

Sâr Dubnotal took a deep, cleansing breath, focused his thoughts and brought his palms together in a loud clap. The sound thundered through the attic, cast upwards and away by his will. The Eagle jerked around, something pink and slimy dangling from its beak. Inhuman eyes fixed on him and narrowed speculatively.

"El Tebib, Doctor to the World's Pain, bids you go from this place, beast," Sâr Dubnotal roared. "He will not ask again!" He spread his arms and gripped the air, feeling the magic that had made this place twitch at his touch. There was still power here; he could feel the remnants of the mystic bindings Cassave had woven whispering across his fingertips. If he could draw the frayed skein tight, he might be able to banish the creature—or, at the very least, severely inconvenience it.

The Eagle shrieked in rage and flapped its wings, stirring the air to hurricane fierceness. Sâr Dubnotal felt the wind tear at him, but he remained firm. Having planted himself, he would not be moved. Not by anything in the world. He began to murmur the chant of Hloh, and move his fingers in the second and third gestures. The Eagle responded with another shriek and sprang into the air with a snap of its wings.

It swooped past him, its feathers rattling like the spears of a hostile army as it did so. The stink of it enveloped him; not an avian smell, but the rancid odor of something unhealthy—a gangrenous wound or a spreading cancer. It circled him, the beating of its wings drowning out his voice and his thoughts alike. He wondered if it were curious about him, or whether it merely regarded him as another potential meal.

When it dove, he was ready. He leapt lightly aside as its talons tore deep gouges in the floorboards. Regaining his footing instantly, he finished the Hloh chant and made the final gestures, letting loose the magic he had collected. There was an incandescent flash and the Eagle screamed—not in fury now, but pain. Normally, the chant would have served to banish it, but in this place, it only served to annoy it. But that was fine; he had its attention now. He turned and ran, knowing the beast would follow.

It came after him with a shrill cry, wings flapping. It slashed at him with its beak or clawed at him, but he was never where it struck. Though it was not wholly a thing of the world, its attacks were of a physical nature. That meant they could be avoided, with a bit of foresight and a lot of luck. But luck was finite. He could but hope that Euryale had grasped the essence of his plan, and was making haste to free Lampernisse.

He leapt over a fallen armoire, ignoring a group of tiny homunculi who scattered in his shadow. He trusted the small creatures were smart enough to stay out of this affair. He all but danced across the dusty floorboards, jeering at his pursuer. The Eagle redoubled its pursuit with all the fury of a frustrated animal, but always he stayed just out of its reach.

Suddenly, a board split beneath Sâr Dubnotal's foot and he pitched headlong to the floor. More boards gave way, nails popping loose from the joists. An abyss of unidentifiable colors swirled beneath him, and a rush of cold wind seared him to the bone. He cried out and tried to drag himself free, but the Eagle was already upon him. A talon slammed down, catching hold of him, and he found himself wrenched into the air.

The Eagle's claw tightened about him, crushing the air from his lungs. He pushed past the pain and tried to concentrate on working his limbs free, but to little avail. The beast was too strong—unless... he pried an arm free and clasped his tiepin. Pulling it loose, he jammed the sharp end of the pin into the creature's talon. As he'd hoped, the Eagle shrieked, albeit in surprise rather than pain. While the holiness within the pin wasn't enough to banish it, it did cause it to release its hold on him.

He dropped to the floor, rolling painfully across the boards until he bumped into the armoire he'd dodged over earlier. He spied the homunculi watching fearfully from the open doors and nudged the latter shut as he rose to his feet, brushing dirt from his clothing. Out of the corner of his eye, he caught a glimpse of Euryale ghosting silently towards him.

The Eagle had perched on a nearby beam, and was attempting to use its beak to pluck the stickpin from its talon. He marched towards the creature, a stern expression on his face. "I did warn you, beast," he called out. "And the words of the Great Psychagogue must be heeded—even by creatures such as yourself." As he'd hoped, its malign gaze fixed on him. If it noticed Euryale's approach, it gave no sign.

Sâr Dubnotal cleared his throat. "I say again… leave this place. Your time is ended and your task completed. The time of wrath is long past. Soar back into the empty places between the stars, where one like yourself might find more appropriate prey." He held up his hands, as if in prayer. "Or else you will pay the price hubris demands!" He slammed his palms together, and felt the air twist at his command. The Eagle felt it as well, and ceased its attempt to minister to its talon. Instead, it readied itself to swoop upon him again.

A moment later, it dove from its perch and he thrust his hands out as if to push it away. A stiff wind sprang up and caught the Eagle in its embrace. The beast wailed as its lunge was halted, and its wings beat the air frantically. As he'd hoped, its physicality made it vulnerable. But how vulnerable—that was the question. One it was up to Euryale to answer.

Yet it was not Euryale who appeared next; rather it was Lampernisse who sprang up and caught his tormentor by the wings and dragged it bodily to the floor. "Down, glutton," he bellowed hoarsely. "Down, thief of light! No more shall you steal my colors!" For the next few moments, titan strove against monster and there was no saying who might be the victor. Then, the Eagle's beak slashed out and Lampernisse reeled, clutching his eyes.

The giant fell and the Eagle pounced. But Sâr Dubnotal was there, drawing up the wind and sending the great beast hurtling backwards into a beam. Its form frayed and shivered like a splash of water, ripping apart and coalescing as it recovered to lunge forward in a swirl of feathers.

Sâr Dubnotal braced himself to meet its charge, but at the last moment a hand caught the back of his shirt and flung him aside as if he weighed no more than a ragdoll. The Eagle, unable or unwilling to stop itself, met his savior in the center of the attic.

Time slowed; the torrent shrank to a trickle. Moments dripped. The great Eagle rose over the small form of Euryale, talons extended, beak spread, wings stretched in a welcoming curve. But Euryale was no longer Euryale; or rather, she was her true self, stripped of all human frailty. All that remained was a monstrous lethality. The gorgon unbound.

In the slow moments that followed, Euryale stared at the beast, and a jade radiance grew about her. Sâr Dubnotal turned away and busied himself with Lampernisse's injuries, which were already healing. The giant squeezed his bloody eyes shut. "The gorgon... the gorgon..." he muttered. "We must not look at her light..."

Sâr Dubnotal said nothing. Behind him, there was a sound like a rising storm, and all the windows rattled as the beams creaked and the joists groaned. The whole attic shook, as if it might judder to pieces around them and cast them into the void. The Eagle screeched and there was no hunger in that sound, nor triumph. Only fear. Euryale screamed as well—a cry of challenge, he thought, as one elemental power met another in combat.

Then, all at once, it was done. Silence fell, save for the thudding of a great form against the floor of the attic. Sâr Dubnotal turned. The Eagle was dying. Or perhaps simply... departing. Its form collapsed in on itself as pieces of it stiffened and crumbled to dust. Wingtips broke and shattered like weakened escarpments. The beak bent and slid down until it broke into a thousand fragments on the floor. Soon, there was nothing left of the creature's physical form but a pile of grey dust.

Sâr Dubnotal was on his feet, arms outstretched as Euryale sank back, human once more. He caught her as she swooned, and felt her shudder. He heard a whisper of sound, the distant beating of wings, growing fainter with every passing moment. Then—nothing. "Gone," Euryale murmured, her eyes tightly shut. "I think... I think it was a prisoner too. Like us. It had no more choice in what it did than any of the others."

"Dead or simply gone, it matters little," Sâr Dubnotal said. He helped her to stand and went to aid the giant, who was looking about him with the air of one who had awakened from a long, unhappy slumber. "The Eagle will no longer torment you, Lampernisse. You are free."

"Free?" Lampernisse rumbled. He looked at his hands, and then at the others. "Free?"

"Yes," Euryale said. Her lips quirked into a smile. "As, I suppose, am I."

Sâr Dubnotal returned the gorgon's smile. "Yes. But first—I believe you mentioned something about a library?"

On vole des enfants à Paris [*Someone is Stealing Children in Paris*][35] *by Louis Forest was first published in the daily newspaper* Le Matin *as a feuilleton serial from 25 June to 23 September 1906. Then, a shorter version appeared in book form in 1909. The serial version, entitled* Le Voleur d'enfants [*The Child-Stealer*]*, was a novel told in the form of daily reportage, using subheadings similar to those in the paper's news articles instead of regular chapter headings. Day by day, Forest recounted the history of an "Affair" that was occurring in a kind of parallel world, similar in every way to the actual one, except with respect to the events described by the hypothetical reportage. This groundbreaking serial about the artificial creation of supermen through radium-based brain surgery is given here a sequel of sorts by Chris Roberson...*

## Chris Roberson: *The Same Peculiar Tint*

*Paris, 1913*

The newspapers at the time had all reported that the children had been returned to normal, whatever that meant. In her nearly twenty years' experience heading a private school, Miss Violet Hunter knew all too well that "normal" was entirely a matter of perspective. "Average" was perhaps a better descriptor for the state to which the children had supposedly been returned, after the subtle alterations worked upon their minds and bodies by the surgical techniques of the infamous Dr. Flax. But while the thirty-one students who were now under her charge were all inarguably "average," it was precisely that point that made Miss Hunter suspicious. They were, if anything, entirely too average. Exactingly so.

It had been some years since newspapers all over Europe had been filled with sensational reports of the "child-stealer" abducting children from the streets of Paris, and how they had been later discovered to have been subjected to experimental "transcendent surgery" by Dr. Flax designed to uplift them to their fullest potential, and the scandal that arose until they were ultimately released from his charge and returned to their worried families. Soon after and at the insistence of the authorities further operations were performed on the children to reverse these changes, so that they might resume their normal lives.

Or so it was believed at the time.

Miss Violet Hunter was preparing for the end of another school term in Walsall when she was approached by an agent working on behalf of the parents of the children, who had all been six or seven when operated on by Dr. Flax, and

[35] Black Coat Press, ISBN 978-1-61227-252-8.

the youngest of whom was now twelve years-old, with most of them already thirteen.

Upon their release they had returned to their former schools, and while it had been anticipated that there might be a period of adjustment as they once more reacclimatized to the classroom environment, after several years of prolonged difficulties, their concerned parents had decided that they might be better served being educated as a group in isolation from other students. A former graduate of Miss Hunter's private school in Walsall had gone on to be a business associate of one of the children's fathers, and had spoken highly of her qualifications as an educator with experience dealing with unusual circumstances. And given that Miss Hunter had grown restless and was already considering seeking a new position, she was only too happy to accept their quite generous offer.

The children abducted by Flax and his associates had been drawn from wealthy families, and so the parents had spared no expense in purchasing and refurbishing a disused abbey to use as their new private school, to say nothing of the generous salary that they offered to Miss Hunter, who was to serve not only as the head of the new school but also as its only educator on staff. All thirty-one children lived at their respective family homes in various corners of Paris, while Miss Hunter resided on the premises in the former quarters of the Abbess.

When she first arrived at the new school and was introduced to the thirty-one students for which she would be responsible, Miss Hunter assumed that the case had been overstated, as they didn't appear to have any particularly difficulty in socializing with one another, and their performance and comportment in the classroom was above reproach. But as the weeks and months wore on, and she familiarized herself with each student's past academic performance, suspicions began to arise.

Even before they were transformed into geniuses by Flax's surgical techniques, each of the children had been extremely bright, and in fact it was their evident intelligence that had singled them out for Flax's schemes. Looking at their early transcripts from before their abductions, Miss Hunter could see that there were inarguably prodigies among their number. Young Ange Pompaigne had been noted by his teachers as being possessed of astonishing intelligence, as had Frantz Vertyolle and Fernand Pig, while at the age of six years and seven months Nicolas Barlatescu already spoke four languages fluently. To have been so academically precocious at such young ages suggested that they would doubtless soar to even greater heights.

But such was not the case with the thirty-one children whom Miss Hunter taught every weekday. Now ranging from twelve to thirteen years-old, these were children who performed well in mathematics and science, who read proficiently and possessed large vocabularies which they were able to spell with accuracy more often than not, but it was not as if they never made mistakes. When they sat for exams they scored well, but always with a certain percentage of wrong answers or incorrect responses. Miss Hunter couldn't escape the nagging sensation that she was missing something, that something vital was passing right before her eyes and she had not yet noticed it. It was then that she realized that the students repeatedly and consistently answered ten percent of the questions incorrectly. Across the board, and without variation or deviation, they were correct ninety percent of the time and wrong the remaining ten. On every exam, and on every assignment.

And there was something about the children's appearance that nagged at Miss Hunter's thoughts. There were twenty-five boys and six girls, all of average height and build for their ages, and their hair coloration ranged from blond so pale it was almost white to hair as black as pitch. But in addition to the scar that each of them bore beneath their left ear, where Dr. Flax had made his incisions, each of them shared another feature in common: while their eyes were in all colors and hues, when the light hit them in just such a way Miss Hunter would swear that she caught a particular tint to each of them. So that whether their eyes were blue or brown or hazel or green or amber, in those brief moments she could discern the slightest tinge of a purplish highlight. A hint of indigo, or violet.

At the time, the papers had reported that each of the children had been endowed with a distinct form of genius, or rather that Flax's transcendent surgery had unlocked a different capacity in each of them. One became especially skilled in fashioning jewelry, while another became an unrivaled chef, or became an extremely gifted poet. One might be suddenly able to leap prodigious lengths, while another suddenly possessed the gift to tame and train any animal. One became a master of aerostatics, while another was able to unlock all the secrets of chemistry. But while Flax had painstakingly documented and detailed the specific forms of genius for each of the twenty-five boys in his study, for the six girls he simply noted that they each possessed what he called "the genius of maternity."

Miss Hunter did not know precisely what Flax had meant by the "genius of maternity," but knowing that he had indicated that it would not come into full flower until the girls had reached the age of sixteen or seventeen years-old, she could easily draw inference. But she suspected that in this, as in so many things, Dr. Flax had been blinded by his own preconceptions and prejudices. He might have stumbled into a previously unknown technique for unlocking a child's potential, but he had little understanding of what that potential might actually be. And she was beginning to suspect that he might not have understood the resulting changes as fully as he had claimed, and overstated his own abilities to reverse the process.

The more time she spent with the children, the more that Miss Hunter suspected that they were simply playing the part, pretending to be average, hiding their true capabilities. The six girls in particular—Germaine, Victorine, Fernande, Louise, and the two Alices—sitting prim and proper at their desks, immaculately dressed and with their hair carefully coiffed. Miss Hunter rarely heard them speak, and then scarcely above a whisper, and only when called upon directly to answer a question. At mealtimes or when the children were sent out for exercise in the courtyard the six girls would stick close to one another, but always in silence.

The boys hardly seemed to take notice of the girls among them, neither to tease them, or to argue, or to flirt, or any of the multitude of ways that schoolboys interact with their female counterparts. That is, until the day that the engine of a passing automobile backfired directly in front of the school, sounding uncannily like a gunshot, and all twenty-five pairs of male eyes turned to look in the direction of the six girls sitting at the back of the classroom, as if awaiting instruction. The six girls sat in silence for a moment, their eyes downcast, until Germaine looked up and gave a brief shake of her head, at which point the mood in the classroom returned to normal. The whole event went without a word being spoken, over the course of just a few seconds, but in that time, Miss Hunter could not help noticing that the thirty-one children had acted in perfect unison, seeming to determine whether the sound that they had heard represented a threat, and if so how they should react.

And Miss Hunter couldn't help wondering just what the response might have been, had the children believed themselves to be in actual danger.

There was the time when Miss Hunter found herself lapsing unconsciously back into English when addressing the students. Among the subjects that she had taught in Walsall over the years was the French language, and over the years she had gone from having a blushing familiarity to being a completely fluent speaker, and she had no difficulty carrying out each day's instruction in the students' native tongue. But when she did address the students in English by accident, she noticed that each of the thirty-one of them clearly understood what she had said, even if based on their past academic performance no more than half of them was fluent in the English language. And that was just one of the areas where they clearly possessed skills or knowledge that they otherwise pretended they didn't.

She devised little tests and trials, intending to catch them out. She might sneak a particularly advanced calculus problem in amongst entirely ordinary arithmetic problems, or an incredibly obscure scientific principle in with a list of otherwise mundane terms to define, or address the class in a phrase from Swahili or Xhosa or Tibetan to see if any of them might respond. But after the one occasion on which she'd accidentally spoken English to the class and they'd all clearly understood, none of them ever fell into any of the little traps she laid for them. The arcane and obscure questions went unanswered, and only silence greeted her when she addressed them in some obscure tongue.

Then Miss Hunter changed her tactic. Rather than simply putting absurdly difficult or obscure questions on exams for them to answer, she created extensive exams made up entirely of true-or-false questions, the vast majority of them drawn from subjects that no twelve or thirteen year-old could possibly know. And as she had expected, when the exams were graded, every one of the thirty-one students had answered the difficult questions incorrectly. Every single time. Had they simply been guessing at random, they should have at least gotten roughly half of the questions correct, but the students in her classroom had chosen the incorrect response each and every time. And the only way that they could possibly have answered every question incorrectly was to have known the correct answer every time and chosen the wrong answer on purpose.

Some expression must have flitted across Miss Hunter's face as she graded the exams, while the students worked on their next assignment, because when she looked up from the marked papers she saw the six girls at the back of the room looking in her direction, studying her closely. And when she repeated the experiment with another set of extremely difficult true-false questions the following week, each student answered exactly half of the questions correctly and half incorrectly, to the dot.

The families of the students were primarily interested in them being able once more to socialize with their peers. Education was an important end in and of itself, of course, but paled in importance with the question of whether their children would one day be able successfully to navigate the wealthier strata of Parisian society. And so, whenever Miss Hunter found herself in conference with any of the parents, she found that their questions to her about their children's progress was entirely along the lines of whether they were behaving "normally" or "appropriately" or as generally befitted their station in life. And whenever she would try to broach the subject of her suspicions regarding the children's true natures and capabilities, the parents would express a profound disinterest. So long as their sons and daughters were able to rejoin polite society without causing difficulty or scandal, it scarcely seemed to matter to the parents if there were aspects about themselves that the children chose to keep hidden from view.

By the end of the first year together under Miss Hunter's tutelage, the youngest of the children had reached their thirteenth year while the rest were all fourteen years of age. The time that they had spent away from other students seemed to have given them the opportunity to perfect their performance as "average" children, sometimes even allowing themselves to be seen as even less or greater than average in various ways. Sometimes, they would get only seven or eight percent of their responses on an exam incorrect while other times answering as much as fourteen or fifteen percent wrong. A few of them gradually displayed ostensibly newfound facilities with foreign languages, or slowly showed evidence of mastery of some more complicated area of study. The six girls in the class began to speak up more frequently in social situations, exchanging carefully practiced small talk and idle gossip. But Miss Hunter felt that it was all still a performance, albeit a more subtle one.

With the school out of session for the summer months, Miss Hunter returned to England to handle some personal matters, expecting to return to her duties in Paris soon. At the end of June, however, came the news of the assassination of the Archduke of Austria, and within a month war was declared. Miss Hunter received word from the parents that the private school would not be reopening in the fall and her services would no longer be required.

Soon after, Miss Hunter was contacted by Sir Walter Bullivant, a former associate who was now affiliated with the Foreign Section of the Secret Service Bureau, and thereafter spent the war years working in various educational positions throughout Europe and elsewhere—teacher, school mistress, governess, et cetera—while secretly providing intelligence for the war effort.

And increasingly in the latter days of the war and in the years that followed, Miss Hunter would occasionally spot what she thought was a familiar face in the corridors of power or in rooms where significant decisions were being made. Seemingly anonymous and otherwise entirely average young people in rooms with government leaders and captains of industry, shoulder-to-shoulder with warlords and tycoons. Young men and women who were rarely at the center of the action, but were never far from it; seldom noticed by those in authority but clearly in close enough proximity to have an influence, quietly accruing power to themselves. Whenever one of those familiar faces realized that Miss Hunter had glimpsed them, they would quickly depart, so that she was never able to get close enough to address them directly. But in every case, she always caught a familiar tinge of color in their eyes when they looked in her direction, that same peculiar tint of violet.

*Robert Robinson returns to his signature character, Judex, this time taking him into the* film noir *genre as our shadowy hero crosses the Atlantic and goes Hollywood...*

## Robert L. Robinson, Jr.: *The Hollywood Affair*

*Hollywood, 1920*

The midday sun pierced through the grey canopy of Chicago, casting shadows along the magnificent train station platforms. From a distance, the rhythmic clatter of locomotives and the distant calls of porters blended into a harmonious urban symphony. It was in the midst of this cacophony that one traveler found a peculiar solace, a welcome intermission from the eight-day journey that had begun on the decks of the elegant *Aquitania*, crossing the Atlantic, and now continued upon the 20th Century Limited.

The grand ship had carried the tall and serious man along with his younger brother from Europe's shores, across the vast Atlantic, with all the grandeur and elegance that one of his social standings would expect—delightful traveling companions found upon each leg. However, this trip was business, not personal, as their family holdings required new ventures. So the French millionaire, Jacques de Trémeuse and his brother Roger had left their beloved France to promising opportunities awaiting them in America.

The two men set up a two full days' worth of meetings in New York that Jacques would attend while Roger would continue immediately on to Los Angeles. The plan was that Jacques would follow out at the end of the week, to join Roger after his meetings with the banker, J. P Morgan. The allure of the burgeoning movie industry had tempted the Trémeuse brothers as an extension for their family investments, and Roger was to be their herald, while Jacques met with Morgan to oversee many of their numerous holdings and investments.

After two successful days in New York with Morgan, and a new relationship established, Jacques had boarded the private car he'd ordered on the esteemed train, The 20th Century Limited, and raced across the United States, bound for Chicago first, then Los Angeles.

After twenty hours of traveling, the grand train had arrived in Chicago, granting the Frenchman a few hours of leisure as it would leave later that evening on the final leg of its journey for Los Angeles. The Palmer House's famed restaurant, mere blocks from the station, promised and delivered a delectable lunch, almost worthy of a Parisian restaurant. After the lovely repast, Jacques retraced his steps, the crimson carpet of the terminal soft underfoot, relishing the fresh memory of the culinary delight of roasted duck, before he was drawn from his reverie by an insistent porter.

"Mr. de Trémeuse?" the man inquired.

As a nod in return acknowledged the question, the porter held out a sealed envelope with a telegram bore with measured reverence. "This arrived for you, sir." The beige paper felt oddly heavy in Jacques' hand. Unfolding it, he read the short and to the point message:

*September 11, 1920.*
*Mr. Jacques de Trémeuse.*
*Urgent. Your brother, Mr. Roger de Trémeuse, has been missing for the past two days. No word at the Chateau Marmont. Please advise upon receipt.*

A cold dread settled over Jacques, his thoughts racing, each one more dire than the last. Whatever enemies they had in France, were no longer an issue. Was this a simple mistake, or was it more? Could it be related to the Trémeuse family fortune, or perhaps to that secret Jacques had—that he was the cloaked legend of the night, the whispered about crime-fighter, Judex?

As Judex, he'd made sure that he was seen more as a whispered legend than a real creature- so what was this about? Who might be behind Roger's vanishing?

His impromptu culinary excursion suddenly felt frivolous, even foolish. Chicago's industrial symphony now played a haunting tune. The journey ahead had taken on a new, grave importance.

The 20th Century Limited awaited, not just as a marvel of locomotive engineering, but as the vessel that would carry him closer to the truth, whatever it was. The glittering prospects of Hollywood suddenly seemed draped in shadows, and the man who was Judex was heading straight into its enigma.

The rhythmic clatter of the steel on steel below the riders gradually became a soothing backdrop, allowing the passengers a semblance of peace amidst their travels. As the train approached Los Angeles, the landscape outside morphed, blending urban sprawl with the sun-soaked Californian vistas. Jacques, for the last forty-five hours, had thought of nothing else but the mysterious telegram, his thoughts constantly drifting to his dear brother Roger's enigmatic disappearance.

An unexpected bond he had forged on this journey was with none other than Charlie Chaplin, the masterful comic of the silver screen. Their adjacent private cars had led to shared meals in the dining car and extended conversations about the intricacies of Hollywood's rapidly evolving film industry, and a welcomed distraction. Charlie's quick wit and poignant insights provided a welcome distraction from Jacques' growing concerns.

Upon their arrival, Charlie, ever the gentleman, insisted, "You must come with me, Jacques. My driver will take us to the Chateau Marmont. We'll get to the bottom of this."

579

The Chateau, with its castle-like presence amidst the Hollywood Hills, emanated an aura of international elegance. However, beneath its majestic facade, the pair soon discovered a tale of distress. The hotel manager, a polished man named Albert E. Smith, greeted the pair with a tense demeanor. "Monsieur de Trémeuse, your brother, did indeed check in, but he has not been seen for days."

The weight of Roger's disappearance bore heavily upon Jacques, and the grandeur of the Chateau did little to assuage his growing anxiety. "Perhaps," Smith ventured cautiously, "it might be wise to involve the local authorities?"

Not knowing much of Los Angeles, Jacques hesitated momentarily, but then Charlie spoke. "The local coppers have the ability to get to the bottom of things, but sometimes not as quickly as we'd like."

Jacques nodded and replied, "Very well, let's call them."

Smith placed a call, speaking in whispers which led, in a short time, to the pair coming face to face with a man sent by the District Attorney's office. He looked at Jacques, then at Chaplin, who was the only person excited by his presence.

"My name is Marlowe," he began while lighting a cigarette. "Philip Marlowe. I understand that your brother is missing?"

"That is correct," said Jacques.

"Hm. Probably on a bender, or he met a broad," Marlowe said. "Hollywood's full of them, and if he has money like you, that's likely to be the story. Case closed."

"But that is not at all like Roger," Jacques argued. "He was here on family business, and when he sets his sights on a goal, nothing will deter him from it."

"Then, we must work backwards," Marlowe said.

"Backwards?" asked Chaplin.

"Yeah," said Marlowe, not taking the actor overly serious, but smart enough to know he was a man with great power due to his fame. "Backwards. Start with when he was last seen." He turned towards the hotel manager who was still standing there and asked, "He checked in, right?"

"Yes, he did," Smith responded, wiping his brow.

"Was he alone? Did he have meetings here? What can you tell me?"

"I don't know, Mr. Marlowe. We provide all the amenities that our guests could want, but not personal babysitting."

"Don't start getting wise with me," said Marlowe. "Just gimme straight answers, and we'll get along fine." The investigator looked about at the opulence of the hotel then asked Jacques, "Who was he meeting here? Any ideas?"

"*Oui*, I mean, yes," replied the Frenchman. "He was meeting with Mr. Lasky at Paramount and then with Mr. Mayer at Metro-Goldwyn-Mayer."

"Two gems, that's for sure," laughed Marlowe. "I wish I could help you, but my plate is full at the moment at the D.A.'s office. Personally, I think they only sent me because of your buddy here." He pointed at Chaplin. "However, I do know someone who might be of assistance. Where should I have him come to, this dump or…?"

"The Coconut Grove," said Chaplin. "I will make the reservations for 7 p.m. Who will be coming?"

"A good egg I used to work with who set out as a private dick about a year ago," stated Marlowe. "He's smart, tough and won't be intimated by the likes of Lasky or Mayer. And I wouldn't have him go to some ritzy joint. If you need to meet somewhere fancy, at least do Musso & Frank. Better bar for chatting."

"And who is your friend?" asked Jacques.

"Sorry," laughed Marlowe. "Picturing him at the Grove had me laughing. His name is Spade, Sam Spade. You'll like him. And by the way. I know what '*Oui*' means." And with that, Marlowe turned and left.

And thus, under the neon lights of Hollywood, in the dim ambiance of a bar where producers, aspiring actors and world-weary souls converged, Jacques de Trémeuse met Sam Spade. The budding detective's reputation preceded him. His sharp features and hawk-like eyes promised a mind that missed no detail.

As the golden liquid swirled in their glasses, the Frenchman relayed his tale, every nuance of Roger's disappearance laid bare. Spade listened, the faintest hint of intrigue lighting up his eyes.

"We'll find your brother, Mr. de Trémeuse," the detective murmured, raising his glass, "Hollywood hides many secrets, but they can't remain in the shadows forever."

With Chaplin's sympathetic presence and Spade's determination bolstering his spirits, the search for Roger had truly begun.

"How about we do this?" suggested Spade. "I will work my contacts, see what the undercurrent is. You visit the movie guys, Lasky and Mayer. Read them, see what you feel, if anything. But remember, they work in selling dreams and lies, so believe half of what you see and none of what you hear."

The next day, Chaplin had his driver take Jacques to the MGM lot after personally setting up the meeting with its head, Louis B. Mayer. Ushered into the oversized office, the Frenchman sat in the chair before the other most powerful man in Hollywood.

"I appreciate your situation, Mr. de Trémeuse," said Mayer. "I truly do, but I am not sure what I can do to help."

"Thank you," replied Jacques, "but as a recent acquaintance of mine said, 'let's work backwards.' Did you meet with Roger?"

"I did. A delightful man, and our conversation explored your joining forces with our New York backers in MGM. I proposed a larger number than he was prepared to commit to, but what he was prepared to invest was still significant."

"There, we have a start," smiled Jacques. "When was this meeting?"

"If I am not mistaken, he came here immediately after checking into his hotel."

"And next," asked the man who was holding Judex within his beating chest for the moment, "do you recall who he was seeing or where he was going after your meeting?"

"I'm not sure I remember, or even if he shared that information."

"Come now, Mr. Mayer," said Trémeuse standing, his large shadow looming over the executive who was used to being in charge. "We are both men of considerable power. There is no way you didn't know where a visitor with the resources that Roger commanded was going, or who else he was meeting with. So, I ask you again, where was he going?"

Mayer was not used to being spoken like this, but he was also not used to having anyone as impressive as Jacques de Trémeuse before him. "Now that I think of it, I believe he mentioned Lasky at Paramount," he muttered.

"And who else? Who don't I know about, that might have gotten wind of Roger's visit?"

"Well, I did ask one of our, er, employees to do a, er, follow up," sweated Mayer. "Your brother had hired a driver—someone named Allard, I believe. Yes, that's it. Kent Allard. An always broke pilot, but he knows how to charm the visitors."

Meanwhile, on the bustling boulevards of Hollywood, Spade strode with purpose. He made his way to The Gilded Lantern, a speakeasy known for its secretive clientele, and, most importantly, its even more secretive barkeep, a man named Eddie Mars.

Eddie's eyes, always observing, flicked up as Spade entered. "Been a while," he murmured, putting down a glass he was drying to pour a bourbon neat in a glass and sliding it over to Spade.

Spade leaned on the bar, nodded his thanks, and finished the drink in one sip. "Hear there's a new player in town, Eddie. Someone from France with lots of money."

Eddie's gaze never left the glass. "France? Well, this is the dream capitol of the world, so who knows."

"My guy went missing a few days ago."

"You don't say."

"I don't say a lot. What I will say is that you know every fart in this town and what ass it came from so I don't want to not have to say anything again."

"How about another while I think?" asks Eddie, reaching for a bottle.

"Sure, but reach higher. I don't want to die from rot gut today."

Eddie poured another glass, this time a little fuller than the one before, and slid it to Spade. "Lots of folks come from all over, Sam. Hollywood's a magnet. You know that."

"I know lots of things," snarled Spade. "For instance, I know that I have a couple of more stops to make and then I'll be coming back. To talk to you again."

"Tomorrow?"

"Tonight."

Eddie's brow crinkled as he popped a Camel in his mouth and lit it up. "You know, Sam," he began. "I can save you a trip. One of my regulars, some burnt out pilot got himself a cushy driving gig for some French guy. Was taking him all around."

"You have a name for this guy?"

"Allard. Kent Allard. But I haven't seen him in a while. He's mixed into something that I don't want any part of."

"What?"

"Some crime lord from China."

"Stop the nonsense."

"On the level, Sam, on the level. He's some boogie man from the East and he runs all the opium dens and half the underground in LA, and a whole lot of other cities. He has something on Allard, and all the sudden, he's a different guy, get me?"

"No," replied Spade lighting up a smoke. "This smoke and mirrors character is according to you, real and the secret power here?"

"Now you got it."

"Where's Allard?"

"No idea. He's a hard man to track down."

Spade took out a five and started to push it across the bar. "Think really hard."

For a moment, the clinking of glasses and murmurs of the patrons were the only sounds in the room. Eddie Mars finally leaned in, voice barely a whisper. And said, "Word is there's a shadow weaving through Tinseltown's circles. But it's just whispers, Spade. Whispers and shadows."

Spade sighed. "I need more, Eddie. I need an address."

Eddie hesitated, then jotted something down on a piece of paper.

"Visit the Lotus Theater in Chinatown. Midnight show. You might find what you're looking for. Show girl named Victoria. Allard bunks down with her from time to time."

Spade nodded his appreciation and left the establishment with the weight of Eddie Mars's words pressing down on him.

Sitting in the back of the chauffeured car, Jaques de Trémeuse was lost in thought as he reran the conversation with Louis B. Mayer through his mind. It seemed that the powerful studio head was almost afraid of Allard, and had hesitated to mention his name. But what would someone want with Roger? There had been no ransom demand and he hadn't been carrying any funds, nor had he requested any to be transferred. What would the next man he has to visit have to say?

That answer was coming shortly, as Jacques walked into a restaurant near the Paramount offices for his meeting with Jesse L. Lasky. The studio boss was in a booth near the bar and waved him over. "Monsieur de Trémeuse," the dark-haired man said, "I'm Jesse Lasky. What can I do for you?"

"Right to it then," smiled Jacques. "Fine. I am looking for my brother, Roger. You were one of the last people to see him."

"Me and the old man."

"The old man?"

"Yeah," explained Lasky. "I chatted with your brother, understood what you two wanted, and brought in Zukor. He runs the place. I thought it was clear they had a good meeting. The old man would rather you two invest with him than Mayer."

"Is there anything else you can tell me?"

"Only that the guy taking him around LA is a rat bastard by the name of Allard. A pilot with his fingers in a lot of things we don't want around our studio."

"Where can I find this Allard?"

"I don't keep tabs on every creep out here, but I will tell you this. I know he's part of some new group from China bringing opium in. In fact, I told Roger not to trust him."

"You did?"

"Of course. I liked him. And dead men don't invest. Now is there anything else I can help you with? I've a busy day ahead."

"No," replied Jacques. "You have been most helpful. Thank you."

Back at his office, Spade began digging. Stacks of newspapers lay scattered, each one hinting at curious occurrences. Studio mishaps, hushed meetings with foreign investors, and peculiar accidents involving anyone who might have asked too many questions. But names were absent or obscured, making his search even more challenging.

Hours turned into evening as Spade pieced together snippets. His research was interrupted by a soft knock on his door. Before him stood a woman draped in a long coat, a veiled hat obscuring her features.

"Mr. Spade," she began, her voice tinged with an accent he couldn't quite place, "be wary of the path you're walking. Heed the words of Kâramanèh. Some shadows are best left undisturbed."

And as quickly as she had appeared, she vanished into the night, with Spade lighting a cigarette as he contemplated her visit. And from across the street, watching Spade's office from a distance, stood the man who, for the time being, was no longer Jacques de Trémeuse, but instead Judex. Watching and waiting.

Midnight found Spade at the Lotus Theater, the neon lights painting the streets in a soft, otherworldly glow. The show was a mesmerizing blend of Eastern tales, but it was the final act that left him transfixed. The Lotus Theater's chandeliers bathed the room in a soft glow, their light dancing off sequined dresses and polished cufflinks. The rhythm of a jazz number pulsed through the air, setting the atmosphere alight with a mix of anticipation and nonchalance. In this den of glamour, the elite of Hollywood sipped their drinks and exchanged whispers, their laughter interspersed with the sultry notes of the saxophone.

At the bar, the detective's silhouette was unmistakable, even in the dimmed ambiance. His eyes were always observing, always calculating. Tonight, they were fixed on one man: Kent Allard.

Allard, exuding an air of discreet confidence, held court at a corner table, his conversation partners hanging on to his every word. Yet, there was an undercurrent of urgency to his demeanor, a subtle tension that Spade picked up on.

As the evening wore on, Allard began to display signs of restlessness. With a final word to his companions, he subtly motioned for the bill. Spade, ever alert, took this as his cue. He downed the last of his whiskey, threw some bills on the counter, and prepared to tail his target.

Allard's exit was quiet, almost inconspicuous, a stark contrast to the opulence of the Lotus. As the side door clicked shut behind him, Spade, moving with a feline grace, was hot on his trail. But they were not alone. Judex, the silent sentinel, had been watching, waiting for the right moment to make his move.

Los Angeles' streets, bathed in the soft glow of streetlamps and the deeper shades of night, provided the perfect canvas for the unfolding drama. Allard's measured steps sounded out a rhythm against the cobbled pathways. He believed he walked alone—one soon shattered. Behind him, Spade shadowed every move, every turn, his eyes hawk-like. And a few paces behind was another presence—the wraith-like Judex, hidden within his cloak's embrace, following them, unseen and unknown.

He'd barely gone a few yards when the soft whisper of another set of footsteps layered into the night's soundscape. Allard, perhaps driven by some uncanny sixth sense, paused momentarily. He glanced over his shoulder, but saw nothing amiss. With a barely perceptible nod, he proceeded towards a plain, brick-faced building. Its only noteworthy feature was a heavy wooden door, partially hidden in the shadows. Without hesitation, Allard slipped through.

Within the doorway was a world apart. The room, bathed in the warm, flickering glow of lanterns, buzzed with quiet conversations in various languages. Men with sharp eyes sat around low tables, exchanging whispered secrets. The scent of exotic incense wafted through the room, mingling with the sharp tang of spilt alcohol.

Allard wasted no time. Striding to the center, he began urgently, "They know we have the Frenchman. Time to move out of here, Li Po."

A loud banging sound at a door that was never knocked upon turned all heads. Li Po said to a man standing behind him, "Send whoever it is away."

Opening the door, Spade, entered roughly, pushing past the man sent to greet him and announced with a smirk, "Quite the office you've got here, Allard. Where's Trémeuse?"

"Kill him!" shouted Li Po.

Within a heart beat, bullets were whizzing past the private eye, their deadly intent clear. Spade dived for cover, his gun drawn, returning fire as he tried to pinpoint his assailants in the dim light.

Away from the blazing guns and smoke, Allard, sensing an opportunity, quickly looked to make a silent exit. But, as he neared another exit, a shadowy figure emerged, suddenly blocking his path. The soft whisper of a cloak and the glint of piercing, determined eyes was all he got before he found himself engaged in a fierce hand-to-hand combat with Judex. Fists flew before they found themselves in each other's arms, struggling in battle that was both intense and intimate in its ferocity.

Still struggling, the two large combatants crashed through a weak partition, revealing a room beyond—one thick with the haze of opium. Languid figures lay strewn about, trapped in their narcotic dreams. Among them was Roger de Trémeuse, pipe in hand, his eyes devoid of their usual spark. His capturers did not need any longer the steel chain they once used to force him to stay—just the hideous lure of the pipe.

Seizing the momentary distraction as Judex's gaze fell upon his brother, Allard grunted, "You might have found him, but the game's just begun," and quickly retreated, melting into the shadows once more.

As Judex went to Roger, trying to wake him from his stupor, Spade joined him, having temporarily dealt with the more immediate threats.

"Trémeuse," Spade muttered, catching his breath. "What took you so long?"

"You knew I was following you?"

"You're good," laughed Spade. "Very good. But I made you at the Lotus. Figured you had a reason for staying behind. Now, let's get out of here before the coppers arrive. I'll square this with Marlowe tomorrow. Your brother needs help."

Roger, still dazed, managed a weak smile at his brother. "They wanted the location, Jacques... of the mines."

Pulling his brother close, Jacques whispered, "We'll deal with it together. And I will find Allard."

"He's a pawn," whispered Roger with a rough and weary voice. "Only an agent of someone who's forcing him to do his bidding."

"Do you know who?" asked Spade.

"Just a name whispered I heard."

"What name, Roger?" asks his concerned brother.

"Fu Manchu."

"Never heard of him," said Spade.

"Then," said Jacques, "This Fu Manchu has an enemy."

"You?" asked Spade.

"No, Judex."

And with that, Sam Spade and Jacques de Trémeuse put their arms about Roger and helped him as they rushed to get him out of the building and put this tragic Hollywood Affair behind them. For the moment, at least, as somewhere to the East Judex's thoughts went...

*Frank Schildiner is currently at work on a novel that will feature the green-masked Fantômas, who was the star of a trilogy of French films in the 1960s starring Jean Marais and Louis de Funès. Recognizing that this version of the character owed more to James Bond than the original dark-clad psychopath created by Allain & Souvestre, Frank has been practicing by penning a series of humorous homages, of which this is the latest...*

## Frank Schildiner: *No Child of Mine*

The meeting of the Sons and Daughters of Fantômas came to order just after dinner, a sumptuous meal of stolen beef, chicken, vegetables, and wine. The members had paid double the cost of every item, having bought everything from those dirty shadowy men who lurk on the edge of markets. That was one of their credos, having decided when they made their pledge in the Prince of Evil's name to only buy illegal goods for club business.

Club President, Monsieur Louis Castaigne, stood and raised his glass and began with the traditional opening toast.

"To the Master of Men, the Prince of Evil, the Lord of Terror, our Father in Spirit, gentlemen and ladies, to Fantômas!"

The others, having risen, repeated the last word, clinked glasses, and downed their cheap wine in one gulp. The beverage had a distinctly vinegarish flavor, probably having gone bad prior to being bought by Madame Morcata and her bratty nephew. Said nephew, Damien, was not present, having decided that the club wasn't as enjoyable as the one run by a crone named Helena Markos.

"Now, to business, I move that we waive the reading of the old business and move on to current events. Do I have a second? Thank you, Monsieur Gower. All in favor? And nays? No, excellent, the motion passes!"

A smattering of light applause from the eleven members present followed as a waiter emerged from the single door. He was a hunched figure with long, damp, tendrils of grayish, black hair and a lined face that appeared aged and infirmed. Hands shaking with unconcealed palsy, he placed a silver serving tray with a huge dome shaped covering upon the center table. He bowed several inches and backed away, closed the door firmly shut behind him a moment later.

"Ah, now we are alone. As the Sons and Daughters of Fantômas, I believe we have a need to distinguish ourselves from our former colleagues, the Children of Darkness. Their rejection of the core principle of wearing the costumes of our adopted father, the great Fantômas, remains a permanent point of contention. Also, their insistence of the use of Lord of Evil and Prince of Terror means we shall no longer conduct joint enterprises," Castaigne said, adjusting his domino mask and top hat as he completed his report.

Monsieur Pierre De la Poer, a short, portly figure who dressed in flowing red robes that did not hide his love of wine and fromage, rose from his seat, lifting his red hood as he said, "I believe three of their group are preparing a demand for the return of the proper order of Father Fantômas's titles. Should their rebellion fail, I suggest we offer them places among our august body."

Madame Juliet D'Urfe, a young, petite pretty girl who always dressed in a striped shirt, blank pantaloons, a domino mask, and a men's fedora, rose and bowed, "Unless they agree to the proper garb in all meetings, this discussion is moot, Monsieur. We must not yield our proper respect to the Lord of Terror! I think... did someone spill a carafe; my feet feel wet...?"

"Mine too," Castaigne said, stepping back as he pulled the tablecloth aside.

Below the table he and the others soon observed a rapidly rising flow of clear, warm water. Without pause, he walked to the door to complain to the restaurant staff, only to find the door locked.

"Locked!" he cried and hammered on the door with both gloved hands, "Garçon! Let us out! A pipe must have broken!"

Silence only greeted him as the water rose and was soon above their ankles. Three other members soon joined Castaigne at the door, their yells and rapidly weakening blows to the portal yielding no response.

Within five minutes, they abandoned this endeavor as the hip-deep water flowed into the small chamber. The Sons and Daughters of Fantômas were soon standing on the room's chairs as the rising tide of fluid continued, ceasing only when Mesdames Morcata and D'Urfe, the shortest members of the organization, were forced to stand upon their tip toes.

Oddly, the bright silver serving tray with its massive silver dome, did not sink. The metal palaver floated in place in the center of the room, bobbing as the members of the group moved about in the water.

"I think it stopped," Castaigne said, "How could this happen?"

"A good question," a silken voice said, from above where they bobbed, "with a simple answer..."

They looked up, gaping as the elderly face of the waiter gazed down upon them with glee. A black gloved hand reached up, pulling off the wig and wizened face, revealing a visage somehow hidden among the newly-appearing shadows.

"...Fantômas," he said as his hooded eyes narrowed, "the one you claim is your father..."

"Oh! Oh my! It is he, the Lord of Terror!" several voices said.

"The Prince of Evil..."

"He comes to us, not to anyone else! Oh, Fantômas, we are most honored by your..." Castaigne said.

"Silence," Fantômas said, never raising his voice, but hushing them without effort, "Do you believe I consider your worship an honor? You, who follow my deeds with glee and feel mighty for your knowledge? The lot of you and your friends who call themselves the Children of Darkness are truly the most pathetic pack of hyenas I have ever had the misfortune to encounter! I would call you vultures, but you have not the will to soar as those carrion-eating birds do for their meal! You are maggots, feasting upon the flesh of corpses and believe you are royalty!"

"But, great Fantômas, we admire your destruction of the laws that bind each of us..." De la Poer said, but ceased when the Prince of Evil performed a chopping gesture.

"Cease your prattle! You insult me by claiming I am your parent," Fantômas said, "Even a metaphorical comparison disgusts me, De la Poer! Yes, I know your name and shall empty your safe later tonight. You and your worms are no child of mine and I shall teach you, and the rest of the world, what occurs when you take the name of Fantômas in vain!"

The silver dome that lay upon the bobbing platter tipped over and red fluid appeared. It fell into the water and a rusty metallic scent permeated the water-filled chamber.

"Blood?" Madame Morcata asked, "I do not understand."

"It is the blood of your compatriots, the Children of Darkness. I executed them earlier this evening. I find it fitting that their *vitae* bring about your end... observe..." the Lord of Terror said as a panel in the wall slid aside.

The panel revealed a glass wall with dozens of silver and red fish within. The animals were about the size of a man's hand, and they moved about their tank with inhuman indifference.

"Allow me to introduce you to the Red-Bellied Piranha. Normally a placid animal whose diet consists of small animals... unless they scent blood... they become ravenous, maddened, killers who can strip a cow clean in minutes... we shall see how long it takes my little friends when consuming maggots!" Fantômas said as the glass wall vanished, depositing the fish into the room.

Fantômas smiled as the screams of fright rose, soon followed by the wails of agony. Straightening, he walked away from the scene, knowing Hélène and Vladimir would have emptied the homes of those below and their fellows on the other side of Paris.

"I wonder how Juve and Fandor will react to these actions," he thought as he leaped across the rooftops. "Then we shall confront Lupin. I think that silly man is in need of a lesson in horror, curtesy of Fantômas!"

*"Artikel Unbekannt" is the nom-de-plume of a French writer-editor (including for our sister imprint Rivière Blanche) who is also a respected figure in the field of horror literature & film criticism. In this amusing vignette, he asks the question: what if Mario Bava's classic 1968 film* Danger: Diabolik *was not fiction but a biopic?*

## Artikel Unbekannt: *The Dark Demon*

*Clerville police station, September 29, 1967.*

It was long past midnight, but Inspector Ginko still hadn't gone home. Alone in the deserted building, the policeman paced up and down the corridors, mentally reviewing the events of the last few days.

Although the case had been solved, and he had been congratulated by his superiors, he remained unsatisfied. And the more he thought about the situation, the more something eluded him. It was as if he'd been playing an extra in a film the script of which he hadn't read...

*Two weeks earlier.*

Ginko was distractedly examining a few cold case files when the telephone rang. He picked it up after three rings.

"Inspector Ginko?" asked a voice that sounded familiar.

"Yes. To whom am I speaking...?"

"My name is Dino De Laurentiis. Perhaps you've heard of me?"

In spite of himself, the inspector gasped slightly. Dino De Laurentiis was a famous film producer. He had never met him, but he knew that the tycoon owned a lavish villa in Clerville.

"Yes, I know who you are, Mr. De Laurentiis. How can I be of help?"

"I'd rather tell you in person, if you don't mind. May I drop by your office?"

"Of course. Any time. I look forward to seeing you."

"Thank you! I'll be there as soon as I can."

Half an hour later, the mogul entered the Inspector's office. Ginko knew the producer's reputation, and that he was not the type of man to be easily intimidated. So he was surprised to see De Laurentiis trembling slightly as they shook hands.

"Thank you for seeing me, Inspector. The reason I'm here is this: As you can imagine, a man in my position doesn't only have friends. I often receive insulting or even threatening letters. But this is the first time I've received one like this," he explained, handing Ginko an envelope.

591

The Inspector took it and read the letter inside. It was both clear and laconic:

*Dear sir,*
*I hereby inform you that I desire your property. You're much too rich, and I'm determined to seize a portion of your fortune. I will use all the means at my disposal to do so, and these are substantial. I look forward to impoverishing you soon.*
*Best regards,*
*K.*

Who was the dark figure behind this mysterious initial? And who had the audacity of claiming responsibility for a crime before it was committed, thus warning his intended victim who would surely inform the police?

Ginko decided to take the threat seriously, and did his best to reassure De Laurentiis. The producer thanked him profusely, especially since the shooting of his next film was due to start in Clerville in a few days.

"I'll leave it with you, Inspector., but I'm counting on your discretion," he said. "Obviously, neither I, nor my director, Mario Bava, need this kind of publicity."

"Of course, Mr. De Laurentiis. I'll keep you informed of my progress. You can count on me to be the soul of discretion."

As he said this, Ginko had no idea what he would soon be facing...

The first incident happened the next day, but against all expectations, the producer was not the target.

Ginko was contacted by Renato Polselli, a notorious film director. He, too, had received a letter identical to the one sent to De Laurentiis.

The next day, a fire broke out at the Central Bank of Clerville. It was followed by yet another letter, this time addressed to the city's most famous lawyer. The same thing happened three days later, with an explosion in the town's main shopping mall and a letter sent in parallel to Andrea Bianchi, one of its owners.

And so it went for the next few days: each attack followed by a new letter. Although there were no serious casualties, the public was shocked. The town was on the verge of a collective psychosis, because while firefighters and the police were mobilized to the scene of the disasters, burglaries targeting the people who had received the letters were being committed! Indeed, although the letters had been sent in no particular order, it turned out that each of the individuals concerned had had a direct link with the attacks.

Like nesting dolls, the letters heralded an explosion, which in turn heralded a burglary. Paintings, sculptures, jewelry, cash... The total haul was proportional to the damage caused by the fire, and it was considerable.

A week later, the richest people in the region had all received the same threats, all carried out. Or almost. Because seven letters had been sent, followed by only six attacks and burglaries. The letter received by De Laurentiis could not be linked to any mischief...

At least, not directly. The situation in Clerville was so out of control that the producer had been forced to postpone the shooting of Mario Bava's film. The director was reportedly unhappy about the postponement, and made no bones about it in the press. So much for the negative publicity the tycoon had been determined to avoid...

*So much for the negative publicity he said he wanted to avoid*, thought Ginko.

Almost immediately, the policeman retracted this thought, which had no basis in fact.

"Just because I haven't been able to apprehend any suspects doesn't mean I have to invent a new one, for God's sake!"

But the facts were even more stubborn than the Inspector—which was saying something. A mysterious individual had set out to spread chaos in Clerville, following a plan that was as insane as it was Machiavellian. It was as if some obscure evil genius had taken inspiration from the various criminals whose exploits were romanticized in the *fumetti*. In spite of himself, Ginko thought of them: *Kriminal, Killing*, even *Satanik*... So many featuring the letter K which had served as the signature on all threatening letters...

"But none of these have any connection with the present situation," grumbled the Inspector, chastising himself for this flight of fancy, even more far-fetched than his earlier thought

A knock on his door drew him out of his thoughts. Seconds later, a young policewoman appeared.

"The media are waiting, Inspector. Are you ready?"

"No... Er, yes, of course," grumbled Ginko. "Let's do it."

Caught between his superiors' expectations and public pressure, the policeman had finally resolved to face the media. He hated it, especially when, like now, he had nothing to report. Worse yet, it wasn't impossible that one of these busybodies might be a step ahead of him!

Fortunately for Ginko, the media were no more informed than he was. He was able to deliver a skillful blend of lies of omission and half-truths that enabled him to avoid answering the most embarrassing questions.

*The same evening, at the luxurious villa of Dino de Laurentiis.*

Edwige Hossegor had arrived in Clerville with Teddy Verano a few days before the attacks. The actress, finally free of Mephista's evil grip, had decided to relaunch her career. Thanks to an Italian agent who had fond memories of her earlier performances, she had been cast to replace Catherine Deneuve in Mario Bava's new film. A real godsend, especially as it was a Dino de Laurentiis production.

Delighted with Edwige's commitment, the mogul had insisted on letting her and her chaperone stay with him until filming began. But, because of the attacks, the initial good mood had soon given way to a gloomy atmosphere. As a result, the two French guests hadn't lingered long after dinner that evening. They wished the producer and his wife, the actress Silvana Mangano, a good night, then went back to their respective rooms.

At around 3 a.m., Edwige tossed about in her sleep, coughed, and woke up. She noticed that the temperature had risen noticeably, and saw a few wisps of smoke coming from under the door. There was a fire somewhere in the house!

Throwing back her sheets, the actress dressed hastily and hurried down the corridor. She was about to knock on Verano's door when her attention was caught by a movement on the staircase leading to the first floor.

Instinctively, she turned around and immediately recognized Dino de Laurentiis. But as she moved towards him, he ran down the stairs at an incredible speed.

Edwige set off in pursuit, but was unable to reach the producer, who ignored her calls. In a few quick strides, he left the burning house, reached the edge of the woods adjacent to the property, and disappeared amongst the trees.

Moments later, Teddy Verano and Silvana Mangano, both unharmed, emerged from the mansion. Extremely worried, the actress told her guests that her husband had disappeared. Edwige didn't have time to tell them what she had seen, as the police and the fire department were arriving on the scene.

Silvana was taken to hospital, while Edwige and Teddy accompanied Ginko back to the police station.

"Are you absolutely certain of what you saw, Mademoiselle Hossegor?" asked the Inspector after Edwige had reported her story. "Could it have been a nightmare? Perhaps even a hallucination?"

"I was wide awake and very lucid, Inspector. I realize that my account may seem strange, especially as I don't understand it myself, but I stand by what I said: I saw Dino de Laurentiis run away shortly after the fire started. I give you my word."

Ginko let a few moments pass. He knew Edwige Hossegor by reputation, and was well aware of the role that Mephista had played in her life. However, he didn't want to appear indelicate by doubting her.

Sensing the policeman's indecision, Verano stepped in.

"I can vouch for Mademoiselle Hossegor, Inspector. Yes, it is true that she and I have been through a number of ordeals as strange and mysterious as this one in the recent past, but she has never been affected to the point of distorting reality. She's telling you the truth."

Ginko nodded politely, then showed his visitors out, after thanking them and assuring them that he would keep them informed of any further developments.

The next day, Dino de Laurentiis was found haggard, wandering along a country road. He remembered nothing, and had no idea what had happened to him.

In addition, several cans of petrol were found in the vicinity of the producer's home. And each of them bore his fingerprints...

All roads now led to Dino de Laurentiis, but Ginko still hesitated to connect the dots in this murky affair. The producer's involvement seemed incomprehensible. For one thing, the man was not a crook. Second, he was rich and had no need of money. Why would he have burned down his own house? On the other hand, Edwige Hossegor had no reason to lie, or even frame him, especially after signing a contract to appear in his film. Something just didn't add up.

*Clerville, September 30, 1967.*

Lying on the edge of a swimming pool in the garden of a secluded, sumptuous estate, a couple were enjoying the last days of the Indian summer, sipping a Martini. The ominous metallic glint in the man's eyes softened when he turned to his companion, a gorgeous blonde with the look of a femme fatale—in every sense of the word.

"So, Eva, what do you think of my ploy?"

"It worked beyond our expectations. Not only has Bava's film been abandoned, but all those letters completely led the police astray. It weas easy to relieve our seven victims of a substantial portion of their wealth, and as an added bonus, De Laurentiis is suspected of having orchestrated the whole affair, not forgetting insurance fraud!"

"Letting him make that ridiculous film about us was out of the question. With it gone, we can go back to our life of crime and remain as an urban legend. I'm not worried about Dino; he is quite resourceful."

"Your idea of impersonating him by wearing that mask after setting fire to his villa was excellent."

"Thank you, my dear. The trickiest part was kidnapping him first, but the fact that the villa was unguarded helped. All I had to do was inject him with a drug of my own composition, place his fingerprints on the jerrycans, and set fire to the house..."

"Yes, but you still had to be spotted at the right time, and by the right person. The testimony of that French actress did us a great service. Now we're rich enough to take a vacation. A long one..."

"A vacation?" replied Diabolik, feigning outrage. "You can't mean it! There are still a lot of rich people in Clerville, and I have many more masks."

*The problem with Nathalie Vidalinc's tale is that it is like* The Empire Strikes Back, *i.e.: the second instalment of a trilogy that begun with "The Music Box" in our Volume 18. I hesitated before publishing this tale, despite the fact that it ends on quite a revelation, because this is our last volume, and therefore I won't be able to offer its conclusion to our readers. Its third and last instalment will eventually appear in our French edition,* Les Compagnons de l'Ombre, *and I do intend to find a way to squeeze in its English translation somewhere in a future project... Or you could learn French...*

## Nathalie Vidalinc: *The Noose of the Phansigars*

*India, Spring 1932*

The woman who called herself Joséphine Balsamo, a.k.a. Countess Cagliostro, arrived in Benares with two acolytes. The older one, her right-hand man, she called Leonard according to some obscure family tradition; the other was a young American, the scion of a wealthy Floridan family, was named Randolph March. The city was even more exotic than she remembered from her first visit. More crowded too. She immediately thought that competition here would be fierce.

The three visitors made their way to the European Quarter and settled in a comfortable hotel before embarking on their adventure. Leonard had become even more skeptical about the viability of their enterprise since discovering India, and aired his grievances.

"I still think that that no piece of art is valuable enough for us to waste time in such a god-forsaken place!"

"Until we learn the origins of the music box, we can't know its real value," replied Joséphine.

Leonard looked doubtful.

"Speak!" ordered the young woman.

But her second-in-command didn't want to have an argument.

"Speak!" she insisted.

"Are you really after the treasure—or its owner?" he finally muttered.

Joséphine smiled ambiguously.

"There's no reason I can't combine work and pleasure. But I'm convinced that there's something real behind all this. I can feel it."

She spoke the truth: there was something here that intrigued her. Perhaps it was that Rama Tamerlane—the man known as Felifax—had suddenly departed, right in the middle of his honeymoon. That was striking. It couldn't be a coincidence...

Randolph joined the discussion. Joséphine had come up with a plan of action during their trip. She knew they'd have to blend in, so the young American had been asked to find Indian clothing to wear upon their arrival.

"I think I have everything we need," he said. "I even have this little extra for you, Mademoiselle. The saleswoman thought that Western women don't realize how lucky they are with their hair..."

It was a type of henna.

"A fine initiative, Randolph," said Joséphine.

"There's no way I'm dying my hair," Leonard said grumpily.

"The only thing I ask you to do is to go about unnoticed," Joséphine insisted. "You and I will be making our first visit to the temple posing as tourists. You, Randolph, will be trying to locate Baber Tamerlane's house."

The lushness of the Bengal jungle had surprised Felifax as much as it had pleased him. The villagers who had shown him where he might have the best chance of finding the one he was looking for, had urged him to travel armed. When they saw him leave empty-handed, they thought they'd never see him again...

He had entered the jungle without fear. He was familiar with the strange noises coming from all directions, which would have scared off many a visitor. The forest was chattering, but he knew that he was the cause of it. When silence suddenly fell, he decided to settle down and wait for whatever the forest also waited...

A man approached. In his fifties, he was impressively slim and athletic, with an affable appearance. He walked towards Felifax alone, but discreet shadows followed behind him showing that he had not come unprepared. When he reached Rama, he stopped, suddenly looking uncertain. Rama understood why and answered his unvoiced question.

"Yes, it is I, Felifax," he said. "I smell like a tiger because that beast is part of my nature."

"You're the one who's been stirring up trouble in my jungle," stated the newcomer.

"I'm afraid so," replied the tiger-man. "I've come to find a companion in adventure, and I thought a man like you, with such a thorough understanding of the animal kingdom, could be of great help to me."

"I'm always ready to listen to anyone who needs my help," replied the other man, extending his hand in friendship.

"My friends call me Rama," said Felifax, taking the hand and shaking it.

"And mine call me Mowgli."

A few days later, at the palace, behind the thick walls of the Ramnagar fort, the high society of Benares had come to toast Maharajah Prahbhu Narayan Singh. Nightfall was starting to push some of the sybarites towards the exit.

Joséphine Balsamo had found the right contacts to introduce her to the local potentate. As the salons gradually emptied, she remained behind in the company of an old man who had unwittingly given her some interesting information that might prove useful in her projects.

Leonard had already gone ahead. He staved off boredom by nonchalantly observing his surroundings. Suddenly, he noticed something unusual moving quickly in the shadows. He thought he had seen a stealthy figure walk by, but where had it gone? He was relatively sure it was their man. He rushed to the palace to alert his boss.

On seeing him arrive, Joséphine gracefully took leave of her guide. She knew from the look on Leonard's face that something serious has happened.

"Someone is trying to walk in the shadows of Ramnagar unnoticed," reported her henchman. "I bet it's our guy. What do we do?"

"Can you follow him?" asked Joséphine, looking at the place Leonard had indicated.

"But what will happen if he confronts me...?"

"We'll worry about that later. Go quickly! And follow him when he comes out."

"What if he leaves via the Ganges?"

"Then you'll go through the Ganges."

The Sepoys in charge of guarding the royal apartments had left without having found anything suspicious. However, the Maharajah paused as he took the first step into his suite. He had noticed something unusual: prominently displayed on the central table was a music box he knew well, and which he had sent away several months ago. Now it was back and seemed to be taunting him.

The sovereign didn't call his men back; in fact, he didn't even blink.

"I thank you, O merciful Son of Kali, for answering my call," he said simply.

The shadow of a man, bearded, with loose hair, dressed in a simple *langouti*, stepped from behind the sumptuous curtains. The two men bowed slightly, their hands clasped in salute.

The Maharajah took the music box and showed his visitor into a small, secluded room. There, he invited the newcomer to sit down.

"Nobody will hear us here," said the Maharajah.

"At least, not without my sensing their presence," replied Felifax.

The Maharajah moved the carvings of the two tigers decorating the top of the music box from right to left, then turned a key. Finally, he slid one edge open to reveal a small space containing a tiny opaline vial. He took it out.

"This was not mentioned in the report you received, Rama Tamerlane. This is what the criminal Edward Sexton called eSx22 in the file you received. We don't know what it is, but my scientist suspects it's behind the strange alterations of the body we have discovered, and which are the cause of my concern."

Felifax took the vial and looked at it thoughtfully for a moment. Then he put it back in the box.

"Things have gotten worse here since you came into possession of the box," continued the Maharajah. "Young girls entering puberty have been disappearing from across my kingdom. I'm afraid they're the next victims of the abominable surgeons who left a dead body in their wake. But those monsters have disappeared!"

"That is disturbing. If they're abducting young girls, they must have found a place big enough to hold them. My investigator mentioned a lot of new equipment—that should help us locate them. I've enlisted a new ally who might make a difference."

The Maharajah, who until then had maintained a position of equals with the son of Kali, suddenly assumed a more solemn posture.

"I must speak to you of another matter of great importance to India," he said gravely. "There's a strange rumor going around about a child—a monkey god."

"A god?" said Rama, surprised. The news came as a great surprise to the tiger-man. "What are the English saying?" he asked.

"Those godless heathens do not understand the importance of this. They don't believe it. Do you think this might be the result of another experiment by whoever is Edward Sexton's successor?"

"Well, we need to find out more," replied Rama.

He stood up, preparing to take his leave. The Maharajah joined him.

"I've told you of the suspicions I harbor about the people around me," he said. "I've received death threats. You are the best person able to help me."

"Rest assured I'll do my best, Sire."

"Then, let me show you something..."

The Maharajah opened a small, beautifully inlaid cupboard with a key he was carrying. He took a long tie with a skull on it out of a box and handed it to Felifax.

"Impossible!" was all the tiger-man could think of saying

"Why are Kali's servants angry with me?" asked the old man with obvious concern.

"Since returning to Benares, I've had the opportunity to observe the temple Brahmins. I've seen nothing suspicious. Besides, only a totally insane Brahmin would want to resurrect the Thugee sect."

"I can't help worrying. It's so easy for them to kill," said the Maharajah.

Felifax took a long look at what he recognized as the noose of the Phansigars, wondering what it meant. It couldn't have anything to do with the Sexton case. Thugee would never disembowel a woman; they used this type of weapon precisely because it didn't draw blood. But he knew that, in the past, some had taken liberties with the mission of Kali's divine army.

"But why you, Majesty?" he asked, still puzzled. "They're always acting on orders; they're the arm of the goddess."

"I imagine that they, like many of our people, blame me for making a pact with the English," replied the Maharajah. "But I did what I thought was best for my people. I remain faithful to our religion."

Felifax handed the noose back to the potentate.

"I'll find out who is behind this threat," he said, placing his hand on the sovereign's. He could feel his confidence soothe the old man.

"Now I need some trace of the creatures' scent," he added. "Can you provide me with something of the kind?"

The Maharajah thought for a while, then nodded.

"Would you like to meet my investigators, or would you like me to send you what they have?" he asked.

"I know what would be best," answered Rama. "Lead on, Sire."

As he approached the old caravanserai where the monstrous creatures had stayed, Felifax sensed peril. Since he'd been back in India, he was no longer undergoing the treatment that moderated his tiger nature. It troubled him to feel so different. More powerful. And, surprisingly, better. Everything felt more immediate, more real. The smells were becoming clearer. He had been expecting it, but thought it best to call out a song of *jerdon verdin*, rare in the region. Another voice replied.

When he entered the caravanserai enclosure, Felifax found himself surrounded by wolves. Mowgli stepped out of the darkness to meet him. An impressive black wolf was escorting him.

"Rama, I'd like to introduce you to Naka, the eldest of the last wolf sires." Then, turning to the wolf, he addressed him in his own language.

"Thank you for the incomparable help you've agreed to give us, Naka," said the tiger-man.

The wolf sneezed in contempt.

"My brother speaks a plain language, Rama," noted Mowgli, trying to translate the tiger-man's words to the wolf.

While they were getting to know each other, another wolf came from outside.

"You've been followed," said Mowgli after listening to the newcomer. "By a woman."

"I know who she is. She is interested in the music box I told you about. But I am surprised she came all the way from Europe to get her hands on it."

"Do you want us to mislead her?"

After considering his options, Felifax answered in the affirmative. He was curious to see how far Joséphine would go.

"The Maharajah has given me a means to track our fugitives," he added, opening a cardboard box he had brought along.

Naka sniffed attentively and gathered his pack together to share the scents.

"It's the same smell I detected in the enclosure," commented Mowgli. Then, he reported Naka's 'words: "He said we're looking for animals. But they also smell human like you... What do you want us to do?"

"I'll trust your brothers' sense of smell and follow them," replied Felifax.

Leonard was up in the early hours of the morning. He took his binoculars and grabbed a cup of coffee. Seeing no movement at the caravanserai, he became concerned. Knowing Joséphine, he knew he'd have to bring her back some kind of information, even if it meant risking being torn to shreds by the wolves.

Their targets had obviously left. He knew this would upset Joséphine, but deep down he was relieved. But contrary to his expectations, Joséphine didn't fly into a rage when she heard the news. She decided to rely on Mowgli's wolves. Their presence would surely not go unnoticed by the natives. So they went door-to-door and asked questions, and although the wolves had been discreet, their approach paid off. They soon found where Felifax had gone.

Joséphine immediately gave the order to pack. Soon, the three of them were in a car, heading for the unknown. Their route took them over increasingly bumpy roads, and the tires eventually failed to keep up. They were forced to stop.

"The tires are shot," said Randolph. "We won't be able to get very far like this."

Joséphine ranted and raved. Finally, she took some money and handed it to Randolph.

"Randolph, go find a horse and another car. Leonard, let's go!"

Since Naka and his pack had found a scent, the trackers had been working hard to follow it. They had forgotten Joséphine and her henchmen.

"Naka, the smell has been stronger for the last few miles," noted Mowgli as they stopped for food.

"We're close to Agra," observed Felifax, "and heading further and further north."

"Does that concern you?"

"Yes. I think it's increasing the odds of our soon meeting a group of hybrids."

"Hybrids—like you... How were these beings made?" asked Mowgli.

"A mad scientist introduced an animal seed into a woman's womb," replied Felifax.

"What a horrible idea. But why?" asked a deeply troubled Mowgli.

"I don't know. But I know we should be very careful."

Naka, who had gone hunting, suddenly returned.

"We found one of their houses," he growled.

Felifax tried to ask the wolf questions in his own language, but Naka just made a scornful noise.

"He's still learning, so please be understanding," Mowgli apologized.

In an abandoned hut, they found the body of a woman, her insides lacerated by the being that had been born from her.

"There's no doubt we're on the right track," said Felifax dryly.

Without dwelling further on the matter, he set off with Mowgli to find out more about the hut's former occupants.

They were surprised by the attitude of the natives. In the first village, the old chief was reluctant to talk, but his wife, sensitive to Felifax's youthful beauty, was more forthcoming.

"These barbarians treated her like a thing, yet she was high caste," she volunteered.

"Who were they?" asked Rama.

"Foreigners—Asians with cruel faces. They always carried weapons as if the poor child could have threatened them!"

"How many were there?" asked Mowgli.

"Four."

"In your opinion," asked Felifax, "which way did they go?"

"That way," replied the chief, gesturing towards Simla.

"Very well. We'll be staying in your village until dawn," concluded the tiger-man in a tone that left no room for discussion.

As the train approached Benares Station, the heart of Grace Tamerlane *née* Palmer began to beat faster. She could no longer bear the separation from her husband. Every minute spent without him was painful. Impatience drove her.

Getting off the train, she immediately spotted Reverend Douglas, a former pastor who had been her father's friend. He came over to help her with her luggage.

"It's such a pleasure to see you again, Miss Grace," he said with unabashed sincerity. "Would you like to rest a little from the journey?"

"Oh, no! I can't wait to see Rama again. I'm going to look for him right away."

"I tried to see him while he was in the city, but received no response..."

They left in the pastor's automobile, and, according to Grace's wishes, he dropped her at Baber's house in the native quarter. The young woman thought she'd find her husband in the old dwelling, but like Joséphine before her, she was unsuccessful. She found the place too dusty for anyone to have lived there, and bravely decided to go looking for him in the few places where they had been together.

These visits, which brought back only memories and melancholy, dulled Grace's resolution. In the evening, at her hotel, her tears were overcome only by her tiredness, and she fell asleep.

In the morning, a new resolve had rekindled her courage. Surely, Rama must have seen the Maharajah; she decided to go ask the potentate.

She began by securing an audience with the great king. She understood she was something of a problem. She had diverted Kali's son from his sacred mission and she had profaned him by sharing his bed. She would have to summon great courage to face the courtiers and the clerics of the Court.

In the late morning, she received a card from the palace; a car would pick her up in front of her hotel.

The Maharajah's Rolls arrived on time and took her to a discreet palace entrance from where she could go to meet the sovereign with a minimum of fuss.

Unfortunately, neither the Maharajah's measured words, nor English tea and scones, could prevent Grace from feeling dismay when she realized he didn't know where her husband was either.

Despite the vast expanse of the country, Randolph had succeeded in finding a horse that pleased him. Then, he had made his way to the wealthy city of Lucknow, where he'd found an all-terrain car, a Citroën P10, not very comfortable, but suitable for their journey. He made his way back slowly, the horse tied behind the car, and soon found his two friends in the middle of nowhere.

The car swallowed all obstacles, and soon they arrived at the same village where Felifax and his companions had found the woman's body.

Joséphine visited the hut and understood what had triggered Felifax's wrath. She then searched the ashes of the small funeral pyre where two villagers had burned the woman's corpse, but found nothing. The whole thing exasperated her. Felifax appeared to be following some kind of trail, but she couldn't guess where it led.

After offering a small gratuity, she learned from the village chief that her targets were only a day ahead of her, and that they were following the tracks of another vehicle that was headed northwest.

Joséphine liked the horse Randolph had bought and was better at getting around on it than in the car. A superb rider since childhood, she crossed the nearly impassable terrain with skill, and it didn't take her long to locate her prey.

Remaining out of sight, she watched Felifax and Mowgli through binoculars. The two seemed to have lost the trail of their target. The heavy rains had washed away the tire tracks. For the first time since arriving in India, she smiled.

Meanwhile in Benares, Grace acted like an automaton, her reddened eyes seemingly looking at nothing. She had finished packing and, like a ghost, she headed for the hotel's exit. As the servants carried her suitcases, a Western-dressed native discreetly stopped them. Another man approached Grace and whispered a few words in her ear. The young woman paled, stepped back, her face, her whole being, expressing the tumult of her feelings.

"Where is he?" she asked breathlessly.

"Follow me," replied the man, pushing her towards an automobile, in the trunk of which the servants hurriedly dropped her bags.

Grace slipped into the car, where she was surprised to find a Brahmin. The first man pushed her out of the way and took a seat on the other side. The car started up. Grace had now come to her senses and couldn't help feeling worried.

"What happened?" she asked the Brahmin. "How did Rama get hurt?"

Grace only had time to see the Brahmin smile kindly at her before recognizing the distinctive smell of chloroform.

Felifax felt that they had reached a dead end. Several of the wolves had randomly left along the trail. The stubborn Joséphine, whom he had spotted, was also a source of concern, as she moved without taking any precautions.

It had now been ten days since they had left the outskirts of Agra, and they were not far from Simla, when Mowgli's remaining 'brothers' were able to detect a promising scent.

Back at Joséphine's camp, Randolph was trying to relax by telling his companions some uplifting tales, when suddenly, the chilling howl of a wolf instantly put them on guard.

In the darkness, the camp was barely lit by a storm lamp waving in the wind; their tents were pitched between the restless horse and the Citroën. They suddenly made out shadows. Emerging from the darkness, armed men were rushing towards them. But they paused in surprise as several wolf-like figures suddenly appeared around the camp.

This frightening double threat made the three Europeans stand back to back, their weapons drawn. Men leaped, wolves howled, shots rang out. Bursts of gunfire illuminated the night.

Felifax heard the first howls, then the shots.

"It's coming from Joséphine's camp. They need help."

He straightened up, ready to act, but Mowgli stopped him, pointing at two shining eyes in the night.

"Naka is already here," he said.

In the wolf's mouth was a braid of black hair.

"It's all over," the wolf growled. "It was very quick! Two of my brothers died. The attackers were too heavily armed, so I chose to protect my tribe."

"Let's follow their trail," said Felifax.

What they saw at the camp was carnage. The throats of many of the attackers—who looked as if they were Chinese—had been torn out by the jaws of the wolves. Next to them lay several of Mowgli's brothers, blood still spurting from their severed carotids.

Felifax immediately looked for the bodies of the three Europeans, but they had vanished. One of the wolves found the direction taken by the vehicle that had disappeared along with Joséphine and her two assistants.

"Let's not waste any time," said Felifax. "We must follow their tracks."

Luck seemed to be smiling on them, as they made rapid progress. On the second day, they had to split up for a while in order to follow separate trails. Unsurprisingly, the wolves were the best at this. On the evening of the third day, this was confirmed by Mowgli's vulture friend, Chil, who came to tell them that he had spotted the strange vehicle. And so they arrived at their enemies' camp.

It was a fortified farmhouse, a seemingly impregnable eagle's nest. Felifax and Mowgli began to look for the best vantage point before setting up their own camp.

In her sleep, Joséphine Balsamo heard voices; her fierce spirit commanded her to awaken. Her brain was giving her terrifying new information. She opened her eyes.

She was naked; her legs were spread wide open and tied up in some kind of gynecological stirrups, displaying her in an unbearably obscene position. Everything inside her revolted. A scream of rage rose up inside her throat, but she was well aware that, in order to save her life, she had to do everything in her power to regain control of herself.

Her body trembling with rage, her heart aching, her mind overwhelmed by hate, she vowed to kill all the men who had raped her.

When she was finally able to reopen her eyes, she began to look for a way out of her hellish predicament. Two men stood nearby, chatting in German. They were busy with some unfamiliar piece of equipment and had their backs turned to her. She examined the room, looking for a solution. It was a laboratory and also, it seemed, a surgery. Instruments taunted her from a few inches too far away. There seemed to be no one else in the room, but an area behind her remained out of her sight.

"What a fine specimen she is!" said one of the Germans. "I wonder what the Master will do with her?"

"I can't stand the idea of someone wasting such a beautiful girl. She wasn't made for science," replied his companion with a gravelly laugh.

Calmly and cautiously, the athletic Joséphine managed to lift her feet out of the stirrups, while keeping a watchful eye on the backs of the two men. Then she straightened up on the examination table. Reaching for one of the surgical instruments would require greater concentration in order to balance her precarious sitting position. With determination, Joséphine managed to grab a pair of scissors with a sharp, curved tip. There was no need to be picky; they would do the job just fine.

In an instant, she leapt towards the two men, scissors firmly in hand. But suddenly, she felt herself caught from behind. However, her assailant had not counted on her rage. With her hands, she knocked him over and plunged the scissors deep into his chest.

Then she felt a needle stab her shoulder...

Joséphine opened her eyes in a dark and uncomfortable room. She was fully clothed again. The thought made her shiver. She rose from her straw mattress. The only source of light, a peephole in her door, opened onto a brightly lit corridor with many other doors. She hoped that Leonard and Randolph were in one of the other rooms. She was about to call out when she saw two frighteningly unnatural female creatures pass by. They were both strange and animal-like.

With her mind on fire, the young woman sat down to think. She was surely in the presence of what Felifax has been looking for. A surreptitious smile lit up her face.

When Grace opened her eyes, she was no longer in the car. She was stretched out, on a litter under a canvas tent, her hands and feet bound. The aftereffects of chloroform still clouded her thoughts. She then realized that it wasn't a canvas tent. The jolts that rocked her made her think she was inside a truck. She drifted back to sleep.

At last, she awoke. Through a crack between two planks, she could see that the truck she was being held in was traveling at high speed along a dusty high road. It took a few more hours before her journey came to an end.

Several natives untied her limbs and guided her swiftly into a courtyard. The layout reminded her of an ashram. Her captors took her into a luxurious mansion. She was going to meet her captor.

There, in a vast white room, sitting on a cushioned throne, the young Englishwoman gagged in shock and fear. She found herself face to face with a ghost.

She was forced to kneel and bow before him. He clapped his hands.

"You!" he ordered one of the men. "Go and get the beverage to make her talk! I have a lot of questions about Felifax. I'm told he's here, in India, but I can't find out where. I'm counting on you, impure woman, to tell me more..."

A strong wind was blowing across the cliff where Felifax and Mowgli had eventually set up their camp, between two massive boulders. The tiger-man was studying the fortified farmhouse through binoculars, while Mowgli stood watch. They were aided by the acuity of Chil's piercing eyes. They were trying to gauge the enemy's strength, the resilience of its defenses, and anticipate any unpleasant surprises that might be in store for them.

Meanwhile, spurred by her hatred, Joséphine had called her companions and, to her relief, they had responded. They were held in other cells in the same corridor. But she knew that her cries might also have raised the alarm. She purposefully told them her plan in German, so as to be understood by any prying ears.

"I've got things to tell you that you don't know," she said. "We're just ahead of Felifax. The problem is getting our jailers to understand that we're here on business. They are, after all, Europeans like us. But the circumstances of our meeting put us in the worst possible situation. I had to kill one of them..."

His companions voiced their surprise.

"They mistook me for a prey, so I did what I could to disabuse them of that notion," continued the young woman. "Now it's going to be difficult to meet their master for a chat. They'll have a hard time admitting that I'm the one they should be talking to. Did they ask you anything?"

"No, boss," Randolph replied.

"If they're Europeans, they can't leave us here to rot," declared Leonard.

"Let's hope not," concluded Joséphine.

Later, as Leonard and Randolph were taken out of their cells, Joséphine reflected that her plan seemed to be going along well. She had every confidence in her men's intelligence.

They didn't pass by her cell, so she couldn't see the faces of the guards who were taking them away. Both men had recoiled at their sight. They were young, almost children; one was a woman covered in fur with clawed hands; the other, a male who could barely stand on his own legs, his face twisted by animalistic features, with a mouth filled with sharp teeth.

As Leonard and Randolph crossed the courtyard on their way to what might have been a refurbished outbuilding, they could only reflect upon their unhuman guards. Their thoughts were filled with fear.

They were taken into a dark, empty room and tied up in two chairs. They didn't have time to settle down, as two men entered through a door opening onto a strange, ghastly laboratory, the sight of which only added to their anxiety. The two men wore white coats and sat down opposite them. They looked unsympathetic, as well as unhealthy. They each sported a long scar on their bald heads.

"Let's begin, Wilhelm!" said the first man who sported a moustache worthy of the Kaiser.

"Yes, Karl," replied Wilhelm, who had a moon-like face. Then, turning towards Joséphine's henchmen, he asked: "What were you doing in the middle of nowhere?"

"We were looking for you," answered Leonard.

The two Germans laughed sardonically.

"No one knows we exist," replied Karl curtly.

"When I say you, I meant your creations," added Leonard.

"How did you find out about them?" growled Wilhelm.

"Our boss doesn't tell us her secrets. We just obey," cut in Randolph, judging that it was better to say as little as possible.

"Your boss?" asked Wilhelm.

"The woman we're with," replied Randolph.

"You've met her, I believe," added Leonard smugly, thinking of the man Joséphine had stabbed

"Ah yes, indeed, we have!" chuckled the two Germans so wickedly that Leonard wanted to leap up in a fit of rage, but was stopped by the ties binding him to the chair. Randolph had stiffened. Suddenly, he shouted:

"What do you want from us?"

"Why are our creatures of interest to your boss?" asked Wilhelm.

"I don't know. We're her tools; she's the brain of the operation, and everything works fine that way," replied Randolph.

"I don't think subordinates like you would understand her plans anyway," added Leonard, who had calmed down.

Karl leapt up, furious, but his companion held him back.

"Calm down. We've got to report this to the Master," he said.

The two Germans went inside the central building that stood opposite the massive gate that closed off the fortified compound. They kept a low profile. They soon found themselves in a luxurious office in front of a tall Chinese man in traditional dress sitting behind a desk, and his servant, standing up straight behind the back of his master's carved chair.

"Interesting," said the Master. "How did this woman make you feel?"

"She's a real fury; she killed our technician," replied Wilhelm.

"She's their boss; we've heard her talk to the men," added Karl.

"Leave now. I need to think about this," said the tall Chinese man, dismissing the two Germans with a wave of his hand.

Sitting cross-legged under a waterproof tarpaulin, Felifax saw, through his binoculars, the large gate of the compound open and a lone man ride away at full speed.

On a not-too-distant hillside, another pair of binoculars were tracking the same movements. On one of the hands holding them, the brown wrist was encircled by a thick leather lace that barely hid a small coin.

"The village chief was right. These are the men we've been tracking. But we're not alone in our quest. The One We Seek is also here. We must send a carrier pigeon to alert the Great One as soon as possible!" said the watcher to his companion.

Thanks to his feline nature, with every meter he ran, Felifax covered a little more ground as he climbed the steep hillside where the fortified farmhouse was located. Mowgli followed in his footsteps, the scent of their enemies growing stronger by the minute. He wondered what Felifax would look like once they got to the compound.

Behind them, the wolves followed, but more cautiously. They wouldn't be joining in the battle—too many firearms were likely to be involved.

Mowgli caught up with Felifax on the narrow walkway overlooking the compound. He quickly understood why he'd been so outrageously outdistanced when he met the terrible yellow gaze of his companion. The jungle man felt an unpleasant sensation and decided to keep his distance.

Felifax headed for the refurbished outbuilding. It wasn't locked. The tiger-man felt his rage rise again when he saw the laboratory. The sight of the tiger-man came as a shock to the first one who saw him enter. The incongruous sound of metallic instruments crashing to the floor was soon replaced by an alarm, which the hapless man had time to give before he fell beneath Felifax's claws.

Karl stopped when he saw Felifax. He turned around and quickly locked himself in an adjacent office, but Felifax wasn't in the mood to play...

Mowgli headed for the main building, which they had identified as the one where the abducted women were being kept. It was well guarded, with a sentry earnestly pacing in front. But instead, the wolf-brother elected to climb onto the roof, where only the sentries from the main gate could see him.

The building was unadorned, quadrilateral in shape, with only small, high windows. It was dark inside. Armed with a dagger, Mowgli attacked the nearest window next to the least exposed gable.

The dimly-lit interior stank like a stable, and occasional moans could be heard. Mowgli approached one of the doors. Through the peephole, he saw pregnant women shackled on straw mattresses. He set about to freeing them. The shackles meant minimal surveillance. This explained the calmness of the place. He quickly convinced the women that silence was vital.

Twenty women or so, in various stages of pregnancy, had already been re-leased when the wolf-brother came to a separating door that opened onto another row of cells. The exit was on the other side. He heard words being spoken in a foreign tongue.

Suddenly, out of the depths of the building came a creature Mowgli had never seen before. A strange being, savage and menacing, who frightened him. The beast knocked on the doors of several cells and bellowed orders for silence.

The massive oaken office door shattered like balsa wood. Felifax grabbed the first man ahead of him and threw him at a Chinese guard who, surprised, fired at him. Karl aimed his gun at the tiger man's chest and shot.

The gunshots had now alerted the entire garrison. Shots were also heard coming from the sentries at the main gate and from the pregnant women's prison.

Everyone, armed men and monsters alike, seemed to be converging upon the main building.

Meanwhile, Mowgli had seized the opportunity to lead the women towards the exit. But a woman's voice calling for help made him retrace his steps. It was Joséphine's voice that had pierced the sounds of chaos.

The unopposed women rushed towards the main gate but when they opened the only exit to flee, they found themselves facing a small army of native men arriving on horses. Listening to one of them, they took off running towards the now wide-open central building. The newcomers took no notice of them.

Without waiting, nooses in hand, the Phansigars—for it was they—entered the building and immediately got down to business. Protected by the asphyxiated bodies of their victims, they moved expertly from neck to neck.

Felifax, wounded by Karl's bullet, was enraged and the thugees' interruption did not soften his mood. He crossed the room in two strides. Faced with his wrath, the Phansigars crouched down and bent over, heads bowed, hands clasped over their third eyes.

"Grant us thy mercy, O revered son of Kali!" they begged.

This plea stopped Felifax in his tracks. His troubled mind turned to the religion that had ennobled him. As he calmed down, the assault came to an end. The house troops were dead, or in flight; their commanders kept a low profile. The trouble seemed to have died down

The thugees rose to their feet.

"Will you follow us, my lord? They're waiting for us outside," said the man in charge of the assault, while his fellow soldiers tied up the remaining prisoners.

"These men must be taken to Benares," ordered Felifax, before following the thugee.

"I understand," was the man's laconic reply.

The sight of the muddy courtyard where the surviving parties had instinctively gathered filled Mowgli and Felifax's hearts with a sense of failure.

The horsemen guarding the gate stepped aside to let a magnificent new rider enter. The rain seemed to have had no effect on him. Wearing a handsome, gray turban in which a blood-red ruby seemed to light up the day, he had a victorious smile on his lips.

Felifax blushed. The sight of this brahmin almost overwhelmed him. The man was none other than Sourina, once the chief Brahman of the temple of Kali, the one who had turned him into a hybrid to fulfill his warlike obsessions, a man

610

who had not hesitated to become an assassin in order to satisfy his old grievances.

Sourina was supposed to have taken his own life in order to escape English justice. But now, at the sight of this revenant, rage completely overtook Felifax. He leapt towards Sourina, roaring.

Nooses flew like fronds from the four corners of the courtyard. Lacking air, the tiger-man collapsed, almost asphyxiated.

Sourina passed by him without a glance and guided his mount towards the nondescript creatures, the wounded, and the abnormal number of pregnant women.

When he saw Joséphine Balsamo, still stunningly beautiful despite everything that had happened, he stopped to observe her. She seemed to be daring him to do anything more.

Sourina, impassive, went towards the house.

"Bring me the leaders!" he ordered with a sweep of his hand, encompassing the entire compound.

The Phsansigars obeyed and quickly gathered the few surviving German and Chinese prisoners. But their Master had disappeared.

Gradually, Felifax regained consciousness and air once again filled his lungs. Rehaining his human form, weakened, he approached Mowgli.

"We're outnumbered," he said. "We must withdraw. But we're only temporarily out of the game."

"I'm with you."

They left surreptitiously. Outside, Naka, having seen the unexpected reinforcements arrive at the fortified farmhouse, had taken the initiative to summon his brothers. Together, they set off for the temporary camp.

Chil circled high above the compound.

Back to their waterproof tarpaulin, Felifax kept watch. Shortly afterwards, he saw Sourina setting off again with his men, Joséphine at his side, followed by Leonard and Randolph. Further on, a covered wagon was taking away the prisoners and the women. The tiger-man was upset; he had hoped to save them. He could not let the evil Brahmin triumph.

But Sourina suddenly moved up the column of prisoners. He looked in Felifax's direction and, as if the tiger-man could see him, ostentatiously planted a spear with something attached to it floating in the wind. Then, he laughed and waved goodbye.

Mowgli called Naka and issued some quick instructions. Soon, the wolf returned with the spear, although he guessed that the little bun of hair hanging from it was the real message.

Felifax snatched it away furiously. His anger made Mowgli recoil, and he waited at a distance until the tiger-man was ready to talk. Then he saw Rama silently weeping over the little bun.

"This is my wife's hair and her wedding ring," explained Felifax. "This monster is holding Grace prisoner. I must free her, my friend, for who knows what he can do to her just to break me."

"Naka will soon find their trail and we shall follow, Rama," replied Mowgli.

The = next day, the two companions resumed their hunt, now with a sense of urgency.

"If Sourina meddles in Edward Sexton's legacy, he could become even more dangerous," explained Felifax. "If he got wind of the avatar, he'll do any-thing to make it his own. This might finally allow him to wage a holy war against the British."

Sourina hadn't been on horseback for a long time, but his pride forbade him to show his tiredness, especially as the woman accompanying him rode her mount as if she'd been born on it.

Everyone entered the temple on the outskirts of Simla completely exhaust-ed. The waters of one of the women had broken and her companions were rush-ing to help her.

The Brahmin ordered his men to sort things out: the prisoners were to be locked up, but Joséphine and her two acolytes were to be installed in comforta-ble apartments. Then he took a well-deserved rest.

When Sourina awoke, he wrote a few letters, then went to the stables. There, sitting on a bed of straw, Grace Palmer, her head shaved, looked at him without lowering her eyes. Sourina reveled in her angry look.

"You'll be happy to know that I've bumped into your husband," he said. "Obviously, he didn't know at first that you're my prisoner, but I informed him of the fact."

*At last!* thought Grace. *It wouldn't be much longer now.*

Then Sourina left her, carefully closing the *gurbi* that was her prison. He had no empathy and couln't imagine how much learning of Felifax's nearby presence had brought balm to Grace's heart. He then headed for the prison and asked one of his new prisoners to come along.

"My name's Karl," said the man.

Sourina made a gesture of annoyance.

"You'll leave with one of my men. Take him to the one you call 'Master' and give him this," the Brahmin said, holding out a letter. "My man will bring me back his answer."

Karl thought the Brahmin was unlikely to receive an answer, but looked forward to being free again.

Sourina opened his eyes. It took him a moment to realize that it wasn't his ceiling he was looking at. This was not his room, and, through the window, it became clear that this was not his familiar landscape. He swore; he sat up on his bed. Who had dared! A terrible rage tinged with fear overcame him.

The door curtain parted and a man entered, carrying a meal on a stove.

"The Master welcomes you to this humble abode," said the servant.

He clapped his hands and a woman came in carrying a breakfast tray.

"Who is he? Where am I? Answer!" the Brahmin shouted.

"Take your time. Eat. the Master wants you to feel at home. He'll see you later."

But Sourina would have none of it. He grabbed the servant by the shoulder, but, without knowing how, he flew over the man's shoulder and fell hard to the ground.

"The Master will see you later," repeated the man. "Please take your time."

Although his rage and curiosity were undiminished, Sourina thought it best to act in a more civilized manner.

When he felt restored and ready, feeling more confident, he went out the way the servants had come in. Another servant had been waiting for him to come out.

"This way, please," said the man, inviting him to follow.

Sourina nodded.

They arrived in a room worthy of China's most lavish imperial palace. On a throne at the back, a child was lazing about. At this unexpected arrival, he straightened up and looked bravely at the Brahmin. Then, discreetly, he appeared to change.

Sourina stared at him, transfixed. He approached the prodigy and, overcome with emotion, greeted the monkey-child.

He was in the middle of his meditation when men came from all sides, looking menacing. Annoyed by this disturbance, Sourina turned sharply, ready to complain, when he saw a majestic, austere and sinister figure standing in the middle of the vast room.

The Brahmin had no trouble recognizing him, as his face had often appeared on the front pages of the English press. For the West, he was the embodiment of evil. He was Doctor Fu Manchu.

*Translated by Jean-Marc & Randy Lofficier.*

*David Vineyard's latest clever caper is, as usual, a perfect little thriller that fits neatly in both Arsène Lupin's later years, left relatively unchronicled by Maurice Leblanc, and, this case, Sexton Blake's adventures. Also, kudos for bringing in Paul Temple from the rather forgotten 1938 BBC radio serial...*

## David L. Vineyard: *The Thief of Light and Shadows*

*Paris, 1922*

Arsène Lupin, his white tie and tails and scarlet-lined cloak impeccable, moved across the room quickly and quietly. His hands were gloved in white silk and a jaunty angled top hat sat on his head—the only jarring piece of his wardrobe—and a domino mask that had replaced his famous monocle.

The room consisted of heavy furniture and a vaguely Asian motif, filled with an eclectic variety of antiquities and artistic pieces ranging from Ming vases to delicate carved ivory and jade figures, but Lupin ignored all of these and instead closed in on a Chinese silk screen depicting cranes upon a calm lake among the reeds obscuring part of one damasked papered wall.

Reaching that screen Lupin quickly moved it, revealing a formidable looking wall safe in the wall behind it. Lupin swiftly bent his ear to it and his white gloved fingers began to turn the dial.

Bright light suddenly filled the room.

Lupin, ever Lupin, as if expecting this sudden interference, turned toward the figure across the room from him. It was a man, a remarkable man, tall, but bent and twisted, a Chinese dressed in the long robes of his culture, moving oddly as if gliding across the floor like a serpent, his fangs a Browning automatic which pointed unwavering at the white expanse of Lupin's immaculate dress shirt.

"I think I have you," said Hanoi Shan, one-time governor of a province in Indochina, now the wealthiest and most dangerous fence in Paris. "A pleasure long delayed, Monsieur Lupin."

"Alas," Lupin said, "not delayed as long as I might like."

A twisted smile curled Shan's lip. "I take your point, but quite timely for me. You are after the Louis XIV Emerald I presume?"

Lupin shrugged, careful not to lower his raised hands enough to tempt Shan to shoot. "The pride of your collection, set in diamonds and emeralds, carved of pure ivory with gold inlay and, of course, priceless because of its provenance."

"You know it well. I am impressed, indeed. I have long wanted to meet you... I have made inroads of course."

"So I noticed. But I fear doing business with you comes at too high a price.

Too many who have done so seem to have been found floating face down in the Seine, or betrayed to Madame Guillotine. However much pleasure doing business with you might have been, it is not worth losing my head over it."

"Perhaps it is as you say. My business requires certain sacrifices to the gods of law and order, I fear."

"Ah, is that my fate? A sacrifice to the law?"

Hanoi Shan shook his head. "Pointless in your case. No, I am sorry, Monsieur Lupin, but in your case, the solution must be permanent. A pity, but there is no other choice. Farewell, Arsène Lupin."

And with that, Hanoi Shan raised his automatic and fired at point blank range at Lupin's chest.

*"Cut!"*

"Excellent, excellent ! Bravo, Monsieur Novello! Your Lupin is perfection, and Monsieur Pratt, your Hanoi Shan shall make you a star."

Ivor Novello, the British matinée idol, removed the top hat, mask, gloves, cloak, and white silk scarf, handing them to the costumer; his handsome features were marked by a sheen of perspiration. It was close and hot under the lights on the set. "You are too generous, Monsieur Feuillade, but I do agree that Mr. Pratt was superb."

William Henry Pratt blushed, though no one noticed beneath his heavy makeup. In his own soft near lisp, rather than the sing song of Hanoi Shan, he accepted the compliment and added how happy he was to be on the screen with Ivor Novello, the actor and song writer. "No one will recognize me under all this, but I will know I did a solid job."

Dismissing both actors with praise, and sending them off set as this was the last shot of the day, film director Louis Feuillade turned to his three guests who sat behind the cameras watching, as the crew shut down for the night.

"Well, Monsieur Blake, what do you think of our little endeavor?"

"Fascinating," said Sexton Blake, the other master sleuth of Baker Street. "Of course, I never crossed swords—so to speak—with Lupin, at least not as far as I know, but I must admit Novello captures him as I picture him in my mind. And this fellow Pratt is a real discovery. His Hanoi Shan sent chills down my spine."

"Mine as well," said a younger Englishman rising from next to Blake. This was Paul Temple, fairly recently down from Oxford and already making a reputation as a mystery writer and expert on crime. "Tell me, Ashton-Wolfe, you at least knew Hanoi Shan. How well does Mr. Pratt do at capturing him?" Temple asked of the third man.

H. Ashton-Wolfe, the man who had captured Hanoi Shan, seen him guillotined, and written of him in his book *Warped in the Making*, smiled and rose from his chair as well. "Physically, perhaps not a true match, but he has the man's presence down perfectly. I admit, merely watching him move with that peculiar serpent-like gait poor Shan had after an elephant broke his back sent shivers along my spine."

"Tell me," Blake asked, "this Louis XIV emerald mentioned in the script, I recall reading about it at the time as one of Shan's treasures, but was it ever recovered? I don't suppose Lupin actually stole it?"

"Not that he didn't want to," Ashton-Wolfe said, "but the Emerald disappeared after Shan was arrested, and he never spoke of it during his trial, not even before his death. I myself interrogated him over it. We hoped when we found Shan's safe that the Emerald would be in it, but no such luck. We never cracked it and were too afraid to blow it and risk destroying what might be in it. If that fellow Lanyard, the they call the Lone Wolf, hadn't reformed, we might have had to go shopping to find a cracksman capable of getting into it. We were already letting out feelers all over the world for one equal to the job from old Smiler Bunn to that American they call the Gray Seal—set a crook to catch a crook as the old saying goes."

"As a matter of fact, gentlemen, the safe you see before you is the actual safe from Hanoi Shan's living quarters," Feuillade added. "In fact, this entire set is a recreation of the room we found it in, save that Shan's quarters actually had a ceiling, of course. Even the silk screen is taken from the rooms and stands exactly where police photos showed it. Almost all the items on the set, down to the rugs, have been loaned to us by the authorities. As far as it can be, these are Hanoi Shan's rooms, down to the matte paintings of the view from his windows. We called in Monsieur Aston-Wolfe as a technical expert but, though the Sûreté, he informed us he was departing for the Far East on a matter for the Foreign Office. Luckily for us, the very next morning he called us himself to tell us his departure would be delayed and he would be delighted to help."

"And what detective wouldn't want one of his greatest triumphs celebrated on screen by Monsieur Louis Feuillade, the director of so many masterpieces of crime," Ashton-Wolfe commented, bowing slightly toward the director. "Don't you agree, Mr. Blake?"

Blake was fiddling with his pipe, "Oh, I dare say, certainly. Can't say I've been quite so lucky. The films based on my exploits tend to be all blood and thunder, and no detective work. You would think all I had to do was send Tinker, my assistant, out for pipe tobacco, and the next thing you know, I'm up to my neck in attractive ladies in distress and colorful criminal masterminds chasing them down foggy London alleys with old Toby, my hound, baying after them on a leash."

"Considering that rogues' gallery of yours, it's no surprise," Temple remarked. "Rhymer, Waldo, Zenith, that Plummer chap... Monsieur Feuillade should take up your casebook next, you and that American Carter seem to have a corner on exotic crime and colorful adversaries."

"Ah," the director said before Blake could speak, "You expose my further motive, Monsieur Temple. I hoped that once Monsieur Blake saw us at work on this film, he would be intrigued enough to let me film one his adventures."

Ivor Novello had just rejoined them, wearing his own clothes with a white silk scarf at his neck. "Monsieur Feuillade would invite that infamous Chinese doctor to watch a filming if he thought he could get the inside track on filming one of his adventures, no doubt. He practically kidnapped me in London to play Lupin in this one, though I must admit it is a fascinating role. I only hope the real Lupin likes my performance. I shouldn't want to get on his wrong side."

"You?" joined Pratt who, back to his normal appearance, was tall and slender with dramatic eyebrows, hauntingly shadowed eyes, and a long high cheeked boned face. "I'm the one playing a murderer."

"A quite dead one, I assure you," Aston-Wolfe said. "I was at his execution and he pulled none of Monsieur Feuillade's Fantômas-like tricks with the guillotine. Monster he may have been, even, as we suspected, an associate of the Si Fan, but he was no Devil Doctor. No, Monsieur Pratt, he rests comfortably in his grave."

"Good to know," Pratt said. "I fear I may not be cut out for playing murderers and monsters. Perhaps drawing room comedy is my true forte."

"Well, gentlemen," Feuillade said. "Much as I would love to pick all your brains, I have rushes to watch, and Messrs. Novello and Pratt are due in make-up at 5 a.m. If you, gentlemen, wish to join us for the big scene tomorrow ,when Lupin cracks the safe only to find there's no King's Emerald inside, you should get some rest."

"Yes, yes," Ashton-Wolfe said hurriedly. "I have some pressing business on my desk I must deal with this very night."

The group broke up. The two actors went back to their hotel to study the script and go to bed early; the director to see his rushes, and Ashton-Wolfe to return to 13 Quai de Orfèvres and his offices to work on "criminal matters," as he said, leaving Blake and Temple to go their own way.

"I've booked an early table at Maxim's on the Rue Royale," Temple said. "Why don't we repair to our rooms and change and meet for drinks at the Savoy's Bar before heading out to dinner?"

Blake nodded his agreement. He rather wanted to think about the events of the day, but Paris was no city for dining alone in a hotel room, and the young man seemed to have a good head on him to bounce ideas off of.

The two men met for drinks, then shared a cab to the restaurant, and after returning to their hotel, found a quiet corner and ordered brandy to sip with after dinner cigars.

"I'm here as a writer," Temple said, "but I must admit to some curiosity as to what brings the famous Sexton Blake to watch a film being made. I have trouble believing that mere curiosity about how films are being made is all there is to your presence. You could do that in any studio in England."

"You should become a detective yourself, Temple," Blake said, twirling his brandy in the bubble glass. "You might find yourself just as successful at solving crime as writing about it. Of course, you are absolutely right. I am here because of far more than just watching a film being made."

"Ah," Temple said. "May I hazard the Louis XIV emerald and Arsène Lupin..."

"Precisely! The jewel, when it was originally stolen by the Italian Dr. Nikola and found its way into the hands of Hanoi Shan, was insured by Lloyds of London for some quarter of a million pounds. After the theft, I was asked to try to negotiate a return of the stone for a percentage of its value, but before I could reach Paris, Ashton-Wolfe and the police had pounced on Hanoi Shan and arrested him. Like many I'd hoped the jewel would be found in Shan's safe, but it was not, and Shan went to his grave without revealing so much as a word about its location. When I heard this film was being made, and that the actual rooms Shan lived in were being recreated, it seemed like one final shot at the thing."

"And Lupin?"

"The fly in the ointment, Temple, and a particularly annoying one. If I thought the film might be an opportunity to find the jewel, it would be sheer folly to imagine Lupin would think any less. You have no doubt read of his obsession with the treasures of the Kings of France. Can you imagine he would let any chance for seizing this one pass?

"And when Lupin strikes...?"

"I intend to be right there. Perhaps I'll have better luck than my former neighbor, now beekeeping in Sussex. In any case, it is my belief that, sometime tomorrow, Lupin will make a try for the jewel, and hopefully reveal its hiding place to me and himself at the same time. Now, I'm afraid I have to beg off. I have an early meeting in the morning with some government officials and I can't afford to be dozing when Lupin does make his move—assuming he makes one at all."

Blake rose and said his goodnight, but Temple sat in his chair and exchanged his cigar for a more contemplative pipe. When he was invited to observe the filming of the latest Louis Feuillade epic, he had been at a cocktail party in Paris, celebrating his latest book. Aside from his curiosity about the process, and the opportunity to do some pleasurable research, like Blake, he had been intrigued about the unanswered questions surrounding Hanoi Shan and Arsène Lupin.

There were rumors, nothing more than that, but still intriguing, that Lupin had encountered Shan long before in Indochina, when he'd impersonated M. Lenormand, but then, rumors about men like Lupin and Shan always circulated.

Temple, as a crime writer, had long followed Lupin's career—a gentleman adventurer, a master criminal, and a more than fair detective in the same category as Blake and his former neighbor. He was to modern crime what Houdini was to magic. Lupin was far more than a clever criminal, he was the prince of crime, a figure almost too fantastic to be real, his exploits reading like fantastic fictions when they were, in fact, absolutely true.

Whether or not any of those questions would be answered or not, the next day was still open. With a sigh, Temple knocked his pipe out in a heavy glass ashtray and took a last sip of the brandy. Whatever else tomorrow was going to be, it would be an interesting day.

Temple rose. He had already signed the bill. He was suddenly tired, but he didn't imagine he would sleep all that well. A mysterious Chinese with a gait like a serpent and a faceless man in a jaunty top hat and monocle were going to haunt his dreams.

Feeling more refreshed than he expected, Temple rose early, but a call to Blake's rooms to see if he wanted to join him for breakfast revealed the detective was already gone. He had said he was leaving early, and meant it.

After a light breakfast of a brioche and coffee, while reading the London papers the hotel provided, Temple was just putting the last touches to his appearance when the phone rang, telling him that the studio had sent a car for him.

Once at the studio, he was escorted to the set and found the director waiting for him, but no Blake and no Ashton-Wolfe.

"I can't imagine what is keeping Monsieur Blake, but I'm sure Ashton-Wolfe has been called away on duty. A shame really. Anyway, you are here to enjoy the day," said Feuillade.

Temple nodded.

"I admit," the director went on, "I prefer shooting on location as I did for so much of *Fantômas* during the War or for *Les Vampires*, but with the chance to recreate Hanoi Shan's apartments, a studio was necessary. There is no way to crowd my cameras into the actual location. In any case, I think we can offer you an exciting day, Mr. Temple."

*More exciting than you may expect*, Temple thought, if Blake is right, but he saw no need to disturb the director.

It was still sometime before the actual filming and Temple wandered around the set, occasionally asking one of the crew questions. They were busy setting up the cameras and lighting, making sure every item was in its place and the actors' marks had been clearly designated.

Novello, he was told, was still having the final touches to his makeup applied, and Feuillade was busy discussing with him what he wanted. Today, all eyes and the camera would be on Novello's Lupin.

Temple checked his watch several times, wondering what was keeping Blake, who had been so interested in observing the filming of this scene. And whatever Ashton-Wolfe was up to, Temple doubted that he had been called away on any business not related to this set and this film.

Temple was not superstitious, but the hair at the nape of his neck was tickling, and he found he was anticipating much more than watching a film being made. The closer it got to filming the scene, the more he wished Blake was there. For a writer who dabbled in mystery, he had little patience with unsolved ones.

An air of anticipation hung over the film set, and Temple found himself looking at every shadow, studying the faces of every crew member as if one of them might by Lupin in disguise, and knowing that, with Lupin, that was entirely possible.

Did Lupin linger behind some drapery, just beyond his sight, ready to pounce? Was he above in the scaffolding, with one of the men manning the lights? Was Lupin even here, or were Blake and Ashton-Wolfe wrong and Lupin had somehow already obtained the jewel—if a jewel even existed and hadn't been cut and sold in pieces a decade earlier?

Now, the stage was set. Feuillade took his chair after checking with the cameraman and the lighting. The light on the set was lowered, a single spot focused stage right, and as the clip board snapped shut and the director ordered action, the room became silent.

A figure slowly appeared in the light. It was Novello, again dressed in white tie, cloak, top hat, and this time, the familiar monocle rather than a domino mask. He advanced slowly across the set as he had before, paused to remove the silk screen with its cranes standing in calm waters...

A hand gripped Temple's shoulder.

He almost cried out, but instead turned. Behind him stood Sexton Blake, holding one finger to his lips for silence. His grip on Temple's shoulder was tight. His lean features were tense and his whole body seemed as if he might spring like a tiger at the least provocation.

Removing his finger from his lips, he nodded his head toward Novello now listening as he opened the safe and formed one word.

"Lupin."

Temple turned, riveted now to the figure twirling the dials of the safe.

It couldn't be. Even Lupin would not be that brazen. And anyway, everyone knew the safe was empty. The whole point was that the safe was empty. This was the story of Lupin's single failure, not his triumph.

And yet, Blake poised to strike had formed one word, one word that changed everything, that sent Temple's head spinning and opened up avenues of speculation that flashed like fireworks in his head. The whole world seemed to pivot on that single unspoken words:

"Lupin"

Lupin the criminal. Lupin the thief. Lupin the extraordinary. Arsène Lupin...

Now, the safe was opening. Novello, or Lupin, whoever, seemed to savor taking forever to open its door. Then, a small spot light illuminated the interior of the safe—revealing that it was empty.

Here, the script called for Lupin/Novello to pause. Show surprise, and then turn to the camera for a close up showing him smiling raffishly at the big joke that and been played on him.

But the cloaked figure did not pause or turn to the camera. Instead, he reached into the safe, his hand and arm blocking Temple from seeing what he was doing. Blake's hand was like a vise on his shoulder.

Slowly, so slowly to be painful, Lupin—for now, Temple had no doubt Blake was right and it was Lupin—withdrew his hand and turned it up for the spotlight, holding forth the Louis XIV emerald, intact and sparkling brilliantly.

There were gasps in the room.

Feuillade cried out, "For the love of God, keep the camera turning!"

Blake had let go of Temple's shoulder. A policeman's whistle blew loudly behind Temple.

"Lupin," shouted Blake. "It's Lupin."

Now, Temple saw several gendarmes who had been standing in the darkness just off set spring toward Lupin, who still held the jewel in his right hand. But it was Lupin's right hand that moved and caught Temple's eye.

And suddenly, as his eye focused on it, the hand lifted and something was thrown.

Blinding light and heavy smoke filled the room.

An illusionist's trick, a simple glass globe that, when broken, spewed a flash of blinding light and smoke. Absolutely harmless as anyone who had ever seen a magician work would know, but startling enough to stun everyone in the room, just long enough for Lupin to vanish.

The place was chaotic for nearly three hours as police questioned everyone and searched every nook and cranny of the set, from the scaffolding to the broom closets. In the end, they found Ivor Novello in his dressing room, gagged and tied up, but unharmed. That and nothing more—not a single thing.

No sign that Lupin had ever been on the set; no sign that he had ever entered the studio. Not a single witness, not a single clue.

Temple was drawn to the safe and was examining it when Blake walked over to his side after most of the gendarmes had left.

"A shame Ashton-Wolfe missed this," Temple said. "In some ways, it all started with his arrest of Hanoi Shan."

"I suppose," Blake said, "but then, he might have had a difficult time getting here from Saigon."

"Saigon?"

"Yes, Saigon, where Ashton-Wolfe has been for the last month on the orders of the Foreign Office. That was my appointment this morning, cutting through the bureaucratic red tape to finally find one senior Minister who would confirm that Ashton-Wolfe has indeed been in Saigon, busy with government business the entire time this film has been in development."

"Then Ashton-Wolfe was..."

"Arsène Lupin, yes. He must have known I suspected him. That's why he disappeared last night. Once I was sure, I contacted the police and was assigned the gendarmes you saw to cover the studio, but alas..."

"So the charade today was some last minute bit of business?"

"A backup perhaps, but certainly not his original plan. I imagine he planned to remove the stone as Ashton-Wolfe without anyone ever knowing it, likely after the set had been struck when there would have been fewer people about, and as Ashton-Wolfe, he could also claim he was overseeing the collection of Hanoi Shan's flat. But last night, he must have caught a hint that I was visiting the Foreign Office this morning, and decided his plans had to change. However brazenly, he would have to steal the jewel on camera in front of the crew, the police, and if I may sound immodest, me."

"Sounds like Lupin, audacious and blatant, but what I still don't get is the jewel. We've all seen inside this safe, it was empty, it has been empty since Hanoi Shan was arrested."

"It has also been inaccessible since Shan was arrested, locked away where even Lupin might hesitate to tread. No, this was the best chance he would get, and Ashton-Wolfe the perfect disguise. As for the jewel, it was where it always was, where Shan kept it all along... I don't know how Lupin found out... Did he deduce it as being the most obvious place where it could be? Or did he investigate the manufacturer of the safe, the Dale Company in the United States, and discover it that way? Perhaps both. He's thorough I'll give him that."

Temple shook his head, "I still don't see..."

"Take a look inside the safe," Blake said, handing Temple a small cigarette lighter to illuminate its interior.

Temple took the lighter and flicking the flame on peered into the safe. "There's a second door," he finally said. "A false back. All this time..."

"All this time the jewel was kept in a secret compartment in the back of the safe. How long has Lupin known this, how long has he been frustrated, unable to get to the jewel... It must have been irksome, to say the least, and how delighted he must be with today's exploit."

"I'd like to know how he got away," Temple said.

"Oh, that I can tell you," Blake replied. "You noticed that Mr. Pratt was in none of the scenes filmed today. Yet, while we were frantically searching the studio, a security guard informed me that Pratt had left shortly after all the commotion. I made a call and Mr. Pratt informed me that he was enjoying his day away from filming and had not even considered coming in to watch the filming..."

"Lupin."

"Lupin"

Temple was still examining the safe when he paused. "What's this then?" he asked pulling something out of the safe.

It was an envelope addressed to Sexton Blake of Baker Street. Blake took it and opened it carefully. A single piece of paper was folded shut. Blake withdrew it, opened it and read it aloud:

*Dear Sexton Blake,*

*I apologize for today's theatrics, I really had no intention to act so dramatically, but when I realized you were so close on my heels I had to innovate. I regret my attack on Mr. Novello whose impersonation of myself I greatly admire—something = which I hope you will inform him of—but needs must...*

*I had looked forward to matching wits with you, but I fear I nearly overplayed my hand and underestimated you. I must watch that in the future. Our friend the Beekeeper is not the only sharp mind in our line of work.*

*By the time you read this, I shall be well away, and the Louis XIV emerald will join those other treasures of the Kings of France under my protection. I may one day donate my collection for the enjoyment of the people of France, but as long as there are rogues like myself around, I feel that would be reckless.*

*Extend my thanks to Monsieur Feuillade and my best wishes for his film. I really can't wait to see how it plays out on screen. I still don't know how Lupin escaped that bullet Hanoi Shan fired at him in yesterday's filming, and I shan't rest until that is resolved.*

*With deepest regards,*
(and the letter was signed with the sprawling initials *A.L.*

Sexton Blake chuckled. "You mentioned my colorful collection of adversaries, did you not Temple? I think I have a new one to add at the top of the list, and a most distinguished one, wouldn't you say? Now,, we owe our host an explanation of the day's activities, then I think you and I should find a table at the Moulin Rouge, like two good English tourists, and toast our friend Lupin with a Brut of champagne as he is entitled to. What say you, my friend."

"I say," Paul Temple replied, "the first bottle is on me."

Blake laughed. "As our friend Lupin wrote, needs must when the devil drives."

# CREDITS

## *Essays & Reminiscences*

**Stephen R. BISSETTE** is a comic book artist and publisher with a focus on the horror genre. He is best known for his multiple award-winning collaborations with writer Alan Moore. He later published the horror anthology *Taboo* and created *Tyrant*, a comic book biography of a Tyrannosaurus rex. More recently, he has edited and published *Green Mountain Cinema* as well as five volumes of *Blur*, collecting his film reviews and criticism.

**Neil GAIMAN** is a British author of short fiction, novels, comic books, graphic novels, audio theatre, and a screenwriter. His works include the award-winning *Sandman* series and the novels *Good Omens, Stardust, Anansi Boys, American Gods, Coraline,* and *The Graveyard Book.* He has won numerous awards, including the Hugo, Nebula, and Bram Stoker awards, as well as the Newbery and Carnegie medals.

**Stuart GELZER** has translated Paul Féval's *The Hunchback* (2021), two *Harry Dickson* collections, Paul d'Ivoi's *Miss Musketeer* (2022) and *Queen of Illusions* (2023) for Black Coat Press. He is currently working on Frédéric Soulié's *The Devil's Memoirs.*

Margaret Astrid Lindholm Ogden, known by her pen names of **Robin HOBB** and Megan Lindholm is known for her fantasy novels set in the Realm of the Elderlings, which comprise the *Farseer, Liveship Traders* and *Tawny Man* trilogies, the *Rain Wild* chronicles, and the *Fitz and the Fool* trilogy. As Lindholm, she has written the urban fantasy novel *Wizard of the Pigeons* and several science fiction short stories.

**Stephen JONES** is a British editor of horror anthologies, and the author of several book-length studies of horror and fantasy films as well as an account of H. P. Lovecraft's early British publications. He and Kim Newman have edited several books together, including *Horror: 100 Best Books*, the 1988 horror volume in Xanadu's 100 Best series, *and Horror: Another 100 Best Books*, a 2005 sequel from Carroll & Graf.

**K. A. LAITY** is an award-winning author, scholar, filmmaker, critic, editor, and arcane artist. Current research includes medieval Scots, crime fiction/films, and the writings of Leonora Carrington. Her short film *Pomegranate* has had its first festival selection, and *A Fire Ritual for the Heart* was featured in the *Silent Fire* exhibition co-curated by the Yale Institute of Sacred Music and Nasty Women Connecticut. Her art has been appearing in galleries across the northeast.

**Randy LOFFICIER** has written a number of animation teleplays, including episodes of *Duck Tales* and *The Real Ghostbusters*, as well as collaborated with Jean-Marc on original comic-book series such as *Robur* and *Tiger & The Eye.* She is a member of the Writers Guild of America West and a lapsed member of the Mystery Writers of America.

**Tim LUCAS** is a film critic, biographer, novelist, screenwriter, blogger, and publisher and editor of the video review magazine *Video Watchdog*. In 2006, he became a published poet when he placed several poems in issues 13 and 14 of the British journal *The Ugly Tree*. In 2013, his first published short story, *Banishton*, appeared in the first issue of the British literary magazine *The Imperial Youth Review*.

**Frank J. MORLOCK** is a prolific translators of stage plays who has authored *Sherlock Holmes: The Grand Horizontals* (2006) for Black Coat Press and adapted the following: *Arsène Lupin vs Sherlock Holmes: The Stage Play; Cheri-Bibi; Frankenstein Meets the Hunchback of Notre-Dame; Gentlemen of the Night; Nick Carter vs. Fantômas; Lord Ruthven the Vampyre; The Return of Lord Ruthven; Lord Ruthven Begins; Rocambole; Sherlock Holmes vs Fantômas; Sherlock Holmes vs. Jack the Ripper; Sherlock Holmes, Fantomas, Lupin, Raffles and More: The Spanish Plays; Vidocq and the Lemonade Girl*; and *The Madwoman of Melun.*

**Kim NEWMAN**'s literary career began as a film reviewer and critic. His first stories were published in *Interzone*. In 1985, he wrote two non-fiction books, *Ghastly Beyond Belief* (with Neil Gaiman) and *Nightmare Movies*. His first novels were *The Night Mayor* (1989) and *Bad Dreams* (1990). The publication of *Anno Dracula* (1992) established him as a major name in horror fiction. That series continued with *The Bloody Red Baron* (1995) and *Judgment of Tears* (1998). Other novels by Kim include *Jago* (1991), *The Quorum* (1994) and *Life's Lottery* (1999). Kim's short story collections include *The Original Dr. Shade* (1994), *Famous Monsters* (1995), *Seven Stars* (2000), *Where the Bodies are Buried* (2000) and *Unforgivable Stories* (2000).

**Sharan NEWMAN** is a medieval historian and author. Rather than teach, she chose to write novels set in the Middle Ages, including three Arthurian fantasies and ten mysteries set in 12th-century France, featuring Catherine Levendeur, a one-time student of Heloise at the Paraclete; her husband, Edgar, an Anglo-Scot; and Solomon, a Jewish merchant of Paris. The Levendeur series has been nominated for many awards. Sharan won the Macavity Award for best first mystery for *Death Comes As Epiphany* and the Herodotus Award for best historical mystery of 1998 for *Cursed in the Blood*. The most recent book in the series *The Witch in the Well* won the Bruce Alexander award for best historical mystery of 2004.

**Henry Lion OLDIE** is the pen name of Ukrainian science fiction and fantasy writers Dmitry Gromov and Oleg Ladyzhensky. Both authors reside in Kharkiv, Ukraine, and write in Russian. At Eurocon 2006 in Kyiv, the European Science Fiction Society named them Europe's best writers of 2006.

**David J. SCHOW** is the author of many horror novels, short stories, and screenplays. His credits include films such as *Leatherface: The Texas Chainsaw Massacre III, The Crow* and *The Hills Run Red*. Most of his work falls into the subgenre splatterpunk, a term he is sometimes credited with coining. In the 1990s, Schow wrote a regular column for *Fangoria* magazine, later collected in the book *Wild Hairs*, which won the International Horror Guild's award for best non-fiction in 2001.

**Michael SHREVE** is a prolific translator who has adapted the following titles for Black Coat Press: *Enemy Force* (2008), *Spiridon* (2009), *Lamekis* (2010), nine *Madame Atomos* novels, *The Child Who Walked on the Sky* (2012), *The Masters of Silence* (2015), *Mephista* (2016), *The Polarian-Denebian War* (2016), *Lost!* (2017), *The Nyctalope and The Tower of Babel* (2018), *Zigomar* (2019), *Sibilla: Deadly Circles* (2020), *The Nyctalope and The Master of Life* (2022), *The Improbables* (2023), and *Kobor Tigan't* (2023).

**John SKIPP** is a splatterpunk horror and fantasy author and anthology editor, as well as a songwriter, screenwriter, film director, and film producer. He collaborated with Craig Spector on multiple novels. He worked as editor-in-chief of both Fungasm Press and Ravenous Shadows. Skipp has also been a past contributor to liner notes for cult film distributors Grindhouse Releasing/Box Office Spectaculars on the North American Blu-ray/DVD release of *An American Hippie in Israel*.

**Brian M. STABLEFORD** has been a professional writer since 1965. He has published more than 50 novels and 200 short stories, as well as several non-fiction books, thousands of articles for periodicals and reference books and a number of anthologies. He is also a part-time Lecturer in Creative Writing at King Alfred's College Winchester. Brian's novels include *The Empire of Fear*

(1988), *Young Blood* (1992), *The Wayward Muse* (2005), *The Stones of Camelot* (2006), and *The New Faust at the Tragicomique* (2007). His non-fiction includes *Scientific Romance in Britain* (1985), *Yesterday's Bestsellers* (1998) and *Glorious Perversity: The Decline and Fall of Literary Decadence* (1998). Brian's translations for Black Coat Press include numerous Paul Féval titles, Jean de La Hire's *The Nyctalope vs. Lucifer* and *The Nyctalope on Mars*; and many others.

**Antifaz de TORQUEMADA** is the *nom-de-plume* of a visual development artist and graphic designer from Columbia.

**Rob WALTON** is a Canadian comic book artist who illustrated the comic *Predator: God's Truth* and the *Devil's Hammer* installment of the *Grendel Tales* anthology series. In 2006, he wrote and illustrated his own 464-page graphic novel, *Ragmop*. Walton has also worked in animation and storyboarding on such projects as the popular children's show *The Backyardigans*.

**Lance WEILER** is a filmmaker and writer from Pennsylvania, and the Director of the Digital Storytelling Lab at Columbia University School of the Arts. He first was known for *The Last Broadcast*, a found footage horror film which he co-wrote, co-produced, co-directed, and co-starred in with Stefan Avalos.

**Douglas E. WINTER** is a writer, critic and lawyer, currently working at Bryan Cave Leighton Paisner LLP. He has also taught legal writing at the University of Iowa. Winter edited the horror anthologies *Prime Evil* (1988) and *Revelations* (1997) as well as the Hugo Award-nominated and World Fantasy Award-winning interviews collection *Faces of Fear* (1985, revised 1990). He has also written the authorized critical biographies of Stephen King and Clive Barker. His novel *Run* (2000) was selected as the Best Suspense Novel of the Year by the Book of the Month Club and was nominated for the World Mystery Award.

**Thomas YEATES** is a comic strip and comic book artist best known for illustrating the comic strips *Prince Valiant* and *Zorro* and for working on characters created by Edgar Rice Burroughs.

## Stories

### *The Hunter and the Grubber*

| Starring: | Created by: |
|---|---|
| Mateo Falcone | Prosper Mérimée |
| Orlando | Alexandre Dumas |
| Colona | Alexandre Dumas |
| Alfred Kurtz | based on Joseph Conrad, |
| | John Milius |
| | & Francis Ford Coppola |
| The Savoli boy | Walter B. Gibson |
| Elizabeth Quatermain | based on H. Rider Haggard |
| Monsieur Leblanc | H. Rider Haggard |
| **Co-Starring:** | |
| The Carsons | H. Rider Haggard |
| Solomon Kane | Robert E. Howard |
| The Clarkes | Arthur Conan Doyle |
| Allan Quatermain | H. Rider Haggard |

**Jason Scott AIKEN** is a freelance writer who enjoys penning fantasy and horror fiction. He has had short stories published by Black Coat Press, Cirsova, Meteor House, and Paizo Publishing. In addition to writing, Aiken has hosted and produced Pulp Crazy, a podcast dedicated to pulp authors, literature, and themes. He can be found online at jasonscottaiken.com and pulpcrazy.com.

### *The Exquisite Corpse*

| Starring: | Created by: |
|---|---|
| Simone Desroches (Belphegor) | Arthur Bernède |
| Leo Saint-Clair (The Nyctalope) | Jean de La Hire |
| **Co-Starring:** | |
| Fantômas | Pierre Souvestre |
| | & Marcel Allain |
| The Vampires | Louis Feuillade |
| Maldoror | Lautréamont |
| Melmoth | Charles Maturin |
| The Black Coats | Paul Féval |
| Eve | Villiers de L'Isle-Adam |
| The Martians | H.G. Wells |

| | |
|---|---|
| Laurence Saint-Clair *née* Païli | Jean de La Hire |
| Jacques Bellegarde | Arthur Bernède |
| Phillipe Roget | Tim Newton Anderson |
| Jérôme Fandor | Pierre Souvestre |
| | & Marcel Allain |
| Philippe Guérande | Louis Feuillade |
| Joseph Joséphin (Rouletabille) | Gaston Leroux |
| Glô Von Warteck (Lucifer) | Jean de La Hire |
| Zigomar | Léon Sazie |
| Satanas | Gabriel Bernard |
| Joséphine Balsamo | Maurice Leblanc |
| Arsène Lupin | Maurice Leblanc |

**Also Starring:**
Louis Mandrin
André Breton
Yvan Goll
Tristan Tzara
Pierre Albert-Birot
Francis Picabia
Guillaume Apollinaire
Louis Aragon
Antonin Artaud
Paul Eluard
Robert St Onge
Arthur Cravan
Thomas Edison
Louis Feuillade
Félix Fénéon
Adrienne Monner
Sylvia Beach
René Clair
Nikola Tesla
Alfred Jarry

**Tim Newton ANDERSON** is a former journalist and PR manager who recently started writing fiction. His story *The Pataphysical Detectives* was published in *Emanations 9: When a Planet Was a Planet*. *Letters to my Daughter* appeared in *Parsec* magazine and several other stories in the MX Anthology of New Sherlock Holmes Stories. He is a member of the London Institute of Pataphysics and an enthusiastic collector of science fiction and fantasy. His blog is at https://wordpress.com/posts/atjentertainments.wordpress.com

## When Worlds Collide

| Starring: | Created by: |
|---|---|
| Marc DuQuesne | E.E. "Doc" Smith |
| Chevalier Bruno Coqdor | Maurice Limat |
| Râx | Maurice Limat |
| Dr. Stewe | Maurice Limat |
| Richard Seaton | E.E. "Doc" Smith |
| **Co-Starring:** | |
| Masters of the Island | K.H. Scheer |
| Robin Muscat | Maurice Limat |
| Stephanie de Marigny | E.E. "Doc" Smith |
| Kimball Kinnison | E.E. "Doc" Smith |
| The Chlorans | E.E. "Doc" Smith |
| Brainiac | Otto Binder & Al Plastino |
| **And:** | |
| AKKA Weapon | Jack Williamson |
| Disruptor | Edmond Hamilton |
| Martervenux | Maurice Limat |
| Interpol/Interplan | Maurice Limat |
| Dzô | Maurice Limat |
| Zero Particle/Chronon | Maurice Limat |
| Great White Beam | Maurice Limat |

**Jean-Michel ARCHAIMBAULT** is a retired rocket scientist who lives with his wife in the pine forests near Bordeaux on the Atlantic coast. He is the author of several novels and short story collections published by Rivière Blanche and was the Managing Editor of the *Perry Rhodan* imprint for Editions Fleuve Noir.

## The Staffel from Yuggoth

| Starring: | Created by: |
|---|---|
| James Bigglesworth (Biggles) | W.E. Johns |
| Jack Powell (The Shooting Star) | John Monk Saunders |
| Jack Clayton (Korak) | Edgar Rice Burroughs |
| Major Brand | John Monk Saunders |
| Patrick O'Malley | Jon Cleary |
| Leo Saint-Clair (The Nyctalope) | Jean de La Hire |
| Marco Pagot (Porco Rosso) | Hayao Miyazaki |
| Philip Strange (The Brain Devil) | Donald Keyhoe |
| Heinrich | Matthew Baugh |
| Karl Von Juntz | based on Robert E. Howard |
| The Mi-Gou | H.P. Lovecraft |

| | |
|---|---|
| Erich Von Stalhein | W.E. Johns |
| Bruno Satchel | Jack D. Hunter |
| Ernst Kessler | George Roy Hill |
| | & William Goldman |
| Heinrich Von Fruelich | Charles Hoffman |
| | & Doug Wildey |
| Algernon Montgomery Lacey | W.E. Johns |
| Doktor Krueger | Robert J. Hogan |
| Kalakaperi of the Pfifltriggi | C.S. Lewis |
| Kent Allard (The Dark Eagle) | Walter B. Gibson |
| Sylvia Lewis | John Monk Saunders |
| Gina | Hayao Miyazaki |
| Dr. John H. Watson | Arthur Conan Doyle |
| Karol von Marlow | Donald Keyhoe |
| **And:** | |
| Yuggoth | H.P. Lovecraft |
| Tok'l metal | H.P. Lovecraft |

**Matthew BAUGH** is the author of oodles and oodles of short stories and several novels, who aspires to keep writing until there are no more stories left to tell. He is represented by Rebecca Angus of the Golden Wheat agency. He is also the author of *The Vampire Count of Monte-Cristo.*

## *The Society of the Phantom*

| **Starring:** | **Created by:** |
|---|---|
| Eugenia Ronder | Arthur Conan Doyle |
| Baron Adelbert Gruner | Arthur Conan Doyle |
| René Marot | Christopher Wicking |
| | & Henry Slesar |
| Ivan Igor | Don Mullaly |
| | & Carl Erickson |
| Roger Vigers | W.F. Morris |
| Janos Szabo | Allen Vincent, Paul Jarrico |
| | & Arthur Levinson |
| Nora Goodrich | Mindret Lord, |
| | Lewis Herman |
| | & Anne Wigton |
| Erik (Phantom of the Opera) | Gaston Leroux |
| **Co-Starring:** | |
| Sherlock Holmes | Arthur Conan Doyle |
| Henry Jarrod | Crane Wilbur |

| | |
|---|---|
| Raoul de Chagny | Gaston Leroux |
| The Persian | Gaston Leroux |
| Christine Daae | Gaston Leroux |
| Pretty Boy Murphy | Robert Creighton Williams |
| Karl Verloc | Charles Bennett |
| Ted Spencer | Charles Bennett |
| Charles Larousse Dreyfus | Maurice Richlin |
| | & Blake Edwards |
| The Man in Black | Dario Argento, Lamberto |
| | Bava, Dardano Sacchetti, |
| | & Franco Ferrini |
| Eve Gill | Whitfield Cook, Alma |
| | Reville & Selwyn Jepson |
| Doctor Omega | Arnould Galopin |
| Helen Selleck (Cathy) | John D. Lamond, |
| | John-Michael Howson |
| | & Colin Eggleston |
| Austin Johnson | Stu Segall, John F. Goff |
| | & George Buck Flower |
| Irving Wallace (The Night Owl) | Lew Cooper |
| | & Sheila Goldberg |
| **And:** | |
| Bijou Theater | Charles Bennett |
| Freiburg Tanz Akademie | Dario Argento |
| | & Daria Nicolodi |
| Spotlite Theater | Rick Sloane |

**Atom Mudman BEZECNY** is the editor-in-chief of the independent press Odd Tales Productions, a position she has occupied for seven years. Her previous publications include the novels *The New Adventures of the Flash Avenger*, *Flint Golden and the Thunderstrike Crisis*, and *So Be It...Desecrator*. She has written two official movie tie-ins: *The Return of the Amazing Bulk*, a sequel to Lewis Schoenbrun's superhero film *The Amazing Bulk*, and *The Bryan Gospels*, an expansion of Seth Landau's horror movie *Bryan Loves You*—she has also contributed stories to R. Paul Sardanas' Doc Talos series of adult literary pulp tales. A full list of her work can be found on www.oddtalesofwonder.com.

## *Holy Water*

| **Starring:** | **Created by:** |
|---|---|
| Jacques de Trémeuse (Judex) | Louis Feuillade |
| | & Arthur Bernède |
| Matthieu Cordère | P.C. Wren |

633

| | |
|---|---|
| André de Saint-Avit | Pierre Benoit |
| Father Comusse | Pierre Véry |
| Father Lankester Merrin | William Peter Blattty |
| Alfred Cocantin | Louis Feuillade |
| | & Arthur Bernède |
| Jean Cocantin (The Kid) | Louis Feuillade |
| | & Arthur Bernède |
| Chevalier Auguste Dupin | Edgar Allan Poe |
| Lord Ruthven | John William Polidori |

**Co-Starring:**

| | |
|---|---|
| Maurice-Ernest Favraux | Louis Feuillade |
| | & Arthur Bernède |

**Also Starring:**
Philippe Pétain
**And:**

| | |
|---|---|
| Fort Zinderneuf | P.C. Wren |

**Thom BRANNAN** (est.1976) was a nuclear submariner and offshore oilfield electrician, and now works on automated equipment in Texas for whomever will allow it. He's the author of the *Tales of the Century* urban fantasy series and *World of Trouble: Tribulation of Dax*, a post-post-apocalyptic crime/zombie romp. He's aided and abetted by Kitty (his wife) and a couple of kids and a dog.

## *Get Fantômas*

| **Starring:** | **Created by:** |
|---|---|
| Graf Hugo von der Drache | Ian Fleming |
| Fantômas | Jean Halain |
| | & Pierre Foucaud |
| | based on Pierre Souvestre |
| | & Marcel Allain |
| Nick Carter (Agent N3 / Kill- | Michael Avallone |
| master) | & Valerie Moolman |
| | based on Ormand G. Smith |
| | & John R. Coryell |
| Tyrone Tackett | George Armitage |
| | based on Ted Lewis |
| Cleopatra Jones | Max Julien |
| | & Sheldon Keller |
| Neil Burnside | Ian Macintosh |
| George Smiley (C) | John Le Carré |
| G. Joubert | James Grady |
| Bolo | Michael Allin |

| | |
|---|---|
| Lady Maud Beltham | Pierre Souvestre |
| | & Marcel Allain |
| The Jackal | Frederick Forsyth |
| Pavane | Doug Moench |
| | & Paul Gulacy |
| **Co-Starring:** | |
| Senator Thomas Jordan | Richard Condon |
| Jeeves | P.G. Wodehouse |
| Zorro | Johnston McCulley |
| **Also Starring:** | |
| Al Jolson | |
| J. Edgar Hoover | |
| Charlton Heston | |
| **And:** | |
| AXE | Michael Avallone |
| | & Valerie Moolman |
| Double-0 Section | Ian Fleming |
| Sandbaggers | Ian Macintosh |
| IMF | Bruce Gellar |
| UNCLE | Sam Rolfe |
| | & Norman Felton |
| Omega Sector | James Cameron |

**Nathan CABANISS** is a writer based in Atlanta, GA, where he lives a life consisting primarily of danger, intrigue and Netflix. His stories have appeared in various publications, in both English and French. 2016 saw the release of his first collection of short fiction, *Mares in the Night*, and in 2018 his short novel *The Mummy's Hand At the Center of the Universe* was released by Pro Se Press.

## *The Midnight Train to Paris*

| **Starring:** | **Created by:** |
|---|---|
| John Talbot | Andrew Kevin Walker |
| | & David Self |
| | based on Curt Siodmak |
| Irma Vep | Louis Feuillade |
| The Vampires | Louis Feuillade |
| Docteur Génessier | Jean Redon |
| The *Kommandant* (Dracula) | Bram Stoker |
| Lieutenant Sturmer | Gérard Oury, Danièle |
| | Thompson & Marcel Jullian |
| Flick | Jeremy Lloyd |
| | & David Croft |

| | |
|---|---|
| Fantômas | Pierre Souvestre |
| | & Marcel Allain |
| Hélène Fandor *née* Gurn | Pierre Souvestre |
| | & Marcel Allain |
| Vladimir | Pierre Souvestre |
| | & Marcel Allain |
| Pierre Martin | Noël-Noël |
| Dr. Victor Frankenstein | Mary Shelley |
| Anneke Frankenstein | based on Mary Shelley |

**Co-Starring:**

| | |
|---|---|
| M | Ian Fleming |
| Jérôme Fandor | Pierre Souvestre |
| | & Marcel Allain |

**Also Starring:**
Eugène Bullard
Helmut Knochen
Hans Kiefer
Willi Herold

**Bill CUNNINGHAM** is a writer, graphic designer and producer of pulp entertainment. He is the co-editor (with Bob Deis) of the *Men's Adventure Quarterly*, and *The Art of Ron Lesser Vol. 1: Deadly Dames and Sexy Sirens*. He publishes through his own imprint Pulp 2.0 Press and can be contacted through his website www.pulp2ohpress.com.

## *A Greener Future*

| Starring: | Created by: |
|---|---|
| Nicolas Vermont | Maurice Renard |
| Emma Bourdichet | Maurice Renard |
| Sâr Dubnotal | Norbert Sevestre |
| Frank | Norbert Sevestre |
| Eric von Emmelman (The Heap) | Harry Stein, Mort Leav |
| | & Ed Cronin |
| Otto Klotz | Maurice Renard |
| Ronald LeBay | Stephen King |
| Alex Olsen | Len Wein |
| | & Bernie Wrightson |
| Alcide | Maurice Renard |

**Co-Starring:**

| | |
|---|---|
| Doctor Francis Ardan | Guy d'Armen |
| His Assistant (Monk Mayfair) | Lester Dent |
| Doctor Frédéric Lerne | Maurice Renard |

| | |
|---|---|
| Monsieur de Gambertin | Maurice Renard |
| Flaxman Low | E. & E. Heron |
| Christine | Stephen King |
| Ted Sallis (Man-Thing) | Stan Lee, Roy Thomas, |
| | Gerry Conway |
| | & Gray Morrow |
| Alec Holland (Swamp Thing) | Len Wein |
| | & Bernie Wrightson |

**Matthew DENNION** lives in South Jersey with his beautiful wife and daughters. He currently works as a teacher of students with autism at a Special Services School. Matthew writes giant monster stories for *G-Fan* magazine and he has recently published three giant monster novels, *Chimera: Scourge of the Gods, Operation R.O.C.: A Kaiju Thriller, The Atomic Rex Series, Raptor Retribution of the Revenants, Kaiju Faithful, Agent 666, The Final Host* and numerous other novels. All of his books are available on amazon..

## *The Steam House in Innsmouth*

| **Starring:** | **Created by:** |
|---|---|
| Henri Maucler | Jules Verne |
| Captain Blake Hood | Jules Verne |
| Freddy Fox | Jules Verne |
| Colonel Sir Edward Munro | Jules Verne |
| Lady Beverly Munro | Jules Verne |
| Sergeant Jake McNeil | Jules Verne |
| Josiah Banks | Jules Verne |
| Wilberforce Phillips | Jules Verne |
| Mathias van Guitt | Jules Verne |
| Jenny Arbutus | Jules Verne |
| The White Apes | H.P. Lovecraft |
| Zadok Allen | H.P. Lovecraft |
| The Deep Ones | H.P. Lovecraft |
| **Co-Starring:** | |
| Etienne Drouet | Jules Verne |
| Monsieur Parazard | Jules Verne |
| Jermyn Family | H.P. Lovecraft |
| Captain Obed Marsh | H.P. Lovecraft |
| Professor Tyler Freeborn | H.P. Lovecraft |
| **Also Starring:** | |
| Darling, Brown and Sharp | |
| Phineas Taylor Barnum | |
| William Cameron Coup | |

Professor Louis Agassiz
Nathaniel B. Shurtleff
**And:**

| | |
|---|---|
| The Steam House | H.P. Lovecraft |
| Miskatonic University | H.P. Lovecraft |
| Innsmouth | H.P. Lovecraft |

**Paul DI FILIPPO**'s career began either in 1977, when his first story appeared in *Unearth* magazine; or in 1982, when he quit his job as a COBOL programmer to devote himself fulltime to writing; or in 1985, when his second and third stories appeared in *The Magazine of Fantasy & Science Fiction* and *The Twilight Zone Magazine*; or in 1995, when his first book, *The Steampunk Trilogy*, debuted. Whichever date one chooses, 2024 will see the publication of his 49th book, *Vangie's Ghosts,* a milestone he is very proud of. He intends to retire now in stages over the next 20 years.

## *The Secret Archive of Vienna*

| **Starring:** | **Created by:** |
|---|---|
| Captain Nemec | Brian Gallagher |
| Simon Hart | Jules Verne |
| Dr. Cornelius Kramm | Gustave Le Rouge |
| The Red Hand | Gustave Le Rouge |
| Hamilton | Leslie Charteris |
| Percy Phelps | Arthur Conan Doyle |
| Countess Irina Petrovski | Arnaud d'Usseau & Julian Zimet |
| | |
| Tamas Varga | Brian Gallagher |
| Corporal Simon Fischer | Brian Gallagher |
| Felix Lechner | Brian Gallagher |
| Lieutenant Mayr | Brian Gallagher |
| Captain Vuljanić | Brian Gallagher |
| Kata | Brian Gallagher |
| Lord Astor Burydan | Gustave Le Rouge |
| Private Brunner | Brian Gallagher |
| Professor Saxton | Arnaud d'Usseau & Julian Zimet |
| | |
| Dr. Wells | Arnaud d'Usseau & Julian Zimet |
| | |
| Dr. Cerral | Maurice Renard |
| **Co-Starring:** | |
| Count Dracula | Bram Stoker |
| Von Bork | Arthur Conan Doyle |

| | |
|---|---|
| Prince Wilhelm | Arthur Conan Doyle |
| The Creature | Arnaud d'Usseau |
| | & Julian Zimet |
| Count Petrovski | Arnaud d'Usseau |
| | & Julian Zimet |
| The Jovians | Pierre Lavaur |
| Captain Marić | Lazić |
| The Saturnians | Cesare Zavattini |
| | & Federico Pedrocchi |
| | & Giovanni Scolari |

**Also Starring:**
Emperor Karl I
President Woodrow Wilson
General Józef Piłsudski
Count von Czernin
President Tomáš Masaryk
Karl Renner
Vladimir Lenin
Karl Marx
Friedrich Engels
The Romanov
Stjepan Radić
Adolf Hitler
**And:**

| | |
|---|---|
| Planet 10 | Derrick Sherwin |

**Brian GALLAGHER** has a BA in Politics and Society and lives in London. He works in the media and for many years has written on the politics, economics and many other aspects of Croatia and has been quoted in Croatian and international media. In relation to that he has written extensively on Croatian-related cases at the International Criminal Tribunal for the Former Yugoslavia. He has always been interested in SF, classic horror, comics and is proud to be a lifelong *Doctor Who* fan. His latest BCP collection is *The Return of Captain Vampire*.

## *Shadowmen* (*illustration*)

| **Starring from Left to Right:** | **Created by:** |
|---|---|
| Rouletabille | Gaston Leroux |
| Belphegor | Arthur Bernède |
| Arsène Lupin | Maurice Leblanc |
| Irma Vep | Louis Feuillade |
| Sâr Dubnotal | Norbert Sevestre |

John **GALLAGHER** is a freelance artist living in the North West of England . He divides his time between working on his own comic strip projects and painting fantasy subjects. Amongst other things, he has published, in collaboration with 'Archaic' Alan Hewetson, *The Complete Saga of the Victims*; a graphic novel compilation of the old Skywald *Horror-Mood* comic strip.

## *Young Robur and The Masada Pattern*

| **Starring:** | **Created by:** |
|---|---|
| Artemisia | Martin Gately |
| Dr. Johnson | Martin Gately |
| Mayor of Rock Ridge | Martin Gately |
| Robur | Jules Verne |
| Idaho Jones | Luci Ward & Morgan Cox |
| Walter Trump | John Robinson |
| Tom Turner | Jules Verne |
| Trina Dressard | Luci Ward & Morgan Cox |
| Major McIntosh | James A. Michener |
| Seraphina | Martin Gately |
| Gideon Spilitt | Jules Verne |
| Airman Alistair | Martin Gately |
| Sergeant Duignan | Martin Gately |
| Steve Clark | Luci Ward & Morgan Cox |
| Grand Pater Platanus (Albert Trump) | Martin Gately |
| Carpinus | Martin Gately |
| Chef François Tapage | Jules Verne |
| Sister Avellana | Martin Gately |
| Airman Shanks | Martin Gately |
| **Co-Starring:** | |
| Professor Oxalis | Martin Gately |
| Thaddeus Frycollin Sr | Martin Gately based on Jules Verne |
| Sister Myrtle | Martin Gately |
| Uncle Prudent | Jules Verne |
| Phil Evans | Jules Verne |
| Thaddeus Frycollin Jr | Jules Verne |
| **Also Starring:** | |
| The Anu Sinom | Hopi Legends |
| **And:** | |
| Woodlanders Haven | Martin Gately |
| Dunn & Duffy Combined | George Lucas, |
| Circus | Menno Meyjes |

                                                            & Jeffrey Boam

Weldon Institute                                        Jules Verne

**Martin GATELY** is the author of the official prequel to Philip José Farmer's *The Green Odyssey (Samdroo and the Grassman* in *The Worlds of Philip José Farmer 4—Voyages to Strange Days)*. His writing career commenced in 1988 when he wrote for D C Thomson's legendary *Starblazer* comic. He is also a contributor to the UK's journal of strange phenomena *Fortean Times.* For Black Coat Press, he has provided stories for two collections, *Exquisite Pandora* and *The New Exploits of Joseph Rouletabille*, and contributed to the following anthologies: *Night of the Nyctalope, Harry Dickson Vs. The Spider* and *The Vampire Almanac Vol. 1.* His latest work is an adaptation of Edgar Rice Burroughs' *Pirate Blood* into comic strip form, drawn by Anthony Summey and available on the official ERB website.

### *Masters of the World*

| **Starring:** | **Created by:** |
|---|---|
| Professor Pierre Aronnax | Jules Verne |
| James West | Michael Garrison |
| Artemus Gordon | Michael Garrison |
| Captain Nemo (Prince Dakkar) | Jules Verne |
| Robur | Jules Verne |
| John Strock | Jules Verne |
| Captain Nicholl | Jules Verne |
| John Hart | Jules Verne |
| **Co-Starring:** | |
| The Gun Club | Jules Verne |
| William Boltyn | Gustave Le Rouge |
| | & Gustave Guitton |
| **And:** | |
| Hotel de la Plage | Jacques Tati |
| The *Nautilus* | Jules Verne |
| The *Great Eastern* | Jules Verne |
| The *Terror* | Jules Verne |
| The Columbiad cannon | Jules Verne |
| Propeller Island | Jules Verne |

**Lex GIL** is a physically disabled writer, still waiting for his awards. Besides writing, this international man of mystery has a deep interest in photography, martial arts, archery, fencing, and the outdoors. One's favorite movies are too many to name, and most of his favorite books just happen to be sci-fi. He has been an assembly line worker, a mailman, a soldier, a bartender, a janitor, a screenwriter and even homeless, among a couple of other things. Lex has an eclectic list of musical tastes, from classic to jazz to techno to Japanese drums, and so on.

## *The Secret Alchemy of Very Bad Balloons*

| Starring: | Created by: |
|---|---|
| Teddy Verano (*père & fils*) | Maurice Limat |
| Angerona (Angie Rona | Micah Harris based on |
| /Theodora) | Roman Mythology |
| The Firemen | David Lynch & Mark Frost |
| Lt .Margaret O'Houlihan | Richard Hooker |
| Norman Nash | Ian Fleming |
| Auric Goldfinger | Ian Fleming |
| Velda Wickman | Robert Aldrich |
| | & A.I. Bezzerides |
| | based on Mickey Spillane |
| Carl Evello | Robert Aldrich |
| | & A.I. Bezzerides |
| | based on Mickey Spillane |
| Dr. G.E. Soberin | Robert Aldrich |
| | & A.I. Bezzerides |
| | based on Mickey Spillane |
| Mike Hammer | Robert Aldrich |
| | & A.I. Bezzerides |
| | based on Mickey Spillane |
| Gabrielle | Robert Aldrich |
| | & A.I. Bezzerides |
| | based on Mickey Spillane |
| BOB | David Lynch & Mark Frost |
| John Drake | Patrick McGoohan |
| | & George Markstein |
| | based on Ralph Smart |
| Rover | Patrick McGoohan |
| | & George Markstein |

| Co-Starring: | |
|---|---|
| Marco | Maurice Limat |
| Lionella | Maurice Limat |
| The League of Ten Thousand | Honoré Balzac |
| Jacques Collin | Honoré Balzac |
| Marcus Marsellus | Quentin Tarentino |
| | & Roger Avary |
| Prosper Lepicq | Pierre Véry |

| | |
|---|---|
| Quentin Moretus Cassave | Jean Ray |
| Judy (Jowday) | David Lynch & Mark Frost |
| The Dugpas | Talbot Mundy |
| Christina Bailey | Robert Aldrich |
| | & A.I. Bezzerides |
| | based on Mickey Spillane |
| James Bond | Ian Fleming |

**Also Starring:**
Alexander Korda
Pierre Véry
Charlie Parker
Niccolo Machiavelli
Sir Alfred Russell Wallace
Sir William Crookes
Jack Parsons
Aleister Crowley
**And:**

| | |
|---|---|
| Galerie du Zodiaque | *Historical* |
| W.A.S.T.E. | Thomas Pynchon |
| Thurn and Taxis | *Historical* |
| Trystero | Thomas Pynchon |
| The Village | Patrick McGoohan |
| | & George Markstein |
| The Black Lodge | David Lynch & Mark Frost |
| | based on Talbot Mundy |
| Project Babalon | Aleister Crowley |
| Experiment IV | Kate Bush |
| M&D Funeral Coach | The Beatles |

**Micah S. HARRIS'** recent publications include *Incognito*, a steam punk novella in his *Chronicles of Aarastad*. Other volumes in this series include *The World Queen Awakens, The Dark Lord Lurking* and *Royals, Rogues, and Dragons Arise!* His *Ravenwood, the Stepson of Mystery: Return of the Dugpa* won the 2016 Pulp Ark Award for Best Novel. He is also the author (with artist Michael Gaydos) of the 2003 graphic novel *Heaven's War*, which pits the Oxford Inklings against Aleister Crowley. His other novels include *The Eldritch New Adventures of Becky Sharp* (now in an expanded edition) and *Jim Anthony: the Hunters*, written with fellow *TOTS* contributor Joshua Reynolds.

## The Ghosts of Gascony

| **Starring:** | **Created by:** |
|---|---|
| M. du Vallon de Bracieux de | Alexandre Dumas |

| | |
|---|---|
| Pierrefonds (Porthos) | |
| Orlando | based on Virginia Wolfe and Alan Moore |
| Solomon Kane | Robert E. Howard |
| Rotwang | Fritz Lang & Thea Von Harbou |
| Hélène | Travs Hiltz Based on Fritz Lang & Thea Von Harbou |
| The Volkites | Maurice Geraghty & Oliver Drake |
| Doctor Omega | Arnould Galopin |
| Lotte | Paul Féval |
| **Co-Starring:** | |
| Isaac Laquedem (The Wandering Jew) | Paul Féval |
| Athos | Alexandre Dumas |
| Aramis | Alexandre Dumas |
| Mousqueton | Alexandre Dumas |
| The Morlocks | H.G. Wells |
| **Also Starring:** | |
| D'Artagnan | |

**Travis HILTZ** started making up stories at a young age. Years later, he began writing them down. In high school, he discovered that some writers actually got paid and decided to give it a try. He has since gathered a modest collection of rejection letters and a shelf full of books with his name on them. Travis lives in the wilds of New Hampshire with his very loving and tolerant wife and a staggering amount of comic books and *Doctor Who* novels.

## *The Epicurean Slaughter*

| Starring: | Created by: |
|---|---|
| Lord Horace Chiltern | based on Oscar Wilde |
| Tom Wills | Anonymous |
| Harry Dickson | Anonymous |
| Samuel Goodfield | Anonymous |
| Jules de Grandin | Seabury Quinn |
| Lady Julia Chiltern | based on Oscar Wilde |
| Lord Algernon Lorton | based on Oscar Wilde |
| Doris | Riley Hogan |
| Mrs. Crown | Anonymous |
| Sir Cecil Arnheim | based on Oscar Wilde |

| Igor Samsa | based on Franz Kafka |
|---|---|
| **Co-Starring:** | |
| Fantômas | Pierre Souvestre |
| | & Marcel Allain |
| The Vampires Gang | Louis Feuillade |
| **Also Starring:** | |
| Joseph Bell | |
| **And:** | |
| The Pink Panther | Blake Edwards |
| | & Maurice Richlin |

**Riley HOGAN** is the author of *As Tartary Burns*. He lives in Alaska away from any nuisances.

## *The Nyctalope at the Earth's Core*

| **Starring:** | **Created by:** |
|---|---|
| Jan Bjelke | based on Jules Verne |
| Leo Saint-Clair (The Nyctalope) | Jean de La Hire |
| John Rutherford | based on Philip José Farmer |
| The Lidenbrock Society | based on Jules Verne |
| Dr. Abner Perry | Edgar Rice Burroughs |
| Igor Trukhanov | based on Vladimir Obruchev |
| The Unseen Ones | Wyllis Cooper |
| Jacques de Mésange | based on Simon Tyssot de Patot |
| **Co-Starring:** | |
| Otto Lidenbrock | Jules Verne |
| Hans Bjelke | Jules Verne |
| Dr. George Challenger | Arthur Conan Doyle |
| Clairancy | Jacques Collin de Plancy |
| Sebastian Moran | Arthur Conan Doyle |
| Sherlock Holmes | Arthur Conan Doyle |
| The Mahars | Edgar Rice Burroughs |
| **And:** | |
| Pellucidar | Edgar Rice Burroughs |
| The Maple White Land | Arthur Conan Doyle |
| The Heart of Ahriman | Robert E. Howard |

**Matthew ILSEMAN** was born in Texas and currently lives in Colorado. He started writing before he could actually write. His mother would write down stories he dictated to her. He has been writing ever since and has had four stories published in *Swords and Sorcery* Magazine.

## *Executioners Also Die*

| Starring: | Created by: |
|---|---|
| Jezebel Garvin | based on Tito Carpic, Alessandro Continenza, Massimiliano Capriccioli, & Giovanni Simonelli |
| Glen "Jangles" Garvin | Tito Carpic, Alessandro Continenza, Massimiliano Capriccioli, & Giovanni Simonelli |
| Tom Garvin | Tito Carpic, Alessandro Continenza, Massimiliano Capriccioli, & Giovanni Simonelli |
| Ken Kluster | Tito Carpic, Alessandro Continenza, Massimiliano Capriccioli, & Giovanni Simonelli |
| Luther Ringo | Tito Carpic, Alessandro Continenza, Massimiliano Capriccioli, & Giovanni Simonelli |
| Django | Sergio Corbucci, Bruno Corbucci, Franco Rossetti, José Gutiérrez Maesso & Piero Vivarelli |
| Louise Lupin | based on Maurice Leblanc |
| Jeffrey Kluster | Tito Carpic, Alessandro Continenza, Massimiliano Capriccioli, & Giovanni Simonelli |
| Jessica Texar-Kluster | based on Jules Verne & Tito Carpic, Alessandro Continenza, Massimiliano Capriccioli, & Giovanni Simonelli |
| Texar Brothers | Jules Verne |
| Theodore "Doc" Marley | Tito Carpic, |

Alessandro Continenza,
Massimiliano Capriccioli,
& Giovanni Simonelli

Messalina — based on Walter B. Gibson

Fergus Lupin — based on Maurice Leblanc

Penny Bannington — Sergio Sollima
& Pompeo De Angelis

Issachar Coffran — based on Walter B. Gibson

Maude Allinghame — Frank E. Smedley

Jedediah Trigardo (Delay) — Sergio Corbucci,
Sabatino Ciuffini
& Mario Amen

Bill Norton — Adriano Bolzoni
& Franco Rossetti

Nathaniel Cassidy, Jr. — Sergio Sollima
& Pompeo De Angelis

Thelma "Amula" Cronin — based on Walter B. Gibson
& Ambrose Bierce

Colette Mordaunt — based on Alexandre Dumas

William "Billy" Skelton — Tito Carpic,
Alessandro Continenza,
Massimiliano Capriccioli,
& Giovanni Simonelli

Louella Burbank — based on Jules Verne

Gilbert Burbank — Jules Verne

Glenda Gordon — based on Tito Carpic,
Alessandro Continenza,
Massimiliano Capriccioli,
& Giovanni Simonelli

Fred "One Sleeve" Gordon — Tito Carpic,
Alessandro Continenza,
Massimiliano Capriccioli,
& Giovanni Simonelli

Branwen Skelton — based on Magdalen
King-Hall

Barney Maguire — E.W. Hornung

The Black Coats — Paul Féval

Juanita Brown — Robert Hamner,
Preston Woods
& Michael Garrison

Lizzie Ringo — based on Tito Carpic,
Alessandro Continenza,
Massimiliano Capriccioli,

|  |  |
|---|---|
|  | & Giovanni Simonelli |
| John Obadiah Brown | Robert Hamner, |
|  | Preston Woods |
|  | & Michael Garrison |
| Carma Vasquez | Robert Hamner, |
|  | Preston Woods |
|  | & Michael Garrison |
| Ezekial Bingham | Walter B. Gibson |
| Captain Jerry Jackson | Magdalen King-Hall |
| Barbara Worth (Lady Skelton) | Magdalen King-Hall |
| Sir Ralph Skelton | Magdalen King-Hall |
| Lucy Skelton | based on Tito Carpic, |
|  | Alessandro Continenza, |
|  | Massimiliano Capriccioli, |
|  | & Giovanni Simonelli |
|  | & Magdalen King-Hall |
| Sonia "Sonny" Trigardo (Delay) | Sergio Corbucci, |
|  | Sabatino Ciuffini |
|  | & Mario Amen |

**Also Starring:**
Julius Caesar
Maria Isabella "Belle" Boyd
Ambrose Bierce
Ben Franklin
**And:**

|  |  |
|---|---|
| Silver Creek | Tito Carpic, |
|  | Alessandro Continenza, |
|  | Massimiliano Capriccioli, |
|  | & Giovanni Simonelli |
| Burton City | Sergio Sollima |
|  | & Pompeo De Angelis |
| Garvin-Kluster Partners | Tito Carpic, |
|  | Alessandro Continenza, |
|  | Massimiliano Capriccioli, |
|  | & Giovanni Simonelli |

**Rick LAI** is an authority on pulp fiction and the Wold Newton Universe concepts of Philip José Farmer. His speculative articles have been collected in *Rick Lai's Secret Histories*: *Daring Adventurers*, *Rick Lai's Secret Histories*: *Criminal Masterminds*, *Chronology of Shadows: A Timeline of The Shadow's Exploits* and *The Revised Complete Chronology of Bronze*. Rick's fiction has been collected in *Shadows of the Opera*, *Shadows of the Opera: Retribution in Blood* and *Sisters of the Shadows: The Cagliostro Curse* (the last two titles are available from Black Coat Press). He has also translated Arthur Bernède's *Judex* and *The Return of Judex* into English for Black Coat Press. Rick resides in Bethpage, New York, with his wife and children.

## The Legacy of a Man

| Starring: | Created by: |
|---|---|
| Leo Saint-Clair (The Nyctalope) | Jean de La Hire |
| Carmilla Karnstein | J. Sheridan Le Fanu |
| Malai | Roman Leary |
| Khin | Roman Leary |
| Thalia Tomasis | Based on Morton S. Fine, |
| | Nico Mastorakis |
| | & Win Wells |
| | Arthur Conan Doyle |
| Tommy Vargas | Roman Leary |
| Françoise Cordier | Jacques Champreux |
| Brigade des Maléfices | Claude Guillemot |
| | & Claude-Jean Philippe |
| Hubert de Mauvouloir | Jacques Champreux |
| Henchmen (Foley, Chapman, | Roman Leary |
| Miller, Stevens) | |
| Niran | Roman Leary |
| Mrs. Davika Chaiya | Roman Leary |

**Roman LEARY** was eight years old when a family friend gave him an Ace paperback of *Conan* stories. He has been a devotee of pulp fiction ever since. Today, he is a librarian living in the small town of Washington, North Carolina, with his lovely wife Ana and their equally lovely daughter Joana.

## The Vampire and the Air Pirate

| Starring: | Created by: |
|---|---|
| Philippe Guérande | Louis Feuillade |
| Oscar Mazamette | Louis Feuillade |
| Irma Vep | Louis Feuillade |
| Filibus | Giovanni Bertinetti |
| Kyrios Papopolous | Agatha Christie |
| **Co-Starring:** | |
| Elstir | Marcel Proust |
| The Vampires | Louis Feuillade |
| Jane Brémontier | Louis Feuillade |
| Arsène Lupin | Maurice Leblanc |

| | |
|---|---|
| Fantômaa | Pierre Souvestre |
| | & Marcel Allain |
| Kutt-Hendy | Giovanni Bertinetti |
| Leonora Kutt-Hendy | Giovanni Bertinetti |
| Robur | Jules Verne |
| Kutt Hardy | Herbert Bennet |
| Sherlock Holmes | Arthur Conan Doyle |
| Silvio Montalbano | based on Andrea Camilleri |
| Don Ciccio | Matio Puzo |
| Jacques de Trémeuse (Judex) | Louis Feuillade |
| | & Arthur Bernède |
| Leo Saint-Clair (The Nyctalope) | Jean de La Hire |
| Ténébras | Arnould Galopin |
| Mircalla Karnstein | J. Sheridan Le Fanu |
| René Batroc | based on Stan Lee |
| | & Jack Kirby |
| Georges Batroc | Stan Lee & Jack Kirby |
| Zia Papopolous | Agatha Christie |
| Lewin Lockridge Gayle | Raymond Chandler |
| **And:** | |
| *Le Mondial* | Louis Feuillade |
| Rue Maule | Edgar Rice Burroughs |
| Jade necklace | Raymond Chandler |
| Dale safe | Frank L. Packard |
| International Bank | Giovanni Bertinetti |

**Sean Lee LEVIN** is a member of the New Wold Newton Meteoritic Society, and the author of _*Crossovers Expanded: A Secret Chronology of the World* (Volumes 1 and 2), the authorized companions to Win Scott Eckert's *Crossovers: A Secret Chronology of the World*. He is currently working on a third *Crossovers Expanded*.

## *A Scepter in a Child's Hand*

| **Starring:** | **Created by:** |
|---|---|
| Arsène Lupin | Maurice Leblanc |
| Joseph Joséphin (Rouletabille) | Gaston Leroux |
| Dr. Francis Ardan | Guy d'Armen |
| Rose L'Ange (Phantom Angel) | Randy Lofficier |
| | based on the fairy tale |
| Hareton Ironcastle | J.H. Rosny *Aîné* |
| Leo Saint-Clair (The Nyctalope) | Jean de La Hire |
| Jacques de Trémeuse (Judex) | Louis Feuillade |

| | & Arthur Bernède |
|---|---|
| Sâr Dubnotal | Norbert Sevestre |
| Jérôme Clampin (Pistolet) | Paul Féval |
| Henriette Lupin *née* d'Andrésy | Maurice Leblanc |
| Hulet | Charles Rabou |
| **Co-Starring:** | |
| *Société Secrète des Aventuriers* | Randy Lofficier |
| Athanase Pamplemousse | based on Michael Bond |
| Théophraste Lupin | Maurice Leblanc |
| The Black Coats | Paul Féval |
| The *Cabinet Noir* | Charles Rabou |
| Marquis de Lupiano | Charles Rabou |
| Victoire | Maurice Leblanc |
| **Also Starring:** | |
| Maurice Leblanc | |
| Prosper-Olivier Lissagaray | |
| Vidocq | |
| Louise Michel | |
| **And:** | |
| Inramonda | Guy d'Armen |
| Kadath | H.P. Lovecraft |

**Jean-Marc LOFFICIER** (with his wife **Randy**) have collaborated on five screenplays, a dozen books and numerous translations, including *Arsène Lupin, Doc Ardan, Doctor Omega, The Phantom of the Opera* and *Rouletabille*. Their latest novels include *Edgar Allan Poe on Mars, The Katrina Protocol* and *Return of the Nyctalope*. Jean-Marc has written numerous comics featuring such popular heroes as *Superman* and *Doctor Strange*, and is currently the publisher and editor-in-chief of Hexagon Comics.

## Scarlet Petals, Crimson Flames

| **Starring:** | **Created by:** |
|---|---|
| Maurice Lindey | Alexandre Dumas |
| Sir Percy Blakeney (The Scarlet Pimpernel) | Charles Hamilton |
| Gaston | David McDonald |
| Georges Lemaître | Dennis Spooner |
| Aline de Kercadiou, Comtesse de Gavrillac | Rafael Sabatini |
| *Enragés* (Raoul, Henri, Antoine) | David McDonald |
| **Also Starring:** | |
| Maximilien Robespierre | |

**David McDONALD** is a mild-mannered editor by day, and a wild-eyed writer by night. In 2013 he won the Ditmar Award for Best New Talent, and in 2014 won the William J. Atheling Jr. Award for Criticism or Review and was shortlisted for the WSFA Small Press Award. His short fiction has appeared in anthologies from publishers such as Moonstone Books, Crazy 8 Press, and Fablecroft Publishing. In 2015, his first movie novelization, Backcountry, was released by Harper Collins, and his first Marvel novel—*Guardians of the Galaxy: Castaways*—was published in August 2016. David is a member of Science Fiction and Fantasy Writers of America, the Horror Writers Association, and the International Association of Media Tie-In Writers.

## Shadows of the Past

| Starring: | Created by: |
|---|---|
| Bob Morane | Henri Vernes |
| René Mathis | Ian Fleming |
| Antoinette Vague | Georges Simenon |
| Basil & Kratt | Ian Fleming |
| Le Chiffre | Ian Fleming |
| James Bond | Ian Fleming |
| **Co-Starring:** | |
| Henri Leblanc | Rod McFadyen |
| **Also Starring:** | |
| Hermann Goering | |
| Friedrich-Wilhelm Krüger | |
| **And:** | |
| *Reflets* magazine | Henri Vernes |
| Casino Royale | Ian Fleming |

**Rod McFADYEN** has been dabbling in creative writing for a number of years now, although generally doing more dabbling than writing. While an avid reader of books of history, science fiction and fantasy, he is also a fan of the pulp genre and was delighted to come across the French pulp heroes. He's also a sucker for a good crossover.

## Sow the Wind

| Starring: | Created by: |
|---|---|
| Harry Dickson | *Anonymous* |
| Lieutenant Dimitri Klebb | based on Ian Fleming |
| Professor Bernard Quatermass | Nigel Kneale |
| Captain Kronsteen | based on Ian Fleming |

| The Triffids | John Wyndham |
| **Co-Starring:** | |
| Minerva Campbell | Jean Ray |
| Control | John Le Carré |

**Nigel MALCOLM** lives in Kent, England. He works as a Teacher of English as a Foreign Language. He is a long-term *Doctor Who, Star Trek* and *Prisoner* fan, long before all the new-fangled versions came along. As well as being a regular contributor to *Tales of the Shadowmen,* he is working on various novels and audio plays.

## *The Recerebration Machine*

| **Starring:** | **Created by:** |
| Mazelier | Eugène Thebault |
| Gribal | Eugène Thebault |
| **Co-Starring:** | |
| Adenoid Hynkel | Charlie Chaplin |
| Doctor Faustroll | Alfred Jarry |
| **Also Starring:** | |
| Bernard Grasset | |
| Louis Brun | |
| Henry Muller | |
| Maurice Renard | |
| Alfred Jarry | |
| **And:** | |
| Tomainia | Charlie Chaplin |
| Xenobiotic Invasion | Théo Varlet |
| Radio-Terror | Eugène Thebault |

**Xavier MAUMÉJEAN** won the renowned Gerardmer Award in 2000 for his psychological thriller *The Memoirs of the Elephant Man*. His other works include *Gotham*, another thriller, *The League of Heroes*, which won the 2003 Imaginaire Award of the City of Brussels and was translated by Black Coat Press in 2005, and the recent *La Vénus Anatomique*, which won the 2005 Rosny Award. Xavier has a diploma in philosophy and the science of religions and works as a teacher in the North of France, where he resides, with his wife and his daughter, Zelda.

## *Malice and Snares*

| **Starring:** | **Created by:** |
| Sidney Thomas | William Patrick Maynard |

| | |
|---|---|
| | & Anna Victoria Maynard |
| Fantômas | Pierre Souvestre |
| | & Marcel Allain |

**William Patrick MAYNARD** was born and raised in Northeast Ohio. An avid reader of classic detective and horror fiction and a keen student of film and comic art, he has been writing fiction since childhood. Since 2009, he has been authorized by The Sax Rohmer Literary Estate to continue the Fu Manchu series. Apart from his novels, he also writes mystery, thriller, and sci-fi short fiction and screenplays. He has authored nearly 300 pop culture articles and has contributed DVD commentaries to classic films of the last century.

**Anna Victoria MAYNARD** was born and raised in Northeast Ohio. She is a published author, professional photographer, and artist. Anna is also active in entertainment marketing. She is currently completing her Professional Writing degree as a University student.

## *The Fall of Scientific City*

| Starring: | Created by: |
|---|---|
| Zohra (Tamenokatl) | Jess Nevins |
| Atbir & Other students | Jess Nevins |
| Jack Wright | Luis P. Senarens |
| Bradley Drake | Tom Curtin |
| Philip Strange | Donald Keyhoe |
| **Co-Starring:** | |
| Walther Spurtzheim | H. de Volta |
| Daniel Dorteuil (Miraculas) | H. de Volta |
| Cosgrove | H. Bedford-Jones |
| Lundgren | H. Bedford-Jones |
| Suzanne Dorteuil | H. de Volta |
| Dr. Flax | Louis Forest |
| Ortiz | Horacio Quiroga |
| Sivel | Horacio Quiroga |
| Thomas Alva Edison | John Merriman |
| Joe West | *Anonymous* |
| Professor Fringe | H.-J. Magog |
| Sweeney | Jules d'Ottange |
| The Black Panther | Stan Lee & Jack Kirby |
| Mack Wan | José Canellas Casals |
| | & Marc Farell |
| Bara | J. Nemo |
| Charlemagne Sale-Trou | José Moselli |
| Meztli Xocoyotzin | Otfird von Hanstein |

| | |
|---|---|
| Mboya Kapinga | Robert Murray Graydon |
| Professeur Mephisto | André-René Jolly |
| Khünbish (Shiwan Khan) | Walter B. Gibson |

**Also Starring:**
Patrice Lumumba
Rafael Trujillo
Achmed Sukarno
Aristide Briand
Calvin Coolidge,
Frank B. Kellogg,
Dwight Filley Davis,
Mary Catherine Phee
Herbert Yardley
Pancho Villa
Paul Painlevé
Saigō Takamori

**And:**

| | |
|---|---|
| Arrĕm | Jess Nevins |
| Wakanda | Stan Lee & Jack Kirby |
| Scientific-City | H. de Volta |
| Goël Island | H. de Volta |
| Experiment Nine Ninety-Nine/chrono-viewer | H. Bedford-Jones |
| Wrightstown | Luis P. Senarens |
| Readestown | Harry Enton & Luis P. Senarens |
| Haiti-sous-la-Mer | José Moselli |
| Cuahuitl Itzimpazoliuhca | Otfird von Hanstein |
| Science City | Robert Murray Graydon |
| Tessha Okoku | Oshikawa Shunro |
| Métropole Électrique | André-René Jolly |
| Xanadu | Walter B. Gibson |

**Written by:**

**Jess NEVINS** is a reference librarian at Lone Star College in Tomball, TX. He is the author of a number of books on popular culture and popular literature, including *The Encyclopedia of Fantastic Victoriana, The Encyclopedia of Pulp Heroes, The Evolution of the Costumed Avenger: the 4000 Year History of the Superhero*, and *Horror Fiction in the 20th Century: Exploring Literature's Most Chilling Genre*. Jess lives outside of Houston with his wife Alicia and his son Henry.

# Full Circle

| Starring: | Created by: |
|---|---|
| Gouroull (Monster of Franken-stein) | Jean-Claude Carrière<br>based on Mary Shelley |
| Colonel Ernst Vogel | Jeffrey Boam,<br>George Lucas<br>& Menno Meyjes |
| Cochinelle | E.T.A. Hoffman,<br>Jules Barbier<br>& Jacques Offenbach |
| Erik (Phantom of the Opera) | Gaston Leroux |
| Jacques Courbé | Tod Robbins |
| St. Eustache | Tod Robbins |
| Quasimodo (Hunchback of Notre-Dame) | Sean Todd<br>based on Victor Hugo |
| Zam (Monster of Frankenstein) | Charles Nodier,<br>Antoine Beraud<br>& Jean Toussaint-Merle<br>based on Mary Shelley |
| Charles (Monster of Franken-stein) | J. Searle Dawley<br>based on Mary Shelley |

**Co-Starring:**

| | |
|---|---|
| Victor Frankenstein | Mary Shelley |
| Dr. Herbert West | H.P. Lovecraft |
| Wou Ling | Jean-Claude Carrière |
| Basil Frankenstein | Donald F. Glut<br>& Chic Stone<br>& Jean-Marc Lofficier<br>based on Mary Shelley |
| Jeanne-Marie Courbé | Tod Robbins |
| The Persian (*Daroga*) | Gaston Leroux |
| Spalanzani | E.T.A. Hoffman<br>Jules Barbier<br>& Jacques Offenbach |
| Dr. Omega | Arnould Galopin |
| Rosemary | J.-M. & Randy Lofficier |
| Zametti Pretorius | Charles Nodier<br>Antoine Beraud<br>Jean Toussaint-Merle<br>& William J. Hurlbut |
| Charles Frankenstein | J. Searle Dawley<br>based on Mary Shelley |

| | |
|---|---|
| Ludwig Frankenstein | Christofer Nigro |
| | based on Stan Lee |
| | & John Buscema |
| | & Jean- Marc Lofficier |
| | based on Mary Shelley |
| Julianne Frankenstein | Christofer Nigro |
| Leo Saint-Clair (The Nyctalope) | Jean de La Hire |
| The Genie of the Black Rock | Charles Nodier |
| | Antoine Beraud |
| | & Jean Toussaint-Merle |
| Hezekiah Whateley | Frank Schildiner |
| | based on H.P. Lovecraft |
| The Creeper | Dwight V. Babcock |
| | & George Bricker |

**Also Starring:**
Grigori Yefimovich Rasputin
Adolph Hitler
**And:**

| | |
|---|---|
| The Spear of Destiny | *Historical* |
| The Black Rock | Charles Nodier |
| | Antoine Beraud |
| | & Jean Toussaint-Merle |

**Christofer NIGRO** is a writer of both fiction and non-fiction with a strong interest in pulps, comic books and fantastic cinema, and a regular contributor to *Tales of the Shadowmen*. He may be known to some by his websites *The Godzilla Saga* and *The Warrenverse*, as he is an authority on the subject of *dai kaiju eiga* (the sub-genre of cinema specializing in giant monsters), and the characters featured in the comic magazines published by Warren. He has recently revived and expanded Chuck Loridans' classic site MONSTAAH, and has since been published in the anthologies *Aliens Among Us* and *Carnage: After the Fall*.

## *A Singular Haunting*

| **Starring:** | **Created by:** |
|---|---|
| Thomas Carnacki | William Hope Hodgson |
| Roger Danglars | based on Alexandre Dumas |
| The Servants (Henry, Ruby, | John Peel |
| Mrs. Mullins) | |
| Myra Vidal *née* Roderich | Jules Verne |
| **Co-Starring:** | |
| Wilhelm Storitz | Jules Verne |
| Marc Vidal | Jules Verne |

| Joe Rollon | Jean de La Hire |
|---|---|
| **Also Starring:** | |
| Henry Irving | |

**John PEEL** was born in Nottingham, England, and moved to the U.S. in 1981 to marry his pen-pal. He and his wife ("Mrs. Peel") and their rescue dog Dickens (named for as favorite author!) live on Long Island, New York. He has written more than a hundred novels, including tie-ins based on shows like *Doctor Who, Star Trek* and *The Avengers* (the one with the *other* Mrs. Peel!). His most popular works are the *Diadem* series and the *Dragonhome* series. Two volumes of his collected short stories are now available from Black Coat Press: *Return to the Center of the Earth* and *Twenty Thousand Years Under the Sea.*

## *115,200 Seconds*

| Starring: | Created by: |
|---|---|
| Phileas Fogg | Jules Verne |
| James Strand | Jules Verne |
| James Forster | Jules Verne |

**Neil PENSWICK** was a successful theater writer in the North of England. He was on the short-list to write for *Doctor Who* when it was cancelled in 1989. He adapted his script entitled *Hostage* as one of Virgin's *New Adventures* (1993). In recent years, Neil has written for a range of television series including thrillers, Sunday-night family viewing, a drama-documentary, and, for the first time, and contradicting his Leonard Cohen type reputation, a situation comedy. He is currently short-listed to write for a popular BBC TV children's series and has also been mentored by the brilliant and hugely talented Phil Ford and written an original three-part scary children's series.

## *Judgment Knight*

| Starring: | Created by: |
|---|---|
| Julie Ziegler | Aaron Sorkin |
| Jacques de Trémeuse (Judex) | Louis Feuillade |
| | & Arthur Bernède |
| The Gangsters (Walter, Will, Mike, Eric, Hank, Paul, Reno, Dan) | Anthony Perconti |
| Jonas Yard | based on Dashiell Hammett |
| Commissioner Stanley Kirkpatrick | Grant Stockbridge |
| The Dumont-Warrens (Aaron, | Jean de La Hire |

Miriam & Ruth)
**Co-Starring:**

| | |
|---|---|
| Kent Allard (The Shadow) | Walter B. Gibson |
| Doctor Francis Ardan | Guy d'Armen |
| Richard Wentworth (The Spider) | Grant Stockbridge |

**Also Starring:**
Fritz Julius Kuhn
Father Coughlin
Fiorello La Guardia

**Anthony PERCONTI** lives and works in the hinterlands of New Jersey with his wife and kids. He enjoys well-crafted and engaging stories from across a variety of genres and mediums.

### The School of Hard Knocks

| **Starring:** | **Created by:** |
|---|---|
| Jacques d'Etraille | based on Guy de Maupassant |
| Jean Passepartout | Jules Verne |
| Censor Severin | based on Leopold von Sacher-Masoch |
| Doktor Krogh | based on Willis Cooper |
| Ming Tai Tsu (The Yellow Shadow) | Henri Vernes |
| Théophraste Dupin (Lupin) | Maurice Leblanc |
| **Co-Starring:** | |
| Phileas Fogg | Jules Verne |
| Chevalier Auguste Dupin | Edgar Allan Poe |
| Rocambole | P.-A. Ponson du Terrail |
| Inspector Paul Picard | William Kotzwinkle |
| Victor Rougon | Emile Zola |
| **Also Starring:** | |
| Otto Von Bismarck | |
| Pai Mei | |

**Dennis E. POWER** has a B.A. in History and lives in Saint Louis, Missouri. In 1998, his interests in history, popular entertainment and literature led to the creation of the second internet site dedicated to Philip Jose Farmer's Wold Newton Universe concept He was a contributor to *Myths for the Modern Age, Doctor Omega and the Shadowmen, The Shadow of Judex* and *The Worlds Philip Jose Farmer: Protean Dreams*. He also wrote the afterword to the Titan edition of *Flesh* by Philip Jose Farmer.

### The Deposition of Randolph Carter

| Starring: | Created by: |
|---|---|
| Randolph Carter | H.P. Lovecraft |
| Etienne-Laurent de Marigny | H.P. Lovecraft |
| Khagnon Faugn | based on Frank Belknap Long |
| Jules Maigret | Georges Simenon |
| **Co-Starring:** | |
| Crismus Bonus | René Goscinny & Albert Uderzo |

**Pete RAWLIK** is a collector of Lovecraftian fiction, and in 1985 stole a car to go see the film *Reanimator*. He successfully defended himself by explaining that his father had regularly read him *The Rats in the Wall* as a bedtime story. His first professional sale was in 1997 but didn't begin to write seriously until 2010. Since then, he has authored more than fifty short stories and the Cthulhu Mythos novels *Reanimators, The Weird Company, Reanimatrix,* and *The Eldritch Equations*. In 2014 his short story *Revenge of the Reanimator* was nominated for a New Pulp Award. In 2015 he co-edited *The Legacy of the Reanimator* for Chaosium. Somewhere along the line he became known as the Reanimator guy, but he fervently denies being obsessed with the character. He lives in southern Florida where he works on Everglades issues and does a lot of fishing.

**Sal CIANO** wears many hats in his everyday life. When not writing, Sal can be found working an ever-growing set of jobs or spending his time dog-dadding; all while he gives silent thanks to the powers that be for the strange parade of the completely absurd, utterly delightful, and wildly weird events and people that he has had the pleasure of experiencing and meeting over the years. He cannot wait to see where this journey through life and literature will take him next.

### The House of Malice

| Starring: | Created by: |
|---|---|
| Sar Dubnotal | Norbert Sevestre |
| Rudolph | Norbert Sevestre |
| Euryale | Jean Ray |
| Lampernisse (Prometheus) | Jean Ray |
| The Eagle | Jean Ray |
| The Borrrowers/The Homonculi | Mary Norton & Jean Ray |
| | |
| **Co-Starring:** | |
| Thomas Carnacki | William Hope Hodgson |

| | |
|---|---|
| Naini | Norbert Sevestre |
| Quentin Moretus Cassave | Jean Ray |
| Oliver Haddo | W. Somerset Maugham |
| Rowley Thorne | Manly Wade Wellman |
| John Silence | Algernon Blackwood |
| Jean-Jacques Grandsire | Jean Ray |
| Professor Meister | John Gilling |
| | Anthony Nelson Keys |
| | & J. Llewellyn Divine |
| Count Manzeppi | Charles Bennett |
| | & Michael Garrison |
| Doctor Nikola | Guy Boothby |
| Eisengott | Jean Ray |
| **Also Starring:** | |
| Alceister Crowley | |
| **And:** | |
| Malpertuis | Jean Ray |
| Belasco House | Richard Matheson |
| The House on the Borderland | William Hope Hodgson |
| Castle Borski | John Gilling |
| | Anthony Nelson Keys |
| | & J. Llewellyn Divine |
| Shandor Building | Dan Aykroyd |
| | & Harold Ramis |

**Joshua REYNOLDS** is a professional author since 2007, Josh has over thirty novels to his name, as well as numerous short stories, novellas, and audio scripts. Born and raised in South Carolina, he now resides in Sheffield with his wife and daughter, as well as a highly excitable dog and something he hopes is a cat.

## *The Same Peculiar Tint*

| | |
|---|---|
| **Starring:** | **Created by:** |
| Violet Hunter | Arthur Conan Doyle |
| The Children (Ange Pompaigne, | Louis Forest |
| Frantz Vertyolle, Fernand Pig, | |
| Nicolas Barlatescu, Germaine, | |
| Victorine, Fernande, Louise, | |
| and the two Alices) | |
| Sir Walter Bullivant | John Buchan |
| **Co-Starring:** | |
| Dr. Flax | Louis Forest |

**Chris ROBERSON**'s novels include *Here, There & Everywhere, The Voyage of Night Shining White, Paragaea: A Planetary Romance*, and the forthcoming *Set the Seas on Fire, End of the Century, Iron Jaw & Hummingbird* and *The Dragon's Nine Sons*. His short stories have appeared in such magazines as *Asimov's Science Fiction, Postscripts* and *Subterranean*, and in anthologies such as *Live Without a Net, The Many Faces of Van Helsing, FutureShocks* and *Forbidden Planets*. Along with his business partner and spouse Allison Baker, he is the publisher of MonkeyBrain Books, an independent publishing house specializing in genre fiction and nonfiction genre studies, and he is the editor of the *Adventure* anthology series. He has been a finalist for the World Fantasy Award three times—once each for writing, publishing and editing—twice a finalist for the John W. Campbell Award for Best New Writer, and twice for the Sidewise Award for Best Alternate History Short Form (winning in 2004 with his story "O One"). Chris and Allison live in Austin, Texas with their daughter Georgia.

## The Hollywood Affair

| Starring: | Created by: |
|---|---|
| Jacques de Trémeuse (Judex) | Louis Feuillade & Arthur Bernède |
| Roger de Trémeuse | Louis Feuillade & Arthur Bernède |
| Philip Marlowe | Raymond Chandler |
| Sam Spade | Dashiell Hammett |
| Eddie Mars | Raymond Chandler |
| Kent Allard (The Shadow) | Walter B. Gibson |
| Kâramanèh | Sax Rohmer |
| Li Po | Lloyd Corrigan, Florence Ryerson, George Marion, Jr., Joseph L. Mankiewicz based on Sax Rohmer |

| **Co-Starring:** | |
|---|---|
| Fu Manchu | Sax Rohmer |

**Also Starring:**
J.P. Morgan
Charlie Chaplin
Albert E. Smith
Louis B. Mayer
Jesse L. Lasky
Adolph Zukor

**Robert L. ROBINSON, Jr.** is a lifetime entrepreneur, successfully founding, developing, and exiting a series of companies before pivoting to pursue his passion for entertainment and storytelling. Residing just outside Philadelphia, his journey was initially inspired by an early exposure to the arts and literature in the 1960s, a foundation laid by his parents. Robinson has since contributed two tales featuring Judex for Black Coat Press and eagerly returned with his new story. In the television industry, his breakthrough as a producer came to the forefront in 2020 with the creation and executive production of "The Talk," a Channel 4 documentary that delved into race relations and earned recognition, being shortlisted for two British Broadcast Awards (Best Documentary Feature & Best Lockdown Feature). Currently, Robinson is at the helm of "The Dinner Salon," a conversational series he created and is the executive producer for PBS. This series brings together six distinguished minds per episode for insightful discussions, showcasing his commitment to fostering intelligent discourse and enlightenment for audiences. Behind the scenes, he finds unwavering support from his wife Ann, and together they have nurtured a family with their four children, Abby, Rob, Matt, and Kara and their grandchildren, Lando and Declan, forming a strong personal network that complements his professional endeavors.

## *No Child of Mine*

| **Starring:** | **Created by:** |
|---|---|
| Louis Castaigne | Robert W. Chambers |
| Madame Morcata | Dennis Wheatley |
| Ralph Gower | Robert Wynne-Simmons |
| | & Piers Haggard |
| Pierre de La Poer | H.P. Lovecraft |
| Juliet D'Urfe | Dennis Wheatley |
| Fantômas | Pierre Souvestre |
| | & Marcel Allain |
| **Co-Starring:** | |
| Damien Morcata | Dennis Wheatley |
| Helena Markos | Dario Argento& |
| | Daria Nicolodi |
| Hélène | Pierre Souvestre |
| | & Marcel Allain |
| Vladimir | Pierre Souvestre |
| | & Marcel Allain |
| Juve | Pierre Souvestre |
| | & Marcel Allain |
| Fandor | Pierre Souvestre |
| | & Marcel Allain |
| Arsène Lupin | Maurice Leblanc |

**Frank SCHILDINER** has been a pulp fan since a friend gave him a gift of Philip Jose Farmer's *Tarzan Alive*. Since that time he has written the *Frankenstein* trilogy, the *Napoleon's Vampire Hunters* series (3 vols.), *Irma Vep and the Great Brain of Mars*, and *The Last Days of Atlantis* fantasy series, all for Black Coat Press. Frank has been published in many other anthologies. He works as a martial arts instructor at Amorosi's Mixed Martial Arts and resides in New Jersey with his wife Gail, who is his top supporter.

## The Dark Demon

| Starring: | Created by: |
|---|---|
| Inspector Ginko | Angela & Luciana Giussani |
| Edwige Hossegor (Mephista) | Maurice Limat |
| Teddy Verano | Maurice Limat |
| Diabolik | Angela & Luciana Giussani |
| Eva Kant | Angela & Luciana Giussani |
| **Co-Starring:** | |
| Kriminal | Magnus & Max Bunker |
| Killing | *Anonymous* |
| Satanik | Magnus & Max Bunker |
| **Also Starring:** | |
| Dino De Laurentiis | |
| Mario Bava | |
| Renato Polselli | |
| Andrea Bianchi | |
| Silvana Mangano | |
| **And:** | |
| Clerville | Angela & Luciana Giussani |

**Artikel UNBEKANNT** (not his real name!) lives in Berlin and is the author and/or editor of many books published by Black Coat Press' French sister imprint, Rivière Blanche, as well as a horror novel, *Bloodfist*, released in 2013.

## The Noose of the Phansigars

| Starring: | Created by: |
|---|---|
| Joséphine Balsamo | Maurice Leblanc |
| Leonard | based on Maurice Leblanc |
| Randolph March | Leslie Charteris |
| Rama Tamerlane (Felifax) | Paul Féval, *fils* |
| Mowgli | Rudyard Kipling |
| Grace Tamerlane *née* Palmer | Paul Féval, *fils* |

| | |
|---|---|
| Naka | Rudyard Kipling |
| Chil | Rudyard Kipling |
| Karl | Maurice Renard |
| Wilhelm | Maurice Renard |
| Sourina | Paul Féval, *fils* |
| Fu-Manchu | Sax Rohmer |
| **Co-Starring:** | |
| Reverend Douglas | Paul Féval, *fils* |
| Eric Palmer | Paul Féval, *fils* |
| Edward Sexton | Paul Féval, *fils* |
| Baber | Paul Féval, *fils* |
| **Also Starring:** | |
| Maharajah Prahbhu Narayan Singh | |

Nathalie **VIDALINC** is a graphic designer who lives in the Périgord region of France. She is an eclectic reader who loves detective novels, history books, science fiction & fantasy and pretty much everything except poetry. Her favorite English-language author is P. G, Wodehouse. She has written half-a-dozen short stories published in genre magazines and anthologies.

## *The Thief of Light and Shadows*

| **Starring:** | **Created by:** |
|---|---|
| Arsène Lupin | Maurice Leblanc |
| Hanoi Shan | H. Ashton-Wolfe |
| Sexton Blake | Harry Blyth |
| Paul Temple | Francis Durbridge |
| **Co-Starring:** | |
| Michael Lanyard (The Lone Wolf) | Joseph Louis Vance |
| Smiler Bunn | Bertram Atkey |
| Jimmy Dale (The Gray Seal) | Frank L. Packard |
| Sexton Blake's Cast of characters (Tinker, Toby, Dr. Huxton Rhymer, Zenith the Albino, Waldo the Wonderman, George Marsden Plummer) | Various, including William Murray Graydon, Maxwell Scott, Norman Goddard, Cecil Hayter, D. H. Parry, E. W. Alais, W. J Lomax, and Michael Storm |
| Nick Carter | John Coryell |
| Dr. Fu Manchu | Sax Rohmer |
| Fantômas | Pierre Souvestre & Marcel Allain |

| Dr. Nikola | Guy Boothby |
| Sherlock Holmes | Arthur Conan Doyle |

**Also Starring:**
Ivor Novello
William Henry Pratt (Boris Karloff)
Louis Feuillade
H. Ashton-Wolfe

**And:**

| Dale safe | Frank L. Packard |

**David L. VINEYARD** is a fifth generation Texan (named for his gunfighter/Texas Ranger great-grandfather) currently living in Oklahoma City, OK, where the tornadoes come sweeping down the plains. He has useless degrees in history, politics, and economics, and is the author of several tales about Buenos Aires private eye Johnny Sleep, two novels, several short stories, some journalism, and various non-fiction. He is currently working on several ideas while battling with his cat for household dominance and the keyboard of his PC.

# Last Word

## By Wun Scott Eckert

Jean-Marc Lofficier planted the seeds.

We had met online in the early 2000s through our mutual admiration of Philip José Farmer's Wold Newton mythology, and both had newfangled websites dedicated to hosting speculative "non-fiction" Wold Newton articles, character genealogies and timelines, and other information on pulp and pop heroes. But whereas my site was necessarily angled toward American and British pulp lit, JM's site pulled back the veil on a fascinating—and daunting!—plethora of French characters, some of which were known to me through some well-known French classics (Verne's Captain Nemo and Phileas Fogg; Arsène Lupin; the Phantom of the Opera; Fantômas; Monsieur Lecoq), but most of which were brand new to me.

The Black Coats! Madame Atomos! Doctor Omega! Nestor Burma! Judex! Doc Ardan!

Still, my efforts were contained to a fan site, whereas JM was a well-known comic book and prose writer. Why did he want to spend his time playing in a sandbox with *us*?

Because he cared about these characters, this largely forgotten literature, and us. He wanted to share these characters and see them grown again, and generously gave us Wold Newton fans the opportunity to write our own stories set in this French pulp fiction world—this world of *Tales of the Shadowmen*.

I'll never forget the first and only time I had the opportunity to meet JM in person, at the San Diego ComicCon in 2004. There, he breathlessly explained his idea for an ongoing French pulp fiction, Wold-Newtonesque anthology, and encouraged me to participate. I was honestly taken aback, for I hadn't seen myself as a prose fiction writer. But JM did.

My first published story was a Doc Ardan-Dr. Natas mashup, "The Vanishing Devil" in *Tales of the Shadowmen #1: The Modern Babylon*. JM's fascinating "non-fiction" essay "Will There Be Light Tomorrow?" which provided a framework for my Wold Newton Origins tales appearing in *Shadowmen #1: Heroes and Villains of French Pulp Fiction*.

JM gave me—gave us—the chance. He planted the seeds. He nurtured and watered them.

Cheers, and congratulations to both Jean-Marc and Randy Loffcier on the magnificent accomplishment of twenty annual volumes of top-notch pulp fiction enjoyment.

And thank you for planting the seeds.